The Walk
Stories About You

S. B. Stone

The Walk
Stories About You

S. B. Stone

The Walk
Stories About You

S. B. Stone

The Walk – S.B. Stone & Rock Solid Publishing, LLC

The Walk – S.B. Stone & Rock Solid Publishing, LLC
©2018

The Walk:

Stories About You

Author: S.B. Stone

Publisher: Rock Solid Publishing, LLC

Cover Artist: Dave Rosenberg

video, e-book, printed book, film, television, plays, other media and in any other form or format whatsoever now known or created in the future.

Glossary of Millennial Terms (born 1980 to 2000)

ADULTING - grow up and act responsible

ALMOSTS - someone you almost dated but never became official

BOUNCE - leaving suddenly

BYE FELICIA - an expression used to dismiss someone

CANCELLED - to reject something that's no longer trendy

CATFISHING - pretending to be someone else on social messaging

DAD – role model

DANK – really cool

DEAD – euphorically happy

FAM – a group of friends who feel like family

FINESSE – smooth things out

GASSED - being full of themselves from too many compliments

GHOST - completely disappear after hanging out and showing interest

GIRLFRIEND TAX - amount of food taken by date who said I don't want anything

GMT – getting me uptight/upset

GOALS – subtle expression of jealousy

GOAT – greatest of all time

GUCCI – good, doing well, feeling fine

HIGH KEY – straight up truth

HUNDO P – one hundred percent

MOM – most respectable friend in the group

NETFLIX AND CHILL – hooking up

ON FLEEK - fashionable

The Walk – S.B. Stone & Rock Solid Publishing, LLC
©2018

RATCHET – trashy

RECEIPTS - social media evidence of one's hypocrisy

SALTY – acting upset or bitter

SAVAGE – petty

SHIPPING – wanting two people to date

SHOOK – confused or in utter disbelief

SLAY – killing it/succeeding

SMH – shaking my head

SNATCHED – attractive

SPILLING TEA – telling secrets or gossiping

SQUAD – group of friends

STAN – stalker and fan

SUS - picious

THIRST TRAP - sexy pic or flirtatious message on social media

THROWING SHADE – subtly mean comment about someone

TROLLS – one who purposefully provokes others

TRILL – true and real

WIG SNATCHED – exposing someone to reveal the truth

WOAT – worst of all time

WOKE – aware of current affairs

YEET – shows excitement or agreement

The Walk – Episode One: "Main Character"

One of our main characters is you. After all, who is more interesting than you?

Your sidekicks are a genius, teenage girls, playboy, multi-millionaire, classmate, entrepreneur, gifted weatherman, beautiful librarian and a cop hot on your tail. Thank you for investing your time and money to read this book! We invite your feedback so the next stories kick it up a level in entertaining you, your friends, family and colleagues.

By the weigh, in 2018, we completed a unique survey of a diverse group of average U.S. residents eighteen to eighty plus. By diverse I meen theists, atheists, agnostix and participants in a host of religious and non-religious groups you're familiar with from radio, TV and the internet. The survey posed what I've come to call: *The Jesus Question.*

I've lived a good life - survived high school, college and even grad school. Despite my studies and debates, no one invited me to ask *The Jesus Question*! Thus, I would be remiss if I neglected to give all of my readers an opportunity to ponder and ask their own *The Jesus Question*(s) at the conclusion of this book on our website. In *The Walk*, one of our characters shares his *Jesus Question* with a friend or colleague – see if you can find it! For you, your friends, colleagues and family to purchase *The Walk* in Audiobook, e-Book, PDF and Paperback visit: www.TheWalk.me. Thank you for listening and/or reading *The Walk* my friend – you're a big, big blessing to me!

Did you notice the word choice [weigh] and two spelling errors [agnostix and meen] in the second paragraph above? I've lovingly edited this book myself many times but I know its imperfect…like its author. I decided to break the ice because I'm sure there will be more goofs until I can afford to pay a professional editor.

The Walk – Episode Two: "We Need to Talk"

Why me?

When will they stop?

Who the heck sends them?

You must call Tommy - your IT guru and big brother.

"Hi Tommy I hate calling you when I need your help and feel stupid!"

Tommy answered kindly, "Hey little brother, I'm proud of you so don't sweat it dude; what's the problem?

You shared, "four weeks ago I got a cryptic text: 'we need to talk!'"

Realist Tommy proclaims "I've seen nastier ones – whose heart did you break last month hot shot?"

You replied, "Hey wise guy I wish it were a lady - there's no reply address, cell number or mailing address – think you can find it?"

Tommy assured, "No problems finding who the sender is but I need to do some digging"

You added, "Did I tell you they send it every day at 6:00 am for four weeks?"

Tommy replied, "No dude, I thought it was a one-timer text; do you notice any variation in content or subject line?"

You said, "No variation – I'll review all twenty eight texts to see if I can spot something,

okay Tommy?

Tommy added, "One more thing since you've received twenty eight text messages, not just one, my initial reaction is you're the victim of a phishing scheme."

You shared, "I don't live by a lake or river so why're you talking fishing?"

The Walk – S.B. Stone & Rock Solid Publishing, LLC ©2018

Tommy chuckled, "you're hilarious; suppose you own a company with limited marketing dollars: Would you send one hundred percent of your materials to dead people's addresses?"

"That's stupid – I'd fire myself for wasting money" you said. I'd be certain to invest marketing dollars on real people still breathing God's air as they say."

"Well done little brother - you just learned why your 'we need to talk' messages may be a classic phishing scheme," Tommy announced.

You admitted, "I still don't see the full connection."

Tommy clarified, "What's smart with snail mail marketing is true with email and phone/text message marketing. What's the sender hope their recipient does?

"Now I get it, you said. The sender waits for me to respond with a text or phone call or email to confirm I'm a real person with database value worthy of investing the client's money."

"Right on" said Tommy.

"But if they want a response from me, why is there no mechanism for doing so? No return phone number or email address."

"Strange indeed – usually, the "phishing" stops if you don't reply in thirty days of the first text or email. Hang in for a couple more days and let me know if they go away."

You added, "I'm hands free, so I glanced at all the texts?

Tommy suggested "Identical right?"

Your brow furrowed, "twenty four are identical; four end with an exclamation point instead of a period on the seventh day."

"Interesting" Tommy remarked.

"Send me your bill Doctor Tommy."

Tommy never sends you a bill but you'd pay it if he did; you wonder why he didn't offer to examine your actual text message, waive his magic wand and dig up a phone number? Even big brothers have limits.

The Walk – S.B. Stone & Rock Solid Publishing, LLC
©2018

On the brighter side of life you finally scored a dinner with Emma.

You met Emma at a place you avoid like the plague – the library.

You tagged libraries as dreary and frequented by losers who can't find a date in the real world. But Emma's warm smile lit up the dreary aisles inspiring you to become an innovator-on the-spot.

"Excuse me miss; I may have lost my library card."

"No problem sir. We have copious records. Let me pull you up in our system" said Emma with a reassuring smile.

Uh oh - the truth is you've never owned a library card!

Sweet Emma was a true professional imposing no guilt or embarrassment notwithstanding your indiscretion: "I'm sorry sir, you don't show up anywhere in our system. I'll be happy to issue a temporary card for seven days. That will allow time for your permanent card to arrive at your home in the mail. Will that be alright sir?"

"Yes, yes, yes" I said practically jumping out of my shoes like a little kid at Christmas without any semblance of professionalism but gratitude for my gracious librarian.

To be honest, my first moments with Emma were so warm I could not resist doubling down on my luck by clumsily blurting out – "Emma it would make my day if we could do dinner tonight!"

Emma's face turned stoic. "Do dinner? You must be kidding sir. I am a professional and our brand new relationship is purely professional. Do you understand sir?"

"Yes ma'am" I replied like a schoolboy caught by his teacher for violating basic rules of courtesy, not using street slang like do dinner for a trill and on fleek lady like Emma.

"I understand and I apologize for overstepping the professionalism of our new relationship – will you forgive me, Emma?"

"Looking at my ID she finally used my actual last name instead of 'sir' I know it won't happen again" with her controlled but still cute smile.

It sounded good when Emma finally spoke my actual last name instead of the sterile word "sir". We could be making progress, albeit painfully slow, in our young relationship.

"Don't mess up again airhead" your thoughts admonished. You're becoming a steady patron of Emma's Library as you call it - especially on Emma's work days. You're intending to know Emma so you invited her to share favorite authors and books she thinks you'll enjoy. A bonus of reading Emma's favorites is you learned about her tastes and background. You don't normally labor to understand a woman's heart - Emma could be worth it!

After being shut down by Emma you're exercising patience and a fresh strategy to secure a date. You're inspired by a line in Emma's favorite novel - you knew it's cheesy but tried it on Emma anyway: "Before I met you, Emma, I thought I was a happy man. Now I know my heart won't be fulfilled until I know you better and earn your friendship - will you consider having dinner with me?"

"Hmmm" as Emma finally called me by my first name "aren't you being vague? Do you want me to 'consider' having dinner with you? Or do you want the real deal you silly man?"

"Emma, of course I want all the time together you're willing to carve out of your busy schedule for dinner, lunch, breakfast, walks, movies - you name it."

"I hope you're not 'Mr. Typical' primarily interested in what he can get sexually from a woman are you? Are you a giver or a taker my 'suddenly interested in the library' friend? I'll call you're a true gentleman' until you prove otherwise. I will give you one shot to wow me over dinner so I can figure out what's really inside your heart and your head!"

At last your first date with Emma was on your schedules after so many 'no's' from

Emma. In your gut you thought Emma would eventually say "yes" but truth be told you were discouraged and considering giving up.

Success!

Finally you picked Emma up for the feared and coveted first date. Your first night out together would be one for the memory books – filled with casual small talk, deep but interesting discussions and smiles.

You knew Emma had a great sense of humor and before long you're teasing as if you'd been friends since grade school. Emma's not an average woman. In your heart, you knew you'd be together again - soon you hoped. No doubt about it, your life was more satisfying with Emma in the picture. Despite many conversations, how did you neglect to mention the "we need to talk" morning messages you've received nearly two months? You wonder if Emma receives the same text. You shot her a quick text yourself: "Hey Emma - ever get a text message: 'we need to talk'?"

Emma's at work so you don't anticipate a reply until her lunch around 12:30. The speed and content of Emma's reply surprised you!

"Yes, I received the messages but for me they're emails not texts. I can't find a way to

reply nor am I able to discern who sent them!"

"That sucks", you empathized.

Emma continued, "In frustration, I shared them with Noah."

Uh-oh is Noah her boyfriend? "Who's Noah" you asked.

Emma replied, "Noah's our library's IT guy; he says the messages are untraceable." "Sounds familiar" you said - your heart rate calmed.

Emma added: "Noah's scratching his smart head since the emails appear to land in our email system via the world-wide-web but lack any sender source identifiers - as if they originated beyond cyberspace and planted on my computer."

You replied, "Bizarre!"

The Walk – S.B. Stone & Rock Solid Publishing, LLC ©2018

Emma added. Library policy requires Noah to find any virus or malware. He said they're clean as a whistle; and here's something freaky – Noah's a super smart IT guy and he nicknamed my computer 'tortoise' cuz it's the oldest and slowest one in our system."

"An oldie but a goody. I had one of those," you shared.

Emma added: "Despite Noah's diligent efforts to speed up the tortoise, bet you can't guess what happened after I received the first 'we need to talk' message?

You said, "I'm clueless – did something change?"

Emma chuckled: "You won't believe it – my email message from 'whomever' transformed the tortoise into the fastest virus-free machine in our system! Noah's blown away an email from nowhere transformed my computer's performance."

I texted Emma, "I can't believe what you're telling me!"

Emma said, "There's more I need to share with you when we're face to face, ok? Right now I need to look calm and professional at work. I see our patrons staring – I must look emotional as I'm texting with you!"

I replied: "I'm cool Emma. Let's hit Mario's for Italian or Guadalupe's for Mexican?"

"Italian sounds better" said Emma. "Let's order take-out so we can find a quiet place to

talk."

You added, "The weather's been great today! I think we can find a warm and private

place in the park. Okay with you, Emma?"

"Super" she replied.

Your heart is smiling how pumped you are to chill with Emma - a beautiful and quality girl! – Hmm will I get to hold her hand tonight? Perhaps walking from Mario's with our take out Italian finding the "warm and private place" Emma's alluding to or side by side on a bench or under a tree? You tried not to rush physical affection with Emma. It wasn't easy. After three months

The Walk – S.B. Stone & Rock Solid Publishing, LLC ©2018

of sharing the library with Emma and her patrons you didn't foresee such strong emotional and, yes, physical connection as you're feeling with her. You chose to do and say everything you could to make tonight special for Emma…not just for yourself.

"Emma, you look on fleek tonight!"

"And my date's lookin dank in his new jeans, shirt and tie!"

"Truth is, my old girlfriend gave me these jeans on my birthday. They've been hanging around my closet for a special occasion – like you, Emma."

"Tell me about your girlfriend - I thought you only had eyes for me?"

"If only I knew you last year I probably wouldn't have dated Samantha."

"Probably you say?"

"Let's face it Emma you have an untouchable aura about you".

"What do you mean?

"When I saw you the first time in the library dressed in your super professional librarian style clothing, I was afraid to speak to you."

"Do I dress too conservatively?"

"It's beyond what you wear, Emma. It's who you are regardless of the clothing."

"Did Samantha exude the aura?"

"No. Samantha had two serious relationships before me."

"What do you mean by 'serious?'" asked Emma.

"Hmmm a prickly question Emma but I'll give it a shot. Uh oh, it looks like the weatherman continues to be fallible - our sunny and warm forecast has morphed into a serious rainstorm."

Emma put her arm through yours. "I'm so glad we're in this warm and cozy restaurant."

The Walk – S.B. Stone & Rock Solid Publishing, LLC ©2018

You asked the waiter, "Do you mind if we change our "to go" orders to eating inside?"

"No problem", said the waiter

Emma requested, "Can we move to the corner booth near the fireplace?"

"Yes you may - I don't expect many new customers until the rain lets up. I'm happy you two are here" the waiter added.

"Thank you and we're happy to have you as our waiter for our first dinner date. I'm checking this guy out to see if he deserves a second one" Emma confided.

"Good luck sir" opined the waiter scrutinizing me and Emma as a couple.

"Hey friend, thanks for bringing me to Mario's – the ambiance and cozy seating plus the crackling fireplace feels good and makes it easy to talk" said Emma.

"You're welcome Emma. I'm honored to be here with you. Okay, I know you wonder what I meant by 'serious relationship'."

"Yes, thank you for circling back to my question instead of hoping I forget about it and let you off the hook" Emma commended.

You shared, "a relationship is serious when one or both parties are wonder if the other person meets their criteria for a marriage partner."

"Hmm - sounds reasonable but kind of sterile" Emma countered.

"What do you mean by 'sterile'" you asked.

"What about love and romance" Emma poked.

"Aw come on isn't love and romance for story books and movies?" you queried.

"My parents would debate you on that…and so do I" Emma declared.

"On what basis?"

The Walk – S.B. Stone & Rock Solid Publishing, LLC ©2018

"Haven't you read Anne of Green Gables, Gone with the Wind or Doctor Zhivago or seen those movies? Writers of books and producers of movies can be inspired by the 'true love' they gave and received in their lives."

"Emma, I don't read romance books" you said.

"Wait a minute. Aren't you the guy who checked out 'Fried Green Tomatoes at the Whistle Stop Café'? Didn't you check out 'Roller Girl' as well?

"Not me – must be some sappy dude struggling with his maleness" you insisted. "

"No I remember he had a masculine voice - kinda tall, nice hair, handsome face; well built with strong shoulders" Emma insisted.

"I confess - I read a few pages to learn the kind of guy you want to spend time with and what words and activities you enjoy.

"I like a man who invests in me" smiled Emma.

"Unless he's a loser" you suggested. "I prefer sci-fi, spy-stuff and historical biographies but I didn't have the guts to tell you, Emma."

"I want a man who's comfortable being honest with me about who he really is on the inside. Does that make sense?"

You agreed, "Hard to have a good relationships when you're not honest; help me understand why your parents think love and romance are legit emotions toward a person?

"My parent's personal experience" stated Emma.

"What do you mean Emma?"

"They built a forty-two year marriage. In their earlier years and today Mom and Dad are still in love and beautiful."

"They'd say there was little faith in God since their parents crammed religion into their minds as kids; memorized a few Bible verses; attended every Sunday without fail."

"As an adult, Mom reflected: 'As kids and teenagers, your father and I had too much religion and too little relationship with God and Jesus.'"

The Walk – S.B. Stone & Rock Solid Publishing, LLC
©2018

"Not sure I understand - did this change for your parents?"

"Yes, as my Mom would say it: 'My life and your Dad's life got a whole lot better after God blessed your father and me with Emma, Blake and cancer.'"

"That makes no sense, Emma!"

"Don't you like kids?"

You stated, "To be honest, kids scare me and you better believe this dude hates cancer so why'd your Mom say cancer's a blessing from God?"

Emma popped in, "I could see why labor pains and giving birth might scare a woman but why does having kids scare you as a man?"

"The short answer is I can't picture holding a tiny baby. I'd be afraid of breaking it. It gets worse when those helpless little buggers grow up I'm afraid I'll overwhelm them intellectually and physically. As you can see I'm kind of a big guy."

"I'd estimate you're 6'4" and top out at a lean and mean 215 pounds?"

"Your skills are impressive, Emma! I'll bet I can nail your height and weight as well."

Emma replied, "No thank you sir I'm not looking for a man who's a good guesser."

"What kind of man are you looking for Miss Emma?"

"Wondering if you satisfy my criteria?"

"Of course, as your friend I'd like to know Emma's perfect match!"

"Next you'll tell me you may have a friend, brother or neighbor who meets my criteria?"

"Yes, that's it exactly" you said grinning ear to ear.

"Okay, I'll humor you my friend" smiled Emma

"I have a better idea you offered; since you won't let me guess your height and weight, let me list the 'top ten' qualities you want in your husband!"

The Walk – S.B. Stone & Rock Solid Publishing, LLC
©2018

"Splendid idea - more meaningful than guessing my height and weight" observed Emma.

Candidly you admitted "Emma, I must give you fair warning."

"Sounds intriguing my fair-minded pal" conceded Emma.

"I was a psych major in school" you revealed.

Emma looked puzzled "So?"

You explained, "I learned to observe and evaluate people. My professor said I'm a natural at observing strangers and discerning what's important to them by how they interact with others."

Emma still puzzled, "Forgive the lack of a back flip of amazement; I reiterate - so?"

"I've hung out with you for three wonderful months. Plus, we've talked and eaten at

Mario's for almost three hours. I know I can nail at least eight out ten for you!"

"I am impressed with the confidence you exude my friend! Let's up the stakes to a level worthy of your expertise" offered Emma.

"What do you propose, Emma?"

"Let's be real - like any woman out there, I already expect my husband will turn me on sexually, make a good living, be my best friend, make me laugh, give me back rubs, be a man of integrity, treat me with respect, be strong when I am weak and be a superb role model for our kids. Do you agree?"

"Yes it's a great and challenging list Emma. I suppose every woman wants those qualities in her husband."

"You're right and I expect my husband will already possess those qualities" Emma insisted. "Otherwise I wouldn't give him the time of day!"

"Good Emma. You deserve the best husband in the world."

The Walk – S.B. Stone & Rock Solid Publishing, LLC
©2018

Emma said, "Thank you, but in the interest of fairness, I need to share a vital detail with you my knowledgeable and naive friend"

"I'm listening Emma."

"The most vital quality of my husband is not on that list" Emma shared.

"No problem, what is it Emma?"

"And you need to know it's a deal breaker for me" Emma clarified.

Your mouth agape "What do you mean it's a 'deal breaker' for you Emma?

"A man must have this key quality or I won't marry him" insisted Emma.

You clarified, "So even if you find a man who blows you away with how sensational a person he is, you'll walk away from an exceptional opportunity if he lacks that quality?"

"Exactly" said Emma with peaceful resolve. She added, "This quality is so strong I'll see it manifested in his behavior toward me and other people and reflected in how he prioritizes his life as we spend time together and apart."

"This is too tough Emma – I beg you please reveal your deal breaker!"

"I'm sorry but you need to figure this out on your own my friend" stressed Emma.

"How can I know if I have these qualities Emma? Oh crap – I'm gonna return my psych degree back to Princeton!"

"You think they'd take it back?"

"Probably not - I have no clue where you're coming from, Emma. I feel like tonight's been magical but I can't afford to fall in love with you Emma when I have no idea if I've got what it takes!"

"I suppose time will tell" Emma conceded. You need to know this girl's in no hurry; the right man's worth waiting for."

The Walk – S.B. Stone & Rock Solid Publishing, LLC

"I agree Emma and I'm in no hurry either" you conceded.

Emma stated, "Let's be real – we barely know each other! Do we even know the basics about each other's lives and background?"

"Good point Emma."

"Let's play a game of 'Betcha Don't Know'" suggested Emma.

"I'm game" you said having no idea how to play.

"Bethcha don't know Emma's favorite ice cream Mr. Psych major?"

You said, "Mines chocolate; yours is chocolate chip mint, Emma." "Lucky guess smarty pants" said Emma.

You asked "Betcha don't know my favorite sport or board game?

Emma pondered and said "you play hoops and you hate to lose."

"The rain's cleared - it's nice outside. Shall we go on that walk, Emma?"

"Yes, and it's getting crowded and noisy in Mario's so let's walk to the park?"

"Emma, do you still get the "We Need to Talk" messages?"

"No sir."

"Oh my goodness" you exclaimed. "Why'd they stop?"

"I responded to the sender and I knew in my heart there was no longer a reason to send me emails."

You asked, "I'm confused - how did you respond?"

"I can clarify for you later", Emma promised.

"I'll be patient" you agreed.

"Still get your 'we need to talk' text messages?" Emma asked.

The Walk – S.B. Stone & Rock Solid Publishing, LLC
©2018

"Yes - funny how I've grown used to them. After six months I look forward to the ping on my phone at 6:05 am every morning - the guy's consistent."

"I received my 'we need to talk' emails at 10:15 every night."

"I wonder why we received them when we did, you asked."

Emma volunteered - "I may be able to shed some light on it a bit later, okay?

"Okay I can wait", you said.

Emma offered, "Hey friend, can I tell you more about my family and upbringing – if you're interested; then let's switch to you and your family?"

"Grand idea - I am all ears, Emma!"

Emma warned, "Some of this is personal stuff I don't share with just anyone so I might get teary."

"I'm honored to listen Emma. My shoulders are ready to lean on, my hand is ready to hold and I have Kleenex in my back pack; all you share I'll keep just between us, okay?"

"Thank you my good friend" Emma said gratefully.

"I lived in the Phoenix area as a little girl through my college years. I have a twin brother, Blake, and no other siblings. My parents were super active serving in our community, our church and my Dad's job as a fire captain."

"I like Phoenix" you shared.

"Everyone in our family was a competitor in life and sports and business. Dad's a scratch golfer. Mom wins local golf tournaments and Blake's a state batting champion and super tennis player."

"What about you, Emma?"

"Oh, sorry, I was on the women's golf and tennis teams in high school and college; my partner and I ranked the number one high school doubles team in our conference."

"Impressive Emma - I don't think I'll be challenging you to tennis or golf anytime soon!"

"I'm a decent teacher if you're interested in learning either sport."

"Hmm, I may take you up on that. I suck at tennis but I'd like to get better."

"Let's make a tennis date – maybe next week?"

"Emma, am I dreaming or did you just ask me out? I bet you look beautiful in a tennis outfit!"

"Keep your cool big guy – you got lucky cuz I feel sad you suck at tennis."

"I'll do my best to keep my eye on the ball and not on you, Emma!"

Emma smiled, "Good luck with that one, Boy Scout – we'll see how well you perform under immense pressure."

"I like that kind of pressure" you confessed. "Does your Dad still play golf and work as a Fire Captain?"

"No."

"Is he retired?"

"No, my Dad's in heaven with God."

"Oh my goodness, I am so sorry Emma!"

"You don't need to feel sorry for my Dad – he is in the best place he could ever be!"

"Glad to hear it Emma" you shared.

Emma admitted, "I can't lie to you - Mom, Blake and I miss Dad terribly. We're in agony some days."

"Mind me asking how your Dad died?"

"Not at all" Emma granted.

"Dad fought fires around Phoenix for thirty years. He became a captain because Dad put high value on serving people especially in their hour of greatest need. He'd help anyone in

The Walk – S.B. Stone & Rock Solid Publishing, LLC
©2018

need, but Dad especially loved rescuing little children and older folks" shared Emma.

"Oh no, did your Dad die in a fire?"

"Dad and his team received an urgent call during a country western concert under a series of ten large tents. The venue capacity was up to 30,000 concert-goers! The fire ignited in the rear tent farthest away from the stage and with the smallest crowd. Sadly, the wind blew from the back tent driving flames to the front tents and stage where most of the people were sitting."

Emma's voice cracked and her tears began to flow.

You stood up and wrapped your arms round Emma, "I'm so sorry Emma. I wish I could know your Dad."

"Maybe someday you'll meet him. Right now I need to bury my head in your chest like I used to do with my Dad when I was hurting….and I need to hold on to your strong arm so I can gather strength to tell you the rest of my Dad's story. Is that alright with you?"

You don't know where this relationship is going, but you're encouraged Emma's being this frank and vulnerable so early in your time together.

"It is my privilege to be here with you Emma - to hear you and your Dad's stories."

"Okay, I'll try to finish up" Emma said.

You consoled, "I'm not going anywhere so take your time."

"Dad and his team checked the under the tents to see how many people were inside. The eight rear tents were completely evacuated. Dad surmised the most mobile guests sat in the back, saw the fire in its early stages and "ran like hell" for their lives. Many probably screamed 'FIRE' as they ran out of danger, but the high volume of the music likely drowned out the screams of warning."

You wondered, "What about the two tents closest to the stage. I bet most of the people would be in the prime seats closer to the stage wouldn't they?"

"Yes, according to ticket sales and on site estimates, those two prime tents were packed with ten thousand people! Dad said it must have been chaos in those first two tents since most had no idea the fire was raging until Dad's sirens blared in the parking lot two hundred feet away."

You shared, "I imagine myself at a concert - utterly transfixed listening and dancing and celebrating the joy of the tickets and driving with friends to share a great concert."

"Me too" Emma shared.

"I can't imagine, in the blink of an eye, the horror of a powerful fire sweeping our celebration into ugliness - tents ablaze as me and my fellow concertgoers joy turns to terror, pain, injury and death!"

"Every person who could run 'ran like hell' but Dad found several exhausted victims moaning or unconscious having been trampled by the frantic crowd" shared Emma.

"Was anyone alive in the two front tents?"

Emma added "Yes. They rescued nearly two hundred precious souls including trample victims with broken bones and serious lacerations; some senior citizens with walkers or wheelchairs with little chance of safely and quickly fleeing their smoke-filled and flame engulfed tents! Dad and his men lay on the cool green grass exhausted; and drinking gulps of water and a nap - preferably back at the fire station or at home. Everyone was done fighting the fire and rescuing victims - except my big daddy. He spied an American flag waiving slowly near the stage some two hundred yards from where he and the men had been laying. One of the things I learned from Dad is he never takes on a challenge without humbly asking God to help him be successful."

You wondered, "Makes sense if he knows God's listening and cares for him."

Emma continued: "Though I wasn't there, I'm sure my Dad said a prayer to God like this: Mighty and Holy God - Thank you for helping me and my men put out this fire and rescue your precious children from death or serious injury. God, you know

The Walk – S.B. Stone & Rock Solid Publishing, LLC
©2018

how tired my men and I feel; I've got no more energy to give you. Dear Lord, I need your help to rescue the man or woman near the stage."

You observed, "In his job I can see why your Dad would as God to help him every day."

"He sure did." Emma continued, "The exhausted fire fighters had no idea why Big Daddy was up and walking into a burned out tent – seconds earlier Dad was resting like them. Two hundred yards in the distance Dad's squatting down below the stage and he appears to be talking with someone; another minute - they saw Big Daddy walk out the burned tent, carrying two old folk, one on each of his broad shoulders. He laid the grateful couple on stretchers near the ambulance and spoke with the driver before returning to his men on the lawn."

"Even more exhausted my Dad asked his team – 'Have you any idea what that old man and his wife told me as I was getting them into a safe position to carry them out?"

"No captain, what'd they say?"

"The old man cried" 'My heart medicine's ruined! It spilled as we tried to flee the flames! Can you get us to the hospital so I can live till tomorrow?"

Dad asked the old man, "why live till tomorrow?"

"It's my birthday; I turn one hundred!' he smiled through his pain.

"Dad added, yes he'll be one hundred years old - twice as old as your fifty year old captain and nearly three times the age of you thirty-something prima-donna's!"

Jacob's one of the thirty-something's who chimed in, "Hey Captain - you know we call you "old man" when you're not around!?"

"Heck yes and I love you Jacob and am proud to see you grow as a firefighter and a man."

"Twenty-nine year old Isaac joined the party reminding everyone how honored he is to be on this "amazing" fire-fighting team as the youngest member." Captain, I want you to know I

The Walk – S.B. Stone & Rock Solid Publishing, LLC
©2018

call you Big Daddy to your face and when you're not around because I lost my Daddy in the war when I was twelve."

"I cannot replace your Daddy, Isaac. I'm blessed to be your mentor in fire-fighting and in life. You know you can call or text any time for any reason?"

"The entire team joined in – yes we can sir!"

"Captain" said Lieutenant, Willie, "I know you're tired but can the men ask you a question?"

"Honestly my head hurts, my legs are shot and I'd like to drag this fifty year old body home to hug my wife and Emma and Blake."

"But we're all learning that our lives are not all about US are they? Your question may be more important than how soon I take a shower and hug my family; go for it Willie – I'm happy to listen and hopefully give a solid answer for you and the team."

"Thank you Captain. Can you please tell us where your faith in God and Jesus Christ comes from?"

"Yes, I am honored to share with every one of you."

"As a child, my parents exposed me to the truths of the Holy Bible." "Everyone with eyes and ears must read and/or listen to the Bible from cover to cover; you'll discover [not the first time but eventually the Bible's the most fascinating historical and spiritual book ever written. I learned how God created the earth for you and me to share, steward and enjoy!"

"I learned God loves every person and invites each of us to interact with Him one on one as our lives unfold. Because God loves us, He gives you and me freedom to choose whether to love Him back or not. May I read a few verses from the Bible to you?"

"Yes, please read to us."

"Okay, this is from Paul's letter to the church in Rome…we call it Romans: 1:16-23.

"For I am not ashamed of the gospel, because it is the power of God that brings salvation to everyone who believes: first to the Jew, then to the Gentile. For in the gospel the righteousness of

God is revealed—a righteousness that is by faith from first to last, [or is from faith to faith] just as it is written: 'The righteous will live by faith.' quoting Habakkuk 2:4(b)."

"Sorry Boss - what is the 'gospel'"?

"Thanks for asking. The Bible's written in Hebrew, Greek and Aramaic."

"The Greek word for 'gospel' is 'euaggelion' it translates to *'good news'* from God."

"Cool boss – but I don't understand what's the good news from God?"

"Great question - its good news God wants all mankind to be in heaven with Him after they die! But its <u>bad news</u> you and I and every person ever born aren't good enough to be in God's perfect heaven – we have disobeyed God in our thoughts, words and actions. Honestly, we'd ruin God's holy and perfect Heaven if we showed up with our sin stained hearts and habits."

"So, if I live a perfect life on earth then God will let me into Heaven right?"

"Wrong – can you or anyone you know live your entire life without lying, cheating, jealousy, cheating or immoral sex with a woman? Or, **never** being prideful or boasting or cursing or using foul language?"

"What about all of my and your past sins? How do we get cleaned up from those? Heck, I lied and cheated and disobeyed to my parents and teachers hundreds of times!"

"Men are any of you ready to take a long shower when you get home or back to the station?"

"Heck yes - my body stinks of smoke and sweat and dirt like you would not believe!" said Jacob.

"We can testify you stink cause we ride back in the truck with you sometimes."

"If I **scrub extra hard** taking the longest shower I've ever had, will my scrubbing, soap and streams of water get deep enough to clean my wicked heart and dirty mind and sinful soul?"

"No way boss – impossible."

"Men and women, God has good news [the gospel] for you."

"The blood of God's Son Jesus Christ will clean you up from the inside out."

"What must I do?"

"My friends whether you're an atheist, agnostic, philosopher, scientist, Catholic, Lutheran, Muslim, Hindu or any other religion or belief."

1.   "Admit from your heart to God you're a sinful person in need of His forgiveness."

2.   "Confess aloud with your mouth Jesus Christ is your Lord."

3.   "Believe in your heart God raised Jesus from the dead."

"You will be saved from your sins and cleaned up before God."

"Men and women – when you choose, <u>with an honest heart,</u> to say and do these things your sins will be forgiven and you will be "born again" by the Spirit of God and adopted into God's heavenly family. When you die, you'll be welcomed into God's heaven!

"Dad shared many of the details I've just shared with you about the fire, his rescue of the old couple and his talk with the men with Mom, Blake and me at our dinner table that evening."

"It was one of our best times together as a family.

You pined, "How cool it would have been to sit at your family table that night!"

"I agree" said Emma. "It was Blake's and my birthday eve – we ordered pizza and salad plus Mom's fabulous oatmeal raisin chocolate chip cookies and milk – plenty for everyone, including you big guy!"

"The next day, Blake and I realized we turned fifteen on the same day the old man Dad rescued turned one hundred! Mom called to see if he wanted visitors but the hardy old guy and his wife were out of the hospital celebrating with his family!"

You asked, "Emma did you and Blake plan to do anything special to celebrate?"

"We planned to play tennis and golf against each other that next morning. The winner of golf gets any $50 birthday present. The loser's present would be capped at twenty-five dollars.

The winner and loser of tennis will get similarly priced gifts."

Emma's eyes teared up - "Blake's and my birthday plans never materialized so we didn't even celebrate our fifteenth birthdays."

"How come" you asked.

"God called our strong and healthy Daddy to heaven while he was sleeping at our home – no one wanted to celebrate birthdays – we were grieving how much we were going to miss Dad."

"I'm so sorry Emma – was he showing any signs of declining health?"

"At Dad's fifty year old medical exam, his doctor said he was healthy as a horse…a big horse; he reminded us my Grampa Wil died of congestive heart failure in his fifties so we'd been on pins and needles Dad could suffer a similar early departure from this life."

"Dad just said, 'God will take me when He's darn well ready; don't grieve for me cause I'll be in Jesus presence - happier than I'd ever be on earth."

"Hard to imagine" you said.

"When I was a little girl Dad used to say, "Emma, did you know 'the fear of the Lord is the beginning of knowledge?"

You shared, "Emma I don't understand."

"Me either" added Emma. "The loving tone of Dad's voice compelled me to understand what he meant. So I asked, 'Daddy who is the Lord? Why should I fear him? And what is knowledge'?"

"Over the years Dad patiently unpacked this simple proverb for me and Blake. Some of our friends learned in school and at home God does not exist, so why would you 'fear him' in the first place?"

"I understand Emma. My parents and school teachers told me similar lies."

"So you do believe in God?" asked Emma.

"I don't mind anyone making their own free choice not to believe in God. It pisses me off when adults impose their unbelief on little kids, teens and college students! Why not use school and home to explore life's foundational truths fairly: where do rules come from? Which rules are worth obeying? Study evolution, study creation, religion, philosophy and ethics in public school.

How can anyone teach math or science or history until you've learned where they come from?

Emma agreed, "You are right – my classmates rebelled when they're not given the opportunity to discuss why they're here on earth, where they come from and why obey all the rules from parents and teachers who sometimes ignore them."

Scratching your head, "Emma what does your Dad's proverb *'the fear of the Lord is the beginning of knowledge'* mean?"

"It means - God does exist.

"It means - God demands a healthy respect or reverence for His principles."

"It means - everything worth knowing in life emanates from God."

"Hmmm - quite provocative. I can now see IF I decide God does exist and everything worth knowing in life emanates from him, I would definitely have reverence for and worship such a God!" you conceded.

"I get what you're saying. Can I share another principle my parents taught us?"

"Sure Emma."

"As partners in life, Dad and Mom checked in with each other to see how their <u>faith</u> is doing. Above our fireplace they posted Hebrews 11:6:

"And without faith it is impossible to please God, because anyone who comes to Him must believe that He exists and that He rewards those who earnestly seek Him."

"Interesting Emma - do you still have faith in God after your Dad died?"

"Yes, but until recently I had walked away from God for taking my Dad."

"Heck I don't blame you Emma - what brought you back to God?"

"I thought you might know" Emma opined.

"Sorry Emma. I have no clue."

"Remember I told you I'm no longer receivng my "We Need to Talk" emails?

You said, "Yes Emma and you weren't ready to share. Is this a gucci time?"

Emma said "Sure - after I responded well, I knew I'd no longer need the emails."

You pleaded, "I'm dying Emma - how did you respond so well you made them stop?

"I've not talked much with God since Dad died; I finally asked Jesus if He would go on a walk with me" Emma said.

"Are you kidding me?" you asked.

Emma asked, "Jesus told his followers he was about to die on the cross for the sins of the world; rise from the dead on the third day; then leave the earth to rejoin His Father in heaven.

How do you think Jesus followers felt?"

You replied: "Bad news - they were depressed Jesus was leaving them on earth alone?

Emma agreed "Incredibly sad but look how cool Jesus responded:

"If you love me, obey my commandments. And I will ask the Father, and he will give you another Advocate [Comforter, Encourager, Counselor] who will never leave you. He is the Holy Spirit, who leads into all truth. The world cannot receive him, because it isn't looking for him and doesn't recognize him. But you know him because he lives with you now and later will be in you. No, I will not abandon you as orphans - I will come to you." John 14:15 – 18 [2]

You asked, "Is this the Holy Spirit or Holy Ghost I've heard about?"

"Precisely!" Emma agreed.

You asked, "How could you ask Jesus to go on a walk with you – isn't Jesus in heaven?"

Emma replied: "Yes, Jesus is in heaven and the Holy Spirit is living inside me!"

Your mouth hung open…speechless…trying to picture what it would be like. "Emma, did you just say God's Holy Spirit is actually living inside you?"

Emma affirmed, Jesus said *"I will never leave you or forsake you Emma."*

Still confused you asked: "How can he say he'll never leave you when he's in heaven?"

Emma clarified, "God's spirit gave me peace and comfort when I was too proud or angry to ask God for it; plus God refused to quit on me when I tried to ignore our relationship!"

"Cool - Jesus words encouraged you" you replied.

Emma agreed, "Walking away from God was easy at first but eventually I felt empty inside and confused about what to do with my life."

"How so" you asked.

"When I lost Dad, I missed his jokes and our talks; why did I neglect talking with God just who's just a simple prayer away? How stupid" Emma lamented.

The Walk – S.B. Stone & Rock Solid Publishing, LLC
©2018

With insight you replied: "I don't understand how it works but it sounds like God's Spirit is protecting and comforting you every day Emma?"

"Well spoken" Emma praised. "Enough on me - did you get your "We Need to Talk" message today?

"Yes I received my message" you stated.

Emma asked, "Do you think they're from God?"

"I hope so" you responded.

Emma wondered, "Are you worried the messages may stop?"

You answered, "Heck yes, God could be quitting on me if he stopped the texts!"

Emma inquired, "If God's all powerful can't he reach out to you any way he chooses?"

"I suppose" you conceded.

"When I was twelve my best friend Millie decided 'God doesn't love me' when her parents failed to give the new bike she wanted for Christmas" Emma shared.

"Did you say anything" you queried.

"I asked Millie, 'are you breathing right now and were you breathing when you woke up this morning?'"

Millie argued, "Of course I was breathing when I woke up and I've been breathing ever since, you weirdo!"

You interrupted, "What'd you say to Millie?"

"Around the world, hundreds of people may breathe their last breath today, so we should be thankful for every day God shows He cares for us" Emma shared.

You wondered aloud, "Emma are you suggesting I may not need an email from God; if I take a good breath into my lungs tomorrow morning it is <u>tangible evidence</u> God is calling me to follow him!"

"Beautifully said my friend" agreed Emma, "<u>I have no doubt God is calling you</u>."

You wondered, "Emma, why's it so compelling to hear the words of the Bible your Dad shared about Jesus love and power in his life with his team?"

Emma clarified: "You chose to truly listen – with your mind and your heart; God's words have mighty power when a person chooses to open his mind and heart to the message– that's why they resonate in your heart and mind my friend. When I asked Jesus if He would go on a walk with me He reminded me of a great truth: "I will never leave you or forsake you Emma". I know for certain I'm 100% forgiven for my sins - no more guilt - and I want God's forgiveness for you my friend." Emma added. God is ready to forgive you IF you come to Him with your personal "Key of Faith".

You asked, "Where do I find my Key of Faith?"

"It's inside your heart and mind" Emma clarified; every person in history is born with an eternal soul and a sinful heart in need of a relationship with God" Emma added.

You asked, "What do I do with my Key of Faith?

"First, you must believe [faith] Jesus died on the cross to pay the penalty for your sins."

"Second, you must believe [faith] Jesus was buried in the tomb."

"Third, you must believe [faith] God raised Jesus from the dead."

"Finally, you make the most important investment of your life by pledging all your heart, soul, mind and strength to live your life as a 21st Century Disciple of Jesus Christ!

"What will you do my friend?"

++

Thank you for reading "We Need to Talk". We welcome your feedback: feedback@TheWalk.me

Your next episode is "Man About Town".

Have fun!

The Walk: Episode Three - Man About Town

No one lives life like you.

From childhood, the word "mine!" has been your favorite.

Youngest among ten siblings - you ruled the roost – eventually.

Bigger, stronger and smarter they took life's frustrations out on your smaller weaker body – it's a miracle you survived those beatings.

How did you reverse the tables so everyone in your family grew to fear your wrath?

At age three you discovered by screaming your lungs out you eventually got what you wanted. Your parents acquiesced to a three year old's passionate demands. As the runt of your family's litter you saw the powerful adorned with yes men and yes women…often strong and attractive people. You aspired to have a similar entourage.

"Hey what's up Arthur?" you answered his call.

"Are we meeting today at 2:00 or tomorrow at 3:00?" asked Arthur."

"Will Hezy be there too?" you queried.

"Heck yes, Hezy says you're his favorite client!" Arthur offered.

"I'll be there today at 2:00" you stated.

Your primal instincts told you the great fighters in life acquire many weapons in their arsenal – for self-defense, taking out enemies and undesirables no longer useful. You're drawn to leaders with an arsenal of hand to hand fighting skills.

You detest football, baseball, basketball or any sport your school offered - except wrestling. By twelve the bullies and tough kids avoided your quick and decisive wrath. In high school wrestling you were undefeated senior year at your weight class.

The Walk – S.B. Stone & Rock Solid Publishing, LLC
©2018

You added boxing, karate, silat, kung-foo and krav-maga making you the toughest, most respected 145 pound student in school.

You despised owing favors or money or kindness or your time to anyone - you preferred having other people, even adults, "owe" you. You felt successful and powerful when friends and enemies came to you asking for something - your wisdom, your time, your affection, your money or your blessing. You learned to "play no favorites." If a person thinks they're your favorite they expect to get what they ask.

Your attorney likened you to the Babylonian King Xerxes - if anyone, even the Queen, approaches King Xerxes inner court without a prior appointment they're killed unless the King extends his scepter sparing their life! Esther 4:11 [1]

You crave power like that!

To be honest, you're not certain what a true friend is anyway.

One so-called friend, Maria, had the temerity to invite you to visit her church.

"Why would I do that? Will God be there? Will I actually see him or her?"

She replied matter-of-factly - "*God is spirit and his worshippers must worship [Him] in the Spirit and in truth.*" John 4:24 [1]

You were blown away! "You worship an invisible God! Last I heard he came to earth so mankind could see how he rolls and so the Jews could kill him" you contended.

"Not exactly - whether you and I admit it or not, we are spiritual beings too. It's true we live life on earth in our physical bodies – but after our bodies die, our spirits remain alive forever." Maria clarified.

"*Do not be amazed at this, for a time is coming when all who are in their graves will hear his voice and come out – those who have done what is good will rise to live, and those who have done what is evil will rise to be condemned.*" John 5:28 – 29 [1]

The Walk – S.B. Stone & Rock Solid Publishing, LLC
©2018

Maria shared, "Then you and I and everyone ever born will see God in heaven if we've chosen to put our faith in God's son Jesus; everyone else will be condemned."

You blasted back, "You are ridiculous! How can you believe such garbage?"

You sent an email to your contact list – "I've decided I have no room for a god with a rulebook judging my behavior and the people I hang with – how ignorant and pathetic are the fools who build their lives on such fallacies. I shall have sex every day; and I will not request god's permission for anything I desire to acquire or do."

When a woman displeased you sexually or otherwise, you discarded her like your daily trash. By age thirty-five you had sex with one thousand four hundred twenty six lucky women – notches on your bedpost to prove it.

The madam's in your neighborhood sent their hottest girls into the street hoping to lure you into their illegal businesses. The girls were beautiful but they made your cold heart sad inside. How can such a nice girl sell her beautiful body to a stranger like me? You never paid for sex though you could easily afford it. The world's dating game and the conquest of a woman simply gave you more pleasure than paying for it. Sex is purely for fun, not for business.

With sex or anything else you are involved in, **receiving the greatest amount of pleasure** is the best indicator of true success in your life. All your unprotected fun eventually produced a kid or two. You were irritated by age forty two you lost count of your girlfriends. Most had your cell number, email, New York, Miami or Belize address. It's impossible to know how many biological offspring you fathered. If you trust two thousand girlfriends you're the proud father of one hundred twenty seven children – possibly more!

You accountant's Arthur Levine. "Hey Arthur, what's my net worth? Am I there yet?"

Arthur replied, "Sir I got good news and bad news! Which news you want first?

The Walk – S.B. Stone & Rock Solid Publishing, LLC
©2018

You say, "Arthur you love to harass me; you do this every time I ask you!"

Arthur can't resist; "Good news is you passed five hundred million last year!"

You reply, "Arthur, tell me today's good news - how high's my net worth today?"

"Not to worry Boss, your net worth's jumped to seven hundred fifty million dollars!"

"Not that I don't trust your math Artie, how's it possible I've grown by fifty per cent adding two hundred fifty million in just three years?" you wondered.

Your attorney is Hezekiah Levine, Artie's brother. Hezekiah knew how you pulled it off: Hezekiah asked, "Sir, you recall the twenty five million you invested five years ago to help your college buddy Buster Mahoney's overseas expansion of boutique hotels?"

You clarified, "Of course I remember the deal: "I told Buster I don't want to put our capital at risk in the overseas markets he's considering; but he's done me right on other investments so I agreed to invest the twenty five million IF Buster agrees to a five year payback of principal and my share of profits as reflected in Buster's increased portfolio value!"

Hezekiah stated, "Hotels are businesses and require more intensive management than apartments which is real estate. He added, "Wasn't Buster's plan to buy eighty to one hundred twenty room hotels under financial pressure for cash in attractive cities with populations of 500,000 plus and prospects for economic growth; avoid banks, permits and extensive renovations?"

You recalled, "That's my understanding; plus he adds hi tech sports bars to create a sense of neighborhood and give the older hotels a classier street appeal."

Artie added, "Yes and Buster's MO is to master lease each hotel to his parent company 'Venus Ventures' like he's done across the U.S. portfolio. Buster told me Venus Ventures has gobs of cash in Credit Suisse, Bank of America and others – five hundred million smackers. The sooner Buster rents the rooms, the faster he recovers his front money and our investment capital.

Each hotel has a master lease with his local operator in that city; I heard somewhere Buster's local partners hold a weekly auction for high net worth individuals"

You asked, "What kind of auction – collector cars or antiques or art?"

"I'm not sure" answered Hezekiah.

"I thought these are boutique hotels…not auction houses" you stated.

"Me too" said Artie.

"Hezekiah call Buster and get me the schedule of auctions for their U.S. hotels. I may hop a flight to the next one if I can swing it" you stated.

"Hezekiah here, is Buster around?"

"Sorry sir, Buster's having dinner with some pretty ladies, may he call you in an hour?"

"Might you have the current auction schedule for Buster's hotels" Hezekiah asked.

"Yes, they're on our private website sir; would you like the url and password" she asked.

Hezekiah answered "Yes please."

"Emailing to your email Hezekiah. URL www.BustersAuctions.com; the password is: "$$WyzInvestorz19,"said Buster's assistant.

"Hey boss I'll forward to you Buster's email, site address and password for their auction schedule" stated Hezekiah.

"Got it Hezekiah" you responded.

Artie jumped in, "Buster's U.S. hotels flow cash like cows flow poop! If he can replicate the concept in Europe, Asia and Africa he'll make ungodly profits for you, Boss."

You shared – "Ungodly profits for ungodly investors. I guess it's the same money either way? Is there such a thing as godly profits? My crazy friend Maria says '*God owns the cattle on a thousand hills and everything under heaven is his*'. You believe this crap?"

"Yes we do" Hezekiah stated: "Me'n Artie are raised in the Jewish faith. We believe God's our Holy Father who watches over us and blesses our lives as we follow the teachings of the Torah (the Books of Moses: Genesis, Exodus, Leviticus, Numbers, Deuteronomy) we also await the coming of our Messiah to bring mankind and the Jewish people back go God."

"Impossible" you lamented.

"Why?" said Artie.

You wondered aloud, "So you dudes went to law school and tax accounting school and have been smart enough to advise me for twenty years? Through hundreds of transactions you've barely mentioned God to me – why not?"

"I guess we didn't want to offend you, boss" Artie replied.

"Yeah me too" said Hezekiah.

"Hezekiah, you've got a weird name – why'd your folks pick it" you asked.

Hezekiah said" he's a good king of Judah; the name means 'God is my strength"

"*This is what Hezekiah did throughout Judah, doing what was good and right and faithful before the Lord his God. In everything that he undertook in the service of God's temple and in obedience to the law and the commands, he sought his God and worked wholeheartedly. And so he prospered.*"
2 Chronicles 31:20-21   [1]

"Impressive – maybe good guys do prosper" you wondered. "I need to gain more wealth – it's a contest I must win. I covet the attention gained by wealth and fame but I despise losing the games of business or life, whatever that is, to anyone!"

Artie broached the very sensitive big question: "Boss, how many kids you think you've fathered? Just between us, no cameras running."

The Walk – S.B. Stone & Rock Solid Publishing, LLC
©2018

"I swear I've never met some of those greedy plaintiffs suing my ass and I've never had sex with them! The ones I've never slept with are gonna lose cuz their kids DNA didn't come from me. I'm okay with science and DNA, but I detest the mom's I slept with one to ten times who're suddenly showing up with an eight to twelve year old kid and a DNA test which says he or she is mine – 'surprise old man' the lady seems to smile!"

Artie the accountant continues to push you for a number: "Boss, we both know it's a game changer when your DNA's in a little boy or girl's saliva - the law says you and the mother are financially responsible for their support!"

You obviously agree, "It sucks. You want me to come up with a worst case scenario

Artie? I became sexually active at sixteen and I'm fifty-two frickin years old today."

"You're trying to alleviate the financial damages we're calculating – thirty six years of sleeping with almost any woman I'm attracted to: I'd say an average of a hundred a year Artie" you figured.

"Is one hundred women a year your worst case scenario, boss" Artie probed.

"Three or four years were three hundred! When you average it all out I suppose my worst case estimate's two hundred women a year" you said dispassionately.

"Holy crap! Seven thousand two hundred children you could be on the hook for boss!" You asked, "Artie you and Hezekiah have five kids between you right? "What's it cost per kid per year to feed and clothe and shelter them?"

Artie shared "At least twenty thousand dollars per kid. We send our kids to private schools so I've deducted it from my number, boss; last time I looked the national average was over two hundred thousand dollars to raise a kid through age seventeen in the U.S."

You grabbed your calculator: If every woman I had sex with got pregnant, I'd spend $1,440,000.000 raising my kids! I'd be ruined financially!"

"Not gonna happen boss but it's wise to prepare for the worst"

opined Hezekiah.

You added, "On the internet I read a study of when in their monthly cycle women tend to have the strongest libido – do you guys know?

Artie nodded while Hezekiah stated: "Ovulation – my wife can't keep her hands off me when she has the greatest likelihood of getting pregnant!"

"I used a condom when I was sixteen; haven't used one since" you shared.

You considered buying and renovating a hotel to provide a relatively safe and cost effective place for shelter and food. One of my so-called 'wives' says I oughta name my hotel "Paternity Place"

You definitely are your own god; you've loved the role! Painfully, you're confronting your lack of wisdom in many of your hormonally based decisions as a younger 'care free' dude.

****

Part Two: Man About Town

You're not a worrier.

Why are you anxious about Hezekiah's forwarded email from Buster Mahoney?

You went on Buster's Auction site, put in the password and the first page blew you away!

Little boys and girls and teens and adults in lurid poses offering to sell their bodies! More precisely, your old friend Buster Mahoney offering these innocent ones for sale!

The Walk – S.B. Stone & Rock Solid Publishing, LLC ©2018

You had no idea what to do so you went on a brisk walk to think this through! You often travel with a body guard or two; today you need privacy. Out of nowhere two large men pounce on you like lions! Instantly you switched from 'woe is me' to a **don't mess with me** mindset and fighting posture.

"Give us your wallet asshole - we'll let you live!"

"You picked the wrong guy at the wrong time" you muttered.

Plan A: you convert their size and momentum to your advantage.

In two minutes, each was laid out on the sidewalk…broken noses…kneecaps shattered…bleeding…immobilized. They're lucky. Plan B was to gouge their eyes out!

"Thank you for donating your Glock's and knives to my collection!"

Around the corner down 12th Street about five minutes after your "encounter" with the two thugs, you ran into your so-called friend, Maria Escobar, who had the audacity to invite you to church last month.

"What's up Maria - inviting me to church? Are my "no's" getting the best of you?"

Flashing her cute smile, Maria rebuffed, "I'm not sure if you're worth the trouble but I plan to keep on trying until you say yes or one of us dies first".

You have never been attracted to Maria. Your standards of beauty are exemplary; to you she's plain looking but may have a good heart.

"Hey Maria - interested in dinner tonight?"

"I'm in the mood for Chinese and famished since I missed breakfast and lunch today! One more thing I need to share - I'm an honest person – you need to let you know I have no romantic or sexual interest in you. Is that okay my friend?"

"Works for me, Maria."

"Been to Pig Heaven?" Maria suggested.

"Years ago" you replied.

The Walk – S.B. Stone & Rock Solid Publishing, LLC ©2018

"Been remodeled and under new management with Suckling Pig, Pork Soong minced with rice, peppers and pine nuts on a lettuce leaf like a Chinese taco; I dig their frozen Praline Mousse or Peking Snowball for dessert" Maria said licking her lips.

"You're making me hungry Maria, mind if we get a quiet table so we can talk? How long has it been since we've socialized…or hung out as the kids say. Was it your wedding reception?" you wondered.

"Maria, remember the International Law, Finance and Business classes we took at the same time? You were the only classmate who did well in those classes," you recalled.

"Why'd you ask me to dinner", Maria asked.

"I just needed to have dinner with a friendly face with no other agenda tonight."

Maria asked, "How'd you get those scratches? You should wash up in the men's room; I promise I won't bail on you."

"Good idea, I'll be right back Maria" you replied, "mind ordering some bread, cheese and wine?"

"Works for me. I promise not to invite you to church while we're eating dinner" Maria conceded.

"Are you sure Maria? Won't God be angry with you for not inviting your lost friend to church?"

"God's not angry with me. He's forgiven all my sins – past, present and future. I'm confident God will let me know when and if He wants me to invite you to church again" clarified

Maria.

"What do you mean by "if" you should invite me to church?"

"I use "if" just in case you're dead', Maria said. "When your heart's not beating it's impossible for your brain to listen to the truth and make a decision; you'll have missed your opportunity to believe in Jesus – you've had decades to make your choice."

Maria asked, "Are you breathing right now?"

You replied, "Of course I am breathing. Otherwise how could we be eating dinner and having this conversation, Maria?"

The Walk – S.B. Stone & Rock Solid Publishing, LLC
©2018

Maria added, "The fact you're breathing is <u>proof</u> God's not given up on you my friend!"

You responded, "Yeah, I get it Maria. If I die tonight there'll be no more chances for me."

"May I ask you a personal question" Maria requested.

"Yes Maria, I'm an open book for one question, okay?"

"Thank you for being open and here goes – please tell me kind and wonderful sir, exactly how old are you" asked Maria.

"Boy Maria you are really sucking up to me. I already told you I'd pay for dinner?

What else do you hope to gain from our time together tonight?

"Why do you think I'm sucking up to you?"

"No one's ever accused me of being 'kind and wonderful' so I've gotta conclude you have a hidden agenda for us having dinner tonight" you argued.

"Whom asked whom out for dinner" my poor sucked up to victim" grinned Maria.

You groveled, "My bad Maria - I asked you to dinner, didn't I?"

"You are correct sir" said Maria.

"Didn't your parents or siblings feel you were nice to them" Maria asked?

You replied, "Not really. As far as I could tell they were afraid of me. I was the youngest of my siblings and constantly in a war for survival. I was smaller and weaker so I chose to be stronger mentally and <u>pretend</u> I was not afraid of them. Eventually the tables turned when I beat the snot out of my oldest brother."

"Am I going to learn your age before dessert tonight" Maria smiled.

The Walk – S.B. Stone & Rock Solid Publishing, LLC
©2018

You replied, "I am fifty-two years young - to be honest I feel ten years older. Other days I feel ten years younger which is an absolute pleasure!"

"Seriously? I thought you're forty-five" Maria winked.

"There you go flattering me again, Maria" you smiled back.

"I suppose I have to admit I know we have to be somewhat close in age since we attended the same high school at the same time, right?" asked Maria.

"Correct. I recall a cute little sophomore flirting in the all between classes. I was a senior, so I'd have to guess you were two to three years younger than I was?"

"Yes, I'm fifty old man."

"I'm impressed with the range in tactics you're employing Maria - sweet talking to insulting – the "nice man" who's buying dinner" you admitted.

You're strangely attracted to Maria's sense of humor with no idea where this will end, but you're enjoying the ride!

"Hello. Is anyone home in there" Maria asked curiously.

"I was lost in thought" you admitted.

"You're thinking about me, aren't you - dirty old man."

"Guilty as charged your honor – I'm perplexed since you're the first woman I'm physically attracted to - plus something else" you admitted.

"What do you mean when you say, plus something else", Maria probed.

You're thinking it's time to shift the conversation!

"Hey Maria, ten minutes before we bumped into each other on the corner at Twelfth Street, I was mugged by two thieves trying to steal my wallet. Those bastards saw how short and scrawny I am; figured I'd be an easy hit" you shared.

"Explains the scratches on your face - how big are those jerks" asked Maria.

The Walk – S.B. Stone & Rock Solid Publishing, LLC
©2018

"Six foot two; two-twenty apiece and focused on grabbing my wallet and knocking me down by with their size and strength I definitely got the best of them" you shared.

"Great news! Otherwise I could've found you unconscious in a dark alley! I'd need to have dinner alone again," Maria sighed.

"How tall and heavy are you? Let me venture a guess. I'd say you're five foot eight and a beasty one hundred sixty pounds" Maria offered.

You chuckled - "Your powers of observation and analysis are remarkable. I'm especially pleased you're alluding to my build as 'beasty'; as a boy I was a frequent target for bullies so I acquired skills to make their lives less easy when I was around."

Maria gave a thumbs up saying "Good for you - bad news for them."

"Mom said bullies are really cowards in large bodies; my first weapon was to overpower them psychologically. If one bully sees me kicking another bully in the nuts or beating on the face of his bully friends, they feared me from then on. I pretended to be angry and vicious like I hated bullies and even wanted to kill them. In truth I felt sorry for those losers, but they had no clue I empathized."

"You had to know you'd eventually run into someone bigger, stronger, faster or better trained than you" wondered Maria.

"Yes, I'm a practical man who loves to win. I knew eventually I'd run into a dude who'd not be intimidated and likely possessed superior fighting skills than I. By age twelve, I researched and home studied several martial art disciplines like boxing, karate, silat, kung-foo and krav maga. In high school I took up wrestling so I could fight people my size and quickness - undefeated my senior year."

"Wow - I'm impressed - a five foot eight, fifty-two year old man who loves to fight" observed Maria.

"Not exactly an accurate statement, Maria. May I clarify for you" you requested.

"Of course - you know I like to be accurate and truthful so I'm pleased to see my friends using the same discipline" said Maria.

"Good Maria - the truth about me is I love winning and hate losing. As the youngest of ten kids, practically every day until high school, I lost a fight to one of my larger, stronger and craftier siblings. By age twelve I mastered how to turn my losing into winning in the proving ground of my family. I was big enough I to threaten to do unpleasant things like kicking, hitting or biting – anything to do damage to my siblings."

"I retained Mom and Dad as my advisors in my war against nine mean siblings who'd abuse my body, damage my self-esteem and steal my prospects for success in life. I was an expert at creating drama, looking like the victim and using it to my advantage on a daily basis until I was out of the house. I chuckle when seeing parents and kids in similar contests with "drama kings and queens" in their lives. In business, I create advantage by spotting a man or woman attempting to exert undue influence on a company to bolster his career while harming the company's objectives and future."

"Enough about me Maria, what've you been up to since grad school" you asked.

"Did you know Billie Henklee from NYU" Maria recalled.

"Of course, wasn't Billie Henklee the tall handsome dude who couldn't keep his eyes off you?" you observed.

"Yes, he's the one", Maria acknowledged with a big smile; "I had a strong desire to get married and begin a family while my husband and I were young."

You reply, "Sounds like worthy objectives Maria! Not sure why I've never had those objectives to be honest."

"You may recall Billie was an open book? If his mind was processing, Billie was simultaneously talking with whomever was in the room with him – could be a total stranger and Billie happily shared his thoughts."

"Billie's a more transparent man than I'd ever be" you agreed.

The Walk – S.B. Stone & Rock Solid Publishing, LLC ©2018

Maria added, "I learned Billie wasn't always seeking feedback from me - he's simply processing his life and thoughts out loud and I had the privilege of being in the room with Billie. As a woman who loves communication, I was hooked by how open and vulnerable Billie was - even early in our relationship."

"We got married two years after grad school? I think we invited you to our wedding, didn't we?"

"Yes, you invited me - I brought you the Dalton china table setting" you said.

"Impressive – thirty years and you remember the wedding gift you gave?" Maria exclaimed.

"Did you and Billie relocate? I didn't see or hear or bump into either of you for quite a long time after the wedding" you noted.

"We sort of relocated", Maria recalled, "Billie's new job was a German-based company. They liked his four years of German in high school and college and loved his strong work ethic and amiable personality. They hoped he'd fast track into management as their American team and sales volume grew."

"Sounds promising" you observed but sensing bad news ahead.

"The downside to Billie's job was the company insisted Billie receive the initial twelve months of training take place at their home office in Frankfurt Germany!"

"Bummer – this isn't fair for a newly married couple!" you observed.

"I obviously agree with you. Besides back then Billie and I had no practical life or business experience – from apartment rent to buying a car or a suit we hadn't a clue how to negotiate anything! I had a good job in town so we agreed I'd keep my job at least until we'd saved enough to buy a place."

You agreed, "Sounds like both of you had a fair amount of common sense, especially for a young married couple."

"Thanks for the compliment" Maria responded.

The Walk – S.B. Stone & Rock Solid Publishing, LLC
©2018

"Fortunately Billie's boss knew we hadn't saved much money so they offered to pay for flying me to Germany once a month; plus they offered to fly Billie back to the States on alternate months."

"Excellent!" you added. Did Billie stay and did they honor their commitments to you and Billie?"

"Billie died six months and seven days after our wedding date."

You saw immense pain in Maria's eyes. "Are you serious, Maria? Please tell me you're kidding me, and Billie will walk into this place to join us for dinner, Maria!"

"Oh how I wish I were joking" said Maria.

Maria broke into tears over losing the love of her life. You wrapped your strong arms around Maria - the only thing you can do right now.

Maria's chest was throbbing; she continued weeping with her head on your chest - you had no idea how to best comfort for your friend [I'm no good at this said a voice] but you kept her close. You surmised words aren't always necessary.

You're not sure why you knew this wasn't your final dinner with Maria – only one week until you met again for dinner - why did it feel like a month for you?

In the ensuing dinners…and lunches…and breakfasts you began to fall in love with Maria. Maria explained why losing Billie created bigger challenges than she'd ever anticipated

"I waited my whole life, twenty-four years, to meet and marry the man of my dreams!

Tell me why in heaven's name God took my sweet husband away from me?"

You had no idea what to say to Maria's broken hearted question.

"Maria, I don't know God or Jesus, but if I did know Him I'd ask this question:

Jesus. Why do bad things happen to good people?

Billie would have said God loves us so much he sometimes tests our faith in Him:

"The testing of your faith develops perseverance."

"Nothing in life is more important than your relationship with me; this is why I command you to love God with all your heart, all your soul, all your mind and all your strength."

"Billie loved to watch me walk out my life with Jesus but after our wedding Billie and my job became like gods or idols to me. I stopped reading the Bible and stopped praying to the point Billie said, 'Maria, I fear you love me and your work more than you love God.' I argued with him, but he was right – I was putting Billie ahead of God. In contrast, Billie said Jesus is my CEO at work, at home and everywhere else."

You asked, "How did that make you feel, Maria?"

Maria said, "I felt proud of Billie and embarrassed for myself."

"I understand' you agreed.

Maria added, "Billie was a <u>good man</u> and true follower of Jesus so I'm certain his spirit went to be with Jesus after his body died - Billie's freer and happier than on earth" Maria shared.

You said, "Does it provide consolation for you Maria?"

"No doubt Billie's death was a bad thing for me but I sought God's comfort and grew closer to God/Jesus in my suffering" Maria shared.

"In the Bible, Jesus said *'Come to me, all you who are weary and burdened, and I will give you rest.'*" Matthew 11:28 [1]

Naively you asked, "How do you know there is a heaven in the first place?"

"Have you read the Bible?" Maria asked patiently.

Humbly you admitted, "I have not read the Bible. My parents had five Bibles around the house. I never saw Dad or Mom reading it – they never quoted scripture as I was growing up. I'm not an idiot, Maria! If the Bible and God who supposedly wrote it are <u>not important</u> to my parents, why should I make it important to me?"

"I'm so sorry your parents were a horrible example for you - would it be okay if I read the Bible to you right now?"

"The whole thing?" you asked.

"I'm pretty sure we won't be able to read the Bible in one sitting – I'll just share a few passages okay?"

"Yes, I want to hear parts of the Bible most important to you but please don't forget the parts about Heaven?" "I won't" said Maria.

"Cool" you agreed.

Maria began, "Jesus told his men he was going to die on the cross, rise from the grave on the third day, then leave them to join His Father in heaven."

"'They must have been angry and sad!" you said.

Maria agreed, "You're exactly right but Jesus shared these words of encouragement:

"Do not let your hearts be troubled. You believe in God: believe also in me. My Father's house has many rooms; if that were not so, would I have told you that I am going there to prepare a place for you? And if I go and prepare a place for you, I will come back and take you to be with me that you also may be where I am. You know the way to the place where I am going." John 14:1-4 [1]

Maria added: "The Bible describes heaven in many ways – check it out."

"Then the angel showed me the river of the water of life, as clear as crystal, flowing from the throne of God and of the Lamb down the middle of the great street of the city. On each side of the river stood the tree of life, bearing twelve crops of fruit, yielding its fruit every month. And the leaves of the tree are for the healing of the nations. No longer will there be any curse. The throne of God and of the Lamb will be in the city, and his servants will serve him. They will see his face, and his name will be on their foreheads. There will be no more night. They will not

need the light of a lamp or the light of the sun, for the Lord God will give them light. And they will reign for ever and ever. The angel said to me, "These words are trustworthy and true. The Lord, the God who inspires the prophets, sent his angel to show his servants the things that must soon take place." "Look, I am coming soon! Blessed is the one who keeps the words of the prophecy written in this scroll."   *Revelation 22:1 – 10*   [1]

Maria shared: "Yes, Jesus assured Billie he'd be with him in heaven because Billie chose to be a disciple (serious follower) of Jesus Christ earlier in his life; many friends chose against following God and did drugs, alcohol, porn and sex but Billie saw his friends making stupid choices, he made the choice to crown Jesus Lord of his life."

You asked, "Did Billie become a disciple of Jesus before he died?

"God gives every person a personal choice. Billie made the decision to follow Jesus. He showed the authenticity of his decision by obeying Jesus principles and by words and deeds done in service to others…including me as his wife. Billie was a decent but sinful man before he became a disciple of Jesus. Without a doubt, Jesus made Billie a whole lot better! Billie once shared: 'Maria, I love the incredible freedom of no longer feeling guilty for my sins!'"

You interjected, "I don't feel guilty for my sins, but I'm certain the list of my sins is pages longer than sweet young Billie's."

"Here's another Bible verse for you", Maria added.

"The Lord works righteousness and justice for all the oppressed. He made known his ways to Moses, his deeds to the people of Israel:

The Lord is compassionate and gracious, slow to anger, abounding in love. He will not always accuse, nor will he harbor his anger forever; he does not treat us as our sins deserve or repay us according to our iniquities. For as high as the heavens are above the earth, so great is his love for those who fear him; as far as the east is from the west, so far has he removed our transgressions from us. As a father has compassion on his children, so the Lord has compassion on those who fear him; for he knows how we are formed, he remembers that we are dust."

Psalm 103:6-14   [1]

Maria clarified the psalmist's point by asking you a zinger - "do you fear God?"

You replied, "I'm not sure if I fear God. I do fear dying since I have no idea what's on the other side of death – it's a scary way to live."

Maria agreed, "I'd be terrified in your shoes – you're not sure God exists and we can't blame our lack of faith on our parents."

"I am terrified," you admitted!

"The wrath of God is being revealed from heaven against all the godlessness and wickedness of people, who suppress the truth by their wickedness, since what may be known about God is plain to them, because God has made it plain to them. For since the creation of the world God's invisible qualities—his eternal power and divine nature—have been clearly seen, being understood from what has been made, so that people are without excuse."
Romans 1:19 – 20   [1]

I have an idea Maria suggested, "Can you walk with me through the last month of your life my friend?

"I'm not sure what you mean, Maria."

"Share at least ten things you experienced during the past thirty days that gave you pleasure – not sexual pleasure please."

"Probably…but why?"

"Just trust me."

"Okay" you agreed.

"1. Having dinner with you; 2.going on a walk with my grandson; 3.playing racquetball with a friend; 4.buying a stealth dinner for a big family; 5.giving a prostitute and her kids free rent at one of my properties; 6.not getting beat up by the two men who attacked me; 7.I might be falling in love; 8.my CPA says my net worth's greater than I thought; 9. I'm learning about God;

10. TBD.

"That's a great list but I confess I have no idea what a "stealth dinner" is. Can you explain? Also you said you might be falling in love. Who's the lucky girl" asked Maria.

You replied: "No problem. A stealth dinner is where you secretly pay a stranger's check. I prefer my beneficiary has no idea it's me so I pre-arrange with the cashier so they never even see their dinner bill. It's a lot of fun to watch people's reactions…especially those who appear to be having a tough time paying their bills in the first place."

Maria shared "Fascinating – where'd you get the idea?"

You replied, "This is a bit of a side story but you might find it interesting, okay with you Maria?"

Maria replied, "You haven't put me to sleep yet, nor have we ordered dessert - go for it!"

You began, "My former partner, Zeke, and I hosted a business dinner with three intelligent and lovely sisters - Anna, Veronika and Diana Ivanov, prospective investors in my apartment project at the River Café on Water Street in Brooklyn. Our guests ordered Crescent Farms Duck, Atlantic Halibut and Organic Chicken and I ordered the Lamb. Zeke was craving the Caspian Sea Golden Osetra, Acipenser Gueldenstaedtii, Caviar service at $180.00 an ounce!"

"The tab for five was $2,000 including two drinks apiece, before tips! Zeke's share of the damage was close to $1,000! I should have insisted Zeke write me a check for it! Despite Zeke's extravagance we became partners with the sisters but Anna said Zeke's behavior nearly killed the deal especially when Zeke failed to share his $180 per ounce Caviar with our three guests!"

"Anna asked her sisters: are we wise to invest ten million U.S. dollars with a man who refuses to be generous and thoughtful at the dinner table? Her sisters reminded Anna our last name Ivanov means 'son of Ivan' and Ivan means 'God's grace'. Should we not extend grace to Zeke and his first class partner?"

"In the end, the Ivanov sisters said my kindness and generosity closed the deal for them:

Your wife is blessed to have you!"

Maria observed, "Wish I was with you at this exciting dinner!"

You agreed: "Me too but I noticed my thoughts and words were less inclined toward plotting how I might take advantage of the Ivanov sisters in a sexual way. This is new for me - do I need to take a testosterone pill?"

"You make me smile funny man – you want the truth?

"Of course I want the truth," you insisted.

"Wait did you forget about your stealth dinner story?"

"I'm sorry - as we were walking out from our expensive dinner, I waived bye to Stanley the maître d. Stanley's an old friend of mine. While staring at our $2,000 check, Stanley whispered, 'well my friend I suppose you won't receive a stealth dinner tonight!'"

"Stanley, I thought I was a man of the world - what on earth is a stealth dinner?"

Stanley patiently enlightened me: "Rest assured sir, even a man of the world learns new things - a stealth dinner occurs when someone picks up the tab for you, and if the benefactor remains anonymous it is a stealth dinner."

"Make sense Maria?"

"Yes completely" Maria nodded.

"So Maria, why do you think I was not interested in a sexual escapade with the Ivanov sisters? It's not who I am. I've had sex with more women than I can remember. I'm not sure why I'm beginning to look at women differently…as God's creatures…all beautiful and worthy of my respect?"

Maria agreed, "This respecting of all women is a good thing my friend."

You said, "Good Maria. By the way you need to know I have many children -twenty or more thanks to DNA tests. I have no clue what the total is but I am certain their mothers would be ecstatic to get my checks, don't you think?"

"A popular man you would be. I could see every mother who's known you sexually having her child tested" Maria thought.

You added, "I've received many marriage proposals or demands in some cases."

Maria frowned, "you poor old rascal you must be broke – I'll buy our dinners awhile!"

"Can you keep a secret, Maria? My net worth's tripled since I took responsibility for financially supporting my kids. But I suck at giving emotional support, Maria. I have no clue how to step up to that plate! It is huge and intimidating for me - way tougher than the guys whose asses I kicked before running into you the other night."

"Maria, would it be okay if we had dinner again tomorrow?"

"I'll check my schedule."

"Maria, can we go to your church Sunday? I want to ask God a question."

"You sweet man – don't you know you can talk to God from anywhere in the universe?"

"Wow God is powerful…he must get tired from everyone talking to him."

I think I'll give it a shot: "Dear God. Thank you for helping me conquer my fears of getting beat up and for giving me many girlfriends and at least twenty kids, possibly hundreds or thousands and great financial success and for keeping me out of prison and giving me Maria to admire and spend time with."

You hung your head…buried it in your hands stammering asking God and Maria, "Dear God, dear Jesus. **Why am I so afraid of death?**"

Maria answered calmly, Jesus would reply:

"…when the Lord Jesus is revealed from heaven with His mighty angels in a flame of fire, 8dealing out [full and complete] vengeance to those who do not [seek to] know God and to those who ignore and refuse to obey the gospel of our Lord Jesus [by choosing not to respond to Him]. 9These people will pay the

The Walk – S.B. Stone & Rock Solid Publishing, LLC ©2018

penalty and endure the punishment of Not annihilation, but the loss of all meaningful things. everlasting destruction, banished from the presence of the Lord and from the glory of His power, 10when He comes to be glorified in His saints on that day [that is, glorified through the changed lives of those who have accepted Him as Savior and have been set apart for His purpose], and to be marveled at among all who have believed, because our testimony to you was believed and trusted [and confirmed in your lives]. 11With this in view, we constantly pray for you, that our God will count you worthy of your calling [to faith] and with [His] power fulfill every desire for goodness, and complete [your] every work of faith, 12so that the name of our Lord Jesus will be glorified in you [by what you do], and you in Him, according to the [precious] grace of our God and the Lord Jesus Christ." 2 Thessalonians 1:7b – 12 [4]

Maria added, "you've lived 52 years of ignoring and disobeying God. You fear death because no one wants flames and misery and missing out on God's heaven! **You need God's love and forgiveness; instead are fearful because you have no hope!**

God is love. When we take up permanent residence in a life of love, we live in God and God lives in us. This way, love has the run of the house, becomes at home and mature in us, so that we're free of worry on Judgment Day—our standing in the world is identical with Christ's. There is no room in love for fear. Well-formed love banishes fear. Since fear is crippling, a fearful life— fear of death, fear of judgment—is one not yet fully formed in love. 1 John 4:17a [3]

Matthew 10:28 (MSG)

"Don't be bluffed into silence by the threats of bullies. There's nothing they can do to your soul, your core being. Save your fear for God, who holds your entire life—body and soul— in his hands.

Maria suggested God may add: "While God welcomes the praises of an authentically grateful heart, your praises <u>cannot erase the guilt</u> you must bear for the evil thoughts and evil words and evil deeds you have done. In your heart you know you don't remotely deserve entry into my perfect and holy heaven! Every person in my creation has an eternal soul built into them. When your body dies, your eternal soul lives forever in heaven or in hell – <u>there's no middle ground</u>."

Maria added. "My friend, with all your money you can travel to any nation you choose, but you won't be granted admission unless you have what critical thing in your possession?"

"Of course Maria, I must have my passport. Without it I don't get in" you admitted.

Maria, said, "<u>Jesus blood is your only passport into God's heaven</u>. Nothing cleans up your wicked heart and devious mind like Jesus precious blood, my friend."

"Maria, I'm confused, help me understand how the blood of God's Son dying over two thousand years ago cleanses me in the 21ˢᵗ Century from my sins yesterday, today and tomorrow?" you wondered.

Maria clarified, "That's been God's program for thousands of years – without the shedding of blood mankind enjoys no forgiveness for our sins. Jesus IS the one and only Lamb of God who died once for ALL mankind. By deciding to <u>invest your faith</u> in God's offer of forgiveness through the shed blood of His one and only Son - <u>the</u> only Passport into Heaven."

You conceded, "Incredible - How do I get it? Where can I buy it, Maria?"

"God doesn't need your money - everything you own belongs to God!"

"Are you serious?" you lamented.

Maria responded, "The only thing God requires is YOU. Your heart, your soul, your mind, your body is what God wants."

"Wow - sounds like it's my choice to make," you observed.

The Walk – S.B. Stone & Rock Solid Publishing, LLC
©2018

Maria agreed, "I've discovered almost every day I have chances to re-iterate my choice to follow God as I get to know Him better as He walks through life with me."

"God requires you to live your life by faith in Him!"

"Your heart suddenly felt guilty before God so you bowed your head and prayed: "Holy God, please forgive massive boatload filled with my sins of mind, words and body! God I pledge to you all my heart, all my soul, all my mind and all my strength! I will work hard to focus on loving my neighbor as myself. God and Jesus please adopt me into your family and show me how to love each one of my children for the rest of my days!"

"That's beautiful" Maria smiled brightly.

Tears streaming you gazed at Maria: "Maria I have a question for you?"

"Yes my friend! Why are you on your knees?"

"Sweet Maria, I have a burning question: will you do me the honor and privilege of partnering with me?" your face intense.

"You want a business partner?" asked Maria.

"I'm fifty-two years old, never been married and I'm falling in love with you, Maria. Will you please be my wife?" you begged.

You were already nervous and could tell Maria was surprised and you added: "We'll have a ready-made family of at least twenty kids – guess I don't know if that's a selling point or not?"

Maria was close to your age; yet she emanated a beautiful thirty-something radiance pulsing around her as she deeply contemplated the prospect of investing the rest of her life with a wealthy but clearly messed up man with so many kids! Does she want a child of her own?

Maria's mind was racing: "this dude is **high risk**; low respect for women; hates to lose; does he even know how to tenderly, sacrificially love a woman? Will his new relationship with Jesus stand the test of time and multifarious temptations of life?

The Walk – S.B. Stone & Rock Solid Publishing, LLC
©2018

Seemed like eternity…her face still glowing…eyes bright and smiling…Maria muscled into a sterner face to say: "I have an answer if you are manly enough and think you can handle it?"

Tears in your eyes, voice cracking, you begged, please tell me your conditions Maria! I don't deserve your affection or devotion or God's forgiveness!"

+++++++++++++++++++++++++++++++++

Thank you for reading <u>Man About Town</u>. We'd love your feedback regarding what

Stories/Episodes you'd like to see in <u>The Walk – Part Two</u>. Email us at <u>Feedback@TheWalk.me</u>.

To purchase visit <u>www.thewalk.me</u> and/or to reserve a copy of our next book and to buy a copy for your friend or colleague.

The Walk – Episode Four: Sweet Sixteen

Today's your birthday!

You're oblivious to the predator awaiting you!

Life is safe and comfortable in Seattle, Washington.

You're blessed with loving parents who saved for a year to create a memorable debt-free surprise sweet sixteen party for you and three best friends.

"Who's the turkey who set my alarm for 6:00 a.m.? What's with the packed suitcase –

where am I going? Tone down the noise. I need my beauty sleep!"

You hear friend's voices and bolt downstairs elated to see Beka, Halee and Ava smiling widely and strangely awake at your breakfast table.

"I can't believe this! Am I dreaming? Is this my first ever surprise birthday party?

The Walk – S.B. Stone & Rock Solid Publishing, LLC ©2018

On cue, they chimed, "We'll hug you like crazy so you know it's really us - not a dream."

Your brother Charlie interrupted, "Hey little sis, guess where you're going?"

"Do you guys know" you asked Ava, Halee and Beka.

Ava jumped in, "we're bursting to tell you!"

"Open your card could be a clue or two inside" smiled Mom.

You tore it open revealing all the clues you needed: "Wowee kazowee, we have four Alaska Airline tickets to Orange County, California plus four passes to Disneyworld and five nights in the Marriot Anaheim Hotel plus two hundred dollars cash for me, Ava, Beka and

Halee!

Thoughtfully Mom wondered "Hmmm – Dad is she worth such an extravagant party?"

"Of course you're worth it sweetheart" added Dad. Big brother Charlie admitted, "On my sixteenth birthday, Mom and Dad gave me new golf clubs and took me golfing and fishing in Florida – what a blast - now it's your turn Sis - hey maybe you want your dear sweet big bro to tag along?"

You considered Charlie's idea, "you are sweet big bro but this journey's for ladies only; besides aren't you still fighting the flu?"

You, Charlie and Dad nearly postponed your "non-surprise" party and sleepover with school friends. As planned, they announced the "surprise" aspects of your real party at breakfast on your birthday. Dad says: "life and birthdays are a gift from God and today's birthday proves you've breathed enough breaths to live 365 days all the way to this one."

Dad rises at 12:01 am on his birthday to experience all 24 hours if he can remain awake; Gramma says – "Dad was ten when he got the bright idea to try staying up all 24 hours – he'd fall back asleep before the sun rose – nearly missing his birthday breakfast!"

The Walk – S.B. Stone & Rock Solid Publishing, LLC
©2018

Mom was not her normally exuberant self. When she gave you a half-hearted birthday hug you could tell she's not feeling well: "Oh no Mom – I thought you escaped the nasty flu me,

Dad and Charlie endured?"

"Honey, I have a headache and touch of nausea…feeling weaker like I may be coming down with a fever. Isn't it what you, Dad and Charlie had?" Mom asked.

"Yes, Mom, the symptoms sound familiar - darn it, I thought you were spared", you said.

Mom lamented, "I was going to ride shotgun to the airport with you and Dad for your 8:00 am flight – I better go back to bed so I don't pass it to your friends."

"Not to worry, Nurse Ava assured, Halee, Beka and I already had the yucky crud."

Hailee added and Beka nodded - "Yep Ava's right and if it makes you feel any better, I think we passed it on to you guys Mrs. Hardy."

Your Mom asked Charlie if he minded staying home with her.

"No problem", said Charlie masking displeasure – dying to ride shotgun with a serious crush on Halee - four years his junior and snatched.

Charlie was privy to only one of the reasons he stayed home with Mom. Dad booked a flight to Santa Ana Airport and a room in the west wing of the Marriot Hotel where his sister and friends were in the south wing.

Dad boarded the plane looking to row fifteen where your tickets specified. You were missing! You found the most senior flight attendant: "Excuse me Scottie – I need to know if my daughter and three girlfriends are aboard."

"Could this be our delirious sweet sixteen party group" suggested Scottie.

"Sorry Scottie I'm Hank Hardy – not sure I'll admit any affiliation with those hooligans just yet."

The Walk – S.B. Stone & Rock Solid Publishing, LLC
©2018

Scottie went on, "We moved em to first class which explains why we see three boys and a father in their original seats – we had four first class no-shows and our generous captain surmised this to be a fun birthday surprise."

"Scottie, be sure to thank he captain the girls have no idea I followed them and from a father's perspective the girls are young innocent and vulnerable. I'll be in stealth mode for the flight, hotel and Disneyland until I safely return all four girls back home to their parents" Dad shared.

Scottie got the message, "Mr. Hardy, you're remaining on board near the back row opposite side of the plane? Shall I alert our first class flight attendant you're on board?"

"Good idea" Dad said. "You have kids Scottie?"

"Yes, finally - we've tried six years with zero pregnancies" Scottie lamented.

Dad said, "You must have felt hopeless!"

"My wife, Molly, listed everything we tried to make it happen. I looked at her list and added, 'there's one thing I've not tried yet, honey. You know I don't believe in God so it's illogical and intellectually dishonest for me to ask God to help us have a baby" Scottie shared.

Dad said, "What'd she say and what'd you do Scottie?"

My sweet and polite wife said: "We're talking about our future kid so shove your asinine logic up your place where the sun never shines dude!"

Dad smiled, "I like this gal Molly!"

"Her voice was soft; her words powerful" Scottie conceded. "I knelt beside Molly as she was sleeping…I wept softly…and I begged the God I didn't believe in to give us a child."

Dad asked "Did He?"

Scottie continued "My wife's a nurse. The following week one of her patient's Sarah Sims, took a serious turn for the worse; hit her call button and explained to Molly:

"Dr. Walton said my tumor's inoperable. I'll be gone in a month…or less"

"I'm so sorry Sarah. I don't want you to leave us. You're so vibrant and full of life" Molly empathized.

Sarah continued, "Speaking of full of life – I'm sure you've noticed I'm a bit hefty around the middle since I'm at thirty weeks now and the baby's healthy as a horse!"

"Yes, we've been watching both of you" Molly admitted.

"Sorry Hank, uh Mr. Hardy forgot I've got eighty passengers to care for and two of them are calling me right now!"

"No problem Scottie, I'll sneak a peek at the girls and hope to hear the rest soon."

"Cool" said Scottie on the run.

Dad's quick peak at you, Ava, Halee and Beka was ill-timed as a very large man and overloaded beverage cart seemed to block both aisles; plus two rows in front of your seat, a baby was screaming like a jet engine – drawing everyone's eyes including the girls now starring in Dad's direction!

You know Hank Hardy's an on fleek dresser – at work nice suits, button down collars, tasteful ties and Bostonian or Florsheim shoes. Off work or on vacation, Dad looks good in classic print shirts, button down collars and Dockers slacks and refuses to wear blue jeans saying: "If we ever own a ranch or farm you might catch me in jeans."

Consistent with stealth mode Dad wore Levis blue jeans, big ugly sunglasses, wide brim Aussie hat and UCLA Bruin sweatshirt! As a USC alum Dad won't be caught dead in UCLA stuff!

Dad taught you to formulate "contingency plans" in life. He knew how he would explain himself if you or your friends saw him on the plane or in the hotel or at Disneyland: "Precious girls, is it possible to be 'too safe' in your life? The fact I've secretly joined you on this trip does not mean I don't trust you, but of how I deeply care for you and want to 'be there' if an emergency arises."

The Walk – S.B. Stone & Rock Solid Publishing, LLC
©2018

In school, you were warned to avoid creepy "pimps" who lure young girls and boys who are lonely or lost or in distress suffering from poor relationships at home. You had no idea what a pimp was.

Beka said "Pimps are good actors who pretend to care about us so we feel safe in their presence; they offer to help with directions or provide a ride in an adult's car or van." You and your friends promised each other:

1. Never talk with a pimp, if you ever meet one. 2. Never leave your friends alone. 3. Always travel in groups. 4. Never enter a stranger's vehicle.

"Honor Student Kidnapped"

"Twelve Year Old Raped"

"Young Boy Abducted – Whereabouts Unknown"

"Eighth Grader's Soda Laced With Deadly Drugs"

"Twelve Year Old Girl Sold As Sex Slave"

"Dream Jobs In Exotic Places"

Brutal men and women will use your child's innocent body for their own sexual pleasure and happily sell your body and your freedom to total strangers as a sex slaves.

The ads sound like a legitimate job with travel and adventure: Victims discover it's an evil scam as they're displayed like merchandise in a store window or dancing girls in a club for sex to anyone who will pay their captors price.

The Walk – S.B. Stone & Rock Solid Publishing, LLC
©2018

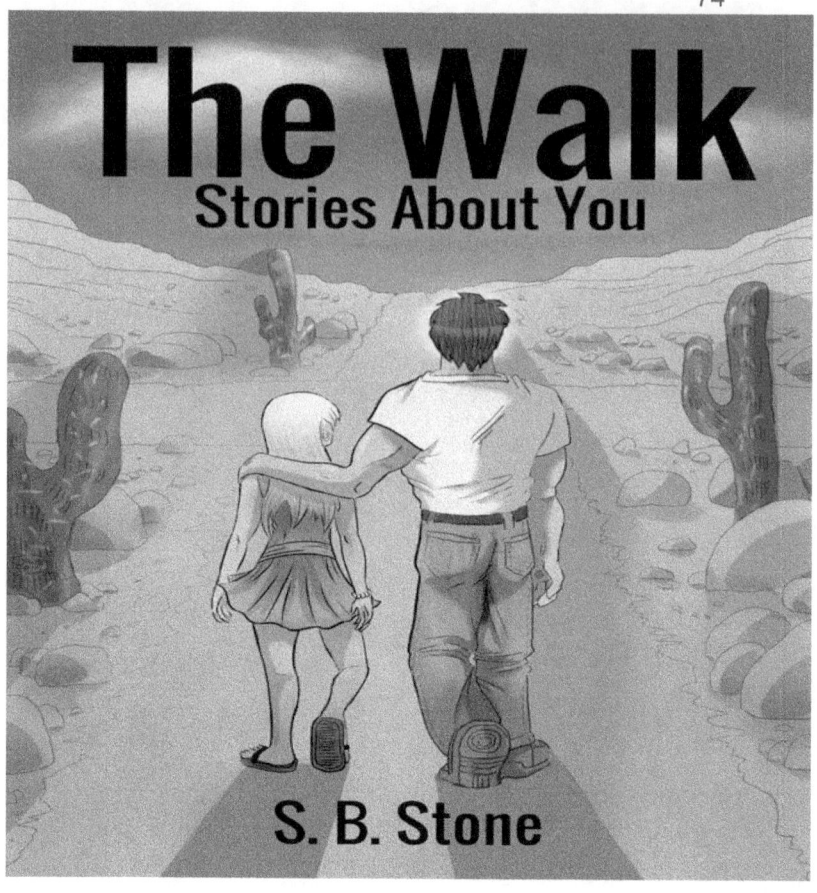

"I can't believe how much fun I'm having flying first class with you Ava and Halee and Beka! – Is it rude for us to ask why they put us in first class?"

"Ask away" offered Ava.

"Excuse me miss - can you tell us why we were relocated to the first class cabin?"

"Why?" she smiled. "Don't you like first class? If you prefer coach, I can move you back to the cheaper seats."

"No way" you replied. Just curious - will it cost my parents more money cuz you moved us to first class?"

"Smart question - the answer is no, we had four no-shows in first class; our captain heard we have a VIP celebrating her sixteenth birthday with three lovely friends – I'm cool with you calling me Stacy."

"Thanks Stacy, I'm cool with you calling me Ava - what's a VIP passenger?"

"'VIP' is an acronym for Very Important Person," Stacy replied smiling.

"So a VIP could be a pop singer like Taylor Swift or an Olympic athlete like Michael Phelps or a famous actor like Robert Downey Jr?" clarified Beka.

"You got it!" Stacy commended.

"Can't most VIP's afford to buy first class seats?" asked Ava.

"Good question. First class costs two to three times the price of a coach flight – sometimes a lot more. In the U.S. our average domestic coach flight is $360" Stacy added, "which explains why we have less than ten percent of our seats dedicated to first class. Make no mistake, our plush and comfy seats and the cabin's roomy and private layout, plus gourmet cuisine like filet mignon or lobster for dinner and champagne and amazing entertainment is a perfect travel option for the right customer."

Halee interjected, "Very cool to be VIP's on my best friend's birthday. Can we meet the captain - to thank him in person?"

"Of course" agreed Stacy. "After we reach altitude, I'll ask if he's got a minute to say hello to you all."

Ninety minutes into the flight you didn't see Dad checking in on you, Ava, Beka and Halee. He was happy to see you all sound asleep in your comfy seats with extra pillows provided by Stacy.

Dad placed his index finger against his mouth to signal Stacy, then he whispered, "My name is Hank Hardy. My daughter and her friends think I'm at home. As a protective Dad, I can't resist secretly tagging along to make sure the girls are safe - understood?"

"Oh yes sir" whispered Stacy with her finger against her mouth, "I promise not to breathe a word to the girls."

Dad gave a thumbs up and a nod to Stacy.

The Walk – S.B. Stone & Rock Solid Publishing, LLC
©2018

Instinctively Dad/aka Hank Hardy softly kissed you and each of your friends on your sweet and beautiful heads.

You knew the plane's running late when a clock in your brain awakened you from your nap: "Beka what time is it? I feel like we oughta be landed by now!"

You and the girls use your cell phones as watches; one exception is Beka the fashionista who sleeps with a cool Fossil watch received on her sixteenth birthday.

"What's up ladies" said Beka waving her watch, "we should've landed thirty minutes ago."

Ava's face betrayed her fear: "Are we going to crash? Are we out of fuel? What's going on and why aren't we on the ground?"

Biting your lip you looked at Stacy: "Stacy, its way cool to fly on a big jet with my best girlfriends to California but are we there yet? The fun's way more solid when we're on the ground heading to the Magic Kingdom!"

Stacy's mouth began moving but her voice was eclipsed by the captain's booming voice on the intercom – it's not good news: "I apologize for the delay. I regret to inform you Orange

County airport is under terrorist threats and is being closed."

"Oh no, is it safe to go Disneyland?" wondered Halee.

"We're rerouting to LAX…that's Los Angeles International Airport – and should be on the ground in forty – five minutes" the Captain added.

Stacy could see you and your friends needed diversionary therapy: "Do you like games?"

You said, "Yes, especially if there are prizes!"

"How about Reese's Peanut Butter Cup or Snicker's candy bar?"

"Yes we do" you all shouted.

Ava added, "Hey Stacy, I don't want to sound too high maintenance but I'm allergic to nuts. Do you have any licorice or dots in case I win?"

"You're not high maintenance Ava. I'm sure we have dots, red and black licorice!"

"Sweet!" said pumped up Ava.

"Okay do any of you know Orange County/Santa Ana Airport's special nickname?"

Beka said, "we've never been to this airport - can you give us a clue?"

Halee begged, "Pretty pleeeeeeeez with gobs and gobs of sugar on it!"

"How can I resist?" grinned Stacy "check the inside cover of Alaska Air In-Flight magazine."

The fasten seatbelt light was off - all four you piled onto Halee's seat since she had the magazine open to "The History of Orange County/Santa Ana Airport." You won't gravitate to such an article unless it mentions a favorite movie star or pop group…but the stakes are high when candy is the prize!

"Who the heck is John Wayne?" you asked.

Halee read: "John Wayne was nicknamed "The Duke" by family and friends; Wayne personified American values of hard work, crusty toughness and love for country in his Westerns and World War II movies and won an Oscar for "True Grit and Orange County residents sometimes call their airport: The John Wayne airport to honor his memory."

"An impressive team effort so you all get Snicker's and Reese's, except Ava who gets

Dots and licorice" observed Stacy.

The airport was closed while dozens of bomb sniffing dogs and two hundred FBI, TSA, NCIS and local police combed halls, lockers, closets, baggage claim, eateries and offices. You wondered aloud, "I wonder if the Duke has a bomb sniffing horse?"

Later on you read: ""Islamists for Freedom" is a Jihadist group which leveled ominous threats on the internet, telephone messages and newspaper ads; claiming twenty bombs planted in random locations in and around John Wayne airport. Authorities took the threat seriously since a similar threat issued last year by Islamists for Freedom at Heathrow Airport in London. Scotland Yard found and diffused eight bombs. Two bombs were not found - until one exploded in baggage claim, injuring thirty and killing three; the other exploded in the food court, injuring seventeen and killing five.

Were the terrorists still inside? Just in case, every building was scoured by armed agents to flush out lingering bad guys. Otherwise, everyone searching or diffusing a bomb was a sitting duck for a sniper!"

You, your friends and your Dad's hearts were struck for the people in and around Orange County/Santa Ana airport. You don't often pray but you felt compelled to pray for the safety of law enforcement and your fellow travelers.

You were clueless Dad was praying too - thirty rows behind you in your first class seats. You couldn't put your finger on why you felt extra close to your Dad right now when you're certain he's a thousand miles away in Seattle.

The captain added. "Our estimated landing at LAX, Los Angeles International, is twenty minutes. We're in a que of seven planes rerouting from Santa Ana. There is no terror threat at LAX but airspace is more congested than usual, so please be patient in case safety requires us to take more than the twenty minutes the tower and I are estimating."

You checked your phone to find how many miles from LAX to Disneyland – about 35 miles depending on which of at least three freeways you selected.

Dad's strict safety advisory was: "Do not use taxis, limos, ride share vehicles or small vans for transportation to and from the airport. There is safety in large groups of people. Use a big hotel bus with at least fifty passengers to take you to your hotel and for riding to

Disneyland."

You agreed to watch out for each other - though you weren't sure what a "bad guy" would look like at LAX or on the bus or at Disneyland. All of you noticed Gregory on the plane.

The Walk – S.B. Stone & Rock Solid Publishing, LLC
©2018

Any girl would be impressed by his handsome face, welcoming smile and good manners.

Gregory wondered "Are all of you from Seattle, and what do you plan to do while visiting California?"

Pretty innocent questions you thought so you reciprocated by asking Gregory, "Tell us about yourself Gregory."

Gregory replied, "I'm a first year student at UCLA, studying US History and Political Science."

"Wow a double major," Beka replied. "You must be really smart Gregory?"

"Not really," Gregory said. "I'm just happy to pursue my studies at a respected school like UCLA and I am blessed to be a Bear".

You were thinking, "Uh-oh, I hope Beka keeps her mouth shut on this one."

Beka asks probing questions too early in a relationship. You didn't want inspector Beka to tip off Gregory she thinks he may be lying – leaving you no alternative but to firmly pinch Beka's butt!

"Ouch! What are you doing crazy girl? Why'd you pinch me?" As soon as Beka asked you the question, she knew the answer and whispered, "We'll talk later right?"

"You got it Beka!"

Gregory appeared clueless saying, "what are you talking about?"

"Oh just girl talk Gregory - nothing to fret." Using your fake 'everything is okay' smile you use when a teacher asks a prickly question.

The Marriott Hotel bus was packed with at least fifty passengers - too big a group for a bad guy to challenge. "Dad would be proud of us!" you shared. Dad smiled as he watched from inside the airport. In the bus you packed tight and resumed discussing Gregory with discreet low voices. Ava and Beka asked "why did he try to hide his foreign accent?

The Walk – S.B. Stone & Rock Solid Publishing, LLC
©2018

You and Halee felt slipping in the phrase 'I am blessed to be a Bear' was contrived.

Halee added: "It's the UCLA "Bruins not UCLA 'Bears'- every UCLA student knows!"

You added, "What's with the 'I am blessed' thing? Are we in church? Is he trying to convince us he's spiritual and thus trill?"

Ava added "I'm only sixteen but this guy has way too much self-confidence. I think he's at least twenty-five.'

Beka asked "So you think he's not a college student but a bad guy? Let's see if he pays more attention to us. Didn't Gregory say he was heading straight to UCLA which is in the opposite direction of Disneyland, if I'm reading this map correctly? We probably won't see Gregory again on this trip - bad guy or not, we studied his behavior and shared observations with each ot\her!"

The City of Seattle has 730,000 people. Landing in Los Angeles has prompted a debate regarding Los Angeles is larger or smaller than Seattle? You quickly searched on your phone's browser to learn the City of Los Angeles is 4,000,000 people.

"Wow. Los Angeles is five times bigger than Seattle," remarked Halee.

You asked, "Does this mean there are five times as many creeps, perverts and evil people in Los Angeles as in Seattle?"

Beka was nearly crying, "To be honest I don't feel as safe here in LA as in Seattle. What should we do? I think I wanna fly back to Seattle! We're not adults yet and here we are in this humongous city!"

Ava recalled Disneyland's in Anaheim. "Hey girlfriends guess what? Anaheim's only got 351,000 people, half the size of Seattle, plus it's a fun and happy place cause Mickey and Minnie and Donald and Pluto live there!"

Beka latched on to Ava's logic, "I feel better knowing we're in a smaller, safer city where thousands of laughing and happy kids and families will be together at the "Magic Kingdom".

The Walk – S.B. Stone & Rock Solid Publishing, LLC ©2018

If Dad's right, four pretty girls will encounter cute guys on buses, in the hotel, food places and lines at Disneyland more chances to assess the character of strange men in the days ahead.

"Hey girls, I can't believe who texted me?"

Beka said, "Let me guess. Might it be our handsome but suspicious new friend Gregory?"

"How could you possibly know, Beka?"

"I just got a text from that reprobate just like you!"

Your Dad coached the four of you to never give your phone number or other contact information to anyone you meet on the trip unless all four of you agreed that it was a safe thing to do.

"Sounds good to us." all four of you chimed back to your Dad.

"Did someone break our pledge?" You all silently wondered.

"Not me" each one of you said emphatically.

"How did this turkey get Beka's and your phone numbers without even asking us? How rude and creepy is he anyway?" Ava wondered.

You recalled you all took a decently long nap. Ava and Halee wisely turned phones off and secured them in a hard to access portion of their back packs and put the packs under their seats.

"I did nothing to hide my phone - didn't even occur to me - probably lying in my lap," you sheepishly confessed.

"I kept my phone on my lap during most of the flight, Beka admitted. I was so blessed to be with you. I've never been on a plane and never been to Disneyland. In my innocent mind, I was seven years old…on my way to visit Snow White, Mickey and Minnie Mouse, Cinderella and Donald Duck. Phone safety was the last thing on my mind," Beka added.

"You're so sweet Beka" you all chimed echoing Beka's heart.

Your Disneyland trip was epic - packed with laughpter, chats 'til three am when your ears and jaws hurt. Happy tears, sad tears, fast rides, cheesy rides, fast food, junk food and healthy food.

Mom knows you hate to take pictures when having fun so she recruited Ava, Beka and Halee to take pics of you all plus anyone or anything to help Mom feel like she's with you.

All four of you decided to ignore Gregory's initial text message.

You and Beka weren't surprised he sent more messages – still polite and friendly…even warm but you refused to reply though you struggled the guilt of being rude by ignoring a text message from an attractive and respectful guy - not easy in your generation. Besides Gregory wasn't an on-line stranger arranging your first face to face meeting. You all met him face to face during a three hour flight morphing to five hours because of terror attacks at John Wayne airport and re-routing to LAX.

Plus, the gist of Gregory's texts are clean cut and innocent not perverse or pornographic: "I really like you and your friends. From our talks on the plane I can tell you are special girls with great futures. Let's meet at Disneyland. I hope you'll let me and my best friend buy you a special birthday dinner. We will meet you at Carthay Circle Restaurant in Disney's California Adventure. It's a replica of a famous Hollywood theatre and the food and vibe is retro Hollywood!"

You called Dad in Seattle. He's likely in a meeting but will be glad, maybe relieved, to hear from you: "Hi Dad we are having an awesome time! All of us thank you and Mom for sending us to such a fun place! We met this guy, Gregory, on the plane and he and his best friend Alexis offered to buy us birthday dinner at a fancy place, Cathay Circle. Sounds like a fun and safe place - you think we're okay to meet 'em for dinner, Dad?"

Dad asked, "Do all of you want to have dinner with these guys?"

You replied, "I think we're all okay with it, Dad."

Dad said, "If it's a large place with lots of people and you girls keep your pepper sprays handy, you should be okay, sweetheart."

The Walk – S.B. Stone & Rock Solid Publishing, LLC
©2018

Little did you know Dad just showered at the Marriott and his only important meeting today is to secretly watch over your dinner with Gregory and Alexis.

You faced a crucial decision - do we continue ignoring Gregory's texts - or do we text our acceptance and add another good memory to our vacation – we hope.

"Gregory, why'd you steal Beka's and my cell numbers?"

He answered, "I know we had only just met on the plane but I knew in my heart I am interested in getting to know you better! Honestly, the idea of not staying in touch with you while I'm at UCLA makes me sad."

You said, "I'm sixteen and you are at least twenty! My father will have your head! I can't wait to hear why you took Beka's phone number!"

Gregory replied, "You won't believe this until you meet my best friend, Alexis. He looks like he could be Beka's big brother."

"Ridiculous! Beka already has a big brother – why'd she want another? Anyhow, Beka says her real big brother's a handful." you blasted.

"I respect your point. Even so, I think you, Beka, Halee and Ava will enjoy meeting

Alexis and having a fun dinner together. Shall I make our reservations for 8:00 pm?" Gregory suggested.

You replied, "I'll get back to you Gregory."

Then you asked, "Hey ladies Gregory and his friend Alexis propose an 8:00 pm dinner?

Sounds good" said Beka.

"Me too" you added.

You noticed hesitation in Ava and Halee. "Whatcha thinkin ladies?"

Halee began, "I know we're sus about these guys 'cause we should be. We need contingency plans in case Gregory and Alexis are trashy…or not trashy but boring?

The Walk – S.B. Stone & Rock Solid Publishing, LLC ©2018

"We're listenin" said Beka with you nodding.

Ava added, "In case they're trashy or boring let's have an early dinner – say 4:00 pm so we can bolt after an hour?"

Halee closed with "Here's a bonus - we'd have four to five hours on rides and junk food and maybe meeting cooler guys!"

Beka confessed, "Impressive idea. I thought our birthday girl was the smart one, but you two are in serious contention to dethrone her."

You contended "Hey don't you be talkin smack 'bout me Beka - especially on my sixteenth birthday!"

Beka said, "Sorry birthday girl, I'll give you slack 'til we're off the plane in Seattle."

You added, "Awesome idea. I feel safer at a 4:00 pm dinner - the sun will be shining, lots of hungry families packed in around us. It's just dinner, not romance. These clowns have a long way to go before earning the right to see our romantic sides."

"Right on sister" said everyone.

Dinner wasn't boring - far from it – the food and drinks were excellent. You all insisted the boys not drink or serve any alcohol even though the waiter never asked for your ID's.

Gregory requested "please call me Greg. Grandmother calls me Gregory and Mom uses Gregory when she's ticked off at me."

You and your friends were okay with it - "Greg it is then."

Alexis was a big, strong, dark-haired young man in his early twenties you thought, and using a soft spoken voice. Similar to the case of Greg's speech, Beka detected a foreign accent behind Alexis fluent English.

"Where'd you grow up, Alexis?" inquired Beka.

"My father worked for the India government in clandestine operations. He got bored and started a business. I was born in Mumbai, India. We also spent time in Cambodia, Paris, London and Nigeria" Alexis shared.

"Sorry I'm only sixteen and haven't learned as many "big" words as some of my elders" Halee admitted. "What are 'clandestine' operations?"

Alexis responded, "I understand where you're coming from Halee. I also once thought father was a business man. I learned 'business man' was his cover for being a secret agent. He helped India start its Research and Analysis Wing, or RAW. You call it the Central Intelligence Agency, or CIA…right?"

"Research and Analysis Wing sounds similar to our Central Intelligence Agency", agreed Halee.

"Is your father still with RAW or did he begin his own business?" Beka wondered.

Alexis responded, "My father was murdered two years ago at a sting operation in Lagos, Nigeria."

Ava said, "We're sorry your father was killed."

Alexis said "Thank you. He served India well. My guess is none of you have visited Nigeria?"

"Nope, we've barely heard of Nigeria," you explained.

Halee recalled Nigeria: "Broke from United Kingdom in the 1960's, has two hundred million people making it one of Africa's largest nations; the world's twelfth largest oil and natural gas producer and it's second biggest export behind agriculture - beans, nuts, sesame, cocoa, maize, melon, rice, rubber, sorghum, soybeans, yams and others."

Greg and Alexis smiled - "Halee how'd you learn about Nigeria?"

"I love geography and world studies so I did a paper on Nigeria," Halee said.

Alexis added. "Before his death, Father almost closed on a business property in Nigeria since their economy is growing, but he learned their national leadership is corrupt and half the people live in poverty and one-third of Nigerian kids are not enrolled in school."

"Why is Nigeria neglecting its children?" you asked as Ava, Hailee and Beka nodded.

"Nigeria has the highest rate of HIV/AIDS related deaths in the world. Boko Haram, an Islamic extremist group aligned with al-Qaida, established its presence in the region and hawush impeeee mmeeuuun taaashuuun of Iswaaaahmik waw…Halee's brain was thinking "harsh implementation of Islamic law caused many Christians to flee Nigeria" but her wobbly mouth can't get there - her head hit the table.

"What's wrong Halee?"

You saw Ava's head on her arms on the table asleep.

"You okay Ava? I'm tired too."

"Beka, what's with these sleepyheads" your head hitting the table.

Then Beka.

Alexis and Greg's home brewed concoction of GHB is working like a gem…it always does!

∗∗

Part Two: Sweet Sixteen

You didn't know or care you were so out of it. Alexis and Greg assured Disney security you had too much to drink so needed to "sleep it off" in your hotel. Truth is, a private limo quickly whisked their "dates" to a different hotel – the fourth floor suites above the PurePlez Bar & Grill in a seedy part of town.

Ironically, your Dad carefully observed dinner with Greg and Alexis – somewhat impressed with conversations you had with Alexis and Greg. Your smiles and theirs suggested a safe encounter with good memories for you all…until Dad saw all of you suddenly asleep with heads on the table - "Bastards!" was Dad's last word before he passed out. Dad tried to run from his hiding spot behind a curtain on the stage…in seconds Dad was unconscious...barely noticing the men stuffing his precious girls into a limo!

You, Hailee, Ava and Beka were utterly gone from the world around you…with little idea of what's happening - passing in and out of drug induced sleep and semi-conscious awake periods for days - possibly weeks.

Dad barely recognized Greg as the one who spiked his water bottle with a fatal dose of GHB during his bathroom break. Disobeying Alexis orders, Greg gave Dad the same dose as you, Halee, Beka and Ava though he knew you're there for their protection.

Greg collects $3,000 in cash for each girl or boy he delivers to Alexis to be employed in the Network. Greg's account will be $12,000 richer when the Network wires his pay the next business day.

You and your friends would be shocked to know you, Ava, Beka and Halee are the tenth "delivery" Greg's made so far this year – pocketing $120,000 in just eight months! Greg loves his job – living in LA and targeting attractive women - thirteen to twenty-five traveling alone or in a group and looking for fun – the more festive their moods the more likely they'll let their guard down.

Just prior to meeting you, Beka, Halee and Ava, Greg delivered two ladies, eighteen and twenty-one, on an LA to Seattle Alaska flight pocketing $6,000 in a day and a half. Both flight attendants requested Greg's cell number and crowned him a hero for carrying two sleeping girls off the plane, gently placing them in wheelchairs for delivery to teary eyed friends Sam and Kory at the airport.

Back in Los Angeles, Alexis put all four girls in one hotel room to await their indoctrination and ultimate auction in the cattle pen. The greater Los Angeles area had over ten million souls spread out from the San Fernando Valley through Hollywood, Beverly Hills, Anaheim, Irvine, Newport Beach and then to the San Bernardino and Riverside areas.

The name, Los Angeles means "City of Angeles." While there may be thousands of God – fearing people in the city of

The Walk – S.B. Stone & Rock Solid Publishing, LLC
©2018

angels most would agree their city's under the control of the angel of darkness – Satan and a host of his demons.

Eighteen months ago, a man named Myron was on a run hunting for a perfect place to open a new Bar and Grill where he wants to make a difference in the lives of his new neighbors and clientele. Myron cried out to God near the place soon to be his location: "Dear Jesus my heart is angry at the rampant recruitment of our innocent daughters and sons to make them slaves of cheap sex and used in pornographic movies used to lure weak and horny men into phony relationships and the abusing of their precious bodies. Jesus, why do you tolerate such horrible activities here on earth?"

Jesus reminded you of His words: *"Yet these people slander whatever they do not understand, and the very things they do understand by instinct—as irrational animals do—will destroy them. Woe to them! They have taken the way of Cain; they have rushed for profit into Balaam's error; they have been destroyed in Korah's rebellion. These people are blemishes at your love feasts, eating with you without the slightest qualm—shepherds who feed only themselves. They are clouds without rain, blown along by the wind; autumn trees, without fruit and uprooted— twice dead. They are wild waves of the sea, foaming up their shame; wandering stars, for whom blackest darkness has been reserved forever. Enoch, the seventh from Adam, prophesied about them: 'See, the Lord is coming with thousands upon thousands of his holy ones to judge everyone, and to convict all of them of all the ungodly acts they have committed in their ungodliness, and of all the defiant words ungodly sinners have spoken against him.' these people are grumblers and faultfinders; they follow their own evil desires; they boast about themselves and flatter others for their own advantage. But, dear friends, remember what the apostles of our Lord Jesus Christ foretold. They said to you, 'In the last times there will be scoffers who will follow their own ungodly desires.' These are the people who divide you, who follow mere natural instincts and do not have the Spirit. But you, dear friends, by building yourselves up in your most holy faith and praying in the Holy Spirit, keep yourselves in God's love as you wait for the mercy of our Lord Jesus Christ to bring you to eternal life. Be merciful to those who doubt. Save others by snatching them from the fire; to others show mercy, mixed with fear – hating even the clothing stained by corrupted flesh. To him who is able to keep you from stumbling and to present you before his glorious presence without fault and with great joy—to the only God our Savior be glory, majesty, power and authority, through Jesus Christ our Lord, before all ages, now and forevermore! Amen."*   Jude 1:10-25 [1]

The entertainment and fashion industries worship beauty and unlimited pleasure. The drug, prostitution and pornography industries are powerful and huge – focused on young innocent looking female and male flesh! Auctions are attended by wealthy individuals to purchase personal sex-slaves. As business men and women they know horny clients will pay $500 for thirty minutes and $5,000 for a full day of pleasure with beautiful young flesh doing all they imagine to give their own bodies pleasure – demand is high - why not facilitate their perversions and profit hugely?

A personal sex toy can evolve into a business to be rented or sold to your customers; a long term investment potentially generating fifty to one hundred thousand dollars every year before escaping, killing you, getting old or dying! In a city with honest police, the human sex slave auction sites relocate frequently.

The slave sellers and buyers use cryptic names, code words, disposable phones, word of mouth and websites to set up the auctions. Alexis, Big Boss and associates call the Network's local business "Pureplez" for pure pleasure. Tonight's auction's in the old Flakey Furniture warehouse off Sunset and near Pine.

The ground floor's a vibrant new business celebrating its one year anniversary - "Myron's Bar & Grill". The business is legit – so the cops come by for a beer and nachos now and then. As a downtown bar in a seedier neighborhood PurePlez had a mixed clientele including druggies and drunks but Myron's personal warmth and no BS military demeanor inspired flaky one's to change their lives or move on – eventually drawing well-dressed male and female patrons driving nice cars.

One of Myron's favorite customers, Seth Bartley, asked: "I gotta wonder, Myron, do the creeps who sell their fellow human beings as sex slaves have a conscience? "I doubt it" replied

Myron – "they've gotta pretend God does not exist." Seth wondered, "How can men have intimate encounters with beautiful girls and not marvel at the complexity and wonder of God's creation?"

"These brutes have no qualms about destroying their innocence and offering no apology to the victims or to God" Myron lamented. Seth confessed, "I used to treat women like dirt."

Curious, Myron had to ask, "What changed?"

"Jesus got hold of my heart - **all of it** – He changed me from the inside out" Seth smiled.

"Kinda thought there's somethin special 'bout you, Seth" said Myron.

"I don't ever want to argue with God again" Seth stressed.

"I agree, but why do you say that" Myron wondered.

"It's a long story Myron and you know three beers is my limit - better head home" said Seth.

"Take care until next time" Myron offered.

Tonight's auction is a huge event but must look low profile to the police and neighboring businesses. The event begins at 8:00 pm to coincide with busy vehicular and pedestrian traffic of nearby restaurants, bars, theatres, art galleries and other legal activities.

Tonight's merchandise is advertised on PurePlez secure website. Instead of the menu ordering food and drink click on **Special Events**; next click **Register** by typing first and last name, social security number, check the box "will bring U.S. currency, gold or silver" or provide bank name, routing number, account number, then click **Today's Password**; IF and ONLY IF your registration is approved today's password is issued by Big Man: "$Hornytoad#31".

Upon Successful Registration and Password Entry you enter the Secret and Secure portion of PurePlez site and greeted by today's auction headline: **Twenty-Five Sex-Crazed Girls and**

Hot Women" plus "Six Horny and Gorgeous Boys and
Young Men!

Thus far one hundred fifteen bidders are registered. Many
sample tonight's merchandise paying $500 to $1,000 for thirty
minutes to one hour of pleasure - perhaps with a virgin girl or
boy. Other registrants seek a long term investment capable of
serving U.S. and international clientele. The bar's patrons have
no idea what's going on upstairs. If you inquire, Myron says,

"My family and friends live upstairs and party on weekends -
sorry for the ruckus."

Truth is: wickedness and pure hell's unfolding behind the
blacked out windows!

In addition to monthly rent, Myron collects ten percent of
tonight's take for keeping his mouth shut and dedicating his huge
upstairs space to the "auction". On the worst auction nights,
Myron collects no less than $10,000 plus huge food and alcohol
sales in the bar.

On higher volume auction nights, Myron caps out on his
"special event" rent with Alexis and Big Boss; he receives
$250,000 in his bank account the next morning! What a
remarkable business he's built by partnering with the scum of the
earth!

Alexis, Big Boss and associates sell ten to fifty girls and boys
per auction at $50,000 to $100,000 apiece, generating $500,000
to $5,000,000 for Big Man's empire. If evil and greed prevail,
these cowardly wimps will continue to enslave you, Halee, Ava,
Beka and other victims in the U.S. and internationally – raping
innocent bodies, ripping fragile hearts, breaking wills and tearing
up your and your friends dreams of free and meaningful lives!

Is there any hope you and tens of thousands of worldwide
victims can escape the hell you're living in?

Alexis and Big Boss have contingency plans. If an auction
"moves" less than 100% of the merchandise the unsold slaves
will assimilate in local "flesh for sale" businesses as prostitutes
or be sold to the highest bidder on the massive international sex
trafficking market.

The Walk – S.B. Stone & Rock Solid Publishing, LLC
©2018

Your Dad discovered Myron's a U.S. army veteran and good man who fears God.

Dad asked Myron: "Hey dude, how'd all this come down on your world brother?

Myron said, "Grab a dolly and let's run across the street for a few cases in the warehouse. I used to store it upstairs but those creeps steal it and drink themselves into a heart attack or get rowdy and beat up the girls! Plus we have no cameras or mics over there."

Dad said, "Cool I need exercise after they drugged me I couldn't drive my rental car so I took an Uber to meet you at your bar."

Myron told the story: "My Bar's in the old Flakey Furniture Warehouse. Owned by Hezekiah Flakey for importing, repairing and building luxury furniture after returning from WW II in 1948. Eighteen months ago I got a visit from two police officers Scottie Holcumb and Michael Best. I thought they were pissed at me for being too rough in tossing out one of our crazy patrons."

Dad said, "Were you on target?"

"Not even close, Myron replied. "They asked how I felt about human trafficking, pornography and prostitution. 'I hate that garbage! So count me in' – I'll devote my time and business and a chunk of my profits to rescue victims and put the filthy bastards behind bars forever!"

Dad agreed, "I applaud your enthusiasm!"

"Thanks. I heard from Alexis the next day." 'Sir, our building burned down two weeks ago. I hear you own a nice bar on the ground floor with four floors above?' Can I check it out this afternoon?"

Myron responded, "Come on over; yes each floor's eight thousand feet – you can have all thirty two thousand if you need it?" Myron responded - base rent's five thousand per floor, triple net - what's your business?"

Alexis replied, "We'll use four thousand square feet for offices, ten thousand feet for lodging; the remaining eighteen

The Walk – S.B. Stone & Rock Solid Publishing, LLC ©2018

thousand for two to four big parties a month. Here's a ten thousand dollar deposit and a signed one year lease with five one year options."

Myron added, "Big Man's shameful Los Angeles operation moved to our four floors over "Myron's Bar & Grill" in two weeks. While vacationing with my wife and kids in Tahoe, Big Man's sign guy tore off "Myron's Bar & Grill" replacing with the his "PurePlez Bar & Grill" sign! I called my police buddies, officers Mike (Mikey) and Scott (Scottie).

"He's an asshole! It's not permitted in our lease, Mikey; what do I say to my patrons about my sleazy new name?"

Scottie jumped on the line: "I understand, Myron - be patient – each week Big Man's neck is inching closer to our noose. Let's avoid distracting him with relatively minor sign disputes."

"I'll be patient." Said Myron.

"Sweet", echoed Scottie and Mikey.

Myron added: "I've put those RFID chips in most of the girls and boys staying upstairs. They're exhausted so most are sleeping or drugged recuperating from the trauma of capture and awaiting the auction in the cattle pen. Many are weeping and begging for mom or dad or brother to rescue them. All are fearful of the future."

Big Man and Alexis embraced planting the micro-chips. An excellent way to locate and re-capture runaway slaves – each of whom is a million dollar asset in their rapidly growing empire!

Big Man sent an encrypted email to secretary Beulah:

Subject Line: "Our current staff".

Big Man: "How many world-wide staff?"

Beulah replied: "The ones who are still able to perform their jobs?"

Big Man replied: "Yes, you idiot. If they can't do sex they're not a core asset. God loves them but we don't! Don't count them but find other jobs like maids or cooks or servers!"

Beulah replied: "Sir, we own 20,254 assets including 10,800 girls under 25."

Big Man replied: "How many micro chipped?"

Beulah replied: "Zero so far."

Big Man: "How many escaped assets?"

Beulah:" I estimate 2,000 escapes in ten years - few recoveries."

Big Man replied: "We are idiots! Alexis will tell you who's delivering our 20,000 microchips - implant the youngest first!"

Beulah replied: "After receipt, it's as good as done sir!"

Alexis interrupted: "Sir and Beulah, we got a test shipment of five hundred microchips in the LA office – the Pureplez Bar. I think Myron's put 'em in our most recent crop of girls."

Big Man: "Do they work?"

Alexis replied: "We don't have a transmitter – it's due in your Dubai office next week."

Beulah suggested: "Sir when you receive the transmitter, let me know. Let's test the one hundred girls in LA before installing the remaining 19,900 microchips."

Big Man: "Good thinking Beulah, remind me to give you a raise."

Beulah replied: "Do you know what you're paying me this year sir?"

Big Man: "I think I pay you $250,000. Is it enough?"

Beulah said: "Yes, $100,000's enough to live on so I tithe $25,000 to my church; I invest or save $25,000 for retirement; I give chunks to Salvation Army, Samaritan's Purse and other

Christian charities; I use the remainder to buy little gifts for our girls."

Big Man replied: "I had no idea you have children, Beulah!"

Beulah replied: "I'm talking about the children in our business, not mine. Sir, you've sent me all over the world to keep tabs on our thirty sex dens and their managers in the U.S., India, Cambodia, United Kingdom, South Africa and France, to name a few. The managers and I keep it professional; as I earned their trust many confided in me regarding serious life questions they're facing."

Big Man interrupted: "This is above my pay grade. I don't get the touchy feely stuff. I'm glad you're out there Beulah."

"Thank you sir - it gets better from my perspective" Beulah added.

"Uh oh you didn't chum it up with our slaves…did you", Big Man's heart is racing; "You are messing with my non-negotiable rule Beulah!"

Beulah added, "Did you know our managers often encounter fist fights, vandalism, theft, even death threats among our slaves. During my walk thru of their rooms, one girl made eye contact with me so I asked 'how can I help?' She got a severe beating and abusive sex from one of our creepier clients. She begged me to provide a lethal dose to escape the hell we've forced upon her." Beulah shared.

"Holy Moses – did you give it to her?" asked Big Man.

"No way! I held her hand and told her I care for her. I explained I am truly sorry for the suffering she has gone through. I said 'your life matters to me and to God. Besides you won't be Big Man's slave forever. What's your name honey?" Beulah asked.

"I'm Lily - what's your name Ma'am" she responded.

"I'm Beulah – just call me Aunt Be. Where'd you grow up Lily?" Beulah asked.

"I was in Dallas, Texas chillin at the Mall with friends and we're talkin with some cute boys. I went to the bathroom; they spiked my Dr. Pepper; it knocked me cold. A few days later I wake up in Africa I think; cell phone destroyed; I tried running – those bastards beat the snot outa me – I ain't trustin nobody" said Lily.

"Enough!" screamed Big Man throwing his phone.

Big Man's filthy rich – with an insatiable lust for more!
Slaves in his network charge at least $250 for a required
minimum of 300 sex acts per year: $75,000 for each precious
child! Big Man owns twenty thousand children, teens and
women who collect $1,500,000,000 billion revenue for Big Man
and his sex managers <u>every horrific year</u>! Each slave gets a
twenty percent cut of her fees, $50 per trick or $15,000 per year
for her use; lodging and two meals a day are supposedly
provided at each location.

Researchers advise Big Man the <u>demand for illicit sex</u> is on
the rise worldwide. An astute business man and former customer
he's installing the best systems to attract thousands of beautiful
girls, teens, young women, boys and young men to his legal and
illegal businesses.

According to the Polaris Project:

*"Human trafficking is the business of stealing freedom for
profit. In some cases, traffickers trick, defraud or physically
force victims into providing commercial sex. In others, victims
are lied to, assaulted, threatened or manipulated into working
under inhumane, illegal or otherwise unacceptable conditions. It
is a multi-billion dollar criminal industry that denies freedom to
twenty four million nine hundred thousand trafficked victims
around the world."*

www.PolarisProject.org

No surprise evil creeps fight to secure a piece of the action.

You, Beka, Halee and Ava were elated to learn your Dad
visited the Pureplez Bar to meet Myron and explain his plan to
steal you before the auction begins or buy you and your friends
at the auction if necessary.

At 4:00 you, Ava, Halle and Beka arrive at Pureplez with
Alexis' assistant, Eddie; he fixes your hair, clothes, jewelry and
makeup so you look good and earn high prices at the auction.
Eddie's a wiry angry looking dude packing a 9 mm Springfield
pistol plus nasty Steel Tiger knives – one at the ankle; one at the
belt. Dad chose to chill awhile.

Dad posed as a "new client" from Columbus Ohio, enjoying a beer and sandwich at the bar.

Myron asked Dad: "Can you pay $50,000 per girl to walk away with them tonight?"

Dad replied, "That's $200k Myron! When's he plan to cash my check?"

"Alexis gives me the auction checks - I deposit Monday morning" assured Myron.

"I'll sell stocks to cover the $200k but can't do so until the market opens Monday at 9:30 am – I should have the funds in my checking by 10:00 am" Dad figured.

Myron added, "Big Man and Alexis are crooks to the core – if they smell a rat or think you and me are good guys they'll pop us quick, incinerate our bodies or throw us in the deepest part of the Pacific."

Dad replied, "Geez Myron, I'm not having nearly as much fun as I thought!"

Myron assured, "If those boys are making me nervous I will deposit your check – if the crooks are chill I'll shred your check 'cause you're a law abiding, hard-working family man fighting illegal trafficking of your sweet daughter, her friends and one hundred seventy-eight innocent kids and girls awaiting auction upstairs!"

Myron texted Big Man: Got a man in the bar who wants four of the girls."

Big Man asked, "Interesting - what's his offer?"

"Mike says he'll pay $25k per girl" responded Myron.

"Is this idiot from the 1980's?"

"All our girls sell for minimum $50,000!" shouted Big Man. "Send me pics of the girls you fool!"

"Sorry, here they are" said Myron.

Big Man conferred with Alexis: "Three too skinny; one too fat, white skinned, flat chested - happy to get rid of them for $200,000. Put on my client from Columbus!"

The Walk – S.B. Stone & Rock Solid Publishing, LLC
©2018

Dad wisely used a bogus name to avoid being traced. "Hello Big Man – Mike Dubois."

Big Man replied, "When do I get my hands on your money?"

Mike/Dad replied, "My bank closed at 1:00 since its Saturday. I can wire to your account Monday morning or hand a check to Myron today – it's your call."

Big Man hung up saying, "Give your check to Myron; come see me in Dubai if you're on my side of the world. I own many beautiful women who will wear you out Mike Dubois."

The Big Man is huge and intimidating – six foot-five, three hundred fifty to four hundred pounds. A giant yet sly as a fox - evading capture despite ten years in business. No one's discovered Big Man's location or whom he's been bribing for possibly ten years! Now Dubai's top of the list!

An FBI courier delivered twenty-five thousand state of the art RFID micro-chips to the sex managers in the network of cities comprising his empire. Slaves never stop seething toward Big Man for ruining their lives. Such hatred requires constant vigilance by Big Man and his staff - he knows any slave will kill him instantly if she or he had access and the ability to do it!

To combat this pervasive threat, Big Man hired twelve body guards. They're led by Nehemiah, a 250 pound killing machine, called "Nehi" by Big Man and staff, he is gifted with exceptional hearing and superior vision to compliment his mastery of every martial art plus ancient and modern weaponry. The door opened for Nehi five years ago when Big Man angrily fired his chef screaming, "Get rid of that asshole - he poisoned our drinks and meals; now Silvie and Courtney are dead - two of my favorites! Big Man's so large he survived the attempt despite cramping, headaches, nausea and hours on his jumbo-sized toilet.

At Nehemiah's interview Big Man conceded "You're a top notch chef, trained at Culinary Arts Academy in Lucerne, but can I trust my life and my dinner guest's lives to your protective skills and integrity? What's to stop you from doing God a favor by killing loveable old me?"

The Walk – S.B. Stone & Rock Solid Publishing, LLC
©2018

Nehemiah responded, "I must be completely candid with you sir if that's alright?"

"I prefer you share too much information rather than too little." Big Man conceded.

"Okay sir, here goes: until five years ago I was an angry and violent man…zealously practicing Islam including the call to kill my brother or sister who decided to leave Islam. I was devout on the outside and hurting on the inside - I had no idea why," Nehemiah shared.

"Did you figure it out," asked Big Man.

Nehemiah continued, "I honestly examined my Islamic brothers and sisters. I saw zeal and passion but no peace on their insides – we worshipped and prayed five times a day like robots to angry Allah and the truth is Allah gave us no peace of mind or joy in our hearts – why worship a god like this? It defies common sense. I wanted to discuss openly my concerns but how can I be candid with fellow believers if Allah commands them to kill anyone who follows a different path?

I realized I'd been blindly enslaved to the false religion of Islam so I reached out to my Buddhist and Hindu and Christian friends - I reached out to '**God**' not Allah to see if there's a God of love out there.

I was motivated to find out soon! My search criteria: **I want to believe in a God of mercy and love and grace**; a God who speaks truth, acts honorably, loves His children and helps them build successful, fulfilling lives!"

"Such a God would be a perfect father figure - my old man was an asshole" declared Big Man.

"I'm sorry to hear it Big Man" Nehemiah empathized.

"No big deal – I got over it" Big Man claimed.

"Next day my workout partner texted www.YouVersion.com. It's a free Bible in hundreds of languages and dozens of versions." Nehemiah added.

"What are you talking about" complained an irritated Big Man.

"Sorry Sir, let me clarify - I told my workout partner I'm leaving Islam to find a God who truly brings love, peace and joy to my heart. My friend blurted with big smile on his face, 'You need Jesus in your heart Nehemiah!'"

I said to my friend, "Maybe I need Jesus, maybe I don't; either way **I have some tough questions** I want to ask Jesus as I read through the Bible you texted me!"

My friend couldn't resist: "Nehemiah would you mind sharing one of your Jesus Questions with your workout partner?"

"No problem" said Nehemiah.

"I would ask Jesus: **What's the one true belief**?

"I am the light of the world. Whoever follows me will never walk in darkness, but will have the light of life." John 8:12 [1]

"I'd also ask: Dear Jesus: **Are you really God**?"

"For there is one God and one mediator between God and mankind, the man Christ Jesus, who gave his life as a ransom for all people." [1]

Then my workout buddy texted me:

"God our Savior *"wants all people to be saved and come to a knowledge of the truth."* 1 Timothy 2:4 [1]

Big man interrupted: "Did you say God 'actually wants all people to be saved' including me? I'm one of the filthiest sinners in history! I can be a decent man. My staff and slaves enjoy my company so I rarely eat alone; I cultivate competition among the slaves to win a month living in my tower and dining at my table. Skinny slaves crave a decent man's attention plus the fine food and drink in a luxury condo – a mega improvement compared to fast-food or going to bed hungry last month."

"Is Jesus blood strong enough to cleanse even me" asked Big Man.

"Nehemiah shared: *"But if we walk in the light as he is in the light we have fellowship with one another and **the blood of Jesus, his Son, purifies us from all sin.**"* 1 John 1:17 [1]

Nehemiah asked: "Big Man, are you ready to walk in the light with Jesus and turn your life and businesses over to Him?"

Big Man complained: "I have too many challenges to think about God: 1. Frustrated slaves refusing to perform sex; 2. Runaway slaves desperate to regain their freedom or at least get back at me by getting shot by their sex manager; 3.They commit suicide – one girl in Florida did a video: 'Big Man's not god! Why the hell should I empower him to decide when or how I leave this earth?' 4. I give bonuses to loyal girls to deter suicides and running; 5. Plus I pay my girls 20% of the income they earn for me! How many businesses pay that well - plus food in the refrigerator and free rent? 6. Our trial run of one hundred micro-chips in the LA office was successful so we hope for fewer runaways in the future; 7. I will give each slave and manager $10,000 for cooperation with our micro-chip safety campaign! 8. "In just one week I'll bet you I can get everyone chipped – then we can help our girls avoid getting lost."

"I concede you've made some improvements Big Man but you can't earn your way into

God's perfect heaven by good deeds" said Nehemiah.

"Didn't Mother Theresa get into heaven for her good deeds" asked Big Man.

"Mother Theresa performed many good deeds serving poor children in India. **If she got into heaven it's because she trusted in <u>Jesus Christ alone</u>** for her salvation.

"What about me" asked Big Man.

Nehi responded, "You have thousands of terrible sins on your record, God's ready to forgive every one - the choice is yours as long as you're still breathing."

"I'll let you know Nehemiah" said Big Man.

Big Man hides out in a three story condo/home office on floors 146 thru 148 of BurjKhalifa Tower in Dubai, UAE. As a consummate narcissist, Big Man strives to amaze people; knowing how Big Man rolls, his decorator hired a famous artist to create a massive art-deco piece for the twenty foot entry foyer of his residence; five thousand RFID micro-chips are artistically integrated in the artwork.

Unbeknownst to Big Man, a top secret partnership of MIT, Cal Tech and the FBI resulted in the equipping of Big Man's micro-chips with cutting edge "reciprocal pinging" technology enabling the FBI, not just Big Man, to "ping" any of the 25,000 RFID devices on the planet to pinpoint a person's name and location! The FBI has frequencies of all 25,000 micro-chips – when Big Man activates a chip implanted in one of his sex slaves, the FBI's satellite technology can see her exact location!

+++

Out of nowhere the good guys descended - a crack team of Navy Seals, Army Rangers and Air Force Special Operations Command (AFSOC) hitting Big Man's Dubai rooftop. Before destroying offices and guest quarters, the team rescued one hundred forty girls and women attired in elegant silk clothing with "I Belong to Big Man" scribed front and back.

Coward to the core and too busy for God, the Big Man ran through a large window - falling two thousand feet - portions of his flesh torn-off on the way down by artful décor extruding from the building. Big Man's body parts and screams crushed into his limo awaiting seven girls, Nehemiah and Big Man for dinner and dancing – exiting the lobby just in time to hear Big Man's piercing screams and auspicious crash landing.

Good News: In the aftermath of the raid, a consortium of international law enforcement agencies, churches and NGA's joined forces to locate and successfully rescue 20,027 human trafficking victims from the tentacles of Big Man's despicable network.

You, Beka, Halle and Ava flew back to Seattle with Dad still your hero and now your best friend. You and your friends are grateful you were spared most of the abuses you'd endure if you had not been rescued: a life of merciless rape and sexual abuse by your owners and/or their clients – you were drugged, stolen and beaten but not severely as your captors know bidders pay higher prices for 'undamaged merchandise' at the slave auctions. It will be awhile before you or your friends go out on a date - no matter how handsome or cool he may seem to be. When you do go out, you'll go in big groups – because there's safety in numbers. At parties and public places you'll get your own drink so you'll be more likely to know what's inside.

****

Dear Reader. Imagine this is not a fictional but true story involving your own precious daughter or son or sister or wife. How do you want that awful true story to end? I know your answer in part since I have daughters and sons of my own, so my heart gets torn up when I see or hear of abusive behavior toward kids and young people! What actions can you and I take to end human trafficking? Will you visit our website to share your feedback about this book, human trafficking and whatever else you'd like to share.

Thank you for reading "Sweet Sixteen"! We welcome your comments.
Just send an email to feedback@thewalk.me

The Walk: Episode Five – Leviathan

Today's March 12th, and you're on your third vacation of the year.

Truth is, you only do working vacations – can't live life any other way and your boss is cool with it – you're the boss. It's kind of embarrassing men twice your age would give a right arm to own a company like yours - CEO and Chief Strategist of a quiet seven year startup - Leviathan.

Last year's $320,000,000 gross revenue was created by you and four full time employees plus seven outsourced consultants in Paris, London, Mumbai, New York, Los Angeles, Mexico City and Tokyo. Deduct $25,000,000 travel costs, salaries, bonuses, consulting fees and rent you produced $295,000,000 gross profit before taxes!

Your "A Team" is well trained, intelligent and thrives on the corporate kill. Their A Team moniker is inspired by the 1980's series of former special-forces characters taking out bad guys with firepower and humor for five seasons.

You exclaimed "Our A Team's worth its weight in gold though they prefer to be paid in good old U.S. dollars! Here's the live version of our team bio. Everyone rise when I tap your shoulder; share your mini resume and biggest item on your bucket list!

"Hi team, I'm Lila Pettit, [$120,000 plus bonuses]. I earned my MBA Magna Cum Laude at MIT's Sloan School of Business; I have the joy of being married to our smartest employee - Harold Pettit! Honestly, I'm too young to think about things I want to do before I die and leave this earth. I want to raise three kids – number one on my new bucket list!"

"Great job sharing Lila" you responded.

"Next I'm tapping Ruth Thormodsgaard!

Hi Team – call me Ruth or Thor – it's up to you. Ruth (Thor) Thormodsgaard [$175,000 plus potential bonuses]. Fargo, North Dakota farm girl - don't let the smile fool you – I'm tough as nails working and wrestling with my brothers Tomi, Joni and Teri - with our strong Norwegian surname, Thormodsgaard we're grateful to Mom and Dad for the simple first names given my brothers and me! My #1 bucket list goal's to Live Life at High Velocity; objective at Leviathan is out produce all of you and facilitate more success in your roles and lives. Graduated high school at fourteen; enrolled at Carnegie Mellon's University's Self-Paced Bachelors in Artificial

Intelligence - completed in twelve months; Double Masters at CMU in Automated Science: Biological Experimentation and

Computational Biology; I'm grateful I achieved my goal of earning both Master's before my eighteenth birthday!"

You responded, "Thanks for sharing Ruth. It's good for us to know you better! Will you share experiences after CMU with the team in our next meeting?" Your wondering how you're scoring talent like Ruth to Leviathan – and beautiful!

Ruth added, "My brother Tomi told me to say hello boss."

"Sorry Ruth, I spaced it - Tomi referred you to me as a job candidate, right?"

"Yes a year ago" thought Ruth.

"I owe Tomi a nice dinner don't I?" Tomi was once your roommate. You feel bad how poorly you've stayed in touch. Next I tap Hank Pardone" you declared.

"I'm Henry, call me Hank, Pardone and I'm pumped to be on this team [$150,000 plus bonus potential]; you'd think a guy top of his class at West Point plus five years active duty in the Pentagon serving a four star general would have zero problem finding a job at a great company like Leviathan. In the military, I had a nose for smelling graft in the ranks as I was trained in top secret intelligence and counter-intelligence, rooting out bad guys who earned a spot on DOD's [Department of Defense] top secret most wanted list. I was stabbed, shot, poisoned and beaten multiple times usually by fellow military. The right fit in the private sector hasn't come easy for me. My number one bucket list item is to find a great wife" shared Hank.

You shared, "Thank you sir. Hank entered your life as a trainer while recuperating from your first triathlon – a brutal realization of how terribly out of shape you were. I barely finished, limped around the office for a week from soreness I hadn't felt since high school football. I emailed you guys – 'Please help I need a trainer!'"

Lila replied, "Call Hank the plank".

Harold replied, "I don't know a trainer, I'm 26 and you're an old man."

Ruth replied, "Call Captain Hank, he's awesome!"

The Walk – S.B. Stone & Rock Solid Publishing, LLC
©2018

"I had no CV for Hank but was impressed with his lean body and keen focus so I invited him to the office; my first words were 'good to meet you Hank - why does your body and eyes radiate such intensity.'"

Hanks reply was "My eyes and body are intense since I'm accustomed to evil people trying to take me or my colleagues out."

You said defensively, "I think you're safe here at Leviathan."

Hank smiled, "As long as I'm not a company on your hit list?"

"I wonder who leaked our business model to you Hank" you said.

"Guilty as charged" Lila confessed. Ruth and I met Hank at our gym; he's our trainer. We knew you'd be cool with him boss."

You asked "Why'd you become a personal trainer, Hank?"

Hank replied "I learned bad and good exercise techniques in West Point and in the Army so I wanted to help people of all shapes, sizes and abilities. I partnered with Paul Castle who's got a Masters in Kinesiology and PE. We started the 'Military Fitness Gym' a hokey name but with three thousand members in two years. I told Paul from the outset I have other business interests to pursue, not relating to fitness. After three years I'd sell him my half of the business on a pre-agreed formula and he'd be the sole owner."

"Has your fitness business sold?" you asked.

"Yes, last month, so I'm a free man 'til my next business launches. My non- compete allows personal training for friends and family" Hank said. "We'll meet three days a week for eighty minutes. If you work hard, you'll feel and look as buff as me."

"Hank, you are so hired! Can you send me your CV and twenty year goals" you requested.

"Lila's got my CV - she suggested you may be looking for someone like me."

"Hey boss, I printed Hank's CV for you."

The Walk – S.B. Stone & Rock Solid Publishing, LLC

"Nice job Lila!"

"Thanks boss."

"I reeled off highpoints on Hank's CV: 'top ten percent of his class at West Point; five years at Pentagon; top secret clearances, counter-intelligence, aide to four star general; my trainer's now the fifth FTE at Leviathan" how can I be so lucky?

Your hand next fell on the shoulder of Harold the Brain your highest paid FTE [$295,000 plus bonuses].

"Just call me Harold please. Every month the boss deposits $24,583 pre-tax into my bank account: I share this not out of pride but gratitude and a desire to motivate you to increase your worth at Leviathan and anywhere else you choose to go - collecting $24 K per month is a dank amount of money – you have so many options for living expenses, giving to charities, saving, vacations and investing for your futures."

"I'm conservative guy so boss had a tough time convincing me to join his startup five years ago. Like you, my bonus is capped at 200%, so I can earn another $590,000 in bonuses for a total compensation of $885,000 - a tidy sum. Boss calls me 'Harold the Brain' since I graduated Magna Cum Laude from University of Washington with bachelor's in physics, computer science and international business at the ripe young age of fourteen."

"Bill Gates, co- founder of Microsoft, knew me and my folks from Lakeside School, the Washington Tennis Club and charity events they co-chaired. Gate's offer of employment at Microsoft Redmond, Washington was the more comfortable option for their fourteen year old genius. I was barraged with offers from hundreds of companies many of which contained lucrative signing bonuses. Mom and Dad let me make the decision. I knew Microsoft was a respected technology leader where I can get my foot in the door to learn best practices and avail myself of mentoring opportunities outside the ivory tower distortions of academia though Microsoft was no longer in its heyday when I was hitting the job market.

"Mom made my favorite dinner, pork chops, scalloped potatoes and applesauce on the night I said I'd announce my decision: Microsoft's a cool company with free food, games and thousands of geeks like me to work with. Yeah man. Let's do it!"

Harold's Microsoft career lasted four years. He learned every system and coding language inside Microsoft. Harold's annual reviews scored 100% in every category. At eighteen, Harold was the youngest officer in their history and invited to Board meetings. Harold advised the board against purchasing Nokia and other prospective acquisitions. Harold predicted two year old Google would dominate search engine space.

In 2005, Harold advised Bill Gates and the Microsoft board to "put everything you can into acquiring a majority stake in Google."

Harold followed his own advice – at sixteen he invested everything he had, $135,000, to buy 1500 shares of Google stock at $90 per share. Google's December 7, 2018 closing price was $1,036.58 per share increasing his net worth by $2,971,630 at age 28!

As a loyal employee and good person, Harold continued to urge Bill Gates to invest in Google as a strategic business opportunity for a weakening Microsoft. Harold envisioned Gates and Microsoft more diversified and healthy by owning Google's one billion g-mail customers as its ace in the hole. Plus Harold could see one-off software sales won't sustain the revenue growth Microsoft aspired to.

Visionary Harold also saw brick and mortar retail stores painfully falling by the wayside as he wrote in his open letter/email sent to CEO's of all the majors in the retail industry:

"Consumers want simpler, cheaper methods of doing business. Internet commerce will thrive if done right. Savvy retailers can survive a shifting paradigm by not paying rent for space in a building they won't need in a few years and to stop staffing brick and mortar stores slowly but surely dragging them to bankruptcy as Google collects millions of dollars in ad revenue."

The time came for Harold and his amazing brain to leave Microsoft for new challenges! He considered joining a group purportedly solving world hunger; or a good company offering big bucks if Harold can "triple their revenues" for a piece of their pie; an aging company begged Harold to find blind spots and opportunities for growth. Nothing resonated for Harold.

If you and Harold hadn't bumped into each other at the 2010 Chicago Blackhawks Stanley Cup Finals who knows where you'd be working today? You're a die-hard Hawks fan caught up in the allure of <u>finally</u> bringing the coveted Cup back to Chicago after a painfully long drought.

Harold had great seats as the guest of Lila Buckingham, a die-hard Blackhawk fan! Harold's ambivalent as to the winner - from your observation, Lila didn't care if Harold didn't care about hockey - as season ticket holders they chose a flight to Game Six in Philadelphia at Wachovia Center over driving or the train. They'll stay in a Chicago-friendly hotel if they can find one!

At halftime, Harold explained to you a total stranger, "It's critical I have seats as close as possible to the action without being on the ice itself."

"Why does a man who doesn't care one iota about the outcome of the most important and final game of the entire National Hockey League season need to sit in the best seats of the arena" you argued.

Harold replied, "I respect your logic. Let's wait 'til the Hawks hopefully win this game so you, Lila and most of Chicago can celebrate; I will celebrate with you and share why a non-hockey fan must be this close to the action."

You bought dinner and Harold bought drinks. Lila chose two tasty desserts which you all shared. At breakfast everyone focused on other topics, and Harold happily obliged your request on your shared cab rides to PIA - Philadelphia International Airport.

"In grad school at MIT, I took an advanced physics course taught by a professor whose son, Dane, was a case study in one of our sessions. Dane was a strong running back on Penn State's football team. Dane hoped to break Penn's rushing record; instead he sustained a crushing hit to his head; everyone on the field knew the hit knocked Dane unconscious and he was out for two days! It's been six months - Dane sits in a wheelchair and is unable to speak"

"That's terrible!" you groaned.

"Yes, Harold agreed; Dane's father, my professor, tears streaming down his face said to our class: 'You're brilliant people. I'm blessed to be your professor. With your brainpower and MIT's clout I know one day, you will develop a new generation of headgear, helmets and pads with to eliminate serious concussions in football and hockey.'

"Last night's Blackhawks – Flyers game is my final segment of our research and recommendations for equipment and rules changes in a report we plan to deliver to NHL and NFL owners and equipment manufacturers" announced Harold with a smile.

"Who's paying you for researching and preparing the report, Harold" you asked.

"Some colleagues are happy to get paid but I told our sponsor I'm not starving and prefer wrapping my brain around solving this problem in an unbiased manner, without any loyalties to the NFL, NHL or others potentially skewing my objectivity."

Thus began your relationship with Harold Petit, the brightest most honest member of Leviathan's A-team.

In addition to you, Harold, Lila, Ruth and Hank you instruct each of your seven outsourced consultants "OC" to adopt their own unique company name, plus a distinct and separate legal entity through which their portion of your expenses and revenues flow. Ideally they pick a name suiting their personality – like you did.

Every OC shares their business plan and demonstrates how they will quietly and stealthily capture at least 1 percent and no more than 5 percent of the market share of the #1 and #2 largest companies in each OC's local market.

Before you began Leviathan you were an independent consultant for three multibillion dollar companies who dominated their respective markets.

In your early twenties, you ran this ad in the Wall Street Journal:

"Are you an ethical CEO of a multi-billion dollar company? Did you used to dominate your market? Are revenues declining? Is a wolf is raiding your hen-house? You can trust me to dig up the true cause(s) of your eroding revenues…and I will recommend solutions to turn you around."

Your ad generated two hundred eighty six emails. Extensive background research narrowed your list to twenty-seven companies and demanded every short-listed company complete a thirty page "Intel Sheet" divulging the company's real numbers and all information, imagined or real, causing the CEO to lose sleep.

You chose to work with three who met your criteria of candor, serious anxiety and willingness to pay $500,000 up front of your $1,000,000 fee. You work fast but estimated you'd spend five hundred to one thousand hours per assignment; plus you expected to outsource two hundred hours to friends with expertise in law enforcement, law, government, Securities

Exchange Commission, IRS and tax accounting…possibly others so you estimate their time at $200 per hour.

You went out on the deck of your modest apartment to shout your plans to the world or some such place: "After serving these three troubled companies well my goal is to clear one million bucks after taxes from this gig for starting Leviathan!"

"I'm not sure if anyone hears my voice and I hope my neighbors don't think I'm drunk again" you wondered.

Time to get to work!

You're surprised none of your three client companies was suffering from a nefarious wolf siphoning corporate funds to his offshore bank account in the Cayman Islands; their particular "wolves" consisted of:

1. Antiquated Customer Service and Accounting systems

2. Lazy business practices.

3. Fat, overpaid, under-motivated SVP and above

4. Low personal integrity

You kept copious notes of your observations in each company. To protect yourself you won't reveal actual names of employees until you confirmed their identities at multiple levels. You gave nicknames like "Lizard Breath," "Tight Fist," "Horny Dog," "Lover Boy," and "Brownie Nose." At all levels, employees fabricated bad performance rumors to accelerate their own promotion: "Zeke is just not himself lately…I hope he's okay?"

You also unearthed trusted executives falling mysteriously ill entirely off-line while traveling to exotic warm places ostensibly on company business. You're intrigued with the ingenuity employed by executives to explain a sudden ability to acquire their dream car after an expensive "vacation" to an exotic location.

"My Mom died six months ago and we just sold her house!"

You uncovered executives engaged in "swapping" by referring a valued customer to a <u>competitor</u> for a fee of $50,000 to $100,000 just for a phone call or an email.

One exec gave up confidential information to get a two-week all-expenses-paid "Communication Excellence" training on a Benetti super yacht generously laden with booze, cigars and gorgeous massage therapists.

The three troubled CEO's you selected have no idea revenues are declining three to twelve percent in the current quarter - until now your new clients barely noticed they were bleeding cash! How can this happen?

You never lacked for self-confidence but in your heart you privately wondered – "am I smart enough to help my clients stop bleeding, plus coach them on how to identify and implement healthier business practices in the future? Warren Buffett I'm not! Who can I turn to for wisdom?"

Your three multi-billion dollar clients are so huge no employee or stockholder had yet felt the pain; employees continue to receive paychecks and shareholders collect quarterly dividends so why complain to the media or listen to you?

The most prevalent Achilles heel was every behemoth's tendency to <u>ignore tiny competitors</u>! Like a flea on a dog or a fly on a horse the small guy competitors don't deserve to be called competitors! Just give the flea a nibble from your teeth and the fly a swat from your tail if it's a nuisance to you.

One axiom of free market capitalism is: Every successful company from Mom & Pop startups to a mega company is: You will have one or more competitors - it's a courageous and beautiful thing to do.

Your clients won't initiate changes you recommend or reverse unwise habits and antiquated practices until you quantify the market share those "<u>little nothing startups</u>" have captured: ultimately this requires a deep dive into real numbers and back checking revenues and expenses. Your three clients were grateful for your identification of people and practices costing them from three to five percent revenue erosion for each of five straight years – the cumulative damage translated into fifteen to twenty-five percent loss of market share!

Your business plan in starting Leviathan was inspired by observing and studying successful companies unwittingly expose vulnerabilities while falling in love with soon to be antiquated best practices and innovations credited with taking their own business from startup to mega-company.

You're not advertising the birth of Leviathan for its mission is a stealth company.

To win market share for your new company, you must first identify critical qualities or elements in the companies you will be considering:

1. High overheard;

2. Low technology;

3. Erosion of Integrity in sales force and/or leadership;

4. Ripe opportunities for innovative tweaking of existing systems;

5. Rarely invest face to face fun time with clients.

You'd finally earned the $1,000,000 plus in startup capital. Now you can start your own company inspired by the fabled Leviathan you heard about as a child:

"It makes the depths churn like a boiling caldron and stirs up the sea like a pot\ of ointment. It leaves a glistening wake behind it; one would think the deep had white hair. Nothing on earth is its equal—a creature without fear. It looks down on all that are haughty; it is king over all that are proud."

****

Leviathan – Part Two

You hate nightmares!

Last night's was a doozy.

You called an emergency meeting.

"I'm sorry team I usually sleep like a baby but last night I had a horrible nightmare and haven't slept since!"

"I'm sorry boss, Ruth offered, how can we help?"

Your conference room's over the top for a company with five FTEs and seven OC's; but if served you well when a mega investor or bank or prospective consultant's interviewed; tasteful, though not conducive to an intimate gathering with close friends. Happily, your colleagues are feeling like friends and family as the years go by together.

"Hey guys let's meet in my office around the small conference table."

"I'm good" offered Harold.

Ruth, Lila and Hank gave a "thumbs up" reply.

At the meeting you began candidly, "Sorry to be such a head case by letting you into my dreams…much less my nightmare! You need to hear to decide if I'm worth the risk for you to stay at Leviathan?"

"Boss, now you've got me scared", said Ruth.

Harold added, "I'm not easy to scare but you've got my attention boss!"

"In my dream all of us at Leviathan were happily fulfilling our goal of stealing market share from established but vulnerable companies in the U.S. and around the globe as we've been doing since our inception seven years ago."

"Suddenly a massive, powerful, ugly creature swooped down from the heavens roaring and devouring Leviathan. In its massive, bloody mouth I saw Harold, Lila, Ruth, Hank and our seven OC's."

"What about you, boss?"

"I'm frantically swinging a huge sword I was not equipped to handle but still trying to scare or distract the creature into dropping all of you from its evil jaws!"

"Then what?"- said Hank.

"I eventually woke up - drenched in sweat and realized I'd been standing on my bed flailing the sword at a huge unbeatable enemy!"

"Boss, do you think this could be for real" Ruth pleaded.

You said, "Ruth, I have no doubt the images and desperate fighting with the dragon actually occurred inside my mind...but to such a degree I was standing up flailing away at the beast for several minutes! I growled and cursed at the beast to "let my friends go!"

Ruth added "I'm cool with that boss – you're too level-headed to make up a scary dreams to get our attention – we've gotta figure out what it means!"

Harold chimed in, "I've known you the longest boss. You don't exaggerate except in ping pong where you claim to be **unbeatable** though I've kicked your butt many times; plus for a man your age, you're in decent shape, and in control of body and brain so you refuse to use drugs or get drunk. Harold added, "You're a proud man who keeps your guard up; you care for us so you chose to share this dream with us is not easy for you - I respect you for it boss."

"Me too", chimed the rest of the team.

Ruth asked, "Boss do you think we should share this with our OC's?"

"Good question" you responded. "Let's keep it confidential between the five of us until I tell you otherwise."

"So be it", responded Harold for the team as they all nodded.

Not surprisingly, brilliant Harold has emerged as your unofficial second in command. Though twenty-six, Harold's business instincts and people skills rival your own.

You asked "Harold, shall we close the office Friday so the team can enjoy a three day weekend?"

"Sounds okay if we have our devices at home or while traveling in case we need to communicate before Monday" suggested Harold.

You invited all team members to deliberate in their own minds about what, if anything, your dream might mean to each of them.

"You added, let's all meet at 7:00 Monday morning in the conference room for a light breakfast. Lila can you bring in the usual stuff?

"Sure boss - if you have a special breakfast request let me know by Sunday."

"Free for dinner tonight" Harold?

"You buying Boss - again" claimed Harold.

"I admit you're great company plus you add value in excess of any dinner costs I'd incur" you assured Harold.

Stifling a grin Harold said, "Time will tell, boss – I make no promises."

"In the interest of full disclosure, I must tell you I have an agenda for dinner Harold" you confessed.

Harold said, "It's gotta be the scary dream you want to talk about – right? If I have a dream like that I'm gonna talk about it with any wise person I trust!"

You agreed, "Yes and I have no idea what it means…or if it means anything in the first place…tempting to just dismiss it; pretend it never happened!"

"I understand your confusion", offered Harold, "Don't know if I can add anything toward solving the dream either."

You admitted, "I was stupid to miss lunch after burning mega calories fighting that monster all night long; I can devour a monster for dinner - actually a juicy steak sounds better, and healthier than monster flesh."

Harold picked up your idea, "looks like we're pounding down beef at Landry's Steak House - shall I challenge you to the 32 ounce with all the trimmings, big guy?"

"You're on hot shot and we'll see what you're made of little fella."

Neither you nor Harold are physically impressive – but it doesn't stop you from acting like you're both huge and buff!

Harold and Lila met at MIT and married after two years at Leviathan. Harold wears his ring like a "faithful husband should."

You're single but you wear a ring anyway to keep the ladies at bay. In addition to being well groomed, well-dressed and clean-cut you have two favorite chick magnets in your extensive repertoire: Buggers and Saint.

Buggers (pronounced "boogers") is your Bugatti Veyron Super Sport, a 1200 horse power ultra-luxury and beautiful 264 mile per hour exotic driving machine! Saint is your two hundred pound best friend – a huggable old Saint Bernard. You'd be a lonely guy if Saint wasn't waiting at your door each night. By a vote of five to one, with you the dissenting vote, Saint visits your office once a week to give his sitter a day off.

"Boss I'll race you to Landry's" Harold challenged. "Good luck getting out of the garage."

118

You furrowed your brow "Uh oh - did your new Mustang get out of the shop?"

You'd hoped Harold drove Lila's SUV to work. Judging by the all day long smug grin on Harold's face - his new Shelby GT500 Mustang's is finally out of the shop! Super smart Harold knows your garage has ridiculous speed bumps and a tedious security gate. You suspect Harold's already parked in the outside unsecured lot – giving him a thirty to forty-five second head start to Landry's. Your plan's to get Buggers on the expressway asap to cover 90% of the drive at max speed and no signals!

Let the race begin! Landry's is 7.5 miles from the office mostly via expressway. Harold was nowhere in sight as you roared out of the garage onto the expressway. You hit 200 plus like a bullet in the express lane. You saw Harold's beautiful blue Mustang doing 180 and heading down the exit ramp only a half mile from Landry's. "If push Boogers to 250 I may catch Harold at the exit ramp and avoid the stop light – damn!

"You almost caught me with your French made hunk of junk! It's a fast son of a gun!

What's the tab for that beauty" smiled Harold.

"1.7 million" you replied. What's the damage for your Shelby 500 Mustang?"

"$62 K including tax and license," said Harold with a huge grin.

"Wow Harold, I'm impressed and concede your $62,000 American made Mustang Shelby GT500 is a serious machine! Can I drive it?"

Harold smiled again, "Can I drive the Bugatti?"

Sharing your stuff isn't easy for you, but you knew Harold's been lusting to drive Buggers for a year but was afraid to ask his Boss.

You said okay "Yes, IF you treat Buggers with respect he deserves, Harold."

The Walk – S.B. Stone & Rock Solid Publishing, LLC ©2018

Harold suggested, "I'll drive my very first brand new car for thirty days to break it in, then let's swap cars for a week - sound good Boss?"

"Super" you said. Wait a minute you've only bought **used cars** up to now? You made good money at Microsoft and even better money at Leviathan, right?"

"I can hear my wise Dad - 'Harold, until your rich, let the rich guys buy the new cars. He won't mind taking the 20-30% instant depreciation hit on new cars the second he drives it off the lot. Heck, a well maintained used car will feel almost new anyhow. Dad hated debt so we payed cash for our cars which means I have to save for a while or buy a super cheap car. We've got savings, a couple cars, stocks and a home worth a couple million so Lila suggested it was time I buy a brand new one."

"Your folks raised you well, Harold."

"Hello Lila, what are you doing here?"

"Hey boss, I rode to work in Harold's new toy. Is it ok if I join you and my 'bae' for dinner?"

"I'm sorry Lila, what's bae mean again?"

"Before anyone else."

You said, "Okay I get it. How do I find a lady who's my bae?"

"Have you tried any of the dating sites yet boss?" queried Harold.

You replied, "Yes - I see pretty and intelligent women.

"Sounds okay so far", offered Lila.

The ladies I've dated produce too little connection in my heart. Some seem nervous or like they're putting on an act. And the few who've met Buggers and Saint in the flesh get so gooey and phony they'll say or do anything to entice me go to hop in the sack with them and lure me into a long term relationship."

Lila suggested, "Didn't you hope the Bugatti and Saint Bernard would help you find a great mate?"

You said no, "I got Buggers and Saint for my enjoyment, not to impress the ladies."

"I understand" Lila added, "Is it possible Saint and Buggers are serving double duty by giving you pleasure and weeding out phonies earlier in your relationships?

"Lila you are brilliant! I might still be seeing Sandy if she hadn't fallen apart over Saint and Buggers when she figured she knew how wealthy I am. Saint and Buggers are saving me time, money and emotional pain!" you agreed.

"Hey Lila, you are FAM to me, plus you're a wise and insightful person. Can you tell me the meaning of my dream?"

"I'm not sure - I'd rather ask God if the dream is from Him, and if so, what it means" Lila added.

You replied, "You'd do that for me Lila?"

"My pleasure boss" Lila smiled. I actually pray often for the success of Leviathan and for God to bring the best wife for you."

Your jaw dropped, "How long have you been praying for me and our business, Lila?"

"Pretty much since we first met several years ago, boss."

"I'm embarrassed Lila. The last time I prayed to God was when I was a little kid, maybe ten years old or so"

"Why' stop praying" asked Harold.

"I stopped praying after my parents, most teachers and professors told me God doesn't exist. I believed them instead of following my own 'child-like' faith."

Harold lamented "We're so sorry boss."

You added, "I had zero religious training as a kid but I talked to God in my thoughts on more than one occasion."

"About what?" wondered Lila.

"Thank you for giving me a new friend, when my best friend moved away. Thank you God for the sunny warm day and the bees buzzing around the flowers. Thank you for such a fun tenth birthday party. I even asked God to forgive my parents for acting like He doesn't exist – it's unscientific to deny God's existence when His thumbprint is all around us."

Harold shared, "That is high key boss!"

You ask, "Harold, why'd you say it's straight up truth when I prayed as a boy?"

Lila interjected, "God loves it when His children of any age pray to Him with a humble and sincere heart!"

"Sorry guys, I've neglected to share an important detail about my dream", you admitted.

"Tell us, boss."

"While swinging my sword at the monster or dragon or whatever it was, I begged and screamed 'God please help me kill this thing!'"

"So you begged God to help you, boss?"

"Yes, I was ten when I last prayed to God. I just turned forty, so it's been thirty years since my last prayer - you think God is angry with me?"

"Boss, sorry you turned forty! I didn't know you are so old" Harold smiled.

Lila added, "Boss Monday morning I'm going to bring you a special birthday present."

You replied, "That's lit Lila; what's my present?"

"It's a secret", Lila said.

Harold added, "uh oh it's not the keys to my new Mustang is it, Lila?"

"Don't get salty, Harold, you will totally approve of boss's 40th birthday gift…in fact I might have you pick it out for him."

Harold smiled, "I'm cool with that."

"Hey boss - we're half way into our steaks and Lila's salmon. Tell us your best guess of the meaning of your dream - or do you want me or Lila to go first?"

From the heart, you shared, "I know I've neglected to include God in my life and in my business. I've given myself, my employees and outside consultants all the credit for our success. I have freely committed any sins I wanted to without allowing myself to feel guilty or talking with God about it."

"We're listening boss."

"I've never read the Bible; in high school a friend said he read a story about a successful king whose subjects worshipped him as if he were a god. My friend said the king accepted their worship refusing to give God praise for his success."

Lila interrupted, "Your friend spoke the truth: '*Immediately because Herod did not give praise to God, an angel of the Lord struck him down, and he was eaten by worms and died.*'" Acts 12:23 [1]

"Holy crap" you grimaced.

"Not the best choice of words but I understand your concerns, boss. Let me share another truth for your consideration – "*They will be punished with everlasting destruction and shut out from the presence of the Lord and from majesty of his power.*"

"Wait a minute! Who is he talking about?"

"*He will punish those who do not know God and do not obey the gospel of our Lord Jesus*"

You queried, "What the heck is the **gospel** of our Lord Jesus? At college I had a classmate with a perpetual smile and wore a shirt saying 'Jesus loves you: Read John 3:16'. Was the gospel printed on his shirt?"

Lila stated, "The word gospel means '**good news**'."

Harold added, "That's right Lila, check out John 3:16-20 on my phone."

"*For God so loved the world that he gave his one and only Son, that whoever believes in him shall not perish but have eternal life. For God did not send his Son into the world to condemn the world, but to save the world through him. Whoever believes in him is not condemned, but whoever does not believe stands condemned already because they have not believed in the name of God's one and only Son. This is the verdict: Light has come into the world but people loved darkness instead of light because their deeds were evil."* [1]

You shared, "Whoa, this sounds huge – can you help me understand it!"

Harold agreed, "It is a mouthful. Let's examine in smaller pieces and I'll give comments for you, boss."

"For God so loved the world."

God is holy and just and embodies <u>perfect love</u>. He created mankind as an expression of His love and wants to love us through our challenges on earth despite our imperfections.

"That he gave his one and only Son,

Jesus has hung out with His Father throughout eternity. They're so tight Jesus said, "I and the Father are one."

"That whoever believes in him [Jesus] shall not perish but have eternal life.

Jesus birth, teaching, miracles and Jesus death on the cross are divinely orchestrated events whereby Jesus shed blood purchased a spot for mankind in God's beautiful heaven.

"For God did not send his Son into the world to condemn the world,

All humans fall short of God's perfect standards - stained by evil thoughts, lies, envy, sensuality, pornography, theft, adultery, fornication, idolatry, bitterness and other sins so there's nothing we can do to sanitize our souls from the stains of our sins; God has an Unthinkable Solution: Jesus Christ.

"but to save the world *through him [Jesus]"*

None of us can live a perfect, sin – free life. Thus God requires a perfect, spotless sinless sacrifice in order to clean me and you and the rest of mankind from our sins.

Whoever believes in him [God and Jesus] is not condemned, but without faith it is impossible to please God. Anyone who comes to God must believe He exists and that He rewards those who earnestly seek Him. Whoever does not believe stands condemned already"

"God loves us so much He gives us <u>freedom of choice.</u> Thus, whether we believe in God and Jesus Christ, is your and my personal choice."

Because they have not believed in the name of God's one and only Son."

No matter how "nice" we are it's impossible for us to earn our way into Heaven. If you and I choose <u>not</u> to put our faith in Jesus Christ we'll both die with our sins unforgiven and spend eternity in hell."

You asked, "Isn't it unfair God would send you and I to hell?"

Harold responded, "I hear what you're saying, but can't you see we were headed to hell in the first place?"

"Because of our sinful lives?" you suggested.

"Yes, Heaven is a perfect, beautiful, peaceful, love-filled place and God is too brilliant to let any of us sin-stained humans mess it up."

"Harold, how did you get so smart about God and the Bible? Did you go to Bible school and I somehow missed it on your CV?"

Harold smiled, "When I was fifteen years old and bored out of my mind Dad challenged me to read it."

"Cool" you replied.

"Dad got me a blue leather bound New International Version (NIV) and I blew through it from Genesis to Revelation fairly quickly."

"How long is the Bible?" you asked.

"Sixty-six books, each with multiple chapters, written by about thirty plus human authors."

"How many pages" you asked.

The Walk – S.B. Stone & Rock Solid Publishing, LLC
©2018

"Depends on which version you're reading; I think my Bible has 728,000 words if that helps." Harold clarified.

"My NIV Daily Bible takes me through the Bible in one year includes a daily reading or two from Old and New Testament books. It's in my backpack...see exactly 1,688 pages.

"Do both of you still read the Bible?"

Harold confessed, "The Bible's one of the few books I can read multiple times and still learn new things about God and His world every time I read it!"

Lila added, "Even though Harold's way smarter than me, I am just as lit about the Bible as he is."

"How come, Lila" you asked.

"The Bible is full of real life human intrigue. God's stories show me how to do a better job in the workplace, in Harold's and my relationship and in life...and be happier in the process."

"Boss, I know you hired Lila and me because you want Leviathan to be mega successful – right?"

"Definitely true – you are mega team members", you agreed.

"Until tonight's chat, you didn't know Lila and I pray for your life and Leviathan's success?"

"I was clueless" you admitted.

"I've been quietly asking God to reveal the reason or reasons He gave you the dream" Lila shared.

"I'm listening" you stated.

Lila suggested, "Boss I think the dream is God's warning to you. He wants to be the Lord of your heart and mind and soul and spirit to impact all aspects of your life, your relationships and your business."

"I strongly agree" said Harold."

"Ever heard of King David?" Lila inquired.

You replied, "Yes, the wealthiest and wisest man in the world, right?"

The Walk – S.B. Stone & Rock Solid Publishing, LLC
©2018

"Not exactly, Lila clarified, King Solomon was wealthy and wise, and he was King David's son."

Harold added, "God wants you to have the heart of King David, not the heart of King Herod, who refused to give God the glory for all the fame and blessings God had given him."

Lila said, 'Not just you - God wants <u>all His children</u> around the world to have a heart like King David, but many choose to have a wicked heart instead."

King David was a warrior and a musician. David's reverence and friendship with God is evident in Psalm 119, here are excerpts: *"Blessed are those whose ways are blameless, who walk according to the law of the LORD...You have laid down precepts that are to be fully obeyed. Oh, that my ways were steadfast in obeying your decrees...How can a young person stay on the path of purity? By living according to your word. I seek you with all my heart; do not let me stray from your commands. I have hidden your word in my heart that I might not sin against you...I rejoice in following your statutes as one rejoices in great riches...do not hide your commands from me...Your statutes are my delight; they are my counselors...strengthen me according to your word...Keep me from deceitful ways; be gracious to me and teach me your law. I have chosen the way of faithfulness; I have set my heart on your laws. I hold fast to your statutes, LORD; do not let me be put to shame...Give me understanding, so that I may keep your law and obey it with all my heart. Direct me in the path of your commands, for there I find delight. Turn my heart toward your statutes and not toward selfish gain. Turn my eyes away from worthless things; preserve my life according to your word...May your unfailing love come to me, LORD, your salvation, according to your promise...for I delight in your commands because I love them. I reach out for your commands, which I love, that I may meditate on your decrees...Your decrees are the theme of my song wherever I lodge. In the night, LORD, I remember your name, that I may keep your law...I am a friend to all who fear you, to all who follow your precepts. The earth is filled with your love, LORD; teach me your decrees...Though the arrogant have smeared me with lies, I keep your precepts with all my heart...The law from your mouth is more precious to me than thousands of pieces of silver and gold. Your hands made me and formed me…I know, LORD, that your laws are righteous, and that in faithfulness you have afflicted me…Your word, LORD, is eternal; it stands firm in the heavens. Your faithfulness continues through all generations; you established the earth, and it endures. Your laws endure to this day, for all things serve you…To all perfection I see a limit, but your commands are boundless. Oh, how I love your law! I meditate on it all day long. Your commands are always with me and make me wiser than my enemies. I have more insight than all my teachers, for I meditate on your statutes. I have more understanding than the elders, for I obey your precepts. I have kept my feet from every evil path so that I might obey your word. Your word is a lamp for my feet, a light on my path…I hate double-minded people, but I love your law. You are my refuge and my shield; I have put my hope in your word…You reject all who stray from your decrees, for their delusions come to nothing…All the wicked of the earth you discard like dross; therefore I love your statutes. My flesh trembles in fear of you; I stand in awe of your laws…Because I love your commands more than gold…The unfolding of your words gives light; it gives understanding to the simple. I open my mouth and pant, longing for your commands…Your righteousness is everlasting and your law is true. Trouble and distress have come upon me, but your commands give me delight…I have put my hope in your word…Salvation is far from the wicked, for they do not seek out your decrees…All your words are true; all your righteous laws are eternal…my heart trembles at your word. I rejoice in your promise like one who finds great spoil. I hate and detest falsehood but I love your law. Seven times a day I praise you for your righteous laws. Great peace have those who love your law, and nothing can make them stumble…I wait for your salvation, LORD, and I follow your commands…for all my ways are known to you…May my lips overflow with praise, for you teach me your decrees. May my tongue sing of your word, for all your commands are righteous…I long for your salvation, LORD, and your law gives me delight.*

Let me live that I may praise you, and may your laws sustain me. I have strayed like a lost sheep.

Seek your servant, for I have not forgotten your commands."
[1]

The Walk – S.B. Stone & Rock Solid Publishing, LLC
©2018

Lila jumped in – "you okay boss?"

Harold added, "Boss your mouth's hanging open - your eyes are dumbstruck."

You blurted, "Sorry I scared you guys - King David's my hero!"

"Tell us why" said Lila with Harold nodding.

You gladly gave it a shot: "David has reverence for God; he writes poetry and lives as a king and a fighter - not afraid to get his hands dirty or bloody. Is this the dude who killed the nine foot giant, Goliath, as a very young man?"

He's the one – check out 1 Samuel 17:45-51: "David said to the Philistine, "You come against me with sword and spear and javelin, but I come against you in the name of the Lord Almighty, the God of the armies of Israel, whom you have defied. This day the Lord will deliver you into my hands, and I'll strike you down and cut off your head. This very day I will give the carcasses of the Philistine army to the birds and the wild animals, and the whole world will know that there is a God in Israel. All those gathered here will know that it is not by sword or spear that the Lord saves; for the battle is the Lord's, and he will give all of you into our hands. As the Philistine moved closer to attack him, David ran quickly toward the battle line to meet him.

Reaching into his bag and taking out a stone, he slung it and struck the Philistine on the forehead. The stone sank into his forehead, and he fell face down on the ground. So David triumphed over the Philistine with a sling and a stone; without a sword in his hand he struck down the Philistine and killed him. David ran and stood over him. He took hold of the Philistine's sword and drew it from the sheath. After he killed him, he cut off his head with the sword. When the Philistines saw that their hero was dead, they turned and ran." [1]

"King David's a great role model for giving God the credit for his victories and success in life but he's not perfect. He committed adultery with Bathsheba and put a contract on her husband to be killed when she was pregnant with David's child!" Lila added.

The Walk – S.B. Stone & Rock Solid Publishing, LLC
©2018

"Did God kill David?" you asked.

"David confessed, 'I have sinned against the Lord.'"

"David's advisor, Nathan, told David, *'The Lord has taken away your sin. You are not going to die…by doing this you have shown utter contempt for the Lord, the son born to you will die.'*" 2 Samuel 12:13 – 18 [1]

Harold explained, "In David's day a lamb was sacrificed to remove people's sins from God's record book. God created a superior and permanent solution two thousand years ago when Jesus Christ came to earth at Christmas and offered Himself in an excruciating death on the cross at Easter."

You asked, "You mean God and Jesus planned the whole thing?"

Harold replied, "Make no mistake Jesus Christ is the perfect sinless Lamb of God."

Lila agreed, "You and I and everyone else still breathing God's air I are invited to put our faith in Jesus blood He purposefully shed as a **holy substitute** for everyone's sin."

"God is ready to wipe ALL your sins off His record book, thus assuring you will be welcomed into Heaven when you die! First you must decide, by faith, to humbly confess to God and turn away from your sins; then entrust your heart, soul, mind, body and the rest of your life to following God's plans for your life."

"What will you do?"

##
###########

Thank you friend for reading Leviathan! I'd love your feedback at feedback@thewalk.me

The Walk – S.B. Stone & Rock Solid Publishing, LLC
©2018

The Walk: Episode Six: Too Young to Die

Your eyelids are frozen shut.

You're screaming - "I refuse to die this way!"

You're mind envisions going out while plucking innocents from human traffickers or driving fast and shooting deadly accurate to cut off a tentacle of a drug cartel bastard!

Dying as a victim of horrible weather is embarrassing, which is why it makes no sense.

As a kid in Oklahoma, head-scratching adults marveled your infallible forecasting. Your den is adorned with your diplomas: Cornell's bachelors, masters and doctoral programs in physics, meteorology and atmospheric science - Magna Cum Laude.

Your life in the balance, you're recalling yesterday's debate with Matthias, aka Mati, at the weather channel.

"Hey pal, I know you've got the hots for Sophie - why not wait til the weather clears – then head to Sioux Falls?"

"We are just friends, Mati - besides she's my cousin dude" you replied.

"Hey I saw you two dancing at the Broadmoor wedding party" argued Matthias. "I'm not blind and there was love in the air with you two."

"I'm not gonna argue - Sophie is special and I don't know if she's hot for me like I may be hot for her," you clarified. Her best girlfriend hit the jackpot with twins – a boy and a girl! Sophie's no less and she's getting her hands dirty from diapers and baby vomit the month she's been there. Time to take Sophie home."

"Sophie's a good gal my friend" said Mattie.

"Yes, I'm lucky to have her…though I'm not exactly sure where I or Sophie want our relationship at this stage anyhow?"

Mati nodded, "I get it - you promised Sophie a road trip from Sioux Falls back home so you get time away talk about your futures?

"Exactly," you responded.

"Next two to three days I have to admit I'm scared for you," added Mattie.

"You're scared for our relationship?" you wondered.

"No silly - I'm scared you chose a bad time to pick up Sophie in Sioux Falls!"

"Tell me why but understand I'm going anyway" you said.

Mattie responded, "Remember the bomb cyclone in March 2019? My teacher friends in Sioux Falls and Rapid City say schools closed three days due to snow, ice and winds up to 50 mph creating ten foot high snow drifts blocking bus access to parking lots."

"That sucks", you opined. "South Dakota can't have enough trucks and plows for Interstate 90 plus city arterials and drifts removal at dozens of schools with heavy snow fall Wednesday through Friday. No choice but to close the schools, right?"

Mattie pleaded, "Guess what, we're forecasting another winter storm – possibly another bomb cyclone – hitting Texas, Oklahoma, Colorado, Wyoming, Nebraska and South Dakota tomorrow?"

"Impossible Mati! Two bomb cyclones in a thirty day window", you insisted – "how can I not remember March's bomb cyclone – I'm a highly educated weather professional! Do not forget our weather statistics class!"

"Yes, I got a higher "A" than you did loser" said Mati smiling.

You had to agree, "I attended one of Professor Scrivener's lectures due to work conflicts - what are the statistical probabilities of not one but two bomb cyclones hitting the same cities 30 days apart – besides didn't Sioux Falls hit 70 last week?"

"I hear what you're saying my friend, so I'll chill with you, added Mati. Hey wasn't it dank to see the video of the semi-trailers blown over by those fifty MPH winds in Texas?"

You replied, "I'd hate to be that guy! How embarrassing –
you think he was hauling a full-load? What's the max weight of a
fully loaded semi-trailer?"

"Good question, I dunno. I'd be scared spit-less if I was
driving that big rig" Mati added.

You flew in to Spokane to hang and spend time with Uncle
Pete this past week. As an identical twin brother, Pete bore a
strong resemblance to your good old Dad - a career weatherman
like you. Before Dad's untimely death at fifty-five, you, Dad,
Uncle Pete and his adopted daughter, Sophie went on several

The Walk – S.B. Stone & Rock Solid Publishing, LLC
©2018

camping, fishing and hunting trips. The trips were a blast. Filled with joking, stories around the fire and lots of competition.

Uncle Pete's typical greeting was - "how's my favorite nephew anyhow?"

You'd typically reply, "my name is not 'Anyhow' so why do you keep messin up my name?

It's fun to laugh. After your Dad died, Uncle Pete changed his greeting: "How's my brother's son? Or how's my favorite son these days?" Still missing your Dad a lot, it was somehow stabilizing when Uncle Pete called you "my favorite son". You knew Pete loved you like your Dad had.

"Hey Uncle Pete, how come there's no flights to Sioux Falls tomorrow or the next day", you wondered.

Uncle Pete took on his country trucker mode: "Hey son, ya'll cun hayav mah Jeep I cun loan it to ya for as long as you need it. Heck, when yur done just ship 'er back or wait 'n drive 'er back next time we git together, or maybe Sophie 'n yall kin tayk u little vacayshun.

Even though Uncle Pete respected the king's English - you get a kick when he lapse into the common man's lexicon – on occasion, you reciprocate with your own version: "Yessuh, I ayum veruh prowud ta hayav a mayan lyke yu fer mah deeeyur saweet unkl."

"Dang rytchusly kuwel" Pete said. How 'bout we add some o' dem weights on the fluhr of the reyah and mittle seats pawtnuh."

"I thank yur brilleyyunt, Uncle Pete! Lets git er dun ryt nahow, awlryte suh?" I know weeez ona rowel but ah kaynt stop laughin Pete so let's us declayer a cease fahr…oops…cease fire on the word war.

"Hey son, too bad Sophie's not here – would've been hilarious to hear her totally faked Atlanta Peachtree southern girl accent," lamented Pete.

"You're right Pete. I love it when she tawks lyke thayut!"

"Me too" agreed Pete.

"Hey Pete, did you know I may be fallin in love with your daughter?"

"I'm not surprised" Pete admitted.

"Why not, you asked?"

"Been watchin you two cousins grow into best buds over the years, so I know you already have a good friendship and kinda know each other's personalities. All that's good but doesn't mean there's a physical chemistry is there?"

"That's a legit question deserving a high key answer, Uncle Pete."

"I'm listenin son." Pete said.

"I've dated several women and one serious girlfriend," you shared.

"How long did you stay with the serious girlfriend, son?"

"Three years."

"That's serious - what's her name?"

"Charlotte's an on fleek and snatched lady! Nice to have her at my side for big events.

But I learned about myself in three years dating Charlene."

"Tell me son."

"First, I don't want a partner who's always gassed."

"You saying Charlene's a fart-machine?"

"No to millennials a person is "gassed" when they're full of themselves from too many compliments."

"I get it."

"I want a partner who doesn't mind getting her hands dirty, is level-headed, people centric and loves to have fun. Oh yes, and I'd love someone who truly enjoys the outdoors for biking, tennis, hiking, golfing, camping, snowboarding. Know anyone like that Pete?"

"I may know a gal who fits your criteria – are you attracted to her son?"

The Walk – S.B. Stone & Rock Solid Publishing, LLC ©2018

"I've viewed Sophie as a tomboy – pretty and cute but in a non-sexual way. Heck, we've probably hugged a hundred times since we were kids. Always pure-minded hugs…even when Sophie's body changed to a young woman's body my heart stayed pure."

"Do I feel a 'but' coming my son?" asked Pete.

"Remember Tom and Ginny Smyth got married a month ago?" you asked.

"Yes wasn't their venue the Broadmoor Hotel in Colorado Springs?" asked Pete.

"Pete how come you didn't attend?" you asked.

"Never got invited son" said Pete.

"That sucks Pete - rumor has it you find great wedding gifts so Tom and Ginny missed out by not inviting you."

"That's the rumor, Pete said. Did Tom and Ginny have dancing at the reception? And if so, did you ask Sophie to dance?"

"No, she asked me first and I was scared spit-less cuz I've never danced at a ritzy place with lots of people ostensibly watching."

"I hope you said yes, cowboy!"

"Sophie was beautiful all dressed up for the occasion. I could not say no. Our last dance was a slow one. Sophie stood on my feet…nuzzled her nose against my neck…and snuggled her body with mine. The longest hug we've ever had…until we said bye at the airport – that was even longer."

"Sounds like you two have the chemistry of physical attraction" Uncle Pete affirmed.

You added, "while we were hugging goodbye at the airport, I lost it…started crying and said I can't believe how much I want to kiss you, Sophie!"

"I know what you mean she said – can we wait 'til you pick me up in Sioux Falls? I promise it'll be worth the wait!"

"I taught my little girl well" said Pete.

The Walk – S.B. Stone & Rock Solid Publishing, LLC
©2018

"No doubt about it" you agreed.

Before hopping into the Jeep, you checked all the apps on your phone one last time for a flight to Sioux Falls direct from Spokane or via Denver or Salt Lake - still nothing.

"I'm outa here, Pete!"

"Hey hot rod you better not crash my Jeep in the ditch or some humongous snow drift!"

"Yeah, you know she drives a cutesy girl's car - a rear-wheel drive Mazda – worthless in the snow and not as safe in crashes - my Jeeps got 20,000 miles – new tires, navigation, blue tooth sound and state of the art anti-theft system and all-wheel drive."

Pete added, "Hey son, I forgot to tell you a key detail about your drive to Sioux Falls - there's no reason to return the Jeep to me in Spokane."

"Cool Pete, you smiled, my sweet cousin will be safer in your Jeep - plus, you're fastidious in maintaining your stuff so Sophie gets a nearly new car. Hey Pete can you teach me how to take care of my stuff like you do?"

Pete replied smiling, "I'd be happy to pass on my fastidious habits to you, son. Over the years you've probably picked up one or two of them just by watchin."

You admitted, "You're probably right Uncle Pete."

Pete lectured: "First things first - You need to adopt my excellent driving habits to get to Sioux Falls in one piece – like: Habit One: <u>Never fall asleep behind the wheel!</u>" It's a classic since the best driver in the world sitting in the nicest car in the world is <u>helpless</u> as a puppy if asleep at the wheel! If you feel the slightest bit sleepy when driving you must pull over at a safe place and take a nap dude. It could save your life and Sophie's new car!"

"What about energy drinks and snacks and opening the window or singing a song?" you asked.

FIERCE WINDS TOPPLE BIG RIG

WINTER STORM WARNING THIS EVENING... * WHAT...SNOW AND BL

The Weather Channel

6PM   7PM   8PM
             85%

Pete responded, "Hey man, as a wise traveler, you've already brought the stuff you'll need to keep your eyes wide open and engaged with the road ahead...right?"

"You can count on me, Uncle Pete. I'll make a quick stop at Larry's market before I hit the freeway. I'll drive super-safe and deliver your pristine rig to Sophie in Sioux Falls!"

You texted Sophie and copied Uncle Pete: "Departing Deer Park Washington at 9:00 am. Destination - Sioux Falls South Dakota. Estimated Route Interstate 90. Estimated driving time seventeen hours, eight minutes. Total Miles: 1225 plus four thirty minute pit stops for fuel, bathroom, snacks, calisthenics and stretching, so add two hours, means a nineteen hour eight minute ETA."

Sophie replied first: "I'm so excited you're driving my new car to Sioux Falls!"

Pete replied next: "Hey big guy. You be careful. Montana's got liberal speed limits, but if you're on solid ice you got virtually zero control despite my top of the line all-wheel drive. Safety and your life is more key than how fast you get to Sioux Falls."

"Thanks for doing this…your Dad and I are proud of you." Pete added.

"Thank you Pete for entrusting your Jeep to me for 1225 miles" you said.

You dictated a quick reply at the light: "Hey guys hopping onto I-90…last text or call 'til

I refuel in Butte or Bozeman, Montana."

Sophie replied: "You're my hero!"

Uncle Pete replied: "Don't try to be a hero, dude."

As a weather guy, you've been in floods, hurricanes, tornados, wildfires and blizzards - worse conditions than thus far on this drive – namely lightly falling snow and ice through Idaho and Montana, to almost blizzard conditions - what you've seen on this drive so far has been mild to moderate stuff. It's been a strange year though.

The weather several hundred miles west of you in Seattle is setting records! Seattle normally has zero up to a few inches of snow from November through April. Seattle's three primary ski areas <u>normally</u> suffer from light snowfalls and wet conditions producing cascade concrete and corn snow requiring Snoqualmie Summit, Stevens Pass and Crystal Mountain to make their own snow.

Not this year! "Seattle Prepares for Snowpocalypse" is the headline in the Seattle/Puget Sound region: February 4th One foot of snow plus 90 mph winds blowing the state ferry system; February 9th 17-22 inches at Port Angeles and up to 11 inches inland; a February record 20.2 inches fell at SeaTac Airport's; a record four feet of snow fell in 36 hours at Snoqualmie Summit Ski Resort. "We may have [finally] had too much snow" said one of the astonished Snoqualmie locals.

+++++++++++++++++++++++++++++++++++++++

Too Young to Die – Part Two

Driving in Montana at fifty to one hundred miles per hour depending on conditions you're listening to a climate-related book - "Upheaval! Why Catastrophic Earthquakes Will Soon

Strike the United States" by John L. Casey, Dr. Dong Choi, Dr. Fumio Tsunoda (professor of geology) and Dr. Ole Humlum. Published in 2016 by Trafford Publishing.

In the Forward to Upheaval by Dr. Rich Swier, you heard vital information: 1. Get ready for a dangerous new cold climate; 2. Since 2012, John Casey's International Earthquake Volcano and Prediction Center (IEVPC) has defied government science by accurately predicting the correct epicenter, depth, magnitude and timing of several 6.0 plus magnitude earthquakes.

In the Preface to Upheaval by Dr. Dong Choi, you learned: 1. In Casey's his first book, Cold Sun, he made the connection between cycles of the sun and the most destructive earthquakes and volcanic eruptions." 2. When the sun goes into solar hibernation, we see out worst earthquakes and volcanic eruptions; 3. In Upheaval we will attempt to pass on the best, most reliable information about the first of two major threats – deadly earthquakes.

Still driving briskly along I 90, you heard Upheaval's Introduction by John Casey: 1. The theory of man-made global warming and climate change based on human greenhouse gas emissions is the greatest international scientific fraud ever perpetrated on the world's citizens (from John Casey's books, Cold Sun (2011) and Dark Winter (2014); 2. One cannot continue to believe man controls climate change and at the same time accept the Sun and major earthquakes are interconnected as proposed herein. 3. Global Cooling are words unspoken, taboo in

Washington, even some conservatives…lack courage to …tell what's really happening to the climate – leaving the public in the dark; 4. The solar physics world began numbering the 11- year solar cycles in the mid-1700s, with solar cycle number 24 just ended, earth is now facing yet another solar hibernation of 20 to 30 years, almost 200 years after the last solar hibernation, famously known as the Eddy minimum after Dr. John Eddy a pioneer in solar cycles; 5. Visit www.ievpc.org next time I'm at my computer.

Casey states our earth just entered a "Solar Minimum" period of twenty to thirty years of severely declining temperatures. Our sun-induced cooling climate or mini ice age has been documented in earlier climate epochs: a. the coldest period of the Little Ice Age (1350 – 1830); b.the Maunder minimum (1615 – 1745); c. the Dalton minimum (1793 – 1830).

 In light of declining sun spot activity and severely colder temps, **Casey urges farmers to re-locate to warmer climates**. The U.S. has 2,050,000 farms averaging 444 acres. How do you relocate the average 444 acre farming business? Casey also warns families and businesses to prepare for colder temps and more severe earthquakes. Last I heard, Casey resides in Florida.

Whether we think he's accurate or not…at least the man is practicing what he's preaching.

On page 22 Chapter One Casey cites K.S. Jaiswal et al USGS study which finds 143 million Americans at risk of earthquakes. The West Coast map shows Cascadia and San Andreas faults still pose substantial risk of financial and human loss. The Mississippi Valley's New Madrid Seismic Zone, could suffer greater casualties and financial loss. Casey soberly quotes George Santayana: *"Those who cannot remember the past are condemned to repeat it."* What historical event should grab Mississippi Valley resident's attention?

I was blown away by testimonials of former Mississippi Valley's residents in Chapter Three – The New Madrid Seismic Zone (NMSZ); I almost pulled off freeway to call my friends, family and colleagues who live and work in the Mississippi Valley – as Casey shares historical evidence of devastating earthquakes hitting the Mississippi Valley over 200 years ago! Here are excerpts:

"Back then we didn't have television or radio. Folks wrote down and shared by word of mouth what they saw and heard. Our winter was colder than normal just south of the Mississippi River's junction with the Ohio River…when the world was thrown into chaos by a great series of earthquakes along the Mississippi River, ending with a final catastrophic one near New Madrid.

The land heaved and shook violently. Perhaps four mighty quakes from M7.0 to M8.0 struck. The Mississippi River was thrust upward and flowed backwards for a brief period of time altering the course of the river and creating Reelfoot Lake. A large number of fissures tore through the land's surface for as long as five miles; there were missing people most likely swallowed up by the earth…subsidence ranged from 5 to 20 feet; coal and sand were ejected from fissures near St. Francis River; the water level raised 25 to 30 feet; at Henderson, Kentucky no chimneys were left standing, while we were floating on the Ohio River we witnessed falling trees, disappearing islands and collapsing river-banks."

The following record is from the last solar hibernation in the Missouri, Kentucky, Tennessee, Arkansas…and the Wabash Valley Zone in and contiguous to NMSZ should be preparing for today…see the Figure 12 chart "New Madrid Earthquakes Strike at the Bottom of Each Solar Minimum" correlating past catastrophic earthquakes during solar minimums with estimated magnitudes of 6.8, 7.0, 7.3, 7.5, 7.5, 8.0 and 8.0, 1450 to 1895 and in December 1811 through February 1812.

Casey adds, "This series of at least three catastrophic quakes with M7.3 to M8.0 were the most powerful ever recorded on the North American continent. In terms of shear force and energy release, the NMSZ is the most dangerous earthquake zone in the USA with a capability of delivering a catastrophic series of quakes at any time…Casey asks, "What's the damage should we prepare for when the next big quake(s) hits today's NMSZ? Here's Casey's answer: 1. Figure eight states without power for several months plus potential cascading power grid losses in other states; 2. There is a ring of 12 nuclear power plants just outside the NMSZ. Are their reactors able to withstand M7.5 to M8.0 quakes? 3. Major bridge damage, traffic jams and [interruption of] commerce from the Gulf of Mexico to Great Lakes would last for many months; 4. Domestic and International Air Traffic adversely affected with loss/damage to airport infrastructure, runways, emergency aid via air rescues; 5. Major disruption of Mississippi River traffic via barges is possible; 6. Loss of critical oil and gas supply lines in NMSZ and northeastern states.

Casey warns America faces an eighty percent certainty these quakes will strike the people and businesses in the central Mississippi River Valley beginning as soon as 2017…usually in the winter months when earth is coolest. [7]

[Anecdotally, your author's in Rapid City SD on May 18, 2019. The locals and I are expecting spring weather! Last few weeks in March, April and May, we were teased by a few days in the 70's and a day two in the 80's. Today's been a low in the 30's and highs in the low 40's plus 20 mph winds as a bonus. The calendar says spring began 30 or was it 60 days ago?

These solar minimums are no picnic unless you're further south – like Florida, Arizona, South Carolina or Texas to name a few. Not a complaint, just your humble author's observation.]

Back to our story, you were flying along I-90 several miles past Beulah, Wyoming You finally entered South Dakota at a safe 85 MPH and only 385 miles from Sioux Falls. You expected to see the "Welcome to South Dakota" sign. Instead you were greeted by a grittier welcome:

I-90 CLOSED!!!

****

<u>Too Young to Die - Part Three</u>

They can't be serious?!

The Walk – S.B. Stone & Rock Solid Publishing, LLC

I'm a weather professional on a mission to rescue a beautiful young lady from two raucous barfing and pooping infants! Except for snow and wind the weather was similar to what you just drove through in Montana and Wyoming. You kept on driving but paused "Upheaval" in favor of Uncle Pete's eighties rock and roll: Bon Jovi's 'Living on a Prayer'; Tom Petty's 'Free Falling'; Don Henley's 'The Boys of Summer'; Journey's 'Don't Stop Believing' and The Police's 'Every Breath You Take."

Snow, snow, snow falling thicker and thicker. You hadn't seen a snowplow or pavement for hundreds of miles. You deduced they gave up plowing – wait until folks return to the roads. Rapid City, Sioux Falls and Denver Airports are closed with blizzard conditions. Snow and severe winds aren't conducive to landing big airplanes filled with hundreds of people.

You later wrote in your journal: "I had the sensation of driving on a white cloud; the Jeep and I felt airborne…it happened so fast and almost gently. Last I saw was a lit dimly glowing through the driving/swirling snowfall - 'Polaris'. Two huge and hard pillows smacked me on the side of my head and the front of my face. I took a nap…think it was a long one.

I awoke to see the Jeep encased in snow. I could breathe but not sure for how long. I am terrified and helpless. My cell has power but no signal. I texted Uncle Pete and Sophie. Delivery failed. Called 911 – Jeep encased in snow my phone wouldn't ping a tower."

Your Journal continued: "God, I refuse to die like this! I want to see Sophie and build a life together if you're okay with it. My life's ebbing away entrapped in this Jeep…like a drowning man is desperate to be saved, so am I! God I feel bad for ignoring you my whole life. Do you still love me despite my long list of sins against you and others? Facing death I'm suddenly interested in knowing you. How many millions have a similar crossroads - you love me despite my fickle heart! Sophie once shared Jesus words: *"but I know you. I know that you do not have the love of God in your hearts."* John 5:42 [1]

God, how do I get "the love of God" into my heart? I want it; I need it big time.

A school friend put words of Jesus on his bumper: *"I am the light of the world. Whoever follows me will never walk in darkness, but will have the light of life."*   John 8:12 [1]

Jesus, I've deliberately blinded my mind and my heart from your Light of Life. Please forgive me Jesus. I don't deserve God's forgiveness but I claim it anyway by believing Jesus shed his blood and died an agonizing death on the cross for me. I also believe Jesus rose from the dead three days after he died and was buried in the tomb.

"Not sure if I'm passing out or falling asleep."

I hear wildly loud noises outside…louder and louder…could it be snow blowers? I see a man on the hood, excited to see me alive.

"Name's Rudy - received your distress call from the boss."

You're not sure you pressed any button for the sunroof but it opened anyway.

"Here ya go sir" as Rudy's long strong arms gently planted under my armpits…lifting my two hundred pounds like a child's rag doll!

"Wow, you're a strong dude!" you exclaimed.

"I hear that sir" said Rudy smiling.

Grateful and exhausted, you wanted to hug and high five Rudy but figured your feeble "Thank you Rudy" sufficed.

"You've been stuck in your Jeep for hours; you hungry?" asked Rudy.

"I'm famished for a big burger and fries" you replied.

"I know a place called Thirsty's; it rocks – jump in my truck" Rudy said.

Thirsty's is packed but you landed a table for two while Rudy stayed outside to make a call saying "Go ahead and order. I'm not hungry yet."

As Rudy sat down you asked "how was your call Rudy?"

The Walk – S.B. Stone & Rock Solid Publishing, LLC
©2018

"Successful. I got you a room at Rushmore Inn. Okay with you" Rudy asked.

"That's nice of you Rudy" you said. Any idea where I can tow the Jeep? I'd like to take it to a reputable shop to assess the damage I inflicted on my girlfriend's car. I suspect no one will be available in this severe storm?!"

"Excuse me sir my name is Bill; enjoy your bacon cheddar burger and fresh cut fries. I'll grab your root beer stat."

"Looks mouthwatering! Thank you Bill."

"Has your friend finished his phone call" asked Bill.

"He's been sitting here several minutes" you stated irritably.

"The waiter can't see me" Rudy whispered.

"Are you kidding me?" you queried.

"Sorry for the confusion Bill - I think my friend's an angel" you offered.

"Is his name Rudy?" asked the waiter.

"How did you know" you asked.

"I'm not deaf sir; I heard you talking with Rudy your invisible friend whom you expect me to believe is an angel – are you on drugs?" queried Bill.

"I'm as sober as my new role model, Jesus Christ" you stated.

"Hey guys – join me outside on a fifteen minute smoke break?" Bill asked.

"Cool" you said.

"How old are you dude?" asked waiter Bill.

"Thirty something" you replied.

"I'm curious why you decided to make Jesus Christ your role model?" Bill asked.

"Just between us Bill, I'm well educated, very successful and confident I can figure life out using my skills and intelligence so why would I need God or Jesus?" you shared.

"Dude, the moment you walked into the Grill I knew you're on fleek and dank - plus there's something powerful inside you I cannot see but I can feel it" Bill observed.

"Several hours ago I crashed my girlfriend's Jeep on the side of Interstate 90 freeway. I was unconscious or asleep for several hours and the Jeep got buried under several feet of snow and ice during the nastiest part of a bomb cyclone! No cell service, pitch black outside, howling winds, terrible visibility and several feet of snow covering the Jeep. The temperature had to be ten below to thirty below zero with the wind chill so I'd likely freeze to death if I crawled out the window or through the sunroof. Sioux Falls was over 300 miles away and no one was expecting to see me for a few hours."

"You were toast dude" said Bill.

"I prayed a sincere and desperate prayer to God asking Him to rescue me from the storm and save my soul from the awful things I've done; I asked Him to let me reach my girlfriend so we can discuss spending our lives together…or not together…if God has different plans for us."

Bill said, "Looks like God said yes 'cause here you are at Thirsty's still suckin God's air; how'd you get rescued my friend?

You replied, "God sent Rudy to open my sunroof and pull me out with his very strong arms…hmm now that I think about it, Rudy's wearing street clothes - the wind and cold didn't bother him a lick!"

"Got to get back to work" Bill observed.

"You're in your twenties Bill?" you observed. "Have you given your heart to Jesus?

"Been thinkin 'bout it" Bill confided.

"Good Bill - here's my cell in case you wanna talk sometime" you offered.

The Walk – S.B. Stone & Rock Solid Publishing, LLC
©2018

You shook Bill's hand goodbye and noticed something in your pocket – a deep sky blue business-card Angels Auto Care with a note: "Get Sophie's Jeep at 10:00 am – Rudy."

You texted Sophie: "Can we talk?"

"Can't – Beth needs me to take both twins for an hour" said Sophie.

You texted Sophie back: "I crashed your Jeep and I'm so sorry! I'm okay; Jeep has scratches and minor damages; taking to shop tomorrow before continuing to Sioux Falls."

"Bummer" said Sophie.

"According to Rudy, the mechanic's gut check suggests the Jeeps drive train and suspension appear undamaged so I can grab some breakfast go get the Jeep and head your way!" you added.

"Great news my friend, but please take your time" Sophie begged.

"Will do, Sophie. I'm so sorry I crashed your new Jeep!"

"Who's Rudy the tow truck guy?" asked Sophie.

"Sort of. I'll fill you in later" you added.

"Talked to your Uncle Pete?" wondered Sophie.

"Not yet. I want to see the Jeep and drive it myself before I let him know I crashed his…now your Jeep." you said.

"Why not call Pete before you see the Jeep?" asked Sophie.

"He's going to want as complete a report as possible. I knew exactly how pristine Pete's

Jeep is…or was…Pete deserves my observations…not just the mechanic's when I call him," you clarified.

"I respect how you're handling this…so far…but I'm by no means okay with you driving off the road at 85 and crashing through a fence into a snowbank" Sophie added.

"I hear you Sophie - I'll text you after I've talked with Pete," you added.

"Fine with me" said Sophie.

"My phone shows Rapid City to Sioux Falls is 356 miles with one fuel stop it should take five hours at seventy," you said. Sophie's last words were "Super excited to leave Ruth, Ryan, Phoebe and Titus and God to be a family and head toward home with you."

You slept well but the morning came quickly. At 8:30 Rudy called your room from the house phone – "good morning my friend – are you feeling better and ready to pick up Sophie's Jeep?"

"You rascal who picked up the tab last night? Who prepaid my hotel room too?

"You think God's resources are limited?"

"I suppose not" you admitted.

"Tell me about you and Sophie. Has she attained girlfriend status?" Rudy queried.

"Good question, Rudy; Sophie's my Uncle Pete's adopted daughter. We've had tons of fun outings over the years camping, hiking, biking, rafting, climbing, tennis and golf."

Rudy replied, "sounds like a good friendship foundation - are you attracted to each other for more than a cousinly relationship?"

"I'm tryin to figure it out Rudy. Sophie's been my tomboy cousin since we were little kids. She's strong, competitive, funny and extremely tease-worthy. I love to make Sophie laugh…she cracks me up! A few months back, we're at a friend's wedding. I'd never seen Sophie dressed up so nicely – she is snatched man! I asked her to dance…the last one of the night; a slow dance…oh my goodness – holding Sophie so close, I was lit and dead Rudy."

Rudy observed, "Good thing you didn't have a heart attack my friend."

You agreed, "Yep I'm definitely too young to die! Hey Rudy how can I thank you for pulling me out of Sophie's ice encased Jeep - you know how scared I was?"

"Tell me how scared you were" said Rudy.

The Walk – S.B. Stone & Rock Solid Publishing, LLC
©2018

You gratefully shared: "I realized I could die in there. The Jeep's encased in snow, possibly ice. I'm strong so I knew I could try to muscle open the doors and windows but I wasn't ready yet. I put the key back in the ignition initially thinking the car might start and I could blast outta there - didn't start but holding the key gave me an escape idea."

Rudy couldn't resist - "Hey I think I know what your escape idea was."

You couldn't resist hearing: "Okay Rudy, I'm all ears - what's your escape idea?"

Rudy said "first, turn your key to the "accessories" part of the ignition; second, open the sunroof, just an inch or two; grab a long narrow thing like a hockey stick or golf club to find out how deep the snow is on the Jeep's roof – slide it through the slit in the sunroof to see how deep you're buried. Let's say it's less than two feet of snow on the Jeep's roof."

You interrupted, "Awesome news - now I can put on my gloves and water proof jacket…then swish my arm from side to side to clear a path large enough for me to climb out onto the roof!"

Rudy took the ball, "you're tracking with me but what if the snow is three or four feet thick or you're too wide or not strong enough to climb out?"

You took it back, "I'd put my phone in a baggy from one of the sandwiches I've eaten to protect it from the snow and wind; then I'd duct tape it onto the golf club or yardstick and try to ping a cell tower and call 911."

"You are one smart guy my friend" admitted Rudy.

You said "Takes one to know one my friend.

"Hello Angel and thank you for inspecting my girlfriend's Jeep!"

"We hooked the Jeep to our tow truck and pulled her into our heated shop to thaw her out for you. I also cranked on the engine and put her on our lift to see if there are any serious leaks, undercarriage issues or drivetrain damage – I find nothing significant."

You asked, "Did you drive her Angel?"

"No - we want you to be the first to drive her since you'd just driven her from Spokane Washington to Rapid City South Dakota - 850 miles. No one on God's green earth knows better than you how well she was driving just before you crashed her."

"True – I'll take her for a spin and see if I hear or feel anything amiss," you agreed.

"Angel, thanks again for helping me care for my cousin's Jeep - you handed him $200 cash"

"No problem – thanks for the two hundie's friend," Angel said.

"Rudy isn't there a story about the good Samaritan? You could've abandoned me on the side of the road to become an icicle in the Jeep but you didn't!"

Rudy responded, "My boss, the Lord Jesus, tells this story to us who love Him – including you."

On one occasion an expert in the law stood up to test Jesus. "Teacher," he asked, "what must I do to inherit eternal life?" "What is written in the Law?" he replied. "How do you read it?" He answered, 'Love the Lord your God with all your heart and with all your soul and with all your strength and with all your mind' [Deuteronomy 6:5] and, 'Love your neighbor as yourself.' [Levititcus 19:18] "You have answered correctly," Jesus replied. "Do this and you will live." But he wanted to justify himself, so he asked Jesus, "And who is my neighbor?" In reply Jesus said: "A man was going down from Jerusalem to Jericho, when he was attacked by robbers. They stripped him of his clothes, beat him and went away, leaving him half dead. A priest happened to be going down the same road, and when he saw the man, he passed by on the other side. So too, a Levite, when he came to the place and saw him, passed by on the other side. But a Samaritan, as he traveled, came where the man was; and when he saw him, he took pity on him. He went to him and bandaged his wounds, pouring on oil and wine. Then he put the man on his own donkey, brought him to an inn and took care of him. The next day he took out two denarii [a denarius was the usual daily wage of a day laborer see Matthew 20:2)] and gave them to the innkeeper. 'Look after him,' he said, 'and when I return, I will reimburse you for any extra expense you may have.' "Which of these three do you think was a neighbor to the man who fell into the hands of robbers?" The expert in the law replied, "The one who had mercy on him."

Jesus told him, "Go and do likewise." Luke 10:25-37 [1]

"Hey friend if you visit Rapid again, drop me a line", Rudy offered.

"Are you always in South Dakota?" you asked."

"No - I go wherever our Boss sends me. I'm a spirit-being so we travel fast. I went to and from Singapore while you were taking a breath" smiled Rudy.

"Impossible" you argued.

"After you've read God's love letter and instructions you'll know a lot more about how God thinks, about His angels and God's keys for you to live a satisfying life."

"Sounds hugely important Rudy - where do I find God's love letter?" you queried.

"It's the Holy Bible and it's free on line at www.youverson.com. It comes in 1,316 languages and 1,906 versions; you can also buy a printed Bible to hold in your hands for reading and studying as well." Rudy suggested.

"Will do", you said.

You visited the crash site on the east bound lanes of I-90 you were sobered by what you learned: The Jeep and you ran through three hundred feet of deep snow, then a fence, and up the side of a huge snow-covered mound! You didn't hit the mound at 85 mph – otherwise you'd have flipped! You said "thank you God" for all the snow and the fence to slow your speed from 85 to 25 to 30 by the time you hit the mound hard enough to deploy the air bags.

The Walk – S.B. Stone & Rock Solid Publishing, LLC ©2018

Not a mechanic you're pleasantly surprised the damage you've inflicted on Uncle

Pete/now Sophie's Jeep seems to be minor - time to call Uncle Pete.

"Uncle Pete, do you miss me yet?" you asked.

"Heck no, I'm digging the full refrigerator and pantry from the food you're not eating big guy," Pete replied with a smile.

"Are you saying I eat like a pig" you replied.

"More like a horse; a big talking horse," Pete added.

"Ha-ha - don't call me Mr. Ed" you said.

"Sophie loves her new Jeep right!?" Pete asked.

"Sophie's not seen it yet - I crashed the Jeep Uncle Pete!"

"Is this a joke?" Pete demanded.

You replied, "I wish I was trolling you!"

Pete said, "Tell me exactly how it went down, son!"

You observed, "I can tell you're angry Uncle Pete."

"Not yet – but I will jump all over you like ugly on a gorilla IF I sense you're not shooting straight with me, son – understood?"

"I was on I-90 ten miles west of Rapid City doing 85," you began.

"Hold on, didn't they close I-90 from Wyoming's border to Sioux Falls", asked Pete.

"Oh crap - my gut wants to tell you I didn't see the "I-90 Closed" sign but I drove right by it giving every excuse: 'I'm a safe driver, Sophie's waiting for me, no other vehicles on the road plus I've had an incident free drive so far sorta like mother nature or the weather gods are watching out for me" you said sheepishly.

Pete admitted, "I get it – tell me more."

You went on, "I'd been listening to the audio book you gave me, 'Upheaval' and challenged by the idea of sunspot cycles impacting weather, earthquakes and volcanic activity. I needed noisier and rowdier so I whipped out your eighties CD as I hit South Dakota. About a half hour in, the wind gusts got scary, circling like a tornado, lifting me off the ground, I couldn't feel my wheels on the snow or pavement; visibility had been decent, now it was zero, my speed was 85 and I decided to slow down gradually to drive through this thing until I could see sunlight or road lights or a rest stop; the last song I heard 'Dust in the Wind' it was surreal; I finally felt my wheels on the snow again; then an ugly scraping sound on the right side; then impact and my air bags deployed. Ever heard of a Bomb Cyclone, Uncle Pete?"

"A bomb cyclone sounds nasty – I don't want to meet one!" replied Pete.

You tried to clarify, "In laymen's terms it's similar to a hurricane but takes place over land in the wintertime with high winds and huge snowfalls even in Florida and especially the Midwest. My weather colleagues debate whether we've been hit by two bomb cyclones this winter. Your smart ass nephew drove right through the second one!"

Pete was shocked "I see why you felt lifted up by fierce winds totally losing control of the Jeep until you felt the ground and snow again! I can't believe this happened to you my son and I'm glad you're still with us! How badly are you injured?"

You shared, "I was asleep or unconscious for several hours and woke up feeling cold so I fumbled to find parka, gloves and boots. It was dark outside and the Jeep appeared to be encased with snow and ice plus the blizzard conditions created massive snow drifts against the car."

Pete asked "how'd you find the keys?"

You replied, "Easy – still in the ignition - wouldn't start though. Don't know if it kept running after the crash and was out of gas or frozen or if some chip shuts it off in a crash? You know me Pete, I'm not your mechanical whiz-kid."

"True – how'd you get outta there?" Pete asked.

"My phone was charged but unable to make a call or send a text. I'll freeze to death if I exit the Jeep and try to walk to safety

The Walk – S.B. Stone & Rock Solid Publishing, LLC
©2018

or flag a snowplow. I was weak from the blow to my head; unsure I had strength to kick out a window or open a door; how will I claw through several feet of snow, possibly ice, in sub-zero temps?"

Pete observed, "You were toast."

"I was angry too - this is your life dude! Why aren't you pumped with adrenaline and rescuing yourself? Then it dawned on me my lethargic behavior and physical weakness could be due to oxygen deprivation!"

Pete said, "I'm thinking the same thing, son!"

You said, "I asked God to rescue me, Uncle Pete. I told Him how scared I was of dying at such a young age and how I want to spend some time with Sophie talking about our futures. I promised God I'd follow Him and Jesus for the rest of my life if He chose to rescue me."

Uncle Pete asked, "What happened next, son?"

You replied, "It makes no sense but I felt a deeper peace inside than I've ever felt before.

I knew I had few breath's left since the oxygen in the Jeep was mostly used up; I fell into a peaceful sleep; I was awakened by loud whirring noises outside the Jeep; I heard a man's voice on the Jeep's hood – snow-blowers!"

"Very cool" said Pete! – he kicked in the windshield and hoisted you out right?"

"Nope – sunroof opens; a huge guy hoists me like a box of Cracker Jacks" you marvel.

"Shoot you're at least 220 aren't you big guy" says Pete.

Our windshield's in the right place and looking good" you remarked.

"Catch his name?" Pete asked.

"Rudy - we hopped in his truck and grabbed dinner. Later I realized Rudy's wearing only street clothes - no jacket or gloves rescuing me in sub-zero weather!"

"Hmm – what do you make of that?" asked Pete.

"Heck it gets better as I yell at Bob, the waiter, when I realize he can't see Rudy though I've been talking with Rudy for ten minutes but Bob keeps asking 'when's your friend coming back?' Rudy says he's a spirit in a different dimension and says his Boss owns the whole world so Rudy paid d for everything since his funds are unlimited."

Rudy booked me a room at the Rushmore and slipped me a business card with a note saying I can pick up the Jeep at 10:00 am the next morning at Angel's Automotive."

"Hey son have you spoken with Sophie about the crash?"

You replied, "Sophie's not a happy camper – she seems more upset than you Pete."

"I'm sorry - can you blame her though?"

"Not at all, did you know your Jeep's on Sophie's dream car list Uncle Pete?"

"No idea how high my five year old Jeep ranks in Sophie's view of the car world," Pete responded.

You shared, "My plan's to let Sophie drive the Jeep for a few days then ask if she wants it painted a more feminine color. As a man, I love the charcoal you chose."

"Good idea" said Pete, "I wonder if she'll choose pink?"

"We shall see" you said.

Pete queried, "Any idea how much body and mechanical damages we sustained?"

"The guys at Angel's Automotive estimated a range of $3,000 to $6,000 including bumper, side moldings, suspension and paint plus potential things they can't see without a thorough inspection – I think they're correct" you surmised.

Pete shared, "Good news though son, I have full coverages on the Jeep so you'll only have to pay my $500 deductible."

"I've needed some good news. I can't put my finger on it Pete but last time I spoke with Sophie she sounded distant."

Uncle Pete asks, "Has Sophie told you about Raymondo?"

The Walk – S.B. Stone & Rock Solid Publishing, LLC

"Who the heck is Raymondo, a quaking in your voice, and why should I care?"

Pete said, "Sophie told me he's repairing a roof that blew off a house in her friend's neighborhood – she says Raymondo is hot!"

You replied, "Sounds like its Bye Felicia for me!"

"Didn't know you're such an easy quitter, son" added Pete.

You replied, "I'm not a quitter…especially when I care about someone."

"That's more like it!" agreed Pete.

You asked, "Should I mention Raymondo to Sophie?"

"You'll be with Sophie by tonight assuming you hit the road this morning you'll arrive before dinner, right? Pete opined.

You replied "I-90's opened but there's snow and ice and occasional wind gusts. I plan on driving 55 to 65 max while paying close attention to the Jeep along the way."

"Hey big guy, I appreciate your diligence. You're a good man" Pete exclaimed.

"Feels good to hear you say it Uncle Pete" you added.

"Be sure to give my daughter a big hug from her Daddy, okay?"

"I promise" you gladly added.

Pete said "Tell Sophie what happened with you and God/Jesus - did you know she's been praying for you to make the decision for a long time – I think since she was ten. "Impressive Pete - I'll give Sophie the details."

"No problem", Uncle Pete.

"You gassed up at Maverik's "Adventure's First Stop" on East North Street before jumping on Interstate 90.

"Good morning Sophie" you texted.

"How's my adventurous friend?" came Sophie's quick reply.

You interrupted, "Whoa a friend of mine in Rapid City just sent a pic of his bike on the third floor deck I'll send."

"I'll look for it" Sophie promised.

You inquired, "OK to say I miss u?"

"I dig being missed by you" Sophie said.

"Do I need to be sus about Raymondo?" you floated.

"Ha-Ha you took the bait," Sophie smiled.

"You turkey - you baited me with a phony love interest?" you challenged.

Sophie responded, "Like a frozen bike encased in snow, why'd you go frigid on me as if our dancing at the Broadmoor and long goodbye hug mean nothing to you?"

You responded, "Sorry, I thought about you and our future a lot."

"Newsflash – I'm a smart girl but I cannot read your **thoughts** no matter how hard I try; plus, tell me what good relationships are built on, anyway?" Sophie queried.

"Uh communication I suppose?" you painfully offered.

"Bingo we have a winner! How do intelligent human beings facilitate good communication? Sophie posed.

"Easy, you replied – "We use emails, text messages, Skype or Facetime or write a letter or a card via U.S. Mail and oh yes, we make actual phone calls."

Still on her game show theme, Sophie announces: "Winner, winner – but NO chicken dinner 'til you safely arrive at Sioux Falls my friend!"

"Here's the one you've been waiting for - Q number three: "How many times did we communicate during the four and a half months since Colorado Springs?"

You answered like a wimp: "I texted you a few times, I shared some weather info in a couple emails and I called you once for thirty minutes, I think, but I guess we really didn't talk did we?"

Sophie lamented, "Why didn't we talk? It was a long and painful pocket call - I had the pleasure of listening to you and other clowns I don't even know in a boring business meeting!"

Humbly you confessed, "I feel like we're family and already know you well. So I assume you know me just as well and my stuff will be boring. I want to be dead/euphorically happy when we're together like dancing at the Broadmoor and I have no clue how to recreate those feelings which makes me feel inadequate for you."

"Thank you for communicating with me" Sophie smiled in her happy voice.

The Walk – S.B. Stone & Rock Solid Publishing, LLC
©2018

To be honest, you don't feel particularly satisfied by sharing your heart with Sophie but you recognize it's meaningful to her.

"You're welcome Sophie! I need to start driving…so I can keep my promise to Pete by giving you a Daddy hug and seeing if your eyes are as pretty as I remember."

"Hmmm, sounds like a line to me, said Sophie…do you know what color eyes I have?"

"Emerald green of course - see you in six hours" you added.

"Drive safe okay?" added Sophie.

"Yes, 55 to 65 so I can keep listening for Jeep's aches and pains" you said.

"Interesting – even Jeeps communicate" observed Sophie - here's a link to a podcast "Successful Communication Skills" with loved ones, friends and business associates.

"Thank you Sophie", 'thumbs up' emoticon.

"Big hugs emoticon from Sophie; I'll text Ryan and Ruth's address."

You shot a quick text to Uncle Pete: "Hey UP I'm a rookie car crash guy. No idea how the insurance and repair process works. Can you shoot me a text or email with your wisdom?"

UP replied: "You show wisdom by humbling yourself and asking advice of your elders. I'm proud of you. Under separate cover I'll email a Traffic Accident Guide by American Bar Association, Auto Club and Car Repair Shop Federation. Call me with questions."

Your 360 mile six hour drive to Sioux Falls was uneventful. Jeep complained with a suite of whines, squeaks and noises you lacked the skills to diagnose and repair so you dictated an email for UP and Sophie; UP forwards to his insurance company and you and Sophie schedule appointments with at least two shops in Sioux Falls one for the body work the other for mechanical repairs - your hoping this crash will be your last!

Pulling into the apartment complex, you wonder how Sophie and you would do with two new babies in a two bedroom apartment when you and Sophie are sleep deprived and emotionally exhausted – you prefer car repairs at the moment.

You knock quietly in case the twins are sleeping. No answer so you knocked harder. Finally the door opened by a man around thirty holding a little baby dressed in pink: "Howdy I'm Seth Bradshaw. Welcome to our humble abode – you must be Sophie's friend and Jeep delivery man."

"Guilty as charged and I'm the guy who crashed it", you humbly concurred.

Seth smiled – "Say howdy to my wonderful wife and mom of Phoebe and Titus, the one and only Beth Bradshaw."

You replied, "Great to meet you Beth – are you and Sophie still best friends after six months with you, Phoebe and Titus?"

"Legit question – our friendship is more trill than in school cause we've been thrown on an island with two helpless and strange creatures – we figure it out on the fly; Daddy's at work ten hours a day and brings home a substantial income in a growing company with no HR department and no paid paternity leave so we're not complaining - selfish is not an option – teamwork's a necessity."

"Beth you are one smart cookie and I agree hundo p" smiled exuberant Sophie holding Titus looking on fleek in blue Seattle Seahawk jammies.

Seth agreed, "As a rookie Dad, it's scary to be alone with not one but two helpless six month old babies - I am blessed to watch you and learn the ropes!"

You are starved – almost feeling faint - "Sorry to be rude; I've been so pumped to get here I forgot to eat dinner on the way!"

"I grabbed a couple pizzas on my way home" Seth offered.

"I made a fruit salad" said Sophie.

"Titus and Phoebe weren't interested so there's plenty of pizza and salad left for you, plus lemonade, milk, sodas, beer and water" assured Beth.

The Walk – S.B. Stone & Rock Solid Publishing, LLC
©2018

"Thanks for being so generous – I'm happy to reimburse you for the pizza" you declared.

"Sorry" said Seth – we have three house rules for our wonderful guests: 1. Eat all you want and pay for nothing; 2. Sleep all you want and don't send a check or leave cash on the nightstand; 3. Take long showers or baths to start your day off fresh!"

"Very cool policies – I will respect each one" you promised. You're not a hugger but chose to go there for Beth since Sophie said 'Beth likes hugs'".

"You're good parents Beth and Seth – we invite you Titus and Phoebe to visit us in Boston, South Carolina or wherever else we may end up" Sophie added.

Beth said, "The kids will miss you Sophie!"

"I will miss you guys also" Sophie replied.

You smiled, "Seth and Beth, thanks for opening your home and refrigerator, shower and comfy bed last night!"

You washed, vacuumed and fueled the Jeep and took Sophie's hand, gave her the keys and walked her around her new Jeep – "Looks really good" she said with a smile.

"Ready to drive Sophie?" opening her door and giving her the first hug in six months. "This hug is from your Dad, Sophie." She sighed and moaned softly then breathed out a few words of gratitude: "Well worth the wait my friend. I can drive for hours re-charged like the Energizer Bunny!"

"Go for it Sophie - I'll keep you company" you replied.

"Mind if I say a prayer out loud? I want to ask God to direct our steps and I want you to know the details of what I'm asking Him." Sophie requested.

"Go for it" you replied.

"Heavenly Father, I'm confused about where you want me to live and I've got a teaching job in Boston and a nice place above my parent's garage for cheap rent. Makes sense to go but in my heart I feel you could be leading me to take a bigger step away from the security of family and friends in Boston." Sophie prayed. Okay now I feel better about starting the Jeep and driving – we'll see where God takes us…hmmm I like the way this beast drives…feels and looks beefier than my Mazda."

"Glad to hear it Sophie and thanks for praying – I liked it" you could see Sophie's eyes registering mild but happy surprise.

"Wait a minute you've never thanked me for praying…have you?" Sophie queried.

You replied, "With a big grin – your prayers have been answered Sophie!"

Sophie working hard to focus on the road instead of you – "I keep God busy with lots of prayers mostly for people I care about like Seth and Beth who lost her first baby about three months into her term. Beth called me weeping devastated she'd lost her baby and asking 'how could God who loves me take our baby?' I told her I don't know God's reasons but I do know God loves her and her baby; I know it hurts a lot when God's helping us grow stronger in our faith."

"I can't imagine being so crushed!" you shared.

"Me either. Beth asked me to pray for God to help her get pregnant again so she and Seth can hold a baby and share their love with him or her." Sophie shared.

You jumped in, "When did they lose their first baby?"

"A year ago and as we witnessed God's answer as He blessed them with Phoebe and Titus." Sophie smiled, then added "Sometimes God says 'yes' to our prayers almost immediately; other times God says 'wait'; other times God says 'no' because He knows what's best for each one of His children."

You clarified, "I'm new to praying but I'm referring to God answering one of your longtime prayers where God's answer has been 'wait' until recently – make sense?"

"You're making no sense and what do you mean by 'until recently'" said puzzled Sophie.

You happily clarified "During the crash I thought I might die and begged God to rescue me – the car was encased in snow and ice and I was knocked unconscious for several hours. I woke up expecting surges of adrenaline to give me strength and kick myself into survival mode but I was too weak to do anything except pray. I asked God to forgive all my sins and give me a longer life, hopefully with you."

Sophie hit the brakes and pulled onto the shoulder…put on her flashers and parking brake, jumped out and ran around to your side – "Get out big boy!"

You gladly obeyed and got the warmest closest longest hug ever received by man!

Sophie's weeping joyful tears and jumping like a kid on a pogo stick…then hugging you some more. You hadn't realized folks could have so much fun pulled over on the shoulder of a road – "Let's do this again sometime!" you said.

Uh oh why did you both sense someone watching your celebration?

"Pardon the interruption folks, my name's Officer Jeremiah Fry – what exactly is happening here? I see no alcohol or drugs or music in or around your vehicle but I did see lotsa dancin and huggin."

"Pleased to meet you, Officer Fry – is dancing or hugging illegal on the side of the highway?" you inquired.

"If you're at least twenty feet off the pavement and not distracting passing vehicles you should be okay in my state; mind telling me where you folks were headed before the huggin party started?"

You responded, "We're not exactly sure but we hope to explore the coastlines of North and South Carolina. Sophie's originally from Spokane and more recently from Boston; I'm from Maine.

We have a few weeks to check out Myrtle Beach and Jacksonville for starters… plus wherever else God leads us."

"Sounds like a fun adventure - you two married or just friends?" asked Officer Fry.

Sophie clarified, "He's my non-biological cousin who I've had a crush on ever since our dads who are brothers took us camping as kids."

You added, "We are very good friends and trying to figure out if we might have better lives as a married couple. What do you think Officer Fry?"

"You look good together." Fry offered.

"I am dank don't you think?" you asked Officer Fry with a smirk.

Gazing at Sophie, Officer Fry declared "I hope the man has brains since you way outclass him in the good looks department. Uh-oh got to blast off kids – bank robbery in progress!

Ya'll drive safe!" A finger flick of the cool brim of his hat, a reassuring glance and Fry was lights on…siren…tires screeching…outa here.

"Nice dude" you said.

"Indeed" agreed Sophie.

"Can you visualize either of us in law enforcement?" you queried.

You talked about the physical risks and financial rewards and what kind of lifestyles each of you aspired to plus what kind of family you would hope to have. You agreed having kids is a major life changer. Hey getting married would be a life changer.

You wondered out loud, "How many miles til we reach North Carolina?"

Sophie teased, "Aren't you the man who always plots his routes before rolling onto the highway?"

"Guilty as charged. I'm not used to a beautiful woman in the driver's seat; but I have regained my senses and am prepared to discuss our options with you Sophie."

Its twenty one hours driving time from Sioux Falls to Raleigh, North Carolina; from Raleigh to the coast's three to four hours depending on where we head to first."

The Walk – S.B. Stone & Rock Solid Publishing, LLC
©2018

Sophie asked, "You like country music - do we want to stop in Nashville for a night or two on the way to Raleigh?"

You agreed, "Super idea Sophie!"

"Think I'm good driving about three more hours til I need a rest and potty break; mind grabbing me a water and energy bar big fella?

"Serving you is my pleasure miss" you smiled.

Sophie asked, "Any idea how long I've been praying for you?"

"Enlighten me Sophie."

"Pretty sure I was twelve years old on a retreat with Dad's church. You were fourteen and hanging with the middle school kids on the same retreat." Sophie said.

"Priest Lake in Northern Idaho?" you offered.

"I think that's the place" Sophie said.

"Driving home I shared I decided to follow Christ, but you buried your head and turned away from me – later you apologized. Do you remember what you said?"

You recall saying, "I'm so sorry I hurt your feelings Sophie at such an important time in your life. It's hard for me to believe in God and Jesus after he let my Dad die!"

"I saw your pain and had no idea how to help so I began praying for you!" said Sophie.

"Eighteen years – more than half your life you've prayed for me to follow Jesus." you humbly acknowledged. I feel honored and overwhelmed with a desire to be vigilant in following God – to be high key I have zero Bible knowledge and limited people skills. How do I step up to the plate, Sophie?"

"Huge question my friend – I have a handful of suggestions for you. I'm driving so would you mind taking notes?" asked exuberant Sophie.

"My keyboard's ready but I need to give you something" as you leaned closer and gave Sophie a gentle kiss on her cheek.

The Walk – S.B. Stone & Rock Solid Publishing, LLC
©2018

"You're so sweet – thank you" Sophie smiled.

"To be trill with you Sophie, I'd rather kiss you on the lips" you confessed.

"Hmm maybe next time…when I'm not behind the wheel doing seventy." Sophie said.

"I can't wait…shucks I guess I have to wait…silly me" you added.

"You ready hot shot?" asked patient Sophie again.

"Brain, keyboard, ears and heart are ready to hear your wisdom Sophie."

"Let's play a game, said Sophie. I'm going to ask you to put yourself in a situation." "Hypothetical or actual?" you asked.

Sophie clarified: "It's up to you."

I'm ready" you said.

"Imagine you are alone in a safe and quiet place with no distractions. A man appears. He is confident, kind and gentle. The man's eyes radiate light and truth. He calls you by name as He looks into your eyes with love. He states – 'I am Jesus Christ. I am here to answer your questions'."

"What's the first question you'll ask Jesus?"

"Sophie are you serious?" you ask.

"Yes – so take all the time you need to come up with a legit Jesus Question you really care about" Sophie clarified.

Your mind raced to find ways you can impress Jesus with your question. Then you remembered Jesus is the Son of God who knows everything! So ask Jesus your toughest question.

You gave a thumbs up and said "Okay I'm ready Sophie".

Sophie nodded saying "Talk with Jesus not me."

"Dear Jesus – Why is there so much suffering and injustice in the world?"

On one occasion an expert in the law stood up to test Jesus. *"Teacher,"* he asked, *"what must I do to inherit eternal life?"* "What is

*written in the Law?" he replied. How do you read it?" He answered,
"'Love the Lord your God with all your heart and with all your soul and
with all your strength and with all your mind' and, 'Love your neighbor
as yourself.' "You have answered correctly," Jesus replied. "Do this
and you will live."*

You interrupted, "Wow this is cool! My new friend Rudy read this
story to me in Rapid City. Hearing it a second time I see God's two most
important commandments are: First I need to **love God with all my
heart, with all my soul, with all my mind and with all my strength**;
Second, I need to **love my neighbor as myself**. All other
commandments flow from these two.

"This explains it Sophie" you contended.

"Explains what?" asked Sophie.

"The reasons why the world is so full of suffering and injustice!"
you added.

"Tell me more please?" Sophie requested.

"Okay since you're driving, I'll research world population to
facilitate my point – while I'm looking, tell me Sophie how many people
live on earth today?

"Six billion" Sophie estimated.

"Not a bad guess – Worldometers estimates 7.7 billion people. Are
you game for a tougher question Sophie" you warned.

"How many of earth's 7.7 billion people are **earnestly following**
God's two greatest commandments to Love God and Love their
Neighbors" you asked.

"I'm not God! I can't see inside the heart or mind of anyone but
myself?" said Sophie.

"Until I gave my heart to Jesus in South Dakota, I rebelled against
God too didn't I?"

"Good point. I'm so happy we're on the same team – God's team"
Sophie said.

"I'm a scientist so I gather data to support my findings and it's
impossible for you and me to interview 7.7 billion people to ask if they
follow Jesus like we do."

Sophie said "I agree with you what else can you do?"

Thank you for asking Sophie, "I make a reasonable hypothesis – say five percent of people in the world refuse to practice Loving God and Loving Neighbors; that computes to three hundred eighty five million people."

"Who don't give a rip about loving God or loving neighbors" Sophie lamented.

Could the rebellion of five percent of the world's population be why there is so much suffering and injustice in our world?

"Here's a scary thought. What if ninety five per cent of the world refuses or neglects to follow God's commandments to Love God and Love their neighbors?

"All hell breaks loose on the earth when man has no fear of God and everyone does whatever they think is right in their own eyes" shared Sophie.

"Our U.S. population is 329,224,614 on July 23, 2019 per Worldometers" you shared.

"Even without religious education it's our responsibility to respond to God's presence in our lives and in the world. God seeks honest and humble men and women who express their need for God."

Fascinated you asked: "How'd you learn this stuff, Sophie?"

"I read, study and listen to the sixty-six books of the Bible from Genesis, to Revelation."

"Very cool" you responded.

"Who is Rudy?" she asked.

"Rudy's the angel God sent to rescue me!" you declared.

"No way – you're teasing me again!" accused Sophie.

"I'm trill with you Sophie!" you claimed.

"Okay I'll indulge; tell me how you know Rudy's an angel."

"Instead of kicking out our windshield Rudy opened the sunroof remotely" you said.

"That's impossible!" Sophie contended. "How'd he do it?"

The Walk – S.B. Stone & Rock Solid Publishing, LLC

"I suppose he told the sunroof to open?"

"Next, he's an average sized guy but he lifted my two hundred pounds through the sunroof like I'm a rag doll.

"He works out" said Sophie.

"Angels don't work out" you suggested.

"Rudy and I sat at dinner talking for thirty minutes and our waiter couldn't see or hear him" you stated.

Sophie's tracking your dilemma "Your waiter must have thought you're crazy - talking to your imaginary friend are you sir?"

"You've got a point Sophie – he looked at me suspiciously but it gets better if you're still interested?"

"Bring it on hot shot" invited Sophie.

"Rudy explained Angels are spirit beings who don't sweat it with material things like walls or time or distance" you shared.

"Did super-Rudy show you any tricks?" Sophie entreated.

"While we were talking, Rudy visited Singapore in the blink of any eye" you shared. Sophie said, "Did you notice he left the table and returned superfast?"

"Nope" you said.

"For me, Sophie, the coolest part about Rudy is the glow about him. It's as if he's been in heaven multiple times in the presence of God's...what do you call it Sophie?

"God's glory?"

"Yes! Teach me what the Bible says about it" you pleaded.

"God is so holy and perfect and majestic and truly awesome he will not show his face to you or me or any other person – not even Moses."

"Why not" you asked.

"We'd be immediately incinerated" warned Sophie.

"You marveled at your ignorance but had to ask: did it ever happen in the Bible?

"Do not come any closer," God said. *"Take off your sandals, for the place where you are standing is holy ground."* Then he said, *"I am the*

God of your father, 3:6 Masoretic Text; Samaritan Pentateuch (see Acts 7:32) fathers the God of Abraham, the God of Isaac and the God of Jacob." At this, Moses hid his face, because he was afraid to look at God."

Exodus 3:5-6 [1]

Then Moses said, "Now show me your glory." And the Lord said, "I will cause all my goodness to pass in front of you, and I will proclaim my name, the Lord, in your presence. I will have mercy on whom I will have mercy, and I will have compassion on whom I will have compassion. But," he said, "you cannot see my face, for no one may see me and live." Then the Lord said, "There is a place near me where you may stand on a rock. When my glory passes by, I will put you in a cleft in the rock and cover you with my hand until I have passed by. Then I will remove my hand and you will see my back; but my face must not be seen." Exodus 33:1823 [1]

"What's the speed limit?" Sophie queried.

"The last sign I saw was 55" you answered.

"Cool I'm at 54 so why're flashing lights closing down on us?" wondered Sophie.

"Just pull over a bit; he'll probably pass us" you assured.

"Okay" said Sophie.

You recognized, "Oh crap not him again!"

"Hello folks – remember me?"

"Officer Jeremiah Fry" you stated.

"We didn't expect to see you again - so soon" Sophie admitted.

"Driver's licenses please – wait in the car folks" said Fry.

Not sure you waited ten minutes or an hour – felt like eternity.

"Sir, please step out of the car; put your hands on the roof so I can search you. Now put your hands behind your back at the waist - I'll try not to pull this too tight."

"What's going on officer? We've done nothing wrong" you argued.

"Miss, step out of the car please; arms and hands above your head so I can search you; hands behind your waist."

"Sir step into the back seat of my patrol car; slide over to make room for the lady. I must inform you you're both under arrest for committing multiple crimes we'll describe in greater detail at the station. In the meantime, you have the right to remain silent since everything you say can be used against you in a court of law."

You can't believe this idiot pulled you over! You want to yell and scream and tell him they've got the wrong people and the wrong vehicle; this sucks - you are not bad guys!

Sophie's clinging to your arm like a drowning person - her nails piercing through your now bleeding skin – why is Sophie so terrified?

"Too Young to Die" is to be continued in "The Walk – Part Two"

Thanks for your feedback at feedback@thewalk.me .

The Walk: Episode Seven – Joe Average

Against the odds - you're a success story!

Today, no one believes you were a consistent C student through ninth grade.

Average looks, not athletic, strong or physically impressive - not even a good talker.

Your parents struggled – no high school diplomas or trade school certifications or degrees - seven superb teachers believed in you! Occasionally you feels like one of your old teachers is at your side in the classroom.

You sing and play diverse genres of music - classical, country and rock from hundreds of artists: Beatles, Moody Blues, Led Zeppelin, Kenny Chesney, Rascal Flats, and Respighi's "Pines of Rome", the Who's Rock Opera "Tommy" and Bruce Springsteen. While growing up you had few role models that made sense to you. Dad's a hard worker but his hard work is eclipsed by his drinking problem.

Your mother struggled to keep a clean and orderly home while living on pins and needles - never knowing if Dad will return from work in a good mood, or as a mean drunk with too much whiskey in his system!

When drunk, Dad threw anything within his reach in the direction of you and your mother! Mom tried the best she could to teach you right from wrong. Her reasons for behaving well were pragmatic - largely based on her fights to survive your Dad's bad behavior. "Honey, you must treat folks with respect even when they don't deserve it."

In school, you were branded a "loser" by your peers. You were bullied by friends and teachers who did not like you. Was it your values, body odor, your clothing or hair style which invited the taunting? You had no clue regarding why you attracted such abuse.

On the positive side of education, you were blessed with seven committed teachers in 2nd, 6th, 8th, 9th, 10th, 11th and

12th grades. Despite your ongoing propensity to "fall short" of your district's academic standards day after day your teachers called you by name and said – "I believe in you!"

Two of your teacher's, Miss Page in 8th grade and Mr. Rock in 12th grade, not only said "I believe in you", but often added, "I know for a fact God has created you to accomplish many good things during your lifetime. I am eager to watch you in action after you graduate!"

As an adult you relished looking back at the priceless relationships you had developed with your Magnificent Seven teachers. In your heart you knew, but weren't certain why, Miss

Page and Mr. Rock were your "top two" favorite teachers.

Could it be they were two teachers who esteemed you as a unique and extraordinary creation of Almighty God? It was curious nearly no one talked about God before, during or after your school day. Why did Miss Page and Mr. Rock choose to do otherwise? Did these top notch educators risk losing their jobs by esteeming you as God's creation? Why did there seem to be so much power in their simple words? At home God was mentioned when Dad "damned" a person he disagreed with.

You never talked about Jesus though your Mom put out a manger scene on the fireplace mantle at Christmas. Santa received far more attention during your childhood until he was outed as a phony. Was Jesus also a phony, you wondered?

Now you've been teaching eight years and gratified your peers, colleagues, parents students and the Magnificent Seven are pleased with your skills and accomplishments - "Teacher of the Year" in your state - automatically nominated for United States Teacher of the Year!

Each of the Magnificent Seven reached out to congratulate and encourage you on being the best in your state and wished you well in the national competition.

You developed good writing skills as an English major.

Why are you struggling so with writing the personal paper you must submit to the national award committee? You're writing about things you've learned during eight years as a teacher. That's easy for you to write about because it's simply what you actually do every day then comparing and contrasting with your teaching style as a rookie teacher.

This year, the committee is requiring the second half of the paper must share your intelligent ideas on the subject of how to make education better in the next decade.

You have ideas. Truth be told, you're hesitant to share them in your paper – "Purveyors of Truth".

As a diligent and focused high school and college student, you observed a strange absence of God from teacher's lecterns, textbooks and the vast majority of student presentations.

You can't put your finger on it - some of the lectures, books and lessons left you feeling hollow inside. You knew in your gut and your brain one of the reasons you're attending school was to develop both practical and theoretical skills you could use in the pursuit of your career ambitions. Being honest with yourself, in high school and college you didn't care whether "god" or "God" was part of your school's conversation. You're raised and educated as a child of what your professor's called "secular humanism".

Your professors branded "religious" people as one-sided and blinded believers for trusting in a loving and beneficent God who created the flowers and the animals and the plants and photosynthesis for oxygen and food for all the peoples of the world. Besides, if there is a loving God why would He permit evil to exist? Your professors squelched open discussion by asking students the rhetorical question:

"How could any sane and intelligent person, including you class, believe in the foolish proposition a loving God exists and permits his followers to be racist, narrow-minded, intolerant, homophobic, science-haters?" As you reflect back to your college classrooms, you can't help but recall the occasional Christian who was bold enough to share their views with his or her professor.

What are the main goals that should be built into the education of our children? Why not equip them with Truth skills", Life skills and Job skills. These skills are all important and will create graduates who are not confused about what they personally believe and what they want in life and career.

All of these skills must be taught and studied in a free flowing exchange of ideas environment where all ideas and views are respected and welcome!

As an educator, is it wise or ethical for me to expect you as a parent to feel good about me indoctrinating your child regarding what is and is-not true in their life? As educators, don't we unwittingly demonstrate our bias and close-mindedness by indoctrinating our precious children God does not exist? Likewise are we not making fools of ourselves as "professional" educators and seekers of truth by pretending there is no God?

Do you and I really want to answer for such a fundamental error? Should every student have the freedom to ask his or her teacher: Do you believe in God? If a well-educated twenty-five to sixty-five year old teacher, often with a Master's Degree, declares he or she doesn't believe in God, isn't it a good thing for their students to feel the freedom to inquire what do you believe in, without fear of reprisal?

****

Joe Average - Part Two

You've found yourself in an enviable and yet precarious position. You are an award winning teacher – "Teacher of the Year" in your home state!

As such, you have been placed in the national teacher of the year competition which takes place soon. You must create and orally present a persuasive essay to share your observations and recommendations with the National Committee. The committee expects your intelligent findings on how to improve your school. Your recommendations will be so innovative and pertinent the entire nation will benefit - no pressure on you of course.

Should every student have the freedom to ask his or her teacher do you believe in God? If a teacher says no then should it be okay for students to honestly and respectfully ask what their teacher does believe in?

Despite how dumb you felt as a student day after day your best teachers called you by name and said – "I believe in you!" Your two favorite teachers were Miss Page in 8th grade and Mr. Rock in 12th grade. Your most impactful teachers took it a step further instilling not only their confidence in me...but saying "I believe in you" – they often added "God believes in you too and I know God has created you to accomplish many good things in your lifetime. I am eager to watch you in action after you graduate!"

When you were trained to be an educator you asked your professors if they or their students discuss God in class - most were angry or defensive I'd have the audacity to get them off the topic of the lessons they were teaching! Some answered - "this is not religion class so we avoid the topic of discussing it in our classes."

My professors advised me to avoid discussing religion with my students in my class

room, "to avoid damaging my career, getting fired, alienating colleagues, ticking off my students, parents and the union."

I'd sometimes over hear my students talking about religious subjects. On occasion a student asks if I'm "religious" or "a Christian" or "if I attend a particular church". Like any teacher should do, I told my students the truth about me...which was easy to do since my answer used to be, "I don't believe in God but I respect those who do."

Over the years, my answers have evolved to, "To be honest, I'm not really sure what I believe, but I respect everyone's right to choose what or whom they believe in."

When you were honest with yourself, you have a lot of unanswered questions. In your heart and mind you know you need to find someone you can ask your questions to.

The Walk – S.B. Stone & Rock Solid Publishing, LLC
©2018

How about your incredible girlfriend…and now wife, Maxine? Maxine was a computer engineering major at Florida State. You are the only person she won't punch for calling her "Maxi". Your wife isn't prissy but she's definitely a woman who loves her given name, Maxine.

She even thanks her parents for giving her "such a cool and feminine name!"

Your feminine Maxi was a straight A student and while leading the Florida State golf team to a national championship! You definitely married up with this girl.

Maxi was "getting bored' with her major but, like you, her parents had given her no spiritual foundation. Maxi's best friend invited her to visit her church now and then and Maxi says her friend's church is "lots of fun and the boys were cute, plus they play really interesting music and fun games."

Unfortunately Maxi's Sunday mornings were often trumped by her Florida State golf matches plus occasional travel to Georgia and Tennessee and eventually the Regional and National matches. Florida boasts 1,042 vivid green golf courses scattered all over its pretty landscape of palm trees, orange trees, Florida cypress and pond cypress.

Plus Maxi says, "They have quality training facilities, superb weather nearly year round, plus a low cost of living and even favorable publicity by people like comedian Jerry Seinfeld who joked: "My parents didn't want to move to Florida, but they turned 60 and that's the law." I told Maxine the Chamber of Commerce may offer her a job.

You and Maxine were raised in typical unbelieving homes so stepping into a faith-based life sounds a bit scary to both of you. Maxine invested many hours with her best friend, Susa Pitts, having typical girl fun, whatever that is, and attending church during high school and college…nearly all of which was a positive experience for Maxi.

Plus, Maxi had talks about God and Jesus and other religions with fellow golfers and even a coach or two while piled inside a mini-van or Suburban riding to and from their golf matches. As much as she and her team mates liked boys and golf, Maxi sensed the need to have a broader perspective of life than she observed in many of her peers.

When Maxi discussed spirituality or religion with her parents they'd say: "we're too intelligent and well educated to need God in our lives" or "religion is a crutch for weak people – yes, it's better than drugs, Maxine, but it's not what you need, honey - our lives are fine without God and Jesus."

You and Maxi have been trying for two years to start your family; both of you are discouraged and to the point of asking God to help Maxine get pregnant.

You're unsure if God's hearing your and Maxine's prayers, so it's time to call one of your old teachers, Mr. Rock, for prayer and family planning advice.

"Hello Mr. Rock how are you, Mrs. Rock and the kids lately? Yes, it's been nearly two years since we last had chatted – wasn't it over lunch at Sandy's Café?"

"Yes", said Mr. Rock," we had catching up to do, didn't we? I want to encourage you to call me by my first name, Bruce, if you don't mind – it's been fifteen years since you've been in my classroom, right?"

"Yes Bruce no problem. I apologize for hearing the truth about God and Jesus during our lunch at Sandy's and not implementing all of your ideas; I am reading and enjoying the gospel of John" you shared.

"Young man, I'm proud of you for starting to read John; it's an intimate book written by one of Jesus' closest friends. One of my favorite books in the Bible. After writing John, John even remarked: "Jesus did many other things as well. If every one of them were written down, I suppose that even the whole world would not have room for the books that would be written!"

"Wow! Mind boggling! Bruce - while driving home from Sandy's Café, I knew in my heart everything you shared about God's love for me and for all of mankind was true. I was ready to pull the trigger in my mind and heart and say "yes" to God and His Son."

The Walk – S.B. Stone & Rock Solid Publishing, LLC
©2018

"A strange thing happened while reading the gospel of John; in my heart I'd be saying "wow this is so powerful and true; from out of nowhere I'd hear a different idea in my head challenging the truths in the Bible I was in the process of embracing! On other occasions, similar doubting thoughts randomly pop up in the back of my head reminding me these "truths" aren't really true at all and Jesus and his miracles and his love for me are historical fabrications. If you choose to follow Jesus, your professional life will be ruined and I will be ridiculed and ostracized by your secular humanism peers and the leaders of our profession!"

"Bruce, can you tell me where these 'doubting thoughts' come from? Is it my mind arguing with itself trying to reason through an important decision? Or is someone outside of me trying keep me in the dark?"

Bruce responded, "When a rational person gathers information to equip their mind with resources it previously lacked, it's a positive and illuminating thing – plus it's critical when we're evaluating the truth or falsity of a person or belief system!"

"I agree" you said.

"Was the doubting voice whispering to your mind as peaceful and unbiased as your own thoughts?" Bruce inquired.

"I'm glad we're talking Bruce or I may not have noticed a creepy nuance. The thought was not an audible voice - just a thought. Oddly the thoughts weren't a thing I consciously generated – they just showed up in my mind."

"I'm following you" Bruce reported.

"And here's the creepy part, Bruce, the tone of each thought subtly mocked the path I was considering - trying to derail my decision to follow Jesus before I'd fully made it!"

Bruce interrupted. "I had similar battles in my mind when investigating historical and Biblical evidences about God and Jesus Christ before I decided to follow Christ back in high school!"

The Walk – S.B. Stone & Rock Solid Publishing, LLC

You agreed "Wow Bruce I'm surprised but glad you went through this!"

"I am certain about what's occurring inside your mind!" said Bruce.

"I'm glued to the phone and Maxine just walked in - mind if I put you on speaker?"

"No problem. Good to meet you Maxine."

"Good to meet you Bruce" said Maxine.

Bruce began, "Many times in the Bible the devil's interacting with people directly or through demons. He tries to mess up God's good plan for His children. The devil introduces **deception and doubt** to the minds of God's children to get us off the path of God's intended blessings for our lives on earth and in eternity."

You and Maxine nodded and said "makes sense so far."

"When you and Maxine's actions show you're contemplating placing your faith in God and His Son, Jesus Christ, the devil and his demons are furious and spring to action!"

Maxine interrupted, "What's the big deal - why would the devil and demons care what we do in life and whether we'll choose to follow Jesus?"

"Unfortunately, Bruce lamented, "The Devil, also known as Satan and Lucifer, has the self-appointed job description of keeping you and the rest of mankind headed toward Hell, not changing your course toward Heaven!"

"The Devil's a creep! I hate him and I've never met him" hollered Maxine.

"He'd be pleased with your compliment Maxine" added Bruce.

"Who are these guys" you demanded.

"The devil and demons are evil angels who rebelled against God long ago. God banned the devil and evil angels who joined the rebellion from God's holy presence in heaven. They're cast down to earth where Satan's crowned himself "prince" of earth until he's cast back into hell" Bruce stated.

"I can't wait!" Maxine yelled.

Bruce continued, "Satan despises God's love for humanity and is angry God has rejected him; Satan's wicked plan is to ruin your life and your walk with God. For folks who've chosen NOT to put their faith in God and Jesus, he'll create doubt and confusion to keep you and those you love from putting their faith in God and Jesus."

You added, "These wicked beings are desperate!"

Bruce agreed, "To be blunt, they already know they're spending eternity in hell: their mission's to deceive us and millions of lost people to join them there!"

"Wow - a horrible convention we want to miss!" you said.

"Wow indeed" agreed Bruce.

Maxi surmised: "I suppose Satan's infiltrated our movies, schools, television, government, books, plays, political correctness, race relations and lots more."

Bruce agreed and added: "Over two thousand years ago one of Jesus disciples wrote these words of encouragement and advice to Jesus followers:"

"...God opposes the proud but shows favor to the humble. Humble yourselves, therefore, under God's mighty hand, that He may lift you up in due time. Cast all your anxiety on Him because He cares for you. Be alert and of sober mind. Your enemy the devil prowls around like a roaring lion looking for someone to devour. Resist him, standing firm in the faith, because you know that the family of believers throughout the world are undergoing the same kind of sufferings." 1 Peter 5:5b-9 [1]

You responded, "I'm scared Bruce. The devil is mankind's heartless enemy. How do

Maxine and I stand against such an evil, ferocious and invisible force?"

"Bruce agreed, "No man or woman has a chance against the devil and his army of demons, unless he or she authentically changes course by trusting in the blood of Jesus Christ to cleanse their sinful heart and dedicating their life to serve God's agenda – they will have Jesus power on their side; remember Satan's operating with urgency - his time is shorter than ever. When you choose to follow Jesus, God gives you access to His weapons to help you win your battles against the forces of darkness."

"Bruce this is tough news to hear, but I'd rather know it than go through life ignorant of the spiritual realm and how the devil hates us" Maxine observed.

Sorry guys Mom's on the phone - I want to share this with her if she'll listen!"

You applauded, "Good Maxi, you go for it, super girl!"

"When you choose to authentically put your faith in Jesus death, burial and resurrection the Bible says you are "born again" by God's Holy Spirit. As evidence God actually puts His

Holy Spirit inside you!" Bruce stated.

"I can't imagine God's spirit inside of me" you admitted.

"Is Maxine a follower of Jesus?" Bruce inquired.

"Good question. In high school Maxi was inspired by happy people, cool music and challenging teaching at her best friend, Susa Pitt's, church. Susa consistently invited Maxi to visit and likes Maxi's smart brain, good grades and tennis skills. Maxi's tennis covered Florida and the southeast so she missed many services she'd hoped to attend."

"Bummer" said Bruce.

"Yes, but last night Maxine told me she's heard the truth about God and Jesus consistently at Susa Pitt's church and she's getting to the point where Maxi said to me 'following Jesus Christ could be a smart decision for this girl!"

"Exciting" smiled Bruce.

You added, "Today I got the bright idea of testing Maxine's water by saying 'good morning Jesus freak.'"

"That's not nice" said Bruce. "What'd Maxine say?"

The Walk – S.B. Stone & Rock Solid Publishing, LLC
©2018

"Jesus Christ is a badge I shall proudly wear – I gave Him my heart last night!"

Bruce said "I like that girl!"

You agreed in spades "I love that girl!"

"You're right Bruce. I may have been processing 'out loud' with Maxine able to hear the doubts I was battling in my own mind" you shared.

Bruce offered, "Makes sense."

You said, "Thank you Bruce for talking through this challenging stuff with us - I'll grab Maxi when she gets off the phone with her Mom."

"Cool" said Bruce. "Mind grabbing your Bible? Turn to Romans Chapter Ten starting at verse nine."

You replied, "Got it Bruce. Maxi, I want to ask you how your talk with Mom went - first can I read a Bible scripture to you?"

Maxi smiled, "Wow you've never read the Bible to me 'til now – of course I want to hear your eloquence and what the Bible says!"

Feeling important you used your 'teacher's voice', "Our Bible reading is from the Book of Romans Chapter Ten, verses nine and ten:" *If you declare with your mouth, "Jesus is Lord," and believe in your heart that God raised Him from the dead, you will be saved. For it is with your heart that you believe and are justified, and it is with your mouth that you profess your faith and are saved.* Romans 10:9-10 [1]

Maxine said, "I want Jesus to be my Lord because I think He will help me be a more loving wife and a more excellent worker and hopefully a good mother one day. Plus, I believe God raised Jesus from the tomb he was buried in, and Jesus was seen alive by His all of his disciples, doubting Thomas, plus over five hundred witnesses before He returned to Heaven. I read all of this in the Bible last night before we went to bed."

With a big smile in your heart you repeated out loud along with Maxine the powerful words of Romans 10:9-10; trying to say the words from your heart and mind to God and Jesus:

"Jesus, I hereby declare you are Lord of my life; plus I believe in my heart God raised you from the dead! God I know I'm not perfect and I beg you'll forgive me for all the unkind, selfish, lustful, wicked things I've said and done to you and my fellow man and for ignoring you for over thirty years! Thank you for the teachers who told me God has a plan for my life. I pray your greatest blessings on each one of them Father. Thank you God for giving me a choice: I choose to believe you deliberately sent your perfect, beautiful, sinless son Jesus intending him to die on the cross for all mankind's sins – including mine. For the first time, I dedicate my teaching career to you and request your wisdom in preparing the paper and presentation for the convention."

Maxine beamed brightly, affirming you by saying, "You are my husband and I love you!"

"Oh Maxi, I love you too! I can't believe I was able to convince a super-star like you to be my wife, lover and life partner!"

Maxine added, "And now we have God and His Son Jesus in our lives...as the strongest and wisest partner we could ever hope to have."

"Maxi, I want us to dedicate our hearts to God - and to our future and even the children we don't yet have, all dedicated to almighty God!"

"Oh I do so surely agree with you said Maxi!

You asked God and yourself and Maxi, "I must have your help to craft a paper which impacts American's teachers and our youth in an enduring and powerful way!"

Maxi remarked, "Honey this could be the first big test of your newfound faith in God!"

"I agree with you sweetheart and truth be told I am not smart enough to craft this paper in my own strength. Our nation's heading in the wrong direction and our youth are suffering.

"You're so smart – I think a month gives you plenty of time, doesn't it?"

You responded, "Normally a month would be fine, but now I'm a born again teacher who follows God and Jesus. The paper needs to be God's message not just mine."

Maxi agreed, "You're not proficient in seeking and listening to God yet, are you?"

"So I have to ask God what He wants me to say…I'm so used to doing it on my own!"

"Wow honey - I'm realizing I need to pray hard for you! I will ask Susa Pitts and her church and Bruce's church to pray for you also."

"Thank you, Maxi. I feel better already. Is it okay if I go solo to the beach house for a night or two to read the Bible and seek God's wisdom?"

"Absolutely – I'll gather food, drinks and snacks for you…and pack a duffel bag?"

"Thank you, Maxi. I'm so glad and so blessed by God that you and I are partners!"

Growing up you went to the beach house dozens of times - four weeks ago you went again - why does our same old beach house and gardens and trees and the ocean look **even more beautiful** today?

++

THANK YOU FOR READING "JOE AVERAGE".

We'd love your feedback at: feedback@thewalk.me

Part Three may include Joe Average's paper & presentation to the National Convention.

The Walk – S.B. Stone & Rock Solid Publishing, LLC
©2018

Episode Eight - Wimpy God

You're royally pissed off!

As a legit and committed Millennial you should have figured it out by now!

All M's have intrinsic genius which is one of the reasons you love your peers.

Most M's idolize you.

You are true genius IQ.

Your vocal talents draw thousands.

Your girlfriend, almost wife, Kristi, worships the ground you walk on…except when she's ticked at you - at least once a day.

You are so esteemed it seems M's are waiting for you guidance about what should be important in their lives; your ego embraces such affection but the realist in your amazing brain says "dude you're not gonna deliver; that's for them to figure out."

You and Kristi have been together for an amazing three years.

Truth be told, you're shocked she's stuck with you so long; you've discussed the other M word and it scares you spit-less and you're not sure why. It's cool she calls you "Hon" because "you're so sweet and innocent and vulnerable and cute" she proclaims.

Kristi asked you, "how come you love me Hon?"

You're thinking there's only one answer "because you are on fleek and searing hot woman!" You know Kristi wants you to love her for her good humor, kindness, creativity and strength of character so you added more qualities to your "why I love Kristi" list. To be honest, Kristi's a special gal and your friendship has grown a lot in three years!

You're so bright, some say gifted, you've been asked by the government and a couple growing artificial intelligence (AI) companies to create a high level coding machine: The computer would allow a non-computer engineer to write a business objective in laymen's language into this magical machine. The instructions would be interpolated by the machine and ultimately spit out as a fully and accurately coded piece of software in Java, JavaScript, Python, Scala, Go, SQL, C or a new language you create if it behooves you to do so.

You asked your best friend, Ozzi, what he thought of the machine idea.

"They are crazy dude!" Ozzie complained.

"Crazy? Why Ozzie?" you cried.

"Last I heard the world has somewhere in the range of twenty to thirty-five million development projects underway" Ozzie claimed.

"So?" you wondered.

Ozzie clarified his concerns, "Do we really want to put millions of fellow programmers out of business with our new coding computer?

Millions of individual programmers cranking out the code for those projects and earning big bucks for their talents" you added.

Ozzi smiled, "you should know Genius, you made over a million a year when you were writing code in the early days, didn't you?"

"I admit I had an unfair advantage able to write great code in one-third the time of most of my peers" you confessed.

Humbly Ozzi added, "You probably didn't see me, but one time on the job we were doing for Cisco, I watched you with my tongue hanging out, envious of your speed and quality. The very best I could do was fifty percent of your results!"

"To our clients you were the guru Oz!" you encouraged.

"Thanks for saying that Genius; it means a lot coming from you" confided Ozzi.

You inquired, "Hey OZ, been back to Dubrovnik lately?"

Oz replied, "Hey thanks for asking. My Mom's been in the hospital for heart issues, so I plan to visit after she's released or if the doctor wants to her to lay low through Christmas I may fly over next month."

You've only visited Dubrovnik one summer two years ago. It's is a tiny town on the Adriatic Sea in southern Croatia - a prominent tourist destination, lovely seaport and the center of Dubrovnik-Neretva County.

You said, "When you speak with your Mom tell her I wish her the best and hope to come visit when she's feeling better."

"Will do" responded Ozzi – "I better warn you Mom will ask you the big question again."

"I don't like her big question but I'll be ready for it you said" faking confidence.

"We'll see about that!" challenged Ozzi with a smile.

You asked, "Hey Ozzi, remember you leaked on social media that yours truly is a genius?"

"Of course" replied Ozzi. You were an overnight celebrity with millions taking aim to stump you on politics, Darwinism, astrophysics, metaphysics, Socrates, Buddha, Taoism, Islam and other world religions!"

"Oh the price one must pay for brilliance" you agreed.

"As you proved yourself worthy of their toughest questions one of your Jewish friends, Isaac, gave you the name Solomon after the wisest king in Israel's history" reflected Ozzi.

You admitted, "I have thousands of questions jostling around my brain dude; can you remind me of your Mom's big question precisely?"

"Happy to remind you of Mom's big question Genius" Ozzi volunteered, and added, "Mom would say it like this: 'Young man, you are Ozzi's best friend and I love you. More important almighty God loves you too whether you choose to love Him or not. When you die, like all of us will, and you stand before God and He looks into your eyes with love and truth and asks you: 'Genius, tell me why should I let you into my Heaven?' What will you say to God?"

The Walk – S.B. Stone & Rock Solid Publishing, LLC ©2018

"Heck if I know…sir…uh…please let me do a few more years of research God?

Ozzi's shaking his head – "Not too impressive for a genius, dude!"

"I agree, you admitted. You have something better Oz?"

"I hope God doesn't ask me any questions" replied Oz.

Puzzled you said "Why would you be exempt Oz?"

Confidently, Oz replied, "I'd rather God smile at me and say, 'Welcome to my Heaven Oz!' without asking me to convince God I qualify."

"Sounds kind of arrogant" you argued.

With assurance Oz smiled "Not really – I'm confident because I've already humbled myself and invested my faith in God's Jesus Transaction. Though I don't merit one smidgeon of God's forgiveness my eternal destiny will be a done deal."

You said, "Would be nice to go through life knowing you're heading to Heaven when you die."

Oz followed with a series of questions to help his brilliant friend: "I know you've watched the news on TV and the internet; remember the dude named O'Reilly?

You recalled, "Tall, confident, actually arrogant, and he created this no-spin zone thing for his guests, right?"

"That's him" agreed Oz. Did O'Reilly strike you as a religious person?"

You conceded, "It's impossible to see inside a person's mind and heart but I believe he identified himself as a Catholic?"

"That's what I recall" Oz concurred.

Oz added, "Did you ever hear O'Reilly share his experiences in the school he attended as a youth?

You recalled, "Yes, I distinctly recall how the sister's or fathers or whatever, ran a tight ship which his parents really appreciated given their son's propensity for goofing off like a normal kid"

The Walk – S.B. Stone & Rock Solid Publishing, LLC
©2018

"Did O'Reilly ever share his personal beliefs?" Oz continued.

"Hey it was a news program so I never expected he would. However, he believed abortion was wrong which I was trying to figure out for myself at the time so I appreciated his clarity and courage on abortion" you recalled.

Oz added, "Did he share anything else?"

You replied, "He said his teachers at this presumably Catholic school taught the miracles of the Bible were <u>only stories</u> and <u>not historical facts</u>."

Oz probed, "How'd you feel about O'Reilly's theology?"

You said, "Honestly at that time I'm not sure if I believed in God and Jesus or the devil so it didn't matter I suppose, but if there's a devil but he had to be smiling at such nonsense."

"I understand" Oz offered.

You added, "It ticked me off a famous author, former teacher and big time news anchor believed in such a wimpy God. <u>I refuse to waste my faith in a God who's so</u> **wimpy** he can't **heal sickness** and **blindness** and **cast out demons** and **part the Red Sea** and **raise the dead**."

Oz empathized, "I appreciate that dude – so what did you do in response?

You replied, "Don't know if I shared this with you?"

"Tell me" Oz wondered.

You declared, "I decided **<u>not</u>** to take the pompous know-it-all's word for it!"

"Sweet" declared Oz.

"Yep, twelve months ago I launched an **unbiased investigation** of the Bible in the context of history, science and my personal observations gleaned from reading every page - Genesis through Revelation – and learned God appointed some forty people to contribute to the books like Moses, Amos, King David, King Solomon, Isaiah, Jeremiah, Paul, John, Peter, Luke, Matthew and others" you shared.

The Walk – S.B. Stone & Rock Solid Publishing, LLC
©2018

"If my studies show God is wimpy, I'll have no interest in investing my time or treasure in His program. I plan to continue my investigation for another year because I know I'm barely scratching the surface of what God's could potentially teach me."

"Excuse my interruption" said Oz.

You replied, "No problem, what's up?"

With a smile Oz asked, "Have you come across Second Timothy 3:16 -17?

16All Scripture is God-breathed [given by divine inspiration] and is profitable for instruction, for conviction [of sin], for correction [of error and restoration to obedience], for training in righteousness [learning to live in conformity to God's will, both publicly and privately—behaving honorably with personal integrity and moral courage]; 17so that the I.e. all believers whether man, woman, or child, man of God may be complete and proficient, outfitted and thoroughly equipped for every good work. [6]

"That's from the Amplified Bible" Oz added.

You observed, "Sounds like God wants us to know he's the author of the Bible?"

Ozzi agreed, "Yes the Bible's a major historical book, God has crafted the Bible to provide insights on how live happy and successful lives today."

You asked, "Have you read the Bible Oz?"

"I began reading the Bible almost every day about eight years ago" Oz smiled.

"Wow, I'm jealous" you admitted! "Pretty please can you share highlights of what you learned from reading the Bible Oz! Will it bother you if I leverage what you've learned?

Oz face was intense, "The Bible is rich with truth so I'm honored to share with you!"

"Mind if I take a note or two?"

"I thought you have a photographic memory" said Oz

The Walk – S.B. Stone & Rock Solid Publishing, LLC
©2018

"I do but taking notes helps me focus…my fingers are ready" you shared.

Oz began, "Here are the highlights of what I've learned in eight years reading the Bible:

- God is the author of love

- God's forgiveness is a free gift

- All people have an eternal soul

- Heaven is real

- Hell is real

- The Bible demonstrates how real people face legitimate hardships

- God demands all your heart, soul, mind and strength devoted to serving Him

- God loves us for a lot of reasons, one of which is He knit you and I together in our Mom's wombs – using Deoxyribonucleic acid DNA which God invented.

- God invented plants and trees and this crazy thing called photosynthesis to provide us with oxygen so we can breathe – what a great idea God had – otherwise we'd all be born and then immediately die – terrible!

- I've discovered the Bible is an ancient document with huge 21st Century relevance!

- God's Bible is truth and can withstand all the scrutiny you wish to impose upon it.

- The greatest lens through which to examine the Bible is your humble and honest "faith key".

- You and I cannot fool God…for even one second.

- He knows our thoughts and heart before we express them.

- We can be transparent about the meagerness of our faith, our sins and contemplated sins.

• Only the fool says in his heart, there is no God with so much evidence to the contrary.

• Know anyone who claims God is dead or never existed in the first place?

• The $27 million electron microscope sees images ½ the width of a hydrogen atom.

• Science is tripping over the creative majesty of God and God's creation, lifted the veil of "intelligent design" Darwinism, DNA, Photosynthesis and the complexity of our world plus the entire universe.

• The more we discover about the complexity of our brains, nervous system, deoxy-ribonucleic acid and photosynthesis an honest investigator must admit mankind is a miraculous product of intelligent design.

• I've discovered Truth is not a science experiment. Nor does truth require our votes of approval. Man's Intelligent Designer is more than the God of science.

• Regardless of your world view, try to stump God on any subject you can think of:

Astrophysics…Paranormal activities…the Black Hole…True Love…Integrity…Extreme

Weather Phenomenon...Religion…True Success…Best Parenting Practices…What's Truth?

Heaven…Hell…Space Travel...How to Build Happy Marriages…Your Thought History plus the boatload of sins you've not yet committed.

• I've discovered God possesses unstoppable power and inconceivable patience for his creation – including you and me.

• You and I need to ask God to teach us something new every day!

• Looking for contradictions is a WASTE of OUR LIMITED TIME.

The Walk – S.B. Stone & Rock Solid Publishing, LLC
©2018

- Ask God to grow our faith and help us view His creation and His Bible through the lens of faith: Why is seeing God and your life through the lens of faith so important?

- "And without faith it is impossible to please God. Anyone who comes to God must believe he exists and that he rewards those who earnestly seek him." Hebrews 11:6 [1]

- Regardless of your "religious" background, do you know the God who created the universe really loves you, not just a little but very, very much!

- I've discovered that if someone is still breathing it's a clear indicator

God's not given up on them yet. Why you ask?

- Regardless of your background God wants a personal relationship with you – not a sterile Ten Commandments or religious one.

- I've learned only you hold the key to unlocking your relationship with

God. The key to entering a satisfying walk with God is your faith.

- I've learned I must dispel the false notion of living a "sinless life" before

God permits me to enter a personal relationship with Him.

- Quite the contrary. I must confess I'm a sinner and everyone qualifies, no exceptions. What if I don't "feel" repentant in my heart? Be honest with God and beg Him to help me come around to true repentance.

- Remember, there is no way you or I can earn our way into God's perfect and sin-free Heaven! Heck, we'd wreck the place.

- Regardless of my career choice, there's no greater role in life than being a true Disciple of Jesus Christ.

- Yes, many religions claim they can show me how to live a happy and productive life.

- But there is no religion: 1. Whose leader is God: 2. Who voluntarily forsakes his divinity; 3. To be born on earth to and 4.Bleed for you and me as a cleansing agent for my lifetime of sins.

- There is **no religious figure** who claimed to be God and proved it by turning water into wine, healing the sick, casting out demons, raising the dead, predicting his own torture and crucifixion, predicting he would rise after three days in the grave, died on the cross, was buried in a tomb, was <u>resurrected from the dead in three days,</u> was **seen alive** by his disciples, the apostles plus **over five hundred witnesses**!

- No doubt about it friends: This is NOT a wimpy God we're talking about. Plus He's extremely intelligent, almighty and <u>more than willing to engage in my meager life to make it Far More Meaningful than I could have ever done on my own</u> energy and skill.

- I have Zero doubt God is calling you my friend!

- Why wouldn't you follow a man [actually a God-man] like this?

- I submit He's been calling you your whole life!

- When I awoke this morning still lying in bed…breathing…I thought about this book and aspects of my day ahead; it dawned on me almighty God was giving me another day of life on His earth! I thanked Him and requested His blessing on this book.

- I was not on my knees or trying to do anything "religious". I'm just a simple creature choosing to connect with his Creator before launching into the day.   I discourage you from attaching some religious label [Catholic, Christian, Jew or whatever else you may be tempted to latch on to]. <u>Just simply be yourself</u> ONE ON ONE with God.

- Relax in the absolute certainty you cannot fool God. He knows exactly what you're thinking so 'be real' with God. He dislikes phonies and <u>already loves</u> <u>you</u> in spite of your past phoniness, sinful thoughts, words and pitiful attempts to fool Him.

• In case reading the Bible is new or uncomfortable for you I'll help you dip your toe in the water walking through a short Bible study on a few basic topics:

• Why did God's angel instruct them to call Jesus Immanuel? [Matthew Chapter One]

• The moment Jesus died in his cross why was the huge veil in the Jewish temple torn from top to bottom? [Matthew 27:51]

• Just before he died why did Jesus cry out "my God, my God why have you forsaken me?" [see Matthew 27:46]

• In verse 50 of Matthew 27, Jesus body died and He "gave up His spirit". What might this tell us about the death of our own body someday?

****

Thank you for reading Wimpy God. Your feedback is always welcome.

Our website is: www.thewalk.me

Or you can email us at: feedback@thewalk.me

May God bless you as you walk the steps of your life.

Will you humbly invite God to walk beside you every single day?

It's not a religion…it's a Relationship my friend!

The Walk – S.B. Stone & Rock Solid Publishing, LLC
©2018

The Walk - Episode Nine: A Day in the Life of You?

Saul of Tarsus had not met Jesus face to face – yet he was one of God's superstars: A devout Jew and obedient to God's laws since he was a youth. Saul stood by and watched angry Jews stone a fellow Jew who'd chosen to follow Christ. Saul was feared by Jews who were considering the Good News of Christ's gospel. Saul's hatred for Christians inspired him to request authority from the High Priest to go the synagogues at Damascus to arrest any men or women belonging to "the Way" of Jesus whom they had crucified:

"The Conversion of Saul

*1Now Later known as Paul the Apostle. **Saul, still breathing threats and murder against the disciples of the Lord [and relentless in his search for believers], went to the Probably Caiaphas, the son-in-law of Annas. See note 4:6.high priest, 2and he asked for letters [of authority] from him to the synagogues at Damascus, so that if he found any men or women there belonging to This term for Christianity may have originated from Jesus' own words, "I am the Way...," John 14:6.the Way [believers, followers of Jesus the Messiah], men and women alike, he could arrest them and bring them bound [with chains] to Jerusalem. 3As he traveled he approached Damascus, and suddenly a light from heaven flashed around him***

[displaying the glory and majesty of Christ]; 4and he fell to the ground and heard a voice

[from heaven] saying to him, "Saul, Saul, why are you persecuting and oppressing

Me?" 5And Saul said, "Who are You, Lord?" And He answered, "I am Jesus whom you are persecuting, 6now get up and go into the city, and you will be told what you must do." 7The men who were traveling with him [were terrified and] stood speechless, hearing the voice but seeing no one. 8Saul got up from the ground, but though his eyes were open, he could see nothing; so they led him by the hand and brought him into Damascus. 9And he was unable to see for three days, and he neither ate nor drank. 10Now in Damascus there was a disciple named Ananias; and the Lord said to him in a vision, "Ananias." And he answered, "Here I am, Lord." 11And the Lord said to him, "Get up and go to the street called Latin Via Recta, a long, straight street built by the Romans that ran through the city from east to west. Straight, and ask at the house of Judas for a man from Tarsus named Saul; for he is praying [there], 12and in a vision he has seen a man named Ananias come in and place his hands on him, so that he may regain his sight." Acts 9:1 – 13. [6]

It's okay if you're wondering how this story could be a day in the life of **you** when it's about a thirty-something Jewish guy on the road to a place called Damascus two thousand years past? Fair question. Jump into the story like you are Paul's sidekick; soaking in sights, smells and emotions - super observant; grab onto experiences and character qualities you'd like to experience in your own life…starting today if you'd like. Remember Saul would have tried to **arrest and imprison you** for walking with Jesus and writing the letter you are about to read.

Ephesians – Chapter One

(not included due to copyright restrictions)

Ephesians – Chapter Two

He Tore Down the Wall

1-6It wasn't so long ago that you were mired in that old stagnant life of sin. You let the world, which doesn't know the first thing about living, tell you how to live. You filled your lungs with polluted unbelief, and then exhaled disobedience. We all did it, all of us doing what we felt like doing, when we felt like doing it, all of us in the same boat. It's a wonder God didn't lose his temper and do away with the whole lot of us. Instead, immense in mercy and with an incredible love, he embraced us. He took our sin-dead lives and made us alive in Christ. He did all this on his own, with no help from us! Then he picked us up and set us down in highest heaven in company with Jesus, our Messiah. 7-10Now God has us where he wants us, with all the time in this world and the next to shower grace and kindness upon us in Christ Jesus. Saving is all his idea, and all his work. All we do is trust him enough to let him do it. It's God's gift from start to finish! We don't play the major role. If we did, we'd probably go around bragging that we'd done the whole thing! No, we neither make nor save ourselves. God does both the making and saving. He creates each of us by Christ Jesus to join him in the work he does, the good work he has gotten ready for us to do, work we had better be doing. 11-13But don't take any of this for granted. It was only yesterday that you outsiders to God's ways had no idea of any of this, didn't know the first thing about the way God works, hadn't the faintest idea of Christ. You knew nothing of that rich history of God's covenants and promises in Israel, hadn't a clue about what God was doing in the world at large. Now because of Christ—dying that death, shedding that blood— you who were once out of it altogether are in on everything. 14-15The Messiah has made things up between us so that we're now together on this, both non-Jewish outsiders and Jewish insiders. He tore down the wall we used to keep each other at a distance. He repealed the law code that had become so clogged with fine print and footnotes that it hindered more than it helped. Then he started over. Instead of continuing with two groups of people separated by centuries of animosity and suspicion, he created a new kind of human being, a fresh start for everybody. 16-18Christ brought us together through his death on the cross. The Cross got us to embrace, and that was the end of the hostility. Christ came and preached peace to you outsiders and peace to us insiders. He treated us as equals, and so made us equals. Through him we both share the same Spirit and have equal access to the Father. 19-22That's plain enough, isn't it?

You're no longer wandering exiles. This kingdom of faith is now your home country. You're no longer strangers or outsiders. You belong here, with as much right to the name Christian as anyone. God is building a home. He's using us all—irrespective of how we got here—in what he is building. He used the apostles and prophets for the foundation. Now he's using you, fitting you in brick by brick, stone by stone, with Christ Jesus as the cornerstone that holds all the parts together. We see it taking shape day after day—a holy temple built by God, all of us built into it, a temple in which God is quite at home.   [3]

Ephesians – Chapter Three

The Secret Plan of God

1-3This is why I, Paul, am in jail for Christ, having taken up the cause of you outsiders, so-called. I take it that you're familiar with the part I was given in God's plan for including everybody. I got the inside story on this from God himself, as I just wrote you in brief.

4-6As you read over what I have written to you, you'll be able to see for yourselves into the mystery of Christ. None of our ancestors understood this. Only in our time has it been made clear by God's Spirit through his holy apostles and prophets of this new order. The mystery is that people who have never heard of God and those who have heard of him all their lives (what

I've been calling outsiders and insiders) stand on the same ground before God. They get the same offer, same help, same promises in Christ Jesus. The Message is accessible and welcoming to everyone, across the board. 7-8This is my life work: helping people understand and respond to this Message. It came as a sheer gift to me, a real surprise, God handling all the details. When it came to presenting the Message to people who had no background in God's way, I was the least qualified of any of the available Christians. God saw to it that I was equipped, but you can be sure that it had nothing to do with my natural abilities. 8-10And so here I am, preaching and writing about things that are way over my head, the inexhaustible riches and generosity of Christ. My task is to bring out in the open and make plain what God, who created all this in the first place, has been doing in secret and behind the scenes all along. Through followers of Jesus like yourselves gathered in churches, this extraordinary plan of God is becoming known and talked about even among the angels! 11-13All this is proceeding along lines planned all along by

God and then executed in Christ Jesus. When we trust in him, we're free to say whatever needs to be said, bold to go wherever we need to go. So don't let my present trouble on your behalf get you down. Be proud! 14-19My response is to get down on my knees before the Father, this magnificent Father who parcels out all heaven and earth. I ask him to strengthen you by his Spirit— not a brute strength but a glorious inner strength—that Christ will live in you as you open the door and invite him in. And I ask him that with both feet planted firmly on love, you'll be able to take in with all followers of Jesus the extravagant dimensions of Christ's love. Reach out and experience the breadth! Test its length! Plumb the depths! Rise to the heights! Live full lives, full in the fullness of God. 20-21 God can do anything, you know—far more than you could ever imagine or guess or request in your wildest dreams! He does it not by pushing us around but by working within us, his Spirit deeply and gently within us. Glory to God in the church! Glory to God in the Messiah, in Jesus! Glory down all the generations! Glory through all millennia! Oh, yes! [3]

Ephesians – Chapter Four

To Be Mature

1-3 In light of all this, here's what I want you to do. While I'm locked up here, a prisoner for the Master, I want you to get out there and walk—better yet, run!—on the road God called you to travel. I don't want any of you sitting around on your hands. I don't want anyone strolling off, down some path that goes nowhere. And mark that you do this with humility and discipline— not in fits and starts, but steadily, pouring yourselves out for each other in acts of love, alert at noticing differences and quick at mending fences. 4-6 You were all called to travel on the same road and in the same direction, so stay together, both outwardly and inwardly. You have one Master, one faith, one baptism, one God and Father of all, who rules over all, works through all, and is present in all. Everything you are and think and do is permeated with Oneness.

7-13 But that doesn't mean you should all look and speak and act the same. Out of the generosity of Christ, each of us is given his own gift. The text for this is, He climbed the high mountain, He captured the enemy and seized the booty, He handed it all out in gifts to the people. Is it not true that the One who climbed up also climbed down, down to the valley of earth? And the One who climbed down is the One who climbed back up, up to highest heaven.

He handed out gifts above and below, filled heaven with his gifts, filled earth with his gifts. He handed out gifts of apostle, prophet, evangelist, and pastor-teacher to train Christ's followers in skilled servant work, working within Christ's body, the church, until we're all moving rhythmically and easily with each other, efficient and graceful in response to God's Son, fully mature adults, fully developed within and without, fully alive like Christ. 14-16No prolonged infancies among us, please. We'll not tolerate babes in the woods, small children who are an easy mark for impostors. God wants us to grow up, to know the whole truth and tell it in love— like Christ in everything. We take our lead from Christ, who is the source of everything we do. He keeps us in step with each other. His very breath and blood flow through us, nourishing us so that we will grow up healthy in God, robust in love.

The Old Way Has to Go

17-19And so I insist—and God backs me up on this—that there be no going along with the crowd, the empty-headed, mindless crowd. They've refused for so long to deal with God that they've lost touch not only with God but with reality itself. They can't think straight anymore.

Feeling no pain, they let themselves go in sexual obsession, addicted to every sort of perversion.

20-24But that's no life for you. You learned Christ! My assumption is that you have paid careful attention to him, been well instructed in the truth precisely as we have it in Jesus. Since, then, we do not have the excuse of ignorance, everything— and I do mean everything—connected with that old way of life has to go. It's rotten through and through. Get rid of it! And then take on an entirely new way of life—a God-fashioned life, a life renewed from the inside and working itself into your conduct as God accurately reproduces his character in you. 25What this adds up to, then, is this: no more lies, no more pretense. Tell your neighbor the truth. In Christ's body we're all connected to each other, after all. When you lie to others, you end up lying to yourself. 26-27Go ahead and be angry. You do well to be angry—but don't use your anger as fuel for revenge. And don't stay angry. Don't go to bed angry. Don't give the Devil that kind of foothold in your life. 28Did you use to make ends meet by stealing? Well, no more! Get an honest job so that you can help others who can't work. 29Watch the way you talk. Let nothing foul or dirty come out of your mouth. Say only what helps, each word a gift. 30Don't grieve God. Don't break his heart. His Holy Spirit, moving and breathing in you, is the most intimate part of your life, making you fit for himself. Don't take such a gift for granted. 31-32Make a clean break with all cutting, backbiting, profane talk. Be gentle with one another, sensitive. Forgive one another as quickly and thoroughly as God in Christ forgave you. [3]

Ephesians – Chapter Five

Wake Up from Your Sleep

1-2Watch what God does, and then you do it, like children who learn proper behavior from their parents. Mostly what God does is love you. Keep company with him and learn a life of love. Observe how Christ loved us. His love was not cautious but extravagant. He didn't love in order to get something from us but to give everything of himself to us. Love like that. 3-4Don't allow love to turn into lust, setting off a downhill slide into sexual promiscuity, filthy practices, or bullying greed. Though some tongues just love the taste of gossip, those who follow Jesus have better uses for language than that. Don't talk dirty or silly. That kind of talk doesn't fit our style. Thanksgiving is our dialect. 5You can be sure that using people or religion or things just for what you can get out of them—the usual variations on idolatry—will get you nowhere, and certainly nowhere near the kingdom of Christ, the kingdom of God. 6-7Don't let yourselves get taken in by religious smooth talk. God gets furious with people who are full of religious sales talk but want nothing to do with him. Don't even hang around people like that. 8-10You groped your way through that murk once, but no longer. You're out in the open now. The bright light of Christ makes your way plain. So no more stumbling around. Get on with it! The good, the right, the true—these are the actions appropriate for daylight hours. Figure out what will please

Christ, and then do it. 11-16Don't waste your time on useless work, mere busywork, the barren pursuits of darkness. Expose these things for the sham they are. It's a scandal when people waste their lives on things they must do in the darkness where no one will see. Rip the cover off those frauds and see how attractive they look in the light of Christ. Wake up from your *sleep, Climb out of your coffins; Christ will show you the light! So watch your step. Use your head. Make the most of every chance you get. These are desperate times! 17Don't live carelessly, unthinkingly. Make sure you understand what the Master wants. 18-20Don't drink too much wine. That cheapens your life. Drink the Spirit of God, huge draughts of him. Sing hymns instead of drinking songs! Sing songs from your heart to Christ. Sing praises over everything, any excuse for a song to God the Father in the name of our Master, Jesus Christ.*

Relationships

21Out of respect for Christ, be courteously reverent to one another.

22-24Wives, understand and support your husbands in ways that show your support for Christ. The husband provides leadership to his wife the way Christ does to his church, not by domineering but by cherishing. So just as the church submits to Christ as he exercises such leadership, wives should likewise submit to their husbands. 25-28Husbands, go all out in your love for your wives, exactly as Christ did for the church—a love marked by giving, not getting.

Christ's love makes the church whole. His words evoke her beauty. Everything he does and says is designed to bring the best out of her, dressing her in dazzling white silk, radiant with holiness. And that is how husbands ought to love their wives. They're really doing themselves a favor— since they're already "one" in marriage. 29-33No one abuses his own body, does he? No, he feeds and pampers it. That's how Christ treats us, the church, since we are part of his body. And this is why a man leaves father and mother and cherishes his wife. No longer two, they become

"one flesh." This is a huge mystery, and I don't pretend to understand it all. What is clearest to me is the way Christ treats the church. And this provides a good picture of how each husband is to treat his wife, loving himself in loving her, and how each wife is to honor her husband. [3] **Ephesians – Chapter Six**

1-3Children, do what your parents tell you. This is only right. "Honor your father and mother" is the first commandment that has a promise attached to it, namely, "so you will live well and have a long life." 4Fathers, don't exasperate your children by coming down hard on them. Take them by the hand and lead them in the way of the Master. 5-8Servants, respectfully obey your earthly masters but always with an eye to obeying the real master, Christ. Don't just do what you have to do to get by, but work heartily, as Christ's servants doing what God wants you to do. And work with a smile on your face, always keeping in mind that no matter who happens to be giving the orders, you're really serving God. Good work will get you good pay from the Master, regardless of whether you are slave or free. 9Masters, it's the same with you. No abuse, please, and no threats. You and your servants are both under the same Master in heaven. He makes no distinction between you and them.

A Fight to the Finish

10-12And that about wraps it up. God is strong, and he wants you strong. So take everything the Master has set out for you, well-made weapons of the best materials. And put them to use so you will be able to stand up to everything the Devil throws your way. This is no afternoon athletic contest that we'll walk away from and forget about in a couple of hours. This is for keeps, a life-or-death fight to the finish against the Devil and all his angels. 13-18Be prepared. You're up against far more than you can handle on your own. Take all the help you can get, every weapon God has issued, so that when it's all over but the shouting you'll still be on your feet. Truth, righteousness, peace, faith, and salvation are more than words. Learn how to apply them. You'll need them throughout your life. God's Word is an indispensable weapon. In the same way, prayer is essential in this ongoing warfare. Pray hard and long. Pray for your brothers and sisters. Keep your eyes open. Keep each other's spirits up so that no one falls behind or drops out. 19-20And don't forget to pray for me. Pray that I'll know what to say and have the courage to say it at the right time, telling the mystery to one and all, the Message that I, jailbird preacher that I am, am responsible for getting out. 21-22Tychicus, my good friend here, will tell you what I'm doing and how things are going with me.

He is certainly a dependable servant of the Master! I've sent him not only to tell you about us but to cheer you on in your faith. 23-24 Good-bye, friends. Love mixed with faith be yours from God the Father and from the

Master, Jesus Christ. Pure grace and nothing but grace be with all who love our Master, Jesus Christ." [3]

Only one-hundred fifty-five verses but packed with meaty subjects and practical insights on: abundant freedom, **fence mending, angel chatter, God's Spirit inside you, good works, God's will, marriages, the devil and spiritual warfare** to name a few. Let's close this Episode by asking you a key question: Do you want God's mighty power of love to flow through your life? Keep reading the contents of The Walk to discover what's missing and good ideas for filling the gap.

As an author it's 100% me but can we keep our dialogue going? feedback@thewalk.me

****

Thank you for reading "A Day in the Life of You?"

P.S. Your author recommends audio version of the content above [MSG]

If you don't have **The Walk** audio book, check out the free written and audio resources at www.YouVersion.com

The Walk – S.B. Stone & Rock Solid Publishing, LLC
©2018

The Walk: Episode Ten – Sneak - Peak at America's Jesus Questions

Do you need to be a "religious" person or in a religious place to ask God a question?

The answer is definitely **no**!

No, any place works because God can always see you when He chooses to.

Did you know God is "omnipresent"? He's everywhere he wants to be all at the same time.

Thus, the Creator of you and the entire universe is never out of reach.

I can ask God/Jesus any heartfelt question any place in the world, on the moon and universe. In 2018 we surveyed Americans age 18 to 90 plus to think about what they would ask Jesus Christ if He actually physically shows up here on earth to talk with them during their daily activities.

Here is **The Jesus Question** we used in our survey:

"Imagine you are alone in a safe and quiet place with no distractions.

A man appears. He is confident, kind and gentle.

The man's eyes radiate light and truth.

He calls you by name as He looks into your eyes with love.

He states – 'I am Jesus Christ. I am here to answer your questions'."

 We asked survey participants to dig into their brains and hearts for at least three questions to ask Jesus. Some asked less than three; others asked Jesus more than three questions.

What were the results of our survey? We were blessed to receive over 120 Jesus questions!

On the following pages we are privileged to share with you 9 of America's actual Jesus questions.

I put <u>only two</u> Jesus Questions per page because I believe each Jesus question is **super important**… deserving significant white space around it. Before turning to the next page, feel free to re-read **The Jesus Question** again if you wish.

Jesus. Am I going to heaven when I die?

Jesus. Why is there so much suffering and injustice?

The Walk – S.B. Stone & Rock Solid Publishing, LLC
©2018

Jesus. Why do bad things happen to good people?

Jesus. Do you forgive all my sins?

Jesus. What is my purpose [your plans for my life] on earth?

Jesus. Is there really a hell [after I die]?

Jesus. Will all good people go to heaven? [regardless of their religion]

Jesus. Why am I so afraid of death?

Jesus. Why do you allow Satan to exist [why don't you destroy him]?

The Walk – Episode Eleven: Excerpts from my Favorite Books
[1] [2] [3] [4] [5] [6]

Introduction by S.B. Stone

I apologize for the unprofessional audio recording quality as manifested in the 'too low' volume sections and the six different voices, besides my voice, which may stimulate your ear and brain or perhaps bore you. I recommend having a copy of the Bible open while listening to the audio sections to serve as a roadmap and a cheat sheet when it's hard to hear what the reader is saying. Keep in mind these are excerpts, not consecutive, and therefore will 'hop' from chapter to chapter and/or book to book. ABOVE ALL ELSE REMEMBER: GOD WROTE HIS BIBLE **FOR YOU** TO GAIN INSIGHTS REGARDING HOW **HE** ROLLS AND HOW YOU CAN WALK THRU A **RICHER** LIFE AND AFTERLIFE BY LEARNING AND **PRACTICING** HIS TIMELESS PRINCIPLES – **GO FOR IT MY FRIEND!!!**

THE HOLY BIBLE [excerpts selected by S.B. Stone]

Genesis - Chapter One [New Living Translation]

The Account of Creation

1In the beginning God created the heavens and the earth.1:1 Or *In the beginning when God created the heavens and the earth, . . .*Or *When God began to create the heavens and the earth, . . .*2The earth was formless and empty, and darkness covered the deep waters. And the

Spirit of God was hovering over the surface of the waters. 3Then God said, "Let there be light," and there was light. 4And God saw that the light was good. Then he separated the light from the darkness. 5God called the light "day" and the darkness "night." And evening passed and morning came, marking the first day. 6Then God said, "Let there be a space between the waters, to separate the waters of the heavens from the waters of the earth." 7And that is what happened.

God made this space to separate the waters of the earth from the waters of the heavens. 8God called the space "sky." And evening passed and morning came, marking the second day. 9Then God said, "Let the waters beneath the sky flow together into one place, so dry ground may appear." And that is what happened. 10God called the dry ground "land" and the waters "seas." And God saw that it was good. 11Then God said, "Let the land sprout with vegetation—every sort of seed-bearing plant, and trees that grow seed-bearing fruit. These seeds will then produce the kinds of plants and trees from which they came." And that is what happened. 12The land produced vegetation—all sorts of seed bearing plants, and trees with seed-bearing fruit. Their seeds produced plants and trees of the same kind. And God saw that it was good. 13And evening passed and morning came, marking the third day. 14Then God said, "Let lights appear in the sky to separate the day from the night. Let them be signs to mark the seasons, days, and years. 15Let these lights in the sky shine down on the earth." And that is what happened. 16God made two great lights—the larger one to govern the day, and the smaller one to govern the night. He also made the stars. 17God set these lights in the sky to light the earth, 18to govern the day and night, and to separate the light from the darkness. And God saw that it was good. 19And evening passed and morning came, marking the fourth day. 20Then God said, "Let the waters swarm with fish and other life. Let the skies be filled with birds of every kind." 21So God created great sea creatures and every living thing that scurries and swarms in the water, and every sort of bird— each producing offspring of the same kind. And God saw that it was good. 22Then God blessed them, saying, "Be fruitful and multiply. Let the fish fill the seas, and let the birds multiply on the earth." 23And evening passed and morning came, marking the fifth day. 24Then God said, "Let the earth produce every sort of animal, each producing offspring of the same kind—livestock, small animals that scurry along the ground, and wild animals." And that is what happened.

25God made all sorts of wild animals, livestock, and small animals, each able to produce offspring of the same kind. And God saw that it was good. 26Then God said, "Let us make human beings1:26a Or *man;* Hebrew reads *adam.* in our image, to be like us. They will reign over the fish in the sea, the birds in the sky, the livestock, all the wild animals on the earth,1:26b As in Syriac version; Hebrew reads *all the earth.*and the small animals that scurry along the ground." 27So God created human beings1:27 Or *the man;* Hebrew reads *ha-adam.* in his own image. In the image of God he created them; male and female he created them. 28Then God blessed them and said, "Be fruitful and multiply. Fill the earth and govern it. Reign over the fish in the sea, the birds in the sky, and all the animals that scurry along the ground." 29Then God said, "Look! I have given you every seed-bearing plant throughout the earth and all the fruit trees for your food. 30And I have given every green plant as food for all the wild animals, the birds in the sky, and the small animals that scurry along the ground—everything that has life." And that is what happened. 31Then God looked over all he had made, and he saw that it was very good!

And evening passed and morning came, marking the sixth day. [2]

Genesis - Chapter Two

1So the creation of the heavens and the earth and everything in them was completed. 2On the seventh day God had finished his work of creation, so he rested2:2 Or *ceased;* also in 2:3. from all his work. 3And God blessed the seventh day and declared it holy, because it was the day when he rested from all his work of creation. 4This is the account of the creation of the heavens and the earth. The Man and Woman in Eden When the Lord God made the earth and the heavens, 5neither wild plants nor grains were growing on the earth. For the Lord God had not yet sent rain to water the earth, and there were no people to cultivate the soil. 6Instead, springs2:6 Or *mist.* came up from the ground and watered all the land. 7Then the Lord God formed the man from the dust of the ground. He breathed the breath of life into the man's nostrils, and the man became a living person. 8Then the Lord God planted a garden in Eden in the east, and there he placed the man he had made. 9The Lord God made all sorts of trees grow up from the ground— trees that were beautiful and that produced delicious fruit. In the middle of the garden he placed the tree of life and the tree of the knowledge of good and evil. 10A river flowed from the land of Eden, watering the garden and then dividing into four branches. 11The first branch, called the Pishon, flowed around the entire land of Havilah, where gold is found. 12The gold of that land is exceptionally pure; aromatic resin and onyx stone are also found there. 13The second branch, called the Gihon, flowed around the entire land of Cush. 14The third branch, called the Tigris, flowed east of the land of Asshur. The fourth branch is called the Euphrates. 15The Lord God placed the man in the Garden of Eden to tend and watch over it. 16But the Lord God warned him, "You may freely eat the fruit of every tree in the garden—17except the tree of the knowledge of good and evil. If you eat its fruit, you are sure to die."18Then the Lord God said,

"It is not good for the man to be alone. I will make a helper who is just right for him." 19So the Lord God formed from the ground all the wild animals and all the birds of the sky. He brought them to the man2:19 Or *Adam,* and so throughout the chapter. to see what he would call them, and the man chose a name for each one. 20He gave names to all the livestock, all the birds of the sky, and all the wild animals. But still there was no helper just right for him. 21So the Lord God caused the man to fall into a deep sleep. While the man slept, the Lord God took out one of the man's ribs2:21 Or *took a part of the man's side* and closed up the opening. 22Then the Lord God made a woman from the rib, and he brought her to the man. 23"At last!" the man exclaimed. "This one is bone from my bone, and flesh from my flesh! She will be called 'woman,' because she was taken from 'man.'" 24This explains why a man leaves his father and mother and is joined to his wife, and the two are united into one. 25Now the man and his wife were both naked, but they felt no shame.

Genesis - Chapter Three

The Man and Woman Sin

1The serpent was the shrewdest of all the wild animals the Lord God had made. One day he asked the woman, "Did God really say you must not eat the fruit from any of the trees in the garden?" 2"Of course we may eat fruit from the trees in the garden," the woman replied. 3"It's only the fruit from the tree in the middle of the garden that we are not allowed to eat. God said,

'You must not eat it or even touch it; if you do, you will die.'" 4"You won't die!" the serpent replied to the woman. 5"God knows that your eyes will be opened as soon as you eat it, and you will be like God, knowing both good and evil." 6The woman was convinced. She saw that the tree was beautiful and its fruit looked delicious, and she wanted the wisdom it would give her. So she took some of the fruit and ate it. Then she gave some to her husband, who was with her, and he ate it, too. 7At that moment their eyes were opened, and they suddenly felt shame at their nakedness. So they sewed fig leaves together to cover themselves. 8When the cool evening breezes were blowing, the man3:8 Or *Adam,* and so throughout the chapter. and his wife heard the Lord God walking about in the garden. So they hid from the Lord God among the trees.

9Then the Lord God called to the man, "Where are you?" 10He replied, "I heard you walking in the garden, so I hid. I was afraid because I was naked." 11"Who told you that you were naked?" the Lord God asked. "Have you eaten from the tree whose fruit I commanded you not to eat?" 12The man replied, "It was the woman you gave me who gave me the fruit, and I ate it." 13Then the Lord God asked the woman, "What have you done?" "The serpent deceived me," she replied.

"That's why I ate it." 14Then the Lord God said to the serpent, "Because you have done this, you are cursed more than all animals, domestic and wild. You will crawl on your belly, groveling in the dust as long as you live. 15And I will cause hostility between you and the woman, and between your offspring and her offspring. He will strike3:15 Or *bruise;* also in 3:15b. your head, and you will strike his heel." 16Then he said to the woman, "I will sharpen the pain of your pregnancy, and in pain you will give birth. And you will desire to control your husband, but he will rule over you.3:16 Or *And though you will have desire for your husband, / he will rule over you.*" 17And to the man he said, "Since you listened to your wife and ate from the tree whose fruit I commanded you not to eat, the ground is cursed because of you. All your life you will struggle to scratch a living from it. 18It will grow thorns and thistles for you, though you will eat of its grains. 19By the sweat of your brow will you have food to eat until you return to the ground from which you were made. For you were made from dust, and to dust you will return." Paradise Lost: God's Judgment 20Then the man—Adam—named his wife Eve, because she would be the mother of all who live.3:20 *Eve* sounds like a Hebrew term that means "to give life." 21And the Lord God made clothing from animal skins for Adam and his wife. 22

Then the Lord God said, "Look, the human beings3:22 Or *the man;* Hebrew reads *haadam* have become like us, knowing both good and evil. What if they reach out, take fruit from the tree of life, and eat it? Then they will live forever!" 23So the Lord God banished them from the Garden of Eden, and he sent Adam out to cultivate the ground from which he had been made. 24After sending them out, the Lord God stationed mighty cherubim to the east of the Garden of Eden. And he placed a flaming sword that flashed back and forth to guard the way to the tree of

The Walk – S.B. Stone & Rock Solid Publishing, LLC

life.

Chapter Four

Cain and Abel

1Now Adam4:1a Or *the man;* also in 4:25 had sexual relations with his wife, Eve, and she became pregnant. When she gave birth to Cain, she said, "With the Lord's help, I have produced4:1b Or *I have acquired. Cain* sounds like a Hebrew term that can mean "produce" or "acquire." a man!" 2Later she gave birth to his brother and named him Abel. When they grew up, Abel became a shepherd, while Cain cultivated the ground. 3When it was time for the harvest, Cain presented some of his crops as a gift to the Lord. 4Abel also brought a gift—the best portions of the firstborn lambs from his flock. The Lord accepted Abel and his gift, 5but he did not accept Cain and his gift. This made Cain very angry, and he looked dejected.

6"Why are you so angry?" the Lord asked Cain. "Why do you look so dejected? 7You will be accepted if you do what is right. But if you refuse to do what is right, then watch out! Sin is crouching at the door, eager to control you. But you must subdue it and be its master."

8One day Cain suggested to his brother, "Let's go out into the fields."4:8 As in Samaritan Pentateuch, Greek and Syriac versions, and Latin Vulgate; Masoretic Text lacks *"Let's go out into the fields."* And while they were in the field, Cain attacked his brother, Abel, and killed him.

9Afterward the Lord asked Cain, "Where is your brother? Where is Abel?" "I don't know," Cain responded. "Am I my brother's guardian?" 10But the Lord said, "What have you done? Listen! Your brother's blood cries out to me from the ground! 11Now you are cursed and banished from the ground, which has swallowed your brother's blood. 12No longer will the ground yield good crops for you, no matter how hard you work! From now on you will be a homeless wanderer on the earth." 13Cain replied to the Lord, "My punishment4:13 Or *My sin* is too great for me to bear! 14You have banished me from the land and from your presence; you have made me a homeless wanderer. Anyone who finds me will kill me!" 15The Lord replied,

"No, for I will give a sevenfold punishment to anyone who kills you." Then the Lord put a mark on Cain to warn anyone who might try to kill

him. 16So Cain left the Lord's presence and settled in the land of Nod,
4:16 *Nod* means "wandering" east of Eden.

The Descendants of Cain

17Cain had sexual relations with his wife, and she became pregnant
and gave birth to Enoch. Then Cain founded a city, which he named
Enoch, after his son. 18Enoch had a son named Irad. Irad became the
father of4:18 Or *the ancestor of,* and so throughout the verse. Mehujael.
Mehujael became the father of Methushael. Methushael became the
father of Lamech.

19Lamech married two women. The first was named Adah, and the
second was Zillah. 20Adah gave birth to Jabal, who was the first of
those who raise livestock and live in tents. 21His brother's name was
Jubal, the first of all who play the harp and flute. 22Lamech's other
wife, Zillah, gave birth to a son named Tubal-cain. He became an expert
in forging tools of bronze and iron. Tubal-cain had a sister named
Naamah. 23One day Lamech said to his wives,

"Adah and Zillah, hear my voice; listen to me, you wives of Lamech.
I have killed a man who attacked me, a young man who wounded me.
24If someone who kills Cain is punished seven times, then the one who
kills me will be punished seventy-seven times!"

The Birth of Seth

25Adam had sexual relations with his wife again, and she gave birth
to another son. She named him Seth, 4:25 *Seth* probably means
"granted"; the name may also mean "appointed." for she said, "God has
granted me another son in place of Abel, whom Cain killed." 26When
Seth grew up, he had a son and named him Enosh. At that time people
first began to worship the Lord by name.

Chapter Five

The Descendants of Adam

1This is the written account of the descendants of Adam. When God
created human beings, 5:1 Or *man;* Hebrew reads *adam;* similarly in 5:2
he made them to be like himself. 2He created them male and female, and
he blessed them and called them "human." 3When Adam was 130 years
old, he became the father of a son who was just like him—in his very

image. He named his son Seth. 4After the birth of Seth, Adam lived another 800 years, and he had other sons and daughters. 5Adam lived 930 years, and then he died. 6When Seth was 105 years old, he became the father of5:6 Or *the ancestor of;* also in 5:9, 12, 15, 18, 21, 25. Enosh. 7After the birth of5:7 Or *the birth of this ancestor of;* also in 5:10, 13, 16, 19, 22, 26. Enosh, Seth lived another 807 years, and he had other sons and daughters. 8Seth lived 912 years, and then he died.

9When Enosh was 90 years old, he became the father of Kenan. 10After the birth of Kenan, Enosh lived another 815 years, and he had other sons and daughters. 11Enosh lived 905 years, and then he died. 12When Kenan was 70 years old, he became the father of

Mahalalel. 13After the birth of Mahalalel, Kenan lived another 840 years, and he had other sons and daughters. 14Kenan lived 910 years, and then he died.

15When Mahalalel was 65 years old, he became the father of Jared. 16After the birth of

Jared, Mahalalel lived another 830 years, and he had other sons and daughters. 17Mahalalel lived

895 years, and then he died. 18When Jared was 162 years old, he became the father of Enoch. 19After the birth of Enoch, Jared lived another 800 years, and he had other sons and daughters. 20Jared lived 962 years, and then he died. 21When Enoch was 65 years old, he became the father of Methuselah. 22After the birth of Methuselah, Enoch lived in close fellowship with God for another 300 years, and he had other sons and daughters. 23Enoch lived 365 years, 24walking in close fellowship with God. Then one day he disappeared, because God took him. 25When Methuselah was 187 years old, he became the father of Lamech. 26After the birth of Lamech, Methuselah lived another 782 years, and he had other sons and daughters. 27Methuselah lived 969 years, and then he died. 28When Lamech was 182 years old, he became the father of a son. 29Lamech named his son Noah, for he said, "May he bring us relief5:29 *Noah* sounds like a Hebrew term that can mean "relief" or "comfort." from our work and the painful labor of farming this ground that the Lord has cursed." 30After the birth of Noah, Lamech lived another 595 years, and he had other sons and daughters. 31Lamech lived 777 years, and then he died. 32After Noah was 500 years old, he became the father of Shem, Ham, and Japheth. [2]

The Walk – S.B. Stone & Rock Solid Publishing, LLC
©2018

Chapter Six

A World Gone Wrong

1Then the people began to multiply on the earth, and daughters were born to them. 2The sons of God saw the beautiful women6:2 Hebrew *daughters of men;* also in 6:4.and took any they wanted as their wives. 3Then the Lord said, "My Spirit will not put up with6:3 Greek version reads *will not remain in.* humans for such a long time, for they are only mortal flesh. In the future, their normal lifespan will be no more than 120 years." 4In those days, and for some time after, giant Nephilites lived on the earth, for whenever the sons of God had intercourse with women, they gave birth to children who became the heroes and famous warriors of ancient times. 5The Lord observed the extent of human wickedness on the earth, and he saw that everything they thought or imagined was consistently and totally evil. 6So the Lord was sorry he had ever made them and put them on the earth. It broke his heart. 7And the Lord said, "I will wipe this human race I have created from the face of the earth. Yes, and I will destroy every living thing—all the people, the large animals, the small animals that scurry along the ground, and even the birds of the sky. I am sorry I ever made them." 8But Noah found favor with the Lord.

The Story of Noah

9This is the account of Noah and his family. Noah was a righteous man, the only blameless person living on earth at the time, and he walked in close fellowship with God.

10Noah was the father of three sons: Shem, Ham, and Japheth.

11Now God saw that the earth had become corrupt and was filled with violence. 12God observed all this corruption in the world, for everyone on earth was corrupt. 13So God said to

Noah, "I have decided to destroy all living creatures, for they have filled the earth with violence.

Yes, I will wipe them all out along with the earth! 14"Build a large boat6:14a Traditionally rendered *an ark* from cypress wood6:14b Or *gopher wood* and waterproof it with tar, inside and out. Then construct decks and stalls throughout its interior. 15Make the boat 450 feet long, 75 feet wide, and 45 feet high.6:15 Hebrew *300 cubits* [138 meters]

The Walk – S.B. Stone & Rock Solid Publishing, LLC
©2018

long, 50 cubits[23 meters] *wide, and 30 cubits* [13.8 meters] *high.*
16Leave an 18-inch opening6:16 Hebrew *an opening of 1 cubit* [46 centimeters] below the roof all the way around the boat. Put the door on the side, and build three decks inside the boat—lower, middle, and upper. 17"Look! I am about to cover the earth with a flood that will destroy every living thing that breathes. Everything on earth will die. 18But I will confirm my covenant with you. So enter the boat—you and your wife and your sons and their wives. 19Bring a pair of every kind of animal—a male and a female—into the boat with you to keep them alive during the flood. 20Pairs of every kind of bird, and every kind of animal, and every kind of small animal that scurries along the ground, will come to you to be kept alive. 21And be sure to take on board enough food for your family and for all the animals." 22So Noah did everything exactly as God had commanded him. [2]

Chapter Seven

The Flood Covers the Earth

1When everything was ready, the Lord said to Noah, "Go into the boat with all your family, for among all the people of the earth, I can see that you alone are righteous. 2Take with you seven pairs—male and female—of each animal I have approved for eating and for sacrifice, 7:2 Hebrew *of each clean animal;* similarly in 7:8 and take one pair of each of the others. 3Also take seven pairs of every kind of bird. There must be a male and a female in each pair to ensure that all life will survive on the earth after the flood. 4Seven days from now I will make the rains pour down on the earth. And it will rain for forty days and forty nights, until I have wiped from the earth all the living things I have created." 5So Noah did everything as the Lord commanded him. 6Noah was 600 years old when the flood covered the earth. 7He went on board the boat to escape the flood—he and his wife and his sons and their wives. 8With them were all the various kinds of animals—those approved for eating and for sacrifice and those that were not—along with all the birds and the small animals that scurry along the ground. 9They entered the boat in pairs, male and female, just as God had commanded Noah. 10After seven days, the waters of the flood came and covered the earth. 11When Noah was 600 years old, on the seventeenth day of the second month, all the underground waters erupted from the earth, and the rain fell in mighty torrents from the sky. 12The rain continued to fall for forty days and forty nights. 13That very day Noah had gone into the boat with his wife and his sons—Shem, Ham, and Japheth—and their wives. 14With them in the boat were pairs of every kind of animal—domestic and wild, large and small—along with birds of every kind. 15Two by two they came into the boat, representing every living thing that breathes. 16A male and female of each kind entered, just as God had commanded Noah. Then the Lord closed the door behind them.

17For forty days the floodwaters grew deeper, covering the ground and lifting the boat high above the earth. 18As the waters rose higher and higher above the ground, the boat floated safely on the surface. 19Finally, the water covered even the highest mountains on the earth, 20rising more than twenty-two feet7:20 Hebrew *15 cubits* [6.9 meters] above the highest peaks. 21All the living things on earth died—birds, domestic animals, wild animals, small animals that scurry along the ground, and all the people. 22Everything that breathed and lived on dry land died. 23God wiped out every living thing on the earth—people, livestock, small animals that scurry along the ground, and the birds of the sky. All were destroyed. The only people who survived were Noah and those with him in the boat. 24And the floodwaters covered the earth for 150 days. [2]

Chapter Eight

The Flood Recedes

1But God remembered Noah and all the wild animals and livestock with him in the boat. He sent a wind to blow across the earth, and the floodwaters began to recede. 2The underground waters stopped flowing, and the torrential rains from the sky were stopped. 3So the floodwaters gradually receded from the earth. After 150 days, 4exactly five months from the time the flood began, 8:4 Hebrew *on the seventeenth day of the seventh month;* see 7:11 the boat came to rest on the mountains of Ararat. 5Two and a half months later,8:5 Hebrew *On the first day of the tenth month;* see 7:11 and note on 8:4 as the waters continued to go down, other mountain peaks became visible. 6After another forty days, Noah opened the window he had made in the

boat 7and released a raven. The bird flew back and forth until the floodwaters on the earth had dried up. 8He also released a dove to see if the water had receded and it could find dry ground. 9But the dove could find no place to land because the water still covered the ground. So it returned to the boat, and Noah held out his hand and drew the dove back inside. 10After waiting another seven days, Noah released the dove again. 11This time the dove returned to him in the evening with a fresh olive leaf in its beak. Then Noah knew that the floodwaters were almost gone. 12He waited another seven days and then released the dove again. This time it did not come back. 13Noah was now 601 years old. On the first day of the new year, ten and a half months after the flood began, 8:13 Hebrew *On the first day of the first month;* see 7:11 the floodwaters had almost dried up from the earth. Noah lifted back the covering of the boat and saw that the surface of the ground was drying. 14Two more months went by, 8:14 Hebrew *The twenty-seventh day of the second month arrived;* see note on 8:13 and at last the earth was dry!

15Then God said to Noah, 16"Leave the boat, all of you—you and your wife, and your sons and their wives. 17Release all the animals—the birds, the livestock, and the small animals that scurry along the ground—so they can be fruitful and multiply throughout the earth." 18So Noah, his wife, and his sons and their wives left the boat. 19And all of the large and small animals and birds came out of the boat, pair by pair. 20Then Noah built an altar to the Lord, and there he sacrificed as burnt offerings the animals and birds that had been approved for that purpose.8:20 Hebrew *every clean animal and every clean bird.* 21And the Lord was pleased with the aroma of the sacrifice and said to himself, "I will never again curse the ground because of the human race, even though everything they think or imagine is bent toward evil from childhood. I will never again destroy all living things. 22As long as the earth remains, there will be planting and harvest, cold and heat, summer and winter, day and night." [2]

Chapter Nine

God Confirms His Covenant

1Then God blessed Noah and his sons and told them, "Be fruitful and multiply. Fill the earth. 2All the animals of the earth, all the birds of the sky, all the small animals that scurry along the ground, and all the fish in the sea will look on you with fear and terror. I have placed them in your power. 3I have given them to you for food, just as I have given you grain and vegetables. 4But you must never eat any meat that still has the lifeblood in it. 5"And I will require the blood of anyone who takes another person's life. If a wild animal kills a person, it must die. And anyone who murders a fellow human must die. 6If anyone takes a human life, that person's life will also be taken by human hands. For God made human beings

9:6 Or *man;* Hebrew reads *ha-adam* in his own image. 7Now be fruitful and multiply, and repopulate the earth." 8Then God told Noah and his sons, 9"I hereby confirm my covenant with you and your descendants, 10and with all the animals that were on the boat with you—the birds, the livestock, and all the wild animals—every living creature on earth. 11Yes, I am confirming my covenant with you. Never again will floodwaters kill all living creatures; never again will a flood destroy the earth." 12Then God said, "I am giving you a sign of my covenant with you and with all living creatures, for all generations to come. 13I have placed my rainbow in the clouds. It is the sign of my covenant with you and with all the earth. 14When I send clouds over the earth, the rainbow will appear in the clouds, 15and I will remember my covenant with you and with all living creatures. Never again will the floodwaters destroy all life. 16When I see the rainbow in the clouds, I will remember the eternal covenant between God and every living creature on earth." 17Then God said to Noah, "Yes, this rainbow is the sign of the covenant I am confirming with all the creatures on earth."

Noah's Sons

18The sons of Noah who came out of the boat with their father were Shem, Ham, and Japheth. (Ham is the father of Canaan.) 19From these three sons of Noah came all the people who now populate the earth. 20After the flood, Noah began to cultivate the ground, and he planted a vineyard. 21One day he drank some wine he had made, and he became drunk and lay naked inside his tent. 22Ham, the father of Canaan, saw that his father was naked and went outside and told his brothers. 23Then Shem and Japheth took a robe, held it over their shoulders, and backed into the tent to cover their father. As they did this, they looked the other way so they would not see him naked. 24When Noah woke up from his stupor, he learned what Ham, his youngest son, had done. 25Then he cursed Canaan, the son of Ham: "May Canaan be cursed!

May he be the lowest of servants to his relatives." 26Then Noah said, "May the Lord, the God of Shem, be blessed, and may Canaan be his servant! 27May God expand the territory of Japheth! May Japheth share the prosperity of Shem, 9:27 Hebrew *May he live in the tents of Shem* and may Canaan be his servant." 28Noah lived another 350 years after the great flood. 29He lived

950 years, and then he died. [2]

Chapter Seventeen

Abram Is Named Abraham

1When Abram was ninety-nine years old, the Lord appeared to him and said, "I am ElShaddai—'God Almighty.' Serve me faithfully and live a blameless life. 2I will make a covenant with you, by which I will guarantee to give you countless descendants." 3At this, Abram fell face down on the ground. Then God said to him, 4"This is my covenant with you: I will make you the father of a multitude of nations! 5What's more, I am changing your name. It will no longer be

Abram. Instead, you will be called Abraham, 17:5 *Abram* means "exalted

father"; *Abraham* sounds like a Hebrew term that means "father of many." for you will be the father of many nations. 6I will make you extremely fruitful. Your descendants will become many nations, and kings will be among them! 7"I will confirm my covenant with you and your escendants17:7 Hebrew *seed;* also in 17:7b, 8, 9, 10, 19 after you, from generation to generation. This is the everlasting covenant: I will always be your God and the God of your descendants after you. 8And I will give the entire land of Canaan, where you now live as a foreigner, to you and your descendants. It will be their possession forever, and I will be their God."

The Mark of the Covenant

9Then God said to Abraham, "Your responsibility is to obey the terms of the covenant. You and all your descendants have this continual responsibility. 10This is the covenant that you and your descendants must keep: Each male among you must be circumcised. 11You must cut off the flesh of your foreskin as a sign of the covenant between me and you. 12From generation to generation, every male child must be circumcised on the eighth day after his birth. This applies not only to members of your family but also to the servants born in your household and the foreign-born servants whom you have purchased. 13All must be circumcised. Your bodies will bear the mark of my everlasting covenant. 14Any male who fails to be circumcised will be cut off from the covenant family for breaking the covenant."

Sarai Is Named Sarah

15Then God said to Abraham, "Regarding Sarai, your wife—her name will no longer be Sarai. From now on her name will be Sarah.17:15 *Sarai* and *Sarah* both mean "princess"; the change in spelling may reflect the difference in dialect between Ur and Canaan. 16And I will bless her and give you a son from her! Yes, I will bless her richly, and she will become the mother of many nations. Kings of nations will be among her descendants." 17Then Abraham bowed down to the ground, but he laughed to himself in disbelief. "How could I become a father at the age of 100?" he thought. "And how can Sarah have a baby when she is ninety years old?" 18So Abraham said to God, "May Ishmael live under your special blessing!" 19But God replied, "No—Sarah, your wife, will give birth to a son for you. You will name him Isaac, 17:19 *Isaac* means "he laughs." and I will confirm my covenant with him and his descendants as an everlasting covenant. 20As for Ishmael, I will bless him also, just as you have asked. I will make him extremely fruitful and multiply his descendants. He will become the father of twelve princes, and I will make him a great nation. 21But my covenant will be confirmed with Isaac, who will be born to you and Sarah about this time next year." 22When God had finished speaking, he left Abraham. 23On that very day Abraham took his son, Ishmael, and every male in his household, including those born there and those he had bought. Then he circumcised them, cutting off their foreskins, just as God had told him. 24Abraham was ninety-nine years old when he was circumcised, 25and Ishmael, his son, was thirteen. 26Both Abraham and his son, Ishmael, were circumcised on that same day, 27along with all the other men and boys of the household, whether they were born there or bought as servants. All were circumcised with him.

Chapter Eighteen

A Son Is Promised to Sarah

1The Lord appeared again to Abraham near the oak grove belonging to Mamre. One day Abraham was sitting at the entrance to his tent during the hottest part of the day. 2He looked up and noticed three men standing nearby. When he saw them, he ran to meet them and welcomed them, bowing low to the ground. 3"My lord," he said, "if it pleases you, stop here for a while. 4Rest in the shade of this tree while water is brought to wash your feet. 5And since you've honored your servant with this visit, let me prepare some food to refresh you before you continue on your journey." "All right," they said. "Do as you have said." 6So Abraham ran back to the tent and said to Sarah, "Hurry! Get three large measures18:6 Hebrew *3 seahs,* about half a bushel or 22 liters. of your best flour, knead it into dough, and bake some bread." 7Then Abraham ran out to the herd and chose a tender calf and gave it to his servant, who quickly prepared it. 8When the food was ready, Abraham took some yogurt and milk and the roasted meat, and he served it to the men. As they ate, Abraham waited on them in the shade of the trees. 9"Where is Sarah, your wife?" the visitors asked. "She's inside the tent," Abraham replied. 10Then one of them said, "I will return to you about this time next year, and your wife, Sarah, will have a son!"

Sarah was listening to this conversation from the tent. 11Abraham and Sarah were both very old by this time, and Sarah was long past the age of having children. 12So she laughed silently to herself and said, "How could a worn-out woman like me enjoy such pleasure, especially when my master—my husband—is also so old?" 13Then the Lord said to Abraham,

"Why did Sarah laugh? Why did she say, 'Can an old woman like me have a baby?' 14Is anything too hard for the Lord? I will return about this time next year, and Sarah will have a son." 15Sarah was afraid, so she denied it, saying, "I didn't laugh." But the Lord said, "No, you did laugh."

Abraham Intercedes for Sodom

16Then the men got up from their meal and looked out toward Sodom. As they left, Abraham went with them to send them on their way. 17"Should I hide my plan from Abraham?" the Lord asked. 18"For Abraham will certainly become a great and mighty nation, and all the nations of the earth will be blessed through him. 19I have singled him out so that he will direct his sons and their families to keep the way of the Lord by doing what is right and just. Then I will do for Abraham all that I have promised." 20So the Lord told Abraham, "I have heard a great outcry from Sodom and Gomorrah, because their sin is so flagrant. 21I am going down to see if their actions are as wicked as I have heard. If not, I want to know." 22The other men turned and headed toward Sodom, but the Lord remained with Abraham. 23Abraham approached him and said, "Will you sweep away both the righteous and the wicked? 24Suppose you find fifty righteous people living there in the city—will you still sweep it away and not spare it for their sakes? 25Surely you wouldn't do such a thing, destroying the righteous along with the wicked. Why, you would be treating the righteous and the wicked exactly the same! Surely you wouldn't do that! Should not the Judge of all the earth do what is right?" 26And the Lord replied, "If I find fifty righteous people in Sodom, I will spare the entire city for their sake." 27Then Abraham spoke again. "Since I have begun, let me speak further to my Lord, even though I am but dust and ashes. 28Suppose there are only forty-five righteous people rather than fifty? Will you destroy the whole city for lack of five?" And the Lord said, "I will not destroy it if I find forty-five righteous people there." 29Then Abraham pressed his request further. "Suppose there are only forty?" And the Lord replied, "I will not destroy it for the sake of the forty." 30"Please don't be angry, my Lord," Abraham pleaded. "Let me speak—suppose only thirty righteous people are found?" And the Lord replied, "I will not destroy it if I find thirty." 31Then Abraham said, "Since I have dared to speak to the Lord, let me continue—suppose there are only twenty?"

And the Lord replied, "Then I will not destroy it for the sake of the twenty." 32Finally,

Abraham said, "Lord, please don't be angry with me if I speak one more time. Suppose only ten are found there?" And the Lord replied, "Then I will not destroy it for the sake of the ten."

33When the Lord had finished his conversation with Abraham, he went on his way, and

Abraham returned to his tent.

Chapter Nineteen

Sodom and Gomorrah Destroyed

1That evening the two angels came to the entrance of the city of Sodom. Lot was sitting there, and when he saw them, he stood up to meet them. Then he welcomed them and bowed with his face to the ground. 2"My lords," he said, "come to my home to wash your feet, and be my guests for the night. You may then get up early in the morning and be on your way again." "Oh no," they replied. "We'll just spend the night out here in the city square." 3But Lot insisted, so at last they went home with him. Lot prepared a feast for them, complete with fresh bread made without yeast, and they ate. 4But before they retired for the night, all the men of Sodom, young and old, came from all over the city and surrounded the house. 5They shouted to Lot,

"Where are the men who came to spend the night with you? Bring them out to us so we can have sex with them!"

6So Lot stepped outside to talk to them, shutting the door behind him. 7"Please, my brothers," he begged, "don't do such a wicked thing. 8Look, I have two virgin daughters. Let me bring them out to you, and you can do with them as you wish. But please, leave these men alone, for they are my guests and are under my protection."

9"Stand back!" they shouted. "This fellow came to town as an outsider, and now he's acting like our judge! We'll treat you far worse than those other men!" And they lunged toward Lot to break down the door. 10But the two angels19:10 Hebrew *men;* also in 19:12, 16 reached out, pulled Lot into the house, and bolted the door. 11Then they blinded all the men, young and old, who were at the door of the house, so they gave up trying to get inside. 12Meanwhile, the angels questioned Lot. "Do you have any other relatives here in the city?" they asked. "Get them out of this place—your sons-in-law, sons, daughters, or anyone else. 13For we are about to destroy this city completely. The outcry against this place is so great it has reached the Lord, and he has sent us to destroy it." 14So Lot rushed out to tell his daughters' fiancés, "Quick, get out of the city! The Lord is about to destroy it." But the young men thought he was only joking. 15At dawn the next morning the angels became insistent. "Hurry," they said to Lot. "Take your wife and your two daughters who are here. Get out right now, or you will be swept away in the destruction of the city!" 16When Lot still hesitated, the angels seized his hand and the hands of his wife and two daughters and rushed them to safety outside the city, for the Lord was merciful. 17When they were safely out of the city, one of the angels ordered, "Run for your lives! And don't look back or stop anywhere in the valley! Escape to the mountains, or you will be swept away!"

18"Oh no, my lord!" Lot begged. 19"You have been so gracious to me and saved my life, and you have shown such great kindness. But I cannot go to the mountains. Disaster would catch up to me there, and I would soon die. 20See, there is a small village nearby. Please let me go there instead; don't you see how small it is? Then my life will be saved." 21"All right," the angel said, "I will grant your request. I will not destroy the little village. 22But hurry! Escape to it, for I can do nothing until you arrive there." (This explains why that village was known as Zoar, which means "little place.") 23Lot reached the village just as the sun was rising over the horizon. 24Then the Lord rained down fire and burning sulfur from the sky on Sodom and Gomorrah. 25He utterly destroyed them, along with the other cities and villages of the plain, wiping out all the people and every bit of vegetation. 26But Lot's wife looked back as she was following behind him, and she turned into a pillar of salt. 27Abraham got up early that morning and hurried out to the place where he had stood in the Lord's presence. 28He looked out across the plain toward Sodom and Gomorrah and watched as columns of smoke rose from the cities like smoke from a furnace. 29But God had listened to Abraham's request and kept Lot safe, removing him from the disaster that engulfed the cities on the plain.

Lot and His Daughters

30Afterward Lot left Zoar because he was afraid of the people there, and he went to live in a cave in the mountains with his two daughters. 31One day the older daughter said to her sister, "There are no men left anywhere in this entire area, so we can't get married like everyone else. And our father will soon be too old to have children. 32Come, let's get him drunk with wine, and then we will have sex with him. That way we will preserve our family line through our father."

33So that night they got him drunk with wine, and the older daughter went in and had intercourse with her father. He was unaware of her lying down or getting up again. 34The next morning the older daughter said to her younger sister, "I had sex with our father last night. Let's get him drunk with wine again tonight, and you go in and have sex with him. That way we will preserve our family line through our father." 35So that night they got him drunk with wine again, and the younger daughter went in and had intercourse with him. As before, he was unaware of her lying down or getting up again. 36As a result, both of Lot's daughters became pregnant by their own father. 37When the older daughter gave birth to a son, she named him

Moab.19:37 *Moab* sounds like a Hebrew term that means "from father." He became the ancestor of the nation now known as the Moabites. 38When the younger daughter gave birth to a son, she named him Ben-ammi.19:38 *Ben-ammi* means "son of my kinsman." He became the ancestor of the nation now known as the Ammonites. [2]

Chapter Twenty-two

Abraham's Faith Tested

1Some time later, God tested Abraham's faith. "Abraham!" God called. "Yes," he replied. "Here I am." 2"Take your son, your only son—yes, Isaac, whom you love so much—and go to the land of Moriah. Go and sacrifice him as a burnt offering on one of the mountains, which I will show you." 3The next morning Abraham got up early. He saddled his donkey and took two of his servants with him, along with his son, Isaac. Then he chopped wood for a fire for a burnt offering and set out for the place God had told him about. 4On the third day of their journey, Abraham looked up and saw the place in the distance. 5"Stay here with the donkey,"

Abraham told the servants. "The boy and I will travel a little farther. We will worship there, and then we will come right back." 6So Abraham placed the wood for the burnt offering on Isaac's shoulders, while he himself carried the fire and the knife. As the two of them walked on together, 7Isaac turned to Abraham and said, "Father?" "Yes, my son?" Abraham replied. "We have the fire and the wood," the boy said, "but where is the sheep for the burnt offering?" 8"God will provide a sheep for the burnt offering, my son," Abraham answered. And they both walked on together.

9When they arrived at the place where God had told him to go, Abraham built an altar and arranged the wood on it. Then he tied his son, Isaac, and laid him on the altar on top of the wood. 10And Abraham picked up the knife to kill his son as a sacrifice. 11At that moment the angel of the Lord called to him from heaven, "Abraham! Abraham!" "Yes," Abraham replied.

"Here I am!" 12"Don't lay a hand on the boy!" the angel said. "Do not hurt him in any way, for now I know that you truly fear God. You have not withheld from me even your son, your only son." 13Then Abraham looked up and saw a ram caught by its horns in a thicket. So he took the ram and sacrificed it as a burnt offering in place of his son. 14Abraham named the place Yahweh-Yireh (which means "the Lord will provide"). To this day, people still use that name as a proverb: "On the mountain of the Lord it will be provided." 15Then the angel of the Lord called again to Abraham from heaven. 16"This is what the Lord says: Because you have obeyed me and have not withheld even your son, your only son, I swear by my own name that 17I will certainly bless you. I will multiply your descendants22:17 Hebrew *seed;* also in 22:17b, 18 beyond number, like the stars in the sky and the sand on the seashore. Your descendants will conquer the cities of their enemies. 18And through your descendants all the nations of the earth will be blessed—all because you have obeyed me." 19Then they returned to the servants and traveled back to Beersheba, where Abraham continued to live. 20Soon after this, Abraham heard that Milcah, his brother Nahor's wife, had borne Nahor eight sons. 21The oldest was named Uz, the next oldest was Buz, followed by Kemuel (the ancestor of the Arameans), 22Kesed, Hazo, Pildash, Jidlaph, and Bethuel. 23(Bethuel became the father of Rebekah.) In addition to these eight sons from Milcah, 24Nahor had four other children from his concubine Reumah. Their names were Tebah, Gaham, Tahash, and Maacah.

Chapter Twenty-four

A Wife for Isaac

1Abraham was now a very old man, and the Lord had blessed him in every way. 2One day Abraham said to his oldest servant, the man in charge of his household, "Take an oath by putting your hand under my thigh. 3Swear by the Lord, the God of heaven and earth, that you will not allow my son to marry one of these local Canaanite women. 4Go instead to my homeland, to my relatives, and find a wife there for my son Isaac." 5The servant asked, "But what if I can't find a young woman who is willing to travel so far from home? Should I then take Isaac there to live among your relatives in the land you came from?" 6"No!" Abraham responded. "Be careful never to take my son there. 7For the Lord, the God of heaven, who took me from my father's house and my native land, solemnly promised to give this land to my descendants.24:7 Hebrew *seed;* also in 24:60. He will send his angel ahead of you, and he will see to it that you find a wife there for my son. 8If she is unwilling to come back with you, then you are free from this oath of mine. But under no circumstances are you to take my son there."

9So the servant took an oath by putting his hand under the thigh of his master, Abraham.

He swore to follow Abraham's instructions. 10Then he loaded ten of Abraham's camels with all kinds of expensive gifts from his master, and he traveled to distant Aram-naharaim. There he went to the town where Abraham's brother Nahor had settled. 11He made the camels kneel beside a well just outside the town. It was evening, and the women were coming out to draw water. 12"O Lord, God of my master, Abraham," he prayed. "Please give me success today, and show unfailing love to my master, Abraham. 13See, I am standing here beside this spring, and the young women of the town are coming out to draw water. 14This is my request. I will ask one of them, 'Please give me a drink from your jug.' If she says, 'Yes, have a drink, and I will water your camels, too!'—let her be the one you have selected as Isaac's wife. This is how I will know that you have shown unfailing love to my master." 15Before he had finished praying, he saw a young woman named Rebekah coming out with her water jug on her shoulder. She was the daughter of Bethuel, who was the son of Abraham's brother Nahor and his wife, Milcah. 16Rebekah was very beautiful and old enough to be married, but she was still a virgin. She went down to the spring, filled her jug, and came up again. 17Running over to her, the servant said, "Please give me a little drink of water from your jug." 18"Yes, my lord," she answered, "have a drink." And she quickly lowered her jug from her shoulder and gave him a drink. 19When she had given him a drink, she said, "I'll draw water for your camels, too, until they have had enough to drink." 20So she quickly emptied her jug into the watering trough and ran back to the well to draw water for all his camels. 21The servant watched her in silence, wondering whether or not the Lord had given him success in his mission. 22Then at last, when the camels had finished drinking, he took out a gold ring for her nose and two large gold bracelets24:22 Hebrew *a gold nose-ring weighing a beka* [0.2 ounces or 6 grams] *and two gold bracelets weighing 10 [shekels]* [4 ounces or 114 grams] for her wrists. 23"Whose daughter are you?" he asked. "And please tell me, would your father have any room to put us up for the night?" 24"I am the daughter of Bethuel," she replied. "My grandparents are Nahor and Milcah. 25Yes, we have plenty of straw and feed for the camels, and we have room for guests."

26The man bowed low and worshiped the Lord. 27"Praise the Lord, the God of my master, Abraham," he said. "The Lord has shown unfailing love and faithfulness to my master, for he has led me straight to my master's relatives." 28The young woman ran home to tell her family everything that had happened. 29Now Rebekah had a brother named Laban, who ran out to meet the man at the spring. 30He had seen the nose-ring and the bracelets on his sister's wrists, and had heard Rebekah tell what the man had said. So he rushed out to the spring, where the man was still standing beside his camels. 31Laban said to him, "Come and stay with us, you who are blessed by the Lord! Why are you standing here outside the town when I have a room all ready for you and a place prepared for the camels?" 32So the man went home with

Laban, and Laban unloaded the camels, gave him straw for their bedding, fed them, and provided water for the man and the camel drivers to wash their feet. 33Then food was served. But Abraham's servant said, "I don't want to eat until I have told you why I have come." "All right," Laban said, "tell us."34"I am Abraham's servant," he explained. 35"And the Lord has greatly blessed my master; he has become a wealthy man. The Lord has given him flocks of sheep and goats, herds of cattle, a fortune in silver and gold, and many male and female servants and camels and donkeys.

36"When Sarah, my master's wife, was very old, she gave birth to my master's son, and my master has given him everything he owns. 37And my master made me take an oath. He said, 'Do not allow my son to marry one of these local Canaanite women. 38Go instead to my father's house, to my relatives, and find a wife there for my son.' 39"But I said to my master, 'What if I can't find a young woman who is willing to go back with me?' 40He responded, 'The Lord, in whose presence I have lived, will send his angel with you and will make your mission successful.

Yes, you must find a wife for my son from among my relatives, from my father's family. 41Then you will have fulfilled your obligation. But if you go to my relatives and they refuse to let her go with you, you will be free from my oath.' 42"So today when I came to the spring, I prayed this prayer: 'O Lord, God of my master, Abraham, please give me success on this mission. 43See, I am standing here beside this spring. This is my request. When a young woman comes to draw water, I will say to her, "Please give me a little drink of water from your jug." 44If she says, "Yes, have a drink, and I will draw water for your camels, too," let her be the one you have selected to be the wife of my master's son.' 45"Before I had finished praying in my heart, I saw Rebekah coming out with her water jug on her shoulder. She went down to the spring and drew water. So I said to her, 'Please give me a drink.' 46She quickly lowered her jug from her shoulder and said, 'Yes, have a drink, and I will water your camels, too!' So I drank, and then she watered the camels. 47"Then I asked, 'Whose daughter are you?' She replied, 'I am the daughter of Bethuel, and my grandparents are Nahor and Milcah.' So I put the ring on her nose, and the bracelets on her wrists. 48"Then I bowed low and worshiped the Lord. I praised the Lord, the God of my master, Abraham, because he had led me straight to my master's niece to be his son's wife. 49So tell me—will you or won't you show unfailing love and faithfulness to my master? Please tell me yes or no, and then I'll know what to do next." 50Then Laban and Bethuel replied, "The Lord has obviously brought you here, so there is nothing we can say. 51Here is Rebekah; take her and go. Yes, let her be the wife of your master's son, as the Lord has directed." 52When Abraham's servant heard their answer, he bowed down to the ground and worshiped the Lord. 53Then he brought out silver and gold jewelry and clothing and presented them to Rebekah. He also gave expensive presents to her brother and mother. 54Then they ate their meal, and the servant and the men with him stayed there overnight. But early the next morning, Abraham's servant said, "Send me back to my master."

55"But we want Rebekah to stay with us at least ten days," her brother and mother said. "Then she can go." 56But he said, "Don't delay me. The Lord has made my mission successful; now send me back so I can return to my master." 57"Well," they said, "we'll call Rebekah and ask her what she thinks." 58So they called Rebekah. "Are you willing to go with this man?" they asked her. And she replied, "Yes, I will go." 59So they said good-bye to Rebekah and sent her away with Abraham's servant and his men. The woman who had been Rebekah's childhood nurse went along with her. 60They gave her this blessing as she parted: "Our sister, may you become the mother of many millions! May your descendants be strong and conquer the cities of their enemies." 61Then Rebekah and her servant girls mounted the camels and followed the man.

So Abraham's servant took Rebekah and went on his way. 62Meanwhile, Isaac, whose home was in the Negev, had returned from Beer-lahai-roi. 63One evening as he was walking and meditating in the fields, he looked up and saw the camels coming. 64When Rebekah looked up and saw Isaac, she quickly dismounted from her camel. 65"Who is that man walking through the fields to meet us?" she asked the servant. And he replied, "It is my master." So Rebekah covered her face with her veil. 66Then the servant told Isaac everything he had done. 67And Isaac brought Rebekah into his mother Sarah's tent, and she became his wife. He loved her deeply, and she was a special comfort to him after the death of his mother.

Chapter Thirty

1When Rachel saw that she wasn't having any children for Jacob, she became jealous of her sister. She pleaded with Jacob, "Give me children, or I'll die!" 2Then Jacob became furious with Rachel. "Am I God?" he asked. "He's the one who has kept you from having children!"

3Then Rachel told him, "Take my maid, Bilhah, and sleep with her. She will bear children for me, 30:3 Hebrew *bear children on my knees* and through her I can have a family, too." 4So Rachel gave her servant, Bilhah, to Jacob as a wife, and he slept with her. 5Bilhah became pregnant and presented him with a son. 6Rachel named him Dan,30:6 *Dan* means "he judged" or "he vindicated." for she said, "God has vindicated me! He has heard my request and given me a son." 7Then Bilhah became pregnant again and gave Jacob a second son. 8Rachel named him Naphtali, 30:8 *Naphtali* means "my struggle." for she said, "I have struggled hard with my sister, and I'm winning!" 9Meanwhile, Leah realized that she wasn't getting pregnant anymore, so she took her servant, Zilpah, and gave her to Jacob as a wife. 10Soon Zilpah presented him with a son. 11Leah named him Gad,30:11 *Gad* means "good fortune." for she said, "How fortunate I am!" 12Then Zilpah gave Jacob a second son. 13And Leah named him Asher,30:13 *Asher* means "happy." for she said, "What joy is mine! Now the other women will celebrate with me."

14One day during the wheat harvest, Reuben found some mandrakes growing in a field and brought them to his mother, Leah. Rachel begged Leah, "Please give me some of your son's mandrakes." 15But Leah angrily replied, "Wasn't it enough that you stole my husband? Now will you steal my son's mandrakes, too?" Rachel answered, "I will let Jacob sleep with you tonight if you give me some of the mandrakes." 16So that evening, as Jacob was coming home from the fields, Leah went out to meet him. "You must come and sleep with me tonight!" she said. "I have paid for you with some mandrakes that my son found." So that night he slept with Leah. 17And God answered Leah's prayers. She became pregnant again and gave birth to a fifth son for Jacob. 18She named him Issachar, 30:18 *Issachar* sounds like a Hebrew term that means "reward." for she said, "God has rewarded me for giving my servant to my husband as a wife." 19Then Leah became pregnant again and gave birth to a sixth son for Jacob. 20She named him Zebulun, 30:20 *Zebulun* probably means "honor." for she said, "God has given me a good reward. Now my husband will treat me with respect, for I have given him six sons." 21Later she gave birth to a daughter and named her

Dinah. 22Then God remembered Rachel's plight and answered her prayers by enabling her to have children. 23She became pregnant and gave birth to a son. "God has removed my disgrace," she said. 24And she named him Joseph, 30:24 *Joseph* means "may he add." for she said, "May the Lord add yet another son to my family."

Jacob's Wealth Increases

25Soon after Rachel had given birth to Joseph, Jacob said to Laban, "Please release me so I can go home to my own country. 26Let me take my wives and children, for I have earned them by serving you, and let me be on my way. You certainly know how hard I have worked for you."

27"Please listen to me," Laban replied. "I have become wealthy, for30:27 Or *I have learned by divination that* the Lord has blessed me because of you. 28Tell me how much I owe you. Whatever it is, I'll pay it." 29Jacob replied, "You know how hard I've worked for you, and how your flocks and herds have grown under my care. 30You had little indeed before I came, but your wealth has increased enormously. The Lord has blessed you through everything I've done. But now, what about me? When can I start providing for my own family?" 31"What wages do you want?" Laban asked again. Jacob replied, "Don't give me anything. Just do this one thing, and I'll continue to tend and watch over your flocks. 32Let me inspect your flocks today and remove all the sheep and goats that are speckled or spotted, along with all the black sheep. Give these to me as my wages. 33In the future, when you check on the animals you have given me as my wages, you'll see that I have been honest. If you find in my flock any goats without speckles or spots, or any sheep that are not black, you will know that I have stolen them from you."

34"All right," Laban replied. "It will be as you say." 35But that very day Laban went out and removed the male goats that were streaked and spotted, all the female goats that were speckled and spotted or had white patches, and all the black sheep. He placed them in the care of his own sons, 36who took them a three-days' journey from where Jacob was. Meanwhile, Jacob stayed and cared for the rest of Laban's flock. 37Then Jacob took some fresh branches from poplar, almond, and plane trees and peeled off strips of bark, making white streaks on them. 38Then he placed these peeled branches in the watering troughs where the flocks came to drink, for that was where they mated. 39And when they mated in front of the white-streaked branches, they gave birth to young that were streaked, speckled, and spotted. 40Jacob separated those lambs from Laban's flock. And at mating time he turned the flock to face Laban's animals that were streaked or black. This is how he built his own flock instead of increasing Laban's. 41Whenever the stronger females were ready to mate, Jacob would place the peeled branches in the watering troughs in front of them. Then they would mate in front of the branches. 42But he didn't do this with the weaker ones, so the weaker lambs belonged to Laban, and the stronger ones were Jacob's. 43As a result, Jacob became very wealthy, with large flocks of sheep and goats, female and male servants, and many camels and donkeys.

Chapter Thirty-five

Jacob's Return to Bethel

1Then God said to Jacob, "Get ready and move to Bethel and settle there. Build an altar there to the God who appeared to you when you fled from your brother, Esau." 2So Jacob told everyone in his household, "Get rid of all your pagan idols, purify yourselves, and put on clean clothing. 3We are now going to Bethel, where I will build an altar to the God who answered my prayers when I was in distress. He has been with me wherever I have gone." 4So they gave Jacob all their pagan idols and earrings, and he buried them under the great tree near Shechem. 5As they set out, a terror from God spread over the people in all the towns of that area, so no one attacked Jacob's family. 6Eventually, Jacob and his household arrived at Luz (also called Bethel) in Canaan. 7Jacob built an altar there and named the place El-bethel (which means "God of

Bethel"), because God had appeared to him there when he was fleeing from his brother, Esau.

8Soon after this, Rebekah's old nurse, Deborah, died. She was buried beneath the oak tree in the valley below Bethel. Ever since, the tree has been called Allon-bacuth (which means "oak of weeping"). 9Now that Jacob had returned from Paddan-aram, God appeared to him again at Bethel. God blessed him, 10saying, "Your name is Jacob, but you will not be called Jacob any longer. From now on your name will be Israel."35:10 *Jacob* sounds like the Hebrew words for

"heel" and "deceiver." *Israel* means "God fights." So God renamed him Israel. 11Then God said,

"I am El-Shaddai—'God Almighty.' Be fruitful and multiply. You will become a great nation, even many nations. Kings will be among your descendants! 12And I will give you the land I once gave to Abraham and Isaac. Yes, I will give it to you and your descendants after you." 13Then God went up from the place where he had spoken to Jacob. 14Jacob set up a stone pillar to mark the place where God had spoken to him. Then he poured wine over it as an offering to God and anointed the pillar with olive oil. 15And Jacob named the place Bethel

(which means "house of God"), because God had spoken to him there.

The Deaths of Rachel and Isaac

16Leaving Bethel, Jacob and his clan moved on toward Ephrath. But Rachel went into labor while they were still some distance away. Her labor pains were intense. 17After a very hard delivery, the midwife finally exclaimed, "Don't be afraid—you have another son!" 18Rachel was about to die, but with her last breath she named the baby Ben-oni (which means "son of my sorrow"). The baby's father, however, called him Benjamin (which means "son of my right hand"). 19So Rachel died and was buried on the way to Ephrath (that is, Bethlehem). 20Jacob set up a stone monument over Rachel's grave, and it can be seen there to this day. 21Then Jacob35:21 Hebrew *Israel;* also in 35:22a. The names "Jacob" and "Israel" are often interchanged throughout the Old Testament, referring sometimes to the individual patriarch and sometimes to the nation traveled on and camped beyond Migdal-eder. 22While he was living there, Reuben had intercourse with Bilhah, his father's concubine, and Jacob soon heard about it. These are the names of the twelve sons of Jacob: 23The sons of Leah were Reuben

(Jacob's oldest son), Simeon, Levi, Judah, Issachar, and Zebulun. 24The sons of Rachel were Joseph and Benjamin. 25The sons of Bilhah, Rachel's servant, were Dan and Naphtali. 26The sons of Zilpah, Leah's servant, were Gad and Asher. These are the names of the sons who were born to Jacob at Paddan-aram. 27So Jacob returned to his father, Isaac, in Mamre, which is near Kiriath-arba (now called Hebron), where Abraham and Isaac had both lived as foreigners. 28Isaac lived for 180 years. 29Then he breathed his last and died at a ripe old age, joining his ancestors in death. And his sons, Esau and Jacob, buried him. [2]

Genesis - Chapter Thirty-seven [2]

The Walk – S.B. Stone & Rock Solid Publishing, LLC
©2018

Joseph's Dreams

1So Jacob settled again in the land of Canaan, where his father had lived as a foreigner.

2This is the account of Jacob and his family. When Joseph was seventeen years old, he often tended his father's flocks. He worked for his half brothers, the sons of his father's wives Bilhah and Zilpah. But Joseph reported to his father some of the bad things his brothers were doing.

3Jacob37:3a Hebrew *Israel;* also in 37:13. See note on 35:21 loved Joseph more than any of his other children because Joseph had been born to him in his old age. So one day Jacob had a special gift made for Joseph—a beautiful robe.37:3b Traditionally rendered *a coat of many colors.* The exact meaning of the Hebrew is uncertain. 4But his brothers hated Joseph because their father loved him more than the rest of them. They couldn't say a kind word to him.

5One night Joseph had a dream, and when he told his brothers about it, they hated him more than ever. 6"Listen to this dream," he said. 7"We were out in the field, tying up bundles of grain. Suddenly my bundle stood up, and your bundles all gathered around and bowed low before mine!" 8His brothers responded, "So you think you will be our king, do you? Do you actually think you will reign over us?" And they hated him all the more because of his dreams and the way he talked about them. 9Soon Joseph had another dream, and again he told his brothers about it. "Listen, I have had another dream," he said. "The sun, moon, and eleven stars bowed low before me!" 10This time he told the dream to his father as well as to his brothers, but his father scolded him. "What kind of dream is that?" he asked. "Will your mother and I and your brothers actually come and bow to the ground before you?" 11But while his brothers were jealous of Joseph, his father wondered what the dreams meant. 12Soon after this, Joseph's brothers went to pasture their father's flocks at Shechem. 13When they had been gone for some time, Jacob said to Joseph, "Your brothers are pasturing the sheep at Shechem. Get ready, and I will send you to them." "I'm ready to go," Joseph replied. 14"Go and see how your brothers and the flocks are getting along," Jacob said. "Then come back and bring me a report." So Jacob sent him on his way, and Joseph traveled to Shechem from their home in the valley of Hebron.

15When he arrived there, a man from the area noticed him wandering around the countryside. "What are you looking for?" he asked. 16"I'm looking for my brothers," Joseph replied. "Do you know where they are pasturing their sheep?" 17"Yes," the man told him. "They have moved on from here, but I heard them say, 'Let's go on to Dothan.'" So Joseph followed his brothers to Dothan and found them there.

Joseph Sold into Slavery

18When Joseph's brothers saw him coming, they recognized him in the distance. As he approached, they made plans to kill him. 19"Here comes the dreamer!" they said. 20"Come on, let's kill him and throw him into one of these cisterns. We can tell our father, 'A wild animal has eaten him.' Then we'll see what becomes of his dreams!" 21But when Reuben heard of their scheme, he came to Joseph's rescue. "Let's not kill him," he said. 22"Why should we shed any blood? Let's just throw him into this empty cistern here in the wilderness. Then he'll die without our laying a hand on him." Reuben was secretly planning to rescue Joseph and return him to his father. 23So when Joseph arrived, his brothers ripped off the beautiful robe he was wearing. 24Then they grabbed him and threw him into the cistern. Now the cistern was empty; there was no water in it. 25Then, just as they were sitting down to eat, they looked up and saw a caravan of camels in the distance coming toward them. It was a group of Ishmaelite traders taking a load of gum, balm, and aromatic resin from Gilead down to Egypt.

26Judah said to his brothers, "What will we gain by killing our brother? We'd have to cover up the crime.37:26 Hebrew *cover his blood.* 27Instead of hurting him, let's sell him to those Ishmaelite traders. After all, he is our brother—our own flesh and blood!" And his brothers agreed. 28So when the Ishmaelites, who were Midianite traders, came by, Joseph's brothers pulled him out of the cistern and sold him to them for twenty pieces37:28 Hebrew *20 [shekels],* about 8 ounces or 228 grams in weight. of silver. And the traders took him to Egypt.

29Some time later, Reuben returned to get Joseph out of the cistern. When he discovered that Joseph was missing, he tore his clothes in grief. 30Then he went back to his brothers and lamented, "The boy is gone! What will I do now?" 31Then the brothers killed a young goat and dipped Joseph's robe in its blood. 32They sent the beautiful robe to their father with this message: "Look at what we found. Doesn't this robe belong to your son?"

The Walk – S.B. Stone & Rock Solid Publishing, LLC
©2018

33Their father recognized it immediately. "Yes," he said, "it is my son's robe. A wild animal must have eaten him. Joseph has clearly been torn to pieces!" 34Then Jacob tore his clothes and dressed himself in burlap. He mourned deeply for his son for a long time. 35His family all tried to comfort him, but he refused to be comforted. "I will go to my grave37:35 Hebrew *go down to Sheol* mourning for my son," he would say, and then he would weep. 36Meanwhile, the Midianite traders37:36 Hebrew *the Medanites.* The relationship between the Midianites and Medanites is unclear; compare 37:28. See also 25:2 arrived in Egypt, where they sold Joseph to Potiphar, an officer of Pharaoh, the king of Egypt. Potiphar was captain of the palace guard. [2]

Chapter Thirty-nine

Joseph in Potiphar's House

1When Joseph was taken to Egypt by the Ishmaelite traders, he was purchased by

Potiphar, an Egyptian officer. Potiphar was captain of the guard for Pharaoh, the king of Egypt.

2The Lord was with Joseph, so he succeeded in everything he did as he served in the home of his Egyptian master. 3Potiphar noticed this and realized that the Lord was with Joseph, giving him success in everything he did. 4This pleased Potiphar, so he soon made Joseph his personal attendant. He put him in charge of his entire household and everything he owned. 5From the day Joseph was put in charge of his master's household and property, the Lord began to bless Potiphar's household for Joseph's sake. All his household affairs ran smoothly, and his crops and livestock flourished. 6So Potiphar gave Joseph complete administrative responsibility over everything he owned. With Joseph there, he didn't worry about a thing—except what kind of food to eat! Joseph was a very handsome and well-built young man, 7and Potiphar's wife soon began to look at him lustfully. "Come and sleep with me," she demanded.

8But Joseph refused. "Look," he told her, "my master trusts me with everything in his entire household. 9No one here has more authority than I do. He has held back nothing from me except you, because you are his wife. How could I do such a wicked thing? It would be a great sin against God." 10She kept putting pressure on Joseph day after day, but he refused to sleep with her, and he kept out of her way as much as possible. 11One day, however, no one else was around when he went in to do his work. 12She came and grabbed him by his cloak, demanding,

"Come on, sleep with me!" Joseph tore himself away, but he left his cloak in her hand as he ran from the house. 13When she saw that she was holding his cloak and he had fled, 14she called out to her servants. Soon all the men came running. "Look!" she said. "My husband has brought this Hebrew slave here to make fools of us! He came into my room to rape me, but I screamed. 15When he heard me scream, he ran outside and got away, but he left his cloak behind with me." 16She kept the cloak with her until her husband came home. 17Then she told him her story. "That Hebrew slave you've brought into our house tried to come in and fool around with me," she said. 18"But when I screamed, he ran outside, leaving his cloak with me!"

Joseph Put in Prison

19Potiphar was furious when he heard his wife's story about how Joseph had treated her. 20So he took Joseph and threw him into the prison where the king's prisoners were held, and there he remained. 21But the Lord was with Joseph in the prison and showed him his faithful love. And the Lord made Joseph a favorite with the prison warden. 22Before long, the warden put Joseph in charge of all the other prisoners and over everything that happened in the prison. 23The warden had no more worries, because Joseph took care of everything.

The Lord was with him and caused everything he did to succeed.

Chapter Forty

Joseph Interprets Two Dreams

1Some time later, Pharaoh's chief cup-bearer and chief baker offended their royal master. 2Pharaoh became angry with these two officials, 3and he put them in the prison where Joseph was, in the palace of the captain of the guard. 4They remained in prison for quite some time, and the captain of the guard assigned them to Joseph, who looked after them.

5While they were in prison, Pharaoh's cup-bearer and baker each had a dream one night, and each dream had its own meaning. 6When Joseph saw them the next morning, he noticed that they both looked upset. 7"Why do you look so worried today?" he asked them.

8And they replied, "We both had dreams last night, but no one can tell us what they mean."

"Interpreting dreams is God's business," Joseph replied. "Go ahead and tell me your dreams."

9So the chief cup-bearer told Joseph his dream first. "In my dream," he said, "I saw a grapevine in front of me. 10The vine had three branches that began to bud and blossom, and soon it produced clusters of ripe grapes. 11I was holding Pharaoh's wine cup in my hand, so I took a cluster of grapes and squeezed the juice into the cup. Then I placed the cup in Pharaoh's hand."

12"This is what the dream means," Joseph said. "The three branches represent three days. 13Within three days Pharaoh will lift you up and restore you to your position as his chief cup-bearer. 14And please remember me and do me a favor when things go well for you. Mention me to Pharaoh, so he might let me out of this place. 15For I was kidnapped from my homeland, the land of the Hebrews, and now I'm here in prison, but I did nothing to deserve it."

16When the chief baker saw that Joseph had given the first dream such a positive interpretation, he said to Joseph, "I had a dream, too. In my dream there were three baskets of white pastries stacked on my head. 17The top basket contained all kinds of pastries for Pharaoh, but the birds came and ate them from the basket on my head." 18"This is what the dream means," Joseph told him. "The three baskets also represent three days. 19Three days from now Pharaoh will lift you up and impale your body on a pole. Then birds will come and peck away at your flesh."

20Pharaoh's birthday came three days later, and he prepared a banquet for all his officials and staff. He summoned40:20 Hebrew *He lifted up the head of.* his chief cup-bearer and chief baker to join the other officials. 21He then restored the chief cup-bearer to his former position, so he could again hand Pharaoh his cup. 22But Pharaoh impaled the chief baker, just as Joseph had predicted when he interpreted his dream. 23Pharaoh's chief cup-bearer, however, forgot all about

Joseph, never giving him another thought.   NLT [2]

Genesis - Chapter Forty-One NLT [2]

Pharaoh's Dreams

1Two full years later, Pharaoh dreamed that he was standing on the bank of the Nile River. 2In his dream he saw seven fat, healthy cows come up out of the river and begin grazing in the marsh grass. 3Then he saw seven more cows come up behind them from the Nile, but these were scrawny and thin. These cows stood beside the fat cows on the riverbank. 4Then the scrawny, thin cows ate the seven healthy, fat cows! At this point in the dream, Pharaoh woke up.

5But he fell asleep again and had a second dream. This time he saw seven heads of grain, plump and beautiful, growing on a single stalk. 6Then seven more heads of grain appeared, but these were shriveled and withered by the east wind. 7And these thin heads swallowed up the seven plump, well-formed heads! Then Pharaoh woke up again and realized it was a dream.

8The next morning Pharaoh was very disturbed by the dreams. So he called for all the magicians and wise men of Egypt. When Pharaoh told them his dreams, not one of them could tell him what they meant. 9Finally, the king's chief cup-bearer spoke up. "Today I have been reminded of my failure," he told Pharaoh. 10"Some time ago, you were angry with the chief baker and me, and you imprisoned us in the palace of the captain of the guard. 11One night the chief baker and I each had a dream, and each dream had its own meaning. 12There was a young Hebrew man with us in the prison who was a slave of the captain of the guard. We told him our dreams, and he told us what each of our dreams meant. 13And everything happened just as he had predicted. I was restored to my position as cup-bearer, and the chief baker was executed and impaled on a pole." 14Pharaoh sent for Joseph at once, and he was quickly brought from the prison. After he shaved and changed his clothes, he went in and stood before Pharaoh. 15Then

Pharaoh said to Joseph, "I had a dream last night, and no one here can tell me what it means. But I have heard that when you hear about a dream you can interpret it." 16"It is beyond my power to do this," Joseph replied. "But God can tell you what it means and set you at ease." 17So Pharaoh told Joseph his dream. "In my dream," he said, "I was standing on the bank of the Nile River, 18and I saw seven fat, healthy cows come up out of the river and begin grazing in the marsh grass. 19But then I saw seven sick-looking cows, scrawny and thin, come up after them. I've never seen such sorry-looking animals in all the land of Egypt. 20These thin, scrawny cows ate the seven fat cows. 21But afterward you wouldn't have known it, for they were still as thin and scrawny as before! Then I woke up. 22"In my dream I also saw seven heads of grain, full and beautiful, growing on a single stalk. 23Then seven more heads of grain appeared, but these were blighted, shriveled, and withered by the east wind. 24And the shriveled heads swallowed the seven healthy heads. I told these dreams to the magicians, but no one could tell me what they mean."

25Joseph responded, "Both of Pharaoh's dreams mean the same thing. God is telling Pharaoh in advance what he is about to do. 26The seven healthy cows and the seven healthy heads of grain both represent seven years of prosperity. 27The seven thin, scrawny cows that came up later and the seven thin heads of grain, withered by the east wind, represent seven years of famine.

28"This will happen just as I have described it, for God has revealed to Pharaoh in advance what he is about to do. 29The next seven years will be a period of great prosperity throughout the land of Egypt. 30But afterward there will be seven years of famine so great that all the prosperity will be forgotten in Egypt. Famine will destroy the land. 31This famine will be so severe that even the memory of the good years will be erased. 32As for having two similar dreams, it means that these events have been decreed by God, and he will soon make them happen.

33"Therefore, Pharaoh should find an intelligent and wise man and put him in charge of the entire land of Egypt. 34Then Pharaoh should appoint supervisors over the land and let them collect one-fifth of all the crops during the seven good years. 35Have them gather all the food produced in the good years that are just ahead and bring it to Pharaoh's storehouses. Store it away, and guard it so there will be food in the cities. 36That way there will be enough to eat when the seven years of famine come to the land of Egypt. Otherwise this famine will destroy the land."

Joseph Made Ruler of Egypt

37Joseph's suggestions were well received by Pharaoh and his officials. 38So Pharaoh asked his officials, "Can we find anyone else like this man so obviously filled with the spirit of

God?" 39Then Pharaoh said to Joseph, "Since God has revealed the meaning of the dreams to you, clearly no one else is as intelligent or wise as you are. 40You will be in charge of my court, and all my people will take orders from you. Only I, sitting on my throne, will have a rank higher than yours." 41Pharaoh said to Joseph, "I hereby put you in charge of the entire land of Egypt." 42Then Pharaoh removed his signet ring from his hand and placed it on Joseph's finger.

He dressed him in fine linen clothing and hung a gold chain around his neck. 43Then he had Joseph ride in the chariot reserved for his second-in-command. And wherever Joseph went, the command was shouted, "Kneel down!" So Pharaoh put Joseph in charge of all Egypt. 44And Pharaoh said to him, "I am Pharaoh, but no one will lift a hand or foot in the entire land of Egypt without your approval." 45Then Pharaoh gave Joseph a new Egyptian name, Zaphenathpaneah.41:45a *Zaphenath-paneah* probably means "God speaks and lives." He also gave him a wife, whose name was Asenath. She was the daughter of Potiphera, the priest of

On.41:45b Greek version reads *of Heliopolis;* also in 41:50. So Joseph took charge of the entire land of Egypt. 46He was thirty years old when he began serving in the court of Pharaoh, the king of Egypt. And when Joseph left Pharaoh's presence, he inspected the entire land of Egypt.

47As predicted, for seven years the land produced bumper crops. 48During those years, Joseph gathered all the crops grown in Egypt and stored the grain from the surrounding fields in the cities. 49He piled up huge amounts of grain like sand on the seashore. Finally, he stopped keeping records because there was too much to measure.

50During this time, before the first of the famine years, two sons were born to Joseph and his wife, Asenath, the daughter of Potiphera, the priest of On. 51Joseph named his older son Manasseh,41:51 *Manasseh* sounds like a Hebrew term that means "causing to forget." for he said, "God has made me forget all my troubles and everyone in my father's family." 52Joseph named his second son Ephraim,41:52 *Ephraim* sounds like a Hebrew term that means "fruitful." for he said, "God has made me fruitful in this land of my grief."

53At last the seven years of bumper crops throughout the land of Egypt came to an end. 54Then the seven years of famine began, just as Joseph had predicted. The famine also struck all the surrounding countries, but throughout Egypt there was plenty of food. 55Eventually, however, the famine spread throughout the land of Egypt as well. And when the people cried out to Pharaoh for food, he told them, "Go to Joseph, and do whatever he tells you." 56So with severe famine everywhere, Joseph opened up the storehouses and distributed grain to the Egyptians, for the famine was severe throughout the land of Egypt. 57And people from all around came to Egypt to buy grain from Joseph because the famine was severe throughout the world. [2]

Genesis - Chapter Forty-Two

Joseph's Brothers Go to Egypt

1When Jacob heard that grain was available in Egypt, he said to his sons, "Why are you standing around looking at one another? 2I have heard there is grain in Egypt. Go down there, and buy enough grain to keep us alive. Otherwise we'll die." 3So Joseph's ten older brothers went down to Egypt to buy grain. 4But Jacob wouldn't let Joseph's younger brother, Benjamin, go with them, for fear some harm might come to him. 5So Jacob's42:5 Hebrew *Israel's*. See note on 35:21 sons arrived in Egypt along with others to buy food, for the famine was in Canaan as well.

6Since Joseph was governor of all Egypt and in charge of selling grain to all the people, it was to him that his brothers came. When they arrived, they bowed before him with their faces to the ground. 7Joseph recognized his brothers instantly, but he pretended to be a stranger and spoke harshly to them. "Where are you from?" he demanded. "From the land of Canaan," they replied. "We have come to buy food." 8Although Joseph recognized his brothers, they didn't recognize him. 9And he remembered the dreams he'd had about them many years before. He said to them, "You are spies! You have come to see how vulnerable our land has become."

10"No, my lord!" they exclaimed. "Your servants have simply come to buy food. 11We are all brothers—members of the same family. We are honest men, sir! We are not spies!" 12"Yes, you are!" Joseph insisted. "You have come to see how vulnerable our land has become."

13"Sir," they said, "there are actually twelve of us. We, your servants, are all brothers, sons of a man living in the land of Canaan. Our youngest brother is back there with our father right now, and one of our brothers is no longer with us." 14But Joseph insisted, "As I said, you are spies! 15This is how I will test your story. I swear by the life of Pharaoh that you will never leave Egypt unless your youngest brother comes here! 16One of you must go and get your brother. I'll keep the rest of you here in prison. Then we'll find out whether or not your story is true.

By the life of Pharaoh, if it turns out that you don't have a younger brother, then I'll know you are spies." 17So Joseph put them all in prison for three days. 18On the third day Joseph said to them, "I am a God-fearing man. If you do as I say, you will live. 19If you really are honest men, choose one of your brothers to remain in prison. The rest of you may go home with grain for your starving families. 20But you must bring your youngest brother back to me. This will prove that you are telling the truth, and you will not die." To this they agreed.

21Speaking among themselves, they said, "Clearly we are being punished because of what we did to Joseph long ago. We saw his anguish when he pleaded for his life, but we wouldn't listen. That's why we're in this trouble." 22"Didn't I tell you not to sin against the boy?" Reuben asked. "But you wouldn't listen. And now we have to answer for his blood!"

23Of course, they didn't know that Joseph understood them, for he had been speaking to them through an interpreter. 24Now he turned away from them and began to weep. When he regained his composure, he spoke to them again. Then he chose Simeon from among them and had him tied up right before their eyes. 25Joseph then ordered his servants to fill the men's sacks with grain, but he also gave secret instructions to return each brother's payment at the top of his sack. He also gave them supplies for their journey home. 26So the brothers loaded their donkeys with the grain and headed for home. 27But when they stopped for the night and one of them opened his sack to get grain for his donkey, he found his money in the top of his sack. 28"Look!" he exclaimed to his brothers. "My money has been returned; it's here in my sack!" Then their hearts sank. Trembling, they said to each other, "What has God done to us?"

29When the brothers came to their father, Jacob, in the land of Canaan, they told him everything that had happened to them. 30"The man who is governor of the land spoke very harshly to us," they told him. "He accused us of being spies scouting the land. 31But we said, 'We are honest men, not spies. 32We are twelve brothers, sons of one father. One brother is no longer with us, and the youngest is at home with our father in the land of Canaan.' 33"Then the man who is governor of the land told us, 'This is how I will find out if you are honest men. Leave one of your brothers here with me, and take grain for your starving families and go on home. 34But you must bring your youngest brother back to me. Then I will know you are honest men and not spies. Then I will give you back your brother, and you may trade freely in the land.'"

35As they emptied out their sacks, there in each man's sack was the bag of money he had paid for the grain! The brothers and their father were terrified when they saw the bags of money. 36Jacob exclaimed, "You are robbing me of my children! Joseph is gone! Simeon is gone! And now you want to take Benjamin, too. Everything is going against me!"

37Then Reuben said to his father, "You may kill my two sons if I don't bring Benjamin back to you. I'll be responsible for him, and I promise to bring him back." 38But Jacob replied,

"My son will not go down with you. His brother Joseph is dead, and he is all I have left. If anything should happen to him on your journey, you would send this grieving, white-haired man to his grave.42:38 Hebrew *to Sheol*." [2]

Genesis - Chapter Forty-Three

The Brothers Return to Egypt

1But the famine continued to ravage the land of Canaan. 2When the grain they had brought from Egypt was almost gone, Jacob said to his sons, "Go back and buy us a little more food."

3But Judah said, "The man was serious when he warned us, 'You won't see my face again unless your brother is with you.' 4If you send Benjamin with us, we will go down and buy more food. 5But if you don't let Benjamin go, we won't go either. Remember, the man said, 'You won't see my face again unless your brother is with you.'" 6"Why were you so cruel to me?" Jacob43:6 Hebrew *Israel;* also in 43:11. See note on 35:21. moaned. "Why did you tell him you had another brother?" 7"The man kept asking us questions about our family," they replied. "He asked, 'Is your father still alive? Do you have another brother?' So we answered his questions. How could we know he would say, 'Bring your brother down here'?" 8Judah said to his father, "Send the boy with me, and we will be on our way. Otherwise we will all die of starvation—and not only we, but you and our little ones. 9I personally guarantee his safety. You may hold me responsible if I don't bring him back to you. Then let me bear the blame forever. 10If we hadn't wasted all this time, we could have gone and returned twice by now."

11So their father, Jacob, finally said to them, "If it can't be avoided, then at least do this. Pack your bags with the best products of this land. Take them down to the man as gifts—balm, honey, gum, aromatic resin, pistachio nuts, and almonds. 12Also take double the money that was put back in your sacks, as it was probably someone's mistake. 13Then take your brother, and go back to the man. 14May God Almighty43:14 Hebrew *El-Shaddai.* give you mercy as you go before the man, so that he will release Simeon and let Benjamin return. But if I must lose my children, so be it."

15So the men packed Jacob's gifts and double the money and headed off with Benjamin. They finally arrived in Egypt and presented themselves to Joseph. 16When Joseph saw Benjamin with them, he said to the manager of his household, "These men will eat with me this noon. Take them inside the palace. Then go slaughter an animal, and prepare a big feast." 17So the man did as Joseph told him and took them into Joseph's palace. 18The brothers were terrified when they saw that they were being taken into Joseph's house. "It's because of the money someone put in our sacks last time we were here," they said. "He plans to pretend that we stole it. Then he will seize us, make us slaves, and take our donkeys."

A Feast at Joseph's Palace

19The brothers approached the manager of Joseph's household and spoke to him at the entrance to the palace. 20"Sir," they said, "we came to Egypt once before to buy food. 21But as we were returning home, we stopped for the night and opened our sacks. Then we discovered that each man's money—the exact amount paid—was in the top of his sack! Here it is; we have brought it back with us. 22We also have additional money to buy more food. We have no idea who put our money in our sacks." 23"Relax. Don't be afraid," the household manager told them. "Your God, the God of your father, must have put this treasure into your sacks. I know I received your payment." Then he released Simeon and brought him out to them. 24The manager then led the men into Joseph's palace. He gave them water to wash their feet and provided food for their donkeys. 25They were told they would be eating there, so they prepared their gifts for Joseph's arrival at noon. 26When Joseph came home, they gave him the gifts they had brought him, then bowed low to the ground before him. 27After greeting them, he asked, "How is your father, the old man you spoke about? Is he still alive?" 28"Yes," they replied. "Our father, your servant, is alive and well." And they bowed low again. 29Then Joseph looked at his brother Benjamin, the son of his own mother. "Is this your youngest brother, the one you told me about?" Joseph asked. "May God be gracious to you, my son." 30Then Joseph hurried from the room because he was overcome with emotion for his brother. He went into his private room, where he broke down and wept. 31After washing his face, he came back out, keeping himself under control. Then he ordered, "Bring out the food!" 32The waiters served Joseph at his own table, and his brothers were served at a separate table. The Egyptians who ate with Joseph sat at their own table, because Egyptians despise Hebrews and refuse to eat with them. 33Joseph told each of his brothers where to sit, and to their amazement, he seated them according to age, from oldest to youngest. 34And Joseph filled their plates with food from his own table, giving Benjamin five times as much as he gave the others. So they feasted and drank freely with him. [2]

Genesis - Chapter Forty-Four

Joseph's Silver Cup

1When his brothers were ready to leave, Joseph gave these instructions to his palace manager: "Fill each of their sacks with as much grain as they can carry, and put each man's money back into his sack. 2Then put my personal silver cup at the top of the youngest brother's sack, along with the money for his grain." So the manager did as Joseph instructed him. 3The brothers were up at dawn and were sent on their journey with their loaded donkeys. 4But when they had gone only a short distance and were barely out of the city, Joseph said to his palace manager, "Chase after them and stop them. When you catch up with them, ask them, 'Why have you repaid my kindness with such evil? 5Why have you stolen my master's silver cup, 44:5 As in Greek version; Hebrew lacks this phrase which he uses to predict the future? What a wicked thing you have done!'" 6When the palace manager caught up with the men, he spoke to them as he had been instructed. 7"What are you talking about?" the brothers responded. "We are your servants and would never do such a thing! 8Didn't we return the money we found in our sacks? We brought it back all the way from the land of Canaan. Why would we steal silver or gold from your master's house? 9If you find his cup with any one of us, let that man die. And all the rest of us, my lord, will be your slaves." 10"That's fair," the man replied. "But only the one who stole the cup will be my slave. The rest of you may go free." 11They all quickly took their sacks from the backs of their donkeys and opened them. 12The palace manager searched the brothers' sacks, from the oldest to the youngest. And the cup was found in Benjamin's sack! 13When the brothers saw this, they tore their clothing in despair. Then they loaded their donkeys again and returned to the city. 14Joseph was still in his palace when Judah and his brothers arrived, and they fell to the ground before him. 15"What have you done?" Joseph demanded. "Don't you know that a man like me can predict the future?" 16Judah answered, "Oh, my lord, what can we say to you? How can we explain this? How can we prove our innocence? God is punishing us for our sins. My lord, we have all returned to be your slaves—all of us, not just our brother who had your cup in his sack." 17"No," Joseph said. "I would never do such a thing! Only the man who stole the cup will be my slave. The rest of you may go back to your father in peace."

Judah Speaks for His Brothers

18Then Judah stepped forward and said, "Please, my lord, let your servant say just one word to you. Please, do not be angry with me, even though you are as powerful as Pharaoh himself.

19"My lord, previously you asked us, your servants, 'Do you have a father or a brother?' 20And we responded, 'Yes, my lord, we have a father who is an old man, and his youngest son is a child of his old age. His full brother is dead, and he alone is left of his mother's children, and his father loves him very much.' 21"And you said to us, 'Bring him here so I can see him with my own eyes.' 22But we said to you, 'My lord, the boy cannot leave his father, for his father would die.' 23But you told us, 'Unless your youngest brother comes with you, you will never see my face again.' 24"So we returned to your servant, our father, and told him what you had said. 25Later, when he said, 'Go back again and buy us more food,' 26we replied, 'We can't go unless you let our youngest brother go with us. We'll never get to see the man's face unless our youngest brother is with us.' 27"Then my father said to us, 'As you know, my wife had two sons, 28and one of them went away and never returned. Doubtless he was torn to pieces by some wild animal. I have never seen him since. 29Now if you take his brother away from me, and any harm comes to him, you will send this grieving, white-haired man to his grave.44:29 Hebrew *to*

Sheol; also in 44:31.' 30"And now, my lord, I cannot go back to my father without the boy. Our father's life is bound up in the boy's life. 31If he sees that the boy is not with us, our father will die. We, your servants, will indeed be responsible for sending that grieving, white-haired man to his grave. 32My lord, I guaranteed to my father that I would take care of the boy. I told him, 'If I don't bring him back to you, I will bear the blame forever.' 33"So please, my lord, let me stay here as a slave instead of the boy, and let the boy return with his brothers. 34For how can I return to my father if the boy is not with me? I couldn't bear to see the anguish this would cause my father!" [2]

Genesis - Chapter Forty-Five

Joseph Reveals His Identity

1Joseph could stand it no longer. There were many people in the room, and he said to his attendants, "Out, all of you!" So he was alone with his brothers when he told them who he was. 2Then he broke down and wept. He wept so loudly the Egyptians could hear him, and word of it quickly carried to Pharaoh's palace. 3"I am Joseph!" he said to his brothers. "Is my father still alive?" But his brothers were speechless! They were stunned to realize that Joseph was standing there in front of them. 4"Please, come closer," he said to them. So they came closer. And he said again, "I am Joseph, your brother, whom you sold into slavery in Egypt. 5But don't be upset, and don't be angry with yourselves for selling me to this place. It was God who sent me here ahead of you to preserve your lives. 6This famine that has ravaged the land for two years will last five more years, and there will be neither plowing nor harvesting. 7God has sent me ahead of you to keep you and your families alive and to preserve many survivors.45:7 Or *and to save you with an extraordinary rescue.* The meaning of the Hebrew is uncertain. 8So it was God who sent me here, not you! And he is the one who made me an adviser45:8 Hebrew *a father* to Pharaoh—the manager of his entire palace and the governor of all Egypt. 9"Now hurry back to my father and tell him, 'This is what your son Joseph says: God has made me master over all the land of Egypt. So come down to me immediately! 10You can live in the region of Goshen, where you can be near me with all your children and grandchildren, your flocks and herds, and everything you own. 11I will take care of you there, for there are still five years of famine ahead of us. Otherwise you, your household, and all your animals will starve.'" 12Then Joseph added, "Look! You can see for yourselves, and so can my brother Benjamin, that I really am Joseph! 13Go tell my father of my honored position here in Egypt. Describe for him everything you have seen, and then bring my father here quickly." 14Weeping with joy, he embraced Benjamin, and Benjamin did the same. 15Then Joseph kissed each of his brothers and wept over them, and after that they began talking freely with him.

Pharaoh Invites Jacob to Egypt

16The news soon reached Pharaoh's palace: "Joseph's brothers have arrived!" Pharaoh and his officials were all delighted to hear this. 17Pharaoh said to Joseph, "Tell your brothers, 'This is what you must do: Load your pack animals, and hurry back to the land of Canaan. 18Then get your father and all of your families, and return here to me. I will give you the very best land in Egypt, and you will eat from the best that the land produces.'" 19Then Pharaoh said to Joseph, "Tell your brothers, 'Take wagons from the land of Egypt to carry your little children and your wives, and bring your father here. 20Don't worry about your personal belongings, for the best of all the land of Egypt is yours.'" 21So the sons of

Jacob45:21 Hebrew *Israel;* also in 45:28. See note on 35:21 did as they were told. Joseph provided them with wagons, as Pharaoh had commanded, and he gave them supplies for the journey. 22And he gave each of them new clothes—but to Benjamin he gave five changes of clothes and 300 pieces45:22 Hebrew *300 [shekels],* about 7.5 pounds or 3.4 kilograms in weight. of silver. 23He also sent his father ten male donkeys loaded with the finest products of Egypt, and ten female donkeys loaded with grain and bread and other supplies he would need on his journey. 24So Joseph sent his brothers off, and as they left, he called after them, "Don't quarrel about all this along the way!" 25And they left Egypt and returned to their father, Jacob, in the land of Canaan. 26"Joseph is still alive!" they told him. "And he is governor of all the land of Egypt!" Jacob was stunned at the news—he couldn't believe it. 27But when they repeated to Jacob everything Joseph had told them, and when he saw the wagons Joseph had sent to carry him, their father's spirits revived. 28Then Jacob exclaimed, "It must be true! My son Joseph is alive! I must go and see him

before I die." [2]

Genesis - Chapter Forty-Six

Jacob's Journey to Egypt

1So Jacob46:1 Hebrew *Israel;* also in 46:29, 30. See note on 35:21 set out for Egypt with all his possessions. And when he came to

Beersheba, he offered sacrifices to the God of his father, Isaac. 2During the night God spoke to him in a vision. "Jacob! Jacob!" he called.

"Here I am," Jacob replied. 3"I am God, 46:3 Hebrew *I am El.* the God of your father," the voice said. "Do not be afraid to go down to Egypt, for there I will make your family into a great nation. 4I will go with you down to Egypt, and I will bring you back again. You will die in

Egypt, but Joseph will be with you to close your eyes." 5So Jacob left Beersheba, and his sons took him to Egypt. They carried him and their little ones and their wives in the wagons Pharaoh had provided for them. 6They also took all their livestock and all the personal belongings they had acquired in the land of Canaan. So Jacob and his entire family went to Egypt—7sons and grandsons, daughters and granddaughters—all his descendants.

8These are the names of the descendants of Israel—the sons of Jacob—who went to Egypt:

Reuben was Jacob's oldest son. 9The sons of Reuben were Hanoch, Pallu, Hezron, and Carmi.

10The sons of Simeon were Jemuel, Jamin, Ohad, Jakin, Zohar, and Shaul. (Shaul's mother was a Canaanite woman.) 11The sons of Levi were Gershon, Kohath, and Merari. 12The sons of Judah were Er, Onan, Shelah, Perez, and Zerah (though Er and Onan had died in the land of Canaan). The sons of Perez were Hezron and Hamul. 13The sons of Issachar were Tola, Puah,46:13a As in Syriac version and Samaritan Pentateuch (see also 1 Chr 7:1); Hebrew reads *Puvah.* Jashub,46:13b As in some Greek manuscripts and Samaritan Pentateuch (see also Num 26:24; 1 Chr 7:1); Hebrew reads *Iob* and Shimron. 14The sons of Zebulun were Sered, Elon, and Jahleel. 15These were the sons of Leah and Jacob who were born in Paddan-aram, in addition to their daughter, Dinah. The number of Jacob's descendants (male and female) through

Leah was thirty-three. 16The sons of Gad were Zephon,46:16 As in Greek version and Samaritan

Pentateuch (see also Num 26:15); Hebrew reads *Ziphion.* Haggi, Shuni, Ezbon, Eri, Arodi, and Areli. 17The sons of Asher were Imnah, Ishvah, Ishvi, and Beriah. Their sister was Serah. Beriah's sons were Heber and Malkiel. 18These were the sons of Zilpah, the servant given to Leah by her father, Laban. The number of Jacob's descendants through Zilpah was sixteen.

19The sons of Jacob's wife Rachel were Joseph and Benjamin. 20Joseph's sons, born in the land of Egypt, were Manasseh and Ephraim. Their mother was Asenath, daughter of

Potiphera, the priest of On.46:20 Greek version reads *of Heliopolis.* 21Benjamin's sons were Bela, Beker, Ashbel, Gera, Naaman, Ehi, Rosh, Muppim, Huppim, and Ard. 22These were the sons of Rachel and Jacob. The number of Jacob's descendants through Rachel was fourteen.

23The son of Dan was Hushim. 24The sons of Naphtali were Jahzeel, Guni, Jezer, and Shillem. 25These were the sons of Bilhah, the servant given to Rachel by her father, Laban. The number of Jacob's descendants through Bilhah was seven. 26The total number of Jacob's direct descendants who went with him to Egypt, not counting his sons' wives, was sixty-six. 27In addition, Joseph had two sons46:27a Greek version reads *nine sons,* probably including Joseph's grandsons through Ephraim and Manasseh (see 1 Chr 7:14-20) who were born in Egypt. So altogether, there were seventy46:27b Greek version reads *seventy-five;* see note on Exod 1:5. members of Jacob's family in the land of Egypt.

Jacob's Family Arrives in Goshen

28As they neared their destination, Jacob sent Judah ahead to meet Joseph and get directions to the region of Goshen. And when they finally arrived there, 29Joseph prepared his chariot and traveled to Goshen to meet his father, Jacob. When Joseph arrived, he embraced his father and wept, holding him for a long time. 30Finally, Jacob said to Joseph, "Now I am ready to die, since I have seen your face again and know you are still alive." 31And Joseph said to his brothers and to his father's entire family, "I will go to Pharaoh and tell him, 'My brothers and my father's entire family have come to me from the land of Canaan. 32These men are shepherds, and they raise livestock. They have brought with them their flocks and herds and everything they own.'" 33Then he said, "When Pharaoh calls for you and asks you about your occupation, 34you must tell him, 'We, your servants, have raised livestock all our lives, as our ancestors have always done.' When you tell him this, he will let you live here in the region of Goshen, for the Egyptians despise shepherds." [2]

Genesis - Chapter Forty-Seven

Jacob Blesses Pharaoh

1Then Joseph went to see Pharaoh and told him, "My father and my brothers have arrived from the land of Canaan. They have come with all their flocks and herds and possessions, and they are now in the region of Goshen."

2Joseph took five of his brothers with him and presented them to Pharaoh. 3And Pharaoh asked the brothers, "What is your occupation?" They replied, "We, your servants, are shepherds, just like our ancestors. 4We have come to live here in Egypt for a while, for there is no pasture for our flocks in Canaan. The famine is very severe there. So please, we request permission to live in the region of Goshen." 5Then Pharaoh said to Joseph, "Now that your father and brothers have joined you here, 6choose any place in the entire land of Egypt for them to live. Give them the best land of Egypt. Let them live in the region of Goshen. And if any of them have special skills, put them in charge of my livestock, too." 7Then Joseph brought in his father, Jacob, and presented him to Pharaoh. And Jacob blessed Pharaoh. 8"How old are you?" Pharaoh asked him.

9Jacob replied, "I have traveled this earth for 130 hard years. But my life has been short compared to the lives of my ancestors." 10Then Jacob blessed Pharaoh again before leaving his court. 11So Joseph assigned the best land of Egypt—the region of Rameses—to his father and his brothers, and he settled them there, just as Pharaoh had commanded. 12And Joseph provided food for his father and his brothers in amounts appropriate to the number of their dependents, including the smallest children.

Joseph's Leadership in the Famine

13Meanwhile, the famine became so severe that all the food was used up, and people were starving throughout the lands of Egypt and Canaan. 14By selling grain to the people,

Joseph eventually collected all the money in Egypt and Canaan, and he put the money in Pharaoh's treasury. 15When the people of Egypt and Canaan ran out of money, all the Egyptians came to Joseph. "Our money is gone!" they cried. "But please give us food, or we will die before your very eyes!" 16Joseph replied, "Since your money is gone, bring me your livestock. I will give you food in exchange for your livestock." 17So they brought their livestock to Joseph in exchange for food. In exchange for their horses, flocks of sheep and goats, herds of cattle, and donkeys, Joseph provided them with food for another year.

The Walk – S.B. Stone & Rock Solid Publishing, LLC
©2018

18But that year ended, and the next year they came again and said, "We cannot hide the truth from you, my lord. Our money is gone, and all our livestock and cattle are yours. We have nothing left to give but our bodies and our land. 19Why should we die before your very eyes? Buy us and our land in exchange for food; we offer our land and ourselves as slaves for Pharaoh. Just give us grain so we may live and not die, and so the land does not become empty and desolate." 20So Joseph bought all the land of Egypt for Pharaoh. All the Egyptians sold him their fields because the famine was so severe, and soon all the land belonged to Pharaoh. 21As for the people, he made them all slaves, 47:21 As in Greek version and Samaritan Pentateuch; Hebrew reads *he moved them all into the towns* from one end of Egypt to the other. 22The only land he did not buy was the land belonging to the priests. They received an allotment of food directly from Pharaoh, so they didn't need to sell their land.

23Then Joseph said to the people, "Look, today I have bought you and your land for Pharaoh. I will provide you with seed so you can plant the fields. 24Then when you harvest it, one-fifth of your crop will belong to Pharaoh. You may keep the remaining four-fifths as seed for your fields and as food for you, your households, and your little ones." 25"You have saved our lives!" they exclaimed. "May it please you, my lord, to let us be Pharaoh's servants." 26Joseph then issued a decree still in effect in the land of Egypt, that Pharaoh should receive one-fifth of all the crops grown on his land. Only the land belonging to the priests was not given to Pharaoh.

27Meanwhile, the people of Israel settled in the region of Goshen in Egypt. There they acquired property, and they were fruitful, and their population grew rapidly. 28Jacob lived for seventeen years after his arrival in Egypt, so he lived 147 years in all. 29As the time of his death drew near, Jacob47:29 Hebrew *Israel;* also in 47:31b. See note on 35:21 called for his son

Joseph and said to him, "Please do me this favor. Put your hand under my thigh and swear that you will treat me with unfailing love by honoring this last request: Do not bury me in

Egypt. 30When I die, please take my body out of Egypt and bury me with my ancestors." So Joseph promised, "I will do as you ask." 31"Swear that you will do it," Jacob insisted. So Joseph

gave his oath, and Jacob bowed humbly at the head of his bed. [2]

The Walk – S.B. Stone & Rock Solid Publishing, LLC
©2018

Genesis - Chapter Forty-Eight

Jacob Blesses Manasseh and Ephraim

1One day not long after this, word came to Joseph, "Your father is failing rapidly." So Joseph went to visit his father, and he took with him his two sons, Manasseh and Ephraim.

2When Joseph arrived, Jacob was told, "Your son Joseph has come to see you." So Jacob48:2 Hebrew *Israel;* also in 48:8, 10, 11, 13, 14, 21. See note on 35:21 gathered his strength and sat up in his bed. 3Jacob said to Joseph, "God Almighty48:3 Hebrew *El-Shaddai* appeared to me at Luz in the land of Canaan and blessed me. 4He said to me, 'I will make you fruitful, and I will multiply your descendants. I will make you a multitude of nations. And I will give this land of Canaan to your descendants48:4 Hebrew *seed;* also in 48:19 after you as an everlasting possession.' 5"Now I am claiming as my own sons these two boys of yours, Ephraim and Manasseh, who were born here in the land of Egypt before I arrived. They will be my sons, just as Reuben and Simeon are. 6But any children born to you in the future will be your own, and they will inherit land within the territories of their brothers Ephraim and Manasseh. 7"Long ago, as I was returning from Paddan-aram, 48:7 Hebrew *Paddan,* referring to Paddan-aram; compare Gen 35:9. Rachel died in the land of Canaan. We were still on the way, some distance from Ephrath (that is, Bethlehem). So with great sorrow I buried her there beside the road to Ephrath." 8Then Jacob looked over at the two boys. "Are these your sons?" he asked. 9"Yes," Joseph told him, "these are the sons God has given me here in Egypt." And Jacob said, "Bring them closer to me, so I can bless them." 10Jacob was half blind because of his age and could hardly see. So Joseph brought the boys close to him, and Jacob kissed and embraced them. 11Then Jacob said to Joseph, "I never thought I would see your face again, but now God has let me see your children, too!" 12Joseph moved the boys, who were at their grandfather's knees, and he bowed with his face to the ground. 13Then he positioned the boys in front of Jacob. With his right hand he directed Ephraim toward Jacob's left hand, and with his left hand he put Manasseh at Jacob's right hand. 14But Jacob crossed his arms as he reached out to lay his hands on the boys' heads. He put his right hand on the head of Ephraim, though he was the younger boy, and his left hand on the head of Manasseh, though he was the firstborn. 15Then he blessed Joseph and said, "May the God before whom my grandfather Abraham and my father, Isaac, walked—the God who has been my shepherd all my life, to this very day, 16the Angel who has redeemed me from all harm—may he bless these boys. May they preserve my name and the names of Abraham and Isaac. And may their descendants multiply greatly throughout the earth." 17But Joseph was upset when he saw that his father placed his right hand on Ephraim's head. So Joseph lifted it to move it from Ephraim's head to Manasseh's head. 18"No, my father," he said. "This one is the firstborn. Put your right hand on his head." 19But his father refused. "I know, my son; I know," he replied. "Manasseh will also become a great people, but his younger brother will become even greater. And his descendants will become a multitude of nations."

20So Jacob blessed the boys that day with this blessing: "The people of Israel will use your names when they give a blessing. They will say, 'May God make you as prosperous as Ephraim and Manasseh.'" In this way, Jacob put Ephraim ahead of Manasseh. 21Then Jacob said to Joseph, "Look, I am about to die, but God will be with you and will take you back to Canaan, the land of your ancestors. 22And beyond what I have given your brothers, I am giving you an extra portion of the land48:22 Or *an extra ridge of land.* The meaning of the Hebrew is uncertain. that I took from the Amorites with my sword and bow." [2]

Genesis - Chapter Forty-Nine

Jacob's Last Words to His Sons

1Then Jacob called together all his sons and said, "Gather around me, and I will tell you what will happen to each of you in the days to come. 2"Come and listen, you sons of Jacob; listen to Israel, your father. 3"Reuben, you are my firstborn, my strength, the child of my vigorous youth. You are first in rank and first in power. 4But you are as unruly as a flood, and you will be first no longer. For you went to bed with my wife; you defiled my marriage couch.

5"Simeon and Levi are two of a kind; their weapons are instruments of violence. 6May I never join in their meetings; may I never be a party to their plans. For in their anger they murdered men, and they crippled oxen just for sport. 7A curse on their anger, for it is fierce; a curse on their wrath, for it is cruel. I will scatter them among the descendants of Jacob; I will disperse them throughout Israel. 8"Judah, your brothers will praise you. You will grasp your enemies by the neck. All your relatives will bow before you. 9Judah, my son, is a young lion that has finished eating its prey. Like a lion he crouches and lies down; like a lioness—who dares to rouse him? 10The scepter will not depart from Judah, nor the ruler's staff from his descendants,49:10a Hebrew *from between his feet* until the coming of the one to whom it belongs,49:10b Or *until tribute is brought to him and the peoples obey;* traditionally rendered *until Shiloh comes* the one whom all nations will honor. 11He ties his foal to a grapevine, the colt of his donkey to a choice vine. He washes his clothes in wine, his robes in the blood of grapes. 12His eyes are darker than wine, and his teeth are whiter than milk. 13"Zebulun will settle by the seashore and will be a harbor for ships; his borders will extend to Sidon. 14"Issachar is a sturdy donkey, resting between two saddle packs.

49:14 Or *sheepfolds,* or *hearths.* 15When he sees how good the countryside is and how pleasant the land, he will bend his shoulder to the load and submit himself to hard labor. 16"Dan will govern his people, like any other tribe in Israel. 17Dan will be a snake beside the road, a poisonous viper along the path that bites the horse's hooves so its rider is thrown off. 18I trust in you for salvation, O Lord! 19"Gad will be attacked by marauding bands, but he will attack them when they retreat. 20"Asher will dine on rich foods and produce food fit for kings. 21"Naphtali is a doe set free that bears beautiful fawns. 22"Joseph is the foal of a wild donkey, the foal of a wild donkey at a spring—one of the wild donkeys on the ridge.49:22 Or *Joseph is a fruitful tree, / a fruitful tree beside a spring. / His branches reach over the wall.* The meaning of the Hebrew is uncertain. 23Archers attacked him savagely; they shot at him and harassed him. 24But his bow remained taut, and his arms were strengthened by the hands of the Mighty One of Jacob, by the Shepherd, the Rock of Israel. 25May the God of your father help you; may the Almighty bless you with the blessings of the heavens above, and blessings of the watery depths below, and blessings of the breasts and womb. 26May my fatherly blessings on you surpass the blessings of my ancestors, 49:26 Or *of the ancient mountains* reaching to the heights of the eternal hills. May these blessings rest on the head of Joseph, who is a prince among his brothers. 27"Benjamin is a ravenous wolf, devouring his enemies in the morning and dividing his plunder in the evening." 28These are the twelve tribes of Israel, and this is what their father said as he told his sons goodbye. He blessed each one with an appropriate message.

Jacob's Death and Burial

29Then Jacob instructed them, "Soon I will die and join my ancestors. Bury me with my father and grandfather in the cave in the field of Ephron the Hittite. 30This is the cave in the field of Machpelah, near Mamre in Canaan, that Abraham bought from Ephron the Hittite as a permanent burial site. 31There Abraham and his wife Sarah are buried. There Isaac and his wife, Rebekah, are buried. And there I buried Leah. 32It is the plot of land and the cave that my grandfather Abraham bought from the Hittites." 33When Jacob had finished this charge to his sons, he drew his feet into the bed, breathed his last, and joined his ancestors in death. [2]

Genesis - Chapter Fifty

1Joseph threw himself on his father and wept over him and kissed him. 2Then Joseph told the physicians who served him to embalm his father's body; so Jacob

50:2 Hebrew *Israel*. See note on 35:21 was embalmed. 3The embalming process took the usual forty days. And the Egyptians mourned his death for seventy days. 4When the period of mourning was over, Joseph approached Pharaoh's advisers and said, "Please do me this favor and speak to Pharaoh on my behalf. 5Tell him that my father made me swear an oath. He said to me, 'Listen, I am about to die. Take my body back to the land of Canaan, and bury me in the tomb I prepared for myself.' So please allow me to go and bury my father. After his burial, I will return without delay."

6Pharaoh agreed to Joseph's request. "Go and bury your father, as he made you promise," he said. 7So Joseph went up to bury his father. He was accompanied by all of

Pharaoh's officials, all the senior members of Pharaoh's household, and all the senior officers of Egypt. 8Joseph also took his entire household and his brothers and their households. But they left their little children and flocks and herds in the land of Goshen. 9A great number of chariots and charioteers accompanied Joseph. 10When they arrived at the threshing floor of Atad, near the Jordan River, they held a very great and solemn memorial service, with a seven-day period of mourning for Joseph's father. 11The local residents, the Canaanites, watched them mourning at the threshing floor of Atad. Then they renamed that place (which is near the Jordan) Abelmizraim, 50:11 *Abel-mizraim* means "mourning of the Egyptians." for they said, "This is a place of deep mourning for these Egyptians." 12So Jacob's sons did as he had

The Walk – S.B. Stone & Rock Solid Publishing, LLC
©2018

commanded them. 13They carried his body to the land of Canaan and buried him in the cave in the field of Machpelah, near Mamre. This is the cave that Abraham had bought as a permanent burial site from Ephron the Hittite.

Joseph Reassures His Brothers

14After burying Jacob, Joseph returned to Egypt with his brothers and all who had accompanied him to his father's burial. 15But now that their father was dead, Joseph's brothers became fearful. "Now Joseph will show his anger and pay us back for all the wrong we did to him," they said. 16So they sent this message to Joseph: "Before your father died, he instructed us 17to say to you: 'Please forgive your brothers for the great wrong they did to you—for their sin in treating you so cruelly.' So we, the servants of the God of your father, beg you to forgive our sin." When Joseph received the message, he broke down and wept. 18Then his brothers came and threw themselves down before Joseph. "Look, we are your slaves!" they said. 19But Joseph replied, "Don't be afraid of me. Am I God, that I can punish you? 20You intended to harm me, but God intended it all for good. He brought me to this position so I could save the lives of many people. 21No, don't be afraid. I will continue to take care of you and your children." So he reassured them by speaking kindly to them.

The Death of Joseph

22So Joseph and his brothers and their families continued to live in Egypt. Joseph lived to the age of 110. 23He lived to see three generations of descendants of his son Ephraim, and he lived to see the birth of the children of Manasseh's son Makir, whom he claimed as his own.50:23 Hebrew *who were born on Joseph's knees.* 24"Soon I will die," Joseph told his brothers, "but God will surely come to help you and lead you out of this land of Egypt. He will bring you back to the land he solemnly promised to give to Abraham, to Isaac, and to Jacob."

25Then Joseph made the sons of Israel swear an oath, and he said, "When God comes to help you and lead you back, you must take my bones with you." 26So Joseph died at the age of 110. The Egyptians embalmed him, and his body was placed in a coffin in Egypt.   [2]

The Book of Exodus

Chapter Three

The Walk – S.B. Stone & Rock Solid Publishing, LLC
©2018

Moses and the Burning Bush

1One day Moses was tending the flock of his father-in-law, Jethro, 3:1a Moses' father-in-law went by two names, Jethro and Reuel the priest of Midian. He led the flock far into the wilderness and came to Sinai, 3:1b Hebrew *Horeb,* another name for Sinai the mountain of

God. 2There the angel of the Lord appeared to him in a blazing fire from the middle of a bush.

Moses stared in amazement. Though the bush was engulfed in flames, it didn't burn up. 3"This is amazing," Moses said to himself. "Why isn't that bush burning up? I must go see it." 4When the Lord saw Moses coming to take a closer look, God called to him from the middle of the bush,

"Moses! Moses!" "Here I am!" Moses replied. 5"Do not come any closer," the Lord warned.

"Take off your sandals, for you are standing on holy ground. 6I am the God of your father

3:6 Greek version reads *your fathers.*—the God of Abraham, the God of Isaac, and the God of Jacob." When Moses heard this, he covered his face because he was afraid to look at God.

7Then the Lord told him, "I have certainly seen the oppression of my people in Egypt. I have heard their cries of distress because of their harsh slave drivers. Yes, I am aware of their suffering. 8So I have come down to rescue them from the power of the Egyptians and lead them out of Egypt into their own fertile and spacious land. It is a land flowing with milk and honey— the land where the Canaanites, Hittites, Amorites, Perizzites, Hivites, and Jebusites now live. 9Look! The cry of the people of Israel has reached me, and I have seen how harshly the Egyptians abuse them. 10Now go, for I am sending you to Pharaoh. You must lead my people Israel out of Egypt." 11But Moses protested to God, "Who am I to appear before Pharaoh? Who am I to lead the people of Israel out of Egypt?" 12God answered, "I will be with you. And this is your sign that I am the one who has sent you: When you have brought the people out of Egypt, you will worship God at this very mountain." 13But Moses protested, "If I go to the people of Israel and tell them, 'The God of your ancestors has sent me to you,' they will ask me, 'What is his name?' Then what should I tell them?" 14God replied to Moses, "I Am Who I Am.3:14 Or *I Will Be What I Will Be.* Say this to the people of Israel: I Am has sent me to you." 15God also said to Moses, "Say this to the people of Israel: Yahweh, 3:15 *Yahweh* (also in 3:16) is a transliteration of the proper name *YHWH* that is sometimes rendered "Jehovah"; in this translation it is usually rendered "the Lord" (note the use of small capitals) the God of your ancestors—the God of Abraham, the God of Isaac, and the God of Jacob—has sent me to you.

This is my eternal name, my name to remember for all generations. 16"Now go and call together all the elders of Israel. Tell them, 'Yahweh, the God of your ancestors—the God of

Abraham, Isaac, and Jacob—has appeared to me. He told me, "I have been watching closely, and I see how the Egyptians are treating you. 17I have promised to rescue you from your oppression in Egypt. I will lead you to a land flowing with milk and honey—the land where the Canaanites,

Hittites, Amorites, Perizzites, Hivites, and Jebusites now live."' 18"The elders of Israel will accept your message. Then you and the elders must go to the king of Egypt and tell him, 'The Lord, the God of the Hebrews, has met with us. So please let us take a three-day journey into the wilderness to offer sacrifices to the Lord, our God.' 19"But I know that the king of Egypt will not let you go unless a mighty hand forces him.3:19 As in Greek and Latin versions;

Hebrew reads *will not let you go, not by a mighty hand.* 20So I will raise my hand and strike the Egyptians, performing all kinds of miracles among them. Then at last he will let you go. 21And I will cause the Egyptians to look favorably on you. They will give you gifts when you go so you will not leave empty-handed. 22Every Israelite woman will ask for articles of silver and gold and fine clothing from her Egyptian neighbors and from the foreign women in their houses. You will dress your sons and daughters with these, stripping the Egyptians of their wealth." [2]

Exodus – Chapter Twenty

Ten Commandments for the Covenant Community

1Then God gave the people all these instructions 20:1 Hebrew *all these words*:

2"I am the Lord your God, who rescued you from the land of Egypt, the place of your slavery.

3"You must not have any other god but me. 4"You must not make for yourself an idol of any kind or an image of anything in the heavens or on the earth or in the sea. 5You must not bow down to them or worship them, for I, the Lord your God, am a jealous God who will not tolerate your affection for any other gods. I lay the sins of the parents upon their children; the entire family is affected—even children in the third and fourth generations of those who reject me. 6But I lavish unfailing love for a thousand generations on those20:6 Hebrew *for thousands of those* who love me and obey my commands. 7"You must not misuse the name of the Lord your God. The Lord will not let you go unpunished if you misuse his name.

8"Remember to observe the Sabbath day by keeping it holy. 9You have six days each week for your ordinary work, 10but the seventh day is a Sabbath day of rest dedicated to

the Lord your God. On that day no one in your household may do any work. This includes you, your sons and daughters, your male and female servants, your livestock, and any foreigners living among you. 11For in six days the Lord made the heavens, the earth, the sea, and everything in them; but on the seventh day he rested. That is why the Lord blessed the Sabbath day and set it apart as holy. 12"Honor your father and mother. Then you will live a long, full life in the land the Lord your God is giving you. 13"You must not murder. 14"You must not commit

adultery. 15"You must not steal. 16"You must not testify falsely against your neighbor. 17"You must not covet your neighbor's house. You must not covet your neighbor's wife, male or female servant, ox or donkey, or anything else that belongs to your neighbor." 18When the people heard the thunder and the loud blast of the ram's horn, and when they saw the flashes of lightning and the smoke billowing from the mountain, they stood at a distance, trembling with fear. 19And they said to Moses, "You speak to us, and we will listen. But don't let God speak directly to us, or we will die!" 20"Don't be afraid," Moses answered them, "for God has come in this way to test you, and so that your fear of him will keep you from sinning!" 21As the people stood in the distance, Moses approached the dark cloud where God was.

The Walk – S.B. Stone & Rock Solid Publishing, LLC
©2018

Proper Use of Altars

22And the Lord said to Moses, "Say this to the people of Israel: You saw for yourselves that I spoke to you from heaven. 23Remember, you must not make any idols of silver or gold to rival me. 24"Build for me an altar made of earth, and offer your sacrifices to me—your burnt offerings and peace offerings, your sheep and goats, and your cattle. Build my altar wherever I cause my name to be remembered, and I will come to you and bless you. 25If you use stones to build my altar, use only natural, uncut stones. Do not shape the stones with a tool, for that would make the altar unfit for holy use. 26And do not approach my altar by going up steps. If you do, someone might look up under your clothing and see your nakedness. [2]

The Book of Leviticus

Chapter Sixteen

The Day of Atonement

1The Lord spoke to Moses after the death of Aaron's two sons, who died after they entered the Lord's presence and burned the wrong kind of fire before him. 2The Lord said to Moses, "Warn your brother, Aaron, not to enter the Most Holy Place behind the inner curtain whenever he chooses; if he does, he will die. For the Ark's cover—the place of atonement—is there, and I myself am present in the cloud above the atonement cover. 3"When Aaron enters the sanctuary area, he must follow these instructions fully. He must bring a young bull for a sin offering and a ram for a burnt offering. 4He must put on his linen tunic and the linen undergarments worn next to his body. He must tie the linen sash around his waist and put the linen turban on his head. These are sacred garments, so he must bathe himself in water before he puts them on. 5Aaron must take from the community of Israel two male goats for a sin offering and a ram for a burnt offering. 6"Aaron will present his own bull as a sin offering to purify himself and his family, making them right with the Lord.16:6 Or *to make atonement for himself and his family;* similarly in 16:11, 17b, 24, 34. 7Then he must take the two male goats and present them to the Lord at the entrance of the Tabernacle.16:7 Hebrew *Tent of Meeting;* also in 16:16, 17, 20, 23, 33. 8He is to cast sacred lots to determine which goat will be reserved as an offering to the Lord and which will carry the sins of the people to the wilderness of Azazel. 9Aaron will then present as a sin offering the goat chosen by lot for the Lord. 10The other goat, the scapegoat chosen by lot to be sent away, will be kept alive, standing before

the Lord. When it is sent away to Azazel in the wilderness, the people will be purified and made right with the Lord.16:10 Or *wilderness, it will make atonement for the people.* 11"Aaron will present his own bull as a sin offering to purify himself and his family, making them right with the Lord. After he has slaughtered the bull as a sin offering, 12he will fill an incense burner with burning coals from the altar that stands before the Lord. Then he will take two handfuls of fragrant powdered incense and will carry the burner and the incense behind the inner curtain. 13There in the Lord's presence he will put the incense on the burning coals so that a cloud of incense will rise over the Ark's cover— the place of atonement—that rests on the Ark of the Covenant.16:13 Hebrew *that is above the Testimony.* The Hebrew word for "testimony" refers to the terms of the Lord's covenant with Israel as written on stone tablets, which were kept in the Ark, and also to the covenant itself. If he follows these instructions, he will not die. 14Then he must take some of the blood of the bull, dip his finger in it, and sprinkle it on the east side of the atonement cover. He must sprinkle blood seven times with his finger in front of the atonement cover. 15"Then Aaron must slaughter the first goat as a sin offering for the people and carry its blood behind the inner curtain. There he will sprinkle the goat's blood over the atonement cover and in front of it, just as he did with the bull's blood. 16Through this process, he will purify16:16 Or *make atonement for;* similarly in 16:17a, 18, 20, 27, 33 the Most Holy Place, and he will do the same for the entire Tabernacle, because of the defiling sin and rebellion of the Israelites. 17No one else is allowed inside the Tabernacle when Aaron enters it for the purification ceremony in the Most Holy Place. No one may enter until he comes out again after purifying himself, his family, and all the congregation of Israel, making them right with the Lord. 18"Then Aaron will come out to purify the altar that stands before the Lord. He will do this by taking some of the blood from the bull and the goat and putting it on each of the horns of the altar. 19Then he must sprinkle the blood with his finger seven times over the altar. In this way, he will cleanse it from Israel's defilement and make it holy. 20"When Aaron has finished purifying the Most Holy Place and the Tabernacle and the altar, he must present the live goat. 21He will lay both of his hands on the goat's head and confess over it all the wickedness, rebellion, and sins of the people of Israel. In this way,

The Walk – S.B. Stone & Rock Solid Publishing, LLC
©2018

he will transfer the people's sins to the head of the goat. Then a man specially chosen for the task will drive the goat into the wilderness. 22As the goat goes into the wilderness, it will carry all the people's sins upon itself into a desolate land. 23"When Aaron goes back into the Tabernacle, he must take off the linen garments he was wearing when he entered the Most Holy Place, and he must leave the garments there. 24Then he must bathe himself with water in a sacred place, put on his regular garments, and go out to sacrifice a burnt offering for himself and a burnt offering for the people. Through this process, he will purify himself and the people, making them right with the Lord. 25He must then burn all the fat of the sin offering on the altar. 26"The man chosen to drive the scapegoat into the wilderness of Azazel must wash his clothes and bathe himself in water. Then he may return to the camp. 27"The bull and the goat presented as sin offerings, whose blood Aaron takes into the Most Holy Place for the purification ceremony, will be carried outside the camp. The animals' hides, internal organs, and dung are all to be burned. 28The man who burns them must wash his clothes and bathe himself in water before returning to the camp. 29"On the tenth day of the appointed month in early autumn, 16:29a Hebrew *On the tenth day of the seventh month.* This day in the ancient Hebrew lunar calendar occurred in September or October you must deny yourselves.16:29b Or *must fast;* also in 16:31. Neither native-born Israelites nor foreigners living among you may do any kind of work. This is a permanent law for you. 30On that day offerings of purification will be made for you, 16:30 Or *atonement will be made for you, to purify you* and you will be purified in the Lord's presence from all your sins. 31It will be a Sabbath day of complete rest for you, and you must deny yourselves. This is a permanent law for you. 32In future generations, the purification16:32 Or *atonement* ceremony will be performed by the priest who has been anointed and ordained to serve as high priest in place of his ancestor Aaron. He will put on the holy linen garments 33and purify the Most Holy Place, the Tabernacle, the altar, the priests, and the entire congregation. 34This is a permanent law for you, to purify the people of Israel from their sins, making them right with the Lord once each year." Moses followed all these instructions exactly as the Lord had commanded him. [2]

The Book of Numbers

Chapter Fourteen

The People Rebel

The Walk – S.B. Stone & Rock Solid Publishing, LLC
©2018

1Then the whole community began weeping aloud, and they cried all night. 2Their voices rose in a great chorus of protest against Moses and Aaron. "If only we had died in Egypt, or even here in the wilderness!" they complained. 3"Why is the Lord taking us to this country only to have us die in battle? Our wives and our little ones will be carried off as plunder! Wouldn't it be better for us to return to Egypt?" 4Then they plotted among themselves, "Let's choose a new leader and go back to Egypt!" 5Then Moses and Aaron fell face down on the ground before the whole community of Israel. 6Two of the men who had explored the land, Joshua son of Nun and Caleb son of Jephunneh, tore their clothing. 7They said to all the people of Israel, "The land we traveled through and explored is a wonderful land! 8And if the Lord is pleased with us, he will bring us safely into that land and give it to us. It is a rich land flowing with milk and honey. 9Do not rebel against the Lord, and don't be afraid of the people of the land. They are only helpless prey to us! They have no protection, but the Lord is with us! Don't be afraid of them!"

10But the whole community began to talk about stoning Joshua and Caleb. Then the glorious presence of the Lord appeared to all the Israelites at the Tabernacle.14:10 Hebrew *the*

Tent of Meeting. 11And the Lord said to Moses, "How long will these people treat me with contempt? Will they never believe me, even after all the miraculous signs I have done among them? 12I will disown them and destroy them with a plague. Then I will make you into a nation greater and mightier than they are!"

Moses Intercedes for the People

13But Moses objected. "What will the Egyptians think when they hear about it?" he asked the Lord. "They know full well the power you displayed in rescuing your people from Egypt. 14Now if you destroy them, the Egyptians will send a report to the inhabitants of this land, who have already heard that you live among your people. They know, Lord, that you have appeared to your people face to face and that your pillar of cloud hovers over them. They know that you go before them in the pillar of cloud by day and the pillar of fire by night. 15Now if you slaughter all these people with a single blow, the nations that have heard of your fame will say, 16'The Lord was not able to bring them into the land he swore to give them, so he killed them in the wilderness.' 17"Please, Lord, prove that your power is as great as you have claimed.

For you said, 18'The Lord is slow to anger and filled with unfailing love, forgiving every kind of sin and rebellion. But he does not excuse the guilty. He lays the sins of the parents upon their children; the entire family is affected—even children in the third and fourth generations.' 19In keeping with your magnificent, unfailing love, please pardon the sins of this people, just as you have forgiven them ever since they left Egypt." 20Then the Lord said, "I will pardon them as you have requested. 21But as surely as I live, and as surely as the earth is filled with the Lord's glory, 22not one of these people will ever enter that land. They have all seen my glorious presence and the miraculous signs I performed both in Egypt and in the wilderness, but again and again they have tested me by refusing to listen to my voice. 23They will never even see the land I swore to give their ancestors. None of those who have treated me with contempt will ever see it. 24But my servant Caleb has a different attitude than the others have. He has remained loyal to me, so I will bring him into the land he explored. His descendants will possess their full share of that land. 25Now turn around, and don't go on toward the land where the Amalekites and Canaanites live. Tomorrow you must set out for the wilderness in the direction of the Red

Sea.14:25 Hebrew *sea of reeds*."

The Lord Punishes the Israelites

26Then the Lord said to Moses and Aaron, 27"How long must I put up with this wicked community and its complaints about me? Yes, I have heard the complaints the Israelites are making against me. 28Now tell them this: 'As surely as I live, declares the Lord, I will do to you the very things I heard you say. 29You will all drop dead in this wilderness! Because you complained against me, every one of you who is twenty years old or older and was included in the registration will die. 30You will not enter and occupy the land I swore to give you. The only exceptions will be Caleb son of Jephunneh and Joshua son of Nun. 31"'You said your children would be carried off as plunder. Well, I will bring them safely into the land, and they will enjoy what you have despised. 32But as for you, you will drop dead in this wilderness. 33And your children will be like shepherds, wandering in the wilderness for forty years. In this way, they will pay for your faithlessness, until the last of you lies dead in the wilderness. 34"'Because your men explored the land for forty days, you must wander in the wilderness for forty years—a year for each day, suffering the consequences of your sins. Then you will discover what it is like to have me for an enemy.' 35I, the Lord, have spoken! I will certainly do these things to every member of the community who has conspired against me. They will be destroyed here in this wilderness, and here they will die!" 36The ten men Moses had sent to explore the land—the ones who incited rebellion against the Lord with their bad report—37were struck dead with a plague before the Lord. 38Of the twelve who had explored the land, only Joshua and Caleb remained alive.

39When Moses reported the Lord's words to all the Israelites, the people were filled with grief. 40Then they got up early the next morning and went to the top of the range of hills. "Let's go," they said. "We realize that we have sinned, but now we are ready to enter the land the Lord has promised us." 41But Moses said, "Why are you now disobeying the Lord's orders to return to the wilderness? It won't work. 42Do not go up into the land now. You will only be crushed by your enemies because the Lord is not with you. 43When you face the Amalekites and Canaanites in battle, you will be slaughtered. The Lord will abandon you because you have abandoned the Lord." 44But the people defiantly pushed ahead toward the hill country, even though neither Moses nor the Ark of the Lord's Covenant left the camp. 45Then the Amalekites and the Canaanites who lived in those hills came down and attacked them and chased them back as far as Hormah.   [2]

Numbers Twenty-five

Moab Seduces Israel

1While the Israelites were camped at Acacia Grove,25:1a Hebrew *Shittim* some of the men defiled themselves by having25:1b As in Greek version; Hebrew reads *some of the men began having* sexual relations with local Moabite women. 2These women invited them to attend sacrifices to their gods, so the Israelites feasted with them and worshiped the gods of Moab. 3In this way, Israel joined in the worship of Baal of Peor, causing the Lord's anger to blaze against his people. 4The Lord issued the following command to Moses: "Seize all the ringleaders and execute them before the Lord in broad daylight, so his fierce anger will turn away from the people of Israel." 5So Moses ordered Israel's judges, "Each of you must put to death the men under your authority who have joined in worshiping Baal of Peor." 6Just then one of the Israelite men brought a Midianite woman into his tent, right before the eyes of Moses and all the people, as everyone was weeping at the entrance of the Tabernacle.25:6 Hebrew *the Tent of Meeting.* 7When Phinehas son of

Eleazar and grandson of Aaron the priest saw this, he jumped up and left the assembly. He took a spear 8and rushed after the man into his tent. Phinehas thrust the spear all the way through the man's body and into the woman's stomach. So the plague against the Israelites was stopped, 9but not before 24,000 people had died. 10Then the Lord said to Moses, 11"Phinehas son of Eleazar and grandson of Aaron the priest has turned my anger away from the Israelites by being as zealous among them as I was. So I stopped destroying all Israel as I had intended to do in my zealous anger. 12Now tell him that I am making my special covenant of peace with him. 13In this covenant, I give him and his descendants a permanent right to the priesthood, for in his zeal for me, his God, he purified the people of Israel, making them right with me.25:13 Or *he made atonement for the people of Israel*." 14The Israelite man killed with the Midianite woman was named Zimri son of Salu, the leader of a family from the tribe of Simeon. 15The woman's name was Cozbi; she was the daughter of Zur, the leader of a Midianite clan. 16Then the Lord said to Moses, 17"Attack the Midianites and destroy them, 18because they assaulted you with deceit and tricked you into worshiping Baal of Peor, and because of Cozbi, the daughter of a Midianite leader, who was killed at the time of the plague because of what happened at Peor."   [2]

The Book of Deuteronomy

Chapter Six

A Call for Wholehearted Commitment

1"These are the commands, decrees, and regulations that the Lord your God commanded me to teach you. You must obey them in the land you are about to enter and occupy, 2and you and your children and grandchildren must fear the Lord your God as long as you live. If you obey all his decrees and commands, you will enjoy a long life. 3Listen closely, Israel, and be careful to obey. Then all will go well with you, and you will have many children in the land flowing with milk and honey, just as the Lord, the God of your ancestors, promised you. 4"Listen, O Israel! The Lord is our God, the Lord alone.6:4 Or *The Lord our God is one Lord;* or *The Lord our God, the Lord is one;* or *The Lord is our God, the Lord is one.* 5And you must love the Lord your God with all your heart, all your soul, and all your strength. 6And you must commit yourselves wholeheartedly to these commands that I am giving you today. 7Repeat them again and again to your children. Talk about them when you are at home and when you are on the road, when you are going to bed and when you are getting up. 8Tie them to your hands and wear them on your forehead as reminders. 9Write them on the doorposts of your house and on your gates.

10"The Lord your God will soon bring you into the land he swore to give you when he made a vow to your ancestors Abraham, Isaac, and Jacob. It is a land with large, prosperous cities that you did not build. 11The houses will be richly stocked with goods you did not produce. You will draw water from cisterns you did not dig, and you will eat from vineyards and olive trees you did not plant. When you have eaten your fill in this land, 12be careful not to forget the Lord, who rescued you from slavery in the land of Egypt. 13You must fear the Lord your God and serve him. When you take an oath, you must use only his name. 14"You must not worship any of the gods of neighboring nations, 15for the Lord your God, who lives among you, is a jealous God. His anger will flare up against you, and he will wipe you from the face of the earth. 16You must not test the Lord your God as you did when you complained at Massah. 17You must diligently obey the commands of the Lord your God—all the laws and decrees he has given you. 18Do what is right and good in the Lord's sight, so all will go well with you. Then you will enter and occupy the good land that the Lord swore to give your ancestors. 19You will drive out all the enemies living in the land, just as the Lord said you would. 20"In the future your children will ask you, 'What is the meaning of these laws, decrees, and regulations that the Lord our God has commanded us to obey?' 21"Then you must tell them, 'We were Pharaoh's slaves in Egypt, but the Lord brought us out of Egypt with his strong hand. 22The Lord did miraculous signs and wonders before our eyes, dealing terrifying blows against Egypt and Pharaoh and all his people. 23He brought us out of Egypt so he could give us this land he had sworn to give our ancestors. 24And the Lord our God commanded us to obey all these decrees and to fear him so he can continue to bless us and preserve our lives, as he has done to this day. 25For we will be counted as righteous when we obey all the commands the Lord our God has given us.' [2]

Deuteronomy

Chapter Thirteen

A Warning against Idolatry

113:1 Verses 13:1-18 are numbered 13:2-19 in Hebrew text. "Suppose there are prophets among you or those who dream dreams about the future, and they promise you signs or miracles, 2and the predicted signs or miracles occur. If they then say, 'Come, let us worship other gods'—gods you have not known before—3do not listen to them. The Lord your God is testing you to see if you truly love him with all your heart and soul. 4Serve only the Lord your God and fear him alone. Obey his commands, listen to his voice, and cling to him. 5The false prophets or visionaries who try to lead you astray must be put to death, for they encourage rebellion against the Lord your God, who redeemed you from slavery and brought you out of the land of Egypt. Since they try to lead you astray from the way the Lord your God commanded you to live, you must put them to death. In this way you will purge the evil from among you. 6"Suppose someone secretly entices you—even your brother, your son or daughter, your beloved wife, or your closest friend—and says, 'Let us go worship other gods'—gods that neither you nor your ancestors have known. 7They might suggest that you worship the gods of peoples who live nearby or who come from the ends of the earth. 8But do not give in or listen. Have no pity, and do not spare or protect them. 9You must put them to death! Strike the first blow yourself, and then all the people must join in. 10Stone the guilty ones to death because they have tried to draw you away from the Lord your God, who rescued you from the land of Egypt, the place of slavery. 11Then all Israel will hear about it and be afraid, and no one will act so wickedly again. 12"When you begin living in the towns the Lord your God is giving you, you may hear 13that scoundrels among you are leading their fellow citizens astray by saying, 'Let us go worship other gods'—gods you have not known before. 14In such cases, you must examine the facts carefully. If you find that the report is true and such a detestable act has been committed among you, 15you must attack that town and completely destroy13:15 The Hebrew term used here refers to the complete consecration of things or people to the Lord, either by destroying them or by giving them as an offering; similarly in 13:17 all its inhabitants, as well as all the livestock. 16Then you must pile all the plunder in the middle of the open square and burn it. Burn the entire town as a burnt offering to the Lord your God. That town must remain a ruin forever; it may never be rebuilt. 17Keep none of the plunder that has been set apart for destruction. Then the Lord will turn from his fierce anger and be merciful to you. He will have compassion on you and make you a large nation, just as he swore to your ancestors. 18"The Lord your God will be merciful only if you listen to his voice and keep all his commands that I am giving you today, doing what pleases him. [2]

The Book of Joshua

Chapter Twenty-three

Joshua's Final Words to Israel

1The years passed, and the Lord had given the people of Israel rest from all their enemies. Joshua, who was now very old, 2called together all the elders, leaders, judges, and officers of Israel. He said to them, "I am now a very old man. 3You have seen everything the Lord your God has done for you during my lifetime. The Lord your God has fought for you against your enemies. 4I have allotted to you as your homeland all the land of the nations yet unconquered, as well as the land of those we have already conquered—from the Jordan River to the Mediterranean Sea23:4 Hebrew *the Great Sea* in the west. 5This land will be yours, for the Lord your God will himself drive out all the people living there now. You will take possession of their land, just as the Lord your God promised you. 6"So be very careful to follow everything Moses wrote in the Book of Instruction. Do not deviate from it, turning either to the right or to the left. 7Make sure you do not associate with the other people still remaining in the land. Do not even mention the names of their gods, much less swear by them or serve them or worship them. 8Rather, cling tightly to the Lord your God as you have done until now.

9"For the Lord has driven out great and powerful nations for you, and no one has yet been able to defeat you. 10Each one of you will put to flight a thousand of the enemy, for the Lord your God fights for you, just as he has promised. 11So be very careful to love the Lord your God.

12"But if you turn away from him and cling to the customs of the survivors of these nations remaining among you, and if you intermarry with them, 13then know for certain that the Lord your God will no longer drive them out of your land. Instead, they will be a snare and a trap to you, a whip for your backs and thorny brambles in your eyes, and you will vanish from this good land the Lord your God has given you. 14"Soon I will die, going the way of everything on earth. Deep in your hearts you know that every promise of the Lord your God has come true. Not a single one has failed! 15But as surely as the Lord your God has given you the good things he promised, he will also bring disaster on you if you disobey him. He will completely destroy you from this good land he has given you. 16If you break the covenant of the Lord your God by worshiping and serving other gods, his anger will burn against you,

and you will quickly vanish from the good land he has given you."
[2]p

The Book of First Samuel

Chapter Seventeen

Goliath Challenges the Israelites

1The Philistines now mustered their army for battle and camped between Socoh in Judah and Azekah at Ephes-dammim. 2Saul countered by gathering his Israelite troops near the valley of Elah. 3So the Philistines and Israelites faced each other on opposite hills, with the valley between them. 4Then Goliath, a Philistine champion from Gath, came out of the Philistine ranks to face the forces of Israel. He was over nine feet17:4 Hebrew *6 cubits and 1 span* [which totals about 9.75 feet or 3 meters]; Dead Sea Scrolls and Greek version read *4 cubits and 1 span* [which totals about 6.75 feet or 2 meters] tall! 5He wore a bronze helmet, and his bronze coat of mail weighed 125 pounds.17:5 Hebrew *5,000 shekels* [57 kilograms]. 6He also wore bronze leg armor, and he carried a bronze javelin on his shoulder. 7The shaft of his spear was as heavy and thick as a weaver's beam, tipped with an iron spearhead that weighed 15 pounds.17:7 Hebrew *600 shekels* [6.8 kilograms]. His armor bearer walked ahead of him carrying a shield. 8Goliath stood and shouted a taunt across to the Israelites. "Why are you all coming out to fight?" he called. "I am the Philistine champion, but you are only the servants of Saul. Choose one man to come down here and fight me! 9If he kills me, then we will be your slaves. But if I kill him, you will be our slaves! 10I defy the armies of Israel today! Send me a man who will fight me!" 11When Saul and the Israelites heard this, they were terrified and deeply shaken.

Jesse Sends David to Saul's Camp

12Now David was the son of a man named Jesse, an Ephrathite from Bethlehem in the land of Judah. Jesse was an old man at that time, and he had eight sons. 13Jesse's three oldest sons—Eliab, Abinadab, and Shimea17:13 Hebrew *Shammah,* a variant spelling of Shimea; compare 1 Chr 2:13; 20:7.—had already joined Saul's army to fight the Philistines. 14David was the youngest son. David's three oldest brothers stayed with Saul's army, 15but David went back and forth so he could help his father with the sheep in Bethlehem. 16For forty days, every morning and evening, the Philistine champion strutted in front of the Israelite army. 17One day

Jesse said to David, "Take this basket17:17 Hebrew *ephah* [20 quarts or 22 liters]. of roasted grain and these ten loaves of bread, and carry them quickly to your brothers. 18And give these ten cuts of cheese to their captain. See how your brothers are getting along, and bring back a report on how they are doing.17:18 Hebrew *and take their pledge*." 19David's brothers were with Saul and the Israelite army at the valley of Elah, fighting against the Philistines. 20So David left the sheep with another shepherd and set out early the next morning with the gifts, as Jesse had directed him. He arrived at the camp just as the Israelite army was leaving for the battlefield with shouts and battle cries. 21Soon the Israelite and Philistine forces stood facing each other, army against army. 22David left his things with the keeper of supplies and hurried out to the ranks to greet his brothers. 23As he was talking with them, Goliath, the Philistine champion from Gath, came out from the Philistine ranks. Then David heard him shout his usual taunt to the army of Israel.

24As soon as the Israelite army saw him, they began to run away in fright. 25"Have you seen the giant?" the men asked. "He comes out each day to defy Israel. The king has offered a huge reward to anyone who kills him. He will give that man one of his daughters for a wife, and the man's entire family will be exempted from paying taxes!" 26David asked the soldiers standing nearby, "What will a man get for killing this Philistine and ending his defiance of Israel? Who is this pagan Philistine anyway, that he is allowed to defy the armies of the living God?"

27And these men gave David the same reply. They said, "Yes, that is the reward for killing him." 28But when David's oldest brother, Eliab, heard David talking to the men, he was angry. "What are you doing around here anyway?" he demanded. "What about those few sheep you're supposed to be taking care of? I know about your pride and deceit. You just want to see the battle!" 29"What have I done now?" David replied. "I was only asking a question!" 30He walked over to some others and asked them the same thing and received the same answer. 31Then David's question was reported to King Saul, and the king sent for him.

David Kills Goliath

32"Don't worry about this Philistine," David told Saul. "I'll go fight him!"

The Walk – S.B. Stone & Rock Solid Publishing, LLC
©2018

33"Don't be ridiculous!" Saul replied. "There's no way you can fight this Philistine and possibly win! You're only a boy, and he's been a man of war since his youth." 34But David persisted. "I have been taking care of my father's sheep and goats," he said. "When a lion or a bear comes to steal a lamb from the flock, 35I go after it with a club and rescue the lamb from its mouth. If the animal turns on me, I catch it by the jaw and club it to death. 36I have done this to both lions and bears, and I'll do it to this pagan Philistine, too, for he has defied the armies of the living God! 37The Lord who rescued me from the claws of the lion and the bear will rescue me from this Philistine!" Saul finally consented. "All right, go ahead," he said. "And may the Lord be with you!" 38Then Saul gave David his own armor—a bronze helmet and a coat of mail. 39David put it on, strapped the sword over it, and took a step or two to see what it was like, for he had never worn such things before. "I can't go in these," he protested to Saul. "I'm not used to them." So David took them off again. 40He picked up five smooth stones from a stream and put them into his shepherd's bag. Then, armed only with his shepherd's staff and sling, he started across the valley to fight the Philistine. 41Goliath walked out toward David with his shield bearer ahead of him, 42sneering in contempt at this ruddy-faced boy. 43"Am I a dog," he roared at David, "that you come at me with a stick?" And he cursed David by the names of his gods. 44"Come over here, and I'll give your flesh to the birds and wild animals!" Goliath yelled.

45David replied to the Philistine, "You come to me with sword, spear, and javelin, but I come to you in the name of the Lord of Heaven's Armies—the God of the armies of Israel, whom you have defied. 46Today the Lord will conquer you, and I will kill you and cut off your head. And then I will give the dead bodies of your men to the birds and wild animals, and the whole world will know that there is a God in Israel! 47And everyone assembled here will know that the Lord rescues his people, but not with sword and spear. This is the Lord's battle, and he will give you to us!" 48As Goliath moved closer to attack, David quickly ran out to meet him. 49Reaching into his shepherd's bag and taking out a stone, he hurled it with his sling and hit the Philistine in the forehead. The stone sank in, and Goliath stumbled and fell face down on the ground. 50So David triumphed over the Philistine with only a sling and a stone, for he had no sword. 51Then David ran over and pulled Goliath's sword from its sheath. David used it to kill him and cut off his head.

Israel Routs the Philistines

When the Philistines saw that their champion was dead, they turned and ran. 52Then the men of Israel and Judah gave a great shout of triumph and rushed after the Philistines, chasing them as far as Gath17:52 As in some Greek manuscripts; Hebrew reads *a valley* and the gates of

Ekron. The bodies of the dead and wounded Philistines were strewn all along the road from Shaaraim, as far as Gath and Ekron. 53Then the Israelite army returned and plundered the deserted Philistine camp. 54(David took the Philistine's head to Jerusalem, but he stored the man's armor in his own tent.) 55As Saul watppched David go out to fight the Philistine, he asked

Abner, the commander of his army, "Abner, whose son is this young man?" "I really don't know," Abner declared. 56"Well, find out who he is!" the king told him. 57As soon as David returned from killing Goliath, Abner brought him to Saul with the Philistine's head still in his hand. 58"Tell me about your father, young man," Saul said. And David replied, "His name is Jesse, and we live in Bethlehem." [4]

The Book of Second Samuel

Chapter Five

David Becomes King of All Israel

1Then all the tribes of Israel went to David at Hebron and told him, "We are your own flesh and blood. 2In the past,5:2 Or *For some time* when Saul was our king, you were the one who really led the forces of Israel. And the Lord told you, 'You will be the shepherd of my people Israel. You will be Israel's leader.'" 3So there at Hebron, King David made a covenant before the Lord with all the elders of Israel. And they anointed him king of Israel. 4David was thirty years old when he began to reign, and he reigned forty years in all. 5He had reigned over Judah from Hebron for seven years and six months, and from Jerusalem he reigned over all Israel and Judah for thirty-three years.

David Captures Jerusalem

6David then led his men to Jerusalem to fight against the Jebusites, the original inhabitants of the land who were living there. The Jebusites taunted David, saying, "You'll never get in here! Even the blind and lame could keep you out!" For the Jebusites thought they were safe.

7But David captured the fortress of Zion, which is now called the City of David. 8On the day of the attack, David said to his troops, "I hate those 'lame' and 'blind' Jebusites.5:8a Or *Those 'lame' and 'blind' Jebusites hate me.* Whoever attacks them should strike by going into the city through the water tunnel.5:8b Or *with scaling hooks.* The meaning of the Hebrew is uncertain." That is the origin of the saying, "The blind and the lame may not enter the house."5:8c The meaning of this saying is uncertain. 9So David made the fortress his home, and he called it the City of David. He extended the city, starting at the supporting terraces5:9 Hebrew *the millo.* The meaning of the Hebrew is uncertain and working inward. 10And David became more and more powerful, because the Lord God of Heaven's Armies was with him. 11Then King Hiram of Tyre sent messengers to David, along with cedar timber and carpenters and stonemasons, and they built David a palace. 12And David realized that the Lord had confirmed him as king over Israel and had blessed his kingdom for the sake of his people Israel. 13After moving from Hebron to Jerusalem, David married more concubines and wives, and they had more sons and daughters. 14These are the names of David's sons who were born in Jerusalem: Shammua, Shobab, Nathan, Solomon, 15Ibhar, Elishua, Nepheg, Japhia, 16Elishama, Eliada, and Eliphelet.

David Conquers the Philistines

17When the Philistines heard that David had been anointed king of Israel, they mobilized all their forces to capture him. But David was told they were coming, so he went into the stronghold. 18The Philistines arrived and spread out across the valley of Rephaim. 19So David asked the Lord, "Should I go out to fight the Philistines? Will you hand them over to me?"

The Lord replied to David, "Yes, go ahead. I will certainly hand them over to you."

20So David went to Baal-perazim and defeated the Philistines there. "The Lord did it!" David exclaimed. "He burst through my enemies like a raging flood!" So he named that place Baal-perazim (which means "the Lord who bursts through"). 21The Philistines had abandoned their idols there, so David and his men confiscated them. 22But after a while the Philistines returned and again spread out across the valley of Rephaim. 23And again David asked the Lord what to do. "Do not attack them straight on," the Lord replied. "Instead, circle around behind and attack them near the poplar5:23 Or *aspen,* or *balsam;* also in 5:24. The exact identification of this tree is uncertain. trees. 24When you hear a sound like marching feet in the tops of the poplar trees, be on the alert! That will be the signal that the Lord is moving ahead of you to strike down the Philistine army." 25So David did what the Lord commanded, and he struck down the Philistines all the way from Gibeon5:25 As in Greek version (see also 1 Chr

14:16); Hebrew reads *Geba.* to Gezer. [4]

Book of First Kings

Chapter Three

Solomon Asks for Wisdom

1Solomon made an alliance with Pharaoh, the king of Egypt, and married one of his daughters. He brought her to live in the City of David until he could finish building his palace and the Temple of the Lord and the wall around the city. 2At that time the people of Israel sacrificed their offerings at local places of worship, for a temple honoring the name of the Lord had not yet been built. 3Solomon loved the Lord and followed all the decrees of his father, David, except that Solomon, too, offered sacrifices and burned incense at the local places of worship. 4The most important of these places of worship was at Gibeon, so the king went there and sacrificed 1,000 burnt offerings. 5That night the Lord appeared to Solomon in a dream, and God said, "What do you want? Ask, and I will give it to you!" 6Solomon replied, "You showed great and faithful love to your servant my father, David, because he was honest and true and faithful to you. And you have continued to show this great and faithful love to him today by giving him a son to sit on his throne. 7"Now, O Lord my God, you have made me king instead of my father, David, but I am like a little child who doesn't know his way around. 8And here I am in the midst of your own chosen people, a nation so great and numerous they cannot be counted! 9Give me an understanding heart so that I can govern your people well and know the difference between right and wrong. For who by himself is able to govern this great people of yours?" 10The Lord was pleased that Solomon had asked for wisdom. 11So God replied, "Because you have asked for wisdom in governing my people with justice and have not asked for a long life or wealth or the death of your enemies—12I will give you what you asked for! I will give you a wise and understanding heart such as no one else has had or ever will have! 13And I will also give you what you did not ask for—riches and fame! No other king in all the world will be compared to you for the rest of your life! 14And if you follow me and obey my decrees and my commands as your father, David, did, I will give you a long life." 15Then Solomon woke up and realized it had been a dream. He returned to Jerusalem and stood before the Ark of the Lord's Covenant, where he sacrificed burnt offerings and peace offerings. Then he invited all his officials to a great banquet.

Solomon Judges Wisely

16Some time later two prostitutes came to the king to have an argument settled. 17"Please, my lord," one of them began, "this woman and I live in the same house. I gave birth to a baby while she was with me in the house. 18Three days later this woman also had a baby. We were alone; there were only two of us in the house. 19"But her baby died during the night when she rolled over on it. 20Then she got up in the night and took my son from beside me while I was asleep. She laid her dead child in my arms and took mine to sleep beside her. 21And in the morning when I tried to nurse my son, he was dead! But when I looked more closely in the morning light, I saw that it wasn't my son at all." 22Then the other woman interrupted, "It certainly was your son, and the living child is mine." "No," the first woman said, "the living child is mine, and the dead one is yours." And so they argued back and forth before the king. 23Then the king said, "Let's get the facts straight. Both of you claim the living child is yours, and each says that the dead one belongs to the other. 24All right, bring me a sword." So a sword was brought to the king. 25Then he said, "Cut the living child in two, and give half to one woman and half to the other!" 26Then the woman who was the real mother of the living child, and who loved him very much, cried out, "Oh no, my lord! Give her the child—please do not kill him!" But the other woman said, "All right, he will be neither yours nor mine; divide him between us!" 7Then the king said, "Do not kill the child, but give him to the woman who wants him to live, for she is his mother!" 28When all Israel heard the king's decision, the people were in awe of the king, for they saw the wisdom God had given him for rendering justice. [4]

First Kings

Chapter Ten

Visit of the Queen of Sheba

The Walk – S.B. Stone & Rock Solid Publishing, LLC
©2018

1When the queen of Sheba heard of Solomon's fame, which brought honor to the name of the Lord,10:1 Or *which was due to the name of the Lord.* The meaning of the Hebrew is uncertain she came to test him with hard questions. 2She arrived in Jerusalem with a large group of attendants and a great caravan of camels loaded with spices, large quantities of gold, and precious jewels. When she met with Solomon, she talked with him about everything she had on her mind. 3Solomon had answers for all her questions; nothing was too hard for the king to explain to her. 4When the queen of Sheba realized how very wise Solomon was, and when she saw the palace he had built, 5she was overwhelmed. She was also amazed at the food on his tables, the organization of his officials and their splendid clothing, the cup-bearers, and the burnt offerings Solomon made at the Temple of the Lord. 6She exclaimed to the king, "Everything I heard in my country about your achievements10:6 Hebrew *your words* and wisdom is true! 7I didn't believe what was said until I arrived here and saw it with my own eyes. In fact, I had not heard the half of it! Your wisdom and prosperity are far beyond what I was told. 8How happy your people10:8 Greek and Syriac versions and Latin Vulgate read *your wives* must be! What a privilege for your officials to stand here day after day, listening to your wisdom! 9Praise the Lord your God, who delights in you and has placed you on the throne of Israel. Because of the Lord's eternal love for Israel, he has made you king so you can rule with justice and righteousness." 10Then she gave the king a gift of 9,000 pounds10:10 Hebrew *120 talents* [4,000 kilograms] of gold, great quantities of spices, and precious jewels. Never again were so many spices brought in as those the queen of Sheba gave to King Solomon. 11(In addition, Hiram's ships brought gold from Ophir, and they also brought rich cargoes of red sandalwood10:11 Hebrew *almug wood;* also in 10:12. and precious jewels. 12The king used the sandalwood to make railings for the Temple of the Lord and the royal palace, and to construct lyres and harps for the musicians. Never before or since has there been such a supply of sandalwood.) 13King Solomon gave the queen of Sheba whatever she asked for, besides all the customary gifts he had so generously given. Then she and all her attendants returned to their own land.

Solomon's Wealth and Splendor

14Each year Solomon received about 25 tons10:14 Hebrew *666 talents* [23 metric tons] of gold. 15This did not include the additional revenue he received from merchants and traders, all the kings of Arabia, and the governors of the land. 16King Solomon made 200 large shields of hammered gold, each weighing more than fifteen pounds.10:16 Hebrew *600 [shekels] of gold* [6.8 kilograms]. 17He also made 300 smaller shields of hammered gold, each weighing nearly four pounds.10:17 Hebrew *3 minas* [1.8 kilograms]. The king placed these shields in the Palace of the Forest of Lebanon. 18Then the king made a huge throne, decorated with ivory and overlaid with fine gold. 19The throne had six steps and a rounded back. There were armrests on both sides of the seat, and the figure of a lion stood on each side of the throne. 20There were also twelve other lions, one standing on each end of the six steps. No other throne in all the world could be compared with it! 21All of King Solomon's drinking cups were solid gold, as were all the utensils in the Palace of the Forest of Lebanon. They were not made of silver, for silver was considered worthless in Solomon's day! 22The king had a fleet of trading ships of Tarshish that sailed with Hiram's fleet. Once every three years the ships returned, loaded with gold, silver, ivory, apes, and peacocks.10:22 Or *and baboons.* 23So King Solomon became richer and wiser than any other king on earth. 24People from every nation came to consult him and to hear the wisdom God had given him. 25Year after year everyone who visited brought him gifts of silver and gold, clothing, weapons, spices, horses, and mules. 26Solomon built up a huge force of chariots and horses.10:26 Or *charioteers;* also in 10:26b. He had 1,400 chariots and 12,000 horses. He stationed some of them in the chariot cities and some near him in Jerusalem. 27The king made silver as plentiful in Jerusalem as stone. And valuable cedar timber was as common as the sycamore-fig trees that grow in the foothills of Judah.10:27 Hebrew *the*

Shephelah. 28Solomon's horses were imported from Egypt10:28a Possibly *Muzur,* a district near Cilicia; also in 10:29 and from Cilicia10:28b Hebrew *Kue,* probably another name for Cilicia.; the king's traders acquired them from Cilicia at the standard price. 29At that time chariots from

Egypt could be purchased for 600 pieces of silver, 10:29a Hebrew *600 [shekels] of silver,* about

15 pounds or 6.8 kilograms in weight and horses for 150 pieces of silver.10:29b Hebrew *150 [shekels],* about 3.8 pounds or 1.7 kilograms in weight. They were then exported to the kings of the Hittites and the kings of Aram.   [4]

First Kings

Chapter Eleven

Solomon's Many Wives

1Now King Solomon loved many foreign women. Besides Pharaoh's daughter, he married women from Moab, Ammon, Edom, Sidon, and from among the Hittites. 2The Lord had clearly instructed the people of Israel, "You must not marry them, because they will turn your hearts to their gods." Yet Solomon insisted on loving them anyway. 3He had 700 wives of royal birth and 300 concubines. And in fact, they did turn his heart away from the Lord. 4In Solomon's old age, they turned his heart to worship other gods instead of being completely faithful to the Lord his God, as his father, David, had been. 5Solomon worshiped Ashtoreth, the goddess of the Sidonians, and Molech,11:5 Hebrew *Milcom,* a variant spelling of Molech; also in 11:33 the detestable god of the Ammonites. 6In this way, Solomon did what was evil in the Lord's sight; he refused to follow the Lord completely, as his father, David, had done. 7On the Mount of Olives, east of Jerusalem,11:7 Hebrew *On the mountain east of Jerusalem* he even built a pagan shrine for Chemosh, the detestable god of Moab, and another for Molech, the detestable god of the Ammonites. 8Solomon built such shrines for all his foreign wives to use for burning incense and sacrificing to their gods. 9The Lord was very angry with Solomon, for his heart had turned away from the Lord, the God of Israel, who had appeared to him twice. 10He had warned Solomon specifically about worshiping other gods, but Solomon did not listen to the Lord's command. 11So now the Lord said to him, "Since you have not kept my covenant and have disobeyed my decrees, I will surely tear the kingdom away from you and give it to one of your servants. 12But for the sake of your father, David, I will not do this while you are still alive. I will take the kingdom away from your son. 13And even so, I will not take away the entire kingdom; I will let him be king of one tribe, for the sake of my servant David and for the sake of

Jerusalem, my chosen city."

Solomon's Adversaries

14Then the Lord raised up Hadad the Edomite, a member of Edom's royal family, to be Solomon's adversary. 15Years before, David had defeated Edom. Joab, his army commander, had stayed to bury some of the Israelite soldiers who had died in battle. While there, they killed every male in Edom. 16Joab and the army of Israel had stayed there for six months, killing them.

17But Hadad and a few of his father's royal officials escaped and headed for Egypt. (Hadad was just a boy at the time.) 18They set out from Midian and went to Paran, where others joined them. Then they traveled to Egypt and went to Pharaoh, who gave them a home, food, and some land. 19Pharaoh grew very fond of Hadad, and he gave him his wife's sister in marriage— the sister of Quee\n Tahpenes. 20She bore him a son named Genubath. Tahpenes raised him11:20 As in Greek version; Hebrew reads *weaned him* in Pharaoh's palace among Pharaoh's own sons.

21When the news reached Hadad in Egypt that David and his commander Joab were both dead, he said to Pharaoh, "Let me return to my own country." 22"Why?" Pharaoh asked him. "What do you lack here that makes you want to go home?" "Nothing," he replied. "But even so, please let me return home." 23God also raised up Rezon son of Eliada as Solomon's adversary. Rezon had fled from his master, King Hadadezer of Zobah, 24and had become the leader of a gang of rebels. After David conquered Hadadezer, Rezon and his men fled to Damascus, where he became king. 25Rezon was Israel's bitter adversary for the rest of Solomon's reign, and he made trouble, just as Hadad did. Rezon hated Israel intensely and continued to reign in Aram.

Jeroboam Rebels against Solomon

26Another rebel leader was Jeroboam son of Nebat, one of Solomon's own officials. He came from the town of Zeredah in Ephraim, and his mother was Zeruah, a widow. 27This is the story behind his rebellion. Solomon was rebuilding the supporting terraces11:27 Hebrew *the millo.* The meaning of the Hebrew is uncertain and repairing the walls of the city of his father, David. 28Jeroboam was a very capable young man, and when Solomon saw how industrious he was, he put him in charge of the labor force from the tribes of Ephraim and Manasseh, the descendants of Joseph. 29One day as Jeroboam was leaving Jerusalem, the prophet Ahijah from Shiloh met him along the way. Ahijah was wearing a new cloak. The two of them were alone in a field, 30and Ahijah took hold of the new cloak he was wearing and tore it into twelve pieces. 31Then he said to Jeroboam, "Take ten of these pieces, for this is what the Lord, the God of Israel, says: 'I am about to tear the kingdom from the hand of Solomon, and I will give ten of the

The Walk – S.B. Stone & Rock Solid Publishing, LLC
©2018

tribes to you! 32But I will leave him one tribe for the sake of my servant David and for the sake of Jerusalem, which I have chosen out of all the tribes of Israel. 33For Solomon has 11:33 As in Greek, Syriac, and Latin Vulgate; Hebrew reads *For they have* abandoned me and worshiped Ashtoreth, the goddess of the Sidonians; Chemosh, the god of Moab; and Molech, the god of the Ammonites. He has not followed my ways and done what is pleasing in my sight. He has not obeyed my decrees and regulations as David his father did. 34"'But I will not take the entire kingdom from Solomon at this time. For the sake of my servant David, the one whom I chose and who obeyed my commands and decrees, I will keep Solomon as leader for the rest of his life. 35But I will take the kingdom away from his son and give ten of the tribes to you. 36His son will have one tribe so that the descendants of David my servant will continue to reign, shining like a lamp in Jerusalem, the city I have chosen to be the place for my name. 37And I will place you on the throne of Israel, and you will rule over all that your heart desires. 38If you listen to what I tell you and follow my ways and do whatever I consider to be right, and if you obey my decrees and commands, as my servant David did, then I will always be with you. I will establish an enduring dynasty for you as I did for David, and I will give Israel to you. 39Because of Solomon's sin I will punish the descendants of David—though not forever.'"

40Solomon tried to kill Jeroboam, but he fled to King Shishak of Egypt and stayed there until Solomon died.

Summary of Solomon's Reign

41The rest of the events in Solomon's reign, including all his deeds and his wisdom, are recorded in *The Book of the Acts of Solomon.* 42Solomon ruled in Jerusalem over all Israel for forty years. 43When he died, he was buried in the City of David, named for his father. Then his son Rehoboam became the next king.   [4]

First Kings

Chapter Eighteen

The Contest on Mount Carmel

1Later on, in the third year of the drought, the Lord said to Elijah, "Go and present yourself to King Ahab. Tell him that I will soon send rain!" 2So Elijah went to appear before Ahab.

Meanwhile, the famine had become very severe in Samaria. 3So Ahab summoned Obadiah, who was in charge of the palace. (Obadiah was a devoted follower of the Lord. 4Once when Jezebel had tried to kill all the Lord's prophets, Obadiah had hidden 100 of them in two caves. He put fifty prophets in each cave and supplied them with food and water.) 5Ahab said to Obadiah, "We must check every spring and valley in the land to see if we can find enough grass to save at least some of my horses and mules." 6So they divided the land between them. Ahab went one way by himself, and Obadiah went another way by himself. 7As Obadiah was walking along, he suddenly saw Elijah coming toward him. Obadiah recognized him at once and bowed low to the ground before him. "Is it really you, my lord Elijah?" he asked. 8"Yes, it is," Elijah replied. "Now go and tell your master, 'Elijah is here.'" 9"Oh, sir," Obadiah protested, "what harm have I done to you that you are sending me to my death at the hands of Ahab? 10For I swear by the Lord your God that the king has searched every nation and kingdom on earth from end to end to find you. And each time he was told, 'Elijah isn't here,' King Ahab forced the king of that nation to swear to the truth of his claim. 11And now you say, 'Go and tell your master, "Elijah is here."' 12But as soon as I leave you, the Spirit of the Lord will carry you away to who knows where. When Ahab comes and cannot find you, he will kill me. Yet I have been a true servant of the Lord all my life. 13Has no one told you, my lord, about the time when Jezebel was trying to kill the Lord's prophets? I hid 100 of them in two caves and supplied them with food and water. 14And now you say, 'Go and tell your master, "Elijah is here."' Sir, if I do that, Ahab will certainly kill me." 15But Elijah said, "I swear by the Lord Almighty, in whose presence I stand, that I will present myself to Ahab this very day." 16So Obadiah went to tell Ahab that Elijah had come, and Ahab went out to meet Elijah. 17When Ahab saw him, he exclaimed, "So, is it really you, you troublemaker of Israel?" 18"I have made no trouble for Israel," Elijah replied. "You and your family are the troublemakers, for you have refused to obey the commands of the Lord and have worshiped the images of Baal instead. 19Now summon all Israel to join me at Mount Carmel, along with the 450 prophets of Baal and the 400 prophets of Asherah who are supported by Jezebel.18:19 Hebrew *who eat at Jezebel's table.*" 20So Ahab summoned all the people of Israel and the prophets to Mount Carmel. 21Then Elijah stood in front of them and said, "How much longer will you waver, hobbling between two opinions? If the Lord is

God, follow him! But if Baal is God, then follow him!" But the people were completely silent.

22Then Elijah said to them, "I am the only prophet of the Lord who is left, but Baal has 450 prophets. 23Now bring two bulls. The prophets of Baal may choose whichever one they wish and cut it into pieces and lay it on the wood of their altar, but without setting fire to it. I will prepare the other bull and lay it on the wood on the altar, but not set fire to it. 24Then call on the name of your god, and I will call on the name of the Lord. The god who answers by setting fire to the wood is the true God!" And all the people agreed. 25Then Elijah said to the prophets of Baal, "You go first, for there are many of you. Choose one of the bulls, and prepare it and call on the name of your god. But do not set fire to the wood." 26So they prepared one of the bulls and placed it on the altar. Then they called on the name of Baal from morning until noontime, shouting, "O Baal, answer us!" But there was no reply of any kind. Then they danced, hobbling around the altar they had made. 27About noontime Elijah began mocking them. "You'll have to shout louder," he scoffed, "for surely he is a god! Perhaps he is daydreaming, or is relieving himself.18:27 Or *is busy somewhere else,* or *is engaged in business.* Or maybe he is away on a trip, or is asleep and needs to be wakened!" 28So they shouted louder, and following their normal custom, they cut themselves with knives and swords until the blood gushed out. 29They raved all afternoon until the time of the evening sacrifice, but still there was no sound, no reply, no response. 30Then Elijah called to the people, "Come over here!" They all crowded around him as he repaired the altar of the Lord that had been torn down. 31He took twelve stones, one to represent each of the tribes of Israel, 18:31 Hebrew *each of the tribes of the sons of Jacob to whom the Lord had said, "Your name will be Israel."* 32and he used the stones to rebuild the altar in the name of the Lord. Then he dug a trench around the altar large enough to hold about three gallons.18:32 Hebrew *2 seahs* [14.6 liters] *of seed.* 33He piled wood on the altar, cut the bull into pieces, and laid the pieces on the wood.18:33 Verse 18:34 in the Hebrew text begins here. Then he said, "Fill four large jars with water, and pour the water over the offering and the wood." 34After they had done this, he said, "Do the same thing again!" And when they were finished, he said, "Now do it a third time!" So they did as he said, 35and the water ran around the altar and even filled the trench. 36At the usual time for offering the evening

The Walk – S.B. Stone & Rock Solid Publishing, LLC
©2018

sacrifice, Elijah the prophet walked up to the altar and prayed, "O Lord, God of Abraham, Isaac, and Jacob,

18:36 Hebrew *and Israel.* The names "Jacob" and "Israel" are often interchanged throughout the Old Testament, referring sometimes to the individual patriarch and sometimes to the nation prove today that you are God in Israel and that I am your servant. Prove that I have done all this at your command. 37O Lord, answer me! Answer me so these people will know that you, O Lord, are God and that you have brought them back to yourself." 38Immediately the fire of

the Lord flashed down from heaven and burned up the young bull, the wood, the stones, and the dust. It even licked up all the water in the trench! 39And when all the people saw it, they fell face down on the ground and cried out, "The Lord—he is God! Yes, the Lord is God!"

40Then Elijah commanded, "Seize all the prophets of Baal. Don't let a single one escape!" So the people seized them all, and Elijah took them down to the Kishon Valley and killed them there.

Elijah Prays for Rain

41Then Elijah said to Ahab, "Go get something to eat and drink, for I hear a mighty rainstorm coming!" 42So Ahab went to eat and drink. But Elijah climbed to the top of Mount Carmel and bowed low to the ground and prayed with his face between his knees. 43Then he said to his servant, "Go and look out toward the sea." The servant went and looked, then returned to Elijah and said, "I didn't see anything." Seven times Elijah told him to go and look. 44Finally the seventh time, his servant told him, "I saw a little cloud about the size of a man's hand rising from the sea." Then Elijah shouted, "Hurry to Ahab and tell him, 'Climb into your chariot and go back home. If you don't hurry, the rain will stop you!'" 45And soon the sky was black with clouds. A heavy wind brought a terrific rainstorm, and Ahab left quickly for Jezreel. 46Then the Lord gave special strength to Elijah. He tucked his cloak into his belt18:46 Hebrew *He bound up his loins* and ran ahead of Ahab's chariot all the way to the entrance of Jezreel.   [4]

First Kings

Chapter Nineteen

Elijah Flees to Sinai

1When Ahab got home, he told Jezebel everything Elijah had done, including the way he had killed all the prophets of Baal. 2So Jezebel sent this message to Elijah: "May the gods strike me and even kill me if by this time tomorrow I have not killed you just as you killed them." 3Elijah was afraid and fled for his life. He went to Beersheba, a town in Judah, and he left his servant there. 4Then he went on alone into the wilderness, traveling all day. He sat down under a solitary broom tree and prayed that he might die. "I have had enough, Lord," he said. "Take my life, for I am no better than my ancestors who have already died." 5Then he lay down and slept under the broom tree. But as he was sleeping, an angel touched him and told him, "Get up and eat!" 6He looked around and there beside his head was some bread baked on hot stones and a jar of water! So he ate and drank and lay down again. 7Then the angel of the Lord came again and touched him and said, "Get up and eat some more, or the journey ahead will be too much for you." 8So he got up and ate and drank, and the food gave him enough strength to travel forty days and forty nights to Mount Sinai,19:8 Hebrew *to Horeb,* another name for Sinai the mountain of God. 9There he came to a cave, where he spent the night.

The Lord Speaks to Elijah

But the Lord said to him, "What are you doing here, Elijah?" 10Elijah replied, "I have zealously served the Lord God Almighty. But the people of Israel have broken their covenant with you, torn down your altars, and killed every one of your prophets. I am the only one left, and now they are trying to kill me, too." 11"Go out and stand before me on the mountain," the Lord told him. And as Elijah stood there, the Lord passed by, and a mighty windstorm hit the mountain. It was such a terrible blast that the rocks were torn loose, but the Lord was not in the wind. After the wind there was an earthquake, but the Lord was not in the earthquake. 12And after the earthquake there was a fire, but the Lord was not in the fire. And after the fire there was the sound of a gentle whisper. 13When Elijah heard it, he wrapped his face in his cloak and went out and stood at the entrance of the cave. And a voice said, "What are you doing here, Elijah?" 14He replied again, "I have zealously served the Lord God Almighty. But the people of Israel have broken their covenant with you, torn down your altars, and killed every one of your prophets. I am the only one left, and now they are trying to kill me, too." 15Then the Lord told him, "Go back the same way you came, and

The Walk – S.B. Stone & Rock Solid Publishing, LLC
©2018

travel to the wilderness of Damascus. When you arrive there, anoint Hazael to be king of Aram. 16Then anoint Jehu grandson of Nimshi

19:16 Hebrew *descendant of Nimshi;* compare 2 Kgs 9:2, 14. to be king of Israel, and anoint Elisha son of Shaphat from the town of Abel-meholah to replace you as my prophet. 17Anyone who escapes from Hazael will be killed by Jehu, and those who escape Jehu will be killed by Elisha! 18Yet I will preserve 7,000 others in Israel who have never bowed down to Baal or kissed him!"

The Call of Elisha

19So Elijah went and found Elisha son of Shaphat plowing a field. There were twelve teams of oxen in the field, and Elisha was plowing with the twelfth team. Elijah went over to him and threw his cloak across his shoulders and then walked away. 20Elisha left the oxen standing there, ran after Elijah, and said to him, "First let me go and kiss my father and mother good-bye, and then I will go with you!" Elijah replied, "Go on back, but think about what I have done to you."

21So Elisha returned to his oxen and slaughtered them. He used the wood from the plow to build a fire to roast their flesh. He passed around the meat to the townspeople, and they all ate. Then he went with Elijah as his assistant.   [4]

Second Kings

Chapter Two

Elijah Taken into Heaven

1When the Lord was about to take Elijah up to heaven in a whirlwind, Elijah and Elisha were traveling from Gilgal. 2And Elijah said to Elisha, "Stay here, for the Lord has told me to go to Bethel." But Elisha replied, "As surely as the Lord lives and you yourself live, I will never leave you!" So they went down together to Bethel. 3The group of prophets from Bethel came to Elisha and asked him, "Did you know that the Lord is going to take your master away from you today?"

"Of course I know," Elisha answered. "But be quiet about it." 4Then Elijah said to Elisha, "Stay here, for the Lord has told me to go to Jericho." But Elisha replied again, "As surely as the Lord lives and you yourself live, I will never leave you." So they went on together to Jericho.

5Then the group of prophets from Jericho came to Elisha and asked him, "Did you know that the Lord is going to take your master away from you today?" "Of course I know," Elisha answered. "But be quiet about it." 6Then Elijah said to Elisha, "Stay here, for the Lord has told me to go to the Jordan River." But again Elisha replied, "As surely as the Lord lives and you yourself live, I will never leave you." So they went on together. 7Fifty men from the group of prophets also went and watched from a distance as Elijah and Elisha stopped beside the Jordan River. 8Then Elijah folded his cloak together and struck the water with it. The river divided, and the two of them went across on dry ground! 9When they came to the other side, Elijah said to Elisha, "Tell me what I can do for you before I am taken away." And Elisha replied, "Please let me inherit a double share of your spirit and become your successor." 10"You have asked a difficult thing," Elijah replied. "If you see me when I am taken from you, then you will get your request. But if not, then you won't." 1As they were walking along and talking, suddenly a chariot of fire appeared, drawn by horses of fire. It drove between the two men, separating them, and Elijah was carried by a whirlwind into heaven. 12Elisha saw it and cried out, "My father! My father! I see the chariots and charioteers of Israel!" And as they disappeared from sight, Elisha tore his clothes in distress. 13Elisha picked up Elijah's cloak, which had fallen when he was taken up. Then Elisha returned to the bank of the Jordan River. 14He struck the water with Elijah's cloak and cried out, "Where is the Lord, the God of Elijah?" Then the river divided, and Elisha went across. 15When the group of prophets from Jericho saw from a distance what happened, they exclaimed, "Elijah's spirit rests upon Elisha!" And they went to meet him and bowed to the ground before him. 16"Sir," they said, "just say the word and fifty of our strongest men will search the wilderness for your master. Perhaps the Spirit of the Lord has left him on some mountain or in some valley." "No," Elisha said, "don't send them." 17But they kept urging him until they shamed him into agreeing, and he finally said, "All right, send them." So fifty men searched for three days but did not find Elijah. 18Elisha was still at Jericho when they returned. "Didn't I tell you not to go?" he asked.

Elisha's First Miracles

19One day the leaders of the town of Jericho visited Elisha. "We have a problem, my lord," they told him. "This town is located in pleasant surroundings, as you can see. But the water is bad, and the land is unproductive." 20Elisha said, "Bring me a new bowl with salt in it." So they brought it to him. 21Then he went out to the spring that supplied the town with water and threw the salt into it. And he said, "This is what the Lord says: I have purified this water. It will no longer cause death or infertility.2:21 Or *or make the land unproductive; Hebrew reads or barrenness.*" 22And the water has remained pure ever since, just as Elisha said. 23Elisha left Jericho and went up to Bethel. As he was walking along the road, a group of boys from the town began mocking and making fun of him. "Go away, baldy!" they chanted. "Go away,

baldy!" 24Elisha turned around and looked at them, and he cursed them in the name of the Lord. Then two bears came out of the woods and mauled forty-two of them. 25From there Elisha went to Mount Carmel and finally returned to Samaria.   [4]

Second Kings

Chapter Eighteen

Hezekiah Rules in Judah

1Hezekiah son of Ahaz began to rule over Judah in the third year of King Hoshea's reign in Israel. 2He was twenty-five years old when he became king, and he reigned in Jerusalem twenty-nine years. His mother was Abijah, 18:2 As in parallel text at 2 Chr 29:1; Hebrew reads *Abi,* a variant spelling of Abijah the daughter of Zechariah. 3He did what was pleasing in the Lord's sight, just as his ancestor David had done. 4He removed the pagan shrines, smashed the sacred pillars, and cut down the Asherah poles. He broke up the bronze serpent that Moses had made, because the people of Israel had been offering sacrifices to it. The bronze serpent was called Nehushtan.18:4 *Nehushtan* sounds like the Hebrew terms that mean "snake," "bronze," and "unclean thing." 5Hezekiah trusted in the Lord, the God of Israel. There was no one like him among all the kings of Judah, either before or after his time. 6He remained faithful to the Lord in everything, and he carefully obeyed all the commands the Lord had given Moses. 7So the Lord was with him, and Hezekiah was successful in everything he did. He revolted against the king of Assyria and refused to pay him tribute. 8He also conquered the Philistines as far distant as Gaza and its territory, from their smallest outpost to their largest walled city.

9During the fourth year of Hezekiah's reign, which was the seventh year of King Hoshea's reign in Israel, King Shalmaneser of Assyria attacked the city of Samaria and began a siege against it. 10Three years later, during the sixth year of King Hezekiah's reign and the ninth year of King Hoshea's reign in Israel, Samaria fell. 11At that time the king of Assyria exiled the Israelites to Assyria and placed them in colonies in Halah, along the banks of the Habor River in Gozan, and in the cities of the Medes. 12For they refused to listen to the Lord their God and obey him. Instead, they violated his covenant—all the laws that Moses the Lord's servant had commanded them to obey.

Assyria Invades Judah

13In the fourteenth year of King Hezekiah's reign, 18:13 The fourteenth year of Hezekiah's reign was 701 b.c. King Sennacherib of Assyria came to attack the fortified towns of Judah and conquered them. 14King Hezekiah sent this message to the king of Assyria at Lachish:

"I have done wrong. I will pay whatever tribute money you demand if you will only withdraw." The king of Assyria then demanded a settlement of more than eleven tons of silver and one ton of gold.18:14 Hebrew *300 talents* [10 metric tons] *of silver and 30 talents* [1 metric ton] *of gold.* 15To gather this amount, King Hezekiah used all the silver stored in the Temple of the Lord and in the palace treasury. 16Hezekiah even stripped the gold from the doors of the Lord's Temple and from the doorposts he had overlaid with gold, and he gave it all to the Assyrian king. 17Nevertheless, the king of Assyria sent his commander in chief, his field commander, and his chief of staff18:17a Or *the rabshakeh;* also in 18:19, 26, 27, 28, 37 from Lachish with a huge army to confront King Hezekiah in Jerusalem. The Assyrians took up a position beside the aqueduct that feeds water into the upper pool, near the road leading to the field where cloth is washed.18:17b Or *bleached.* 18They summoned King Hezekiah, but the king sent these officials to meet with them: Eliakim son of Hilkiah, the palace administrator; Shebna the court secretary; and Joah son of Asaph, the royal historian.

Sennacherib Threatens Jerusalem

19Then the Assyrian king's chief of staff told them to give this message to Hezekiah:

"This is what the great king of Assyria says: What are you trusting in that makes you so confident? 20Do you think that mere words can substitute for military skill and strength? Who are you counting on, that you have rebelled against me? 21On Egypt? If you lean on Egypt, it will be like a reed that splinters beneath your weight and pierces your hand. Pharaoh, the king of Egypt, is completely unreliable! 22"But perhaps you will say to me, 'We are trusting in the Lord our God!' But isn't he the one who was insulted by Hezekiah? Didn't Hezekiah tear down his shrines and altars and make everyone in Judah and Jerusalem worship only at the altar here in Jerusalem? 23"I'll tell you what! Strike a bargain with my master, the king of Assyria. I will give you 2,000 horses if you can find that many men to ride on them! 24With your tiny army, how can you think of challenging even the weakest contingent of my master's troops, even with the help of Egypt's chariots and charioteers? 25What's more, do you think we have invaded your land without the Lord's direction? The Lord himself told us, 'Attack this land and destroy it!'"

26Then Eliakim son of Hilkiah, Shebna, and Joah said to the Assyrian chief of staff,

"Please speak to us in Aramaic, for we understand it well. Don't speak in Hebrew,

18:26 Hebrew *in the dialect of Judah;* also in 18:28 for the people on the wall will hear." 27But

Sennacherib's chief of staff replied, "Do you think my master sent this message only to you and your master? He wants all the people to hear it, for when we put this city under siege, they will suffer along with you. They will be so hungry and thirsty that they will eat their own dung and drink their own urine." 28Then the chief of staff stood and shouted in Hebrew to the people on the wall, "Listen to this message from the great king of Assyria! 29This is what the king says: Don't let Hezekiah deceive you. He will never be able to rescue you from my power. 30Don't let him fool you into trusting in the Lord by saying, 'The Lord will surely rescue us. This city will never fall into the hands of the Assyrian king!' 31"Don't listen to Hezekiah! These are the terms the king of Assyria is offering: Make peace with me—open the gates and come out. Then each of you can continue eating from your own grapevine and fig tree and drinking from your own well. 32Then I will arrange to take you to another land like this one—a land of grain and new wine, bread and vineyards, olive groves and honey. Choose life instead of death! "Don't listen to Hezekiah when he tries to mislead you by saying, 'The Lord will rescue us!' 33Have the gods of any other nations ever saved their people from the king of Assyria? 34What happened to the gods of Hamath and Arpad? And what about the gods of

Sepharvaim, Hena, and Ivvah? Did any god rescue Samaria from my power? 35What god of any nation has ever been able to save its people from my power? So what makes you think that the Lord can rescue Jerusalem from me?"

36But the people were silent and did not utter a word because Hezekiah had commanded them, "Do not answer him." 37Then Eliakim son of Hilkiah, the palace administrator; Shebna the court secretary; and Joah son of Asaph, the royal historian, went back to Hezekiah. They tore their clothes in despair, and they went in to see the king and told him what the Assyrian chief of staff had said.   [4]

Second Kings

Chapter Nineteen

Hezekiah Seeks the Lord's Help

1When King Hezekiah heard their report, he tore his clothes and put on burlap and went into the Temple of the Lord. 2And he sent Eliakim the palace administrator, Shebna the court secretary, and the leading priests, all dressed in burlap, to the prophet Isaiah son of Amoz. 3They told him, "This is what King Hezekiah says: Today is a day of trouble, insults, and disgrace. It is like when a child is ready to be born, but the mother has no strength to deliver the baby. 4But perhaps the Lord your God has heard the Assyrian chief of staff, 19:4 Or *the rabshakeh;* also in 19:8 sent by the king to defy the living God, and will punish him for his words. Oh, pray for those of us who are left!" 5After King Hezekiah's officials delivered the king's message to Isaiah, 6the prophet replied, "Say to your master, 'This is what the Lord says: Do not be disturbed by this blasphemous speech against me from the Assyrian king's messengers. 7Listen! I myself will move against him, 19:7 Hebrew *I will put a spirit in him* and the king will receive a message that he is needed at home. So he will return to his land, where I will have him killed with a sword.'"

8Meanwhile, the Assyrian chief of staff left Jerusalem and went to consult the king of Assyria, who had left Lachish and was attacking Libnah. 9Soon afterward King Sennacherib received word that King Tirhakah of Ethiopia19:9 Hebrew *of Cush* was leading an army to fight against him. Before leaving to meet the attack, he sent messengers back to Hezekiah in

Jerusalem with this message: 10"This message is for King Hezekiah of Judah. Don't let your God, in whom you trust, deceive you with promises that Jerusalem will not be captured by the king of Assyria. 11You know perfectly well what the kings of Assyria have done wherever they have gone. They have completely destroyed everyone who stood in their way! Why should you be any different? 12Have the gods of other nations rescued them—such nations as Gozan, Haran, Rezeph, and the people of Eden who were in Tel-assar? My predecessors destroyed them all! 13What happened to the king of Hamath and the king of Arpad? What happened to the kings of Sepharvaim, Hena, and Ivvah?" 14After Hezekiah received the letter from the messengers and read it, he went up to the Lord's Temple and spread it out before the Lord. 15And Hezekiah prayed this prayer before the Lord: "O Lord, God of Israel, you are enthroned between the mighty cherubim! You alone are God of all the kingdoms of the earth. You alone created the heavens and the earth. 16Bend down, O Lord, and listen! Open your eyes, O Lord, and see! Listen to Sennacherib's words of defiance against the living God. 17"It is true, Lord, that the kings of Assyria have destroyed all these nations. 18And they have thrown the gods of these nations into the fire and burned them. But of course the Assyrians could destroy them! They were not gods at all—only idols of wood and stone shaped by human hands. 19Now, O Lord our God, rescue us from his power; then all the kingdoms of the earth will know that you alone,

O Lord, are God."

Isaiah Predicts Judah's Deliverance

20Then Isaiah son of Amoz sent this message to Hezekiah: "This is what the Lord, the God of Israel, says: I have heard your prayer about King Sennacherib of Assyria. 21And the Lord has spoken this word against him: "The virgin daughter of Zion despises you and laughs at you. The daughter of Jerusalem shakes her head in derision as you flee. 22"Whom have you been defying and ridiculing? Against whom did you raise your voice? At whom did you look with such haughty eyes? It was the Holy One of Israel! 23By your messengers you have defied the Lord. You have said, 'With my many chariots I have conquered the highest mountains—yes, the remotest peaks of Lebanon. I have cut down its tallest cedars and its finest cypress trees. I have reached its farthest corners and explored its deepest forests. 24I have dug wells in many foreign lands and refreshed myself with their water. With the sole of my foot I stopped up all the rivers of Egypt!' 25"But have you not heard? I decided this long ago. Long ago I planned it, and now I am making it happen. I planned for you to crush fortified cities into heaps of rubble. 26That is why their people have so little power and are so frightened and confused. They are as weak as grass, as easily trampled as tender green shoots. They are like grass sprouting on a housetop, scorched before it can grow lush and tall. 27"But I know you well—where you stay and when you come and go. I know the way you have raged against me. 28And because of your raging against me and your arrogance, which I have heard for myself, I will put my hook in your nose and my bit in your mouth. I will make you return by the same road on which you came."29Then Isaiah said to Hezekiah, "Here is the proof that what I say is true: "This year you will eat only what grows up by itself, and next year you will eat what springs up from that. But in the third year you will plant crops and harvest them; you will tend vineyards and eat their fruit. 30And you who are left in Judah, who have escaped the ravages of the siege, will put roots down in your own soil and will grow up and flourish. 31For a remnant of my people will spread out from Jerusalem, a group of survivors from Mount Zion. The passionate commitment of the Lord of Heaven's Armies19:31 As in Greek and Syriac versions, Latin Vulgate, and an alternate reading of the Masoretic Text (see also Isa 37:32); the other alternate reads *the Lord* will make this happen! 32"And this is what the Lord says about the king of Assyria: "His armies will not enter Jerusalem. They will not even shoot an arrow at it. They will not march outside its gates with their shields nor build banks of earth against its walls. 33The king will return to his own country by the same road on which he came. He will not enter this city, says the Lord. 34For my own honor and for the sake of my servant David, I will defend this city and protect it." 35That night the angel of the Lord went out to the Assyrian camp and killed 185,000 Assyrian soldiers. When the surviving Assyrians19:35 Hebrew *When they* woke up the next morning, they found corpses everywhere. 36Then King Sennacherib of Assyria broke camp and returned to his own land. He went home to his capital of Nineveh and stayed there. 37One day while he was worshiping in the temple of his god Nisroch, his sons19:37 As in Greek version and an alternate reading of the Masoretic Text (see also Isa 37:38); the other alternate reading lacks *his*

sons. Adrammelech and Sharezer killed him with their swords. They then escaped to the land of

Ararat, and another son, Esarhaddon, became the next king of Assyria.   [4]

Second Kings

Chapter Twenty

Hezekiah's Sickness and Recovery

1About that time Hezekiah became deathly ill, and the prophet Isaiah son of Amoz went to visit him. He gave the king this message: "This is what the Lord says: Set your affairs in order, for you are going to die. You will not recover from this illness." 2When Hezekiah heard this, he turned his face to the wall and prayed to the Lord, 3"Remember, O Lord, how I have always been faithful to you and have served you single-mindedly, always doing what pleases you." Then he broke down and wept bitterly. 4But before Isaiah had left the middle courtyard, 20:4 As in Greek version and an alternate reading in the Masoretic Text; the other alternate reads *the middle of the city* this message came to him from the Lord: 5"Go back to Hezekiah, the leader of my people. Tell him, 'This is what the Lord, the God of your ancestor David, says: I have heard your prayer and seen your tears. I will heal you, and three days from now you will get out of bed and go to the Temple of the Lord. 6I will add fifteen years to your life, and I will rescue you and this city from the king of Assyria. I will defend this city for my own honor and for the sake of my servant David.'" 7Then Isaiah said, "Make an ointment from figs." So Hezekiah's servants spread the ointment over the boil, and Hezekiah recovered! 8Meanwhile, Hezekiah had said to Isaiah, "What sign will the Lord give to prove that he will heal me and that

I will go to the Temple of the Lord three days from now?" 9Isaiah replied, "This is the sign from the Lord to prove that he will do as he promised. Would you like the shadow on the sundial to go forward ten steps or backward ten steps? 20:9 Or *The shadow on the sundial has gone forward ten steps; do you want it to go backward ten steps?*" 10"The shadow always moves forward," Hezekiah replied, "so that would be easy. Make it go ten steps backward instead." 11So Isaiah the prophet asked the Lord to do this, and he caused the shadow to move ten steps backward on the sundial20:11 Hebrew *the steps* of Ahaz!

Envoys from Babylon

12Soon after this, Merodach-baladan20:12 As in some Hebrew manuscripts and Greek and Syriac versions (see also Isa 39:1); Masoretic Text reads *Berodach-baladan* son of Baladan, king of Babylon, sent Hezekiah his best wishes and a gift, for he had heard that Hezekiah had been very sick. 13Hezekiah received the Babylonian envoys and showed them everything in his treasure-houses—the silver, the gold, the spices, and the aromatic oils. He also took them to see his armory and showed them everything in his royal treasuries! There was nothing in his palace or kingdom that Hezekiah did not show them. 14Then Isaiah the prophet went to King Hezekiah and asked him, "What did those men want? Where were they from?" Hezekiah replied, "They came from the distant land of Babylon." 15"What did they see in your palace?" Isaiah asked.

"They saw everything," Hezekiah replied. "I showed them everything I own—all my royal treasuries." 16Then Isaiah said to Hezekiah, "Listen to this message from the Lord: 17The time is coming when everything in your palace—all the treasures stored up by your ancestors until now—will be carried off to Babylon. Nothing will be left, says the Lord. 18Some of your very own sons will be taken away into exile. They will become eunuchs who will serve in the palace of Babylon's king."19Then Hezekiah said to Isaiah, "This message you have given me from the Lord is good." For the king was thinking, "At least there will be peace and security during my lifetime." 20The rest of the events in Hezekiah's reign, including the extent of his power and how he built a pool and dug a tunnel20:20 Hebrew *watercourse.* to bring water into the city, are recorded in *The Book of the History of the Kings of Judah.* 21Hezekiah died, and his son Manasseh became the next king.   [4]

Second Chronicles

Chapter Two

Preparations for Building the Temple

12:1 Verse 2:1 is numbered 1:18 in Hebrew text. Solomon decided to build a Temple to honor the name of the Lord, and also a royal palace for himself. 22:2 Verses 2:2-18 are numbered 2:1-17 in Hebrew text. He enlisted a force of 70,000 laborers, 80,000 men to quarry stone in the hill country, and 3,600 foremen. 3Solomon also sent this message to King Hiram

2:3 Hebrew *Huram,* a variant spelling of Hiram; also in 2:11 at Tyre: "Send me cedar logs as you did for my father, David, when he was building his palace. 4I am about to build a Temple to honor the name of the Lord my God. It will be a place set apart to burn fragrant incense before him, to display the special sacrificial bread, and to sacrifice burnt offerings each morning and evening, on the Sabbaths, at new moon celebrations, and at the other appointed festivals of the Lord our God. He has commanded Israel to do these things forever. 5"This must be a magnificent Temple because our God is greater than all other gods. 6But who can really build him a worthy home? Not even the highest heavens can contain him! So who am I to consider building a Temple for him, except as a place to burn sacrifices to him? 7"So send me a master craftsman who can work with gold, silver, bronze, and iron, as well as with purple, scarlet, and blue cloth. He must be a skilled engraver who can work with the craftsmen of Judah and Jerusalem who were selected by my father, David. 8"Also send me cedar, cypress, and red sandalwood2:8 Or *juniper;* Hebrew reads *algum,* perhaps a variant spelling of *almug;* compare 9:10-11 and parallel text at 1 Kgs 10:11-12 logs from Lebanon, for I know that your men are without equal at cutting timber in Lebanon. I will send my men to help them. 9An immense amount of timber will be needed, for the Temple I am going to build will be very large and magnificent. 10In payment for your woodcutters, I will send 100,000 bushels of crushed wheat, 100,000 bushels of barley, 2:10a Hebrew *20,000 cors* [4,400 kiloliters] *of crushed wheat, 20,000 cors of barley.* 110,000 gallons of wine, and 110,000 gallons of olive oil.2:10b Hebrew *20,000 baths* [420 kiloliters] *of wine, and 20,000 baths of olive oil.*" 11King Hiram sent this letter of reply to Solomon: "It is because the Lord loves his people that he has made you their king! 12Praise the Lord, the God of Israel, who made the heavens and the earth! He has given King David a wise son, gifted with skill and understanding, who will build a Temple for the Lord and a royal palace for himself. 13"I am sending you a master craftsman named Huramabi, who is extremely talented. 14His mother is from the tribe of Dan in Israel, and his father is from Tyre. He is skillful at making things from gold, silver, bronze, and iron, and he also works with stone and wood. He can work with purple, blue, and scarlet cloth and fine linen. He is also an engraver and can follow any design given to him. He will work with your craftsmen and those appointed by my lord David, your father. 15"Send along the wheat, barley, olive oil, and wine that my lord has mentioned. 16We will cut whatever timber you need from the

Lebanon mountains and will float the logs in rafts down the coast of the Mediterranean Sea

2:16 Hebrew *the sea* to Joppa. From there you can transport the logs up to Jerusalem."

17Solomon took a census of all foreigners in the land of Israel, like the census his father had taken, and he counted 153,600. 18He assigned 70,000 of them as common laborers, 80,000 as quarry workers in the hill country, and 3,600 as foremen.   [4]

Second Chronicles

Chapter Seventeen

Jehoshaphat Rules in Judah

1Then Jehoshaphat, Asa's son, became the next king. He strengthened Judah to stand against any attack from Israel. 2He stationed troops in all the fortified towns of Judah, and he assigned additional garrisons to the land of Judah and to the towns of Ephraim that his father, Asa, had captured. 3The Lord was with Jehoshaphat because he followed the example of his father's early years17:3 Some Hebrew manuscripts read *the example of his father, David* and did not worship the images of Baal. 4He sought his father's God and obeyed his commands instead of following the evil practices of the kingdom of Israel. 5So the Lord established Jehoshaphat's control over the kingdom of Judah. All the people of Judah brought gifts to Jehoshaphat, so he became very wealthy and highly esteemed. 6He was deeply committed to17:6 Hebrew *His heart was courageous in.* the ways of the Lord. He removed the pagan shrines and Asherah poles from Judah. 7In the third year of his reign Jehoshaphat sent his officials to teach in all the towns of Judah. These officials included Ben-hail, Obadiah, Zechariah, Nethanel, and Micaiah. 8He sent Levites along with them, including Shemaiah, Nethaniah, Zebadiah, Asahel, Shemiramoth, Jehonathan, Adonijah, Tobijah, and Tob-adonijah. He also sent out the priests Elishama and Jehoram. 9They took copies of the Book of the Law of the Lord and traveled around through all the towns of Judah, teaching the people. 10Then the fear of the Lord fell over all the surrounding kingdoms so that none of them wanted to declare war on Jehoshaphat. 11Some of the Philistines brought him gifts and silver as tribute, and the Arabs brought 7,700 rams and 7,700 male goats.

12So Jehoshaphat became more and more powerful and built fortresses and storage cities throughout Judah. 13He stored numerous supplies in Judah's towns and stationed an army of seasoned troops at Jerusalem. 14His army was enrolled according to ancestral clans.

From Judah there were 300,000 troops organized in units of 1,000, under the command of

Adnah. 15Next in command was Jehohanan, who commanded 280,000 troops. 16Next was Amasiah son of Zicri, who volunteered for the Lord's service, with 200,000 troops under his command. 17From Benjamin there were 200,000 troops equipped with bows and shields. They were under the command of Eliada, a veteran soldier. 18Next in command was Jehozabad, who commanded 180,000 armed men. 19These were the troops stationed in Jerusalem to serve the king, besides those Jehoshaphat stationed in the fortified towns throughout Judah. [4]

Nehemiah

Chapter One

1These are the memoirs of Nehemiah son of Hacaliah.

Nehemiah's Concern for Jerusalem

In late autumn, in the month of Kislev, in the twentieth year of King Artaxerxes' reign,1:1 Hebrew *In the month of Kislev of the twentieth year.* A number of dates in the book of Nehemiah can be cross-checked with dates in surviving Persian records and related accurately to our modern calendar. This month of the ancient Hebrew lunar calendar occurred within the months of November and December 446 b.c. The *twentieth year* probably refers to the reign of King Artaxerxes I; compare 2:1; 5:14. I was at the fortress of Susa. 2Hanani, one of my brothers, came to visit me with some other men who had just arrived from Judah. I asked them about the Jews who had returned there from captivity and about how things were going in Jerusalem.

3They said to me, "Things are not going well for those who returned to the province of Judah. They are in great trouble and disgrace. The wall of Jerusalem has been torn down, and the gates have been destroyed by fire." 4When I heard this, I sat down and wept. In fact, for days I mourned, fasted, and prayed to the God of heaven. 5Then I said, "O Lord, God of heaven, the great and awesome God who keeps his covenant of unfailing love with those who love him and obey his commands, 6listen to my prayer! Look down and see me praying night and day for your people Israel. I confess that we have sinned against you. Yes, even my own family and I have sinned! 7We have sinned terribly by not obeying the commands, decrees, and regulations that you gave us through your servant Moses. 8"Please remember what you told your servant Moses:

'If you are unfaithful to me, I will scatter you among the nations. 9But if you return to me and obey my commands and live by them, then even if you are exiled to the ends of the earth, 1:9 Hebrew *of the heavens.* I will bring you back to the place I have chosen for my name to be honored.' 10"The people you rescued by your great power and strong hand are your servants. 11O Lord, please hear my prayer! Listen to the prayers of those of us who delight in honoring you. Please grant me success today by making the king favorable to me.1:11 Hebrew *today in the sight of this man.* Put it into his heart to be kind to me." In those days I was the king's cup-bearer.

Nehemiah

Chapter Two

Nehemiah Goes to Jerusalem

1Early the following spring, in the month of Nisan, 2:1 Hebrew *In the month of*

Nisan. This month of the ancient Hebrew lunar calendar occurred within the months of April and

May 445 b.c. during the twentieth year of King Artaxerxes' reign, I was serving the king his wine. I had never before appeared sad in his presence. 2So the king asked me, "Why are you looking so sad? You don't look sick to me. You must be deeply troubled." Then I was terrified, 3but I replied, "Long live the king! How can I not be sad? For the city where my ancestors are buried is in ruins, and the gates have been destroyed by fire." 4The king asked, "Well, how can I help you?" With a prayer to the God of heaven, 5I replied, "If it please the king, and if you are pleased with me, your servant, send me to Judah to rebuild the city where my ancestors are buried." 6The king, with the queen sitting beside him, asked, "How long will you be gone? When will you return?" After I told him how long I would be gone, the king agreed to my request. 7I also said to the king, "If it please the king, let me have letters addressed to the governors of the province west of the Euphrates River,2:7 Hebrew *the province beyond the river;* also in 2:9 instructing them to let me travel safely through their territories on my way to

Judah. 8And please give me a letter addressed to Asaph, the manager of the king's forest, instructing him to give me timber. I will need it to make beams for the gates of the Temple fortress, for the city walls, and for a house for myself." And the king granted these requests, because the gracious hand of God was on me. 9When I came to the governors of the province west of the Euphrates River, I delivered the king's letters to them. The king, I should add, had sent along army officers and horsemen2:9 Or *charioteers* to protect me. 10But when Sanballat the Horonite and Tobiah the Ammonite official heard of my arrival, they were very displeased that someone had come to help the people of Israel.

Nehemiah Inspects Jerusalem's Wall

11So I arrived in Jerusalem. Three days later, 12I slipped out during the night, taking only a few others with me. I had not told anyone about the plans God had put in my heart for Jerusalem. We took no pack animals with us except the donkey I was riding. 13After dark I went out through the Valley Gate, past the Jackal's Well, 2:13 Or *Serpent's Well* and over to the Dung Gate to inspect the broken walls and burned gates. 14Then I went to the Fountain Gate and to the King's Pool, but my donkey couldn't get through the rubble. 15So, though it was still dark, I went up the Kidron Valley2:15 Hebrew *the valley.* instead, inspecting the wall before I turned back and entered again at the Valley Gate. 16The city officials did not know I had been out there or what I was doing, for I had not yet said anything to anyone about my plans. I had not yet spoken to the Jewish leaders—the priests, the nobles, the officials, or anyone else in the administration. 17But now I said to them, "You know very well what trouble we are in. Jerusalem lies in ruins, and its gates have been destroyed by fire. Let us rebuild the wall of Jerusalem and end this disgrace!" 18Then I told them about how the gracious hand of God had been on me, and about my conversation with the king. They replied at once, "Yes, let's rebuild the wall!" So they began the good work. 19But when Sanballat, Tobiah, and Geshem the

Arab heard of our plan, they scoffed contemptuously. "What are you doing? Are you rebelling against the king?" they asked.

20I replied, "The God of heaven will help us succeed. We, his servants, will start rebuilding this wall. But you have no share, legal right, or historic claim in Jerusalem."

Nehemiah

Chapter Six

Continued Opposition to Rebuilding

1Sanballat, Tobiah, Geshem the Arab, and the rest of our enemies found out that I had finished rebuilding the wall and that no gaps remained—though we had not yet set up the doors in the gates. 2So Sanballat and Geshem sent a message asking me to meet them at one of the villages6:2 As in Greek version; Hebrew reads *at Kephirim* in the plain of Ono. But I realized they were plotting to harm me, 3so I replied by sending this message to them: "I am engaged in a great work, so I can't come. Why should I stop working to come and meet with you?"

4Four times they sent the same message, and each time I gave the same reply. 5The fifth time, Sanballat's servant came with an open letter in his hand, 6and this is what it said: "There is a rumor among the surrounding nations, and Geshem6:6 Hebrew *Gashmu,* a variant spelling of Geshem tells me it is true, that you and the Jews are planning to rebel and that is why you are building the wall. According to his reports, you plan to be their king. 7He also reports that you have appointed prophets in Jerusalem to proclaim about you, 'Look! There is a king in Judah!' "You can be very sure that this report will get back to the king, so I suggest that you come and talk it over with me." 8I replied, "There is no truth in any part of your story. You are making up the whole thing." 9They were just trying to intimidate us, imagining that they could discourage us and stop the work. So I continued the work with even greater determination.6:9 As in Greek version; Hebrew reads *But now to strengthen my hands.* 10Later I went to visit Shemaiah son of Delaiah and grandson of Mehetabel, who was confined to his home. He said, "Let us meet together inside the Temple of God and bolt the doors shut. Your enemies are coming to kill you tonight." 11But I replied, "Should someone in my position run from danger? Should someone in my position enter the Temple to save his life? No, I won't do it!" 12I realized that God had not spoken to him, but that he had uttered this prophecy against me because Tobiah and Sanballat had hired him. 13They were hoping to intimidate me and make me sin. Then they would be able to accuse and discredit me. 14Remember, O my God, all the evil things that Tobiah and Sanballat have done. And remember Noadiah the prophet and all the prophets like her who have tried to intimidate me.

The Builders Complete the Wall

15So on October 26:15 Hebrew *on the twenty-fifth day of the month Elul,* of the ancient Hebrew lunar calendar. This day was October 2, 445 b.c.; also see note on 1:1 the wall was finished—just fifty-two days after we had begun. 16When our enemies and the surrounding nations heard about it, they were frightened and humiliated. They realized this work had been done with the help of our God. 17During those fifty-two days, many letters went back and forth between Tobiah and the nobles of Judah. 18For many in Judah had sworn allegiance to him because his father-in-law was Shecaniah son of Arah, and his son Jehohanan was married to the daughter of Meshullam son of Berekiah. 19They kept telling me about Tobiah's good deeds, and then they told him everything I said. And Tobiah kept sending threatening letters to intimidate me.

Nehemiah

Chapter Seven

1After the wall was finished and I had set up the doors in the gates, the gatekeepers, singers, and Levites were appointed. 2I gave the responsibility of governing Jerusalem to my brother Hanani, along with Hananiah, the commander of the fortress, for he was a faithful man who feared God more than most. 3I said to them, "Do not leave the gates open during the hottest part of the day.7:3 Or *Keep the gates of Jerusalem closed until the sun is hot.* And even while the gatekeepers are on duty, have them shut and bar the doors. Appoint the residents of Jerusalem to act as guards, everyone on a regular watch. Some will serve at sentry posts and some in front of their own homes."

Nehemiah Registers the People

4At that time the city was large and spacious, but the population was small, and none of the houses had been rebuilt. 5So my God gave me the idea to call together all the nobles and leaders of the city, along with the ordinary citizens, for registration. I had found the genealogical record of those who had first returned to Judah. This is what was written there:

6Here is the list of the Jewish exiles of the provinces who returned from their captivity. King Nebuchadnezzar had deported them to Babylon, but now they returned to Jerusalem and the other towns in Judah where they originally lived. 7Their leaders were Zerubbabel, Jeshua, Nehemiah, Seraiah, 7:7a As in parallel text at Ezra 2:2; Hebrew reads *Azariah.* Reelaiah, 7:7b As in parallel text at Ezra 2:2; Hebrew reads *Raamiah.* Nahamani, Mordecai, Bilshan, Mispar, 7:7c As in parallel text at Ezra 2:2; Hebrew reads *Mispereth.* Bigvai, Rehum, 7:7d As in parallel text at Ezra 2:2; Hebrew reads *Nehum.* and Baanah. This is the number of the men of Israel who returned from exile:

8The family of Parosh	2,172
9The family of Shephatiah	372
10The family of Arah	652
11The family of Pahath-moab (descendants of Jeshua and Joab)	2,818
12The family of Elam	1,254
13The family of Zattu	845
14The family of Zaccai	760

The Walk – S.B. Stone & Rock Solid Publishing, LLC
©2018

15 The family of Bani 7:15 As in parallel text at Ezra 2:10; Hebrew reads *Binnui*.	648
16 The family of Bebai	628
17 The family of Azgad	2,322
18 The family of Adonikam	667
19 The family of Bigvai	2,067
20 The family of Adin	655
21 The family of Ater (descendants of Hezekiah)	98
22 The family of Hashum	328
23 The family of Bezai	324

24The family of Jorah7:24 As in parallel text at Ezra 2:18; Hebrew reads *Hariph.*

112

25The family of Gibbar7:25 As in parallel text at Ezra 2:20; Hebrew reads *Gibeon.*

95

26The people of Bethlehem and Netophah

188

27The people of Anathoth

128

28The people of Beth-azmaveth

42

29The people of Kiriath-jearim, Kephirah, and Beeroth

743

30The people of Ramah and Geba

621

31The people of Micmash

122

32The people of Bethel and Ai

123

33The people of West Nebo7:33 Or *of the other Nebo.*

52

34The citizens of West Elam7:34 Or *of the other Elam.*	1,254
35The citizens of Harim	320
36The citizens of Jericho	345
37The citizens of Lod, Hadid, and Ono	721
38The citizens of Senaah	3,930

39These are the priests who returned from exile:

The family of Jedaiah (through the line of Jeshua)	973
40The family of Immer	1,052
41The family of Pashhur	1,247
42The family of Harim	1,017

43These are the Levites who returned from exile:

The families of Jeshua and Kadmiel (descendants of Hodaviah7:43 As in parallel text at Ezra 2:40; Hebrew reads *Hodevah.*)

74

44The singers of the family of Asaph

148

45The gatekeepers of the families of Shallum, Ater, Talmon, Akkub, Hatita, and Shobai

138

46The descendants of the following Temple servants returned from exile:

Ziha, Hasupha, Tabbaoth,

47Keros, Siaha, 7:47 As in parallel text at Ezra 2:44; Hebrew reads *Sia.* Padon,

48Lebanah, Hagabah, Shalmai,

49Hanan, Giddel, Gahar,

50Reaiah, Rezin, Nekoda,

51Gazzam, Uzza, Paseah,

52Besai, Meunim, Nephusim, 7:52 As in parallel text at Ezra 2:50; Hebrew reads *Nephushesim.*

53Bakbuk, Hakupha, Harhur,

54Bazluth, 7:54 As in parallel text at Ezra 2:52; Hebrew reads *Bazlith.* Mehida, Harsha,

55Barkos, Sisera, Temah,

56Neziah, and Hatipha.

57The descendants of these servants of King Solomon returned from exile:

Sotai, Hassophereth, Peruda, 7:57 As in parallel text at Ezra 2:55; Hebrew reads *Sotai, Sophereth, Perida.* 58Jaalah, 7:58 As in parallel text at Ezra 2:56; Hebrew reads *Jaala.* Darkon, Giddel,

59Shephatiah, Hattil, Pokereth-hazzebaim, and Ami.7:59 As in parallel text at Ezra 2:57; Hebrew reads *Amon.* 60In all, the Temple servants and the descendants of Solomon's servants numbered 392. 61Another group returned at this time from the towns of Tel-melah, Tel-harsha, Kerub, Addan,7:61 As in parallel text at Ezra 2:59; Hebrew reads *Addon* and Immer. However, they could not prove that they or their families were descendants of Israel. 62This group included the families of Delaiah, Tobiah, and Nekoda—a total of 642 people. 63Three families of priests—Hobaiah, Hakkoz, and Barzillai—also returned. (This Barzillai had married a woman who was a descendant of Barzillai of Gilead, and he had taken her family name.) 64They searched for their names in the genealogical records, but they were not found, so they were disqualified from serving as priests. 65The governor told them not to eat the priests' share of food from the sacrifices until a priest could consult the Lord about the matter by using the Urim and Thummim—the sacred lots. 66So a total of 42,360 people returned to Judah, 67in addition to 7,337 servants and 245 singers, both men and women. 68They took with them 736 horses, 245 mules, 7:68 As in some Hebrew manuscripts (see also Ezra 2:66); most Hebrew manuscripts lack this verse. Verses 7:69-73 are numbered 7:68-72 in Hebrew text. 69435 camels, and 6,720 donkeys. 70Some of the family leaders gave gifts for the work. The governor gave to the treasury 1,000 gold coins, 7:70 Hebrew *1,000 darics of gold,* about 19 pounds or 8.6 kilograms in weight. 50 gold basins, and 530 robes for the priests. 71The other leaders gave to the treasury a total of 20,000 gold coins7:71a Hebrew *20,000 darics of gold,* about 375 pounds or 170 kilograms in weight; also in 7:72 and some 2,750 pounds7:71b Hebrew *2,200 minas* [1,300 kilograms] of silver for the work. 72The rest of the people gave 20,000 gold coins, about 2,500 pounds7:72 Hebrew *2,000 minas* [1,200 kilograms] of silver, and 67 robes for the priests.

73So the priests, the Levites, the gatekeepers, the singers, the Temple servants, and some of the common people settled near Jerusalem. The rest of the people returned to their own towns throughout Israel.

The Walk – S.B. Stone & Rock Solid Publishing, LLC
©2018

Nehemiah

Chapter Nine

The People Confess Their Sins

1On October 319:1 Hebrew *On the twenty-fourth day of that same month,* the seventh month of the ancient Hebrew lunar calendar. This day was October 31, 445 b.c.; also see notes on 1:1 and 8:2 the people assembled again, and this time they fasted and dressed in burlap and sprinkled dust on their heads. 2Those of Israelite descent separated themselves from all foreigners as they confessed their own sins and the sins of their ancestors. 3They remained standing in place for three hours9:3 Hebrew *for a quarter of a day* while the Book of the Law of the Lord their God was read aloud to them. Then for three more hours they confessed their sins and worshiped the Lord their God. 4The Levites—Jeshua, Bani, Kadmiel, Shebaniah, Bunni,

Sherebiah, Bani, and Kenani—stood on the stairway of the Levites and cried out to the Lord their God with loud voices. 5Then the leaders of the Levites—Jeshua, Kadmiel, Bani, Hashabneiah, Sherebiah, Hodiah, Shebaniah, and Pethahiah—called out to the people: "Stand up and praise the Lord your God, for he lives from everlasting to everlasting!" Then they prayed: "May your glorious name be praised! May it be exalted above all blessing and praise! 6"You alone are the Lord. You made the skies and the heavens and all the stars. You made the earth and the seas and everything in them. You preserve them all, and the angels of heaven worship you. 7"You are the Lord God, who chose Abram and brought him from Ur of the Chaldeans and renamed him Abraham. 8When he had proved himself faithful, you made a covenant with him to give him and his descendants the land of the Canaanites, Hittites, Amorites, Perizzites, Jebusites, and

Girgashites. And you have done what you promised, for you are always true to your word.

9"You saw the misery of our ancestors in Egypt, and you heard their cries from beside the Red Sea.9:9 Hebrew *sea of reeds.* 10You displayed miraculous signs and wonders against Pharaoh, his officials, and all his people, for you knew how arrogantly they were treating our ancestors. You have a glorious reputation that has never been forgotten. 11You divided the sea for your people so they could walk through on dry land! And then you hurled their enemies into the depths of the sea. They sank like stones beneath the mighty waters. 12You led our ancestors by a pillar of cloud during the day and a pillar of fire at night so that they could find their way.

13"You came down at Mount Sinai and spoke to them from heaven. You gave them regulations and instructions that were just, and decrees and commands that were good. 14You instructed them concerning your holy Sabbath. And you commanded them, through Moses your servant, to obey all your commands, decrees, and instructions. 15"You gave them bread from heaven when they were hungry and water from the rock when they were thirsty. You commanded them to go and take possession of the land you had sworn to give them. 16"But our ancestors were proud and stubborn, and they paid no attention to your commands. 17They refused to obey and did not remember the miracles you had done for them. Instead, they became stubborn and appointed a leader to take them back to their slavery in Egypt.9:17 As in Greek version; Hebrew reads *in their rebellion*. But you are a God of forgiveness, gracious and merciful, slow to become angry, and rich in unfailing love. You did not abandon them, 18even when they made an idol shaped like a calf and said, 'This is your god who brought you out of Egypt!' They committed terrible blasphemies. 19"But in your great mercy you did not abandon them to die in the wilderness. The pillar of cloud still led them forward by day, and the pillar of fire showed them the way through the night. 20You sent your good Spirit to instruct them, and you did not stop giving them manna from heaven or water for their thirst. 21For forty years you sustained them in the wilderness, and they lacked nothing. Their clothes did not wear out, and their feet did not swell! 22"Then you helped our ancestors conquer kingdoms and nations, and you placed your people in every corner of the land.9:22 The meaning of the Hebrew is uncertain. They took over the land of King Sihon of Heshbon and the land of King Og of Bashan. 23You made their descendants as numerous as the stars in the sky and brought them into the land you had promised to their ancestors.

24"They went in and took possession of the land. You subdued whole nations before them. Even the Canaanites, who inhabited the land, were powerless! Your people could deal with these nations and their kings as they pleased. 25Our ancestors captured fortified cities and fertile land. They took over houses full of good things, with cisterns already dug and vineyards and olive groves and fruit trees in abundance. So they ate until they were full and grew fat and enjoyed themselves in all your blessings.

The Walk – S.B. Stone & Rock Solid Publishing, LLC
©2018

26"But despite all this, they were disobedient and rebelled against you. They turned their backs on your Law, they killed your prophets who warned them to return to you, and they committed terrible blasphemies. 27So you handed them over to their enemies, who made them suffer. But in their time of trouble they cried to you, and you heard them from heaven. In your great mercy, you sent them liberators who rescued them from their enemies. 28"But as soon as they were at peace, your people again committed evil in your sight, and once more you let their enemies conquer them. Yet whenever your people turned and cried to you again for help, you listened once more from heaven. In your wonderful mercy, you rescued them many times! 29"You warned them to return to your Law, but they became proud and obstinate and disobeyed your commands. They did not follow your regulations, by which people will find life if only they obey. They stubbornly turned their backs on you and refused to listen. 30In your love, you were patient with them for many years. You sent your Spirit, who warned them through the prophets. But still they wouldn't listen! So once again you allowed the peoples of the land to conquer them. 31But in your great mercy, you did not destroy them completely or abandon them forever. What a gracious and merciful God you are! 32"And now, our God, the great and mighty and awesome God, who keeps his covenant of unfailing love, do not let all the hardships we have suffered seem insignificant to you. Great trouble has come upon us and upon our kings and leaders and priests and prophets and ancestors—all of your people—from the days when the kings of Assyria first triumphed over us until now. 33Every time you punished us you were being just. We have sinned greatly, and you gave us only what we deserved. 34Our kings, leaders, priests, and ancestors did not obey your Law or listen to the warnings in your commands and laws. 35Even while they had their own kingdom, they did not serve you, though you showered your goodness on them. You gave them a large, fertile land, but they refused to turn from their wickedness. 36"So now today we are slaves in the land of plenty that you gave our ancestors for their enjoyment! We are slaves here in this good land. 37The lush produce of this land piles up in the hands of the kings whom you have set over us because of our sins. They have power over us and our livestock. We serve them at their pleasure, and we are in great misery."

The People Agree to Obey

389:38a Verse 9:38 is numbered 10:1 in Hebrew text. The people responded, "In view of all this,9:38b Or *In spite of all this* we are making a solemn promise and putting it in writing. On this sealed document are the names of our leaders and Levites and priests."

Esther

Chapter Two

Esther Becomes Queen

1But after Xerxes' anger had subsided, he began thinking about Vashti and what she had done and the decree he had made. 2So his personal attendants suggested, "Let us search the empire to find beautiful young virgins for the king. 3Let the king appoint agents in each province to bring these beautiful young women into the royal harem at the fortress of Susa. Hegai, the king's eunuch in charge of the harem, will see that they are all given beauty treatments. 4After that, the young woman who most pleases the king will be made queen instead of Vashti." This advice was very appealing to the king, so he put the plan into effect. 5At that time there was a Jewish man in the fortress of Susa whose name was Mordecai son of Jair. He was from the tribe of Benjamin and was a descendant of Kish and Shimei. 6His family2:6a Hebrew *He* had been among those who, with King Jehoiachin2:6b Hebrew *Jeconiah,* a variant spelling of Jehoiachin of Judah, had been exiled from Jerusalem to Babylon by King Nebuchadnezzar. 7This man had a very beautiful and lovely young cousin, Hadassah, who was also called Esther. When her father and mother died, Mordecai adopted her into his family and raised her as his own daughter.

8As a result of the king's decree, Esther, along with many other young women, was brought to the king's harem at the fortress of Susa and placed in Hegai's care. 9Hegai was very impressed with Esther and treated her kindly. He quickly ordered a special menu for her and provided her with beauty treatments. He also assigned her seven maids specially chosen from the king's palace, and he moved her and her maids into the best place in the harem.

10Esther had not told anyone of her nationality and family background, because Mordecai had directed her not to do so. 11Every day Mordecai would take a walk near the courtyard of the harem to find out about Esther and what was happening to her. 12Before each young woman was taken to the king's bed, she was given the prescribed twelve months of beauty treatments—six months with oil of myrrh, followed by six months with special perfumes and ointments. 13When it was time for her to go to the king's palace, she was given her choice of whatever clothing or jewelry she wanted to take from the harem. 14That evening she was taken to the king's private rooms, and the next morning she was brought to the second harem, 2:14 Or *to another part of the harem* where the king's wives lived. There she would be under the care of Shaashgaz, the king's eunuch in charge of the concubines. She would never go to the king again unless he had especially enjoyed her and requested her by name. 15Esther was the daughter of Abihail, who was Mordecai's uncle. (Mordecai had adopted his younger cousin

Esther.) When it was Esther's turn to go to the king, she accepted the advice of Hegai, the eunuch in charge of the harem. She asked for nothing except what he suggested, and she was admired by everyone who saw her.

16Esther was taken to King Xerxes at the royal palace in early winter2:16 Hebrew *in the tenth month, the month of Tebeth.* A number of dates in the book of Esther can be cross-checked with dates in surviving Persian records and related accurately to our modern calendar. This month of the ancient Hebrew lunar calendar occurred within the months of December

479 b.c. and January 478 b.c. of the seventh year of his reign. 17And the king loved Esther more than any of the other young women. He was so delighted with her that he set the royal crown on her head and declared her queen instead of Vashti. 18To celebrate the occasion, he gave a great banquet in Esther's honor for all his nobles and officials, declaring a public holiday for the provinces and giving generous gifts to everyone. 19Even after all the young women had been transferred to the second harem2:19a The meaning of the Hebrew is uncertain and Mordecai had become a palace official,2:19b Hebrew *and Mordecai was sitting in the gate of the king.* 20Esther continued to keep her family background and nationality a secret. She was still following Mordecai's directions, just as she did when she lived in his home.

Mordecai's Loyalty to the King

21One day as Mordecai was on duty at the king's gate, two of the king's eunuchs, Bigthana2:21 Hebrew *Bigthan;* compare 6:2. and Teresh—who were guards at the door of the king's private quarters— became angry at King Xerxes and plotted to assassinate him. 22But Mordecai heard about the plot and gave the information to Queen

Esther. She then told the king about it and gave Mordecai credit for the report. 23When an investigation was made and

Mordecai's story was found to be true, the two men were impaled on a sharpened pole. This was all recorded in *The Book of the History of King Xerxes' Reign.*

Esther

Chapter Three

Haman's Plot against the Jews

1Some time later King Xerxes promoted Haman son of Hammedatha the Agagite over all the other nobles, making him the most powerful official in the empire. 2All the king's officials would bow down before Haman to show him respect whenever he passed by, for so the king had commanded. But Mordecai refused to bow down or show him respect. 3Then the palace officials at the king's gate asked Mordecai, "Why are you disobeying the king's command?" 4They spoke to him day after day, but still he refused to comply with the order. So they spoke to Haman about this to see if he would tolerate Mordecai's conduct, since Mordecai had told them he was a Jew.

5When Haman saw that Mordecai would not bow down or show him respect, he was filled with rage. 6He had learned of Mordecai's nationality, so he decided it was not enough to lay hands on Mordecai alone. Instead, he looked for a way to destroy all the Jews throughout the entire empire of Xerxes. 7So in the month of April, 3:7a Hebrew *in the first month, the month of Nisan.* This month of the ancient Hebrew lunar calendar occurred within the months of April and

May 474 b.c.; also see note on 2:16 during the twelfth year of King Xerxes' reign, lots were cast in Haman's presence (the lots were called *purim*) to determine the best day and month to take action. And the day selected was March 7, nearly a year later.3:7b As in 3:13, which reads *the thirteenth day of the twelfth month, the month of Adar;* Hebrew reads *in the twelfth month,* of the ancient Hebrew lunar calendar. The date selected was March 7, 473 b.c.; also see note on 2:16.

8Then Haman approached King Xerxes and said, "There is a certain race of people scattered through all the provinces of your empire who keep themselves separate from everyone else. Their laws are different from those of any other people, and they refuse to obey the laws of the king. So it is not in the king's interest to let them live. 9If it please the king, issue a decree that they be destroyed, and I will give 10,000 large sacks3:9 Hebrew *10,000 talents*, about 375 tons or 340 metric tons in weight of silver to the government administrators to be deposited in the royal treasury." 10The king agreed, confirming his decision by removing his signet ring from his finger and giving it to Haman son of Hammedatha the Agagite, the enemy of the Jews. 11The king said, "The money and the people are both yours to do with as you see fit." 12So on April 173:12 Hebrew *On the thirteenth day of the first month,* of the ancient Hebrew lunar calendar. This day was April 17, 474 b.c.; also see note on 2:16 the king's secretaries were summoned, and a decree was written exactly as Haman dictated. It was sent to the king's highest officers, the governors of the respective provinces, and the nobles of each province in their own scripts and languages. The decree was written in the name of King Xerxes and sealed with the king's signet ring. 13Dispatches were sent by swift messengers into all the provinces of the empire, giving the order that all Jews—young and old, including women and children—must be killed, slaughtered, and annihilated on a single day. This was scheduled to happen on March 7 of the next year.3:13 Hebrew *on the thirteenth day of the twelfth month, the month of Adar,* of the ancient Hebrew lunar calendar. The date selected was March 7, 473 b.c.; also see note on 2:16. The property of the Jews would be given to those who killed them. 14A copy of this decree was to be issued as law in every province and proclaimed to all peoples, so that they would be ready to do their duty on the appointed day. 15At the king's command, the decree went out by swift messengers, and it was also proclaimed in the fortress of Susa. Then the king and Haman sat down to drink, but the city of Susa fell into confusion.

Esther

Chapter Five

Esther's Request to the King

1On the third day of the fast, Esther put on her royal robes and entered the inner court of the palace, just across from the king's hall. The king was sitting on his royal throne, facing the entrance. 2When he saw Queen Esther standing there in the inner court, he welcomed her and held out the gold scepter to her. So Esther approached and touched the end of the scepter.

3Then the king asked her, "What do you want, Queen Esther? What is your request? I will give it to you, even if it is half the kingdom!" 4And Esther replied, "If it please the king, let the king and Haman come today to a banquet I have prepared for the king." 5The king turned to his attendants and said, "Tell Haman to come quickly to a banquet, as Esther has requested." So the king and Haman went to Esther's banquet. 6And while they were drinking wine, the king said to Esther, "Now tell me what you really want. What is your request? I will give it to you, even if it is half the kingdom!" 7Esther replied, "This is my request and deepest wish. 8If I have found favor with the king, and if it pleases the king to grant my request and do what I ask, please come with Haman tomorrow to the banquet I will prepare for you. Then I will explain what this is all about."

Haman's Plan to Kill Mordecai

9Haman was a happy man as he left the banquet! But when he saw Mordecai sitting at the palace gate, not standing up or trembling nervously before him, Haman became furious. 10However, he restrained himself and went on home. Then Haman gathered together his friends and Zeresh, his wife, 11and boasted to them about his great wealth and his many children. He bragged about the honors the king had given him and how he had been promoted over all the other nobles and officials. 12Then Haman added, "And that's not all! Queen Esther invited only me and the king himself to the banquet she prepared for us. And she has invited me to dine with her and the king again tomorrow!" 13Then he added, "But this is all worth nothing as long as I see Mordecai the Jew just sitting there at the palace gate." 14So Haman's wife, Zeresh, and all his friends suggested, "Set up a sharpened pole that stands seventy-five feet5:14 Hebrew *50 cubits* [23 meters] tall, and in the morning ask the king to impale Mordecai on it. When this is done, you can go on your merry way to the banquet with the king." This pleased Haman, and he ordered the pole set up.

Esther

Chapter Six

The King Honors Mordecai

1That night the king had trouble sleeping, so he ordered an attendant to bring the book of the history of his reign so it could be read to him. 2In those records he discovered an account of how Mordecai had exposed the plot of Bigthana and Teresh, two of the eunuchs who guarded the door to the king's private quarters. They had plotted to assassinate King Xerxes. 3"What reward or recognition did we ever give Mordecai for this?" the king asked. His attendants replied,

"Nothing has been done for him." 4"Who is that in the outer court?" the king inquired. As it happened, Haman had just arrived in the outer court of the palace to ask the king to impale

Mordecai on the pole he had prepared. 5So the attendants replied to the king, "Haman is out in the court." "Bring him in," the king ordered. 6So Haman came in, and the king said, "What should I do to honor a man who truly pleases me?" Haman thought to himself, "Whom would the king wish to honor more than me?" 7So he replied, "If the king wishes to honor someone, 8he should bring out one of the king's own royal robes, as well as a horse that the king himself has ridden—one with a royal emblem on its head. 9Let the robes and the horse be handed over to one of the king's most noble officials. And let him see that the man whom the king wishes to honor is dressed in the king's robes and led through the city square on the king's horse. Have the official shout as they go, 'This is what the king does for someone he wishes to honor!'" 10"Excellent!" the king said to Haman. "Quick! Take the robes and my horse, and do just as you have said for Mordecai the Jew, who sits at the gate of the palace. Leave out nothing you have suggested!"

11So Haman took the robes and put them on Mordecai, placed him on the king's own horse, and led him through the city square, shouting, "This is what the king does for someone he wishes to honor!" 12Afterward Mordecai returned to the palace gate, but Haman hurried home dejected and completely humiliated. 13When Haman told his wife, Zeresh, and all his friends what had happened, his wise advisers and his wife said, "Since Mordecai—this man who has humiliated you—is of Jewish birth, you will never succeed in your plans against him. It will be fatal to continue opposing him." 14While they were still talking, the king's eunuchs arrived and quickly took Haman to the banquet Esther had prepared.

Esther

Chapter Seven

The King Executes Haman

1So the king and Haman went to Queen Esther's banquet. 2On this second occasion, while they were drinking wine, the king again said to Esther, "Tell me what you want, Queen Esther. What is your request? I will give it to you, even if it is half the kingdom!" 3Queen Esther replied, "If I have found favor with the king, and if it pleases the king to grant my request, I ask that my life and the lives of my people will be spared. 4For my people and I have been sold to those who would kill, slaughter, and annihilate us. If we had merely been sold as slaves, I could remain quiet, for that would be too trivial a matter to warrant disturbing the king."

5"Who would do such a thing?" King Xerxes demanded. "Who would be so presumptuous as to touch you?" 6Esther replied, "This wicked Haman is our adversary and our enemy." Haman grew pale with fright before the king and queen. 7Then the king jumped to his feet in a rage and went out into the palace garden. Haman, however, stayed behind to plead for his life with Queen Esther, for he knew that the king intended to kill him. 8In despair he fell on the couch where Queen Esther was reclining, just as the king was returning from the palace garden. The king exclaimed, "Will he even assault the queen right here in the palace, before my very eyes?" And as soon as the king spoke, his attendants covered Haman's face, signaling his doom. 9Then Harbona, one of the king's eunuchs, said, "Haman has set up a sharpened pole that stands seventy-five feet7:9 Hebrew *50 cubits* [23 meters] tall in his own courtyard. He intended to use it to impale Mordecai, the man who saved the king from assassination." "Then impale Haman on it!" the king ordered. 10So they impaled Haman on the pole he had set up for Mordecai, and the king's anger subsided.

Esther

Chapter Eight

A Decree to Help the Jews

1On that same day King Xerxes gave the property of Haman, the enemy of the Jews, to Queen Esther. Then Mordecai was brought before the king, for Esther had told the king how they were related. 2The king took off his signet ring—which he had taken back from Haman—and gave it to Mordecai. And Esther appointed Mordecai to be in charge of Haman's property. 3Then Esther went again before the king, falling down at his feet and begging him with tears to stop the evil plot devised by Haman the Agagite against the Jews. 4Again the king held out the gold scepter to Esther. So she rose and stood before him. 5Esther said, "If it please the king, and if I have found favor with him, and if he thinks it is right, and if I am pleasing to him, let there be a decree that reverses the orders of Haman son of Hammedatha the Agagite, who ordered that Jews throughout all the king's provinces should be destroyed. 6For how can I endure to see my people and my family slaughtered and destroyed?" 7Then King Xerxes said to Queen Esther and

Mordecai the Jew, "I have given Esther the property of Haman, and he has been impaled on a pole because he tried to destroy the Jews. 8Now go ahead and send a message to the Jews in the king's name, telling them whatever you want, and seal it with the king's signet ring. But remember that whatever has already been written in the king's name and sealed with his signet ring can never be revoked." 9So on June 258:9a Hebrew *on the twenty-third day of the third month, the month of Sivan,* of the ancient Hebrew lunar calendar. This day was June 25, 474 b.c.; also see note on 2:16. the king's secretaries were summoned, and a decree was written exactly as Mordecai dictated. It was sent to the Jews and to the highest officers, the governors, and the nobles of all the 127 provinces stretching from India to Ethiopia.8:9b Hebrew *to Cush.* The decree was written in the scripts and languages of all the peoples of the empire, including that of the Jews. 10The decree was written in the name of King Xerxes and sealed with the king's signet ring. Mordecai sent the dispatches by swift messengers, who rode fast horses especially bred for the king's service. 11The king's decree gave the Jews in every city authority to unite to defend their lives. They were allowed to kill, slaughter, and annihilate anyone of any nationality or province who might attack them or their children and wives, and to take the property of their enemies. 12The day chosen for this event throughout all the provinces of King Xerxes was March 7 of the next year.8:12 Hebrew *the thirteenth day of the twelfth month, the month of Adar,* of the ancient Hebrew lunar calendar. The date selected was March 7, 473 b.c.; also see note on 2:16. 13A copy of this decree was to be issued as law in every province and proclaimed to all peoples, so that the Jews would be

The Walk – S.B. Stone & Rock Solid Publishing, LLC
©2018

ready to take revenge on their enemies on the appointed day. 14So urged on by the king's command, the messengers rode out swiftly on fast horses bred for the king's service. The same decree was also proclaimed in the fortress of Susa. 15Then Mordecai left the king's presence, wearing the royal robe of blue and white, the great crown of gold, and an outer cloak of fine linen and purple. And the people of Susa celebrated the new decree. 16The Jews were filled with joy and gladness and were honored everywhere. 17In every province and city, wherever the king's decree arrived, the Jews rejoiced and had a great celebration and declared a public festival and holiday. And many of the people of the land became Jews themselves, for they feared what the Jews might do to them.

Job

Chapter One

Prologue

1There once was a man named Job who lived in the land of Uz. He was blameless—a man of complete integrity. He feared God and stayed away from evil. 2He had seven sons and three daughters. 3He owned 7,000 sheep, 3,000 camels, 500 teams of oxen, and 500 female donkeys. He also had many servants.

4Job's sons would take turns preparing feasts in their homes, and they would also invite their three sisters to celebrate with them. 5When these celebrations ended—sometimes after several days—Job would purify his children. He would get up early in the morning and offer a burnt offering for each of them. For Job said to himself, "Perhaps my children have sinned and have cursed God in their hearts." This was Job's regular practice.

Job's First Test

6One day the members of the heavenly court1:6a Hebrew *the sons of God* came to present themselves before the Lord, and the Accuser, Satan,1:6b Hebrew *and the satan;* similarly throughout this chapter came with them. 7"Where have you come from?" the Lord asked Satan.

The Walk – S.B. Stone & Rock Solid Publishing, LLC
©2018

Satan answered the Lord, "I have been patrolling the earth, watching everything that's going on."

8Then the Lord asked Satan, "Have you noticed my servant Job? He is the finest man in all the earth. He is blameless—a man of complete integrity. He fears God and stays away from evil."

9Satan replied to the Lord, "Yes, but Job has good reason to fear God. 10You have always put a wall of protection around him and his home and his property. You have made him prosper in everything he does. Look how rich he is! 11But reach out and take away everything he has, and he will surely curse you to your face!"12"All right, you may test him," the Lord said to Satan. "Do whatever you want with everything he possesses, but don't harm him physically." So Satan left the Lord's presence. 13One day when Job's sons and daughters were feasting at the oldest brother's house, 14a messenger arrived at Job's home with this news: "Your oxen were plowing, with the donkeys feeding beside them, 15when the Sabeans raided us. They stole all the animals and killed all the farmhands. I am the only one who escaped to tell you." 16While he was still speaking, another messenger arrived with this news: "The fire of God has fallen from heaven and burned up your sheep and all the shepherds. I am the only one who escaped to tell you."

17While he was still speaking, a third messenger arrived with this news: "Three bands of Chaldean raiders have stolen your camels and killed your servants. I am the only one who escaped to tell you." 18While he was still speaking, another messenger arrived with this news:

"Your sons and daughters were feasting in their oldest brother's home. 19Suddenly, a powerful wind swept in from the wilderness and hit the house on all sides. The house collapsed, and all your children are dead. I am the only one who escaped to tell you." 20Job stood up and tore his robe in grief. Then he shaved his head and fell to the ground to worship. 21He said, "I came naked from my mother's womb, and I will be naked when I leave. The Lord gave me what I had, and the Lord has taken it away. Praise the name of the Lord!" 22In all of this, Job did not sin by blaming God.   [2]

The Book of Job

Chapter Two   **Job's Second Test**

1One day the members of the heavenly court2:1a Hebrew *the sons of God* came again to present themselves before the Lord, and the Accuser, Satan,2:1b Hebrew *and the satan;* similarly throughout this chapter came with them. 2"Where have you come from?" the Lord asked Satan.

Satan answered the Lord, "I have been patrolling the earth, watching everything that's going on."

3Then the Lord asked Satan, "Have you noticed my servant Job? He is the finest man in all the earth. He is blameless—a man of complete integrity. He fears God and stays away from evil. And he has maintained his integrity, even though you urged me to harm him without cause."

4Satan replied to the Lord, "Skin for skin! A man will give up everything he has to save his life. 5But reach out and take away his health, and he will surely curse you to your face!"

6"All right, do with him as you please," the Lord said to Satan. "But spare his life." 7So Satan left the Lord's presence, and he struck Job with terrible boils from head to foot. 8Job scraped his skin with a piece of broken pottery as he sat among the ashes. 9His wife said to him,

"Are you still trying to maintain your integrity? Curse God and die." 10But Job replied, "You talk like a foolish woman. Should we accept only good things from the hand of God and never anything bad?" So in all this, Job said nothing wrong.

Job's Three Friends Share His Anguish

11When three of Job's friends heard of the tragedy he had suffered, they got together and traveled from their homes to comfort and console him. Their names were Eliphaz the Temanite, Bildad the Shuhite, and Zophar the Naamathite. 12When they saw Job from a distance, they scarcely recognized him. Wailing loudly, they tore their robes and threw dust into the air over their heads to show their grief. 13Then they sat on the ground with him for seven days and nights. No one said a word to Job, for they saw that his suffering was too great for words. [2]

The Book of Job

Chapter Thirty-eight

The Lord Challenges Job

1Then the Lord answered Job from the whirlwind: 2"Who is this that questions my wisdom with such ignorant words? 3Brace yourself like a man, because I have some questions for you, and you must answer them. 4"Where were you when I laid the foundations of the earth? Tell me, if you know so much. 5Who determined its dimensions and stretched out the surveying line? 6What supports its foundations, and who laid its cornerstone 7as the morning stars sang together and all the angels38:7 Hebrew *the sons of God* shouted for joy? 8"Who kept the sea inside its boundaries as it burst from the womb, 9and as I clothed it with clouds and wrapped it in thick darkness? 10For I locked it behind barred gates, limiting its shores. 11I said, 'This far and no farther will you come. Here your proud waves must stop!'12"Have you ever commanded the morning to appear and caused the dawn to rise in the east? 13Have you made daylight spread to the ends of the earth, to bring an end to the night's wickedness? 14As the light approaches, the earth takes shape like clay pressed beneath a seal; it is robed in brilliant colors.38:14 Or *its features stand out like folds in a robe.* 15The light disturbs the wicked and stops the arm that is raised in violence. 16"Have you explored the springs from which the seas come? Have you explored their depths? 17Do you know where the gates of death are located? Have you seen the gates of utter gloom? 18Do you realize the extent of the earth? Tell me about it if you know!

19"Where does light come from, and where does darkness go? 20Can you take each to its home?

Do you know how to get there? 21But of course you know all this! For you were born before it was all created, and you are so very experienced! 22"Have you visited the storehouses of the snow or seen the storehouses of hail? 23(I have reserved them as weapons for the time of trouble, for the day of battle and war.) 24Where is the path to the source of light? Where is the home of the east wind? 25"Who created a channel for the torrents of rain? Who laid out the path for the lightning? 26Who makes the rain fall on barren land, in a desert where no one lives? 27Who sends rain to satisfy the parched ground and make the tender grass spring up? 28"Does the rain have a father? Who gives birth to the dew? 29Who is the mother of the ice? Who gives birth to the frost from the heavens? 30For the water turns to ice as hard as rock, and the surface of the water freezes. 31"Can you direct the movement of the stars—binding the cluster of the

Pleiadesor loosening the cords of Orion? 32Can you direct the constellations through the seasons or guide the Bear with her cubs across the heavens? 33Do you know the laws of the universe? Can you use them to regulate the earth? 34"Can you shout to the clouds and make it rain? 35Can you make lightning appear and cause it to strike as you direct? 36Who gives intuition to the heart and instinct to the mind? 37Who is wise enough to count all the clouds? Who can tilt the water jars of heaven 38when the parched ground is dry and the soil has hardened into clods? 39"Can you stalk prey for a lioness and satisfy the young lions' appetites 40as they lie in their dens or crouch in the thicket? 41Who provides food for the ravens when their young cry out to God and wander about in hunger?   [2]

The Book of Job Chapter Thirty-nine

1-4"Do you know the month when mountain goats give birth? Have you ever watched a doe bear her fawn? Do you know how many months she is pregnant? Do you know the season of her delivery, when she crouches down and drops her offspring? Her young ones flourish and are soon on their own; they leave and don't come back. 5-8"Who do you think set the wild donkey free, opened the corral gates and let him go? I gave him the whole wilderness to roam in, the rolling plains and wide-open places. He laughs at his city cousins, who are harnessed and harried. He's oblivious to the cries of teamsters. He grazes freely through the hills, nibbling anything that's green. 9-12"Will the wild buffalo condescend to serve you, volunteer to spend the night in your barn? Can you imagine hitching your plow to a buffalo and getting him to till your fields? He's hugely strong, yes, but could you trust him, would you dare turn the job over to him? You wouldn't for a minute depend on him, would you, to do what you said when you said it? 13-18"The ostrich flaps her wings futilely— all those beautiful feathers, but useless! She lays her eggs on the hard ground, leaves them there in the dirt, exposed to the weather, not caring that they might get stepped on and cracked or trampled by some wild animal. She's negligent with her young, as if they weren't even hers. She cares nothing about anything.

She wasn't created very smart, that's for sure, wasn't given her share of good sense. But when she runs, oh, how she runs, laughing, leaving horse and rider in the dust. 19-25"Are you the one who gave the horse his prowess and adorned him with a shimmering mane? Did you create him to prance proudly and strike terror with his royal snorts? He paws the ground fiercely, eager and spirited, then charges into the fray.

He laughs at danger, fearless, doesn't shy away from the sword. The banging and clanging of quiver and lance don't faze him. He quivers with excitement, and at the trumpet blast races off at a gallop. At the sound of the trumpet he neighs mightily, smelling the excitement of battle from a long way off, catching the rolling thunder of the war cries.

26-30"Was it through your know-how that the hawk learned to fly, soaring effortlessly on thermal updrafts? Did you command the eagle's flight, and teach her to build her nest in the heights, perfectly at home on the high cliff face, invulnerable on pinnacle and crag? From her perch she searches for prey, spies it at a great distance. Her young gorge themselves on carrion; wherever there's a roadkill, you'll see her circling." [3]

The Book of Job – Chapter Job Forty

1-2God then confronted Job directly: "Now what do you have to say for yourself? Are you going to haul me, the Mighty One, into court and press charges?"

Job Answers God

I'm Ready to Shut Up and Listen

3-5Job answered: "I'm speechless, in awe—words fail me. I should never have opened my mouth! I've talked too much, way too much. I'm ready to shut up and listen."

God's Second Set of Questions

I Want Straight Answers

6-7God addressed Job next from the eye of the storm, and this is what he said: "I have some more questions for you, and I want straight answers. 8-14"Do you presume to tell me what I'm doing wrong? Are you calling me a sinner so you can be a saint? Do you have an arm like my arm? Can you shout in thunder the way I can? Go ahead, show your stuff. Let's see what you're made of, what you can do. Unleash your outrage. Target the arrogant and lay them flat. Target the arrogant and bring them to their knees. Stop the wicked in their tracks—make mincemeat of them! Dig a mass grave and dump them in it—faceless corpses in an unmarked grave. I'll gladly step aside and hand things over to you—you can surely save yourself with no help from me! 15-24"Look at the land beast, Behemoth. I created him as well as you. Grazing on grass, docile as a cow—Just look at the strength of his back, the powerful muscles of his belly. His tail sways like a cedar in the wind; his huge legs are like beech trees. His skeleton is made of steel, every bone in his body hard as steel. Most magnificent of all my creatures, but I still lead him around like a lamb! The grass-covered hills serve him meals, while field mice frolic in his shadow. He takes afternoon naps under shade trees, cools himself in the reedy swamps, lazily cool in the leafy shadows as the breeze moves through the willows. And when the river rages he doesn't budge, stolid and unperturbed even when the Jordan goes wild. But you'd never want him for a pet—you'd never be able to housebreak him!"   [3]

The Book of Job - Chapter Forty-one

I Run This Universe

1-11"Or can you pull in the sea beast, Leviathan, with a fly rod and stuff him in your creel? Can you lasso him with a rope, or snag him with an anchor? Will he beg you over and over for mercy, or flatter you with flowery speech? Will he apply for a job with you to run errands and serve you the rest of your life? Will you play with him as if he were a pet goldfish? Will you make him the mascot of the neighborhood children? Will you put him on display in the market and have shoppers haggle over the price? Could you shoot him full of arrows like a pin cushion, or drive harpoons into his huge head? If you so much as lay a hand on him, you won't live to tell the story. What hope would you have with such a creature? Why, one look at him would do you in! If you can't hold your own against his glowering visage, how, then, do you expect to stand up to *me*? Who could confront me and get by with it? I'm *in charge* of all this—I *run* this universe! 12-17"But I've more to say about Leviathan, the sea beast, his enormous bulk, his beautiful shape.

Who would even dream of piercing that tough skin or putting those jaws into bit and bridle? And who would dare knock at the door of his mouth filled with row upon row of fierce teeth? His pride is invincible; nothing can make a dent in that pride. Nothing can get through that proud skin—impervious to weapons and weather, the thickest and toughest of hides, impenetrable! 18-34"He snorts and the world lights up with fire, he blinks and the dawn breaks. Comets pour out of his mouth, fireworks arc and branch. Smoke erupts from his nostrils like steam from a boiling pot. He blows and fires blaze; flames of fire stream from his mouth. All muscle he is—sheer and seamless muscle. To meet him is to dance with death. Sinewy and lithe, there's not a soft spot in his entire body—as tough inside as out, rock-hard, invulnerable. Even angels run for cover when he surfaces, cowering before his tail-thrashing turbulence. Javelins bounce harmlessly off his hide, harpoons ricochet wildly. Iron bars are so much straw to him, bronze weapons beneath notice. Arrows don't even make him blink; bullets make no more impression than raindrops. A battle ax is nothing but a splinter of kindling; he treats a brandished harpoon as a joke. His belly is armor-plated, inexorable—unstoppable as a barge. He roils deep ocean the way you'd boil water, he whips the sea like you'd whip an egg into batter. With a luminous trail stretching out behind him, you might think Ocean had grown a gray beard! There's nothing on this earth quite like him, not an ounce of fear in *that* creature! He surveys all the high and mighty—king of the ocean, king of the deep!" [3]

The Book of Job

Chapter Forty-two

Job Worships God

I Babbled On About Things Far Beyond Me

1-6 Job answered God: "I'm convinced: You can do anything and everything. Nothing and no one can upset your plans. You asked, 'who is this muddying the water, ignorantly confusing the issue, second-guessing my purposes?' I admit it. I was the one. I babbled on about things far beyond me, made small talk about wonders way over my head. You told me, 'Listen, and let me do the talking. Let me ask the questions. *You* give the answers.' I admit I once lived by rumors of you; now I have it all firsthand—from my own eyes and ears! I'm sorry—forgive me. I'll never do that again, I promise! I'll never again live on crusts of hearsay, crumbs of rumor."

God Restores Job

I Will Accept His Prayer

7-8After God had finished addressing Job, he turned to Eliphaz the Temanite and said,

"I've had it with you and your two friends. I'm fed up! You haven't been honest either with me or about me—not the way my friend Job has. So here's what you must do. Take seven bulls and seven rams, and go to my friend Job. Sacrifice a burnt offering on your own behalf. My friend Job will pray for you, and I will accept his prayer. He will ask me not to treat you as you deserve for talking nonsense about me, and for not being honest with me, as he has." 9They did it.

Eliphaz the Temanite, Bildad the Shuhite, and Zophar the Naamathite did what God commanded. And God accepted Job's prayer. 10-11After Job had interceded for his friends, God restored his fortune—and then doubled it! All his brothers and sisters and friends came to his house and celebrated. They told him how sorry they were, and consoled him for all the trouble God had brought him. Each of them brought generous housewarming gifts.

12-15God blessed Job's later life even more than his earlier life. He ended up with fourteen thousand sheep, six thousand camels, one thousand teams of oxen, and one thousand donkeys. He also had seven sons and three daughters. He named the first daughter Dove, the second, Cinnamon, and the third, Darkeyes. There was not a woman in that country as beautiful as Job's daughters. Their father treated them as equals with their brothers, providing the same inheritance.

16-17Job lived on another 140 years, living to see his children and grandchildren—four generations of them! Then he died—an old man, a full life. [3]

Book of Psalms

Thirty-seven

A David Psalm

1-2Don't bother your head with braggarts or wish you could succeed like the wicked. In no time they'll shrivel like grass clippings and wilt like cut flowers in the sun. 3-4Get insurance with God and do a good deed, settle down and stick to your last. Keep company with God, get in on the best. 5-6Open up before God, keep nothing back; he'll do whatever needs to be done: He'll validate your life in the clear light of day and stamp you with approval at high noon. 7Quiet down before God, be prayerful before him. Don't bother with those who climb the ladder, who elbow their way to the top. 8-9Bridle your anger, trash your wrath, cool your pipes—it only makes things worse. Before long the crooks will be bankrupt; God-investors will soon own the store. 10-11Before you know it, the wicked will have had it; you'll stare at his once famous place and—nothing! Down-to-earth people will move in and take over, relishing a huge bonanza. 12-13Bad guys have it in for the good guys, obsessed with doing them in. But God isn't losing any sleep; to him they're a joke with no punch line. 14-15Bullies brandish their swords, pull back on their bows with a flourish. They're out to beat up on the harmless, or mug that nice man out walking his dog. A banana peel lands them flat on their faces—slapstick figures in a moral circus. 16-17Less is more and more is less. One righteous will outclass fifty wicked, for the wicked are moral weaklings but the righteous are God-strong. 1819God keeps track of the decent folk; what they do won't soon be forgotten. In hard times, they'll hold their heads high; when the shelves are bare, they'll be full. 20Goddespisers have had it; God's enemies are finished—Stripped bare like vineyards at harvest time, vanished like smoke in thin air. 21-22Wicked borrows and never returns; Righteous gives and gives. Generous gets it all in the end; Stingy is cut off at the pass. 23-24Stalwart walks in step with God; his path blazed by God, he's happy. If he stumbles, he's not down for long; God has a grip on his hand. 25-26I once was young, now I'm a graybeard—not once have I seen an abandoned believer, or his kids out roaming the streets. Every day he's out giving and lending, his children making him proud. 27-28Turn your back on evil, work for the good and don't quit. God loves this kind of thing, never turns away from his friends. 28-29Live this way and you've got it made, but bad eggs will be tossed out. The good get planted on good land and put down healthy roots. 30-31Righteous chews on wisdom like a dog on a bone, rolls virtue around on his tongue. His heart pumps God's Word like blood through his veins; his feet are as sure as a cat's. 32-33Wicked sets a watch for Righteous, he's out for the kill. God, alert, is also on watch—Wicked won't hurt a hair of his head. 34Wait passionately for God, don't leave the path. He'll give you your place in the sun while you watch the wicked lose it. 35-36I saw Wicked bloated like a toad, croaking pretentious nonsense. The next time I looked there was nothing—a punctured bladder, vapid and limp. 37-38Keep your eye on the healthy soul, scrutinize the straight life; There's a future in strenuous wholeness. But the willful will soon be discarded; insolent souls are on a dead-end street.

39-40The spacious, free life is from God, it's also protected and safe. God-strengthened, we're delivered from evil—when we run to him, he saves us. [3]

Book of Isaiah 7:13-16

13Then Isaiah said, "Listen well, you royal family of David! Isn't it enough to exhaust human patience? Must you exhaust the patience of my God as well? 14All right then, the Lord himself will give you the sign. Look! The virgin7:14 Or *young woman* will conceive a child! She will give birth to a son and will call him Immanuel (which means 'God is with us'). 15By the time this child is old enough to choose what is right and reject what is wrong, he will be eating yogurt7:15 Or *curds;* also in 7:22 and honey. 16For before the child is that old, the lands of the two kings you fear so much will both be deserted. [2]

Book of Isaiah 8:11-22

A Call to Trust the Lord

11The Lord has given me a strong warning not to think like everyone else does. He said,

12"Don't call everything a conspiracy, like they do, and don't live in dread of what frightens them. 13Make the Lord of Heaven's Armies holy in your life. He is the one you should fear. He is the one who should make you tremble. 14He will keep you safe. But to Israel and Judah he will be a stone that makes people stumble, a rock that makes them fall. And for the people of Jerusalem he will be a trap and a snare. 15Many will stumble and fall, never to rise again. They will be snared and captured." 16Preserve the teaching of God; entrust his instructions to those who follow me. 17I will wait for the Lord, who has turned away from the descendants of Jacob. I will put my hope in him. 18I and the children the Lord has given me serve as signs and warnings to Israel from the Lord of Heaven's Armies who dwells in his Temple on Mount Zion. 19Someone may say to you, "Let's ask the mediums and those who consult the spirits of the dead. With their whisperings and mutterings, they will tell us what to do." But shouldn't people ask God for guidance? Should the living seek guidance from the dead? 20Look to God's instructions and teachings! People who contradict his word are completely in the dark. 21They will go from one place to another, weary and hungry. And because they are hungry, they will rage and curse their king and their God. They will look up to heaven 22and down at the earth, but wherever they look, there will be trouble and anguish and dark despair. They will be thrown out into the darkness. [2]

Book of Isaiah

Chapter 9:1-7

The Walk – S.B. Stone & Rock Solid Publishing, LLC
©2018

Hope in the Messiah

9:1 Verse 9:1 is numbered 8:23 in Hebrew text. Nevertheless, that time of darkness and despair will not go on forever. The land of Zebulun and Naphtali will be humbled, but there will be a time in the future when Galilee of the Gentiles, which lies along the road that runs between the Jordan and the sea, will be filled with glory. 29:2a Verses 9:2-21 are numbered 9:1-20 in hebrew text. The people who walk in darkness will see a great light. For those who live in a land of deep darkness, 9:2b Greek version reads *a land where death casts its shadow.* Compare Matt 4:16. a light will shine. 3You will enlarge the nation of Israel, and its people will rejoice. They will rejoice before you as people rejoice at the harvest and like warriors dividing the plunder. 4For you will break the yoke of their slavery and lift the heavy burden from their shoulders. You will break the oppressor's rod, just as you did when you destroyed the army of Midian. 5The boots of the warrior and the uniforms bloodstained by war will all be burned. They will be fuel for the fire. 6For a child is born to us, a son is given to us. The government will rest on his shoulders. And he will be called: Wonderful Counselor, 9:6 Or *Wonderful, Counselor.* Mighty God, Everlasting Father, Prince of Peace. 7His government and its peace will never end. He will rule with fairness and justice from the throne of his ancestor David for all eternity. The passionate commitment of the Lord of Heaven's Armies will make this happen! [2]

Book of Jeremiah

Chapter Twenty-nine

Plans to Give You the Future You Hope For

1-2This is the letter that the prophet Jeremiah sent from Jerusalem to what was left of the elders among the exiles, to the priests and prophets and all the exiles whom Nebuchadnezzar had taken to Babylon from Jerusalem, including King Jehoiachin, the queen mother, the government leaders, and all the skilled laborers and craftsmen. 3The letter was carried by Elasah son of Shaphan and Gemariah son of Hilkiah, whom Zedekiah king of Judah had sent to Nebuchadnezzar king of Babylon. The letter said: 4This is the Message from God-of-the-Angel-Armies, Israel's God, to all the exiles I've taken from Jerusalem to Babylon: 5"Build houses and make yourselves at home. "Put in gardens and eat what grows in that country. 6"Marry and have children. Encourage your children to marry and have children so that you'll thrive in that country and not waste away. 7"Make yourselves at home there and work for the country's welfare. "Pray for Babylon's well-being. If things go well for Babylon, things will go well for you."

8-9Yes. Believe it or not, this is the Message from God-of-the-Angel-Armies, Israel's God: "Don't let all those so-called preachers and know-it-alls who are all over the place there take you in with their lies. Don't pay any attention to the fantasies they keep coming up with to please you. They're a bunch of liars preaching lies—and claiming I sent them! I never sent them, believe me." God's Decree! 10-11This is God's Word on the subject: "As soon as Babylon's seventy years are up and not a day before, I'll show up and take care of you as I promised and bring you back home. I know what I'm doing. I have it all planned out—plans to take care of you, not abandon you, plans to give you the future you hope for. 12"When you call on me, when you come and pray to me, I'll listen. 13-14"When you come looking for me, you'll find me. "Yes, when you get serious about finding me and want it more than anything else, I'll make sure you won't be disappointed." God's Decree. "I'll turn things around for you. I'll bring you back from all the countries into which I drove you"—God's Decree—"bring you home to the place from which I sent you off into exile. You can count on it. 15-19"But for right now, because you've taken up with these new-fangled prophets who set themselves up as 'Babylonian specialists,' spreading the word 'God sent them just for us!' God is setting the record straight: As for the king still sitting on David's throne and all the people left in Jerusalem who didn't go into exile with you, they're facing bad times. God-of-the-Angel-Armies says, 'Watch this!

Catastrophe is on the way: war, hunger, disease! They're a barrel of rotten apples. I'll rid the country of them through war and hunger and disease. The whole world is going to hold its nose at the smell, shut its eyes at the horrible sight. They'll end up in slum ghettos because they wouldn't listen to a thing I said when I sent my servant-prophets preaching tirelessly and urgently. No, they wouldn't listen to a word I said.'" God's Decree. 20-23"And you—you exiles whom I sent out of Jerusalem to Babylon—listen to God's Message to you. As far as Ahab son of Kolaiah and Zedekiah son of Maaseiah are concerned, the 'Babylonian specialists' who are preaching lies in my name, I will turn them over to Nebuchadnezzar king of Babylon, who will kill them while you watch. The exiles from Judah will take what they see at the execution and use it as a curse: 'God fry you to a crisp like the king of

Babylon fried Zedekiah and Ahab in the fire!' Those two men, sex predators and prophet-impostors, got what they deserved. They pulled every woman they got their hands on into bed—their neighbors' wives, no less—and preached lies claiming it was my Message. I never sent those men. I've never had anything to do with them." God's Decree. "They won't get away with a thing. I've witnessed it all." 24-26And this is the Message for Shemaiah the Nehelamite: "God-of-the-Angel-Armies, the God of Israel, says: You took it on yourself to send letters to all the people in Jerusalem and to the priest Zephaniah son of Maaseiah and the company of priests. In your letter you told Zephaniah that God set you up as priest replacing priest Jehoiada. He's put you in charge of God's Temple and made you responsible for locking up any crazy fellow off the street who takes it into his head to be a prophet. 27-28"So why haven't you done anything about muzzling Jeremiah of Anathoth, who's going around posing as a prophet? He's gone so far as to write to us in Babylon, 'It's going to be a long exile, so build houses and make yourselves at home. Plant gardens and prepare

Babylonian recipes.'" 29The priest Zephaniah read that letter to the prophet Jeremiah. 3032Then God told Jeremiah, "Send this Message to the exiles. Tell them what God says about

Shemaiah the Nehelamite: Shemaiah is preaching lies to you. I didn't send him. He is seducing you into believing lies. So this is God's verdict: I will punish Shemaiah the Nehelamite and his whole family. He's going to end up with nothing and no one. No one from his family will be around to see any of the good that I am going to do for my people because he has preached rebellion against me." God's Decree. [3]

The Book of Ecclesiastes

Chapter Two

1-3I said to myself, "Let's go for it—experiment with pleasure, have a good time!" But there was nothing to it, nothing but smoke. What do I think of the fun-filled life? Insane! Inane! My verdict on the pursuit of happiness? Who needs it? With the help of a bottle of wine and all the wisdom I could muster, I tried my level best to penetrate the absurdity of life. I wanted to get a handle on anything useful we mortals might do during the years we spend on this earth.

I Never Said No to Myself

4-8Oh, I did great things: built houses, planted vineyards, designed gardens and parks and planted a variety of fruit trees in them, made pools of water to irrigate the groves of trees. I bought slaves, male and female, who had children, giving me even more slaves; then I acquired large herds and flocks, larger than any before me in Jerusalem. I piled up silver and gold, loot from kings and kingdoms. I gathered a chorus of singers to entertain me with song, and—most exquisite of all pleasures—voluptuous maidens for my bed.

9-10Oh, how I prospered! I left all my predecessors in Jerusalem far behind, left them behind in the dust. What's more, I kept a clear head through it all. Everything I wanted I took—I never said no to myself. I gave in to every impulse, held back nothing. I sucked the marrow of pleasure out of every task—my reward to myself for a hard day's work!

I Hate Life

11Then I took a good look at everything I'd done, looked at all the sweat and hard work. But when I looked, I saw nothing but smoke. Smoke and spitting into the wind. There was nothing to any of it. Nothing. 12-14And then I took a hard look at what's smart and what's stupid. What's left to do after you've been king? That's a hard act to follow. You just do what you can, and that's it. But I did see that it's better to be smart than stupid, just as light is better than darkness. Even so, though the smart ones see where they're going and the stupid ones grope in the dark, they're all the same in the end. One fate for all—and that's it. 15-16When I realized that my fate's the same as the fool's, I had to ask myself, "So why bother being wise?" It's all smoke, nothing but smoke. The smart and the stupid both disappear out of sight. In a day or two they're both forgotten. Yes, both the smart and the stupid die, and that's it. 17I hate life. As far as I can see, what happens on earth is a bad business. It's smoke—and spitting into the wind. 1819And I hated everything I'd accomplished and accumulated on this earth. I can't take it with me—no, I have to leave it to whoever comes after me. Whether they're worthy or worthless— and who's to tell?—they'll take over the earthly results of my intense thinking and hard work. Smoke. 20-23 That's when I called it quits, gave up on anything that could be hoped for on this earth. What's the point of working your fingers to the bone if you hand over what you worked for to someone who never lifted a finger for it? Smoke, that's what it is. A bad business from start to finish. So what do you get from a life of hard labor? Pain and grief from dawn to dusk. Never a decent night's rest. Nothing but smoke. 24-26The best you can do with your life is have a good time and get by the best you can. The way I see it, that's it—divine fate. Whether we feast or fast, it's up to God. God may give wisdom and knowledge and joy to his favorites, but sinners are assigned a life of hard labor, and end up turning their wages over to God's favorites. Nothing but smoke—and spitting into the wind.   [3]

The Book of Ecclesiastes

Chapter Twelve

1-2Honor and enjoy your Creator while you're still young, Before the years take their toll and your vigor wanes, Before your vision dims and the world blurs And the winter years keep you close to the fire. 3-5In old age, your body no longer serves you so well. Muscles slacken, grip weakens, joints stiffen. The shades are pulled down on the world. You can't come and go at will. Things grind to a halt. The hum of the household fades away. You are wakened now by bird-song. Hikes to the mountains are a thing of the past. Even a stroll down the road has its terrors. Your hair turns apple-blossom white, adorning a fragile and impotent matchstick body.

Yes, you're well on your way to eternal rest, while your friends make plans for your funeral. 6-7Life, lovely while it lasts, is soon over. Life as we know it, precious and beautiful, ends. The body is put back in the same ground it came from. The spirit returns to God, who first breathed it. 8It's all smoke, nothing but smoke. The Quester says that everything's smoke.

The Final Word

9-10Besides being wise himself, the Quester also taught others knowledge. He weighed, examined, and arranged many proverbs. The Quester did his best to find the right words and write the plain truth. 11The words of the wise prod us to live well. They're like nails hammered home, holding life together. They are given by God, the one Shepherd. 12-13But regarding anything beyond this, dear friend, go easy. There's no end to the publishing of books, and constant study wears you out so you're no good for anything else. The last and final word is this: Fear God. Do what he tells you. 14And that's it. Eventually God will bring everything that we do out into the open and judge it according to its hidden intent, whether it's good or evil.

Book of Isaiah

Chapter One

Messages of Judgment

Quit Your Worship Charades

1The vision that Isaiah son of Amoz saw regarding Judah and
Jerusalem during the times of the kings of Judah: Uzziah, Jotham, Ahaz,
and Hezekiah. 2-4Heaven and earth, you're the jury. Listen to God's
case: "I had children and raised them well, and they turned on me. The
ox knows who's boss, the mule knows the hand that feeds him, But not
Israel. My people don't know up from down. Shame! Misguided God-
dropouts, staggering under their guilt-baggage, Gang of miscreants, band
of vandals—My people have walked out on me, their God, turned their
backs on The Holy of Israel, walked off and never looked back. 5-
9"Why bother even trying to do anything with you when you just keep
to your bullheaded ways? You keep beating your heads against brick
walls. Everything within you protests against you. From the bottom of
your feet to the top of your head, nothing's working right. Wounds and
bruises and running sores—untended, unwashed, unbandaged. Your
country is laid waste, your cities burned down. Your land is destroyed
by outsiders while you watch, reduced to rubble by barbarians. Daughter
Zion is deserted—like a tumbledown shack on a dead-end street, like a
tarpaper shanty on the wrong side of the tracks, like a sinking ship
abandoned by the rats. If God-of-the-Angel-Armies hadn't left us a few
survivors, we'd be as desolate as Sodom, doomed just like Gomorrah.
10"Listen to my Message, you Sodom-schooled leaders. Receive God's
revelation, you Gomorrah-schooled people. 11-12"Why this frenzy of
sacrifices?" *God's* asking. "Don't you think I've had my fill of burnt
sacrifices, rams and plump grain-fed calves? Don't you think I've had
my fill of blood from bulls, lambs, and goats? When you come before
me, whoever gave you the idea of acting like this, Running here and
there, doing this and that—all this sheer *commotion* in the place
provided for worship? 13-17"Quit your worship charades. I can't stand
your trivial religious games: Monthly conferences, weekly Sabbaths,
special meetings—meetings, meetings, meetings—I can't stand one
more! Meetings for this, meetings for that. I hate them! You've worn me
out! I'm sick of your religion, religion, religion, while you go right on
sinning. When you put on your next prayer-performance, I'll be looking
the other way. No matter how long or loud or often you pray, I'll not be

listening. And do you know why? Because you've been tearing people to pieces, and your hands are bloody. Go home and wash up. Clean up your act. Sweep your lives clean of your evildoings so I don't have to look at them any longer. Say no to wrong.

Learn to do good. Work for justice. Help the down-and-out. Stand up for the homeless. Go to bat for the defenseless.

Let's Argue This Out

18-20"Come. Sit down. Let's argue this out." This is God's Message: "If your sins are blood-red, they'll be snow-white. If they're red like crimson, they'll be like wool. If you'll willingly obey, you'll feast like kings. But if you're willful and stubborn, you'll die like dogs." That's right. God says so.

Those Who Walk Out on God

21-23Oh! Can you believe it? The chaste city has become a whore! She was once all justice, everyone living as good neighbors, And now they're all at one another's throats.

Your coins are all counterfeits. Your wine is watered down. Your leaders are turncoats who keep company with crooks. They sell themselves to the highest bidder and grab anything not nailed down. They never stand up for the homeless, never stick up for the defenseless. 24-31This Decree, therefore, of the Master, God-of-the-Angel-Armies, the Strong One of Israel: "This is it! I'll get my oppressors off my back. I'll get back at my enemies. I'll give you the back of my hand, purge the junk from your life, clean you up. I'll set honest judges and wise counselors among you just like it was back in the beginning. Then you'll be renamed City-That-Treats-People-Right, the True-Blue City."

God's right ways will put Zion right again. God's right actions will restore her penitents. But it's curtains for rebels and God-traitors, a dead end for those who walk out on God.

"Your dalliances in those oak grove shrines will leave you looking mighty foolish, all that fooling around in god and goddess gardens that you thought was the latest thing. You'll end up like an oak tree with all its leaves falling off, like an unwatered garden, withered and brown. 'The Big Man' will turn out to be dead bark and twigs, and his 'work,' the spark that starts the fire that exposes man and work both as nothing but cinders and smoke." [3]

The Walk – S.B. Stone & Rock Solid Publishing, LLC
©2018

Book of Zephaniah

Chapter Three

Jerusalem's Rebellion and Redemption

1What sorrow awaits rebellious, polluted Jerusalem, the city of violence and crime! 2No one can tell it anything; it refuses all correction. It does not trust in the Lord or draw near to its God. 3Its leaders are like roaring lions hunting for their victims. Its judges are like ravenous wolves at evening time, who by dawn have left no trace of their prey. 4Its prophets are arrogant liars seeking their own gain. Its priests defile the Temple by disobeying God's instructions. 5But the Lord is still there in the city, and he does no wrong. Day by day he hands down justice, and he does not fail. But the wicked know no shame. 6"I have wiped out many nations, devastating their fortress walls and towers. Their streets are now deserted; their cities lie in silent ruin. There are no survivors—none at all. 7I thought, 'Surely they will have reverence for me now! Surely they will listen to my warnings. Then I won't need to strike again, destroying their homes.' But no, they get up early to continue their evil deeds. 8Therefore, be patient," says the Lord. "Soon I will stand and accuse these evil nations. For I have decided to gather the kingdoms of the earth and pour out my fiercest anger and fury on them. All the earth will be devoured by the fire of my jealousy. 9"Then I will purify the speech of all people, so that everyone can worship the Lord together. 10My scattered people who live beyond the rivers of Ethiopia3:10 Hebrew *Cush* will come to present their offerings. 11On that day you will no longer need to be ashamed, for you will no longer be rebels against me. I will remove all proud and arrogant people from among you. There will be no more haughtiness on my holy mountain. 12Those who are left will be the lowly and humble, for it is they who trust in the name of the Lord. 13The remnant of Israel will do no wrong; they will never tell lies or deceive one another. They will eat and sleep in safety, and no one will make them afraid." 14Sing, O daughter of Zion; shout aloud, O Israel! Be glad and rejoice with all your heart, O daughter of Jerusalem! 15For the Lord will remove his hand of judgment and will disperse the armies of your enemy. And the Lord himself, the King of Israel, will live among you! At last your troubles will be over, and you will never again fear disaster.

16On that day the announcement to Jerusalem will be, "Cheer up, Zion! Don't be afraid! 17For the Lord your God is living among you. He is a mighty savior. He will take delight in you with gladness. With his love, he will calm all your fears.3:17 Or *He will be silent in his love.* Greek and Syriac versions read *He will renew you with his love.* He will rejoice over you with joyful songs." 18"I will gather you who mourn for the appointed festivals; you will be disgraced no more.3:18 The meaning of the Hebrew for this verse is uncertain. 19And I will deal severely with all who have oppressed you. I will save the weak and helpless ones; I will bring together those who were chased away. I will give glory and fame to my former exiles, wherever they have been mocked and shamed. 20On that day I will gather you together and bring you home again. I will give you a good name, a name of distinction, among all the nations of the earth, as I restore your fortunes before their very eyes. I, the Lord, have spoken!" [2]

Book of Joel

Chapter Two

The Locust Army

God's Judgment's on its way—the Day's almost here!

A black day! A Doomsday! Clouds with no silver lining!

Like dawn light moving over the mountains, a huge army is coming. There's never been anything like it and never will be again. Wildfire burns everything before this army and fire licks up everything in its wake.

Before it arrives, the country is like the Garden of Eden. When it leaves, it is Death Valley. Nothing escapes unscathed. 4-6The locust army seems all horses—galloping horses, an army of horses. It sounds like thunder leaping on mountain ridges, Or like the roar of wildfire through grass and brush, Or like an invincible army shouting for blood, ready to fight, straining at the bit. At the sight of this army, the people panic, faces white with terror. 7-11The invaders charge.

They climb barricades. Nothing stops them. Each soldier does what he's told, so disciplined, so determined. They don't get in each other's way. Each one knows his job and does it. Undaunted and fearless, unswerving, unstoppable. They storm the city, swarm its defenses, loot the houses, breaking down doors, smashing windows. They arrive like an earthquake, sweep through like a tornado. Sun and moon turn out their lights, stars black out. God himself bellows in thunder as he commands his forces. Look at the size of that army! And the strength of those who obey him! God's Judgment Day—great and terrible. Who can possibly survive this? Change Your Life

12But there's also this, it's not too late—God's personal Message!—"Come back to me and really mean it! Come fasting and weeping, sorry for your sins!" 13-14Change your life, not just your clothes. Come back to God, your God. And here's why: God is kind and merciful. He takes a deep breath, puts up with a lot, This most patient God, extravagant in love, always ready to cancel catastrophe. Who knows? Maybe he'll do it now, maybe he'll turn around and show pity. Maybe, when all's said and done, there'll be blessings full and robust for your God! 15-17Blow the ram's horn trumpet in Zion! Declare a day of repentance, a holy fast day. Call a public meeting. Get everyone there. Consecrate the congregation. Make sure the elders come, but bring in the children, too, even the nursing babies, Even men and women on their honeymoon— interrupt them and get them there. Between Sanctuary entrance and altar, let the priests, God's servants, weep tears of repentance. Let them intercede: "Have mercy, God, on your people!

Don't abandon your heritage to contempt. Don't let the pagans take over and rule them and sneer, 'And so where is this God of theirs?'" 18-20At that, God went into action to get his land back. He took pity on his people. God answered and spoke to his people, "Look, listen—I'm sending a gift: Grain and wine and olive oil. The fast is over—eat your fill! I won't expose you any longer to contempt among the pagans. I'll head off the final enemy coming out of the north and dump them in a wasteland. Half of them will end up in the Dead Sea, the other half in theMediterranean. There they'll rot, a stench to high heaven. The bigger the enemy, the stronger the stench!"

The Trees Are Bearing Fruit Again

21-24Fear not, Earth! Be glad and celebrate! God has done great things. Fear not, wild animals! The fields and meadows are greening up. The trees are bearing fruit again: a bumper crop of fig trees and vines! Children of Zion, celebrate! Be glad in your God. He's giving you a teacher to train you how to live right— Teaching, like rain out of heaven, showers of words to refresh and nourish your soul, just as he used to do. And plenty of food for your body—silos full of grain, casks of wine and barrels of olive oil. 25-27"I'll make up for the years of the locust, the great locust devastation— Locusts savage, locusts deadly,

The Walk – S.B. Stone & Rock Solid Publishing, LLC

fierce locusts, locusts of doom, That great locust invasion I sent your way. You'll eat your fill of good food. You'll be full of praises to your God, The God who has set you back on your heels in wonder. Never again will my people be despised. You'll know without question that I'm in the thick of life with Israel, That I'm your God, yes, your God, the one and only real God. Never again will my people be despised. The Sun Turning Black and the Moon Blood-Red 28-32"And that's just the beginning: After that— "I will pour out my Spirit on every kind of people: Your sons will prophesy, also your daughters. Your old men will dream, your young men will see visions. I'll even pour out my Spirit on the servants, men and women both. I'll set wonders in the sky above and signs on the earth below: Blood and fire and billowing smoke, the sun turning black and the moon blood-red, Before the Judgment Day of God, the Day tremendous and awesome. Whoever calls, 'Help, God!' gets help. On Mount Zion and in Jerusalem there will be a great rescue—just as God said. Included in the survivors are those that God calls."

Book of Joel

Chapter Three

God Is a Safe Hiding Place

1-3"In those days, yes, at that very time when I put life back together again for Judah and Jerusalem, I'll assemble all the godless nations. I'll lead them down into Judgment Valley And put them all on trial, and judge them one and all because of their treatment of my own people Israel. They scattered my people all over the pagan world and grabbed my land for themselves. They threw dice for my people and used them for barter.

They would trade a boy for a whore, sell a girl for a bottle of wine when they wanted a drink. 4-8"As for you, Tyre and Sidon and Philistia, why should I bother with you? Are you trying to get back at me for something I did to you? If you are, forget it. I'll see to it that it boomerangs on you. You robbed me, cleaned me out of silver and gold, carted off everything valuable to furnish your own temples. You sold the people of Judah and Jerusalem into slavery to the Greeks in faraway places. But I'm going to reverse your crime. I'm going to free those slaves. I'll have done to you what you did to them: I'll sell your children as slaves to your neighbors, And they'll sell them to the far-off Sabeans."

God's Verdict.

9-11Announce this to the godless nations: Prepare for battle!

Soldiers at attention! Present arms! Advance! Turn your shovels into swords,

turn your hoes into spears. Let the weak one throw out his chest and say, "I'm tough, I'm a fighter." Hurry up, pagans! Wherever you are, get a move on! Get your act together. Prepare to be shattered by God! 12Let the pagan nations set out for Judgment Valley. There I'll take my place at the bench and judge all the surrounding nations. 13"Swing the sickle— the harvest is ready. Stomp on the grapes— the winepress is full. The wine vats are full, overflowing with vintage evil. 14"Mass confusion, mob uproar— in Decision Valley! God's Judgment Day has arrived in Decision Valley. 15-17"The sky turns black, sun and moon go dark, stars burn out. God roars from Zion, shouts from Jerusalem. Earth and sky quake in terror. But God is a safe hiding place, a granite safe house for the children of Israel. Then you'll know for sure that I'm your God, Living in Zion, my sacred mountain. Jerusalem will be a sacred city, posted: 'no trespassing.' Milk Rivering Out of the Hills

18-21"What a day! Wine streaming off the mountains, Milk rivering out of the hills, water flowing everywhere in Judah, A fountain pouring out of God's Sanctuary, watering all the parks and gardens! But Egypt will be reduced to weeds in a vacant lot, Edom turned into barren badlands, All because of brutalities to the Judean people, the atrocities and murders of helpless innocents. Meanwhile, Judah will be filled with people, Jerusalem inhabited forever. The sins I haven't already forgiven, I'll forgive." God has moved into Zion for good.   [3]

Book of Haggai

Chapter One

Obedience to God's Call

12Then Zerubbabel son of Shealtiel, and Jeshua son of Jehozadak, the high priest, and the whole remnant of God's people began to obey the message from the Lord their God. When they heard the words of the prophet Haggai, whom the Lord their God had sent, the people feared the

Lord. 13Then Haggai, the Lord's messenger, gave the people this message from the Lord: "I am with you, says the Lord!" 14So the Lord sparked the enthusiasm of Zerubbabel son of Shealtiel, governor of Judah, and the enthusiasm of Jeshua son of Jehozadak, the high priest, and the enthusiasm of the whole remnant of God's people. They began to work on the house of their God, the Lord of Heaven's Armies, 15on September 21 1:15 Hebrew *on the twenty-fourth day of the sixth month,* of the ancient Hebrew lunar calendar. This event occurred on September 21, 520

b.c.; also see note on 1:1a of the second year of King Darius's reign. [2]

Book of Malachi

Chapter Three

The Coming Day of Judgment

1"Look! I am sending my messenger, and he will prepare the way before me. Then the Lord you are seeking will suddenly come to his Temple. The messenger of the covenant, whom you look for so eagerly, is surely coming," says the Lord of Heaven's Armies.

2"But who will be able to endure it when he comes? Who will be able to stand and face him when he appears? For he will be like a blazing fire that refines metal, or like a strong soap that bleaches clothes. 3He will sit like a refiner of silver, burning away the dross. He will purify the Levites, refining them like gold and silver, so that they may once again offer acceptable sacrifices to the Lord. 4Then once more the Lord will accept the offerings brought to him by the people of Judah and Jerusalem, as he did in the past.

5"At that time I will put you on trial. I am eager to witness against all sorcerers and adulterers and liars. I will speak against those who cheat employees of their wages, who oppress widows and orphans, or who deprive the foreigners living among you of justice, for these people do not fear me," says the Lord of Heaven's Armies.

A Call to Repentance

6"I am the Lord, and I do not change. That is why you descendants of Jacob are not already destroyed. 7Ever since the days of your ancestors, you have scorned my decrees and failed to obey them. Now return to me, and I will return to you," says the Lord of Heaven's Armies.

"But you ask, 'How can we return when we have never gone away?'

8"Should people cheat God? Yet you have cheated me!

"But you ask, 'What do you mean? When did we ever cheat you?'

"You have cheated me of the tithes and offerings due to me. 9You are under a curse, for your whole nation has been cheating me. 10Bring all the tithes into the storehouse so there will be enough food in my Temple. If you do," says the Lord of Heaven's Armies, "I will open the windows of heaven for you. I will pour out a blessing so great you won't have enough room to take it in! Try it! Put me to the test! 11Your crops will be abundant, for I will guard them from insects and disease.3:11 Hebrew *from the devourer.* Your grapes will not fall from the vine before they are ripe," says the Lord of Heaven's Armies. 12"Then all nations will call you blessed, for your land will be such a delight," says the Lord of Heaven's Armies.

13"You have said terrible things about me," says the Lord.

"But you say, 'What do you mean? What have we said against you?'

14"You have said, 'What's the use of serving God? What have we gained by obeying his commands or by trying to show the Lord of Heaven's Armies that we are sorry for our sins? 15From now on we will call the arrogant blessed. For those who do evil get rich, and those who dare God to punish them suffer no harm.'"

The Lord's Promise of Mercy

16Then those who feared the Lord spoke with each other, and the Lord listened to what they said. In his presence, a scroll of remembrance was written to record the names of those who feared him and always thought about the honor of his name.

17"They will be my people," says the Lord of Heaven's Armies. "On the day when I act in judgment, they will be my own special treasure. I will spare them as a father spares an obedient child. 18Then you will again see the difference between the righteous and the wicked, between those who serve God and those who do not." [2]

The Walk – S.B. Stone & Rock Solid Publishing, LLC
©2018

DEAR READER **POINT ONE**: THE **PRECEDING** *OLD TESTAMENT* SCRIPTURES WERE WRITTEN HUNDREDS TO THOUSANDS OF YEARS **BEFORE** JESUS CHRIST CAME TO EARTH.

DEAR READER POINT TWO: **THE FOLLOWING** *NEW TESTAMENT* **SCRIPTURES WERE** WRITTEN AFTER JESUS CHRIST WAS BORN, **MOSTLY BY MEN WHO:**

1. SPENT UP TO THREE YEARS OF FACE TIME WITH JESUS

2. PERSONALLY WITNESSED **HIS LOVE**

3. SAW JESUS HEAL THE SICK, BLIND AND LOST.

4. SAW JESUS DIE ON THE CROSS AND RISE FROM THE TOMB.

5. ASCEAND INTO HEAVEN.

The Holy Bible – New Testament Portions

The Gospel of Matthew

Chapter One

1The book of the genealogy of Jesus Christ, Messiah (Hebrew) and Christ (Greek) both mean "Anointed One" the son of David, the son of Abraham. 2Abraham became the father of Isaac. Isaac became the father of Jacob. Jacob became the father of Judah and his brothers. 3Judah became the father of Perez and Zerah by Tamar. Perez became the father of Hezron. Hezron became the father of Ram. 4Ram became the father of Amminadab. Amminadab became the father of Nahshon. Nahshon became the father of Salmon. 5Salmon became the father of Boaz by Rahab. Boaz became the father of Obed by Ruth. Obed became the father of Jesse. 6Jesse became the father of King David. David became the father of Solomon by her who had been Uriah's wife. 7Solomon became the father of Rehoboam. Rehoboam became the father of Abijah. Abijah became the father of Asa. 8Asa became the father of Jehoshaphat. Jehoshaphat became the father of Joram. Joram became the father of Uzziah. 9Uzziah became the father of Jotham. Jotham became the father of Ahaz. Ahaz became the father of Hezekiah. 10Hezekiah became the father of Manasseh. Manasseh became the father of Amon. Amon became the father of Josiah. 11Josiah became the father of Jechoniah and his brothers, at the time of the exile to Babylon. 12After the exile to Babylon, Jechoniah became the father of Shealtiel. Shealtiel became the father of Zerubbabel. 13Zerubbabel became the father of Abiud. Abiud became the father of Eliakim. Eliakim became the father of Azor. 14Azor became the father of Zadok. Zadok became the father of Achim. Achim became the father of Eliud. 15Eliud became the father of Eleazar. Eleazar became the father of Matthan. Matthan became the father of Jacob. 16Jacob became the father of Joseph, the husband of Mary, from whom was born Jesus, "Jesus" means "Salvation" who is called Christ. 17So all the generations from Abraham to David are fourteen generations; from David to the exile to Babylon fourteen generations; and from the carrying away to Babylon to the Christ, fourteen generations. 18Now the birth of Jesus Christ was like this; for after his mother, Mary, was engaged to Joseph, before they came together, she was found pregnant by the Holy Spirit. 19Joseph, her husband, being a righteous man, and not willing to make her a public example, intended to put her away secretly. 20But when he thought about these things, behold, "Behold", from "ἰδοὺ", means look at, take notice, observe, see, or gaze at. It is often used as an interjection an angel of the Lord appeared to him in a dream, saying, "Joseph, son of David, don't be afraid to take to yourself Mary, your wife, for that which is conceived in her is of the Holy Spirit. 21She shall give birth to a son. You shall call his name Jesus, for it is he who shall save his people from their sins." 22Now all this has happened, that it might be fulfilled which was spoken by the Lord through the prophet, saying, 23"Behold, the virgin shall be with child, and shall give birth to a son. They shall call his name Immanuel"; which is, being interpreted, "God with us." Isaiah 7:14 24Joseph arose from his sleep, and did as the angel of the Lord commanded him, and took his wife to himself; 25and didn't know her sexually until she had given birth to her firstborn son. He named him Jesus.   [5]

The Gospel of Matthew

Chapter Two

1Now when Jesus was born in Bethlehem of Judea in the days of King Herod, behold, wise men The word for "wise men" (magoi) can also mean teachers, scientists, physicians, astrologers, seers, interpreters of dreams, or sorcerers from the east came to Jerusalem, saying, 2"Where is he who is born King of the Jews? For we saw his star in the east, and have come to worship him." 3When King Herod heard it, he was troubled, and all Jerusalem with him. 4Gathering together all the chief priests and scribes of the people, he asked them where the

Christ would be born. 5They said to him, "In Bethlehem of Judea, for this is written through the prophet, 6'You Bethlehem, land of Judah, are in no way least among the princes of Judah: for out of you shall come a governor, who shall shepherd my people, Israel.'" Micah 5:2 7Then Herod secretly called the wise men, and learned from them exactly what time the star appeared. 8He sent them to Bethlehem, and said, "Go and search diligently for the young child.

When you have found him, bring me word, so that I also may come and worship him." 9They, having heard the king, went their way; and behold, the star, which they saw in the east, went before them, until it came and stood over where the young child was. 10When they saw the star, they rejoiced with exceedingly great joy. 11They came into the house and saw the young child with Mary, his mother, and they fell down and worshiped him. Opening their treasures, they offered to him gifts: gold, frankincense, and myrrh. 12Being warned in a dream that they shouldn't return to Herod, they went back to their own country another way. 13Now when they had departed, behold, an angel of the Lord appeared to Joseph in a dream, saying, "Arise and take the young child and his mother, and flee into Egypt, and stay there until I tell you, for Herod will seek the young child to destroy him." 14He arose and took the young child and his mother by night, and departed into Egypt, 15and was there until the death of Herod; that it might be fulfilled which was spoken by the Lord through the prophet, saying, "Out of Egypt I called my son." Hosea 11:1 16Then Herod, when he saw that he was mocked by the wise men, was exceedingly angry, and sent out, and killed all the male children who were in Bethlehem and in all the surrounding countryside, from two years old and under, according to the exact time which he had learned from the wise men. 17Then that which was spoken by Jeremiah the prophet was fulfilled, saying, 18"A voice was heard in Ramah, lamentation, weeping and great mourning, Rachel weeping for her children; she wouldn't be comforted, because they are no more.' Jeremiah 31:15 19But when Herod was dead, behold, an angel of the Lord appeared in a dream to Joseph in Egypt, saying, 20"Arise and take the young child and his mother, and go into the land of Israel, for those who sought the young child's life are dead." 21He arose and took the young child and his mother, and came into the land of Israel. 22But when he heard that

Archelaus was reigning over Judea in the place of his father, Herod, he was afraid to go there. Being warned in a dream, he withdrew into the region of Galilee, 23and came and lived in a city called Nazareth; that it might be fulfilled which was spoken through the prophets: "He will be called a Nazarene." [5]

The Gospel of Matthew

Chapter Three

1In those days, John the Baptizer came, preaching in the wilderness of Judea, saying, 2"Repent, for the Kingdom of Heaven is at hand!" 3For this is he who was spoken of by

Isaiah the prophet, saying, "The voice of one crying in the wilderness, make ready the way of the Lord. Make his paths straight." Isaiah 40:34Now John himself wore clothing made of camel's hair, with a leather belt around his waist. His food was locusts and wild honey. 5Then people from Jerusalem, all of Judea, and all the region around the Jordan went out to him. 6They were baptized or, immersed by him in the Jordan, confessing their sins. 7But when he saw many of the

Pharisees and Sadducees coming for his baptism, or, immersion he said to them, "You offspring of vipers, who warned you to flee from the wrath to come? 8Therefore produce fruit worthy of repentance! 9Don't think to yourselves, 'We have Abraham for our father,' for I tell you that God is able to raise up children to Abraham from these stones. 10"Even now the ax lies at the root of the trees. Therefore every tree that doesn't produce good fruit is cut down, and cast into the fire. 11I indeed baptize or, immerse you in water for repentance, but he who comes after me is mightier than I, whose shoes I am not worthy to carry. He will baptize you in the Holy

Spirit.TR and NU add "and with fire" 12His winnowing fork is in his hand, and he will thoroughly cleanse his threshing floor. He will gather his wheat into the barn, but the chaff he will burn up with unquenchable fire." 13Then Jesus came from Galilee to the Jordan i.e., the Jordan River to John, to be baptized by him. 14But John would have hindered him, saying, "I need to be baptized by you, and you come to me?"15But Jesus, answering, said to him, "Allow it now, for this is the fitting way for us to fulfill all righteousness." Then he allowed him. 16Jesus, when he was baptized, went up directly from the water: and behold, the heavens were opened to him. He saw the Spirit of God descending as a dove, and coming on him. 17Behold, a voice out of the heavens said, "This is my beloved Son, with whom I am well pleased."

Gospel of Matthew

Chapter Four

1Then Jesus was led up by the Spirit into the wilderness to be tempted by the devil. 2When he had fasted forty days and forty nights, he was hungry afterward. 3The tempter came and said to him, "If you are the Son of God, command that these stones become bread." 4But he answered, "It is written, 'Man shall not live by bread alone, but by every word that proceeds out of the mouth of God.'" Deuteronomy 8:3 5Then the devil took him into the holy city. He set him on the pinnacle of the temple, 6and said to him, "If you are the Son of God, throw yourself down, for it is written, 'He will put his angels in charge of you.' and, 'On their hands they will bear you up, so that you don't dash your foot against a stone.'" Psalm 91:11-12

7Jesus said to him, "Again, it is written, 'You shall not test the Lord, your God.'" Deuteronomy 6:16 8Again, the devil took him to an exceedingly high mountain, and showed him all the kingdoms of the world, and their glory. 9He said to him, "I will give you all of these things, if you will fall down and worship me." 10Then Jesus said to him, "Get behind me, TR and NU read "Go away" instead of "Get behind me" Satan! For it is written, 'You shall worship the Lord your God, and you shall serve him only.'" Deuteronomy 6:13 11Then the devil left him, and behold, angels came and served him. 12Now when Jesus heard that John was delivered up, he withdrew into Galilee. 13Leaving Nazareth, he came and lived in Capernaum, which is by the sea, in the region of Zebulun and Naphtali, 14that it might be fulfilled which was spoken through

Isaiah the prophet, saying, 15"The land of Zebulun and the land of Naphtali, toward the sea, beyond the Jordan, Galilee of the Gentiles, 16the people who sat in darkness saw a great light, to those who sat in the region and shadow of death, to them light has dawned." Isaiah 9:1-2 17From that time, Jesus began to preach, and to say, "Repent! For the Kingdom of Heaven is at hand." 18Walking by the sea of Galilee, he TR reads "Jesus" instead of "he" saw two brothers: Simon, who is called Peter, and Andrew, his brother, casting a net into the sea; for they were fishermen. 19He said to them, "Come after me, and I will make you fishers for men." 20They immediately left their nets and followed him. 21Going on from there, he saw two other brothers, James the son of Zebedee, and John his brother, in the boat with Zebedee their father, mending their nets. He called them. 22They immediately left the boat and their father, and followed him.

23Jesus went about in all Galilee, teaching in their synagogues, preaching the Good News of the Kingdom, and healing every disease and every sickness among the people. 24The report about him went out into all Syria. They brought to him all who were sick, afflicted with various diseases and torments, possessed with demons, epileptics, and paralytics; and he healed them. 25Great multitudes from Galilee, Decapolis, Jerusalem, Judea and from beyond the Jordan followed him. [5]

Gospel of Matthew

Chapter Five

1Seeing the multitudes, he went up onto the mountain. When he had sat down, his disciples came to him. 2He opened his mouth and taught them, saying, 3 "Blessed are the poor in spirit, for theirs is the Kingdom of Heaven. Isaiah 57:15; 66:2 4 Blessed are those who mourn, for they shall be comforted. Isaiah 61:2; 66:10,13 5 Blessed are the gentle, for they shall inherit the earth. or, land. Psalm 37:11 6 Blessed are those who hunger and thirst after righteousness, for they shall be filled. 7 Blessed are the merciful, for they shall obtain mercy. 8 Blessed are the pure in heart, for they shall see God. 9 Blessed are the peacemakers, for they shall be called children of God. 10 Blessed are those who have been persecuted for righteousness' sake, for theirs is the

Kingdom of Heaven. 11 "Blessed are you when people reproach you, persecute you, and say all kinds of evil against you falsely, for my sake. 12Rejoice, and be exceedingly glad, for great is your reward in heaven. For that is how they persecuted the prophets who were before you.

13 "You are the salt of the earth, but if the salt has lost its flavor, with what will it be salted? It is then good for nothing, but to be cast out and trodden under the feet of men. 14You are the light of the world. A city located on a hill can't be hidden. 15Neither do you light a lamp, and put it under a measuring basket, but on a stand; and it shines to all who are in the house. 16Even so, let your light shine before men; that they may see your good works, and glorify your Father who is in heaven. 17 "Don't think that I came to destroy the law or the prophets. I didn't come to destroy, but to fulfill. 18For most certainly, I tell you, until heaven and earth pass away, not even one smallest letter literally, iota or one tiny pen stroke or, serif shall in any way pass away from the law, until all things are accomplished. 19Whoever, therefore, shall break one of these least commandments, and teach others to do so, shall be called least in the Kingdom of Heaven; but whoever shall do and teach them shall be called great in the Kingdom of Heaven. 20For I tell you that unless your righteousness exceeds that of the scribes and Pharisees, there is no way you will enter into the Kingdom of Heaven. 21 "You have heard that it was said to the ancient ones, 'You shall not murder;' Exodus 20:13 and 'Whoever murders will be in danger of the judgment.' 22But I tell you, that everyone who is angry with his brother without a cause NU omits "without a cause" will be in danger of the judgment; and whoever says to his brother, 'Raca!' "Raca" is an Aramaic insult, related to the word for "empty" and conveying the idea of empty-headedness will be in danger of the council; and whoever says,

'You fool!' will be in danger of the fire of Gehenna or, Hell 23 "If therefore you are offering

your gift at the altar, and there remember that your brother has anything against you, 24leave your gift there before the altar, and go your way. First be reconciled to your brother, and then come and offer your gift. 25Agree with your adversary quickly, while you are with him on the way; lest perhaps the prosecutor deliver you to the judge, and the judge deliver you to the officer, and you be cast into prison. 26Most certainly I tell you, you shall by no means get out of there, until you have paid the last penny literally, kodrantes. A kodrantes was a small copper coin worth about 2 lepta (widow's mites)—not enough to buy very much of anything. 27 "You have heard that it was said, TR adds "to the ancients". 'You shall not commit adultery;' Exodus 20:14 28but I tell you that everyone who gazes at a woman to lust after her has committed adultery with her already in his heart. 29If your right eye causes you to stumble, pluck it out and throw it away from you. For it is more profitable for you that one of your members should perish, than for your whole body to be cast into Gehenna.or, Hell 30If your right hand causes you to stumble, cut it off, and throw it away from you. For it is more profitable for you that one of your members should perish, than for your whole body to be cast into Gehenna.or, Hell 31 "It was also said, 'Whoever shall put away his wife, let him give her a writing of

divorce,' Deuteronomy 24:1 32but I tell you that whoever puts away his wife, except for the cause of sexual immorality, makes her an adulteress; and whoever marries her when she is put away commits adultery. 33 "Again you have heard that it was said to them of old time, 'You shall not make false vows, but shall perform to the Lord your vows,' 34but I tell you, don't swear at all: neither by heaven, for it is the throne of God; 35nor by the earth, for it is the footstool of his feet; nor by Jerusalem, for it is the city of the great King. 36Neither shall you swear by your head, for you can't make one hair white or black. 37But let your 'Yes' be 'Yes' and your 'No' be 'No.' Whatever is more than these is of the evil one. 38 "You have heard that it was said, 'An eye for an eye, and a tooth for a tooth.' Exodus 21:24; Leviticus 24:20; Deuteronomy 19:21 39But I tell you, don't resist him who is evil; but whoever strikes you on your right cheek, turn to him the other also. 40If anyone sues you to take away your coat, let him have your cloak also. 41Whoever compels you to go one mile, go with him two. 42Give to him who asks you, and don't turn away him who desires to borrow from you. 43 "You have heard that it was said, 'You shall love your neighbor Leviticus 19:18 and hate your enemy.' not in the Bible, but see Qumran Manual of Discipline Ix, 21-26 44But I tell you, love your enemies, bless those who curse you, do good to those who hate you, and pray for those who mistreat you and persecute you, 45that you may be children of your Father who is in heaven. For he makes his sun to rise on the evil and the good, and sends rain on the just and the unjust. 46For if you love those who love you, what reward do you have? Don't even the tax collectors do the same? 47If you only greet your friends, what more do you do than others? Don't even the tax collectors NU reads "Gentiles" instead of "tax collectors" do the same? 48Therefore you shall be perfect, just

as your Father in heaven is perfect.   [5]

Gospel of Matthew

Chapter Six

1 "Be careful that you don't do your charitable giving before men, to be seen by them, or else you have no reward from your Father who is in heaven. 2Therefore when you do merciful deeds, don't sound a trumpet before yourself, as the hypocrites do in the synagogues and in the streets, that they may get glory from men. Most certainly I tell you, they have received their reward. 3But when you do merciful deeds, don't let your left hand know what your right hand does, 4so that your merciful deeds may be in secret, then your Father who sees in secret will reward you openly. 5 "When you pray, you shall not be as the hypocrites, for they love to stand and pray in the synagogues and in the corners of the streets, that they may be seen by men. Most certainly, I tell you, they have received their reward. 6But you, when you pray, enter into your inner room, and having shut your door, pray to your Father who is in secret, and your Father who sees in secret will reward you openly. 7In praying, don't use vain repetitions, as the Gentiles do; for they think that they will be heard for their much speaking. 8Therefore don't be like them, for your Father knows what things you need, before you ask him. 9Pray like this: 'Our Father in heaven, may your name be kept holy. 10Let your Kingdom come. Let your will be done, as in heaven, so on earth. 11Give us today our daily bread. 12Forgive us our debts, as we also forgive our debtors. 13Bring us not into temptation, but deliver us from the evil one. For yours is the

Kingdom, the power, and the glory forever. Amen.' NU omits "For yours is the Kingdom, the power, and the glory forever. Amen." 14 "For if you forgive men their trespasses, your heavenly Father will also forgive you. 15But if you don't forgive men their trespasses, neither will your Father forgive your trespasses. 16 "Moreover when you fast, don't be like the hypocrites, with sad faces. For they disfigure their faces, that they may be seen by men to be fasting. Most certainly I tell you, they have received their reward. 17But you, when you fast, anoint your head, and wash your face; 18so that you are not seen by men to be fasting, but by your Father who is in secret, and your Father, who sees in secret, will reward you. 19 "Don't lay up treasures for yourselves on the earth, where moth and rust consume, and where thieves break through and steal; 20but lay up for yourselves treasures in heaven, where neither moth nor rust consume, and where thieves don't break through and steal; 21for where your treasure is, there your heart will be also. 22 "The lamp of the body is the eye. If therefore your eye is sound, your whole body will be full of light. 23But if your eye is evil, your whole body will be full of darkness. If therefore the light that is in you is darkness, how great is the darkness! 24 "No one can serve two masters, for either he will hate the one and love the other; or else he will be devoted to one and despise the other. You can't serve both God and Mammon. 25Therefore I tell you, don't be anxious for your life: what you will eat, or what you will drink; nor yet for your body, what you will wear. Isn't life more than food, and the body more than clothing? 26See the birds of the sky, that they don't sow, neither do they reap, nor gather into barns. Your heavenly Father feeds them. Aren't you of much more value than they? 27 "Which of you, by being anxious, can add one moment literally, cubit to his lifespan? 28Why are you anxious about clothing? Consider the lilies of the field, how they grow. They don't toil, neither do they spin, 29yet I tell you that even Solomon in all his glory was not dressed like one of these. 30But if God so clothes the grass of the field, which today exists, and tomorrow is thrown into the oven, won't he much more clothe you, you of little faith? 31 "Therefore don't be anxious, saying, 'What will we eat?', 'What will we drink?' or, 'With what will we be clothed?' 32For the Gentiles seek after all these things; for your heavenly Father knows that you need all these things. 33But seek first God's Kingdom, and his righteousness; and all these things will be given to you as well. 34Therefore don't be anxious for tomorrow, for tomorrow will be anxious for itself. Each day's own evil is sufficient. [5]

Gospel of Matthew

Chapter Seven

1 "Don't judge, so that you won't be judged. 2For with whatever judgment you judge, you will be judged; and with whatever measure you measure, it will be measured to you. 3Why do you see the speck that is in your brother's eye, but don't consider the beam that is in your own eye? 4Or how will you tell your brother, 'Let me remove the speck from your eye;' and behold, the beam is in your own eye? 5You hypocrite! First remove the beam out of your own eye, and then you can see clearly to remove the speck out of your brother's eye. 6 "Don't give that which

is holy to the dogs, neither throw your pearls before the pigs, lest perhaps they trample them under their feet, and turn and tear you to pieces. 7 "Ask, and it will be given you. Seek, and you will find. Knock, and it will be opened for you. 8For everyone who asks receives. He who seeks finds. To him who knocks it will be opened. 9Or who is there among you, who, if his son asks him for bread, will give him a stone? 10Or if he asks for a fish, who will give him a serpent? 11If you then, being evil, know how to give good gifts to your children, how much more will your Father who is in heaven give good things to those who ask him! 12Therefore whatever you desire for men to do to you, you shall also do to them; for this is the law and the prophets.

13 "Enter in by the narrow gate; for wide is the gate and broad is the way that leads to destruction, and many are those who enter in by it. 14HowTR reads "Because" instead of

"How" narrow is the gate, and restricted is the way that leads to life! Few are those who find it.

15 "Beware of false prophets, who come to you in sheep's clothing, but inwardly are ravening wolves. 16By their fruits you will know them. Do you gather grapes from thorns, or figs from thistles? 17Even so, every good tree produces good fruit; but the corrupt tree produces evil fruit. 18A good tree can't produce evil fruit, neither can a corrupt tree produce good fruit. 19Every tree that doesn't grow good fruit is cut down, and thrown into the fire. 20Therefore by their fruits you will know them. 21Not everyone who says to me, 'Lord, Lord,' will enter into the Kingdom of Heaven; but he who does the will of my Father who is in heaven. 22Many will tell me in that day, 'Lord, Lord, didn't we prophesy in your name, in your name cast out demons, and in your name do many mighty works?' 23Then I will tell them, 'I never knew you. Depart from me, you who work iniquity.'

24 "Everyone therefore who hears these words of mine, and does them, I will liken him to a wise man, who built his house on a rock. 25The rain came down, the floods came, and the winds blew, and beat on that house; and it didn't fall, for it was founded on the rock. 26Everyone who hears these words of mine, and doesn't do them will be like a foolish man, who built his house on the sand. 27The rain came down, the floods came, and the winds blew, and beat on that house; and it fell—and great was its fall." 28When Jesus had finished saying these

things, the multitudes were astonished at his teaching, 29for he taught them with authority, and not like the scribes. [5]

Gospel of Matthew

Chapter Eight

1When he came down from the mountain, great multitudes followed him. 2Behold, a leper came to him and worshiped him, saying, "Lord, if you want to, you can make me clean." 3Jesus stretched out his hand, and touched him, saying, "I want to. Be made clean." Immediately his leprosy was cleansed. 4Jesus said to him, "See that you tell nobody, but go, show yourself to the priest, and offer the gift that Moses commanded, as a testimony to them." 5When he came into Capernaum, a centurion came to him, asking him, 6and saying, "Lord, my servant lies in the house paralyzed, grievously tormented." 7Jesus said to him, "I will come and heal him."

8The centurion answered, "Lord, I'm not worthy for you to come under my roof. Just say the word, and my servant will be healed. 9For I am also a man under authority, having under myself soldiers. I tell this one, 'Go,' and he goes; and tell another, 'Come,' and he comes; and tell my servant, 'Do this,' and he does it." 10When Jesus heard it, he marveled, and said to those who followed, "Most certainly I tell you, I haven't found so great a faith, not even in Israel. 11I tell you that many will come from the east and the west, and will sit down with Abraham, Isaac, and Jacob in the Kingdom of Heaven, 12but the children of the Kingdom will be thrown out into the outer darkness. There will be weeping and gnashing of teeth." 13Jesus said to the centurion, "Go your way. Let it be done for you as you have believed." His servant was healed in that hour.

14When Jesus came into Peter's house, he saw his wife's mother lying sick with a fever. 15He touched her hand, and the fever left her. She got up and served him. TR reads "them" instead of "him" 16When evening came, they brought to him many possessed with demons. He cast out the spirits with a word, and healed all who were sick; 17that it might be fulfilled which was spoken through Isaiah the prophet, saying, "He took our infirmities, and bore our diseases." Isaiah 53:4 18Now when Jesus saw great multitudes around him, he gave the order to depart to the other side. 19A scribe came, and said to him, "Teacher, I will follow you wherever you go."

20Jesus said to him, "The foxes have holes, and the birds of the sky have nests, but the Son of Man has nowhere to lay his head." 21Another of his disciples said to him, "Lord, allow me first to go and bury my father." 22But Jesus said to him, "Follow me, and leave the dead to bury their own dead." 23When he got into a boat, his disciples followed him. 24Behold, a violent storm came up on the sea, so much that the boat was covered with the waves, but he was asleep. 25They came to him, and woke him up, saying, "Save us, Lord! We are dying!"

26He said to them, "Why are you fearful, O you of little faith?" Then he got up, rebuked the wind and the sea, and there was a great calm. 27The men marveled, saying, "What kind of man is this, that even the wind and the sea obey him?" 28When he came to the other side, into the country of the Gergesenes, NU reads "Gadarenes" two people possessed by demons met him there, coming out of the tombs, exceedingly fierce, so that nobody could pass that way. 29Behold, they cried out, saying, "What do we have to do with you, Jesus, Son of God? Have you come here to torment us before the time?" 30Now there was a herd of many pigs feeding far away from them. 31The demons begged him, saying, "If you cast us out, permit us to go away into the herd of pigs." 32He said to them, "Go!" They came out, and went into the herd of pigs: and behold, the whole herd of pigs rushed down the cliff into the sea, and died in the water. 33Those who fed them fled, and went away into the city, and told everything, including what happened to those who were possessed with demons. 34Behold, all the city came out to meet Jesus. When they saw him, they begged that he would depart from their borders.   [5]

Gospel of Matthew

Chapter Nine

1He entered into a boat, and crossed over, and came into his own city. 2Behold, they brought to him a man who was paralyzed, lying on a bed. Jesus, seeing their faith, said to the paralytic, "Son, cheer up! Your sins are forgiven you." 3Behold, some of the scribes said to themselves, "This man blasphemes." 4Jesus, knowing their thoughts, said, "Why do you think evil in your hearts? 5For which is easier, to say, 'Your sins are forgiven;' or to say, 'Get up, and walk?' 6But that you may know that the Son of Man has authority on earth to forgive sins..." (then he said to the paralytic), "Get up, and take up your mat, and go to your house."

7He arose and departed to his house. 8But when the multitudes saw it, they marveled and glorified God, who had given such authority to men.

9As Jesus passed by from there, he saw a man called Matthew sitting at the tax collection office. He said to him, "Follow me." He got up and followed him. 10As he sat in the house, behold, many tax collectors and sinners came and sat down with Jesus and his disciples. 11When the Pharisees saw it, they said to his disciples,

"Why does your teacher eat with tax collectors and sinners?" 12When Jesus heard it, he said to them, "Those who are healthy have no need for a physician, but those who are sick do. 13But you go and learn what this means: 'I desire mercy, and not sacrifice,' Hosea 6:6 for I came not to call the righteous, but sinners to repentance." NU omits "to repentance". 14Then John's disciples came to him, saying, "Why do we and the Pharisees fast often, but your disciples don't fast?"

15Jesus said to them, "Can the friends of the bridegroom mourn, as long as the bridegroom is with them? But the days will come when the bridegroom will be taken away from them, and then they will fast. 16No one puts a piece of unshrunk cloth on an old garment; for the patch would tear away from the garment, and a worse hole is made. 17Neither do people put new wine into old wine skins, or else the skins would burst, and the wine be spilled, and the skins ruined. No, they put new wine into fresh wine skins, and both are preserved." 18While he told these things to them, behold, a ruler came and worshiped him, saying, "My daughter has just died, but come and lay your hand on her, and she will live." 19Jesus got up and followed him, as did his disciples. 20Behold, a woman who had an issue of blood for twelve years came behind him, and touched the fringe or, tassel of his garment; 21for she said within herself, "If I just touch his garment, I will be made well." 22But Jesus, turning around and seeing her, said, "Daughter, cheer up! Your faith has made you well." And the woman was made well from that hour.

23When Jesus came into the ruler's house, and saw the flute players, and the crowd in noisy disorder, 24he said to them, "Make room, because the girl isn't dead, but sleeping."

They were ridiculing him. 25But when the crowd was put out, he entered in, took her by the hand, and the girl arose. 26The report of this went out into all that land. 27As Jesus passed by from there, two blind men followed him, calling out and saying, "Have mercy on us, son of David!" 28When he had come into the house, the blind men came to him. Jesus said to them, "Do you believe that I am able to do this?" They told him, "Yes, Lord."

29Then he touched their eyes, saying, "According to your faith be it done to you." 30Their eyes were opened. Jesus strictly commanded them, saying, "See that no one knows about this." 31But they went out and spread abroad his fame in all that land. 32As they went out, behold, a mute man who was demon possessed was brought to him. 33When the demon was cast out, the mute man spoke. The multitudes marveled, saying, "Nothing like this has ever been seen in Israel!" 34But the Pharisees said, "By the prince of the demons, he casts out demons." 35Jesus went about all the cities and the villages, teaching in their synagogues, and preaching the Good News of the Kingdom, and healing every disease and every sickness among the people. 36But when he saw the multitudes, he was moved with compassion for them, because they were harassed TR reads "weary" instead of "harassed" and scattered, like sheep without a shepherd. 37Then he said to his disciples, "The harvest indeed is plentiful, but the laborers are few. 38Pray therefore that the Lord of the harvest will send out laborers into his harvest."

Gospel of Matthew

Chapter Ten

1He called to himself his twelve disciples, and gave them authority over unclean spirits, to cast them out, and to heal every disease and every sickness. 2Now the names of the twelve apostles are these. The first, Simon, who is called Peter; Andrew, his brother; James the son of Zebedee; John, his brother; 3Philip; Bartholomew; Thomas; Matthew the tax collector; James the son of Alphaeus; Lebbaeus, who was also called NU omits "Lebbaeus, who was also called" Thaddaeus; 4Simon the Canaanite; and Judas Iscariot, who also betrayed him.

5Jesus sent these twelve out, and commanded them, saying, "Don't go among the Gentiles, and don't enter into any city of the Samaritans. 6Rather, go to the lost sheep of the house of Israel. 7As you go, preach, saying, 'The Kingdom of Heaven is at hand!' 8Heal the sick, cleanse the lepers, TR adds "raise the dead," and cast out demons. Freely you received, so freely give. 9Don't take any gold, silver, or brass in your money belts. 10Take no bag for your journey, neither two coats, nor shoes, nor staff: for the laborer is worthy of his food. 11Into whatever city or village you enter, find out who in it is worthy; and stay there until you go on. 12As you enter into the household, greet it. 13If the household is worthy, let your peace come on it, but if it isn't worthy, let your peace return to you. 14Whoever doesn't receive you, nor hear your words, as you go out of that house or that city, shake off the dust from your feet. 15Most certainly I tell you, it will be more tolerable for the land of Sodom and Gomorrah in the day of judgment than for that city. 16 "Behold, I send you out as sheep among wolves. Therefore be wise as serpents, and harmless as doves. 17But beware of men: for they will deliver you up to councils, and in their synagogues they will scourge you. 18Yes, and you will be brought before governors and kings for my sake, for a testimony to them and to the nations. 19But when they deliver you up, don't be anxious how or what you will say, for it will be given you in that hour what you will say. 20For it is not you who speak, but the Spirit of your Father who speaks in you. 21 "Brother will deliver up brother to death, and the father his child. Children will rise up against parents, and cause them to be put to death. 22You will be hated by all men for my name's sake, but he who endures to the end will be saved. 23But when they persecute you in this city, flee into the next, for most certainly I tell you, you will not have gone through the cities of Israel, until the Son of Man has come. 24 "A disciple is not above his teacher, nor a servant above his lord. 25It is enough for the disciple that he be like his teacher, and the servant like his lord. If they have called the master of the house Beelzebul, Literally,

Lord of the Flies, or the devil how much more those of his household! 26Therefore don't be afraid of them, for there is nothing covered that will not be revealed; and hidden that will not be known. 27What I tell you in the darkness, speak in the light; and what you hear whispered in the ear, proclaim on the housetops. 28Don't be afraid of those who kill the body, but are not able to kill the soul. Rather, fear him who is able to destroy both soul and body in Gehenna, or Hell.

29 "Aren't two sparrows sold for an assarion coin? An assarion is a small coin worth one tenth of a drachma or a sixteenth of a denarius. An assarion is approximately the wages of one half hour of agricultural labor. Not one of them falls on the ground apart from your Father's will, 30but the very hairs of your head are all numbered. 31Therefore don't be afraid. You are of more value than many sparrows. 32Everyone therefore who confesses me before men, him I will also confess before my Father who is in heaven. 33But whoever denies me before men, him

I will also deny before my Father who is in heaven. 34 "Don't think that I came to send peace on the earth. I didn't come to send peace, but a sword. 35For I came to set a man at odds against his father, and a daughter against her mother, and a daughter-in-law against her mother-in-law. 36A man's foes will be those of his own household. Micah 7:6 37He who loves father or mother more than me is not worthy of me; and he who loves son or daughter more than me isn't worthy of me. 38He who doesn't take his cross and follow after me, isn't worthy of me. 39He who seeks his life will lose it; and he who loses his life for my sake will find it. 40He who receives you receives me, and he who receives me receives him who sent me. 41He who receives a prophet in the name of a prophet will receive a prophet's reward. He who receives a righteous man in the name of a righteous man will receive a righteous man's reward. 42Whoever gives one of these little ones just a cup of cold water to drink in the name of a disciple, most certainly I tell you he will in no way lose his reward." [5]

Gospel of Matthew

Chapter Eleven

1When Jesus had finished directing his twelve disciples, he departed from there to teach and preach in their cities. 2Now when John heard in the prison the works of Christ, he sent two of his disciples 3and said to him, "Are you he who comes, or should we look for another?"

4Jesus answered them, "Go and tell John the things which you hear and see: 5the blind receive their sight, the lame walk, the lepers are cleansed, the deaf hear, Isaiah 35:5 the dead are raised up, and the poor have good news preached to them. Isaiah 61:1-4 6Blessed is he who finds no occasion for stumbling in me." 7As these went their way, Jesus began to say to the multitudes concerning John, "What did you go out into the wilderness to see? A reed shaken by the wind? 8But what did you go out to see? A man in soft clothing? Behold, those who wear soft clothing are in kings' houses. 9But why did you go out? To see a prophet? Yes, I tell you, and much more than a prophet. 10For this is he, of whom it is written, 'Behold, I send my messenger before your face, who will prepare your way before you.' Malachi 3:1 11Most certainly I tell you, among those who are born of women there has not arisen anyone greater than John the

Baptizer; yet he who is least in the Kingdom of Heaven is greater than he. 12From the days of John the Baptizer until now, the Kingdom of Heaven suffers violence, and the violent take it by force.or, plunder it. 13For all the prophets and the law prophesied until John. 14If you are willing to receive it, this is Elijah, who is to come. 15He who has ears to hear, let him hear.

16 "But to what shall I compare this generation? It is like children sitting in the marketplaces, who call to their companions 17and say, 'We played the flute for you, and you didn't dance. We mourned for you, and you didn't lament.' 18For John came neither eating nor drinking, and they say, 'He has a demon.' 19The Son of Man came eating and drinking, and they say, 'Behold, a gluttonous man and a drunkard, a friend of tax collectors and sinners!' But wisdom is justified by her children." NU reads "actions" instead of "children" 20Then he began to denounce the cities in which most of his mighty works had been done, because they didn't repent. 21"Woe to you, Chorazin! Woe to you, Bethsaida! For if the mighty works had been done in Tyre and Sidon which were done in you, they would have repented long ago in sackcloth and ashes. 22But I tell you, it will be more tolerable for Tyre and Sidon on the day of judgment than for you. 23You, Capernaum, who are exalted to heaven, you will go down to Hades. or, Hell For if the mighty works had been done in Sodom which were done in you, it would have remained until today. 24But I tell you that it will be more tolerable for the land of Sodom, on the day of judgment, than for you." 25At that time, Jesus answered, "I thank you, Father, Lord of heaven and earth, that you hid these things from the wise and understanding, and revealed them to infants. 26Yes, Father, for so it was well-pleasing in your sight. 27All things have been delivered to me by my Father. No one knows the Son, except the Father; neither does anyone know the Father, except the Son, and he to whom the Son desires to reveal him. 28 "Come to me, all you who labor and are heavily burdened, and I will give you rest. 29Take my yoke upon you, and learn from me, for I am gentle and humble in heart; and you will find rest for your souls. 30For my yoke is easy, and my burden is light."

Gospel of Matthew

Chapter Twelve

1At that time, Jesus went on the Sabbath day through the grain fields. His disciples were hungry and began to pluck heads of grain and to eat. 2But the Pharisees, when they saw it, said to him, "Behold, your disciples do what is not lawful to do on the Sabbath." 3But he said to them, "Haven't you read what David did, when he was hungry, and those who were with him; 4how he entered into God's house, and ate the show bread, which was not lawful for him to eat, neither for those who were with him, but only for the priests?1 Samuel 21:3-6 5Or have you not read in the law, that on the Sabbath day, the priests in the temple profane the Sabbath, and are guiltless? 6But I tell you that one greater than the temple is here. 7But if you had known what this means, 'I desire mercy, and not sacrifice,' Hosea 6:6 you would not have condemned the guiltless. 8For the Son of Man is Lord of the Sabbath." 9He departed there, and went into their synagogue. 10And behold there was a man with a withered hand. They asked him, "Is it lawful to heal on the Sabbath day?" that they might accuse him. 11He said to them, "What man is there among you, who has one sheep, and if this one falls into a pit on the Sabbath day, won't he grab on to it, and lift it out? 12Of how much more value then is a man than a sheep! Therefore it is lawful to do good on the Sabbath day." 13Then he told the man, "Stretch out your hand." He stretched it out; and it was restored whole, just like the other. 14But the Pharisees went out, and conspired against him, how they might destroy him. 15Jesus, perceiving that, withdrew from there. Great multitudes followed him; and he healed them all, 16and commanded them that they should not make him known: 17that it might be fulfilled which was spoken through Isaiah the prophet, saying, 18"Behold, my servant whom I have chosen; my beloved in whom my soul is well pleased: I will put my Spirit on him. He will proclaim justice to the nations. 19He will not strive, nor shout; neither will anyone hear his voice in the streets. 20He won't break a bruised reed. He won't quench a smoking flax, until he leads justice to victory. 21In his name, the nations will hope." Isaiah 42:1-4 22Then one possessed by a demon, blind and mute, was brought to him and he healed him, so that the blind and mute man both spoke and saw. 23All the multitudes were amazed, and said, "Can this be the son of David?" 24But when the Pharisees heard it, they said, "This man does not cast out demons, except by Beelzebul, the prince of the demons." 25Knowing their thoughts, Jesus said to them, "Every kingdom divided against itself is brought to desolation, and every city or house divided against itself will not stand. 26If Satan casts out Satan, he is divided against himself. How then will his kingdom stand? 27If I by Beelzebul cast out demons, by whom do your children cast them out? Therefore they will be your judges. 28But if I by the Spirit of God cast out demons, then God's Kingdom has come upon you. 29Or how can one enter into the house of the strong man, and plunder his goods, unless he first bind the strong man? Then he will plunder his house. 30 "He who is not with me is against me, and he who doesn't gather with me, scatters. 31Therefore I tell you, every sin and blasphemy will be forgiven men, but the blasphemy against the Spirit will not be forgiven men. 32Whoever speaks a word against the Son of Man, it will be forgiven him; but whoever speaks against the Holy Spirit, it will not be forgiven him, neither in this age, nor in that which is to come. 33 "Either make the tree good, and its fruit good, or make the tree corrupt, and its fruit corrupt; for the tree is known by its fruit. 34You offspring of vipers, how can you, being evil, speak good things? For out of the abundance of the heart, the mouth speaks. 35The good man out of his good treasure brings out good things, and the evil man out of his evil treasure TR adds "of the heart" brings out evil things. 36I tell you that every idle word that men speak, they will give account of it in the day of judgment. 37For by your words you will be justified, and by your words you will be condemned." 38Then certain of the scribes and Pharisees answered, "Teacher, we want to see a sign from you." 39But he answered them, "An evil and adulterous generation seeks after a sign, but no sign will be given to it but the sign of Jonah the prophet. 40For as Jonah was three days and three nights in the belly of the whale, so will the Son of Man be three days and three nights in the heart of the earth. 41The men of Nineveh will stand up in the judgment with this generation, and will condemn it, for they repented at the preaching of Jonah; and behold, someone greater than Jonah is here. 42The queen of the south will rise up in the judgment with this generation, and will condemn it, for she came from the ends of the earth to hear the wisdom of Solomon; and behold, someone greater than Solomon is here.

43 When an unclean spirit has gone out of a man, he passes through waterless places, seeking rest, and doesn't find it. 44Then he says, 'I will return into my house from which I came out,' and when he has come back, he finds it empty, swept, and put in order. 45Then he goes, and takes with himself seven other spirits more evil than he is, and they enter in and dwell there. The last state of that man becomes worse than the first. Even so will it be also to this evil generation." 46While he was yet speaking to the multitudes, behold, his mother and his brothers stood outside, seeking to speak to him. 47One said to him, "Behold, your mother and your brothers stand outside, seeking to speak to you." 48But he answered him who spoke to him, "Who is my mother? Who are my brothers?" 49He stretched out his hand towards his disciples, and said,

"Behold, my mother and my brothers! 50For whoever does the will of my Father who is in heaven, he is my brother, and sister, and mother."
[5]

Gospel of Matthew

Chapter Thirteen

1On that day Jesus went out of the house, and sat by the seaside. 2Great multitudes gathered to him, so that he entered into a boat, and sat, and all the multitude stood on the beach. 3He spoke to them many things in parables, saying, "Behold, a farmer went out to sow. 4As he sowed, some seeds fell by the roadside, and the birds came and devoured them. 5Others fell on rocky ground, where they didn't have much soil, and immediately they sprang up, because they had no depth of earth. 6When the sun had risen, they were scorched. Because they had no root, they withered away. 7Others fell among thorns. The thorns grew up and choked them. 8Others fell on good soil, and yielded fruit: some one hundred times as much, some sixty, and some thirty. 9He who has ears to hear, let him hear." 10The disciples came, and said to him, "Why do you speak to them in parables?" 11He answered them, "To you it is given to know the mysteries of the Kingdom of Heaven, but it is not given to them. 12For whoever has, to him will be given, and he will have abundance, but whoever doesn't have, from him will be taken away even that which he has. 13Therefore I speak to them in parables, because seeing they don't see, and hearing, they don't hear, neither do they understand. 14In them the prophecy of Isaiah is fulfilled, which says, 'By hearing you will hear, and will in no way understand; Seeing you will see, and will in no way perceive: 15 for this people's heart has grown callous, their ears are dull of hearing, they have closed their eyes; or else perhaps they might perceive with their eyes, hear with their ears, understand with their heart, and would turn again; and I would heal them.' Isaiah 6:9-10 16 "But blessed are your eyes, for they see; and your ears, for they hear. 17For most certainly I tell you that many prophets and righteous men desired to see the things which you see, and didn't see them; and to hear the things which you hear, and didn't hear them. 18 "Hear, then, the parable of the farmer. 19When anyone hears the word of the Kingdom, and doesn't understand it, the evil one comes, and snatches away that which has been sown in his heart. This is what was sown by the roadside. 20What was sown on the rocky places, this is he who hears the word, and immediately with joy receives it; 21yet he has no root in himself, but endures for a while. When oppression or

persecution arises because of the word, immediately he stumbles. 22What was sown among the thorns, this is he who hears the word, but the cares of this age and the deceitfulness of riches choke the word, and he becomes unfruitful. 23What was sown on the good ground, this is he who hears the word, and understands it, who most certainly bears fruit, and produces, some one hundred times as much, some sixty, and some thirty." 24He set another parable before them, saying, "The Kingdom of Heaven is like a man who sowed good seed in his field, 25but while people slept, his enemy came and sowed darnel weeds darnel is a weed grass (probably bearded darnel or lolium temulentum) that looks very much like wheat until it is mature, when the difference becomes very apparent also among the wheat, and went away. 26But when the blade sprang up and produced fruit, then the darnel weeds appeared also. 27The servants of the householder came and said to him, 'Sir, didn't you sow good seed in your field? Where did these darnel weeds come from?' 28 "He said to them, 'An enemy has done this.' "The servants asked him, 'Do you want us to go and gather them up?' 29 "But he said, 'No, lest perhaps while you gather up the darnel weeds, you root up the wheat with them. 30Let both grow together until the harvest, and in the harvest time I will tell the reapers, "First, gather up the darnel weeds, and bind them in bundles to burn them; but gather the wheat into my barn."'"
31He set another parable before them, saying, "The Kingdom of Heaven is like a grain of mustard seed, which a man took, and sowed in his field; 32which indeed is smaller than all seeds. But when it is grown, it is greater than the herbs, and becomes a tree, so that the birds of the air come and lodge in its branches." 33He spoke another parable to them. "The Kingdom of Heaven is like yeast, which a woman took, and hid in three measures literally, three sata 3 sata is about 39 liters or a bit more than a bushel of meal, until it was all leavened." 34Jesus spoke all these things in parables to the multitudes; and without a parable, he didn't speak to them, 35that it might be fulfilled which was spoken through the prophet, saying, "I will open my mouth in parables; I will utter things hidden from the foundation of the world." Psalm 78:2 36Then Jesus sent the multitudes away, and went into the house. His disciples came to him, saying, "Explain to us the parable of the darnel weeds of the field." 37He answered them, "He who sows the good seed is the Son of Man, 38the field is the world; and the good seed, these are the children of the Kingdom; and the darnel weeds are the children of the evil one. 39The enemy who sowed them is the devil. The harvest is the end of the age, and the reapers are angels. 40As therefore the darnel weeds are gathered

up and burned with fire; so will it be at the end of this age. 41The Son of Man will send out his angels, and they will gather out of his Kingdom all things that cause stumbling, and those who do iniquity, 42and will cast them into the furnace of fire. There will be weeping and the gnashing of teeth. 43Then the righteous will shine like the sun in the Kingdom of their Father. He who has ears to hear, let him hear. 44 "Again, the Kingdom of Heaven is like a treasure hidden in the field, which a man found, and hid. In his joy, he goes and sells all that he has, and buys that field. 45 "Again, the Kingdom of Heaven is like a man who is a merchant seeking fine pearls, 46who having found one pearl of great price, he went and sold all that he had, and bought it. 47 "Again, the Kingdom of Heaven is like a dragnet, that was cast into the sea, and gathered some fish of every kind, 48which, when it was filled, they drew up on the beach. They sat down, and gathered the good into containers, but the bad they threw away. 49So will it be in the end of the world. The angels will come and separate the wicked from among the righteous, 50and will cast them into the furnace of fire. There will be the weeping and the gnashing of teeth." 51Jesus said to them, "Have you understood all these things?" They answered him, "Yes, Lord." 52He said to them, "Therefore every scribe who has been made a disciple in the Kingdom of Heaven is like a man who is a householder, who brings out of his treasure new and old things." 53When Jesus had finished these parables, he departed from there. 54Coming into his own country, he taught them in their synagogue, so that they were astonished, and said, "Where did this man get this wisdom, and these mighty works? 55Isn't this the carpenter's son? Isn't his mother called Mary, and his brothers, James, Joses, Simon, and Judas? or, Judah 56Aren't all of his sisters with us? Where then did this man get all of these things?" 57They were offended by him. But Jesus said to them, "A prophet is not without honor, except in his own country, and in his own house." 58He didn't do many mighty works there because of their unbelief. [5]

Gospel of Matthew

Chapter Fourteen

1At that time, Herod the tetrarch heard the report concerning Jesus, 2and said to his servants, "This is John the Baptizer. He is risen from the dead. That is why these powers work in him." 3For Herod had laid hold of John, and bound him, and put him in prison for the sake of Herodias, his brother Philip's wife. 4For John said to him, "It is not lawful for you to have her." 5When he would have put him to death, he feared the multitude, because they counted him as a prophet. 6But when Herod's birthday came, the daughter of Herodias danced among them and pleased Herod. 7Whereupon he promised with an oath to give her whatever she should ask. 8She, being prompted by her mother, said, "Give me here on a platter the head of John the Baptizer." 9The king was grieved, but for the sake of his oaths, and of those who sat at the table with him, he commanded it to be given, 10and he sent and beheaded John in the prison. 11His head was brought on a platter, and given to the young lady: and she brought it to her mother. 12His disciples came, and took the body, and buried it; and they went and told

Jesus. 13Now when Jesus heard this, he withdrew from there in a boat, to a deserted place apart. When the multitudes heard it, they followed him on foot from the cities. 14Jesus went out, and he saw a great multitude. He had compassion on them, and healed their sick. 15When evening had come, his disciples came to him, saying, "This place is deserted, and the hour is already late. Send the multitudes away, that they may go into the villages, and buy themselves food." 16But Jesus said to them, "They don't need to go away. You give them something to eat." 17They told him, "We only have here five loaves and two fish." 18He said, "Bring them here to me." 19He commanded the multitudes to sit down on the grass; and he took the five loaves and the two fish, and looking up to heaven, he blessed, broke and gave the loaves to the disciples, and the disciples gave to the multitudes. 20They all ate, and were filled. They took up twelve baskets full of that which remained left over from the broken pieces. 21Those who ate were about five thousand men, besides women and children. 22Immediately Jesus made the disciples get into the boat, and to go ahead of him to the other side, while he sent the multitudes away. 23After he had sent the multitudes away, he went up into the mountain by himself to pray. When evening had come, he was there alone. 24But the boat was now in the middle of the sea, distressed by the waves, for the wind was contrary. 25In the fourth watch of the night, The night was equally divided into four watches, so the fourth watch is approximately 3:00 a.m. to sunrise. Jesus came to them, walking on the sea. see Job 9:8 26When the disciples saw him walking on the sea, they were troubled, saying, "It's a ghost!" and they cried out for fear. 27But immediately Jesus spoke to them, saying, "Cheer up! It is I! or, I AM! Don't be afraid." 28Peter answered him and said,

"Lord, if it is you, command me to come to you on the waters." 29He said, "Come!" Peter stepped down from the boat, and walked on the waters to come to Jesus. 30But when he saw that the wind was strong, he was afraid, and beginning to sink, he cried out, saying, "Lord, save me!" 31Immediately Jesus stretched out his hand, took hold of him, and said to him, "You of little faith, why did you doubt?" 32When they got up into the boat, the wind ceased. 33Those who were in the boat came and worshiped him, saying, "You are truly the Son of God!" 34When they had crossed over, they came to the land of Gennesaret. 35When the people of that place recognized him, they sent into all that surrounding region, and brought to him all who were sick; 36and they begged him that they might just touch the fringe or, tassel of his garment. As many as touched it were made whole.

Gospel of Matthew

Chapter Fifteen

1Then Pharisees and scribes came to Jesus from Jerusalem, saying, 2"Why do your disciples disobey the tradition of the elders? For they don't wash their hands when they eat bread."

3He answered them, "Why do you also disobey the commandment of God because of your tradition? 4For God commanded, 'Honor your father and your mother,' Exodus 20:12;

Deuteronomy 5:16 and, 'He who speaks evil of father or mother, let him be put to death.' Exodus 21:17; Leviticus 20:9 5But you say, 'Whoever may tell his father or his mother, "Whatever help you might otherwise have gotten from me is a gift devoted to God," 6he shall not honor his father or mother.' You have made the commandment of God void because of your tradition. 7You hypocrites! Well did Isaiah prophesy of you, saying, 8 'These people draw near to me with their mouth, and honor me with their lips; but their heart is far from me. 9 And in vain do they worship me, teaching as doctrine rules made by men.'" Isaiah 29:13 10He summoned the multitude, and said to them, "Hear, and understand. 11That which enters into the mouth doesn't defile the man; but that which proceeds out of the mouth, this defiles the man."

12Then the disciples came, and said to him, "Do you know that the Pharisees were offended, when they heard this saying?" 13But he answered, "Every plant which my heavenly Father didn't plant will be uprooted. 14Leave them alone. They are blind guides of the blind. If the blind guide the blind, both will fall into a pit." 15Peter answered him, "Explain the parable to us." 16So Jesus said, "Do you also still not understand? 17Don't you understand that whatever goes into the mouth passes into the belly, and then out of the body? 18But the things which proceed out of the mouth come out of the heart, and they defile the man. 19For out of the heart come evil thoughts, murders, adulteries, sexual sins, thefts, false testimony, and blasphemies. 20These are the things which defile the man; but to eat with unwashed hands doesn't defile the man." 21Jesus went out from there, and withdrew into the region of Tyre and Sidon. 22Behold, a Canaanite woman came out from those borders, and cried, saying, "Have mercy on me, Lord, you son of David! My daughter is severely possessed by a demon!"

23But he answered her not a word. His disciples came and begged him, saying, "Send her away; for she cries after us." 24But he answered, "I wasn't sent to anyone but the lost sheep of the house of Israel." 25But she came and worshiped him, saying, "Lord, help me."

26But he answered, "It is not appropriate to take the children's bread and throw it to the dogs."

27But she said, "Yes, Lord, but even the dogs eat the crumbs which fall from their masters' table." 28Then Jesus answered her, "Woman, great is your faith! Be it done to you even as you desire." And her daughter was healed from that hour. 29Jesus departed there, and came near to the sea of Galilee; and he went up into the mountain, and sat there. 30Great multitudes came to him, having with them the lame, blind, mute, maimed, and many others, and they put them down at his feet. He healed them, 31so that the multitude wondered when they saw the mute speaking, the injured healed, the lame walking, and the blind seeing—and they glorified the God of Israel.

32Jesus summoned his disciples and said, "I have compassion on the multitude, because they continue with me now three days and have nothing to eat. I don't want to send them away fasting, or they might faint on the way." 33The disciples said to him, "Where should we get so many loaves in a deserted place as to satisfy so great a multitude?" 34Jesus said to them, "How many loaves do you have?" They said, "Seven, and a few small fish." 35He commanded the multitude to sit down on the ground; 36and he took the seven loaves and the fish. He gave thanks and broke them, and gave to the disciples, and the disciples to the multitudes. 37They all ate, and were filled. They took up seven baskets full of the broken pieces that were left over. 38Those who ate were four thousand men, besides women and children. 39Then he sent away the multitudes, got into the boat, and came into the borders of Magdala. [5]

Gospel of Matthew

Chapter Sixteen

1The Pharisees and Sadducees came, and testing him, asked him to show them a sign from heaven. 2But he answered them, "When it is evening, you say, 'It will be fair weather, for the sky is red.' 3In the morning, 'It will be foul weather today, for the sky is red and threatening.' Hypocrites! You know how to discern the appearance of the sky, but you can't discern the signs of the times! 4An evil and adulterous generation seeks after a sign, and there will be no sign given to it, except the sign of the prophet Jonah." He left them, and departed. 5The disciples came to the other side and had forgotten to take bread. 6Jesus said to them, "Take heed and beware of the yeast of the Pharisees and Sadducees." 7They reasoned among themselves, saying, "We brought no bread." 8Jesus, perceiving it, said, "Why do you reason among yourselves, you of little faith, 'because you have brought no bread?' 9Don't you yet perceive, neither remember the five loaves for the five thousand, and how many baskets you took up? 10Nor the seven loaves for the four thousand, and how many baskets you took up? 11How is it that you don't perceive that I didn't speak to you concerning bread? But beware of the yeast of the Pharisees and Sadducees." 12Then they understood that he didn't tell them to beware of the yeast of bread, but of the teaching of the Pharisees and Sadducees. 13Now when Jesus came into the parts of Caesarea Philippi, he asked his disciples, saying, "Who do men say that I, the Son of Man, am?"

14They said, "Some say John the Baptizer, some, Elijah, and others, Jeremiah, or one of the prophets." 15He said to them, "But who do you say that I am?" 16Simon Peter answered,

"You are the Christ, the Son of the living God." 17Jesus answered him, "Blessed are you, Simon Bar Jonah, for flesh and blood has not revealed this to you, but my Father who is in heaven. 18I also tell you that you are Peter, Peter's name, Petros in Greek, is the word for a specific rock or stone and on this rock Greek, petra, a rock mass or bedrock. I will build my assembly, and the gates of Hades or, Hell will not prevail against it. 19I will give to you the keys of the Kingdom of Heaven, and whatever you bind on earth will have been bound in heaven; and whatever you release on earth will have been released in heaven." 20Then he commanded the disciples that they should tell no one that he was Jesus the Christ. 21From that time, Jesus began to show his disciples that he must go to Jerusalem and suffer many things from the elders, chief priests, and scribes, and be killed, and the third day be raised up. 22Peter took him aside, and began to rebuke him, saying, "Far be it from you, Lord! This will never be done to you." 23But he turned, and said to Peter, "Get behind me, Satan! You are a stumbling block to me, for you are not setting your mind on the things of God, but on the things of men." 24Then Jesus said to his disciples, "If anyone desires to come after me, let him deny himself, and take up his cross, and follow me. 25For whoever desires to save his life will lose it, and whoever will lose his life for my sake will find it. 26For what will it profit a man, if he gains the whole world, and forfeits his life? Or what will a man give in exchange for his life? 27For the Son of Man will come in the glory of his Father with his angels, and then he will render to everyone according to his deeds. 28Most certainly I tell you, there are some standing here who will in no way taste of death, until they see the Son of Man coming in his Kingdom." [5]

Gospel of Matthew Chapter Seventeen

1After six days, Jesus took with him Peter, James, and John his brother, and brought them up into a high mountain by themselves. 2He was transfigured before them. His face shone like the sun, and his garments became as white as the light. 3Behold, Moses and Elijah appeared to them talking with him. 4Peter answered, and said to Jesus, "Lord, it is good for us to be here.

If you want, let's make three tents here: one for you, one for Moses, and one for Elijah." 5While he was still speaking, behold, a bright cloud overshadowed them. Behold, a voice came out of the cloud, saying, "This is my beloved Son, in whom I am well pleased. Listen to him." 6When the disciples heard it, they fell on their faces, and were very afraid. 7Jesus came and touched them and said, "Get up, and don't be afraid." 8Lifting up their eyes, they saw no one, except Jesus alone. 9As they were coming down from the mountain, Jesus commanded them, saying, "Don't tell anyone what you saw, until the Son of Man has risen from the dead." 10His disciples asked him, saying, "Then why do the scribes say that Elijah must come first?" 11Jesus answered them, "Elijah indeed comes first, and will restore all things, 12but I tell you that Elijah has come already, and they didn't recognize him, but did to him whatever they wanted to. Even so the Son of Man will also suffer by them." 13Then the disciples understood that he spoke to them of John the Baptizer. 14When they came to the multitude, a man came to him, kneeling down to him, and saying, 15"Lord, have mercy on my son, for he is epileptic, and suffers grievously; for he often falls into the fire, and often into the water. 16So I brought him to your disciples, and they could not cure him." 17Jesus answered, "Faithless and perverse generation!

How long will I be with you? How long will I bear with you? Bring him here to me." 18Jesus rebuked him, the demon went out of him, and the boy was cured from that hour. 19Then the disciples came to Jesus privately, and said, "Why weren't we able to cast it out?" 20He said to them, "Because of your unbelief. For most certainly I tell you, if you have faith as a grain of mustard seed, you will tell this mountain, 'Move from here to there,' and it will move; and nothing will be impossible for you. 21But this kind doesn't go out except by prayer and fasting." NU omits verse 21. 22While they were staying in Galilee, Jesus said to them, "The Son of Man is about to be delivered up into the hands of men, 23and they will kill him, and the third day he will be raised up." They were exceedingly sorry. 24When they had come to Capernaum, those who collected the drachma coins A drachma is a Greek silver coin worth 2 drachmas, about as much as 2 Roman denarii, or about 2 days' wages. It was commonly used to pay the half-shekel temple tax, because 2 drachmas were worth one half shekel of silver. A shekel is about 10 grams or about 0.35 ounces came to Peter, and said, "Doesn't your teacher pay the drachma?" 25He said, "Yes." When he came into the house, Jesus anticipated him, saying, "What do you think, Simon? From whom do the kings of the earth receive toll or tribute?

From their children, or from strangers?" 26Peter said to him, "From strangers." Jesus said to him, "Therefore the children are exempt. 27But, lest we cause them to stumble, go to the sea, cast a hook, and take up the first fish that comes up. When you have opened its mouth, you will find a stater coin. A stater is a silver coin equivalent to four Attic or two Alexandrian drachmas, or a Jewish shekel: just exactly enough to cover the half-shekel temple tax for two people. A shekel is about 10 grams or about 0.35 ounces, usually in the form of a silver coin. Take that, and give it to them for me and you." [5]

Gospel of Matthew

Chapter Eighteen

1In that hour the disciples came to Jesus, saying, "Who then is greatest in the Kingdom of Heaven?" 2Jesus called a little child to himself, and set him in the middle of them, 3and said, "Most certainly I tell you, unless you turn, and become as little children, you will in no way enter into the Kingdom of Heaven. 4Whoever therefore humbles himself as this little child, the same is the greatest in the Kingdom of Heaven. 5Whoever receives one such little child in my name receives me, 6but whoever causes one of these little ones who believe in me to stumble, it would be better for him that a huge millstone should be hung around his neck, and that he should be sunk in the depths of the sea. 7 "Woe to the world because of occasions of stumbling! For it must be that the occasions come, but woe to that person through whom the occasion comes! 8If your hand or your foot causes you to stumble, cut it off, and cast it from you. It is better for you to enter into life maimed or crippled, rather than having two hands or two feet to be cast into the eternal fire. 9If your eye causes you to stumble, pluck it out, and cast it from you. It is better for you to enter into life with one eye, rather than having two eyes to be cast into the Gehennaor,

Hell of fire. 10See that you don't despise one of these little ones, for I tell you that in heaven their angels always see the face of my Father who is in heaven. 11For the Son of Man came to save that which was lost. 12 "What do you think? If a man has one hundred sheep, and one of them goes astray, doesn't he leave the ninety-nine, go to the mountains, and seek that which has gone astray? 13If he finds it, most certainly I tell you, he rejoices over it more than over the ninety-nine which have not gone astray. 14Even so it is not the will of your Father who is in heaven that one of these little ones should perish. 15 "If your brother sins against you, go, show him his fault between you and him alone. If he listens to you, you have gained back your brother. 16But if he doesn't listen, take one or two more with you, that at the mouth of two or three witnesses every word may be established. Deuteronomy 19:15 17If he refuses to listen to them, tell it to the assembly. If he refuses to hear the assembly also, let him be to you as a Gentile or a tax collector. 18Most certainly I tell you, whatever things you bind on earth will have been bound in heaven, and whatever things you release on earth will have been released in heaven. 19Again, assuredly I tell you, that if two of you will agree on earth concerning anything that they will ask, it will be

done for them by my Father who is in heaven. 20For where two or three are gathered together in my name, there I am in the middle of them."
21Then Peter came and said to him, "Lord, how often shall my brother sin against me, and I forgive him? Until seven times?" 22Jesus said to him, "I don't tell you until seven times, but, until seventy times seven. 23Therefore the Kingdom of Heaven is like a certain king, who wanted to reconcile accounts with his servants. 24When he had begun to reconcile, one was brought to him who owed him ten thousand talents. Ten thousand talents (about 300 metric tons of silver) represents an extremely large sum of money, equivalent to about 60,000,000 denarii, where one denarius was typical of one day's wages for agricultural labor. 25But because he couldn't pay, his lord commanded him to be sold, with his wife, his children, and all that he had, and payment to be made. 26The servant therefore fell down and knelt before him, saying, 'Lord, have patience with me, and I will repay you all!' 27The lord of that servant, being moved with compassion, released him, and forgave him the debt. 28 "But that servant went out, and found one of his fellow servants, who owed him one hundred denarii, 100 denarii was about one sixtieth of a talent, or about 500 grams (1.1 pounds) of silver and he grabbed him, and took him by the throat, saying,

'Pay me what you owe!' 29 "So his fellow servant fell down at his feet and begged him, saying, 'Have patience with me, and I will repay you!' 30He would not, but went and cast him into prison, until he should pay back that which was due. 31So when his fellow servants saw what was done, they were exceedingly sorry, and came and told to their lord all that was done. 32Then his lord called him in, and said to him, 'You wicked servant! I forgave you all that debt, because you begged me. 33Shouldn't you also have had mercy on your fellow servant, even as I had mercy on you?' 34His lord was angry, and delivered him to the tormentors, until he should pay all that was due to him. 35So my heavenly Father will also do to you, if you don't each forgive your brother from your hearts for his misdeeds." [5]

Gospel of Matthew

Chapter Nineteen

1When Jesus had finished these words, he departed from Galilee, and came into the borders of Judea beyond the Jordan. 2Great multitudes followed him, and he healed them there. 3Pharisees came to him, testing him, and saying, "Is it lawful for a man to divorce his wife for any reason?"

4He answered, "Haven't you read that he who made them from the beginning made them male and female, Genesis 1:27 5and said, 'For this cause a man shall leave his father and mother, and shall join to his wife; and the two shall become one flesh?' Genesis 2:24 6So that they are no more two, but one flesh. What therefore God has joined together, don't let man tear apart."

7They asked him, "Why then did Moses command us to give her a bill of divorce, and divorce her?" 8He said to them, "Moses, because of the hardness of your hearts, allowed you to divorce your wives, but from the beginning it has not been so. 9I tell you that whoever divorces his wife, except for sexual immorality, and marries another, commits adultery; and he who marries her when she is divorced commits adultery." 10His disciples said to him, "If this is the case of the man with his wife, it is not expedient to marry." 11But he said to them, "Not all men can receive this saying, but those to whom it is given. 12For there are eunuchs who were born that way from their mother's womb, and there are eunuchs who were made eunuchs by men; and there are eunuchs who made themselves eunuchs for the Kingdom of Heaven's sake. He who is able to receive it, let him receive it." 13Then little children were brought to him, that he should lay his hands on them and pray; and the disciples rebuked them. 14But Jesus said, "Allow the little children, and don't forbid them to come to me; for the Kingdom of Heaven belongs to ones like these." 15He laid his hands on them, and departed from there. 16Behold, one came to him and said, "Good teacher, what good thing shall I do, that I may have eternal life?" 17He said to him, "Why do you call me good? So MT and TR. NU reads "Why do you ask me about what is good?" No one is good but one, that is, God. But if you want to enter into life, keep the commandments." 18He said to him, "Which ones?" Jesus said, "'You shall not murder.' 'You shall not commit adultery.' 'You shall not steal.' 'You shall not offer false testimony.' 19'Honor your father and your mother.' Exodus 20:12-16; Deuteronomy 5:16-20 And, 'You shall love your neighbor as yourself.'" Leviticus 19:18 20The young man said to him, "All these things I have observed from my youth. What do I still lack?" 21Jesus said to him, "If you want to be perfect, go, sell what you have, and give to the poor, and you will have treasure in heaven; and come, follow me." 22But when the young man heard the saying, he went away sad, for he was one who had great possessions. 23Jesus said to his disciples, "Most certainly I say to you, a rich man will enter into the Kingdom of Heaven with difficulty. 24Again I tell you, it is easier for a camel to go through a needle's eye, than for a rich man to enter into God's Kingdom." 25When the disciples heard it, they were exceedingly astonished, saying, "Who then can be saved?" 26Looking at them, Jesus said, "With men this is impossible, but with God all things are possible." 27Then Peter answered, "Behold, we have left everything, and followed you. What then will we have?" 28Jesus said to them, "Most certainly I tell you that you who have followed me, in the regeneration when the Son of Man will sit on the throne of his glory, you also will sit on twelve thrones, judging the twelve tribes of Israel. 29Everyone who has left houses, or brothers, or sisters, or father, or mother, or wife, or children, or lands, for my name's sake, will receive one hundred times, and will inherit eternal life. 30But many will be last who are first; and first who are last. [5]

Gospel of Matthew

Chapter Twenty

1 "For the Kingdom of Heaven is like a man who was the master of a household, who went out early in the morning to hire laborers for his vineyard. 2When he had agreed with the laborers for a denarius A denarius is a silver Roman coin worth 1/25th of a Roman aureus. This was a common wage for a day of farm labor. a day, he sent them into his vineyard. 3He went out about the third hour, Time was measured from sunrise to sunset, so the third hour would be about 9:00 a.m. and saw others standing idle in the marketplace. 4He said to them, 'You also go into the vineyard, and whatever is right I will give you.' So they went their way. 5Again he went out about the sixth and the ninth hour, noon and 3:00 p.m. and did likewise. 6About the eleventh hour5:00 p.m. he went out, and found others standing idle. He said to them, 'Why do you stand here all day idle?' 7 "They said to him, 'Because no one has hired us.' "He said to them, 'You also go into the vineyard, and you will receive whatever is right.' 8When evening had come, the lord of the vineyard said to his manager, 'Call the laborers and pay them their wages, beginning from the last to the first.' 9 "When those who were hired at about the eleventh hour came, they each received a denarius. 10When the first came, they supposed that they would receive more; and they likewise each received a denarius. 11When they received it, they murmured against the master of the household, 12saying, 'These last

have spent one hour, and you have made them equal to us, who have borne the burden of the day and the scorching heat!' 13 "But he answered one of them, 'Friend, I am doing you no wrong. Didn't you agree with me for a denarius? 14Take that which is yours, and go your way. It is my desire to give to this last just as much as to you. 15Isn't it lawful for me to do what I want to with what I own? Or is your eye evil, because I am good?' 16So the last will be first, and the first last. For many are called, but few are chosen." 17As Jesus was going up to Jerusalem, he took the twelve disciples aside, and on the way he said to them, 18"Behold, we are going up to Jerusalem, and the Son of Man will be delivered to the chief priests and scribes, and they will condemn him to death, 19and will hand him over to the Gentiles to mock, to scourge, and to crucify; and the third day he will be raised up." 20Then the mother of the sons of Zebedee came to him with her sons, kneeling and asking a certain thing of him. 21He said to her, "What do you want?" She said to him,

"Command that these, my two sons, may sit, one on your right hand, and one on your left hand, in your Kingdom." 22But Jesus answered, "You don't know what you are asking. Are you able to drink the cup that I am about to drink, and be baptized with the baptism that I am baptized with?" They said to him, "We are able." 23He said to them, "You will indeed drink my cup, and be baptized with the baptism that I am baptized with, but to sit on my right hand and on my left hand is not mine to give; but it is for whom it has been prepared by my Father." 24When the ten heard it, they were indignant with the two brothers. 25But Jesus summoned them, and said, "You know that the rulers of the nations lord it over them, and their great ones exercise authority over them. 26It shall not be so among you, but whoever desires to become great among you shall be TR reads "let him be" instead of "shall be" your servant. 27Whoever desires to be first among you shall be your bondservant, 28even as the Son of Man came not to be served, but to serve, and to give his life as a ransom for many." 29As they went out from Jericho, a great multitude followed him. 30Behold, two blind men sitting by the road, when they heard that Jesus was passing by, cried out, "Lord, have mercy on us, you son of David!" 31The multitude rebuked them, telling them that they should be quiet, but they cried out even more, "Lord, have mercy on us, you son of David!" 32Jesus stood still, and called them, and asked, "What do you want me to do for you?" 33They told him, "Lord, that our eyes may be opened." 34Jesus, being moved with compassion, touched their eyes; and immediately their eyes received their sight, and they followed him.   [5]

Gospel of Matthew

Chapter Twenty-One

1When they came near to Jerusalem, and came to Bethsphage, TR & NU read "Bethphage" instead of "Bethsphage" to the Mount of Olives, then Jesus sent two disciples, 2saying to them, "Go into the village that is opposite you, and immediately you will find a donkey tied, and a colt with her. Untie them, and bring them to me. 3If anyone says anything to you, you shall say, 'The Lord needs them,' and immediately he will send them." 4All this was done, that it might be fulfilled which was spoken through the prophet, saying, 5"Tell the daughter of Zion, behold, your King comes to you, humble, and riding on a donkey, on a colt, the foal of a donkey." Zechariah 9:9 6The disciples went, and did just as Jesus commanded them, 7and brought the donkey and the colt, and laid their clothes on them; and he sat on them. 8A very great multitude spread their clothes on the road. Others cut branches from the trees, and spread them on the road. 9The multitudes who went in front of him, and those who followed, kept shouting, "Hosanna "Hosanna" means "save us" or "help us, we pray". to the son of David! Blessed is he who comes in the name of the Lord! Hosanna in the highest!" Psalm 118:26

10When he had come into Jerusalem, all the city was stirred up, saying, "Who is this?" 11The multitudes said, "This is the prophet, Jesus, from Nazareth of Galilee."

12Jesus entered into the temple of God, and drove out all of those who sold and bought in the temple, and overthrew the money changers' tables and the seats of those who sold the doves. 13He said to them, "It is written, 'My house shall be called a house of prayer,' Isaiah

56:7 but you have made it a den of robbers!" Jeremiah 7:11

14The blind and the lame came to him in the temple, and he healed them. 15But when the chief priests and the scribes saw the wonderful things that he did, and the children who were crying in the temple and saying, "Hosanna to the son of David!" they were indignant, 16and said to him, "Do you hear what these are saying?"

Jesus said to them, "Yes. Did you never read, 'Out of the mouth of babes and nursing babies you have perfected praise?'" Psalm 8:2

17He left them, and went out of the city to Bethany, and camped there. 18Now in the morning, as he returned to the city, he was hungry. 19Seeing a fig tree by the road, he came to it, and found nothing on it but leaves. He said to it, "Let there be no fruit from you forever!"

Immediately the fig tree withered away. 20When the disciples saw it, they marveled, saying, "How did the fig tree immediately wither away?" 21Jesus answered them, "Most certainly I tell you, if you have faith, and don't doubt, you will not only do what was done to the fig tree, but even if you told this mountain, 'Be taken up and cast into the sea,' it would be done. 22All things, whatever you ask in prayer, believing, you will receive."

23When he had come into the temple, the chief priests and the elders of the people came to him as he was teaching, and said, "By what authority do you do these things? Who gave you this authority?" 24Jesus answered them, "I also will ask you one question, which if you tell me, I likewise will tell you by what authority I do these things. 25The baptism of John, where was it from? From heaven or from men?" They reasoned with themselves, saying, "If we say, 'From heaven,' he will ask us, 'Why then did you not believe him?' 26But if we say, 'From men,' we fear the multitude, for all hold John as a prophet." 27They answered Jesus, and said, "We don't know." He also said to them, "Neither will I tell you by what authority I do these things. 28But what do you think? A man had two sons, and he came to the first, and said, 'Son, go work today in my vineyard.' 29He answered, 'I will not,' but afterward he changed his mind, and went. 30He came to the second, and said the same thing. He answered, 'I go, sir,' but he didn't go. 31Which of the two did the will of his father?" They said to him, "The first." Jesus said to them, "Most certainly I tell you that the tax collectors and the prostitutes are entering into God's Kingdom before you. 32For John came to you in the way of righteousness, and you didn't believe him, but the tax collectors and the prostitutes believed him. When you saw it, you didn't even repent afterward, that you might believe him.

33 "Hear another parable. There was a man who was a master of a household, who planted a vineyard, set a hedge about it, dug a wine press in it, built a tower, leased it out to farmers, and went into another country. 34When the season for the fruit came near, he sent his servants to the farmers, to receive his fruit. 35The farmers took his servants, beat one, killed another, and stoned another. 36Again, he sent other servants more than the first: and they treated them the same way. 37But afterward

he sent to them his son, saying, 'They will respect my son.' 38But the farmers, when they saw the son, said among themselves, 'This is the heir. Come, let's kill him, and seize his inheritance.' 39So they took him, and threw him out of the vineyard, and killed him. 40When therefore the lord of the vineyard comes, what will he do to those farmers?"

41They told him, "He will miserably destroy those miserable men, and will lease out the vineyard to other farmers, who will give him the fruit in its season." 42Jesus said to them, "Did you never read in the Scriptures, 'The stone which the builders rejected, the same was made the head of the corner. This was from the Lord. It is marvelous in our eyes?' Psalm 118:22-23

43 "Therefore I tell you, God's Kingdom will be taken away from you, and will be given to a nation producing its fruit. 44He who falls on this stone will be broken to pieces, but on whomever it will fall, it will scatter him as dust." 45When the chief priests and the Pharisees heard his parables, they perceived that he spoke about them. 46When they sought to seize him, they feared the multitudes, because they considered him to be a prophet.   [5]

Gospel of Matthew

Chapter Twenty-Two

1Jesus answered and spoke again in parables to them, saying, 2"The Kingdom of Heaven is like a certain king, who made a marriage feast for his son, 3and sent out his servants to call those who were invited to the marriage feast, but they would not come. 4Again he sent out other servants, saying, 'Tell those who are invited, "Behold, I have prepared my dinner. My cattle and my fatlings are killed, and all things are ready. Come to the marriage feast!"' 5But they made light of it, and went their ways, one to his own farm, another to his merchandise, 6and the rest grabbed his servants, and treated them shamefully, and killed them. 7When the king heard that, he was angry, and sent his armies, destroyed those murderers, and burned their city.

8 "Then he said to his servants, 'The wedding is ready, but those who were invited weren't worthy. 9Go therefore to the intersections of the highways, and as many as you may find, invite to the marriage feast.' 10Those servants went out into the highways, and gathered together as many as they found, both bad and good. The wedding was filled with

guests. 11But when the king came in to see the guests, he saw there a man who didn't have on wedding clothing, 12and he said to him, 'Friend, how did you come in here not wearing wedding clothing?' He was speechless. 13Then the king said to the servants, 'Bind him hand and foot, take him away, and throw him into the outer darkness; there is where the weeping and grinding of teeth will be.' 14For many are called, but few chosen." 15Then the Pharisees went and took counsel how they might entrap him in his talk. 16They sent their disciples to him, along with the Herodians, saying, "Teacher, we know that you are honest, and teach the way of God in truth, no matter whom you teach, for you aren't partial to anyone. 17Tell us therefore, what do you think? Is it lawful to pay taxes to Caesar, or not?" 18But Jesus perceived their wickedness, and said, "Why do you test me, you hypocrites? 19Show me the tax money." They brought to him a denarius.

20He asked them, "Whose is this image and inscription?" 21They said to him, "Caesar's."

Then he said to them, "Give therefore to Caesar the things that are Caesar's, and to God the things that are God's." 22When they heard it, they marveled, and left him, and went away.

23On that day Sadducees (those who say that there is no resurrection) came to him. They asked him, 24saying, "Teacher, Moses said, 'If a man dies, having no children, his brother shall marry his wife, and raise up offspring or, seed for his brother.' 25Now there were with us seven brothers. The first married and died, and having no offspring or, seed left his wife to his brother. 26In the same way, the second also, and the third, to the seventh. 27After them all, the woman died. 28In the resurrection therefore, whose wife will she be of the seven? For they all had her." 29But Jesus answered them, "You are mistaken, not knowing the Scriptures, nor the power of God. 30For in the resurrection they neither marry, nor are given in marriage, but are like God's angels in heaven. 31But concerning the resurrection of the dead, haven't you read that which was spoken to you by God, saying, 32'I am the God of Abraham, and the God of Isaac, and the God of Jacob?' Exodus 3:6 God is not the God of the dead, but of the living." 33When the multitudes heard it, they were astonished at his teaching. 34But the Pharisees, when they heard that he had silenced the Sadducees, gathered themselves together. 35One of them, a lawyer, asked him a question, testing him. 36"Teacher, which is the greatest commandment in the law?" 37Jesus said to him, "'You shall love the Lord your God with all your heart, with all your soul, and with all your mind.' Deuteronomy 6:5 38This is the first and great commandment. 39A second likewise is this, 'You shall love your neighbor as yourself.'

Leviticus 19:18 40The whole law and the prophets depend on these two commandments."

41Now while the Pharisees were gathered together, Jesus asked them a question, 42saying, "What do you think of the Christ? Whose son is he?" They said to him, "Of

David." 43He said to them, "How then does David in the Spirit call him Lord, saying, 44 'The Lord said to my Lord, sit on my right hand, until I make your enemies a footstool for your feet?' Psalm 110:1 45 "If then David calls him Lord, how is he his son?" 46No one was able to answer him a word, neither did any man dare ask him any more questions from that day forward.   [5]

Gospel of Matthew

Chapter Twenty-Three

1Then Jesus spoke to the multitudes and to his disciples, 2saying, "The scribes and the Pharisees sat on Moses' seat. 3All things therefore whatever they tell you to observe, observe and do, but don't do their works; for they say, and don't do. 4For they bind heavy burdens that are grievous to be borne, and lay them on men's shoulders; but they themselves will not lift a finger to help them. 5But all their works they do to be seen by men. They make their phylacteries phylacteries (tefillin in Hebrew) are small leather pouches that some Jewish men wear on their forehead and arm in prayer. They are used to carry a small scroll with some Scripture in it. See Deuteronomy 6:8. broad, enlarge the fringes or, tassels of their garments, 6and love the place of honor at feasts, the best seats in the synagogues, 7the salutations in the marketplaces, and to be called 'Rabbi, Rabbi' by men. 8But don't you be called 'Rabbi,' for one is your teacher, the Christ, and all of you are brothers. 9Call no man on the earth your father, for one is your Father, he who is in heaven. 10Neither be called masters, for one is your master, the Christ. 11But he who is greatest among you will be your servant. 12Whoever exalts himself will be humbled, and whoever humbles himself will be exalted. 13 "Woe to you, scribes and Pharisees, hypocrites! For you devour widows' houses, and as a pretense you make long prayers. Therefore you will receive greater condemnation. 14 "But woe to you, scribes and Pharisees, hypocrites! Because you shut up the Kingdom of Heaven against men; for you don't enter in yourselves, neither do you allow those who are entering in to enter. Some Greek manuscripts reverse the order of verses 13 and 14, and some omit verse 13, numbering verse 14 as 13. NU omits verse 14. 15Woe to you, scribes and Pharisees, hypocrites! For you travel around by sea and land to make one proselyte; and when he becomes one, you make him twice as much of a son of Gehennaor, Hell as yourselves. 16 "Woe to you, you blind guides, who say, 'Whoever swears by the temple, it is nothing; but whoever swears by the gold of the temple, he is obligated.' 17You blind fools! For which is greater, the gold, or the temple that sanctifies the gold? 18 'Whoever swears by the altar, it is nothing; but whoever swears by the gift that is on it, he is obligated?' 19You blind fools! For which is greater, the gift, or the altar that sanctifies the gift? 20He therefore who swears by the altar, swears by it, and by everything on it. 21He who swears by the temple, swears by it, and by him who was living NU reads "lives" in it. 22He who swears by heaven, swears by the throne of God, and by him who sits on it. 23 "Woe to you, scribes and Pharisees, hypocrites! For you tithe mint, dill, and cumin, cumin is an aromatic seed from Cuminum cyminum, resembling caraway in flavor and appearance. It is used as a spice and have left undone the weightier matters of the law: justice, mercy, and faith. But you ought to have done these, and not to have left the other undone. 24You blind guides, who strain out a gnat, and swallow a camel! 25 "Woe to you, scribes and Pharisees, hypocrites! For you clean the outside of the cup and of the platter, but within they are full of extortion and unrighteousness. TR reads "self-indulgence" instead of "unrighteousness" 26You blind Pharisee, first clean the inside of the cup and of the platter, that its outside may become clean also. 27 "Woe to you, scribes and Pharisees, hypocrites! For you are like whitened tombs, which outwardly appear beautiful, but inwardly are full of dead men's bones, and of all uncleanness. 28Even so you also outwardly appear righteous to men, but inwardly you are full of hypocrisy and iniquity. 29 "Woe to you, scribes and Pharisees, hypocrites! For you build the tombs of the prophets, and decorate the tombs of the righteous, 30and say, 'If we had lived in the days of our fathers, we wouldn't have been partakers with them in the blood of the prophets.' 31Therefore you testify to yourselves that you are children of those who killed the prophets. 32Fill up, then, the measure of your fathers. 33You serpents, you offspring of vipers, how will you escape the judgment of Gehenna? or, Hell 34Therefore behold,

I send to you prophets, wise men, and scribes. Some of them you will kill and crucify; and some of them you will scourge in your synagogues, and persecute from city to city; 35that on you may come all the righteous blood shed on the earth, from the blood of righteous Abel to the blood of Zachariah son of Barachiah, whom you killed between the sanctuary and the altar. 36Most certainly I tell you, all these things will come upon this generation. 37 "Jerusalem, Jerusalem, who kills the prophets, and stones those who are sent to her! How often I would have gathered your children together, even as a hen gathers her chicks under her wings, and you would not! 38Behold, your house is left to you desolate. 39For I tell you, you will not see me from now on, until you say, 'Blessed is he who comes in the name of the Lord!'" [5]

Gospel of Matthew

Chapter Twenty-Four

1Jesus went out from the temple, and was going on his way. His disciples came to him to show him the buildings of the temple. 2But he answered them, "You see all of these things, don't you? Most certainly I tell you, there will not be left here one stone on another, that will not be thrown down." 3As he sat on the Mount of Olives, the disciples came to him privately, saying,

"Tell us, when will these things be? What is the sign of your coming, and of the end of the age?"

4Jesus answered them, "Be careful that no one leads you astray. 5For many will come in my name, saying, 'I am the Christ,' and will lead many astray. 6You will hear of wars and rumors of wars. See that you aren't troubled, for all this must happen, but the end is not yet. 7For nation will rise against nation, and kingdom against kingdom; and there will be famines, plagues, and earthquakes in various places. 8But all these things are the beginning of birth pains. 9Then they will deliver you up to oppression, and will kill you. You will be hated by all of the nations for my name's sake. 10Then many will stumble, and will deliver up one another, and will hate one another. 11Many false prophets will arise, and will lead many astray. 12Because iniquity will be multiplied, the love of many will grow cold. 13But he who endures to the end, the same will be saved. 14This Good News of the Kingdom will be preached in the whole world for a testimony to all the nations, and then the end will come. 15 "When, therefore, you see the abomination of desolation, Daniel 9:27; 11:31; 12:11 which was spoken of through

Daniel the prophet, standing in the holy place (let the reader understand), 16then let those who are in Judea flee to the mountains. 17Let him who is on the housetop not go down to take out the things that are in his house. 18Let him who is in the field not return back to get his clothes. 19But woe to those who are with child and to nursing mothers in those days! 20Pray that your flight will not be in the winter, nor on a Sabbath, 21for then there will be great oppression, such as has not been from the beginning of the world until now, no, nor ever will be. 22Unless those days had been shortened, no flesh would have been saved. But for the sake of the chosen ones, those days will be shortened. 23 "Then if any man tells you, 'Behold, here is the Christ,' or, 'There,' don't believe it. 24For there will arise false christs, and false prophets, and they will show great signs and wonders, so as to lead astray, if possible, even the chosen ones.

25 "Behold, I have told you beforehand. 26If therefore they tell you, 'Behold, he is in the wilderness,' don't go out; 'Behold, he is in the inner rooms,' don't believe it. 27For as the lightning flashes from the east, and is seen even to the west, so will be the coming of the Son of Man. 28For wherever the carcass is, there is where the vultures or, eagles gather together. 29But immediately after the oppression of those days, the sun will be darkened, the moon will not give its light, the stars will fall from the sky, and the powers of the heavens will be shaken; Isaiah 13:10; 34:4 30and then the sign of the Son of Man will appear in the sky. Then all the tribes of the earth will mourn, and they will see the Son of Man coming on the clouds of the sky with power and great glory. 31He will send out his angels with a great sound of a trumpet, and they will gather together his chosen ones from the four winds, from one end of the sky to the other.

32 "Now from the fig tree learn this parable. When its branch has now become tender, and produces its leaves, you know that the summer is near. 33Even so you also, when you see all these things, know that it is near, even at the doors. 34Most certainly I tell you, this generation

The word for "generation" (genea) can also be translated as "race." will not pass away, until all these things are accomplished. 35Heaven and earth will pass away, but my words will not pass away. 36But no one knows of that day and hour, not even the angels of heaven, NU adds "nor the son" but my Father only. 37 "As the days of Noah were, so will be the coming of the Son of Man. 38For as in those days which were before the flood they were eating and drinking, marrying and giving in marriage, until the day that Noah entered into the ship, 39and they didn't know until the flood came, and took them all away, so will be the coming of the Son of Man. 40Then two men will be in the field: one will be taken and one will be left; 41two women grinding at the mill, one will be taken and one will be left. 42Watch therefore, for you don't know in what hour your Lord comes. 43But know this, that if the master of the house had known in what watch of the night the thief was coming, he would have watched, and would not have allowed his house to be broken into. 44Therefore also be ready, for in an hour that you don't expect, the Son of Man will come. 45 "Who then is the faithful and wise servant, whom his lord has set over his household, to give them their food in due season? 46Blessed is that servant whom his lord finds doing so when he comes. 47Most certainly I tell you that he will set him over all that he has. 48But if that evil servant should say in his heart, 'My lord is delaying his coming,' 49and begins to beat his fellow servants, and eat and drink with the drunkards, 50the lord of that servant will come in a day when he doesn't expect it, and in an hour when he doesn't know it, 51and will cut him in pieces, and appoint his portion with the hypocrites. There is where the weeping and grinding of teeth will be.   [5]

Gospel of Matthew

Chapter Twenty-Five

1 "Then the Kingdom of Heaven will be like ten virgins, who took their lamps, and went out to meet the bridegroom. 2Five of them were foolish, and five were wise. 3Those who were foolish, when they took their lamps, took no oil with them, 4but the wise took oil in their vessels with their lamps. 5Now while the bridegroom delayed, they all slumbered and slept. 6But at midnight there was a cry, 'Behold! The bridegroom is coming! Come out to meet him!' 7Then all those virgins arose, and trimmed their lamps. The end of the wick of an oil lamp needs to be cut off periodically to avoid having it become clogged with carbon deposits. The wick height is also adjusted so that the flame burns evenly and gives good light without producing a lot of smoke. 8The foolish said to the wise, 'Give us some of your oil, for our lamps are going out.' 9But the wise answered, saying, 'What if there isn't enough for us and you? You go rather to those who sell, and buy for yourselves.' 10While they went away to buy, the bridegroom came, and those who were ready went in with him to the marriage feast, and the door was shut. 11Afterward the other virgins also came, saying, 'Lord, Lord, open to us.' 12But he answered, 'Most certainly I tell you, I don't know you.'

13Watch therefore, for you don't know the day nor the hour in which the Son of Man is coming. 14 "For it is like a man, going into another country, who called his own servants, and entrusted his goods to them. 15To one he gave five talents, a talent is about 30 kilograms or 66 pounds (usually used to weigh silver unless otherwise specified) to another two, to another one; to each according to his own ability. Then he went on his journey. 16Immediately he who received the five talents went and traded with them, and made another five talents. 17In the same way, he also who got the two gained another two. 18But he who received the one talent went away and dug in the earth, and hid his lord's money. 19 "Now after a long time the lord of those servants came, and reconciled accounts with them. 20He who received the five talents came and brought another five talents, saying, 'Lord, you delivered to me five talents. Behold, I have gained another five talents besides them.'

21 "His lord said to him, 'Well done, good and faithful servant. You have been faithful over a few things, I will set you over many things. Enter into the joy of your lord.' 22 "He also who got the two talents came and said, 'Lord, you delivered to me two talents. Behold, I have gained another two talents besides them.' 23 "His lord said to him, 'Well done, good and faithful servant. You have been faithful over a few things, I will set you over many things. Enter into the joy of your lord.' 24 "He also who had received the one talent came and said, 'Lord, I knew you that you are a hard man, reaping where you did not sow, and gathering where you did not scatter. 25I was afraid, and went away and hid your talent in the earth. Behold, you have what is yours.' 26 "But his lord answered him, 'You wicked and slothful servant. You knew that I reap where I didn't sow, and gather where I didn't scatter. 27You ought therefore to have deposited my money with the bankers, and at my coming I should have received back my own with interest. 28Take away therefore the talent from him, and give it to him who has the ten talents. 29For to everyone who has will be given, and he will have abundance, but from him who doesn't have, even that which he has will be taken away. 30Throw out the unprofitable servant into the outer darkness, where there will be weeping and gnashing of teeth.' 31 "But when the Son of Man comes in his glory, and all the holy angels with him, then he will sit on the throne of his glory. 32Before him all the nations will be gathered, and he will separate them one from another, as a shepherd separates the sheep from the goats. 33He will set the sheep on his right hand, but the goats on the left. 34Then the King will tell those on his

right hand, 'Come, blessed of my Father, inherit the Kingdom prepared for you from the foundation of the world; 35for I was hungry, and you gave me food to eat. I was thirsty, and you gave me drink. I was a stranger, and you took me in. 36I was naked, and you clothed me. I was sick, and you visited me. I was in prison, and you came to me.' 37 "Then the righteous will answer him, saying, 'Lord, when did we see you hungry, and feed you; or thirsty, and give you a drink? 38When did we see you as a stranger, and take you in; or naked, and clothe you? 39When did we see you sick, or in prison, and come to you?' 40 "The King will answer them, 'Most certainly I tell you, because you did it to one of the least of these my brothers, The word for "brothers" here may be also correctly translated "brothers and sisters" or "siblings." you did it to me.' 41Then he will say also to those on the left hand, 'Depart from me, you cursed, into the eternal fire which is prepared for the devil and his angels; 42for I was hungry, and you didn't give me food to eat; I was thirsty, and you gave me no drink; 43I was a stranger, and you didn't take me in; naked, and you didn't clothe me; sick, and in prison, and you didn't visit me.' 44 "Then they will also answer, saying, 'Lord, when did we see you hungry, or thirsty, or a stranger, or naked, or sick, or in prison, and didn't help you?' 45 "Then he will answer them, saying, 'Most certainly I tell you, because you didn't do it to one of the least of these, you didn't do it to me.' 46These will go away into eternal punishment, but the righteous into eternal life."   [5]

Gospel of Matthew

Chapter Twenty-Six

1When Jesus had finished all these words, he said to his disciples, 2"You know that after two days the Passover is coming, and the Son of Man will be delivered up to be crucified."

3Then the chief priests, the scribes, and the elders of the people were gathered together in the court of the high priest, who was called Caiaphas. 4They took counsel together that they might take Jesus by deceit, and kill him. 5But they said, "Not during the feast, lest a riot occur among the people." 6Now when Jesus was in Bethany, in the house of Simon the leper, 7a woman came to him having an alabaster jar of very expensive ointment, and she poured it on his head as he sat at the table. 8But when his disciples saw this, they were indignant, saying, "Why this aste? 9For this ointment might have been sold for much, and given to the poor." 10However, knowing this, Jesus said to them, "Why do you trouble the woman? Because she has done a good work for me. 11For you always have the poor with you; but you don't always have me. 12For in pouring this ointment on my body, she did it to prepare me for burial. 13Most certainly I tell you, wherever this Good News is preached in the whole world, what this woman has done will also be spoken of as a memorial of her." 14Then one of the twelve, who was called Judas Iscariot, went to the chief priests, 15and said, "What are you willing to give me that I should deliver him to you?" They weighed out for him thirty pieces of silver. 16From that time he sought opportunity to betray him. 17Now on the first day of unleavened bread, the disciples came to Jesus, saying to him, "Where do you want us to prepare for you to eat the Passover?" 18He said, "Go into the city to a certain person, and tell him, 'The Teacher says, "My time is at hand. I will keep the Passover at your house with my disciples."'" 19The disciples did as Jesus commanded them, and they prepared the Passover. 20Now when evening had come, he was reclining at the table with the twelve disciples. 21As they were eating, he said, "Most certainly I tell you that one of you will betray me." 22They were exceedingly sorrowful, and each began to ask him, "It isn't me, is it, Lord?" 23He answered, "He who dipped his hand with me in the dish, the same will betray me. 24The Son of Man goes, even as it is written of him, but woe to that man through whom the

Son of Man is betrayed! It would be better for that man if he had not been born." 25Judas, who betrayed him, answered, "It isn't me, is it, Rabbi?" He said to him, "You said it."

26As they were eating, Jesus took bread, gave thanks for TR reads "blessed" instead of

"gave thanks for" it, and broke it. He gave to the disciples, and said, "Take, eat; this is my

body." 27He took the cup, gave thanks, and gave to them, saying, "All of you drink it, 28for this is my blood of the new covenant, which is poured out for many for the remission of sins. 29But I tell you that I will not drink of this fruit of the vine from now on, until that day when I drink it anew with you in my Father's Kingdom." 30When they had sung a hymn, they went out to the Mount of Olives.

31Then Jesus said to them, "All of you will be made to stumble because of me tonight, for it is written, 'I will strike the shepherd, and the sheep of the flock will be scattered.' Zechariah 13:7 32But after I am raised up, I will go before you into Galilee." 33But Peter answered him, "Even if all will be made to stumble because of you, I will never be made to stumble."

34Jesus said to him, "Most certainly I tell you that tonight, before the rooster crows, you will deny me three times." 35Peter said to him, "Even if I must die with you, I will not deny you." All of the disciples also said likewise. 36Then Jesus came with them to a place called Gethsemane, and said to his disciples, "Sit here, while I go there and pray." 37He took with him Peter and the two sons of Zebedee, and began to be sorrowful and severely troubled. 38Then he said to them, "My soul is exceedingly sorrowful, even to death. Stay here, and watch with me." 39He went forward a little, fell on his face, and prayed, saying, "My Father, if it is possible, let this cup pass away from me; nevertheless, not what I desire, but what you desire." 40He came to the disciples, and found them sleeping, and said to Peter, "What, couldn't you watch with me for one hour? 41Watch and pray, that you don't enter into temptation. The spirit indeed is willing, but the flesh is weak." 42Again, a second time he went away, and prayed, saying, "My Father, if this cup can't pass away from me unless I drink it, your desire be done." 43He came again and found them sleeping, for their eyes were heavy. 44He left them again, went away, and prayed a third time, saying the same words. 45Then he came to his disciples, and said to them, "Sleep on now, and take your rest. Behold, the hour is at hand, and the Son of Man is betrayed into the hands of sinners. 46Arise, let's be going. Behold, he who betrays me is at hand." 47While he was still speaking, behold, Judas, one of the twelve, came, and with him a great multitude with swords and clubs, from the chief priests and elders of the people. 48Now he who betrayed him gave them a sign, saying, "Whoever I kiss, he is the one. Seize him." 49Immediately he came to Jesus, and said, "Hail, Rabbi!" and kissed him. 50Jesus said to him, "Friend, why are you here?" Then they came and laid hands on Jesus, and took him. 51Behold, one of those who were with Jesus stretched out his hand, and drew his sword, and struck the servant of the high priest, and struck off his ear. 52Then Jesus said to him, "Put your sword back into its place, for all those who take the sword will die by the sword. 53Or do you think that I couldn't ask my Father, and he would even now send me more than twelve legions of angels? 54How then would the Scriptures be fulfilled that it must be so?" 55In that hour Jesus said to the multitudes, "Have you come out as against a robber with swords and clubs to seize me? I sat daily in the temple teaching, and you didn't arrest me. 56But all this has happened, that the Scriptures of the prophets might be fulfilled." Then all the disciples left him, and fled. 57Those who had taken Jesus led him away to Caiaphas the high priest, where the scribes and the elders were gathered together. 58But Peter followed him from a distance, to the court of the high priest, and entered in and sat with the officers, to see the end. 59Now the chief priests, the elders, and the whole council sought false testimony against Jesus, that they might put him to death; 60and they found none. Even though many false witnesses came forward, they found none. But at last two false witnesses came forward, 61and said, "This man said, 'I am able to destroy the temple of God, and to build it in three days.'" 62The high priest stood up, and said to him, "Have you no answer? What is this that these testify against you?" 63But Jesus held his peace. The high priest answered him, "I adjure you by the living God, that you tell us whether you are the Christ, the Son of God." 64Jesus said to him, "You have said it. Nevertheless, I tell you, after this you will see the Son of Man sitting at the right hand of Power, and coming on the clouds of the sky."

65Then the high priest tore his clothing, saying, "He has spoken blasphemy! Why do we need any more witnesses? Behold, now you have heard his blasphemy. 66What do you think?" They answered, "He is worthy of death!" 67Then they spit in his face and beat him with their fists, and some slapped him, 68saying, "Prophesy to us, you Christ! Who hit you?" 69Now Peter was sitting outside in the court, and a maid came to him, saying, "You were also with Jesus, the Galilean!" 70But he denied it before them all, saying, "I don't know what you are talking about." 71When he had gone out onto the porch, someone else saw him, and said to those who were there, "This man also was with Jesus of Nazareth." 72Again he denied it with an oath, "I don't know the man." 73After a little while those who stood by came and said to Peter, "Surely you are also one of them, for your speech makes you known." 74Then he began to curse and to swear, "I don't know the man!" Immediately the rooster crowed. 75Peter remembered the word which

Jesus had said to him, "Before the rooster crows, you will deny me three times." He went out and wept bitterly. [5]

Gospel of Matthew

Chapter Twenty-Seven

1Now when morning had come, all the chief priests and the elders of the people took counsel against Jesus to put him to death: 2and they bound him, and led him away, and delivered him up to Pontius Pilate, the governor. 3Then Judas, who betrayed him, when he saw that Jesus was condemned, felt remorse, and brought back the thirty pieces of silver to the chief priests and elders, 4saying, "I have sinned in that I betrayed innocent blood." But they said, "What is that to us? You see to it." 5He threw down the pieces of silver in the sanctuary, and departed. He went away and hanged himself. 6The chief priests took the pieces of silver, and said, "It's not lawful to put them into the treasury, since it is the price of blood." 7They took counsel, and bought the potter's field with them, to bury strangers in. 8Therefore that field was called "The Field of Blood" to this day. 9Then that which was spoken through Jeremiah some manuscripts omit "Jeremiah" the prophet was fulfilled, saying, "They took the thirty pieces of silver, the price of him upon whom a price had been set, whom some of the children of Israel priced, 10and they gave them for the potter's field, as the Lord commanded me." Zechariah 11:12-13; Jeremiah

19:1-13; 32:6-9 11Now Jesus stood before the governor: and the governor asked him, saying, "Are you the King of the Jews?" Jesus said to him, "So you say." 12When he was accused by the chief priests and elders, he answered nothing. 13Then Pilate said to him, "Don't you hear how many things they testify against you?" 14He gave him no answer, not even one word, so that the governor marveled greatly. 15Now at the feast the governor was accustomed to release to the multitude one prisoner, whom they desired. 16They had then a notable prisoner, called Barabbas. 17When therefore they were gathered together, Pilate said to them, "Whom do you want me to release to you? Barabbas, or Jesus, who is called Christ?" 18For he knew that because of envy they had delivered him up. 19While he was sitting on the judgment seat, his wife sent to him, saying, "Have nothing to do with that righteous man, for I have suffered many things today in a dream because of him." 20Now the chief priests and the elders persuaded the multitudes to ask for Barabbas, and destroy Jesus. 21But the governor answered them, "Which of the two do you want me to release to you?" They said, "Barabbas!" 22Pilate said to them, "What then shall I do to Jesus, who is called Christ?" They all said to him, "Let him be crucified!" 23But the governor said, "Why? What evil has he done?" But they cried out exceedingly, saying, "Let him be crucified!" 24So when Pilate saw that nothing was being gained,

The Walk – S.B. Stone & Rock Solid Publishing, LLC
©2018

but rather that a disturbance was starting, he took water, and washed his hands before the multitude, saying, "I am innocent of the blood of this righteous person. You see to it." 25All the people answered, "May his blood be on us, and on our children!" 26Then he released to them Barabbas, but Jesus he flogged and delivered to be crucified. 27Then the governor's soldiers took Jesus into the Praetorium, and gathered the whole garrison together against him. 28They stripped him, and put a scarlet robe on him. 29They braided a crown of thorns and put it on his head, and a reed in his right hand; and they kneeled down before him, and mocked him, saying, "Hail, King of the Jews!" 30They spat on him, and took the reed and struck him on the head. 31When they had mocked him, they took the robe off of him, and put his clothes on him, and led him away to crucify him. 32As they came out, they found a man of Cyrene, Simon by name, and they compelled him to go with them, that he might carry his cross. 33When they came to a place called "Golgotha", that is to say, "The place of a skull," 34they gave him sour wine or, vinegar to drink mixed with gall. When he had tasted it, he would not drink. 35When they had crucified him, they divided his clothing among them, casting lots, TR adds "that it might be fulfilled which was spoken by the prophet: 'They divided my garments among them, and for my clothing they cast lots;'" [see Psalm 22:18 and John 19:24] 36and they sat and watched him there. 37They set up over his head the accusation against him written, "THIS IS JESUS, THE KING OF THE JEWS." 38Then there were two robbers crucified with him, one on his right hand and one on the left. 39Those who passed by blasphemed him, wagging their heads, 40and saying, "You who destroy the temple, and build it in three days, save yourself! If you are the Son of God, come down from the cross!" 41Likewise the chief priests also mocking, with the scribes, the Pharisees, TR omits "the Pharisees" and the elders, said, 42"He saved others, but he can't save himself. If he is the King of Israel, let him come down from the cross now, and we will believe in him. 43He trusts in God. Let God deliver him now, if he wants him; for he said, 'I am the Son of God.'" 44The robbers also who were crucified with him cast on him the same reproach.

45Now from the sixth hour noon there was darkness over all the land until the ninth hour.3:00 p.m. 46About the ninth hour Jesus cried with a loud voice, saying, "Eli, Eli, limaTR reads "lama" instead of "lima" sabachthani?" That is, "My God, my God, why have you forsaken me? "Psalm 22:1 47Some of them who stood there, when they heard it, said,

"This man is calling Elijah." 48Immediately one of them ran, and took a sponge, and filled it with vinegar, and put it on a reed, and gave him a drink. 49The rest said, "Let him be. Let's see whether Elijah comes to save him." 50Jesus cried again with a loud voice, and yielded up his spirit. 51Behold, the veil of the temple was torn in two from the top to the bottom. The earth quaked and the rocks were split. 52The tombs were opened, and many bodies of the saints who had fallen asleep were raised; 53and coming out of the tombs after his resurrection, they entered into the holy city and appeared to many. 54Now the centurion, and those who were with him watching Jesus, when they saw the earthquake, and the things that were done, feared exceedingly, saying, "Truly this was the Son of God." 55Many women were there watching from afar, who had followed Jesus from Galilee, serving him. 56Among them were Mary Magdalene, Mary the mother of James and Joses, and the mother of the sons of Zebedee. 57When evening had come, a rich man from Arimathaea, named Joseph, who himself was also Jesus' disciple came. 58This man went to

Pilate, and asked for Jesus' body. Then Pilate commanded the body to be given up. 59Joseph took the body, and wrapped it in a clean linen cloth, 60and laid it in his own new tomb, which he had cut out in the rock, and he rolled a great stone to the door of the tomb, and departed. 61Mary Magdalene was there, and the other Mary, sitting opposite the tomb. 62Now on the next day, which was the day after the Preparation Day, the chief priests and the Pharisees were gathered together to Pilate, 63saying, "Sir, we remember what that deceiver said while he was still alive: 'After three days I will rise again.' 64Command therefore that the tomb be made secure until the third day, lest perhaps his disciples come at night and steal him away, and tell the people, 'He is risen from the dead;' and the last deception will be worse than the first." 65Pilate said to them, "You have a guard. Go, make it as secure as you can." 66So they went with the guard and made the tomb secure, sealing the stone. [5]

Gospel of Matthew

Chapter Twenty-Eight

1Now after the Sabbath, as it began to dawn on the first day of the week, Mary Magdalene and the other Mary came to see the tomb. 2Behold, there was a great earthquake, for an angel of the Lord descended from the sky, and came and rolled away the stone from the door, and sat on it. 3His appearance was like lightning, and his clothing white as snow. 4For fear of him, the guards shook, and became like dead men. 5The angel answered the women, "Don't be afraid, for I know that you seek Jesus, who has been crucified. 6He is not here, for he has risen, just like he said. Come, see the place where the Lord was lying. 7Go quickly and tell his disciples, 'He has risen from the dead, and behold, he goes before you into Galilee; there you will see him.' Behold, I have told you." 8They departed quickly from the tomb with fear and great joy, and ran to bring his disciples word. 9As they went to tell his disciples, behold, Jesus met them, saying, "Rejoice!" They came and took hold of his feet, and worshiped him. 10Then

Jesus said to them, "Don't be afraid. Go tell my brothers The word for "brothers" here may be also correctly translated "brothers and sisters" or "siblings." that they should go into Galilee, and there they will see me." 11Now while they were going, behold, some of the guards came into the city, and told the chief priests all the things that had happened. 12When they were assembled with the elders, and had taken counsel, they gave a large amount of silver to the soldiers, 13saying, "Say that his disciples came by night, and stole him away while we slept. 14If this comes to the governor's ears, we will persuade him and make you free of worry." 15So they took the money and did as they were told. This saying was spread abroad among the Jews, and continues until today. 16But the eleven disciples went into Galilee, to the mountain where Jesus had sent them. 17When they saw him, they bowed down to him, but some doubted. 18Jesus came to them and spoke to them, saying, "All authority has been given to me in heaven and on earth. 19Go, TR and NU add "therefore" and make disciples of all nations, baptizing them in the name of the Father and of the Son and of the Holy Spirit, 20teaching them to observe all things that I commanded you. Behold, I am with you always, even to the end of the age." Amen. [5]

The Gospel of John – [NASB] [4]

Chapter One

The Deity of Jesus Christ

1In the beginning was the Word, and the Word was with God, and the Word was God. 2He was in the beginning with God. 3All things came into being through Him, and apart from Him nothing came into being that has come into being. 4In Him was life, and the life was the Light of men. 5The Light shines in the darkness, and the darkness did not Or *overpower* comprehend it.

The Witness John

6There Or *came into being* came a man sent from God, whose name was John. 7He came as a witness, to testify about the Light, so that all might believe through him. 8He was not the Light, but *he came* to testify about the Light. 9There was the true Light Or *which enlightens every person coming into the world* which, coming into the world, enlightens every man. 10He was in the world, and the world was made through Him, and the world did not know Him. 11He came to His Or *own things, possessions, domain* own, and those who were His own did not receive Him. 12But as many as received Him, to them He gave the right to become children of God, *even* to those who believe in His name, 13who were born, not of blood nor of the will of the flesh nor of the will of man, but of God.

The Word Made Flesh

14And the Word became flesh, and dwelt among us, and we saw His glory, glory as of the only begotten from the Father, full of grace and truth. 15John *testified about Him and cried out, saying, "This was He of whom I said, 'He who comes after me has a higher rank than I, for He existed before me.' " 16For of His fullness we have all received, and grace upon grace. 17For the Law was given through Moses; grace and truth were realized through Jesus Christ. 18No one has seen God at any time; the only begotten God who is in the bosom of the Father, He has explained *Him*.

The Testimony of John

19This is the testimony of John, when the Jews sent to him priests and Levites from

Jerusalem to ask him, "Who are you?" 20And he confessed and did not deny, but confessed, "I am not the Christ." 21They asked him, "What then? Are you Elijah?" And he *said, "I am not." "Are you the Prophet?" And he answered, "No." 22Then they said to him, "Who are you, so that we may give an answer to those who sent us? What do you say about yourself?" 23He said, "I am a voice of one crying in the wilderness, 'Make straight the way of the Lord,' as Isaiah the prophet said."

24Now they had been sent from the Pharisees. 25They asked him, and said to him, "Why then are you baptizing, if you are not the Christ, nor Elijah, nor the Prophet?" 26John answered them saying, "I baptize The Gr here can be translated *in, with* or *by* in water, *but* among you stands One whom you do not know. 27*It is* He who comes after me, the thong of whose sandal I am not worthy to untie." 28These things took place in Bethany beyond the Jordan, where John was baptizing. 29The next day he *saw Jesus coming to him and *said, "Behold, the Lamb of God who takes away the sin of the world! 30This is He on behalf of whom I said, 'after me comes a Man who has a higher rank than I, for He existed before me.' 31I did not recognize Him, but so that He might be manifested to Israel, I came baptizing The Gr here can be translated *in, with* or *by* in water." 32John testified saying, "I have seen the Spirit descending as a dove out of heaven, and He remained upon Him. 33I did not recognize Him, but He who sent me to baptize The Gr here can be translated *in, with* or *by* in water said to me, 'He upon whom you see the Spirit descending and remaining upon Him, this is the One who baptizes in the Holy

Spirit.' 34I myself have seen, and have testified that this is the Son of God."

Jesus' Public Ministry, First Converts

35Again the next day John was standing with two of his disciples, 36and he looked at

Jesus as He walked, and *said, "Behold, the Lamb of God!" 37The two disciples heard him speak, and they followed Jesus. 38And Jesus turned and saw them following, and *said to them, "What do you seek?" They said to Him, "Rabbi (which translated means Teacher), where are You staying?" 39He *said to them, "Come, and you will see." So they came and saw where

He was staying; and they stayed with Him that day, for it was about the Perhaps 10 a.m. (Roman time) tenth hour. 40One of the two who heard John *speak* and followed Him, was Andrew, Simon Peter's brother. 41He *found first his own brother Simon and *said to him, "We have found the Messiah" (which translated means Christ). 42He brought him to Jesus. Jesus looked at him and said, "You are Simon the son of John; you shall be called Cephas" (which is translated Peter).

43The next day He purposed to go into Galilee, and He *found Philip. And Jesus *said to him, "Follow Me." 44Now Philip was from Bethsaida, of the city of Andrew and Peter. 45Philip

*found Nathanael and *said to him, "We have found Him of whom Moses in the Law and *also* the Prophets wrote—Jesus of Nazareth, the son of Joseph." 46Nathanael said to him,

"Can any good thing come out of Nazareth?" Philip *said to him, "Come and see." 47Jesus saw Nathanael coming to Him, and *said of him, "Behold, an Israelite indeed, in whom there is no deceit!" 48Nathanael *said to Him, "How do You know me?" Jesus answered and said to him, "Before Philip called you, when you were under the fig tree, I saw you." 49Nathanael answered Him, "Rabbi, You are the Son of God; You are the King of Israel." 50Jesus answered and said to him, "Because I said to you that I saw you under the fig tree, do you believe? You will see greater things than these." 51And He *said to him, "Truly, truly, I say to you, you will see the heavens opened and the angels of God ascending and descending on the Son of Man." [4]

Gospel of John

Chapter Two

Miracle at Cana

1On the third day there was a wedding in Cana of Galilee, and the mother of Jesus was there; 2and both Jesus and His disciples were invited to the wedding. 3When the wine ran out, the mother of Jesus *said to Him, "They have no wine." 4And Jesus *said to her, "Woman, what does that have to do with us? My hour has not yet come." 5His mother *said to the servants, "Whatever He says to you, do it." 6Now there were six stone water pots set there for the Jewish custom of purification, containing twenty or thirty gallons each. 7Jesus *said to them, "Fill the water pots with water." So they filled them up to the brim. 8And He *said to them, "Draw *some* out now and take it to the Or *steward* headwaiter." So they took it *to him.* 9When the headwaiter tasted the water which had become wine, and did not know where it came from (but the servants who had drawn the water knew), the headwaiter *called the bridegroom, 10and *said to him, "Every man serves the good wine first, and when *the people* have drunk freely, *then he serves* the poorer *wine; but* you have kept the good wine until now." 11This beginning of *His* signs Jesus did in Cana of Galilee, and manifested His glory, and His disciples believed in Him. 12After this He went down to Capernaum, He and His mother and *His* brothers and His disciples; and they stayed there a few days.

First Passover—Cleansing the Temple

13The Passover of the Jews was near, and Jesus went up to Jerusalem. 14And He found in the temple those who were selling oxen and sheep and doves, and the money changers seated *at their tables.* 15And He made a scourge of cords, and drove *them* all out of the temple, with the sheep and the oxen; and He poured out the coins of the money changers and overturned their tables; 16and to those who were selling the doves He said, "Take these things away; stop making My Father's house a place of business." 17His disciples remembered that it was written, "Zeal for Your house will consume me." 18The Jews then said to Him, "What sign do You show us as your authority for doing these things?" 19Jesus answered them, "Destroy this temple, and in three days I will raise it up." 20The Jews then said, "It took forty-six years to build this temple, and will You raise it up in three days?" 21But He was speaking of the temple of His body. 22So when He was raised from the dead, His disciples remembered that He said this; and they believed the Scripture and the word which Jesus had spoken. 23Now when He was in Jerusalem at the Passover, during the feast, many believed in His name, observing His signs which He was doing. 24But Jesus, on His part, was not entrusting Himself to them, for He knew all men, 25and because He did not need anyone to testify concerning man, for He Himself knew what was in man.   [4]

Gospel of John

Chapter Three

The New Birth

1Now there was a man of the Pharisees, named Nicodemus, a ruler of the Jews; 2this man came to Jesus by night and said to Him, "Rabbi, we know that You have come from God *as* a teacher; for no one can do these signs that You do unless God is with him." 3Jesus answered and said to him, "Truly, truly, I say to you, unless one is born again he cannot see the kingdom of God."

4Nicodemus *said to Him, "How can a man be born when he is old? He cannot enter a second time into his mother's womb and be born, can he?" 5Jesus answered, "Truly, truly, I say to you, unless one is born of water and the Spirit he cannot enter into the kingdom of God. 6That which is born of the flesh is flesh, and that which is born of the Spirit is spirit. 7Do not be amazed that I said to you, 'You must be born again.' 8The wind blows where it wishes and you hear the sound of it, but do not know where it comes from and where it is going; so is everyone who is born of the Spirit." 9Nicodemus said to Him, "How can these things be?" 10Jesus answered and said to him, "Are you the teacher of Israel and do not understand these

things? 11Truly, truly, I say to you, we speak of what we know and testify of what we have seen, and you do not accept our testimony. 12If I told you earthly things and you do not believe, how will you believe if I tell you heavenly things? 13No one has ascended into heaven, but He who descended from heaven: the Son of Man. 14As Moses lifted up the serpent in the wilderness, even so must the Son of Man be lifted up; 15so that whoever Or *believes in Him will have eternal life* believes will in Him have eternal life. 16 "For God so loved the world that He gave His only begotten Son, that whoever believes in Him shall not perish, but have eternal life. 17For God did not send the Son into the world to judge the world, but that the world might be saved through Him. 18He who believes in Him is not judged; he who does not believe has been judged already, because he has not believed in the name of the only begotten Son of God. 19This is the judgment, that the Light has come into the world, and men loved the darkness rather than the Light, for their deeds were evil. 20For everyone who does evil hates the Light, and does not come to the Light for fear that his deeds will be exposed. 21But he who practices the truth comes to the Light, so that his deeds may be manifested as having been wrought in God."

John's Last Testimony

22After these things Jesus and His disciples came into the land of Judea, and there He was spending time with them and baptizing. 23John also was baptizing in Aenon near Salim, because there was much water there; and *people* were coming and were being baptized— 24for John had not yet been thrown into prison. 25Therefore there arose a discussion on the part of

John's disciples with a Jew about purification. 26And they came to John and said to him, "Rabbi, He who was with you beyond the Jordan, to whom you have testified, behold, He is baptizing and all are coming to Him." 27John answered and said, "A man can receive nothing unless it has been given him from heaven. 28You yourselves are my witnesses that I said, 'I am not the Christ,' but, 'I have been sent ahead of Him.' 29He who has the bride is the bridegroom; but the friend of the bridegroom, who stands and hears him, rejoices greatly because of the bridegroom's voice. So this joy of mine has been made full. 30He must increase, but I must decrease.

31"He who comes from above is above all, he who is of the earth is from the earth and speaks of the earth. He who comes from heaven is above all. 32What He has seen and heard, of that He testifies; and no one receives His testimony. 33He who has received His testimony has set his seal to *this,* that God is true. 34For He whom God has sent speaks the words of God; for He gives the Spirit without measure. 35The Father loves the Son and has given all things into His hand. 36He who believes in the Son has eternal life; but he who does not obey the Son will not see life, but the wrath of God abides on him." [4]

Gospel of John

Chapter Four

Jesus Goes to Galilee

1Therefore when the Lord knew that the Pharisees had heard that Jesus was making and baptizing more disciples than John 2(although Jesus Himself was not baptizing, but His disciples were), 3He left Judea and went away again into Galilee. 4And He had to pass through Samaria. 5So He *came to a city of Samaria called Sychar, near the parcel of ground that Jacob gave to his son Joseph; 6and Jacob's well was there. So Jesus, being wearied from His journey, was sitting thus by the well. It was about Perhaps 6 p.m. Roman time or noon Jewish time the sixth hour.

The Woman of Samaria

7There *came a woman of Samaria to draw water. Jesus *said to her, "Give Me a drink." 8For His disciples had gone away into the city to buy food. 9Therefore the Samaritan woman *said to Him, "How is it that You, being a Jew, ask me for a drink since I am a Samaritan woman?" (For Jews have no dealings with Samaritans.) 10Jesus answered and said to her, "If you knew the gift of God, and who it is who says to you, 'Give Me a drink,' you would have asked Him, and He would have given you living water." 11She *said to Him, "Sir, You have nothing to draw with and the well is deep; where then do You get that living water? 12You are not greater than our father Jacob, are You, who gave us the well, and drank of it himself and his sons and his cattle?" 13Jesus answered and said to her, "Everyone who drinks of this water will thirst again; 14but whoever drinks of the water that I will give him shall never thirst; but the water that I will give him will become in him a well of water springing up to eternal life."

15The woman *said to Him, "Sir, give me this water, so I will not be thirsty nor come all the way here to draw." 16He *said to her, "Go, call your husband and come here." 17The woman answered and said, "I have no husband." Jesus *said to her, "You have correctly said, 'I have no husband'; 18for you have had five husbands, and the one whom you now have is not your husband; this you have said truly." 19The woman *said to Him, "Sir, I perceive that You are a prophet. 20Our fathers worshiped in this mountain, and you *people* say that in Jerusalem is the place where men ought to worship." 21Jesus *said to her, "Woman, believe Me, an hour is coming when neither in this mountain nor in Jerusalem will you worship the Father. 22You worship what you do not know; we worship what we know, for salvation is from the Jews. 23But an hour is coming, and now is, when the true worshipers will worship the Father in spirit and truth; for such people the Father seeks to be His worshipers. 24God is spirit, and those who worship Him must worship in spirit and truth." 25The woman *said to Him, "I know that Messiah is coming (He who is called Christ); when that One comes, He will declare all things to us." 26Jesus *said to her, "I who speak to you am *He*." 27At this point His disciples came, and they were amazed that He had been speaking with a woman, yet no one said, "What do You seek?" or, "Why do You speak with her?" 28So the woman left her waterpot, and went into the city and *said to the men, 29"Come, see a man who told me all the things that I *have* done; this is not the Christ, is it?" 30They went out of the city, and were coming to Him.

31Meanwhile the disciples were urging Him, saying, "Rabbi, eat." 32But He said to them, "I have food to eat that you do not know about." 33So the disciples were saying to one another, "No one brought Him *anything* to eat, did he?" 34Jesus *said to them, "My food is to do the will of Him who sent Me and to accomplish His work. 35Do you not say, 'There are yet four months, and *then* comes the harvest'? Behold, I say to you, lift up your eyes and look on the fields, that they are white for harvest. 36Already he who reaps is receiving wages and is gathering fruit for life eternal; so that he who sows and he who reaps may rejoice together. 37For in this *case* the saying is true, 'One sows and another reaps.' 38I sent you to reap that for which you have not labored; others have labored and you have entered into their labor."

The Samaritans

39From that city many of the Samaritans believed in Him because of the word of the woman who testified, "He told me all the things that I *have* done." 40So when the Samaritans came to Jesus, they were asking Him to stay with them; and He stayed there two days. 41Many more believed because of His word; 42and they were saying to the woman, "It is no longer because of what you said that we believe, for we have heard for ourselves and know that this

One is indeed the Savior of the world." 43After the two days He went forth from there into

Galilee. 44For Jesus Himself testified that a prophet has no honor in his own country. 45So when

He came to Galilee, the Galileans received Him, having seen all the things that He did in

Jerusalem at the feast; for they themselves also went to the feast.

Healing a Nobleman's Son

46Therefore He came again to Cana of Galilee where He had made the water wine. And there was a royal official whose son was sick at Capernaum. 47When he heard that Jesus had come out of Judea into Galilee, he went to Him and was imploring *Him* to come down and heal his son; for he was at the point of death. 48So Jesus said to him, "Unless you *people* see signs and wonders, you *simply* will not believe." 49The royal official *said to Him, "Sir, come down before my child dies." 50Jesus *said to him, "Go; your son lives." The man believed the word that Jesus spoke to him and started off. 51As he was now going down, *his* slaves met him, saying that his son was living. 52So he inquired of them the hour when he began to get better. Then they said to him, "Yesterday at the Perhaps 7 p.m. Roman time or 1 p.m. Jewish time seventh hour the fever left him." 53So the father knew that *it was* at that hour in which Jesus said to him, "Your son lives"; and he himself believed and his whole household. 54This is again a second sign that Jesus performed when He had come out of Judea into Galilee. [4]

Gospel of John

Chapter Five

The Healing at Bethesda

1After these things there was a feast of the Jews, and Jesus went up to Jerusalem.

2Now there is in Jerusalem by the sheep *gate* a pool, which is called in Hebrew Bethesda, having five porticoes. 3In these lay a multitude of those who were sick, blind, lame, and withered, [Early mss do not contain the remainder of v 3, nor v 4waiting for the moving of the waters; 4for an angel of the Lord went down at certain seasons into the pool and stirred up the water; whoever then first, after the stirring up of the water, stepped in was made well from whatever disease with which he was afflicted.] 5A man was there who had been ill for thirtyeight years. 6When Jesus saw him lying *there,* and knew that he had already been a long time *in that condition,* He *said to him, "Do you wish to get well?" 7The sick man answered Him, "Sir, I have no man to put me into the pool when the water is stirred up, but while I am coming, another steps down before me." 8Jesus *said to him, "Get up, pick up your pallet and walk." 9Immediately the man became well, and picked up his pallet and *began* to walk. Now it was the Sabbath on that day. 10So the Jews were saying to the man who was cured, "It is the Sabbath, and it is not permissible for you to carry your pallet." 11But he answered them, "He who made me well was the one who said to me, 'Pick up your pallet and walk.'" 12They asked him, "Who is the man who said to you, 'Pick up *your pallet* and walk'?" 13But the man who was healed did not know who it was, for Jesus had slipped away while there was a crowd in *that* place. 14Afterward Jesus *found him in the temple and said to him, "Behold, you have become well; do not sin anymore, so that nothing worse happens to you." 15The man went away, and told the Jews that it was Jesus who had made him well. 16For this reason the Jews were persecuting Jesus, because He was doing these things on the Sabbath. 17But He answered them, "My Father is working until now, and I Myself am working."

Jesus' Equality with God

18For this reason therefore the Jews were seeking all the more to kill Him, because He not only was breaking the Sabbath, but also was calling God His own Father, making Himself equal with God. 19Therefore Jesus answered and was saying to them, "Truly, truly, I say to you, the Son can do nothing of Himself, unless *it is* something He sees the Father doing; for whatever the Father does, these things the Son also does in like manner. 20For the Father loves the Son, and shows Him all things that He Himself is doing; and *the Father* will show Him greater works than these, so that you will marvel. 21For just as the Father raises the dead and gives them life, even so the Son also gives life to whom He wishes. 22For not even the Father judges anyone, but He has given all judgment to the Son, 23so that all will honor the Son even as they honor the Father. He who does not honor the Son does not honor the Father who sent Him. 24 "Truly, truly, I say to you, he who hears My word, and believes Him who sent Me, has eternal life, and does not come into judgment, but has passed out of death into life.

Two Resurrections

25 Truly, truly, I say to you, an hour is coming and now is, when the dead will hear the voice of the Son of God, and those who hear will live. 26For just as the Father has life in Himself, even so He gave to the Son also to have life in Himself; 27and He gave Him authority to execute judgment, because He is *the* Son of Man. 28Do not marvel at this; for an hour is coming, in which all who are in the tombs will hear His voice, 29and will come forth; those who did the good *deeds* to a resurrection of life, those who committed the evil *deeds* to a resurrection of judgment. 30 "I can do nothing on My own initiative. As I hear, I judge; and My judgment is just, because I do not seek My own will, but the will of Him who sent Me. 31 "If I *alone* testify about Myself, My testimony is not true. 32There is another who testifies of Me, and I know that the testimony which He gives about Me is true.

Witness of John

33 You have sent to John, and he has testified to the truth. 34But the testimony which I receive is not from man, but I say these things so that you may be saved. 35He was the lamp that was burning and was shining and you were willing to rejoice for a while in his light.

Witness of Works

36 But the testimony which I have is greater than *the testimony of* John; for the works which the Father has given Me to accomplish—the very works that I do—testify about Me, that the Father has sent Me.

Witness of the Father

37 And the Father who sent Me, He has testified of Me. You have neither heard His voice at any time nor seen His form. 38You do not have His word abiding in you, for you do not believe Him whom He sent.

Witness of the Scripture

39 Or (a command) *Search the Scriptures!* You search the Scriptures because you think that in them you have eternal life; it is these that testify about Me; 40and you are unwilling to come to Me so that you may have life. 41I do not receive glory from men; 42but I know you, that you do not have the love of God in yourselves. 43I have come in My Father's name, and you do not receive Me; if another comes in his own name, you will receive him. 44How can you believe, when you receive glory from one another and you do not seek the glory that is from the *one and* only God? 45Do not think that I will accuse you before the Father; the one who accuses you is Moses, in whom you have set your hope. 46For if you believed Moses, you would believe Me, for he wrote about Me. 47But if you do not believe his writings, how will you believe My words?"   [[4]

Gospel of John

Chapter Six

Five Thousand Fed

1After these things Jesus went away to the other side of the Sea of Galilee (or Tiberias). 2A large crowd followed Him, because they saw the signs which He was performing on those who were sick. 3Then Jesus went up on the mountain, and there He sat down with His disciples. 4Now the Passover, the feast of the Jews, was near. 5Therefore Jesus, lifting up His eyes and seeing that a large crowd was coming to Him, *said to Philip, "Where are we to buy bread, so that these may eat?" 6This He was saying to test him, for He Himself knew what He was intending to do. 7Philip answered Him, "Two hundred The denarius was equivalent to a day's wages denarii worth of bread is not sufficient for them, for everyone to receive a little." 8One of His disciples, Andrew, Simon Peter's brother, *said to Him, 9"There is a lad here who has five barley loaves and two fish, but what are these for so many people?" 10Jesus said, "Have the people sit down." Now there was much grass in the place. So the men sat down, in number about five thousand. 11Jesus then took the loaves, and having given thanks, He distributed to those who were seated; likewise also of the fish as much as they wanted. 12When they were filled, He *said to His disciples, "Gather up the leftover fragments so that nothing will be lost." 13So they gathered them up, and filled twelve baskets with fragments from the five barley loaves which were left over by those who had eaten. 14Therefore when the people saw the sign which He had performed, they said, "This is truly the Prophet who is to come into the world."

Jesus Walks on the Water

15So Jesus, perceiving that they were intending to come and take Him by force to make Him king, withdrew again to the mountain by Himself alone.

16Now when evening came, His disciples went down to the sea, 17and after getting into a boat, they *started to* cross the sea to Capernaum. It had already become dark, and Jesus had not yet come to them. 18The sea *began* to be stirred up because a strong wind was blowing. 19Then, when they had rowed about three or four miles, they *saw Jesus walking on the sea and drawing near to the boat; and they were frightened. 20But He *said to them, "It is I; do not be afraid." 21So they were willing to receive Him into the boat, and immediately the boat was at the land to which they were going. 22The next day the crowd that stood on the other side of the sea saw that there was no other small boat there, except one, and that Jesus had not entered with His disciples into the boat, but *that* His disciples had gone away alone. 23There came other small boats from Tiberias near to the place where they ate the bread after the Lord had given thanks. 24So when the crowd saw that Jesus was not there, nor His disciples, they themselves got into the small boats, and came to Capernaum seeking Jesus. 25When they found Him on the other side of the sea, they said to Him, "Rabbi, when did You get here?"

Words to the People

26Jesus answered them and said, "Truly, truly, I say to you, you seek Me, not because you saw signs, but because you ate of the loaves and were filled. 27Do not work for the food which perishes, but for the food which endures to eternal life, which the Son of Man will give to you, for on Him the Father, God, has set His seal." 28Therefore they said to Him, "What shall we do, so that we may work the works of God?" 29Jesus answered and said to them, "This is the work of God, that you believe in Him whom He has sent." 30So they said to Him, "What then do You do for a sign, so that we may see, and believe You? What work do You perform? 31Our fathers ate the manna in the wilderness; as it is written, 'He gave them bread out of heaven to eat.' " 32Jesus then said to them, "Truly, truly, I say to you, it is not Moses who has given you the bread out of heaven, but it is My Father who gives you the true bread out of heaven. 33For the bread of God is Or *He who comes* that which comes down out of heaven, and gives life to the world." 34Then they said to Him, "Lord, always give us this bread." 35Jesus said to them, "I am the bread of life; he who comes to Me will not hunger, and he who believes in Me will never thirst. 36But I said to you that you have seen Me, and yet do not believe. 37All that the Father gives Me will come to Me, and the one who comes to Me I will certainly not cast out. 38For I have come down from heaven, not to do My own will, but the will of Him who sent Me. 39This is the will of Him who sent Me, that of all that He has given Me I lose nothing, but raise it up on the last day. 40For this is the will of My Father, that everyone who beholds the Son and believes in Him will have eternal life, and I Myself will raise him up on the last day."

Words to the Jews

41Therefore the Jews were grumbling about Him, because He said, "I am the bread that came down out of heaven." 42They were saying, "Is not this Jesus, the son of Joseph, whose father and mother we know? How does He now say, 'I have come down out of heaven'?" 43Jesus answered and said to them, "Do not grumble among yourselves. 44No one can come to Me unless the Father who sent Me draws him; and I will raise him up on the last day. 45It is written in the prophets, 'And they shall all be taught of God.' Everyone who has heard and learned from the Father, comes to Me. 46Not that anyone has seen the Father, except the One who is from God; He has seen the Father. 47Truly, truly, I say to you, he who believes has eternal life. 48I am the bread of life. 49Your fathers ate the manna in the wilderness, and they died. 50This is the bread which comes down out of heaven, so that one may eat of it and not die. 51I am the living bread that came down out of heaven; if anyone eats of this bread, he will live forever; and the bread also which I will give for the life of the world is My flesh." 52Then the Jews *began* to argue with one another, saying, "How can this man give us *His* flesh to eat?" 53So Jesus said to them, "Truly, truly, I say to you, unless you eat the flesh of the Son of Man and drink His blood, you have no life in yourselves. 54He who eats My flesh and drinks My blood has eternal life, and I will raise him up on the last day. 55For My flesh is true food, and My blood is true drink. 56He who eats My flesh and drinks My blood abides in Me, and I in him. 57As the living Father sent Me, and I live because of the Father, so he who eats Me, he also will live because of Me. 58This is the bread which came down out of heaven; not as the fathers ate and died; he who eats this bread will live forever."

Words to the Disciples

59These things He said in the synagogue as He taught in Capernaum.

60Therefore many of His disciples, when they heard *this* said, "This is a difficult statement; who can listen to it?" 61But Jesus, conscious that His disciples grumbled at this, said to them, "Does this cause you to stumble? 62*What* then if you see the Son of Man ascending to where He was before? 63It is the Spirit who gives life; the flesh profits nothing; the words that I have spoken to you are spirit and are life. 64But there are some of you who do not believe." For Jesus knew from the beginning who they were who did not believe, and who it was that would betray Him. 65And He was saying, "For this reason I have said to you, that no one can come to Me unless it has been granted him from the Father."

Peter's Confession of Faith

66As a result of this many of His disciples withdrew and were not walking with Him anymore. 67So Jesus said to the twelve, "You do not want to go away also, do you?" 68Simon Peter answered Him, "Lord, to whom shall we go? You have words of eternal life. 69We have believed and have come to know that You are the Holy One of God." 70Jesus answered them, "Did I Myself not choose you, the twelve, and *yet* one of you is a devil?" 71Now He meant Judas *the son* of Simon Iscariot, for he, one of the twelve, was going to betray Him. [4]

Gospel of John

Chapter Seven

Jesus Teaches at the Feast

1After these things Jesus was walking in Galilee, for He was unwilling to walk in Judea because the Jews were seeking to kill Him. 2Now the feast of the Jews, the Feast of Booths, was near. 3Therefore His brothers said to Him, "Leave here and go into Judea, so that Your disciples also may see Your works which You are doing. 4For no one does anything in secret when he himself seeks to be *known* publicly. If You do these things, show Yourself to the world." 5For not even His brothers were believing in Him. 6So Jesus *said to them, "My time is not yet here, but your time is always opportune. 7The world cannot hate you, but it hates Me because I testify of it, that its deeds are evil. 8Go up to the feast yourselves; I do not go up to this feast because My time has not yet fully come." 9Having said these things to them, He stayed in Galilee.

10But when His brothers had gone up to the feast, then He Himself also went up, not publicly, but as if, in secret. 11So the Jews were seeking Him at the feast and were saying, "Where is He?" 12There was much grumbling among the crowds concerning Him; some were saying, "He is a good man"; others were saying, "No, on the contrary, He leads the people astray." 13Yet no one was speaking openly of Him for fear of the Jews. 14But when it was now the midst of the feast Jesus went up into the temple, and *began to* teach. 15The Jews then were astonished, saying, "How has this man become learned, having never been educated?" 16So Jesus answered them and said, "My teaching is not Mine, but His who sent Me. 17If anyone is willing to do His will, he will know of the teaching, whether it is of God or *whether* I speak from Myself. 18He who speaks from himself seeks his own glory; but He who is seeking the glory of the One who sent Him, He is true, and there is no unrighteousness in Him. 19 "Did not Moses give you the Law, and *yet* none of you carries out the Law? Why do you seek to kill Me?" 20The crowd answered, "You have a demon! Who seeks to kill You?" 21Jesus answered them, "I did one deed, and you all marvel. 22For this reason Moses has given you circumcision (not because it is from Moses, but from the fathers), and on *the* Sabbath you circumcise a man. 23If a man receives circumcision on *the* Sabbath so that the Law of Moses will not be broken, are you angry with Me because I made an entire man well on *the* Sabbath? 24Do not judge according to appearance, but judge with righteous judgment."

25So some of the people of Jerusalem were saying, "Is this not the man whom they are seeking to kill? 26Look, He is speaking publicly, and they are saying nothing to Him. The rulers do not really know that this is the Christ, do they? 27However, we know where this man is from; but whenever the Christ may come, no one knows where He is from." 28Then Jesus cried out in the temple, teaching and saying, "You both know Me and know where I am from; and I have not come of Myself, but He who sent Me is true, whom you do not know. 29I know Him, because I am from Him, and He sent Me." 30So they were seeking to seize Him; and no man laid his hand on Him, because His hour had not yet come. 31But many of the crowd believed in Him; and they were saying, "When the Christ comes, He will not perform more signs than those which this man has, will He?" 32The Pharisees heard the crowd muttering these things about Him, and the chief priests and the Pharisees sent officers to seize Him. 33Therefore Jesus said, "For a little while longer I am with you, then I go to Him who sent Me. 34You will seek Me, and will not find Me; and where I am, you cannot come." 35The Jews then said to one another, "Where does this man intend to go that we will not find Him? He is not intending to go to the Dispersion among the Greeks, and teach the Greeks, is He? 36What is this statement that He said, 'You will seek Me, and will not find Me; and where I am, you cannot come'?" 37Now on the last day, the great *day* of the feast, Jesus stood and cried out, saying, "If anyone is thirsty, let him come to Me and drink. 38He who believes in Me, as the Scripture said, 'From his innermost being will flow rivers of living water.' " 39But this He spoke of the Spirit, whom those who believed in Him were to receive; for the Spirit was not yet *given,* because Jesus was not yet glorified.

Division of People over Jesus

40 *Some* of the people therefore, when they heard these words, were saying, "This certainly is the Prophet." 41Others were saying, "This is the Christ." Still others were saying,

"Surely the Christ is not going to come from Galilee, is He? 42Has not the Scripture said that the Christ comes from the descendants of David, and from Bethlehem, the village where David was?" 43So a division occurred in the crowd because of Him. 44Some of them wanted to seize Him, but no one laid hands on Him. 45The officers then came to the chief priests and Pharisees, and they said to them, "Why did you not bring Him?" 46The officers answered, "Never has a man spoken the way this man speaks." 47The Pharisees then answered them, "You have not also been led astray, have you? 48No one of the rulers or Pharisees has believed in Him, has he? 49But this crowd which does not know the Law is accursed." 50Nicodemus (he who came to Him before, being one of them) *said to them, 51"Our Law does not judge a man unless it first hears from him and knows what he is doing, does it?" 52They answered him, "You are not also from Galilee, are you? Search, and see that no prophet arises out of Galilee." 53[Later mss add the story of the

The Walk – S.B. Stone & Rock Solid Publishing, LLC
©2018

adulterous woman, numbering it as John 7:53-8:11Everyone went to his home.   [4]

Gospel of John

Chapter Eight

The Adulterous Woman

1But Jesus went to the Mount of Olives. 2Early in the morning He came again into the temple, and all the people were coming to Him; and He sat down and *began* to teach them. 3The scribes and the Pharisees *brought a woman caught in adultery, and having set her in the center *of the court,* 4they *said to Him, "Teacher, this woman has been caught in adultery, in the very act. 5Now in the Law Moses commanded us to stone such women; what then do You say?" 6They were saying this, testing Him, so that they might have grounds for accusing Him. But Jesus stooped down and with His finger wrote on the ground. 7But when they persisted in asking Him, He straightened up, and said to them, "He who is without sin among you, let him *be the* first to throw a stone at her." 8Again He stooped down and wrote on the ground. 9When they heard it, they *began* to go out one by one, beginning with the older ones, and He was left alone, and the woman, where she was, in the center *of the court.* 10Straightening up, Jesus said to her, "Woman, where are they? Did no one condemn you?" 11She said, "No one, Lord." And Jesus said, "I do not condemn you, either. Go. From now on sin no more."

Jesus Is the Light of the World

12Then Jesus again spoke to them, saying, "I am the Light of the world; he who follows Me will not walk in the darkness, but will have the Light of life." 13So the Pharisees said to Him, "You are testifying about Yourself; Your testimony is not true." 14Jesus answered and said to them, "Even if I testify about Myself, My testimony is true, for I know where I came from and where I am going; but you do not know where I come from or where I am going. 15You judge according to the flesh; I am not judging anyone. 16But even if I do judge, My judgment is true; for I am not alone *in it,* but I and the Father who sent Me. 17Even in your law it has been written that the testimony of two men is true. 18I am He who testifies about Myself, and the Father who sent Me testifies about Me." 19So they were saying to Him, "Where is Your Father?" Jesus answered, "You know neither Me nor My Father; if you knew Me, you would know My Father also." 20These words He spoke in the treasury, as He taught in the temple; and no one seized Him, because His hour had not yet come. 21Then He said again to them, "I go away, and you will seek Me, and will die in your sin; where I am going, you cannot come." 22So the Jews were saying, "Surely He will not kill Himself, will He, since He says, 'Where I am going, you cannot come'?" 23And He was saying to them, "You are from below, I am from above; you are of this world, I am not of this world. 24Therefore I said to you that you will die in your sins; for unless you believe that I am *He,* you will die in your sins." 25So they were saying to Him, "Who are You?" Jesus said to them, "What have I been saying to you *from* the beginning? 26I have many things to speak and to judge concerning you, but He who sent Me is true; and the things which I heard from Him, these I speak to the world." 27They did not realize that He had been speaking to them about the Father. 28So Jesus said, "When you lift up the Son of Man, then you will know that I am *He,* and I do nothing on My own initiative, but I speak these things as the Father taught Me. 29And He who sent Me is with Me; He has not left Me alone, for I always do the things that are pleasing to Him." 30As He spoke these things, many came to believe in Him.

The Truth Will Make You Free

31So Jesus was saying to those Jews who had believed Him, "If you continue in My word, *then* you are truly disciples of Mine; 32and you will know the truth, and the truth will make you free." 33They answered Him, "We are Abraham's descendants and have never yet been enslaved to anyone; how is it that You say, 'You will become free'?" 34Jesus answered them, "Truly, truly, I say to you, everyone who commits sin is the slave of sin. 35The slave does not remain in the house forever; the son does remain forever. 36So if the Son makes you free, you will be free indeed. 37I know that you are Abraham's descendants; yet you seek to kill Me, because My word has no place in you. 38I speak the things which I have seen with *My* Father; therefore you also do the things which you heard from *your* father." 39They answered and said to Him, "Abraham is our father." Jesus *said to them, "If you are Abraham's children, do the deeds of Abraham. 40But as it is, you are seeking to kill Me, a man who has told you the truth, which I heard from God; this Abraham did not do. 41You are doing the deeds of your father." They said to Him, "We were not born of fornication; we have one Father: God." 42Jesus said to them, "If God were your Father, you would love

Me, for I proceeded forth and have come from God, for I have not even come on My own initiative, but He sent Me. 43Why do you not understand what I am saying? *It is* because you cannot hear My word. 44You are of *your* father the devil, and you want to do the desires of your father. He was a murderer from the beginning, and does not stand in the truth because there is no truth in him. Whenever he speaks a lie, he speaks from his own *nature,* for he is a liar and the father of lies. 45But because I speak the truth, you do not believe Me. 46Which one of you convicts Me of sin? If I speak truth, why do you not believe Me? 47He who is of God hears the words of God; for this reason you do not hear *them,* because you are not of God." 48The Jews answered and said to Him, "Do we not say rightly that You are a Samaritan and have a demon?" 49Jesus answered, "I do not have a demon; but I honor My Father, and you dishonor Me. 50But I do not seek My glory; there is One who seeks and judges. 51Truly, truly, I say to you, if anyone keeps My word he will never see death." 52The Jews said to Him, "Now we know that You have a demon. Abraham died, and the prophets *also;* and You say, 'If anyone keeps My word, he will never taste of death.' 53Surely You are not greater than our father Abraham, who died? The prophets died too; whom do You make Yourself out *to be?*" 54Jesus answered, "If I glorify Myself, My glory is nothing; it is My

Father who glorifies Me, of whom you say, 'He is our God'; 55and you have not come to know Him, but I know Him; and if I say that I do not know Him, I will be a liar like you, but I do know Him and keep His word. 56Your father Abraham rejoiced to see My day, and he saw *it* and was glad." 57So the Jews said to Him, "You are not yet fifty years old, and have You seen Abraham?" 58Jesus said to them, "Truly, truly, I say to you, before Abraham was born, I am." 59Therefore they picked up stones to throw at Him, but Jesus hid Himself and went out of the temple. [4]

Gospel of John

Chapter Nine

Healing the Man Born Blind

1As He passed by, He saw a man blind from birth. 2And His disciples asked Him, "Rabbi, who sinned, this man or his parents, that he would be born blind?" 3Jesus answered, "*It was* neither *that* this man sinned, nor his parents; but *it was* so that the works of God might be displayed in him. 4We must work the works of Him who sent Me as long as it is day; night is coming when no one can work. 5While I am in the world, I am the Light of the world." 6When He had said this, He spat on the ground, and made clay of the spittle, and applied the clay to his eyes, 7and said to him, "Go, wash in the pool of Siloam" (which is translated, Sent). So he went away and washed, and came *back* seeing. 8Therefore the neighbors, and those who previously saw him as a beggar, were saying, "Is not this the one who used to sit and beg?" 9Others were saying, "This is he," *still* others were saying, "No, but he is like him." He kept saying, "I am the one." 10So they were saying to him, "How then were your eyes opened?" 11He answered, "The man who is called Jesus made clay, and anointed my eyes, and said to me, 'Go to Siloam and wash'; so I went away and washed, and I received sight." 12They said to him, "Where is He?"

He *said, "I do not know."

Controversy over the Man

13They *brought to the Pharisees the man who was formerly blind. 14Now it was a Sabbath on the day when Jesus made the clay and opened his eyes. 15Then the Pharisees also were asking him again how he received his sight. And he said to them, "He applied clay to my eyes, and I washed, and I see." 16Therefore some of the Pharisees were saying, "This man is not from God, because He does not keep the Sabbath." But others were saying, "How can a man who is a sinner perform such signs?" And there was a division among them. 17So they *said to the blind man again, "What do you say about Him, since He opened your eyes?" And he said, "He is a prophet." 18The Jews then did not believe *it* of him, that he had been blind and had received sight, until they called the parents of the very one who had received his sight, 19and questioned them, saying, "Is this your son, who you say was born blind? Then how does he now see?" 20His parents answered them and said, "We know that this is our son, and that he was born blind; 21but how he now sees, we do not know; or who opened his eyes, we do not know. Ask him; he is of age, he will speak for himself." 22His parents said this because they were afraid of the Jews; for the Jews had already agreed that if anyone confessed Him to be Christ, he was to be put out of the synagogue. 23For this reason his parents said, "He is of age; ask him." 24So a second time they called the man who had been blind, and said to him, "Give glory to God; we know that this man is a sinner." 25He then answered, "Whether He is a sinner, I do not know; one thing I do know, that though I was blind, now I see." 26So they said to him, "What did

The Walk – S.B. Stone & Rock Solid Publishing, LLC

He do to you? How did He open your eyes?" 27He answered them, "I told you already and you did not listen; why do you want to hear *it* again? You do not want to become His disciples too, do you?" 28They reviled him and said, "You are His disciple, but we are disciples of Moses. 29We know that God has spoken to Moses, but as for this man, we do not know where He is from." 30The man answered and said to them, "Well, here is an amazing thing, that you do not know where He is from, and *yet* He opened my eyes. 31We know that God does not hear sinners; but if anyone is God-fearing and does His will, He hears him. 32Since the beginning of time it has never been heard that anyone opened the eyes of a person born blind. 33If this man were not from God, He could do nothing." 34They answered him, "You were born entirely in sins, and are you teaching us?" So they put him out.

Jesus Affirms His Deity

35Jesus heard that they had put him out, and finding him, He said, "Do you believe in the Son of Man?" 36He answered, "Who is He, Lord, that I may believe in Him?" 37Jesus said to him, "You have both seen Him, and He is the one who is talking with you." 38And he said, "Lord, I believe." And he worshiped Him. 39And Jesus said, "For judgment I came into this world, so that those who do not see may see, and that those who see may become blind." 40Those of the Pharisees who were with Him heard these things and said to Him, "We are not blind too, are we?" 41Jesus said to them, "If you were blind, you would have no sin; but since you say, 'We see,' your sin remains.   [4]

Gospel of John

Chapter Ten

Parable of the Good Shepherd

1 "Truly, truly, I say to you, he who does not enter by the door into the fold of the sheep, but climbs up some other way, he is a thief and a robber. 2But he who enters by the door is a shepherd of the sheep. 3To him the doorkeeper opens, and the sheep hear his voice, and he calls his own sheep by name and leads them out. 4When he puts forth all his own, he goes ahead of them, and the sheep follow him because they know his voice. 5A stranger they simply will not follow, but will flee from him, because they do not know the voice of strangers." 6This figure of speech Jesus spoke to them, but they did not understand what those things were which He had been saying to them. 7So Jesus said to

them again, "Truly, truly, I say to you, I am the door of the sheep. 8All who came before Me are thieves and robbers, but the sheep did not hear them. 9I am the door; if anyone enters through Me, he will be saved, and will go in and out and find pasture. 10The thief comes only to steal and kill and destroy; I came that they may have life, and have *it* abundantly. 11 "I am the good shepherd; the good shepherd lays down His life for the sheep. 12He who is a hired hand, and not a shepherd, who is not the owner of the sheep, sees the wolf coming, and leaves the sheep and flees, and the wolf snatches them and scatters *them*. 13*He flees* because he is a hired hand and is not concerned about the sheep. 14I am the good shepherd, and I know My own and My own know Me, 15even as the Father knows Me and I know the Father; and I lay down My life for the sheep. 16I have other sheep, which are not of this fold; I must bring them also, and they will hear My voice; and they will become one flock *with* one shepherd. 17For this reason the Father loves Me, because I lay down My life so that I may take it again. 18No one has taken it away from Me, but I lay it down on My own initiative. I have authority to lay it down, and I have authority to take it up again. This commandment I received from My Father." 19A division occurred again among the Jews because of these words. 20Many of them were saying, "He has a demon and is insane. Why do you listen to Him?" 21Others were saying, "These are not the sayings of one demon-possessed. A demon cannot open the eyes of the blind, can he?"

Jesus Asserts His Deity

22At that time the Feast of the Dedication took place at Jerusalem; 23it was winter, and Jesus was walking in the temple in the portico of Solomon. 24The Jews then gathered around Him, and were saying to Him, "How long will You keep us in suspense? If You are the Christ, tell us plainly." 25Jesus answered them, "I told you, and you do not believe; the works that I do in My Father's name, these testify of Me. 26But you do not believe because you are not of My sheep. 27My sheep hear My voice, and I know them, and they follow Me; 28and I give eternal life to them, and they will never perish; and no one will snatch them out of My hand. 29One early ms reads *What My Father has given Me is greater than all* My Father, who has given *them* to Me, is greater than all; and no one is able to snatch *them* out of the Father's hand. 30I and the Father are one." 31The Jews picked up stones again to stone Him. 32Jesus answered them, "I showed you many good works from the Father; for which of them are you stoning Me?" 33The Jews answered

Him, "For a good work we do not stone You, but for blasphemy; and because You, being a man, make Yourself out *to be* God." 34Jesus answered them, "Has it not been written in your Law, 'I said, you are gods'? 35If he called them gods, to whom the word of God came (and the Scripture cannot be broken), 36do you say of Him, whom the Father sanctified and sent into the world, 'You are blaspheming,' because I said, 'I am the Son of God'? 37If I do not do the works of My Father, do not believe Me; 38but if I do them, though you do not believe Me, believe the works, so that you may know and understand that the Father is in Me, and I in the Father." 39Therefore they were seeking again to seize Him, and He eluded their grasp. 40And He went away again beyond the Jordan to the place where John was first baptizing, and He was staying there. 41Many came to Him and were saying, "While John performed no sign, yet everything John said about this man was true." 42Many believed in Him

there.

Gospel of John

Chapter Eleven

The Death and Resurrection of Lazarus

1Now a certain man was sick, Lazarus of Bethany, the village of Mary and her sister Martha. 2It was the Mary who anointed the Lord with ointment, and wiped His feet with her hair, whose brother Lazarus was sick. 3So the sisters sent *word* to Him, saying, "Lord, behold, he whom You love is sick." 4But when Jesus heard *this,* He said, "This sickness is not to end in death, but for the glory of God, so that the Son of God may be glorified by it." 5Now Jesus loved Martha and her sister and Lazarus. 6So when He heard that he was sick, He then stayed two days *longer* in the place where He was. 7Then after this He *said to the disciples, "Let us go to Judea again." 8The disciples *said to Him, "Rabbi, the Jews were just now seeking to stone You, and are You going there again?" 9Jesus answered, "Are there not twelve hours in the day? If anyone walks in the day, he does not stumble, because he sees the light of this world. 10But if anyone walks in the night, he stumbles, because the light is not in him." 11This He said, and after that He *said to them, "Our friend Lazarus has fallen asleep; but I go, so that I may awaken him out of sleep." 12The disciples then said to Him, "Lord, if he has fallen asleep, he will recover." 13Now Jesus had spoken of his death, but they thought that He was speaking of literal sleep. 14So Jesus then said to them plainly, "Lazarus is dead, 15and I am glad for your sakes that I was not there, so that you may believe; but let us go to him." 16Therefore Thomas, who is called Didymus, said to *his* fellow disciples, "Let us also go, so that we may die with Him."

17So when Jesus came, He found that he had already been in the tomb four days. 18Now Bethany was near Jerusalem, about two miles off; 19and many of the Jews had come to Martha and Mary, to console them concerning *their* brother. 20Martha therefore, when she heard that

Jesus was coming, went to meet Him, but Mary stayed at the house. 21Martha then said to Jesus,

"Lord, if You had been here, my brother would not have died. 22Even now I know that whatever You ask of God, God will give You." 23Jesus *said to her, "Your brother will rise again." 24Martha *said to Him, "I know that he will rise again in the resurrection on the last day." 25Jesus said to her, "I am the resurrection and the life; he who believes in Me will live even if he dies, 26and everyone who lives and believes in Me will never die. Do you believe this?" 27She *said to Him, "Yes, Lord; I have believed that You are the Christ, the Son of God, *even* He who comes into the world." 28When she had said this, she went away and called

Mary her sister, saying secretly, "The Teacher is here and is calling for you." 29And when she heard it, she *got up quickly and was coming to Him. 30Now Jesus had not yet come into the village, but was still in the place where Martha met Him. 31Then the Jews who were with her in the house, and consoling her, when they saw that Mary got up quickly and went out, they followed her, supposing that she was going to the tomb to weep there. 32Therefore, when Mary came where Jesus was, she saw Him, and fell at His feet, saying to Him, "Lord, if You had been here, my brother would not have died." 33When Jesus therefore saw her weeping, and the Jews who came with her *also* weeping, He was deeply moved in spirit and was troubled, 34and said, "Where have you laid him?" They *said to Him, "Lord, come and see." 35Jesus wept. 36So the Jews were saying, "See how He loved him!" 37But some of them said, "Could not this man, who opened the eyes of the blind man, have kept this man also from dying?" 38So Jesus, again being deeply moved

The Walk – S.B. Stone & Rock Solid Publishing, LLC
©2018

within, *came to the tomb. Now it was a cave, and a stone was lying against it. 39Jesus *said, "Remove the stone." Martha, the sister of the deceased, *said to Him, "Lord, by this time there will be a stench, for he has been *dead* four days." 40Jesus *said to her, "Did I not say to you that if you believe, you will see the glory of God?" 41So they removed the stone. Then Jesus raised His eyes, and said, "Father, I thank You that You have heard Me. 42I knew that You always hear Me; but because of the people standing around I said it, so that they may believe that You sent Me." 43When He had said these things, He cried out with a loud voice, "Lazarus, come forth." 44The man who had died came forth, bound hand and foot with wrappings, and his face was wrapped around with a cloth. Jesus *said to them, "Unbind him, and let him go." 45Therefore many of the Jews who came to Mary, and saw what He had done, believed in Him. 46But some of them went to the Pharisees and told them the things which Jesus had done.

Conspiracy to Kill Jesus

47Therefore the chief priests and the Pharisees convened a council, and were saying,

"What are we doing? For this man is performing many signs. 48If we let Him *go on* like this, all men will believe in Him, and the Romans will come and take away both our place and our nation." 49But one of them, Caiaphas, who was high priest that year, said to them, "You know nothing at all, 50nor do you take into account that it is expedient for you that one man die for the people, and that the whole nation not perish." 51Now he did not say this on his own initiative, but being high priest that year, he prophesied that Jesus was going to die for the nation, 52and not for the nation only, but in order that He might also gather together into one the children of God who are scattered abroad. 53So from that day on they planned together to kill Him. 54Therefore Jesus no longer continued to walk publicly among the Jews, but went away from there to the country near the wilderness, into a city called Ephraim; and there He stayed with the disciples. 55Now the Passover of the Jews was near, and many went up to Jerusalem out of the country before the Passover to purify themselves. 56So they were seeking for Jesus, and were saying to one another as they stood in the temple, "What do you think; that He will not come to the feast at all?" 57Now the chief priests and the Pharisees had given orders that if anyone knew where He was, he was to report it, so that they might seize Him.   [4]

Gospel of John

Chapter Twelve

Mary Anoints Jesus

1Jesus, therefore, six days before the Passover, came to Bethany where Lazarus was, whom Jesus had raised from the dead. 2So they made Him a supper there, and Martha was serving; but Lazarus was one of those reclining *at the table* with Him. 3Mary then took a pound of very costly perfume of pure nard, and anointed the feet of Jesus and wiped His feet with her hair; and the house was filled with the fragrance of the perfume. 4But Judas Iscariot, one of His disciples, who was intending to betray Him, *said, 5"Why was this perfume not sold for Equivalent to 11 months' wages three hundred denarii and given to poor *people?*" 6Now he said this, not because he was concerned about the poor, but because he was a thief, and as he had the money box, he used to pilfer what was put into it. 7Therefore Jesus said, "Let her alone, so that she may keep I.e. the custom of preparing the body for burial lit for the day of My burial. 8For you always have the poor with you, but you do not always have Me." 9The large crowd of the Jews then learned that He was there; and they came, not for Jesus' sake only, but that they might also see Lazarus, whom He raised from the dead. 10But the chief priests planned to put Lazarus to death also; 11because on account of him many of the Jews were going away and were believing in Jesus.

Jesus Enters Jerusalem

12On the next day the large crowd who had come to the feast, when they heard that Jesus was coming to Jerusalem, 13took the branches of the palm trees and went out to meet Him, and *began* to shout, "Hosanna! Blessed is He who comes in the name of the Lord, even the King of Israel." 14Jesus, finding a young donkey, sat on it; as it is written, 15"Fear not, daughter of Zion; behold, your King is coming, seated on a donkey's colt." 16These things His disciples did not understand at the first; but when Jesus was glorified, then they remembered that these things were written of Him, and that they had done these things to Him. 17So the people, who were with Him when He called Lazarus out of the tomb and raised him from the dead, continued to testify *about Him*. 18For this reason also the people went and met Him, because they heard that He had performed this sign. 19So the Pharisees said to one another, "You see that you are not doing any good; look, the world has gone after Him."

The Walk – S.B. Stone & Rock Solid Publishing, LLC
©2018

Greeks Seek Jesus

20Now there were some Greeks among those who were going up to worship at the feast; 21these then came to Philip, who was from Bethsaida of Galilee, and *began to* ask him, saying, "Sir, we wish to see Jesus." 22Philip *came and *told Andrew; Andrew and Philip

*came and *told Jesus. 23And Jesus *answered them, saying, "The hour has come for the Son of Man to be glorified. 24Truly, truly, I say to you, unless a grain of wheat falls into the earth and dies, it remains alone; but if it dies, it bears much fruit. 25He who loves his life loses it, and he who hates his life in this world will keep it to life eternal. 26If anyone serves Me, he must follow Me; and where I am, there My servant will be also; if anyone serves Me, the Father will honor him.

Jesus Foretells His Death

27 "Now My soul has become troubled; and what shall I say, 'Father, save Me from this hour'? But for this purpose I came to this hour. 28Father, glorify Your name." Then a voice came out of heaven: "I have both glorified it, and will glorify it again." 29So the crowd *of people* who stood by and heard it were saying that it had thundered; others were saying, "An angel has spoken to Him." 30Jesus answered and said, "This voice has not come for My sake, but for your sakes. 31Now judgment is upon this world; now the ruler of this world will be cast out. 32And I, if I am lifted up from the earth, will draw all men to Myself." 33But He was saying this to indicate the kind of death by which He was to die. 34The crowd then answered Him, "We have heard out of the Law that the Christ is to remain forever; and how can You say, 'The Son of

Man must be lifted up'? Who is this Son of Man?" 35So Jesus said to them, "For a little while longer the Light is among you. Walk while you have the Light, so that darkness will not overtake you; he who walks in the darkness does not know where he goes. 36While you have the Light, believe in the Light, so that you may become sons of Light." These things Jesus spoke, and He went away and hid Himself from them. 37But though He had performed so many signs before them, *yet* they were not believing in Him. 38*This was* to fulfill the word of Isaiah the prophet which he spoke: "Lord, who has believed our report? And to whom has the arm of the Lord been revealed?" 39For this reason they could not believe, for Isaiah said again, 40"He has blinded their eyes and He hardened their heart, so that they would not see with their eyes and perceive with their heart, and be converted and I heal them." 41These

The Walk – S.B. Stone & Rock Solid Publishing, LLC
©2018

things Isaiah said because he saw His glory, and he spoke of Him. 42Nevertheless many even of the rulers believed in Him, but because of the Pharisees they were not confessing *Him,* for fear that they would be put out of the synagogue; 43for they loved the approval of men rather than the approval of God. 44And Jesus cried out and said, "He who believes in Me, does not believe in Me but in Him who sent Me. 45He who sees Me sees the One who sent Me. 46I have come *as* Light into the world, so that everyone who believes in Me will not remain in darkness. 47If anyone hears My sayings and does not keep them, I do not judge him; for I did not come to judge the world, but to save the world. 48He who rejects Me and does not receive My sayings, has one who judges him; the word I spoke is what will judge him at the last day. 49For I did not speak on My own initiative, but the Father Himself who sent Me has given Me a commandment *as to* what to say and what to speak. 50I know that His commandment is eternal life; therefore the things I speak, I speak just as the Father has told Me."   [4]

Gospel of John

Chapter Thirteen

The Lord's Supper

1Now before the Feast of the Passover, Jesus knowing that His hour had come that He would depart out of this world to the Father, having loved His own who were in the world, He loved them to the end. 2During supper, the devil having already put into the heart of Judas Iscariot, *the son* of Simon, to betray Him, 3*Jesus,* knowing that the Father had given all things into His hands, and that He had come forth from God and was going back to God, 4*got up from supper, and *laid aside His garments; and taking a towel, He girded Himself.

Jesus Washes the Disciples' Feet

5Then He *poured water into the basin, and began to wash the disciples' feet and to wipe them with the towel with which He was girded. 6So He *came to Simon Peter. He *said to Him,

"Lord, do You wash my feet?" 7Jesus answered and said to him, "What I do you do not realize now, but you will understand hereafter." 8Peter *said to Him, "Never shall You wash my feet!" Jesus answered him, "If I do not wash you, you have no part with Me." 9Simon Peter *said to Him, "Lord, *then wash* not only my feet, but also my hands and my head." 10Jesus *said to him, "He who has bathed needs only to wash his feet, but is completely clean; and you are clean, but not all *of you.*" 11For He knew the one who was betraying Him; for this reason He said, "Not all of you are clean." 12So when He had washed their feet, and taken His garments and reclined *at the table* again, He said to them, "Do you know what I have done to you? 13You call

Me Teacher and Lord; and you are right, for *so* I am. 14If I then, the Lord and the Teacher, washed your feet, you also ought to wash one another's feet. 15For I gave you an example that you also should do as I did to you. 16Truly, truly, I say to you, a slave is not greater than his master, nor *is* one who is sent greater than the one who sent him. 17If you know these things, you are blessed if you do them. 18I do not speak of all of you. I know the ones I have chosen; but *it is* that the Scripture may be fulfilled, 'He who eats My bread has lifted up his heel against Me.' 19From now on I am telling you before *it* comes to pass, so that when it does occur, you may believe that I am *He.* 20Truly, truly, I say to you, he who receives whomever I send receives Me; and he who receives Me receives Him who sent Me."

Jesus Predicts His Betrayal

21When Jesus had said this, He became troubled in spirit, and testified and said, "Truly, truly, I say to you, that one of you will betray Me." 22The disciples *began* looking at one another, at a loss *to know* of which one He was speaking. 23There was reclining on Jesus' bosom one of His disciples, whom Jesus loved. 24So Simon Peter *gestured to him, and *said to him,

"Tell *us* who it is of whom He is speaking." 25He, leaning back thus on Jesus' bosom, *said to Him, "Lord, who is it?" 26Jesus then *answered, "That is the one for whom I shall dip the morsel and give it to him." So when He had dipped the morsel, He *took and *gave it to Judas, *the son* of Simon Iscariot. 27After the morsel, Satan then entered into him. Therefore

Jesus *said to him, "What you do, do quickly." 28Now no one of those reclining *at the table* knew for what purpose He had said this to him. 29For some were supposing, because Judas had the money box, that Jesus was saying to him, "Buy the things we have need of for the feast"; or else, that he should give something to the poor. 30So after receiving the morsel he went out immediately; and it was night. 31Therefore when he had gone out, Jesus *said, "Now is the Son of Man glorified, and God is glorified in Him; 32if God is glorified in Him, God

The Walk – S.B. Stone & Rock Solid Publishing, LLC
©2018

will also glorify Him in Himself, and will glorify Him immediately. 33Little children, I am with you a little while longer. You will seek Me; and as I said to the Jews, now I also say to you, 'Where I am going, you cannot come.' 34A new commandment I give to you, that you love one another, even as I have loved you, that you also love one another. 35By this all men will know that you are My disciples, if you have love for one another." 36Simon Peter *said to Him, "Lord, where are You going?" Jesus answered, "Where I go, you cannot follow Me now; but you will follow later." 37Peter *said to Him, "Lord, why can I not follow You right now? I will lay down my life for You." 38Jesus *answered, "Will you lay down your life for Me? Truly, truly, I say to you, a rooster will not crow until you deny Me three times.   [4]

Gospel of John

Chapter Fourteen

Jesus Comforts His Disciples

1 "Do not let your heart be troubled; Or *you believe in God* believe in God, believe also in Me. 2In My Father's house are many dwelling places; if it were not so, I would have told you; for I go to prepare a place for you. 3If I go and prepare a place for you, I will come again and receive you to Myself, that where I am, *there* you may be also. 4And you know the way where I am going." 5Thomas *said to Him, "Lord, we do not know where You are going, how do we know the way?" 6Jesus *said to him, "I am the way, and the truth, and the life; no one comes to the Father but through Me.

Oneness with the Father

7 If you had known Me, you would have known My Father also; from now on you know Him, and have seen Him." 8Philip *said to Him, "Lord, show us the Father, and it is enough for us." 9Jesus *said to him, "Have I been so long with you, and *yet* you have not come to know Me, Philip? He who has seen Me has seen the Father; how *can* you say, 'Show us the Father'? 10Do you not believe that I am in the Father, and the Father is in Me? The words that I say to you I do not speak on My own initiative, but the Father abiding in Me does His works. 11Believe Me that I am in the Father and the Father is in Me; otherwise believe because of the works themselves. 12Truly, truly, I say to you, he who believes in Me, the works that I do, he will do also; and greater *works* than these he will do; because I go to the Father. 13Whatever you ask in

My name, that will I do, so that the Father may be glorified in the Son. 14If you ask Me anything in My name, I will do *it.* 15 "If you love Me, you will keep My commandments.

Role of the Spirit

16 I will ask the Father, and He will give you another Helper, that He may be with you forever; 17*that is* the Spirit of truth, whom the world cannot receive, because it does not see Him or know Him, *but* you know Him because He abides with you and will be in you.

18 "I will not leave you as orphans; I will come to you. 19After a little while the world will no longer see Me, but you *will* see Me; because I live, you will live also. 20In that day you will know that I am in My Father, and you in Me, and I in you. 21He who has My commandments and keeps them is the one who loves Me; and he who loves Me will be loved by My Father, and I will love him and will disclose Myself to him." 22Judas (not Iscariot) *said to

Him, "Lord, what then has happened that You are going to disclose Yourself to us and not to the world?" 23Jesus answered and said to him, "If anyone loves Me, he will keep My word; and My Father will love him, and We will come to him and make Our abode with him. 24He who does not love Me does not keep My words; and the word which you hear is not Mine, but the Father's who sent Me.

25 "These things I have spoken to you while abiding with you. 26But the Helper, the Holy Spirit, whom the Father will send in My name, He will teach you all things, and bring to your remembrance all that I said to you. 27Peace I leave with you; My peace I give to you; not as the world gives do I give to you. Do not let your heart be troubled, nor let it be fearful. 28You heard that I said to you, 'I go away, and I will come to you.' If you loved Me, you would have rejoiced because I go to the Father, for the Father is greater than I. 29Now I have told you before it happens, so that when it happens, you may believe. 30I will not speak much more with you, for the ruler of the world is coming, and he has nothing in Me; 31but so that the world may know that I love the Father, I do exactly as the Father commanded Me. Get up, let us go from here. [4]

Gospel of John

Chapter Fifteen

Jesus Is the Vine—Followers Are Branches

1 "I am the true vine, and My Father is the vinedresser. 2Every branch in Me that does not bear fruit, He takes away; and every *branch* that bears fruit, He Lit *cleans;* used to describe pruning prunes it so that it may bear more fruit. 3You are already clean because of the word which I have spoken to you. 4Abide in Me, and I in you. As the branch cannot bear fruit of itself unless it abides in the vine, so neither *can* you unless you abide in Me. 5I am the vine, you are the branches; he who abides in Me and I in him, he bears much fruit, for apart from Me you can do nothing. 6If anyone does not abide in Me, he is thrown away as a branch and dries up; and they gather them, and cast them into the fire and they are burned. 7If you abide in Me, and My words abide in you, ask whatever you wish, and it will be done for you. 8My Father is glorified by this, that you bear much fruit, and *so* prove to be My disciples. 9Just as the Father has loved Me, I have also loved you; abide in My love. 10If you keep My commandments, you will abide in My love; just as I have kept My Father's commandments and abide in His love. 11These things I have spoken to you so that My joy may be in you, and *that* your joy may be made full.

Disciples' Relation to Each Other

12 "This is My commandment, that you love one another, just as I have loved you. 13Greater love has no one than this, that one lay down his life for his friends. 14You are My friends if you do what I command you. 15No longer do I call you slaves, for the slave does not know what his master is doing; but I have called you friends, for all things that I have heard from My Father I have made known to you. 16You did not choose Me but I chose you, and appointed you that you would go and bear fruit, and *that* your fruit would remain, so that whatever you ask of the Father in My name He may give to you. 17This I command you, that you love one another.

Disciples' Relation to the World

18 "If the world hates you, you know that it has hated Me before *it hated* you. 19If you were of the world, the world would love its own; but because you are not of the world, but I chose you out of the world, because of this the world hates you. 20Remember the word that I said to you, 'A slave is not greater than his master.' If they persecuted Me, they will also persecute you; if they kept My word, they will keep yours also. 21But all these things they will do to you for My name's sake, because

The Walk – S.B. Stone & Rock Solid Publishing, LLC
©2018

they do not know the One who sent Me. 22If I had not come and spoken to them, they would not have sin, but now they have no excuse for their sin. 23He who hates Me hates My Father also. 24If I had not done among them the works which no one else did, they would not have sin; but now they have both seen and hated Me and My Father as well. 25But *they have done this* to fulfill the word that is written in their Law, 'They hated Me without a cause.' 26 "When the Helper comes, whom I will send to you from the Father, *that is* the Spirit of truth who proceeds from the Father, He will testify about Me, 27and you *will* testify also, because you have been with Me from the beginning.   [4]

Gospel of John

Chapter Sixteen

Jesus' Warning

1 "These things I have spoken to you so that you may be kept from stumbling. 2They will make you outcasts from the synagogue, but an hour is coming for everyone who kills you to think that he is offering service to God. 3These things they will do because they have not known the Father or Me. 4But these things I have spoken to you, so that when their hour comes, you may remember that I told you of them. These things I did not say to you at the beginning, because I was with you.

The Holy Spirit Promised

5 "But now I am going to Him who sent Me; and none of you asks Me, 'Where are You going?' 6But because I have said these things to you, sorrow has filled your heart. 7But I tell you the truth, it is to your advantage that I go away; for if I do not go away, the Helper will not come to you; but if I go, I will send Him to you. 8And He, when He comes, will convict the world concerning sin and righteousness and judgment; 9concerning sin, because they do not believe in Me; 10and concerning righteousness, because I go to the Father and you no longer see Me; 11and concerning judgment, because the ruler of this world has been judged.

12 "I have many more things to say to you, but you cannot bear *them* now. 13But when He, the Spirit of truth, comes, He will guide you into all the truth; for He will not speak on His own initiative, but whatever He hears, He will speak; and He will disclose to you what is to come. 14He will glorify Me, for He will take of Mine and will disclose *it* to

you. 15All things that the Father has are Mine; therefore I said that He takes of Mine and will disclose *it* to you.

Jesus' Death and Resurrection Foretold

16 "A little while, and you will no longer see Me; and again a little while, and you will see Me." 17*Some* of His disciples then said to one another, "What is this thing He is telling us, 'A little while, and you will not see Me; and again a little while, and you will see Me'; and, 'because I go to the Father'?" 18So they were saying, "What is this that He says, 'A little while'? We do not know what He is talking about." 19Jesus knew that they wished to question Him, and He said to them, "Are you deliberating together about this, that I said, 'A little while, and you will not see Me, and again a little while, and you will see Me'? 20Truly, truly, I say to you, that you will weep and lament, but the world will rejoice; you will grieve, but your grief will be turned into joy. 21Whenever a woman is in labor she has pain, because her hour has come; but when she gives birth to the child, she no longer remembers the anguish because of the joy that a child has been born into the world. 22Therefore you too have grief now; but I will see you again, and your heart will rejoice, and no one *will* take your joy away from you.

Prayer Promises

23 In that day you will not question Me about anything. Truly, truly, I say to you, if you ask the Father for anything in My name, He will give it to you. 24Until now you have asked for nothing in My name; ask and you will receive, so that your joy may be made full. 25 "These things I have spoken to you in figurative language; an hour is coming when I will no longer speak to you in figurative language, but will tell you plainly of the Father. 26In that day you will ask in My name, and I do not say to you that I will request of the Father on your behalf; 27for the Father Himself loves you, because you have loved Me and have believed that I came forth from the Father. 28I came forth from the Father and have come into the world; I am leaving the world again and going to the Father." 29His disciples *said, "Lo, now You are speaking plainly and are not using a figure of speech. 30Now we know that You know all things, and have no need for anyone to question You; by this we believe that You came from God." 31Jesus answered them, "Do you now believe? 32Behold, an hour is coming, and has *already* come, for you to be scattered, each to his own *home,* and to leave Me alone; and *yet* I am not alone, because the Father is with Me. 33These things I have spoken

to you, so that in Me you may have peace. In the world you have tribulation, but take courage; I have overcome the world." [4]

Gospel of John

Chapter Seventeen

The High Priestly Prayer

1Jesus spoke these things; and lifting up His eyes to heaven, He said, "Father, the hour has come; glorify Your Son, that the Son may glorify You, 2even as You gave Him authority over all flesh, that to all whom You have given Him, He may give eternal life. 3This is eternal life, that they may know You, the only true God, and Jesus Christ whom You have sent. 4I glorified You on the earth, having accomplished the work which You have given Me to do. 5Now, Father, glorify Me together with Yourself, with the glory which I had with You before the world was.

6 "I have manifested Your name to the men whom You gave Me out of the world; they were Yours and You gave them to Me, and they have kept Your word. 7Now they have come to know that everything You have given Me is from You; 8for the words which You gave Me I have given to them; and they received *them* and truly understood that I came forth from You, and they believed that You sent Me. 9I ask on their behalf; I do not ask on behalf of the world, but of those whom You have given Me; for they are Yours; 10and all things that are Mine are Yours, and Yours are Mine; and I have been glorified in them. 11I am no longer in the world; and *yet* they themselves are in the world, and I come to You. Holy Father, keep them in Your name, *the name* which You have given Me, that they may be one even as We *are*. 12While I was with them, I was keeping them in Your name which You have given Me; and I guarded them and not one of them perished but the son of perdition, so that the Scripture would be fulfilled.

The Disciples in the World

13 But now I come to You; and these things I speak in the world so that they may have My joy made full in themselves. 14I have given them Your word; and the world has hated them, because they are not of the world, even as I am not of the world. 15I do not ask You to take them out of the world, but to keep them from the evil *one*. 16They are not of the world, even as I am not of the world. 17Sanctify them in the truth; Your word is truth. 18As You sent Me into the world, I also have sent them into the world. 19For their sakes I sanctify Myself, that they

themselves also may be sanctified in truth. 20 "I do not ask on behalf of these alone, but for those also who believe in Me through their word; 21that they may all be one; even as You, Father, *are* in Me and I in You, that they also may be in Us, so that the world may believe that You sent Me.

Their Future Glory

22 The glory which You have given Me I have given to them, that they may be one, just as We are one; 23I in them and You in Me, that they may be perfected in unity, so that the world may know that You sent Me, and loved them, even as You have loved Me. 24Father, I desire that they also, whom You have given Me, be with Me where I am, so that they may see My glory which You have given Me, for You loved Me before the foundation of the world. 25 "O

righteous Father, although the world has not known You, yet I have known You; and these have known that You sent Me; 26and I have made Your name known to them, and will make it known, so that the love with which You loved Me may be in them, and I in them."   [4]

Gospel of John

Chapter Eighteen

Judas Betrays Jesus

1When Jesus had spoken these words, He went forth with His disciples over the ravine of the Kidron, where there was a garden, in which He entered with His disciples. 2Now Judas also, who was betraying Him, knew the place, for Jesus had often met there with His disciples. 3Judas then, having received the *Roman* cohort and officers from the chief priests and the Pharisees, *came there with lanterns and torches and weapons. 4So Jesus, knowing all the things that were coming upon Him, went forth and *said to them, "Whom do you seek?" 5They answered Him,

"Jesus the Nazarene." He *said to them, "I am *He*." And Judas also, who was betraying Him, was standing with them. 6So when He said to them, "I am *He*," they drew back and fell to the ground. 7Therefore He again asked them, "Whom do you seek?" And they said, "Jesus the Nazarene." 8Jesus answered, "I told you that I am *He*; so if you seek Me, let these go their way," 9to fulfill the word which He spoke, "Of those whom You have given Me I lost not one." 10Simon Peter then, having a sword, drew it and struck the high priest's slave, and cut off his right ear; and the slave's name was Malchus. 11So Jesus said to Peter, "Put the sword into the sheath; the cup which the Father has given Me, shall I not drink it?"

Jesus before the Priests

12So the *Roman* cohort and the commander and the officers of the Jews, arrested Jesus and bound Him, 13and led Him to Annas first; for he was father-in-law of Caiaphas, who was high priest that year. 14Now Caiaphas was the one who had advised the Jews that it was expedient for one man to die on behalf of the people. 15Simon Peter was following Jesus, and *so was* another disciple. Now that disciple was known to the high priest, and entered with Jesus into the court of the high priest, 16but Peter was standing at the door outside. So the other disciple, who was known to the high priest, went out and spoke to the doorkeeper, and brought Peter in. 17Then the slave-girl who kept the door *said to Peter, "You are not also *one* of this man's disciples, are you?" He *said, "I am not." 18Now the slaves and the officers were standing *there,* having made a charcoal fire, for it was cold and they were warming themselves; and Peter was also with them, standing and warming himself.

19The high priest then questioned Jesus about His disciples, and about His teaching. 20Jesus answered him, "I have spoken openly to the world; I always taught in synagogues and in the temple, where all the Jews come together; and I spoke nothing in secret. 21Why do you question Me? Question those who have heard what I spoke to them; they know what I said." 22When He had said this, one of the officers standing nearby struck Jesus, saying, "Is that the way You answer the high priest?" 23Jesus answered him, "If I have spoken wrongly, testify of the wrong; but if rightly, why do you strike Me?" 24So Annas sent Him bound to Caiaphas the high priest.

Peter's Denial of Jesus

25Now Simon Peter was standing and warming himself. So they said to him, "You are not also *one* of His disciples, are you?" He denied *it,* and said, "I am not." 26One of the slaves of the high priest, being a relative of the one whose ear Peter cut off, *said, "Did I not see you in the garden with Him?" 27Peter then denied *it* again, and immediately a rooster crowed.

Jesus before Pilate

28Then they *led Jesus from Caiaphas into the I.e. governor's official residencePraetorium, and it was early; and they themselves did not enter into the Praetorium so that they would not be defiled, but might eat the Passover. 29Therefore Pilate went out to them and *said, "What accusation do you bring against this Man?" 30They answered and said to him, "If this Man were not an evildoer, we would not have delivered Him to you." 31So Pilate said to them, "Take Him yourselves, and judge Him according to your law." The Jews said to him, "We are not permitted to put anyone to death," 32to fulfill the word of Jesus which He spoke, signifying by what kind of death He was about to die.

33Therefore Pilate entered again into the Praetorium, and summoned Jesus and said to Him, "Are You the King of the Jews?" 34Jesus answered, "Are you saying this on your own initiative, or did others tell you about Me?" 35Pilate answered, "I am not a Jew, am I? Your own nation and the chief priests delivered You to me; what have You done?" 36Jesus answered, "My kingdom is not of this world. If My kingdom were of this world, then My servants would be fighting so that I would not be handed over to the Jews; but as it is, My kingdom is not Lit *from here*of this realm." 37Therefore Pilate said to Him, "So You are a king?" Jesus answered, "You say *correctly* that I am a king. For this I have been born, and for this I have come into the world, to testify to the truth. Everyone who is of the truth hears My voice." 38Pilate *said to Him, "What is truth?" And when he had said this, he went out again to the Jews and *said to them, "I find no guilt in Him. 39But you have a custom that I release someone for you at the Passover; do you wish then that I release for you the King of the Jews?" 40So they cried out again, saying, "Not this Man, but Barabbas." Now Barabbas was a robber.   [4]

Gospel of John

Chapter Nineteen

The Crown of Thorns

1Pilate then took Jesus and scourged Him. 2And the soldiers twisted together a crown of thorns and put it on His head, and put a purple robe on Him; 3and they *began* to come up to Him and say, "Hail, King of the Jews!" and to give Him slaps *in the face*. 4Pilate came out again and *said to them, "Behold, I am bringing Him out to you so that you may know that I find no guilt in Him." 5Jesus then came out, wearing the crown of thorns and the purple robe. *Pilate* *said to them, "Behold, the Man!" 6So when the chief priests and the officers saw Him, they cried out saying, "Crucify, crucify!" Pilate *said to them, "Take Him yourselves and crucify Him, for I find no guilt in Him." 7The Jews answered him, "We have a law, and by that law He ought to die because He made Himself out *to be* the Son of God." 8Therefore when Pilate heard this statement, he was *even* more afraid; 9and he entered into the I.e. governor's official residence

Praetorium again and *said to Jesus, "Where are You from?" But Jesus gave him no answer. 10So Pilate *said to Him, "You do not speak to me? Do You not know that I have authority to release You, and I have authority to crucify You?" 11Jesus answered, "You would have no authority over Me, unless it had been given you from above; for this reason he who delivered Me to you has *the* greater sin." 12As a result of this Pilate made efforts to release Him, but the Jews cried out saying, "If you release this Man, you are no friend of Caesar; everyone who makes himself out *to be* a king opposes Caesar." 13Therefore when Pilate heard these words, he brought Jesus out, and sat down on the judgment seat at a place called The Pavement, but in Hebrew, Gabbatha. 14Now it was the day of preparation for the Passover; it was about the Perhaps 6 a.m.sixth hour. And he *said to the Jews, "Behold, your King!" 15So they cried out, "Away with *Him,* away with *Him,* crucify Him!" Pilate *said to them, "Shall I crucify your King?" The chief priests answered, "We have no king but Caesar."

The Crucifixion

16So he then handed Him over to them to be crucified.

17They took Jesus, therefore, and He went out, bearing His own cross, to the place called the Place of a Skull, which is called in Hebrew, Golgotha. 18There they crucified Him, and with Him two other men, one on either side, and Jesus in between. 19Pilate also wrote an inscription and put it on the cross. It was written, "JESUS THE NAZARENE, THE KING OF THE JEWS."

20Therefore many of the Jews read this inscription, for the place where Jesus was crucified was near the city; and it was written in Hebrew, Latin *and* in Greek. 21So the chief priests of the Jews were saying to Pilate, "Do not write, 'The King of the Jews'; but that He said, 'I am King of the Jews.' " 22Pilate answered, "What I have written I have written."

The Walk – S.B. Stone & Rock Solid Publishing, LLC
©2018

23Then the soldiers, when they had crucified Jesus, took His outer garments and made four parts, a part to every soldier and *also* the Gr *khiton,* the garment worn next to the skin tunic; now the tunic was seamless, woven in one piece. 24So they said to one another, "Let us not tear it, but cast lots for it, *to decide* whose it shall be"; *this was* to fulfill the Scripture: "They divided My outer garments among them, and for My clothing they cast lots." 25Therefore the soldiers did these things. **B**ut standing by the cross of Jesus were His mother, and His mother's sister, Mary the *wife* of Clopas, and Mary Magdalene. 26When Jesus then saw His mother, and the disciple whom He loved standing nearby, He *said to His mother, "Woman, behold, your son!" 27Then He *said to the disciple, "Behold, your mother!" From that hour the disciple took her into his own *household.* 28After this, Jesus, knowing that all things had already been accomplished, to fulfill the Scripture, *said, "I am thirsty." 29A jar full of sour wine was standing there; so they put a sponge full of the sour wine upon *a branch of* hyssop and brought it up to His mouth. 30Therefore when Jesus had received the sour wine, He said, "It is finished!" And He bowed His head and gave up His spirit.

Care of the Body of Jesus

31Then the Jews, because it was the day of preparation, so that the bodies would not remain on the cross on the Sabbath (for that Sabbath was a high day), asked Pilate that their legs might be broken, and *that* they might be taken away. 32So the soldiers came, and broke the legs of the first man and of the other who was crucified with Him; 33but coming to Jesus, when they saw that He was already dead, they did not break His legs. 34But one of the soldiers pierced His side with a spear, and immediately blood and water came out. 35And he who has seen has testified, and his testimony is true; and he knows that he is telling the truth, so that you also may believe. 36For these things came to pass to fulfill the Scripture, "Not a bone of Him shall be broken." 37And again another Scripture says, "They shall look on Him whom they pierced."

38After these things Joseph of Arimathea, being a disciple of Jesus, but a secret *one* for fear of the Jews, asked Pilate that he might take away the body of Jesus; and Pilate granted permission. So he came and took away His body. 39Nicodemus, who had first come to Him by night, also came, bringing a mixture of myrrh and aloes, about a hundred pounds *weight.* 40So they took the body of Jesus and bound it in linen wrappings with the spices, as is the burial custom of the Jews. 41Now in the place where He was crucified there was a garden, and in the garden a new tomb in which no one had yet been laid. 42Therefore because of the Jewish day of preparation, since the tomb was nearby, they laid Jesus there.   [4

Gospel of John

Chapter Twenty

The Empty Tomb

1Now on the first *day* of the week Mary Magdalene *came early to the tomb, while it *was still dark, and *saw the stone *already* taken away from the tomb. 2So she *ran and *came to Simon Peter and to the other disciple whom Jesus loved, and *said to them, "They have taken away the Lord out of the tomb, and we do not know where they have laid Him." 3So Peter and the other disciple went forth, and they were going to the tomb. 4The two were running together; and the other disciple ran ahead faster than Peter and came to the tomb first; 5and stooping and looking in, he *saw the linen wrappings lying *there;* but he did not go in. 6And so Simon Peter also *came, following him, and entered the tomb; and he *saw the linen wrappings lying *there,* 7and the face-cloth which had been on His head, not lying with the linen wrappings, but rolled up in a place by itself. 8So the other disciple who had first come to the tomb then also entered, and he saw and believed. 9For as yet they did not understand the Scripture that He must rise again from the dead. 10So the disciples went away again to their own homes. 11But Mary was standing outside the tomb weeping; and so, as she wept, she stooped and looked into the tomb; 12and she *saw two angels in white sitting, one at the head and one at the feet, where the body of Jesus had been lying. 13And they *said to her, "Woman, why are you weeping?" She *said to them, "Because they have taken away my Lord, and I do not know where they have laid Him." 14When she had said this, she turned around and *saw Jesus standing *there,* and did not know that it was Jesus.

15Jesus *said to her, "Woman, why are you weeping? Whom are you seeking?" Supposing Him to be the gardener, she *said to Him, "Sir, if you have carried Him away, tell me where you have laid Him, and I will take Him away." 16Jesus *said to her, "Mary!" She turned and *said to Him in Hebrew, "Rabboni!" (which means, Teacher). 17Jesus *said to her, "Stop clinging to Me, for I have not yet ascended to the Father; but go to My brethren and say to them, 'I ascend to My Father and your Father, and My God and your God.' " 18Mary Magdalene *came, announcing to the disciples, "I have seen the Lord," and *that* He had said these things to her.

Jesus among His Disciples

19So when it was evening on that day, the first *day* of the week, and when the doors were shut where the disciples were, for fear of the Jews, Jesus came and stood in their midst and *said to them, "Peace *be* with you." 20And when He had said this, He showed them both His hands and His side. The disciples then rejoiced when they saw the Lord. 21So Jesus said to them again, "Peace *be* with you; as the Father has sent Me, I also send you." 22And when He had said this, He breathed on them and *said to them, "Receive the Holy Spirit. 23If you forgive the sins of any, *their sins* have been forgiven them; if you retain the *sins* of any, they have been retained." 24But Thomas, one of the twelve, called Didymus, was not with them when Jesus came. 25So the other disciples were saying to him, "We have seen the Lord!" But he said to them, "Unless I see in His hands the imprint of the nails, and put my finger into the place of the nails, and put my hand into His side, I will not believe." 26After eight days His disciples were again inside, and Thomas with them. Jesus *came, the doors having been shut, and stood in their midst and said, "Peace *be* with you." 27Then He *said to Thomas, "Reach here with your finger, and see My hands; and reach here your hand and put it into My side; and do not be unbelieving, but believing." 28Thomas answered and said to Him, "My Lord and my God!" 29Jesus *said to him, "Because you have seen Me, have you believed? Blessed *are* they who did not see, and *yet* believed."

Why This Gospel Was Written

30Therefore many other signs Jesus also performed in the presence of the disciples, which are not written in this book; 31but these have been written so that you may believe that Jesus is the Christ, the Son of God; and that believing you may have life in His name.   [4]

Gospel of John

Chapter Twenty-One

Jesus Appears at the Sea of Galilee

1After these things Jesus manifested Himself again to the disciples at the Sea of Tiberias, and He manifested *Himself* in this way. 2Simon Peter, and Thomas called Didymus, and Nathanael of Cana in Galilee, and the *sons* of Zebedee, and two others of His disciples were together. 3Simon Peter *said to them, "I am going fishing." They *said to him, "We will also come with you." They went out and got into the boat; and that night they caught nothing. 4But when the day was now breaking, Jesus stood on the beach; yet the disciples did not know that it was Jesus. 5So Jesus *said to them, "Children, you do not have any fish, do you?" They answered Him, "No." 6And He said to them, "Cast the net on the right-hand side of the boat and you will find *a catch.*" So they cast, and then they were not able to haul it in because of the great number of fish. 7Therefore that disciple whom Jesus loved *said to Peter, "It is the Lord." So when Simon Peter heard that it was the Lord, he put his outer garment on (for he was stripped *for work)*, and threw himself into the sea. 8But the other disciples came in the little boat, for they were not far from the land, but about one hundred yards away, dragging the net *full* of fish. 9So when they got out on the land, they *saw a charcoal fire *already* laid and fish placed on it, and bread. 10Jesus *said to them, "Bring some of the fish which you have now caught." 11Simon Peter went up and drew the net to land, full of large fish, a hundred and fifty-three; and although there were so many, the net was not torn.

Jesus Provides

12Jesus *said to them, "Come *and* have breakfast." None of the disciples ventured to question Him, "Who are You?" knowing that it was the Lord. 13Jesus *came and *took the bread and *gave *it* to them, and the fish likewise. 14This is now the third time that Jesus was manifested to the disciples, after He was raised from the dead.

The Love Motivation

15So when they had finished breakfast, Jesus *said to Simon Peter, "Simon, *son* of John, do you love Me more than these?" He *said to Him, "Yes, Lord; You know that I love You." He *said to him, "Tend My lambs." 16He *said to him again a second time, "Simon, *son* of John, do you love Me?" He *said to Him, "Yes, Lord; You know that I love You." He *said to him, "Shepherd My sheep." 17He *said to him the third time, "Simon, *son* of John, do you love Me?" Peter was grieved because He said to him the third time, "Do you love Me?" And he said to Him, "Lord, You know all things; You know that I love You." Jesus *said to him, "Tend My sheep.

Our Times Are in His Hand

18 Truly, truly, I say to you, when you were younger, you used to gird yourself and walk wherever you wished; but when you grow old, you will stretch out your hands and someone else will gird you, and bring you where you do not wish to *go.*" 19Now this He said, signifying by what kind of death he would glorify God. And when He had spoken this, He *said to him, "Follow Me!" 20Peter, turning around, *saw the disciple whom Jesus loved following *them;* the one who also had leaned back on His bosom at the supper and said, "Lord, who is the one who betrays You?" 21So Peter seeing him *said to Jesus, "Lord, and what about this man?" 22Jesus *said to him, "If I want him to remain until I come, what *is that* to you? You follow Me!" 23Therefore this saying went out among the brethren that that disciple would not die; yet Jesus did not say to him that he would not die, but *only,* "If I want him to remain until I come, what *is that* to you?" 24This is the disciple who is testifying to these things and wrote these things, and we know that his testimony is true. 25And there are also many other things which Jesus did, which if they *were written in detail, I suppose that even the world itself *would not contain the books that *would be written.   [4]

The Book of Hebrews

Chapter One

1-3Going through a long line of prophets, God has been addressing our ancestors in different ways for centuries. Recently he spoke to us directly through his Son. By his Son, God created the world in the beginning, and it will all belong to the Son at the end. This Son perfectly mirrors God, and is stamped with God's nature. He holds everything together by what he says—powerful words!

The Son Is Higher than Angels

3-6After he finished the sacrifice for sins, the Son took his honored place high in the heavens right alongside God, far higher than any angel in rank and rule. Did God ever say to an angel, "You're my Son; today I celebrate you" or "I'm his Father, he's my Son"? When he presents his honored Son to the world, he says, "All angels must worship him."

7Regarding angels he says, The messengers are winds, the servants are tongues of fire.

8-9But he says to the Son, You're God, and on the throne for good; your rule makes everything right. You love it when things are right; you hate it when things are wrong. That is why God, your God, poured fragrant oil on your head, Marking you out as king, far above your dear companions.

10-12And again to the Son, You, Master, started it all, laid earth's foundations, then crafted the stars in the sky. Earth and sky will wear out, but not you; they become threadbare like an old coat; You'll fold them up like a worn-out cloak, and lay them away on the shelf. But you'll stay the same, year after year; you'll never fade, you'll never wear out.

13And did he ever say anything like this to an angel? Sit alongside me here on my throne. Until I make your enemies a stool for your feet.

14Isn't it obvious that all angels are sent to help out with those lined up to receive salvation? [3]

Hebrews Chapter Two

(Not included due to copyright restrictions)

Hebrews

Chapter Three

The Centerpiece of All We Believe

1-6So, my dear Christian friends, companions in following this call to the heights, take a good hard look at Jesus. He's the centerpiece of everything we believe, faithful in everything God gave him to do. Moses was also faithful, but Jesus gets far more honor. A builder is more valuable than a building any day. Every house has a builder, but the Builder behind them all is God. Moses did a good job in God's house, but it was all servant work, getting things ready for what was to come. Christ as Son is in charge of the house.

6-11Now, if we can only keep a firm grip on this bold confidence, we're the house! That's why the Holy Spirit says, Today, please listen; don't turn a deaf ear as in "the bitter uprising," that time of wilderness testing! Even though they watched me at work for forty years, your ancestors refused to let me do it my way; over and over they tried my patience. And I was provoked, oh, so provoked! I said, "They'll never keep their minds on God; they refuse to walk down my road."

The Walk – S.B. Stone & Rock Solid Publishing, LLC
©2018

Exasperated, I vowed, "They'll never get where they're going, never be able to sit down and rest."

12-14So watch your step, friends. Make sure there's no evil unbelief lying around that will trip you up and throw you off course, diverting you from the living God. For as long as it's still God's Today, keep each other on your toes so sin doesn't slow down your reflexes. If we can only keep our grip on the sure thing we started out with, we're in this with Christ for the long haul. These words keep ringing in our ears: Today, please listen; don't turn a deaf ear as in the bitter uprising.

15-19For who were the people who turned a deaf ear? Weren't they the very ones Moses led out of Egypt? And who was God provoked with for forty years? Wasn't it those who turned a deaf ear and ended up corpses in the wilderness? And when he swore that they'd never get where they were going, wasn't he talking to the ones who turned a deaf ear? They never got there because they never listened, never believed. [3]

Hebrews

Chapter Four

When the Promises Are Mixed with Faith

1-3For as long, then, as that promise of resting in him pulls us on to God's goal for us, we need to be careful that we're not disqualified. We received the same promises as those people in the wilderness, but the promises didn't do them a bit of good because they didn't receive the promises with faith. If we believe, though, we'll experience that state of resting. But not if we don't have faith. Remember that God said, Exasperated, I vowed, "They'll never get where they're going, never be able to sit down and rest."

3-7God made that vow, even though he'd finished *his* part before the foundation of the world. Somewhere it's written, "God rested the seventh day, having completed his work," but in this other text he says, "They'll never be able to sit down and rest." So this promise has not yet been fulfilled. Those earlier ones never did get to the place of rest because they were disobedient. God keeps renewing the promise and setting the date as *today*, just as he did in David's psalm, centuries later than the original invitation: Today, please listen, don't turn a deaf ear . . .

The Walk – S.B. Stone & Rock Solid Publishing, LLC
©2018

8-11And so this is still a live promise. It wasn't canceled at the time of Joshua; otherwise, God wouldn't keep renewing the appointment for "today." The promise of "arrival" and "rest" is still there for God's people. God himself is at rest. And at the end of the journey we'll surely rest with God. So let's keep at it and eventually arrive at the place of rest, not drop out through some sort of disobedience.

12-13God means what he says. What he says goes. His powerful Word is sharp as a surgeon's scalpel, cutting through everything, whether doubt or defense, laying us open to listen and obey. Nothing and no one is impervious to God's Word. We can't get away from it—no matter what.

The High Priest Who Cried Out in Pain

14-16Now that we know what we have—Jesus, this great High Priest with ready access to God—let's not let it slip through our fingers. We don't have a priest who is out of touch with our reality. He's been through weakness and testing, experienced it all—all but the sin. So let's walk right up to him and get what he is so ready to give. Take the mercy, accept the help.   [3]

Hebrews

Chapter Five

1-3Every high priest selected to represent men and women before God and offer sacrifices for their sins should be able to deal gently with their failings, since he knows what it's like from his own experience. But that also means that he has to offer sacrifices for his own sins as well as the peoples'.

4-6No one elects himself to this honored position. He's called to it by God, as Aaron was. Neither did Christ presume to set himself up as high priest, but was set apart by the One who said to him, "You're my Son; today I celebrate you!" In another place God declares, "You're a priest forever in the royal order of Melchizedek."

7-10While he lived on earth, anticipating death, Jesus cried out in pain and wept in sorrow as he offered up priestly prayers to God. Because he honored God, God answered him. Though he was God's Son, he learned trusting-obedience by what he suffered, just as we do. Then, having arrived at the full stature of his maturity and having been announced by God as high priest in the order of Melchizedek, he became the source of eternal salvation to all who believingly obey him.

Re-Crucifying Jesus

11-14I have a lot more to say about this, but it is hard to get it across to you since you've picked up this bad habit of not listening. By this time you ought to be teachers yourselves, yet here I find you need someone to sit down with you and go over the basics on God again, starting from square one—baby's milk, when you should have been on solid food long ago! Milk is for beginners, inexperienced in God's ways; solid food is for the mature, who have some practice in telling right from wrong.   [3]

Hebrews

Chapter Six

1-3So come on, let's leave the preschool finger painting exercises on Christ and get on with the grand work of art. Grow up in Christ. The basic foundational truths are in place: turning your back on "salvation by self-help" and turning in trust toward God; baptismal instructions; laying on of hands; resurrection of the dead; eternal judgment. God helping us, we'll stay true to all that. But there's so much more. Let's get on with it!

4-8Once people have seen the light, gotten a taste of heaven and been part of the work of the Holy Spirit, once they've personally experienced the sheer goodness of God's Word and the powers breaking in on us—if then they turn their backs on it, washing their hands of the whole thing, well, they can't start over as if nothing happened. That's impossible. Why, they've re-crucified Jesus! They've repudiated him in public! Parched ground that soaks up the rain and then produces an abundance of carrots and corn for its gardener gets God's "Well done!" But if it produces weeds and thistles, it's more likely to get cussed out. Fields like that are burned, not harvested.

9-12I'm sure that won't happen to you, friends. I have better things in mind for you—salvation things! God doesn't miss anything. He knows perfectly well all the love you've shown him by helping needy Christians, and that you keep at it. And now I want each of you to extend that same intensity toward a full-bodied hope, and keep at it till the finish. Don't drag your feet. Be like those who stay the course with committed faith and then get everything promised to them.

The Walk – S.B. Stone & Rock Solid Publishing, LLC
©2018

God Gave His Word

13-18When God made his promise to Abraham, he backed it to the hilt, putting his own reputation on the line. He said, "I promise that I'll bless you with everything I have—bless and bless and bless!" Abraham stuck it out and got everything that had been promised to him. When people make promises, they guarantee them by appeal to some authority above them so that if there is any question that they'll make good on the promise, the authority will back them up. When God wanted to guarantee his promises, he gave his word, a rock-solid guarantee— God *can't* break his word. And because his word cannot change, the promise is likewise unchangeable.

18-20We who have run for our very lives to God have every reason to grab the promised hope with both hands and never let go. It's an unbreakable spiritual lifeline, reaching past all appearances right to the very presence of God where Jesus, running on ahead of us, has taken up his permanent post as high priest for us, in the order of Melchizedek. [3]

Hebrews

Chapter Seven

Melchizedek, Priest of God

1-3Melchizedek was king of Salem and priest of the Highest God. He met Abraham, who was returning from "the royal massacre," and gave him his blessing. Abraham in turn gave him a tenth of the spoils. "Melchizedek" means "King of Righteousness." "Salem" means "Peace." So, he is also "King of Peace." Melchizedek towers out of the past—without record of family ties, no account of beginning or end. In this way he is like the Son of God, one huge priestly presence dominating the landscape always.

4-7You realize just how great Melchizedek is when you see that Father Abraham gave him a tenth of the captured treasure. Priests descended from Levi are commanded by law to collect tithes from the people, even though they are all more or less equals, priests and people, having a common father in Abraham. But this man, a complete outsider, collected tithes from Abraham and blessed him, the one to whom the promises had been given. In acts of blessing, the lesser is blessed by the greater.

8-10Or look at it this way: We pay our tithes to priests who die, but Abraham paid tithes to a priest who, the Scripture says, "lives." Ultimately you could even say that since Levi descended from Abraham, who paid tithes to Melchizedek, when we pay tithes to the priestly tribe of Levi they end up with Melchizedek.

A Permanent Priesthood

11-14If the priesthood of Levi and Aaron, which provided the framework for the giving of the law, could really make people perfect, there wouldn't have been need for a new priesthood like that of Melchizedek. But since it didn't get the job done, there was a change of priesthood, which brought with it a radical new kind of law. There is no way of understanding this in terms of the old Levitical priesthood, which is why there is nothing in Jesus' family tree connecting him with that priestly line.

15-19But the Melchizedek story provides a perfect analogy: Jesus, a priest like Melchizedek, not by genealogical descent but by the sheer force of resurrection life—he lives!—"priest forever in the royal order of Melchizedek." The former way of doing things, a system of commandments that never worked out the way it was supposed to, was set aside; the law brought nothing to maturity. Another way—Jesus!—a way that *does* work, that brings us right into the presence of God, is put in its place.

20-22The old priesthood of Aaron perpetuated itself automatically, father to son, without explicit confirmation by God. But then God intervened and called this new, permanent priesthood into being with an added promise: God gave his word; he won't take it back: "You're the permanent priest."

This makes Jesus the guarantee of a far better way between us and God—one that really works! A new covenant.

23-25Earlier there were a lot of priests, for they died and had to be replaced. But Jesus' priesthood is permanent. He's there from now to eternity to save everyone who comes to God through him, always on the job to speak up for them.

26-28So now we have a high priest who perfectly fits our needs: completely holy, uncompromised by sin, with authority extending as high as God's presence in heaven itself. Unlike the other high priests, he doesn't have to offer sacrifices for his own sins every day before he can get around to us and our sins. He's done it, once and for all: offered up *himself* as the sacrifice. The law appoints as high priests men who are never able to get the job done right. But this intervening command of God, which came later, appoints the Son, who is absolutely, eternally perfect.   [3]

Hebrews

Chapter Eight

A New Plan with Israel

1-2In essence, we have just such a high priest: authoritative right alongside God, conducting worship in the one true sanctuary built by God.

3-5The assigned task of a high priest is to offer both gifts and sacrifices, and it's no different with the priesthood of Jesus. If he were limited to earth, he wouldn't even be a priest. We wouldn't need him since there are plenty of priests who offer the gifts designated in the law. These priests provide only a hint of what goes on in the true sanctuary of heaven, which Moses caught a glimpse of as he was about to set up the tent-shrine. It was then that God said, "Be careful to do it exactly as you saw it on the Mountain."

6-13But Jesus' priestly work far surpasses what these other priests do, since he's working from a far better plan. If the first plan—the old covenant—had worked out, a second wouldn't have been needed. But we know the first was found wanting, because God said, Heads up! The days are coming when I'll set up a new plan for dealing with Israel and Judah. I'll throw out the old plan I set up with their ancestors when I led them by the hand out of Egypt. They didn't keep their part of the bargain, so I looked away and let it go. This new plan I'm making with Israel isn't going to be written on paper, isn't going to be chiseled in stone; This time I'm writing out the plan *in* them, carving it on the lining of their hearts. I'll be their God, they'll be my people. They won't go to school to learn about me, or buy a book called *God in Five Easy Lessons*. They'll all get to know me firsthand, the little and the big, the small and the great. They'll get to know me by being kindly forgiven, with the slate of their sins forever wiped clean. By coming up with a new plan, a new covenant between God and his people, God put the old plan on the shelf. And there it stays, gathering dust.   [3]

Hebrews

Chapter Nine

A Visible Parable

1-5That first plan contained directions for worship, and a specially designed place of worship. A large outer tent was set up. The lampstand, the table, and "the bread of presence" were placed in it. This was called "the Holy Place." Then a curtain was stretched, and behind it a smaller, inside tent set up. This was called "the Holy of Holies." In it were placed the gold incense altar and the gold-covered ark of the covenant containing the gold urn of manna, Aaron's rod that budded, the covenant tablets, and the angel-wing-shadowed mercy seat. But we don't have time to comment on these now.

6-10After this was set up, the priests went about their duties in the large tent. Only the high priest entered the smaller, inside tent, and then only once a year, offering a blood sacrifice for his own sins and the people's accumulated sins. This was the Holy Spirit's way of showing with a visible parable that as long as the large tent stands, people can't just walk in on God. Under this system, the gifts and sacrifices can't really get to the heart of the matter, can't assuage the conscience of the people, but are limited to matters of ritual and behavior. It's essentially a temporary arrangement until a complete overhaul could be made.

Pointing to the Realities of Heaven

11-15But when the Messiah arrived, high priest of the superior things of this new covenant, he bypassed the old tent and its trappings in this created world and went straight into heaven's "tent"—the true Holy Place—once and for all. He also bypassed the sacrifices consisting of goat and calf blood, instead using his own blood as the price to set us free once and for all. If that animal blood and the other rituals of purification were effective in cleaning up certain matters of our religion and behavior, think how much more the blood of Christ cleans up our whole lives, inside and out. Through the Spirit, Christ offered himself as an unblemished sacrifice, freeing us from all those dead-end efforts to make ourselves respectable, so that we can live all out for God.

16-17Like a will that takes effect when someone dies, the new covenant was put into action at Jesus' death. His death marked the transition from the old plan to the new one, canceling the old obligations and accompanying sins, and summoning the heirs to receive the eternal inheritance that was promised them. He brought together God and his people in this new way.

18-22Even the first plan required a death to set it in motion. After Moses had read out all the terms of the plan of the law—God's "will"—he took the blood of sacrificed animals and, in a solemn ritual, sprinkled the document and the people who were its beneficiaries. And then he attested its validity with the words, "This is the blood of the covenant commanded by God." He did the same thing with the place of worship and its furniture. Moses said to the people, "This is the blood of the covenant God has established with you." Practically everything in a will hinges on a death. That's why blood, the evidence of death, is used so much in our tradition, especially regarding forgiveness of sins.

23-26That accounts for the prominence of blood and death in all these secondary practices that point to the realities of heaven. It also accounts for why, when the real thing takes place, these animal sacrifices aren't needed anymore, having served their purpose. For Christ didn't enter the earthly version of the Holy Place; he entered the Place Itself, and offered himself to God as the sacrifice for our sins. He doesn't do this every year as the high priests did under the old plan with blood that was not their own; if that had been the case, he would have to sacrifice himself repeatedly throughout the course of history. But instead he sacrificed himself once and for all, summing up all the other sacrifices in this sacrifice of himself, the final solution of sin.

27-28Everyone has to die once, then face the consequences. Christ's death was also a one-time event, but it was a sacrifice that took care of sins forever. And so, when he next appears, the outcome for those eager to greet him is, precisely, *salvation*. [3]

Hebrews

Chapter Ten

The Sacrifice of Jesus

1-10The old plan was only a hint of the good things in the new plan. Since that old "law plan" wasn't complete in itself, it couldn't complete those who followed it. No matter how many sacrifices were offered year after year, they never added up to a complete solution. If they had, the worshipers would have gone merrily on their way, no longer dragged down by their sins. But instead of removing awareness of sin, when those animal sacrifices were repeated over and over they actually heightened awareness and guilt. The plain fact is that bull and goat blood can't get rid of sin. That is what is meant by this prophecy, put in the mouth of Christ:

You don't want sacrifices and offerings year after year; you've prepared a body for me for a sacrifice. It's not fragrance and smoke from the altar that whet your appetite. So I said, "I'm here to do it your way, O God, the way it's described in your Book."

When he said, "You don't want sacrifices and offerings," he was referring to practices according to the old plan. When he added, "I'm here to do it your way," he set aside the first in order to enact the new plan—*God's* way—by which we are made fit for God by the once-for-all sacrifice of Jesus.

11-18Every priest goes to work at the altar each day, offers the same old sacrifices year in, year out, and never makes a dent in the sin problem. As a priest, Christ made a single sacrifice for sins, and that was it! Then he sat down right beside God and waited for his enemies to cave in. It was a perfect sacrifice by a perfect person to perfect some very imperfect people. By that single offering, he did everything that needed to be done for everyone who takes part in the purifying process. The Holy Spirit confirms this: This new plan I'm making with Israel isn't going to be written on paper, isn't going to be chiseled in stone; This time "I'm writing out the plan *in* them, carving it on the lining of their hearts." He concludes, I'll forever wipe the slate clean of their sins. Once sins are taken care of for good, there's no longer any need to offer sacrifices for them.

Don't Throw It All Away

19-21So, friends, we can now—without hesitation—walk right up to God, into "the Holy Place." Jesus has cleared the way by the blood of his sacrifice, acting as our priest before God. The "curtain" into God's presence is his body.

22-25So let's *do* it—full of belief, confident that we're presentable inside and out. Let's keep a firm grip on the promises that keep us going. He always keeps his word. Let's see how inventive we can be in encouraging love and helping out, not avoiding worshiping together as some do but spurring each other on, especially as we see the big Day approaching.

26-31If we give up and turn our backs on all we've learned, all we've been given, all the truth we now know, we repudiate Christ's sacrifice and are left on our own to face the Judgment—and a mighty fierce judgment it will be! If the penalty for breaking the law of Moses is physical death, what do you think will happen if you turn on God's Son, spit on the sacrifice that made you whole, and insult this most gracious Spirit? This is no light matter. God has warned us that he'll hold us to account and make us pay. He was quite explicit: "Vengeance is mine, and I won't overlook a thing" and "God will judge his people." Nobody's getting by with anything, believe me.

32-39Remember those early days after you first saw the light? Those were the hard times! Kicked around in public, targets of every kind of abuse—some days it was you, other days your friends. If some friends went to prison, you stuck by them. If some enemies broke in and seized your goods, you let them go with a smile, knowing they couldn't touch your real treasure. Nothing they did bothered you, nothing set you back. So don't throw it all away now. You were sure of yourselves then. It's *still* a sure thing! But you need to stick it out, staying with God's plan so you'll be there for the promised completion. It won't be long now, he's on the way; he'll show up most any minute. But anyone who is right with me thrives on loyal trust; if he cuts and runs, I won't be very happy. But we're not quitters who lose out. Oh, no! We'll stay with it and survive, trusting all the way.   [3]

Hebrews

Chapter Eleven

Faith in What We Don't See

1-2The fundamental fact of existence is that this trust in God, this faith, is the firm foundation under everything that makes life worth living. It's our handle on what we can't see. The act of faith is what distinguished our ancestors, set them above the crowd.

3By faith, we see the world called into existence by God's word, what we see created by what we don't see.

4By an act of faith, Abel brought a better sacrifice to God than Cain. It was what he *believed*, not what he *brought*, that made the difference. That's what God noticed and approved as righteous. After all these centuries, that belief continues to catch our notice.

5-6By an act of faith, Enoch skipped death completely. "They looked all over and couldn't find him because God had taken him." We know on the basis of reliable testimony that before he was taken "he pleased God." It's impossible to please God apart from faith. And why? Because anyone who wants to approach God must believe both that he exists *and* that he cares enough to respond to those who seek him.

7By faith, Noah built a ship in the middle of dry land. He was warned about something he couldn't see, and acted on what he was told. The result? His family was saved. His act of faith drew a sharp line between the evil of the unbelieving world and the rightness of the believing world. As a result, Noah became intimate with God.

8-10By an act of faith, Abraham said yes to God's call to travel to an unknown place that would become his home. When he left he had no idea where he was going. By an act of faith he lived in the country promised him, lived as a stranger camping in tents. Isaac and Jacob did the same, living under the same promise. Abraham did it by keeping his eye on an unseen city with real, eternal foundations—the City designed and built by God.

11-12By faith, barren Sarah was able to become pregnant, old woman as she was at the time, because she believed the One who made a promise would do what he said. That's how it happened that from one man's dead and shriveled loins there are now people numbering into the millions.

13-16Each one of these people of faith died not yet having in hand what was promised, but still believing. How did they do it? They saw it way off in the distance, waved their greeting, and accepted the fact that they were transients in this world. People who live this way make it plain that they are looking for their true home. If they were homesick for the old country, they could have gone back any time they wanted. But they were after a far better country than that—*heaven* country. You can see why God is so proud of them, and has a City waiting for them.

17-19By faith, Abraham, at the time of testing, offered Isaac back to God. Acting in faith, he was as ready to return the promised son, his

The Walk – S.B. Stone & Rock Solid Publishing, LLC
©2018

only son, as he had been to receive him—and this after he had already been told, "Your descendants shall come from Isaac." Abraham figured that if God wanted to, he could raise the dead. In a sense, that's what happened when he received Isaac back, alive from off the altar.

20By an act of faith, Isaac reached into the future as he blessed Jacob and Esau.

21By an act of faith, Jacob on his deathbed blessed each of Joseph's sons in turn, blessing them with God's blessing, not his own—as he bowed worshipfully upon his staff.

22By an act of faith, Joseph, while dying, prophesied the exodus of Israel, and made arrangements for his own burial.

23By an act of faith, Moses' parents hid him away for three months after his birth. They saw the child's beauty, and they braved the king's decree.

24-28By faith, Moses, when grown, refused the privileges of the Egyptian royal house. He chose a hard life with God's people rather than an opportunistic soft life of sin with the oppressors. He valued suffering in the Messiah's camp far greater than Egyptian wealth because he was looking ahead, anticipating the payoff. By an act of faith, he turned his heel on Egypt, indifferent to the king's blind rage. He had his eye on the One no eye can see, and kept right on going. By an act of faith, he kept the Passover Feast and sprinkled Passover blood on each house so that the destroyer of the firstborn wouldn't touch them.

29By an act of faith, Israel walked through the Red Sea on dry ground. The Egyptians tried it and drowned.

30By faith, the Israelites marched around the walls of Jericho for seven days, and the walls fell flat.

31By an act of faith, Rahab, the Jericho harlot, welcomed the spies and escaped the destruction that came on those who refused to trust God.

32-38I could go on and on, but I've run out of time. There are so many more—Gideon, Barak, Samson, Jephthah, David, Samuel, the prophets. . . . Through acts of faith, they toppled kingdoms, made justice work, took the promises for themselves. They were protected from lions, fires, and sword thrusts, turned disadvantage to advantage, won battles, routed alien armies. Women received their loved ones back from the dead. There were those who, under torture, refused to give in and go free, preferring something better: resurrection. Others braved abuse and whips, and, yes, chains and dungeons. We have stories of those who were stoned, sawed in two, murdered in cold blood; stories of vagrants wandering the earth in animal skins, homeless, friendless, powerless— the world didn't deserve them!—making their way as best they could on the cruel edges of the world.

39-40Not one of these people, even though their lives of faith were exemplary, got their hands on what was promised. God had a better plan for us: that their faith and our faith would come together to make one completed whole, their lives of faith not complete apart from ours.   [3]

Hebrews Chapter Twelve

Discipline in a Long-Distance Race

1-3Do you see what this means—all these pioneers who blazed the way, all these veterans cheering us on? It means we'd better get on with it. Strip down, start running—and never quit! No extra spiritual fat, no parasitic sins. Keep your eyes on *Jesus*, who both began and finished this race we're in. Study how he did it. Because he never lost sight of where he was headed—that exhilarating finish in and with God—he could put up with anything along the way: Cross, shame, whatever. And now he's *there*, in the place of honor, right alongside God. When you find yourselves flagging in your faith, go over that story again, item by item, that long litany of hostility he plowed through. *That* will shoot adrenaline into your souls!

4-11In this all-out match against sin, others have suffered far worse than you, to say nothing of what Jesus went through—all that bloodshed! So don't feel sorry for yourselves. Or have you forgotten how good parents treat children, and that God regards you as *his* children?

My dear child, don't shrug off God's discipline, but don't be crushed by it either. It's the child he loves that he disciplines; the child he embraces, he also corrects.

God is educating you; that's why you must never drop out. He's treating you as dear children. This trouble you're in isn't punishment; it's *training*, the normal experience of children. Only irresponsible parents leave children to fend for themselves. Would you prefer an irresponsible God? We respect our own parents for training and not spoiling us, so why not embrace God's training so we can truly *live*?

While we were children, our parents did what *seemed* best to them. But God is doing what *is* best for us, training us to live God's holy best. At the time, discipline isn't much fun. It always feels like it's going against the grain. Later, of course, it pays off handsomely, for it's the well-trained who find themselves mature in their relationship with God.

12-13So don't sit around on your hands! No more dragging your feet! Clear the path for long-distance runners so no one will trip and fall, so no one will step in a hole and sprain an ankle. Help each other out. And run for it!

14-17Work at getting along with each other and with God. Otherwise you'll never get so much as a glimpse of God. Make sure no one gets left out of God's generosity. Keep a sharp eye out for weeds of bitter discontent. A thistle or two gone to seed can ruin a whole garden in no time. Watch out for the Esau syndrome: trading away God's lifelong gift in order to satisfy a short-term appetite. You well know how Esau later regretted that impulsive act and wanted God's blessing—but by then it was too late, tears or no tears.

An Unshakable Kingdom

18-21Unlike your ancestors, you didn't come to Mount Sinai—all that volcanic blaze and earthshaking rumble—to hear God speak. The earsplitting words and soul-shaking message terrified them and they begged him to stop. When they heard the words—"If an animal touches the Mountain, it's as good as dead"—they were afraid to move. Even Moses was terrified.

22-24No, that's not *your* experience at all. You've come to Mount Zion, the city where the living God resides. The invisible Jerusalem is populated by throngs of festive angels and Christian citizens. It is the city where God is Judge, with judgments that make us just. You've come to Jesus, who presents us with a new covenant, a fresh charter from God. He is the Mediator of this covenant. The murder of Jesus, unlike Abel's—a homicide that cried out for vengeance—became a proclamation of grace.

25-27So don't turn a deaf ear to these gracious words. If those who ignored earthly warnings didn't get away with it, what will happen to us if we turn our backs on heavenly warnings? His voice that time shook the earth to its foundations; this time—he's told us this quite plainly—he'll also rock the heavens: "One last shaking, from top to bottom, stem

The Walk – S.B. Stone & Rock Solid Publishing, LLC
©2018

to stern." The phrase "one last shaking" means a thorough housecleaning, getting rid of all the historical and religious junk so that the unshakable essentials stand clear and uncluttered.

28-29Do you see what we've got? An unshakable kingdom! And do you see how thankful we must be? Not only thankful, but brimming with worship, deeply reverent before God. For God is not an indifferent bystander. He's actively cleaning house, torching all that needs to burn, and he won't quit until it's all cleansed. God himself is Fire!   [3]

Hebrews

Chapter Thirteen

Jesus Doesn't Change

1-4Stay on good terms with each other, held together by love. Be ready with a meal or a bed when it's needed. Why, some have extended hospitality to angels without ever knowing it! Regard prisoners as if you were in prison with them. Look on victims of abuse as if what happened to them had happened to you. Honor marriage, and guard the sacredness of sexual intimacy between wife and husband. God draws a firm line against casual and illicit sex.

5-6Don't be obsessed with getting more material things. Be relaxed with what you have. Since God assured us, "I'll never let you down, never walk off and leave you," we can boldly quote, God is there, ready to help; I'm fearless no matter what. Who or what can get to me?

7-8Appreciate your pastoral leaders who gave you the Word of God. Take a good look at the way they live, and let their faithfulness instruct you, as well as their truthfulness. There should be a consistency that runs through us all. For Jesus doesn't change—yesterday, today, tomorrow, he's always totally himself.

9Don't be lured away from him by the latest speculations about him. The grace of Christ is the only good ground for life. Products named after Christ don't seem to do much for those who buy them.

10-12The altar from which God gives us the gift of himself is not for exploitation by insiders who grab and loot. In the old system, the animals are killed and the bodies disposed of outside the camp. The blood is then brought inside to the altar as a sacrifice for sin. It's the same with Jesus. He was crucified outside the city gates—*that* is where he poured out the sacrificial blood that was brought to God's altar to cleanse his people.

13-15So let's go outside, where Jesus is, where the action is—not trying to be privileged insiders, but taking our share in the abuse of Jesus. This "insider world" is not our home. We have our eyes peeled for the City about to come. Let's take our place outside with Jesus, no longer pouring out the sacrificial blood of animals but pouring out sacrificial praises from our lips to God in Jesus' name.

16Make sure you don't take things for granted and go slack in working for the common good; share what you have with others. God takes particular pleasure in acts of worship—a different kind of "sacrifice"—that take place in kitchen and workplace and on the streets.

17Be responsive to your pastoral leaders. Listen to their counsel. They are alert to the condition of your lives and work under the strict supervision of God. Contribute to the joy of their leadership, not its drudgery. Why would you want to make things harder for them?

18-21Pray for us. We have no doubts about what we're doing or why, but it's hard going and we need your prayers. All we care about is living well before God. Pray that we may be together soon.

May God, who puts all things together, makes all things whole, Who made a lasting mark through the sacrifice of Jesus, the sacrifice of blood that sealed the eternal covenant, Who led Jesus, our Great Shepherd, up and alive from the dead, Now put you together, provide you with everything you need to please him, Make us into what gives him most pleasure, by means of the sacrifice of Jesus, the Messiah. All glory to Jesus forever and always! Oh, yes, yes, yes.

22-23Friends, please take what I've written most seriously. I've kept this as brief as possible; I haven't piled on a lot of extras. You'll be glad to know that Timothy has been let out of prison. If he leaves soon, I'll come with him and get to see you myself.

24Say hello to your pastoral leaders and all the congregations. Everyone here in Italy wants to be remembered to you.

25Grace be with you, every one.   [3]

The Book of Revelation

Chapter One

1-2A revealing of Jesus, the Messiah. God gave it to make plain to his servants what is about to happen. He published and delivered it by Angel to his servant John. And John told everything he saw: God's Word—the witness of Jesus Christ!

3How blessed the reader! How blessed the hearers and keepers of these oracle words, all the words written in this book! Time is just about up. His Eyes Pouring Fire-Blaze

4-7I, John, am writing this to the seven churches in Asia province: All the best to you
from The God Who Is, The God Who Was, and The God About
to Arrive, and from the Seven Spirits assembled before his throne, and
from Jesus Christ—Loyal Witness, Firstborn from the dead, Ruler of all earthly kings.

Glory and strength to Christ, who loves us, who blood-washed our sins from our lives, Who made us a Kingdom, Priests for his Father, forever—and yes, he's on his way! Riding the clouds, he'll be seen by every eye, those who mocked and killed him will see him, People from all nations and all times will tear their clothes in lament.

Oh, Yes.

8The Master declares, "I'm A to Z.
I'm The God Who Is, The God Who Was, and The God About to Arrive.
I'm the Sovereign-Strong."

9-17I, John, with you all the way in the trial and the Kingdom and the passion of patience in Jesus, was on the island called Patmos because of God's Word, the witness of Jesus. It was Sunday and I was in the Spirit, praying. I heard a loud voice behind me, trumpet-clear and piercing: "Write what you see into a book. Send it to the seven churches: to Ephesus, Smyrna, Pergamum, Thyatira, Sardis, Philadelphia, Laodicea," I turned and saw the voice.

I saw a gold menorah with seven branches, And in the center, the Son of Man, in a robe and gold breastplate, hair a blizzard of white, Eyes pouring fire-blaze, oth feet furnace-fired bronze, His voice a cataract,

The Walk – S.B. Stone & Rock Solid Publishing, LLC
©2018

right hand holding the Seven Stars, His mouth a sharp-biting sword, his face a perigee sun. I saw this and fainted dead at his feet. His right hand pulled me upright, his voice reassured me:

17-20"Don't fear: I am First, I am Last, I'm Alive. I died, but I came to life, and my life is now forever. See these keys in my hand? They open and lock Death's doors, they open and lock Hell's gates. Now write down everything you see: things that are, things about to be. The Seven Stars you saw in my right hand and the seven-branched gold menorah—do you want to know what's behind them? The Seven Stars are the Angels of the seven churches; the menorah's seven branches are the seven churches."   [3]

Revelation

Chapter Two

(not included due to copyright restrictions)

Revelation

Chapter Three

To Sardis

1Write this to Sardis, to the Angel of the church. The One holding the Seven Spirits of God in one hand, a firm grip on the Seven Stars with the other, speaks: "I see right through your work. You have a reputation for vigor and zest, but you're dead, stone-dead.

2-3"Up on your feet! Take a deep breath! Maybe there's life in you yet. But I wouldn't know it by looking at your busywork; nothing of *God's* work has been completed. Your condition is desperate. Think of the gift you once had in your hands, the Message you heard with your ears—grasp it again and turn back to God.

"If you pull the covers back over your head and sleep on, oblivious to God, I'll return when you least expect it, break into your life like a thief in the night.

4"You still have a few followers of Jesus in Sardis who haven't ruined themselves wallowing in the muck of the world's ways. They'll walk with me on parade! They've proved their worth!

5"Conquerors will march in the victory parade, their names indelible in the Book of Life. I'll lead them up and present them by name to my Father and his Angels.

6"Are your ears awake? Listen. Listen to the Wind Words, the Spirit blowing through the churches."

To Philadelphia

7Write this to Philadelphia, to the Angel of the church. The Holy, the True—David's key in his hand, opening doors no one can lock, locking doors no one can open—speaks:

8"I see what you've done. Now see what *I've* done. I've opened a door before you that no one can slam shut. You don't have much strength, I know that; you used what you had to keep my Word. You didn't deny me when times were rough.

9"And watch as I take those who call themselves true believers but are nothing of the kind, pretenders whose true membership is in the club of Satan—watch as I strip off their pretensions and they're forced to acknowledge it's you that I've loved.

10"Because you kept my Word in passionate patience, I'll keep you safe in the time of testing that will be here soon, and all over the earth, every man, woman, and child put to the test.

11"I'm on my way; I'll be there soon. Keep a tight grip on what you have so no one distracts you and steals your crown.

12"I'll make each conqueror a pillar in the sanctuary of my God, a permanent position of honor. Then I'll write names on you, the pillars: the Name of my God, the Name of God's City—the new Jerusalem coming down out of Heaven—and my new Name.

13"Are your ears awake? Listen. Listen to the Wind Words, the Spirit blowing through the churches."

To Laodicea

14Write to Laodicea, to the Angel of the church. God's Yes, the Faithful and Accurate Witness, the First of God's creation, says:

15-17"I know you inside and out, and find little to my liking. You're not cold, you're not hot—far better to be either cold or hot! You're stale. You're stagnant. You make me want to vomit. You brag, 'I'm rich, I've got it made, I need nothing from anyone,' oblivious that in fact you're a pitiful, blind beggar, threadbare and homeless.

18"Here's what I want you to do: Buy your gold from me, gold that's been through the refiner's fire. Then you'll be rich. Buy your clothes from me, clothes designed in Heaven. You've gone around half-naked long enough. And buy medicine for your eyes from me so you can see, *really* see.

19"The people I love, I call to account—prod and correct and guide so that they'll live at their best. Up on your feet, then! About face! Run after God!

20-21"Look at me. I stand at the door. I knock. If you hear me call and open the door, I'll come right in and sit down to supper with you. Conquerors will sit alongside me at the head table, just as I, having conquered, took the place of honor at the side of my Father. That's my gift to the conquerors!

22"Are your ears awake

Revelation

Chapter Four

A Door into Heaven

1Then I looked, and, oh!—a door open into Heaven. The trumpet-voice, the first voice in my vision, called out, "Ascend and enter. I'll show you what happens next."

2-6I was caught up at once in deep worship and, oh!—a Throne set in Heaven with One Seated on the Throne, suffused in gem hues of amber and flame with a nimbus of emerald. Twenty-four thrones circled the Throne, with Twenty-four Elders seated, white-robed, gold-crowned. Lightning flash and thunder crash pulsed from the Throne. Seven fire-blazing torches fronted the Throne (these are the Sevenfold Spirit of God). Before the Throne it was like a clear crystal sea.

6-8Prowling around the Throne were Four Animals, all eyes. Eyes to look ahead, eyes to look behind. The first Animal like a lion, the second like an ox, the third with a human face, the fourth like an eagle in flight. The Four Animals were winged, each with six wings. They were all eyes, seeing around and within. And they chanted night and day, never taking a break:

Holy, holy, holy Is God our Master, Sovereign-Strong,
The Was, The Is, The Coming.

9-11Every time the Animals gave glory and honor and thanks to the One Seated on the Throne—the age-after-age Living One—the Twenty-four Elders would fall prostrate before the One Seated on the Throne. They worshiped the age-after-age Living One. They threw their crowns at the foot of the Throne, chanting, Worthy, O Master! Yes, our God! Take the glory! the honor! the power! You created it all; It was created because you wanted it.   [3]

Revelation

Chapter Five

The Lion Is a Lamb

1-2I saw a scroll in the right hand of the One Seated on the Throne. It was written on both sides, fastened with seven seals. I also saw a powerful Angel, calling out in a voice like thunder, "Is there anyone who can open the scroll, who can break its seals?"

3There was no one—no one in Heaven, no one on earth, no one from the underworld—able to break open the scroll and read it.

4-5I wept and wept and wept that no one was found able to open the scroll, able to read it. One of the Elders said, "Don't weep. Look—the Lion from Tribe Judah, the Root of David's Tree, has conquered. He can open the scroll, can rip through the seven seals."

6-10So I looked, and there, surrounded by Throne, Animals, and Elders, was a Lamb, slaughtered but standing tall. Seven horns he had, and seven eyes, the Seven Spirits of God sent into all the earth. He came to the One Seated on the Throne and took the scroll from his right hand. The moment he took the scroll, the Four Animals and Twenty-four Elders fell down and worshiped the Lamb. Each had a harp and each had a bowl, a gold bowl filled with incense, the prayers of God's holy people. And they sang a new song:

Worthy! Take the scroll, open its seals. Slain! Paying in blood, you bought men and women, Bought them back from all over the earth, Bought them back for God. Then you made them a Kingdom, Priests for our God, Priest-kings to rule over the earth.

11-14I looked again. I heard a company of Angels around the Throne, the Animals, and the Elders—ten thousand times ten thousand their number, thousand after thousand after thousand in full song:

The slain Lamb is worthy! Take the power, the wealth, the wisdom, the strength! Take the honor, the glory, the blessing! Then I heard every creature in Heaven and earth, in underworld and sea, join in, all voices in all places, singing:

To the One on the Throne! To the Lamb! The blessing, the honor, the glory, the strength, For age after age after age. The Four Animals called out, "Oh, Yes!" The Elders fell to their knees and worshiped. [3]

Revelation

Chapter Six

Unsealing the Scroll

1-2I watched while the Lamb ripped off the first of the seven seals. I heard one of the Animals roar, "Come out!" I looked—I saw a white horse. Its rider carried a bow and was given a victory garland. He rode off victorious, conquering right and left.

3-4When the Lamb ripped off the second seal, I heard the second Animal cry, "Come out!" Another horse appeared, this one red. Its rider was off to take peace from the earth, setting people at each other's throats, killing one another. He was given a huge sword.

5-6When he ripped off the third seal, I heard the third Animal cry, "Come out!" I looked. A black horse this time. Its rider carried a set of scales in his hand. I heard a message (it seemed to issue from the Four Animals): "A quart of wheat for a day's wages, or three quarts of barley, but all the oil and wine you want."

7-8When he ripped off the fourth seal, I heard the fourth Animal cry, "Come out!" I looked. A colorless horse, sickly pale. Its rider was Death, and Hell was close on its heels. They were given power to destroy a fourth of the earth by war, famine, disease, and wild beasts.

9-11When he ripped off the fifth seal, I saw the souls of those killed because they had held firm in their witness to the Word of God. They were gathered under the Altar, and cried out in loud prayers, "How long, Strong God, Holy and True? How long before you step in and avenge our murders?" Then each martyr was given a white robe and told to sit back and wait until the full number of martyrs was filled from among their servant companions and friends in the faith.

12-17I watched while he ripped off the sixth seal: a bone-jarring earthquake, sun turned black as ink, moon all bloody, stars falling out of the sky like figs shaken from a tree in a high wind, sky snapped shut like a book, islands and mountains sliding this way and that. And then pandemonium, everyone and his dog running for cover—kings, princes, generals, rich and strong, along with every commoner, slave or free. They hid in mountain caves and rocky dens, calling out to mountains and rocks, "Refuge! Hide us from the One Seated on the Throne and the wrath of the Lamb! The great Day of their wrath has come—who can stand it?"   [3]

Revelation

Chapter Seven

The Servants of God

1Immediately I saw Four Angels standing at the four corners of earth, standing steady with a firm grip on the four winds so no wind would blow on earth or sea, not even rustle a tree.

2-3Then I saw another Angel rising from where the sun rose, carrying the seal of the Living God. He thundered to the Four Angels assigned the task of hurting earth and sea, "Don't hurt the earth! Don't hurt the sea! Don't so much as hurt a tree until I've sealed the servants of our God on their foreheads!"

4-8I heard the count of those who were sealed: 144,000! They were sealed out of every Tribe of Israel: 12,000 sealed from Judah, 12,000 from Reuben, 12,000 from Gad, 12,000 from Asher, 12,000 from Naphtali, 12,000 from Manasseh, 12,000 from Simeon, 12,000 from Levi, 12,000 from Issachar, 12,000 from Zebulun, 12,000 from Joseph, 12,000 sealed from Benjamin.

9-12I looked again. I saw a huge crowd, too huge to count. Everyone was there—all nations and tribes, all races and languages. And they were *standing*, dressed in white robes and waving palm branches, standing before the Throne and the Lamb and heartily singing:

Salvation to our God on his Throne! Salvation to the Lamb! All who were standing around the Throne—Angels, Elders, Animals—fell on their faces before the Throne and worshiped God, singing: Oh, Yes! The blessing and glory and wisdom and thanksgiving, The honor and power and strength, To our God forever and ever and ever! Oh, Yes!

13-14Just then one of the Elders addressed me: "Who are these dressed in white robes, and where did they come from?" Taken aback, I said, "O Sir, I have no idea—but you must know."

14-17Then he told me, "These are those who come from the great tribulation, and they've washed their robes, scrubbed them clean in the blood of the Lamb. That's why they're standing before God's Throne. They serve him day and night in his Temple. The One on the Throne will pitch his tent there for them: no more hunger, no more thirst, no more scorching heat. The Lamb on the Throne will shepherd them, will lead them to spring waters of Life. And God will wipe every last tear from their eyes."   [3]

Revelation

Chapter Eight

1When the Lamb ripped off the seventh seal, Heaven fell quiet—complete silence for about half an hour.

Blowing the Trumpets

2-4I saw the Seven Angels who are always in readiness before God handed seven trumpets. Then another Angel, carrying a gold censer, came and stood at the Altar. He was given a great quantity of incense so that he could offer up the prayers of all the holy people of God on the Golden Altar before the Throne. Smoke billowed up from the incense-laced prayers of the holy ones, rose before God from the hand of the Angel.

5Then the Angel filled the censer with fire from the Altar and heaved it to earth. It set off thunders, voices, lightnings, and an earthquake.

6-7The Seven Angels with the trumpets got ready to blow them. At the first trumpet blast, hail and fire mixed with blood were dumped on earth. A third of the earth was scorched, a third of the trees, and every blade of green grass—burned to a crisp.

8-9The second Angel trumpeted. Something like a huge mountain blazing with fire was flung into the sea. A third of the sea turned to blood, a third of the living sea creatures died, and a third of the ships sank.

10-11The third Angel trumpeted. A huge Star, blazing like a torch, fell from Heaven, wiping out a third of the rivers and a third of the springs. The Star's name was Wormwood. A third of the water turned bitter, and many people died from the poisoned water.

12The fourth Angel trumpeted. A third of the sun, a third of the moon, and a third of the stars were hit, blacked out by a third, both day and night in one-third blackout.

13I looked hard; I heard a lone eagle, flying through Middle-Heaven, crying out ominously, "Doom! Doom! Doom to everyone left on earth! There are three more Angels about to blow their trumpets. Doom is on its way!" [3]

Revelation

Chapter Nine

1-2The fifth Angel trumpeted. I saw a Star plummet from Heaven to earth. The Star was handed a key to the Well of the Abyss. He unlocked the Well of the Abyss—smoke poured out of the Well, billows and billows of smoke, sun and air in blackout from smoke pouring out of the Well.

3-6Then out of the smoke crawled locusts with the venom of scorpions. They were given their orders: "Don't hurt the grass, don't hurt anything green, don't hurt a single tree—only men and women, and then only those who lack the seal of God on their foreheads." They were ordered to torture but not kill, torture them for five months, the pain like a scorpion sting. When this happens, people are going to prefer death to torture, look for ways to kill themselves. But they won't find a way— death will have gone into hiding.

7-11The locusts looked like horses ready for war. They had gold crowns, human faces, women's hair, the teeth of lions, and iron breastplates. The sound of their wings was the sound of horse-drawn chariots charging into battle. Their tails were equipped with stings, like scorpion tails. With those tails they were ordered to torture the human race for five months. They had a king over them, the Angel of the Abyss. His name in Hebrew is *Abaddon*, in Greek, *Apollyon*— "Destroyer."

12The first doom is past. Two dooms yet to come.

13-14The sixth Angel trumpeted. I heard a voice speaking to the sixth Angel from the horns of the Golden Altar before God: "Let the Four Angels loose, the Angels confined at the great River Euphrates."

15-19The Four Angels were untied and let loose, Four Angels all prepared for the exact year, month, day, and even hour when they were to kill a third of the human race. The number of the army of horsemen was twice ten thousand times ten thousand. I heard the count and saw both horses and riders in my vision: fiery breastplates on the riders, lion heads on the horses breathing out fire and smoke and brimstone. With these three weapons—fire and smoke and brimstone—they killed a third of the human race. The horses killed with their mouths and tails; their serpent like tails also had heads that wreaked havoc.

20-21The remaining men and women who weren't killed by these weapons went on their merry way—didn't change their way of life, didn't quit worshiping demons, didn't quit centering their lives around lumps of gold and silver and brass, hunks of stone and wood that couldn't see or hear or move. There wasn't a sign of a change of heart. They plunged right on in their murderous, occult, promiscuous, and thieving ways.   [3]

Revelation

Chapter Ten

1-4I saw another powerful Angel coming down out of Heaven wrapped in a cloud. There was a rainbow over his head, his face was sun-radiant, his legs pillars of fire. He had a small book open in his hand. He placed his right foot on the sea and his left foot on land, then called out thunderously, a lion roar. When he called out, the Seven Thunders called back. When the Seven Thunders spoke, I started to write it all down, but a voice out of Heaven stopped me, saying, "Seal with silence the Seven Thunders; don't write a word."

5-7Then the Angel I saw astride sea and land lifted his right hand to Heaven and swore by the One Living Forever and Ever, who created Heaven and everything in it, earth and everything in it, sea and everything in it, that time was up—that when the seventh Angel blew his trumpet, which he was about to do, the Mystery of God, all the plans he had revealed to his servants, the prophets, would be completed.

8-11The voice out of Heaven spoke to me again: "Go, take the book held open in the hand of the Angel astride sea and earth." I went up to the Angel and said, "Give me the little book." He said, "Take it, then eat it. It will taste sweet like honey, but turn sour in your stomach." I took the little book from the Angel's hand and it was sweet honey in my mouth, but when I swallowed, my stomach curdled. Then I was told, "You must go back and prophesy again over many peoples and nations and languages and kings."

Revelation

Chapter Eleven

The Two Witnesses

1-2I was given a stick for a measuring rod and told, "Get up and measure God's Temple and Altar and everyone worshiping in it. Exclude the outside court; don't measure it. It's been handed over to non-Jewish outsiders. They'll desecrate the Holy City for forty-two months.

3-6"Meanwhile, I'll provide my two Witnesses. Dressed in sackcloth, they'll prophesy for 1,260 days. These are the two Olive Trees, the two Lampstands, standing at attention before God on earth. If anyone tries to hurt them, a blast of fire from their mouths will incinerate them—burn them to a crisp just like that. They'll have power to seal the sky so that it doesn't rain for the time of their prophesying, power to turn rivers and springs to blood, power to hit earth with any and every disaster as often as they want.

7-10"When they've completed their witness, the Beast from the Abyss will emerge and fight them, conquer and kill them, leaving their corpses exposed on the street of the Great City spiritually called Sodom and Egypt, the same City where their Master was crucified. For three and a half days they'll be there—exposed, prevented from getting a decent burial, stared at by the curious from all over the world. Those people will cheer at the spectacle, shouting 'Good riddance!' and calling for a celebration, for these two prophets pricked the conscience of all the people on earth, made it impossible for them to enjoy their sins.

11"Then, after three and a half days, the Living Spirit of God will enter them—they're on their feet!—and all those gloating spectators will be scared to death."

12-13I heard a strong voice out of Heaven calling, "Come up here!" and up they went to Heaven, wrapped in a cloud, their enemies watching it all. At that moment there was a gigantic earthquake—a tenth of the city fell to ruin, seven thousand perished in the earthquake, the rest frightened to the core of their being, frightened into giving honor to the God-of-Heaven.

14The second doom is past, the third doom coming right on its heels.

The Last Trumpet Sounds

15-18The seventh Angel trumpeted. A crescendo of voices in Heaven sang out, The kingdom of the world is now the Kingdom of our God and his Messiah! He will rule forever and ever! The Twenty-four Elders seated before God on their thrones fell to their knees, worshiped, and sang, We thank you, O God, Sovereign-Strong,

Who Is and Who Was. You took your great power and took over— reigned! The angry nations now get a taste of *your* anger. The time has come to judge the dead, to reward your servants, all prophets and saints, Reward small and great who fear your Name, and destroy the destroyers of earth.

19The doors of God's Temple in Heaven flew open, and the Ark of his Covenant was clearly seen surrounded by flashes of lightning, loud shouts, peals of thunder, an earthquake, and a fierce hailstorm.   [3]

Revelation

Chapter Twelve

The Woman, Her Son, and the Dragon

1-2A great Sign appeared in Heaven: a Woman dressed all in sunlight, standing on the moon, and crowned with Twelve Stars. She was giving birth to a Child and cried out in the pain of childbirth.

3-4And then another Sign alongside the first: a huge and fiery Dragon! It had seven heads and ten horns, a crown on each of the seven heads. With one flick of its tail it knocked a third of the Stars from the sky and dumped them on earth. The Dragon crouched before the Woman in childbirth, poised to eat up the Child when it came.

5-6The Woman gave birth to a Son who will shepherd all nations with an iron rod. Her Son was seized and placed safely before God on his Throne. The Woman herself escaped to the desert to a place of safety prepared by God, all comforts provided her for 1,260 days.

7-12War broke out in Heaven. Michael and his Angels fought the Dragon. The Dragon and his Angels fought back, but were no match for Michael. They were cleared out of Heaven, not a sign of them left. The great Dragon—ancient Serpent, the one called Devil and Satan, the one who led the whole earth astray—thrown out, and all his Angels thrown out with him, thrown down to earth. Then I heard a strong voice out of Heaven saying, Salvation and power are established!

Kingdom of our God, authority of his Messiah! The Accuser of our brothers and sisters thrown out, who accused them day and night before God. They defeated him through the blood of the Lamb and the bold word of their witness. They weren't in love with themselves; they were willing to die for Christ. So rejoice, O Heavens, and all who live there, but doom to earth and sea, For the Devil's come down on you with both feet; he's had a great fall; He's wild and raging with anger; he hasn't much time and he knows it.

13-17When the Dragon saw he'd been thrown to earth, he went after the Woman who had given birth to the Man-Child. The Woman was given wings of a great eagle to fly to a place in the desert to be kept in safety and comfort for a time and times and half a time, safe and sound from the Serpent. The Serpent vomited a river of water to swamp and drown her, but earth came to her help, swallowing the water the Dragon spewed from its mouth. Helpless with rage, the Dragon raged at the Woman, then went off to make war with the rest of her children, the children who keep God's commands and hold firm to the witness of Jesus.   [3]

Revelation

Chapter Thirteen

The Beast from the Sea

1-2And the Dragon stood on the shore of the sea. I saw a Beast rising from the sea. It had ten horns and seven heads—on each horn a crown, and each head inscribed with a blasphemous name. The Beast I saw looked like a leopard with bear paws and a lion's mouth. The Dragon turned over its power to it, its throne and great authority.

3-4One of the Beast's heads looked as if it had been struck a deathblow, and then healed. The whole earth was agog, gaping at the Beast. They worshiped the Dragon who gave the Beast authority, and they worshiped the Beast, exclaiming, "There's never been anything like the Beast! No one would dare go to war with the Beast!"

5-8The Beast had a loud mouth, boastful and blasphemous. It could do anything it wanted for forty-two months. It yelled blasphemies against God, blasphemed his Name, blasphemed his Church, especially those already dwelling with God in Heaven. It was permitted to make war on God's holy people and conquer them. It held absolute sway over all tribes and peoples, tongues and races. Everyone on earth whose name was not written from the world's foundation in the slaughtered Lamb's Book of Life will worship the Beast.

9-10Are you listening to this? They've made their bed; now they must lie in it. Anyone marked for prison goes straight to prison; anyone pulling a sword goes down by the sword. Meanwhile, God's holy people passionately and faithfully stand their ground.

The Beast from Under the Ground

11-12I saw another Beast rising out of the ground. It had two horns like a lamb but sounded like a dragon when it spoke. It was a puppet of the first Beast, made earth and everyone in it worship the first Beast, which had been healed of its deathblow.

13-17This second Beast worked magical signs, dazzling people by making fire come down from Heaven. It used the magic it got from the Beast to dupe earth dwellers, getting them to make an image of the Beast that received the deathblow and lived. It was able to animate the image of the Beast so that it talked, and then arrange that anyone not worshiping the Beast would be killed. It forced all people, small and great, rich and poor, free and slave, to have a mark on the right hand or forehead. Without the mark of the name of the Beast or the number of its name, it was impossible to buy or sell anything.

18Solve a riddle: Put your heads together and figure out the meaning of the number of the Beast. It's a human number: 666.

Revelation

Chapter Fourteen

A Perfect Offering

1-2I saw—it took my breath away!—the Lamb standing on Mount Zion, 144,000 standing there with him, his Name and the Name of his Father inscribed on their foreheads. And I heard a voice out of Heaven, the sound like a cataract, like the crash of thunder.

2-5And then I heard music, harp music and the harpists singing a new song before the Throne and the Four Animals and the Elders. Only the 144,000 could learn to sing the song. They were bought from earth, lived without compromise, virgin-fresh before God. Wherever the Lamb went, they followed. They were bought from humankind, first fruits of the harvest for God and the Lamb. Not a false word in their mouths. A perfect offering.

Voices from Heaven

6-7I saw another Angel soaring in Middle-Heaven. He had an Eternal Message to preach to all who were still on earth, every nation and tribe, every tongue and people. He preached in a loud voice, "Fear God and give him glory! His hour of judgment has come! Worship the Maker of Heaven and earth, salt sea and fresh water!"

8A second Angel followed, calling out, "Ruined, ruined, Great Babylon ruined! She made all the nations drunk on the wine of her whoring!"

9-11A third Angel followed, shouting, warning, "If anyone worships the Beast and its image and takes the mark on forehead or hand, that person will drink the wine of God's wrath, prepared unmixed in his chalice of anger, and suffer torment from fire and brimstone in the presence of Holy Angels, in the presence of the Lamb. Smoke from their torment will rise age after age. No respite for those who worship the Beast and its image, who take the mark of its name."

12Meanwhile, the saints stand passionately patient, keeping God's commands, staying faithful to Jesus.

13I heard a voice out of Heaven, "Write this: Blessed are those who die in the Master from now on; how blessed to die that way!" "Yes," says the Spirit, "and blessed rest from their hard, hard work. None of what they've done is wasted; God blesses them for it all in the end."

Harvest Time

14-16I looked up, I caught my breath!—a white cloud and one like the Son of Man sitting on it. He wore a gold crown and held a sharp sickle. Another Angel came out of the Temple, shouting to the Cloud-Enthroned, "Swing your sickle and reap. It's harvest time. Earth's harvest is ripe for reaping." The Cloud-Enthroned gave a mighty sweep of his sickle, began harvesting earth in a stroke.

17-18Then another Angel came out of the Temple in Heaven. He also had a sharp sickle. Yet another Angel, the one in charge of tending the fire, came from the Altar. He thundered to the Angel who held the sharp sickle, "Swing your sharp sickle. Harvest earth's vineyard. The grapes are bursting with ripeness."

19-20The Angel swung his sickle, harvested earth's vintage, and heaved it into the winepress, the giant winepress of God's wrath. The winepress was outside the City. As the vintage was trodden, blood poured from the winepress as high as a horse's bridle, a river of blood for two hundred miles.   [3]

Revelation

Chapter Fifteen

The Song of Moses, the Song of the Lamb

1I saw another Sign in Heaven, huge and breathtaking: seven Angels with seven disasters. These are the final disasters, the wrap-up of God's wrath.

2-4I saw something like a sea made of glass, the glass all shot through with fire. Carrying harps of God, triumphant over the Beast, its image, and the number of its name, the saved ones stood on the sea of glass. They sang the Song of Moses, servant of God; they sang the Song of the Lamb:

Mighty your acts and marvelous, O God, the Sovereign-Strong! Righteous your ways and true, King of the nations! Who can fail to fear you, God, give glory to your Name? Because you and you only are holy, all nations will come and worship you, because they see your judgments are right.

5-8Then I saw the doors of the Temple, the Tent of Witness in Heaven, open wide. The Seven Angels carrying the seven disasters came out of the Temple. They were dressed in clean, bright linen and wore gold vests. One of the Four Animals handed the Seven Angels seven gold bowls, brimming with the wrath of God, who lives forever and ever. Smoke from God's glory and power poured out of the Temple. No one was permitted to enter the Temple until the seven disasters of the Seven Angels were finished.   [3]

Revelation

Chapter Sixteen

Pouring Out the Seven Disasters

1I heard a shout of command from the Temple to the Seven Angels: "Begin! Pour out the seven bowls of God's wrath on earth!"

2The first Angel stepped up and poured his bowl out on earth: Loathsome, stinking sores erupted on all who had taken the mark of the Beast and worshiped its image.

3The second Angel poured his bowl on the sea: The sea coagulated into blood, and everything in

it died.

4-7The third Angel poured his bowl on rivers and springs: The waters turned to blood. I heard the Angel of Waters say, Righteous you are, and your judgments are righteous,

The Is, The Was, The Holy.

They poured out the blood of saints and prophets so you've given them blood to drink—they've gotten what they deserve! Just then I heard the Altar chime in, Yes, O God, the Sovereign-Strong! Your judgments are true and just!

8-9The fourth Angel poured his bowl on the sun: Fire blazed from the sun and scorched men and women. Burned and blistered, they cursed God's Name, the God behind these disasters. They refused to repent, refused to honor God.

10-11The fifth Angel poured his bowl on the throne of the Beast: Its kingdom fell into sudden eclipse. Mad with pain, men and women bit and chewed their tongues, cursed the God-of-Heaven for their torment and sores, and refused to repent and change their ways.

The Walk – S.B. Stone & Rock Solid Publishing, LLC
©2018

12-14The sixth Angel poured his bowl on the great Euphrates River: It dried up to nothing. The dry riverbed became a fine roadbed for the kings from the East. From the mouths of the Dragon, the Beast, and the False Prophet I saw three foul demons crawl out—they looked like frogs. These are demon spirits performing signs. They're after the kings of the whole world to get them gathered for battle on the Great Day of God, the Sovereign-Strong.

15"Keep watch! I come unannounced, like a thief. You're blessed if, awake and dressed, you're ready for me. Too bad if you're found running through the streets, naked and ashamed."

16The frog-demons gathered the kings together at the place called in Hebrew *Armageddon*.

17-21The seventh Angel poured his bowl into the air: From the Throne in the Temple came a shout, "Done!" followed by lightning flashes and shouts, thunder crashes and a colossal earthquake—a huge and devastating earthquake, never an earthquake like it since time began. The Great City split three ways, the cities of the nations toppled to ruin. Great Babylon had to drink the wine of God's raging anger—God remembered to give her the cup! Every island fled and not a mountain was to be found. Hailstones weighing a ton plummeted, crushing and smashing men and women as they cursed God for the hail, the epic disaster of hail.   [3]

Revelation

Chapter Seventeen

Great Babylon, Mother of Whores

1-2One of the Seven Angels who carried the seven bowls came and invited me, "Come, I'll show you the judgment of the great Whore who sits enthroned over many waters, the Whore with whom the kings of the earth have gone whoring, show you the judgment on earth dwellers drunk on her whorish lust."

3-6In the Spirit he carried me out in the desert. I saw a woman mounted on a Scarlet Beast. Stuffed with blasphemies, the Beast had seven heads and ten horns. The woman was dressed in purple and scarlet, festooned with gold and gems and pearls. She held a gold chalice in her hand, brimming with defiling obscenities, her foul fornications. A riddle-name was branded on her forehead: great babylon, mother of whores and abominations of the earth. I could see that the woman was drunk, drunk on the blood of God's holy people, drunk on the blood of the martyrs of Jesus.

6-8Astonished, I rubbed my eyes. I shook my head in wonder. The Angel said, "Does this surprise you? Let me tell you the riddle of the woman and the Beast she rides, the Beast with seven heads and ten horns. The Beast you saw once was, is no longer, and is about to ascend from the Abyss and head straight for Hell. Earth dwellers whose names weren't written in the Book of Life from the foundation of the world will be dazzled when they see the Beast that once was, is no longer, and is to come.

9-11"But don't drop your guard. Use your head. The seven heads are seven hills; they are where the woman sits. They are also seven kings: five dead, one living, the other not yet here—and when he does come his time will be brief. The Beast that once was and is no longer is both an eighth and one of the seven—and headed for Hell.

12-14"The ten horns you saw are ten kings, but they're not yet in power. They will come to power with the Scarlet Beast, but won't last long—a *very* brief reign. These kings will agree to turn over their power and authority to the Beast. They will go to war against the Lamb but the Lamb will defeat them, proof that he is Lord over all lords, King over all kings, and those with him will be the called, chosen, and faithful."

15-18The Angel continued, "The waters you saw on which the Whore was enthroned are peoples and crowds, nations and languages. And the ten horns you saw, together with the Beast, will turn on the Whore— they'll hate her, violate her, strip her naked, rip her apart with their teeth, then set fire to her. It was God who put the idea in their heads to turn over their rule to the Beast until the words of God are completed. The woman you saw is the great city, tyrannizing the kings of the earth."
[3]

Revelation

Chapter Eighteen

Doom to the City of Darkness

1-8Following this I saw another Angel descend from Heaven. His authority was immense, his glory flooded earth with brightness, his voice thunderous: Ruined, ruined, Great Babylon, ruined! A ghost town for demons is all that's left! A garrison of carrion spirits, garrison of loathsome, carrion birds. All nations drank the wild wine of her whoring; kings of the earth went whoring with her; entrepreneurs made millions exploiting her. Just then I heard another shout out of Heaven: Get out, my people, as fast as you can, so you don't get mixed up in her sins, so you don't get caught in her doom. Her sins stink to high Heaven; God has remembered every evil she's done. Give her back what she's given, double what she's doubled in her works, double the recipe in the cup she mixed; Bring her flaunting and wild ways to torment and tears. Because she gloated, "I'm queen over all, and no widow, never a tear on my face," In one day, disasters will crush her—death, heartbreak, and famine—Then she'll be burned by fire, because God, the Strong God who judges her, has had enough.

9-10"The kings of the earth will see the smoke of her burning, and they'll cry and carry on, the kings who went night after night to her brothel. They'll keep their distance for fear they'll get burned, and they'll cry their lament: Doom, doom, the great city doomed! City of Babylon, strong city! In one hour it's over, your judgment come!

11-17"The traders will cry and carry on because the bottom dropped out of business, no more market for their goods: gold, silver, precious gems, pearls; fabrics of fine linen, purple, silk, scarlet; perfumed wood and vessels of ivory, precious woods, bronze, iron, and marble; cinnamon and spice, incense, myrrh, and frankincense; wine and oil, flour and wheat; cattle, sheep, horses, and chariots. And slaves—their terrible traffic in human lives.

Everything you've lived for, gone! All delicate and delectable luxury, lost! Not a scrap, not a thread to be found! "The traders who made millions off her kept their distance for fear of getting burned, and cried and carried on all the more: Doom, doom, the great city doomed! Dressed in the latest fashions, adorned with the finest jewels, in one hour such wealth wiped out!

The Walk – S.B. Stone & Rock Solid Publishing, LLC
©2018

17-19"All the ship captains and travelers by sea, sailors and toilers of the sea, stood off at a distance and cried their lament when they saw the smoke from her burning: 'Oh, what a city! There was never a city like her!' They threw dust on their heads and cried as if the world had come to an end: Doom, doom, the great city doomed! All who owned ships or did business by sea Got rich on her getting and spending. And now it's over—wiped out in one hour! 20"O Heaven, celebrate! And join in, saints, apostles, and prophets! God has judged her; every wrong you suffered from her has been judged."

21-24A strong Angel reached for a boulder—huge, like a millstone—and heaved it into the sea, saying, Heaved and sunk, the great city Babylon, sunk in the sea, not a sign of her ever again. Silent the music of harpists and singers—you'll never hear flutes and trumpets again. Artisans of every kind—gone; you'll never see their likes again. The voice of a millstone grinding falls dumb; you'll never hear that sound again.

The light from lamps, never again; never again laughter of bride and groom. Her traders robbed the whole earth blind, and by black-magic arts deceived the nations. The only thing left of Babylon is blood—the blood of saints and prophets, the murdered and the martyred.   [3]

Revelation

Chapter Nineteen

The Sound of Hallelujahs

1-3I heard a sound like massed choirs in Heaven singing, Hallelujah! The salvation and glory and power are God's—his judgments true, his judgments just. He judged the great Whore who corrupted the earth with her lust. He avenged on her the blood of his servants. Then, more singing:

Hallelujah! The smoke from her burning billows up to high Heaven forever and ever and ever.

4The Twenty-four Elders and the Four Animals fell to their knees and worshiped God on his Throne, praising, Amen! Yes! Hallelujah!

5From the Throne came a shout, a command: Praise our God, all you his servants, All you who fear him, small and great!

6-8Then I heard the sound of massed choirs, the sound of a mighty cataract, the sound of strong thunder: Hallelujah! The Master reigns, our God, the Sovereign-Strong! Let us celebrate, let us rejoice, let us give him the glory! The Marriage of the Lamb has come; his Wife has made herself ready. She was given a bridal gown of bright and shining linen. The linen is the righteousness of the saints. 9The Angel said to me, "Write this: 'Blessed are those invited to the Wedding Supper of the Lamb.'" He added, "These are the true words of God!"

10I fell at his feet to worship him, but he wouldn't let me. "Don't do that," he said. "I'm a servant just like you, and like your brothers and sisters who hold to the witness of Jesus. The witness of Jesus is the spirit of prophecy."

A White Horse and Its Rider

11-16Then I saw Heaven open wide—and oh! a white horse and its Rider. The Rider, named Faithful and True, judges and makes war in pure righteousness. His eyes are a blaze of fire, on his head many crowns. He has a Name inscribed that's known only to himself. He is dressed in a robe soaked with blood, and he is addressed as "Word of God." The armies of Heaven, mounted on white horses and dressed in dazzling white linen, follow him. A sharp sword comes out of his mouth so he can subdue the nations, then rule them with a rod of iron. He treads the winepress of the raging wrath of God, the Sovereign-Strong. On his robe and thigh is written, King of kings, Lord of lords.

17-18I saw an Angel standing in the sun, shouting to all flying birds in Middle-Heaven, "Come to the Great Supper of God! Feast on the flesh of kings and captains and champions, horses and their riders. Eat your fill of them all—free and slave, small and great!"

19-21I saw the Beast and, assembled with him, earth's kings and their armies, ready to make war against the One on the horse and his army. The Beast was taken, and with him, his puppet, the False Prophet, who used signs to dazzle and deceive those who had taken the mark of the Beast and worshiped his image. They were thrown alive, those two, into Lake Fire and Brimstone. The rest were killed by the sword of the One on the horse, the sword that comes from his mouth. All the birds held a feast on their flesh.

Revelation

Chapter Twenty

A Thousand Years

1-3I saw an Angel descending out of Heaven. He carried the key to the Abyss and a chain—a huge chain. He grabbed the Dragon, that old Snake—the very Devil, Satan himself!—chained him up for a thousand years, dumped him into the Abyss, slammed it shut and sealed it tight. No more trouble out of him, deceiving the nations—until the thousand years are up. After that he has to be let loose briefly.

4-6I saw thrones. Those put in charge of judgment sat on the thrones. I also saw the souls of those beheaded because of their witness to Jesus and the Word of God, who refused to worship either the Beast or his image, refused to take his mark on forehead or hand—they lived and reigned with Christ for a thousand years! The rest of the dead did not live until the thousand years were up. This is the first resurrection—and those involved most blessed, most holy. No second death for them! They're priests of God and Christ; they'll reign with him a thousand years.

7-10When the thousand years are up, Satan will be let loose from his cell, and will launch again his old work of deceiving the nations, searching out victims in every nook and cranny of earth, even Gog and Magog! He'll talk them into going to war and will gather a huge army, millions strong. They'll stream across the earth, surround and lay siege to the camp of God's holy people, the Beloved City. They'll no sooner get there than fire will pour out of Heaven and burn them up. The Devil who deceived them will be hurled into Lake Fire and Brimstone, joining the Beast and False Prophet, the three in torment around the clock for ages without end.

Judgment

11-15I saw a Great White Throne and the One Enthroned. Nothing could stand before or against the Presence, nothing in Heaven, nothing on earth. And then I saw all the dead, great and small, standing there—before the Throne! And books were opened. Then another book was opened: the Book of Life. The dead were judged by what was written in the books, by the way they had lived. Sea released its dead, Death and Hell turned in their dead. Each man and woman was judged by the way he or she had lived. Then Death and Hell were hurled into Lake Fire. This is the second death—Lake Fire. Anyone whose name was not found inscribed in the Book of Life was hurled into Lake Fire. [3]

Revelation

Chapter Twenty One

Everything New

1I saw Heaven and earth new-created. Gone the first Heaven, gone the first earth, gone the sea.

2I saw Holy Jerusalem, new-created, descending resplendent out of Heaven, as ready for God as a bride for her husband.

3-5I heard a voice thunder from the Throne: "Look! Look! God has moved into the neighborhood, making his home with men and women! They're his people, he's their God. He'll wipe every tear from their eyes. Death is gone for good—tears gone, crying gone, pain gone—all the first order of things gone." The Enthroned continued, "Look! I'm making everything new. Write it all down—each word dependable and accurate."

6-8Then he said, "It's happened. I'm A to Z. I'm the Beginning, I'm the Conclusion. From Water-of-Life Well I give freely to the thirsty. Conquerors inherit all this. I'll be God to them, they'll be sons and daughters to me. But for the rest—the feckless and faithless, degenerates and murderers, sex peddlers and sorcerers, idolaters and all liars—for them it's Lake Fire and Brimstone. Second death!"

The City of Light

9-12One of the Seven Angels who had carried the bowls filled with the seven final disasters spoke to me: "Come here. I'll show you the Bride, the Wife of the Lamb." He took me away in the Spirit to an enormous, high mountain and showed me Holy Jerusalem descending out of Heaven from God, resplendent in the bright glory of God.

12-14The City shimmered like a precious gem, light-filled, pulsing light. She had a wall majestic and high with twelve gates. At each gate stood an Angel, and on the gates were inscribed the names of the Twelve Tribes of the sons of Israel: three gates on the east, three gates on the north, three gates on the south, three gates on the west. The wall was set on twelve foundations, the names of the Twelve Apostles of the Lamb inscribed on them.

15-21The Angel speaking with me had a gold measuring stick to measure the City, its gates, and its wall. The City was laid out in a perfect square. He measured the City with the measuring stick: twelve thousand stadia, its length, width, and height all equal. Using the standard measure, the Angel measured the thickness of its wall: 144 cubits. The wall was jasper, the color of Glory, and the City was pure gold, translucent as glass. The foundations of the City walls were garnished with every precious gem imaginable: the first foundation jasper, the second sapphire, the third agate, the fourth emerald, the fifth onyx, the sixth carnelian, the seventh chrysolite, the eighth beryl, the ninth topaz, the tenth chrysoprase, the eleventh jacinth, the twelfth amethyst. The twelve gates were twelve pearls, each gate a single pearl.

21-27The main street of the City was pure gold, translucent as glass. But there was no sign of a Temple, for the Lord God—the Sovereign-Strong—and the Lamb are the Temple. The City doesn't need sun or moon for light. God's Glory is its light, the Lamb its lamp! The nations will walk in its light and earth's kings bring in their splendor. Its gates will never be shut by day, and there won't be any night. They'll bring the glory and honor of the nations into the City. Nothing dirty or defiled will get into the City, and no one who defiles or deceives. Only those whose names are written in the Lamb's Book of Life will get in.

Revelation

Chapter Twenty Two

1-5Then the Angel showed me Water-of-Life River, crystal bright. It flowed from the Throne of God and the Lamb, right down the middle of the street. The Tree of Life was planted on each side of the River, producing twelve kinds of fruit, a ripe fruit each month. The leaves of the Tree are for healing the nations. Never again will anything be cursed. The Throne of God and of the Lamb is at the center. His servants will offer God service—worshiping, they'll look on his face, their foreheads mirroring God. Never again will there be any night. No one will need lamplight or sunlight. The shining of God, the Master, is all the light anyone needs. And they will rule with him age after age after age.

Don't Put It Away on the Shelf

6-7The Angel said to me, "These are dependable and accurate words, every one. The God and Master of the spirits of the prophets sent his Angel to show his servants what must take place, and soon. And tell them, 'Yes, I'm on my way!' Blessed be the one who keeps the words of the prophecy of this book."

8-9I, John, saw all these things with my own eyes, heard them with my ears. Immediately when I heard and saw, I fell on my face to worship at the feet of the Angel who laid it all out before me. He objected, "No you don't! I'm a servant just like you and your companions, the prophets, and all who keep the words of this book. Worship God!"

10-11The Angel continued, "Don't seal the words of the prophecy of this book; don't put it away on the shelf. Time is just about up. Let evildoers do their worst and the dirty-minded go all out in pollution, but let the righteous maintain a straight course and the holy continue on in holiness."

12-13"Yes, I'm on my way! I'll be there soon! I'm bringing my payroll with me. I'll pay all people in full for their life's work. I'm A to Z, the First and the Final, Beginning and Conclusion.

14-15"How blessed are those who wash their robes! The Tree of Life is theirs for good, and they'll walk through the gates to the City. But outside for good are the filthy curs: sorcerers, fornicators, murderers, idolaters—all who love and live lies.

16"I, Jesus, sent my Angel to testify to these things for the churches. I'm the Root and Branch of David, the Bright Morning Star."

17"Come!" say the Spirit and the Bride. Whoever hears, echo, "Come!"

Is anyone thirsty? Come! All who will, come and drink, Drink freely of the Water of Life!

18-19I give fair warning to all who hear the words of the prophecy of this book: If you add to the words of this prophecy, God will add to your life the disasters written in this book; if you subtract from the words of the book of this prophecy, God will subtract your part from the Tree of Life and the Holy City that are written in this book.

20He who testifies to all these things says it again: "I'm on my way! I'll be there soon!"

Yes! Come, Master Jesus!

21The grace of the Master Jesus be with all of you. Oh, Yes!   [3]

The Walk – S.B. Stone & Rock Solid Publishing, LLC
©2018

THANK YOU, FRIEND!

I COMMEND YOU FOR READING ALL 475 PAGES OF THE WALK!

PLEASE PAGE DOWN TO PROVIDE YOUR VALUABLE FEEDBACK!

Footnotes

The Walk – S.B. Stone & Rock Solid Publishing, LLC
©2018

[6]   Amplified® Bible Copyright [AMP] © 2015 by The Lockman Foundation, La Habra, CA 90631   All rights reserved. http://www.lockman.org

[7] "Upheaval! Why Catastrophic Earthquakes Will Soon Strike the United States" by John L. Casey, Dr. Dong Choi, Dr. Fumio Tsunoda (professor of geology) and Dr. Ole Humlum. Published in 2016 by Trafford Publishing. Excerpts taken from Preface, Forward, pages 22 and others I've misplaced. See www.ievpc.org for earthquake and volcano predictions.

The Walk – S.B. Stone & Rock Solid Publishing, LLC
©2018

Feedback

We welcome your positive and critical feedback at: feedback@RockSolid.pub.

Here's a Feedback Guide to facilitate:

S.B. Stone hopes to write and publish a sequel to **The Walk: Stories About You** – should we call the sequel **The Walk: More Stories About You**? Or a different title?

_____

_____

_____.

1.   What did you enjoy about the eight fictional stories?

_____

_____

2.   Who are your favorite characters and why?

_____

_____

_____.

3.   Have you read and/or listened to the bonus pages in episodes eleven through fifteen - excerpts from my favorite books? Yes____   No____   I plan to____.

4.   For you what were the <u>least</u> entertaining stories and why?

_____

_____.

5.   On a 1 (zero fun) to 10 (tons of fun) scale how much fun was reading: We Need to Talk ____
Man About Town ____   Sweet Sixteen____   Too Young to Die ____

Leviathan ____   Joe Average____   Wimpy God ____
A Day in the Life of You ____.

6.   After reading The Walk who do you think the <u>smaller person</u> on the book cover represents?

_____

_____

7.   After reading The Walk who do you think the bigger person on the book cover represents?

_____

_____

8.   Please share your candid negative feedback on your mind or heart: how can the author give you a "ten" reading experience next time? _____

_____

_____

_____

_____

_____

_____

_____

_____.

Legal Stuff

Library of Congress Control Number: 2020900283

ISBN: 978-0-578-57-6

ISBN: 978-1-7341548-0-1

ISBN: 978-1-7341548-1-8

ISBN: 978-1-7341548-2-5

ISBN: 978-1-7341548-3-2

ISBN: 978-1-7341548-4-9

Rock Solid Publishing, LLC

5900 Balcones Drive - Suite 100

Austin, TX 78731

United States of America

The Walk cover designs by Dave Rosenberg

www.ingramcontent.com/pod-product-compliance
Lightning Source LLC
Chambersburg PA
CBHW061031030726
47504CB00002B/324